The
Sword
of
Shannara

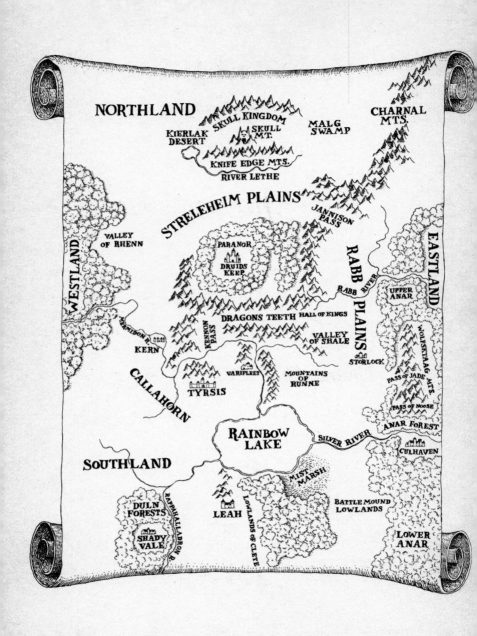

The
Sword
of
Shannara

Terry Brooks

Illustrated by The Brothers Hildebrandt

A Del Rey Book

BALLANTINE BOOKS · NEW YORK

A Del Rey Book
Published by Ballantine Books

Library of Congress Catalog Card Number: 76-53925

ISBN 0-345-24804-X

Manufactured in the United States of America

First Edition: April 1977

Fourth Printing: June 1977

For My Parents,
Who Believed

The
Sword
of
Shannara

I

The sun was already sinking into the deep green of the hills to the west of the valley, the red and gray-pink of its shadows touching the corners of the land, when Flick Ohmsford began his descent. The trail stretched out unevenly down the northern slope, winding through the huge boulders which studded the rugged terrain in massive clumps, disappearing into the thick forests of the lowlands to reappear in brief glimpses in small clearings and thinning spaces of woodland. Flick followed the familiar trail with his eyes as he trudged wearily along, his light pack slung loosely over one shoulder. His broad, windburned face bore a set, placid look, and only the wide gray eyes revealed the restless energy that burned beneath the calm exterior. He was a young man, though his stocky build and the grizzled brown hair and shaggy eyebrows made him look much older. He wore the loose-fitting work clothes of the Vale people and in the pack he carried were several metal implements that rolled and clanked loosely against one another.

There was a slight chill in the evening air, and Flick clutched the collar of his open wool shirt closer to his neck. His journey ahead lay through forests and rolling flatlands, the latter not yet visible to him as he passed into the forests, and the darkness of the tall oaks and somber hickories reached upward to overlap and blot out the cloudless night sky. The sun had set, leaving only the deep blue of the heavens pinpointed by thousands of friendly stars. The huge trees shut out even these, and Flick was left alone in the silent darkness as he moved slowly along the beaten path. Because he had traveled this same route a hundred times, the young man noticed immediately the unusual stillness that seemed to have captivated the entire valley this evening. The familiar buzzing and chirping of insects normally present in the quiet of the night, the cries of the birds that awoke with the setting of the sun to fly in search of food—all were missing. Flick listened intently for some sound of life, but his keen ears could detect nothing. He shook his head uneasily. The deep silence was unsettling, particularly in view of the rumors of a frightening black-winged creature sighted in the night skies north of the valley only days earlier.

He forced himself to whistle and turned his thoughts back to his day's work in the country just to the north of the Vale, where outlying families farmed and tended domestic livestock. He traveled to their homes every week, supplying various items that they required and bringing bits of news on the happenings of the Vale and occasionally the distant cities of the deep Southland. Few people knew the surrounding countryside as well as he did, and fewer still cared to travel beyond the comparative safety of their homes in the valley. Men were more inclined to remain in isolated communities these days and let the rest of the world get along as best it could. But Flick liked to travel outside the valley from time to time, and the outlying homesteads were in need of his services and were willing to pay him for the trouble. Flick's father was not one to let an opportunity pass him by where there was money to be made, and the arrangement seemed to work out well for all concerned.

A low-hanging branch brushing against his head

caused Flick to start suddenly and leap to one side. In chagrin, he straightened himself and glared back at the leafy obstacle before continuing his journey at a slightly quicker pace. He was deep in the lowland forests now and only slivers of moonlight were able to find their way through the thick boughs overhead to light the winding path dimly. It was so dark that Flick was having trouble finding the trail, and as he studied the lay of the land ahead, he again found himself conscious of the heavy silence. It was as if all life had been suddenly extinguished, and he alone remained to find his way out of this forest tomb. Again he recalled the strange rumors. He felt a bit anxious in spite of himself and glanced worriedly around. But nothing stirred on the trail ahead nor moved in the trees about him, and he felt embarrassingly relieved.

Pausing momentarily in a moonlit clearing, he gazed at the fullness of the night sky before passing abruptly into the trees beyond. He walked slowly, picking his way along the winding path that had narrowed beyond the clearing and now seemed to disappear into a wall of trees and bushes ahead. He knew that it was merely an illusion, but found himself glancing about uneasily all the same. A few moments later, he was again on a wider trail and could discern bits of sky peeking through the heavy trees. He was almost to the bottom of the valley and about two miles from his home. He smiled and began whistling an old tavern song as he hurried on. He was so intent on the trail ahead and the open land beyond the forest that he failed to notice the huge black shadow that seemed to rise up suddenly, detaching itself from a great oak tree on his left and moving swiftly toward the path to intercept him. The dark figure was almost on top of the Vale-man before Flick sensed its presence looming up before him like a great, black stone which threatened to crush his smaller being. With a startled cry of fear he leaped aside, his pack falling to the path with a crash of metal, and his left hand whipped out the long thin dagger at his waist. Even as he crouched to defend himself, he was stayed by a commanding arm raised above the figure before him and a strong, yet reassuring voice that spoke out quickly.

"Wait a moment, friend. I'm no enemy and have no wish to harm you. I merely seek directions and would be grateful if you could show me the proper path."

Flick relaxed his guard a bit and tried to peer into the blackness of the figure before him in an effort to discover some semblance of a human being. He could see nothing, however, and he moved to the left with cautious steps in an attempt to catch the features of the dark figure in the tree-shadowed moonlight.

"I assure you, I mean no harm," the voice continued, as if reading the Valeman's mind. "I did not mean to frighten you, but I didn't see you until you were almost upon me, and I was afraid you might pass me by without realizing I was there."

The voice stopped and the huge black figure stood silently, though Flick could feel the eyes following him as he edged about the path to put his own back to the light. Slowly the pale moonlight began to etch out the stranger's features in vague lines and blue shadows. For a long moment the two faced one another in silence, each studying the other, Flick in an effort to decide what it was he faced, the stranger in quiet anticipation.

Then suddenly the huge figure lunged with terrible swiftness, his powerful hands seizing the Valeman's wrists, and Flick was lifted abruptly off the solid earth and held high, his knife dropping from nerveless fingers as the deep voice laughed mockingly up at him.

"Well, well, my young friend! What are you going to do now, I wonder? I could cut your heart out on the spot and leave you for the wolves if I chose, couldn't I?"

Flick struggled violently to free himself, terror numbing his mind to any thought but that of escape. He had no idea what manner of creature had subdued him, but it was far more powerful than any normal man and apparently prepared to dispatch Flick quickly. Then abruptly, his captor held him out at arm's length, and the mocking voice became icy cold with displeasure.

"Enough of this, boy! We have played our little game and still you know nothing of me. I'm tired and hungry and have no wish to be delayed on the forest trail in the chill of the evening while you decide if I am man or beast. I will set you down that you may show me the path. I warn you—do not try to run from me or it will be the worse for you."

The strong voice trailed off and the tone of displeasure disappeared as the former hint of mockery returned with a short laugh.

"Besides," the figure rumbled as the fingers released their iron grip and Flick slipped to the path, "I may be a better friend than you realize."

The figure moved back a step as Flick straightened himself, rubbing his wrists carefully to restore the circulation to his numbed hands. He wanted to run, but was certain that the stranger would catch him again and this time finish him without further thought. He leaned over cautiously and picked up the fallen dagger, returning it to his belt.

Flick could see the fellow more clearly now, and a quick scrutiny of him revealed that he was definitely human, though much larger than any man Flick had ever seen. He was at least seven feet tall, but exceptionally lean, though it was difficult to be certain about this, since his tall frame was wrapped in a flowing black cloak with a loose cowl pulled close about his head. The darkened face was long and deeply lined, giving it a craggy appearance. The eyes were deep-set and almost completely hidden from

view by shaggy eyebrows that knotted fiercely over a
long flat nose. A short, black beard outlined a wide
mouth that was just a line on the face—a line that
never seemed to move. The overall appearance was
frightening, all blackness and size, and Flick had to
fight down the urge building within him to make a
break for the forest's edge. He looked straight into the
deep, hard eyes of the stranger, though not without
some difficulty, and managed a weak smile.

"I thought you were a thief," he mumbled hesitantly.

"You were mistaken," was the quiet retort. Then
the voice softened a bit. "You must learn to know a
friend from an enemy. Sometime your life may
depend upon it. Now then, let's have your name."

"Flick Ohmsford."

Flick hesitated and then continued in a slightly
braver tone of voice.

"My father is Curzad Ohmsford. He manages an
inn in Shady Vale a mile or two from here. You could
find lodging and food there."

"Ah, Shady Vale," the stranger exclaimed suddenly. "Yes, that is where I am going." He paused as if
reflecting on his own words. Flick watched him
cautiously as he rubbed his craggy face with crooked
fingers and looked beyond the forest's edge to the
rolling grasslands of the valley. He was still looking
away when he spoke again.

"You . . . have a brother."

It was not a question; it was a simple statement of
fact. It was spoken so distantly and calmly, as if the tall
stranger were not at all interested in any sort of a reply,
that Flick almost missed hearing it. Then suddenly
realizing the significance of the remark, he started and
looked quickly at the other.

"How did . . .?"

"Oh, well," the man said, "doesn't every young
Valeman like yourself have a brother somewhere?"

Flick nodded dumbly, unable to comprehend what

it was that the other was trying to say and wondering vaguely how much he knew about Shady Vale. The stranger was looking questioningly at him, evidently waiting to be guided to the promised food and lodging. Flick quickly turned away to find his hastily discarded pack, picked it up and slung it over his shoulder, looking back at the figure towering over him.

"The path is this way." He pointed, and the two began walking.

They passed out of the deep forest and entered rolling, gentle hills which they would follow to the hamlet of Shady Vale at the far end of the valley. Out of the woods, it was a bright night; the moon was a full white globe overhead, its glow clearly illuminating the landscape of the valley and the path which the two travelers were following. The path itself was a vague line winding over the grassy hills and distinguishable only by occasional rain-washed ruts and flat, hard patches of earth breaking through the heavy grass. The wind had gathered strength and rushed at the two men with quick gusts that whipped at their clothing as they walked, forcing them to bow their heads slightly to shield their eyes. Neither spoke a word as they proceeded, each concentrating on the lay of the land beyond, as new hills and small depressions appeared with the passing of each traveled knoll. Except for the rushing of the wind, the night remained silent. Flick listened intently, and once he thought he heard a sharp cry far to the north, but an instant later it was gone, and he did not hear it again. The stranger appeared to be unconcerned with the silence. His attention seemed to be focused on a constantly changing point on the ground some six feet in front of them. He did not look up and he did not look at his young guide for directions as they went. Instead, he seemed to know exactly where the other was going and walked confidently beside him.

After a while, Flick began to have trouble keeping

pace with the tall man, who traveled the path with
long, swinging strides that dwarfed Flick's shorter
ones. At times, the Valeman almost had to run to keep
up. Once or twice the other man glanced down at his
smaller companion and, seeing the difficulty he was
having in trying to match strides, slowed to an easier
pace. Finally, as the southern slopes of the valley drew
near, the hills began to level off into shrub-covered
grasslands that hinted at the appearance of new
forests. The terrain began to dip downward at a gentle
slope, and Flick located several familiar landmarks
that bounded the outskirts of Shady Vale. He felt a
surge of relief in spite of himself. The hamlet and his
own warm home were just ahead.

The stranger did not speak a single word during the
brief journey, and Flick was reluctant to attempt any
conversation. Instead, he tried to study the giant in
quick glimpses as they walked, without permitting the
other to observe what he was doing. He was
understandably awed. The long, craggy face, shaded
by the sharp black beard, recalled the fearful Warlocks
described to him by stern elders before the glowing
embers of a late evening fire when he was only a child.
Most frightening were the stranger's eyes—or rather
the deep, dark caverns beneath the shaggy brows
where his eyes should be. Flick could not penetrate the
heavy shadows that continued to mask that entire area
of his face. The deeply lined countenance seemed
carved from stone, fixed and bowed slightly to the
path before it. As Flick pondered the inscrutable
visage, he suddenly realized that the stranger had
never even mentioned his name.

The two were on the outer lip of the Vale, where the
now clearly distinguishable path wound through
large, crowded bushes that almost choked off human
passage. The tall stranger stopped suddenly and stood
perfectly still, head bowed, listening intently. Flick
halted beside him and waited quietly, also listening,

but unable to detect anything. They remained motionless for seemingly endless minutes, and then the big man turned hurriedly to his smaller companion.

"Quickly! Hide in the bushes ahead. Go now, run!"

He half pushed, half threw Flick in front of him as he raced swiftly toward the tall brush. Flick scurried fearfully for the sanctuary of the shrubbery, his pack slapping wildly against his back and the metal implements clanging. The stranger turned on him and snatched the pack away, tucking it beneath the long robe.

"Silence!" he hissed. "Run now. Not a sound."

They ran quickly to the dark wall of foliage some fifty feet ahead, and the tall man hurriedly pushed Flick through the leafy branches that whipped against their faces, pulling him roughly into the middle of a large clump of brush, where they stood breathing heavily. Flick glanced at his companion and saw that he was not looking through the brush at the country around them, but instead was peering upward where the night sky was visible in small, irregular patches through the foliage. The sky seemed clear to the Valeman as he followed the other's intense gaze, and only the changeless stars winked back at him as he watched and waited. Minutes passed; once he attempted to speak, but was quickly silenced by the strong hands of the stranger, gripping his shoulders in warning. Flick remained standing, looking at the night and straining his ears for some sound of the apparent danger. But he heard nothing save their own heavy breathing and a quiet rush of wind through the weaving branches of their cover.

Then, just as Flick prepared to ease his tired limbs by sitting, the sky was suddenly blotted out by something huge and black that floated overhead and then passed from sight. A moment later it passed again, circling slowly without seeming to move, its shadow hanging ominously above the two hidden travelers as if preparing to fall upon them. A sudden feeling of terror raced through Flick's mind, trapping it in an iron web as it strained to flee the fearful madness penetrating inward. Something seemed to be reaching downward into his chest, slowly squeezing the air from his lungs, and he found himself gasping for breath. A vision passed sharply before him of a black image laced with red, of clawed hands and giant wings, of a thing so evil that its very existence threatened his frail life. For an instant the young man thought he would scream, but the hand of the stranger gripped his shoulder tightly, pulling him back from the precipice. Just as suddenly as it had appeared, the giant shadow was gone and the peaceful sky of the patched night was all that remained.

The hand on Flick's shoulder slowly relaxed its grip, and the Valeman slid heavily to the ground, his body limp as he broke out in a cold sweat. The tall stranger seated himself quietly next to his companion and a small smile crossed his face. He laid one long hand on Flick's and patted it as he would a child's.

"Come now, my young friend," he whispered, "you're alive and well, and the Vale lies just ahead."

Flick looked up at the other's calm face, his own eyes wide with fear as he shook his head slowly.

"That thing! What was that terrible thing?"

"Just a shadow," the man replied easily. "But this is neither the place nor the time to concern ourselves with such matters. We will speak of it later. Right now, I would like some food and a warm fire before I lose all patience."

He helped the Valeman to his feet and returned his pack to him. Then with a sweep of his robed arm, he indicated that he was ready to follow if the other was ready to lead. They left the cover of the brush, Flick not without misgivings as he glanced apprehensively at the night sky. It almost seemed as if the whole business had been the result of an overactive imagina-

tion. Flick pondered the matter solemnly and quickly
decided that whatever the case, he had had enough for
one evening: first this nameless giant and then that
frightening shadow. He silently vowed that he would
think twice before traveling again at night so far from
the safety of the Vale.

Several minutes later, the trees and brush began to
thin out and the flickering of yellow light was visible
through the darkness. As they drew closer, the vague
forms of buildings began to take shape as square and
rectangular bulks in the gloom. The path widened into
a smoother dirt road that led straight into the hamlet,
and Flick smiled gratefully at the lights that shone in
friendly greeting through the windows of the silent
buildings. No one moved on the road ahead; if it had
not been for the lights, one might well have wondered
if anyone at all lived in the Vale. As it was, Flick's
thoughts were far from such questions. Already he
was considering how much he ought to tell his father
and Shea, not wishing to worry them about strange
shadows that could easily have been the product of his
imagination and the gloomy night. The stranger at his
side might shed some light on the subject at a later
time, but so far he had not proved to be much of a
conversationalist. Flick glanced involuntarily at the
tall figure walking silently beside him. Again he was
chilled by the blackness of the man. It seemed to reflect
from his cloak and hood over his bowed head and lean
hands, to shroud the entire figure in hazy gloom.
Whoever he was, Flick felt certain that he would be a
dangerous enemy.

They passed slowly between the buildings of the
hamlet, and Flick could see torches burning through
the wooden frames of the wide windows. The houses
themselves were long, low structures, each containing
only a ground floor beneath a slightly sloping roof,
which in most instances tapered off on one side to
shelter a small veranda, supported by heavy poles

affixed to a long porch. The buildings were constructed of wood, with stone foundations and stone
frontings on a few. Flick glanced through the curtained windows, catching glimpses of the inhabitants,
the sight of familiar faces reassuring to him in the
darkness outside. It had been a frightening night, and
he was relieved to be home among people he knew.

The stranger remained oblivious to everything. He
did not bother with more than a casual glance at the
hamlet and had not spoken once since they had
entered the Vale. Flick remained incredulous at the
way in which the other followed him. He wasn't
following Flick at all, but seemed to know exactly
where the Valeman was going. When the road
branched off in opposite directions amid identical
rows of houses, the tall man had no difficulty in
determining the correct route, though he never once
looked at Flick nor even raised his head to study the
road. Flick found himself trailing along while the other
guided.

The two quickly reached the inn. It was a large
structure consisting of a main building and lounging
porch, with two long wings that extended out and
back on either side. It was constructed of huge logs,
cut and laced on a high stone foundation and covered
with the familiar wood shingle roof, this particular
roof much higher than those of the family dwellings.
The central building was well lighted, and muffled
voices could be heard from within, interspersed with
occasional laughter and shouts. The wings of the inn
were in darkness; it was there that the sleeping quarters
of the guests were located. The smell of roasting meat
permeated the night air, and Flick quickly led the way
up the wooden steps of the long porch to the wide
double doors at the center of the inn. The tall stranger
followed without a word.

Flick slid back the heavy metal door latch and pulled
on the handles. The big door on the right swung open

to admit them into a large lounging room, filled with benches, high-backed chairs, and several long, heavy wooden tables set against the wall to the left and rear. The room was brightly lit by the tall candles on the tables and wall racks and by the huge fireplace built into the center of the wall on the left; Flick was momentarily blinded as his eyes adjusted to this new light. He squinted sharply, glancing past the fireplace and lounging furniture to the closed double doors at the back of the room and over to the long serving bar running down the length of the wall to his right. The men gathered about the bar looked up idly as the pair entered the room, their faces registering undisguised amazement at the appearance of the tall stranger. But Flick's silent companion did not seem to see them, and they quickly returned to their conversation and evening drinks, glancing back at the newcomers once or twice to see what they were going to do. The pair remained standing at the door for a few moments more as Flick looked around a second time at the faces of the small crowd to see if his father were present. The stranger motioned to the lounging chairs on the left.

"I will have a seat while you find your father. Perhaps we can have dinner together when you return."

Without further comment, he moved quietly away to a small table at the rear of the room and seated himself with his back to the men at the bar, his face slightly bowed and turned away from Flick. The Valeman watched him for a moment, then moved quickly to the double doors at the rear of the room and pushed through them to the hallway beyond. His father was probably in the kitchen, having dinner with Shea. Flick hurried down the hall past several closed doors before reaching the one that opened into the inn kitchen. As he entered, the two cooks who were working at the rear of the room greeted the young man with a cheerful good evening. His father was seated at the end of a long counter at the left. As Flick had anticipated, he was in the process of finishing his dinner. He waved a brawny hand in greeting.

"You're a bit later than usual, son," he growled pleasantly. "Come over here and have dinner while there's still something to eat."

Flick walked over wearily, lowered the traveling pack to the floor with a slight clatter, and perched himself on one of the high counter stools. His father's large frame straightened itself as he shoved back the empty plate and looked quizzically at the other, his wide forehead wrinkling.

"I met a traveler on the road coming into the valley," Flick explained hesitantly. "He wants a room and dinner. Asked us to join him."

"Well, he came to the right place for a room," the elder Ohmsford declared. "I don't see why we shouldn't join him for a bite to eat—I could easily do with another helping."

He raised his massive frame from the stool and signaled the cooks for three dinners. Flick looked about for Shea, but he was nowhere in sight. His father lumbered over to the cooks to give some special instructions on preparing the meal for the small party, and Flick turned to the basin next to the sink to wash off the dirt and grime from the road. When his father came over to him, Flick asked where his brother had gone.

"Shea has gone out on an errand for me and should return on the moment," his father replied. "By the way, what's the name of this man you brought back with you?"

"I don't know. He didn't say." Flick shrugged.

His father frowned and mumbled something about closemouthed strangers, rounding off his muffled comment with a vow to have no more mysterious types at his inn. Then motioning to his son, he led the way through the kitchen doors, his wide shoulders brushing the wall beyond as he swung to his left toward the lounging area. Flick followed quickly, his broad face wrinkled in doubt.

The stranger was still sitting quietly, his back to the men gathered at the serving bar. When he heard the rear doors swing open, he shifted about slightly to catch a glimpse of the two who entered. The stranger studied the close resemblance between father and son. Both were of medium height and heavy build, with the same broad, placid faces and grizzled brown hair. They hesitated in the doorway and Flick pointed toward the dark figure. He could see the surprise in Curzad Ohmsford's eyes as the innkeeper regarded him for a minute before approaching. The stranger stood up courteously, towering over the other two as they came up to him.

"Welcome to my inn, stranger," the elder Ohmsford greeted him, trying vainly to peer beneath the cloak hood that shadowed the other's dark face. "My name, as my boy has probably told you, is Curzad Ohmsford."

The stranger shook the extended hand with a grip that caused the stocky man to grimace and then nodded to Flick.

"Your son was kind enough to show me to this pleasant inn." He smiled with what Flick could have sworn was a mocking grin. "I hope you will join me for dinner and a glass of beer."

"Certainly," answered the innkeeper, lumbering past the other to a vacant chair where he seated himself heavily. Flick also pulled up a chair and sat down, his eyes still on the stranger, who was in the process of complimenting his father on having such a fine inn. The elder Ohmsford beamed with pleasure and nodded in satisfaction to Flick as he signaled one of the men at the serving bar for three glasses. The tall man still did not pull back the hood of the cloak shading his face. Flick wanted to peer beneath the shadows, but was afraid the stranger would notice, and one such attempt had already earned him sore wrists and a healthy respect for the big man's strength and temper. It was safer to remain in doubt.

He sat in silence as the conversation between his father and the stranger lengthened from polite comments on the mildness of the weather to a more intimate discussion of the people and happenings of the Vale. Flick noticed that his father, who never needed much encouragement anyway, was carrying the entire conversation with only casual questions interjected by the other man. It probably did not matter, but the Ohmsfords knew nothing about the stranger. He had not even told them his name. Now he was quite subtly drawing out information on the Vale from the unsuspecting innkeeper. The whole situation bothered Flick, but he was uncertain what he should do. He began to wish that Shea would appear and see what was happening. But his brother remained absent, and the long-awaited dinner was served and entirely consumed before one of the wide double doors at the front of the lobby swung open, and Shea appeared from out of the darkness.

For the first time, Flick saw the hooded stranger take more than a passing interest in someone. Strong hands gripped the table as the black figure rose silently, towering over the Ohmsfords. He seemed to have forgotten they were there, as the lined brow furrowed more deeply and the craggy features radiated an intense concentration. For one frightening second, Flick believed that the stranger was somehow about to destroy Shea, but then the idea disappeared and was replaced with another. The man was searching his brother's mind.

He stared intently at Shea, his deep, shaded eyes running quickly over the young man's slim countenance and slight build. He noted the telltale Elven features immediately—the hint of slightly pointed ears beneath the tousled blond hair, the pencil-like eyebrows that ran straight up at a sharp angle from the bridge of the nose rather than across the brow, and the slimness of the nose and jaw. He saw intelligence and honesty in that face, and now as he faced Shea across the room, he saw determination in the penetrating blue eyes—determination that spread in a flush over the youthful features as the two men locked their gazes on one another. For a moment Shea hesitated in awe of the huge, dark apparition across the room. He felt unexplainably trapped but, bracing himself with sudden resolve, he walked toward the forbidding figure.

Flick and his father watched Shea approach them, his eyes still on the tall stranger and then, as if suddenly realizing who he was, the two rose from the table. There was a moment of awkward silence as they faced one another, and then all the Ohmsfords began greeting each other at once in a sudden jumble of words that relieved the initial tension. Shea smiled at Flick, but could not take his eyes off the imposing figure before him. Shea was slightly shorter than his brother and was therefore even more in the shadow of the stranger than Flick had been, though he was less nervous about it as he faced the man. Curzad Ohmsford was talking to him about his errand, and his attention was momentarily diverted while he replied to his father's insistent questions. After a few preliminary remarks, Shea turned back to the newcomer to the Vale.

"I don't believe we have met; yet you seem to know me from somewhere, and I have the strangest feeling that I should know you."

The dark face above him nodded as the familiar mocking smile crossed it fleetingly.

"Perhaps you should know me, though it is not surprising that you do not remember. But I know who you are; indeed, I know you well."

Shea was dumbfounded at this reply and, unable to respond, stood staring at the stranger. The other raised a lean hand to his chin to stroke the small dark beard, glancing slowly around at the three men who waited for him to continue. Flick's open mouth was framing the question on the minds of all the Ohmsfords, when the stranger reached up and pulled back the cowl of his cloak to reveal clearly the dark face, now framed by long black hair, cut nearly shoulder length and shading the deep-set eyes, which still showed only as black slits in the shadows beneath the heavy brows.

"My name is Allanon," he announced quietly.

There was a long moment of stunned silence as the three listeners stared in speechless amazement. Allanon—the mysterious wanderer of the four lands, historian of the races, philosopher and teacher, and, some said, practitioner of the mystic arts. Allanon— the man who had been everywhere from the darkest havens of the Anar to the forbidden heights of the Charnal Mountains. His was a name familiar to the people of even the most isolated Southland communities. Now he stood unexpectedly before the Ohmsfords, none of whom had ventured outside their valley home more than a handful of times in their lives.

Allanon smiled warmly for the first time, but inwardly he felt pity for them. The quiet existence they had known for so many years was finished, and, in a way, it was his responsibility.

"What brings you here?" Shea asked at last.

The tall man looked sharply at him and uttered a deep, low chuckle that caught them all by surprise.

"You, Shea," he murmured. "I came looking for you."

II

Shea was awake early the next morning, rising from the warmth of his bed to dress hastily in the damp cold of the morning air. He had arisen so early, he discovered, that no one else in the entire inn, guest or family, was yet awake. The long building was silent as he moved quietly from his small room in the rear of the main section to the large lobby, where he quickly started a fire in the great stone hearth, his fingers almost numb with cold. The valley was always strikingly cold in the early-morning hours before the sun reached the rim of the hills, even during the warmest seasons of the year. Shady Vale was well sheltered, not only from the eyes of men, but from the fury of perverse weather conditions that drifted down from the Northland. Yet while the heavy storms of the winter and spring passed over the valley and Shady Vale, the bitter cold of early morning all year round settled into the high hills, holding until the warmth of the noonday sun filtered down to chase away the chill.

The fire crackled and snapped at the wood as Shea relaxed in one of the high, straight-backed chairs and pondered the events of the previous evening. He leaned back, folded his arms for warmth, and hunched down into the hard wood. How could Allanon have known him? He had seldom been out of the Vale and would certainly have remembered the other man if he had met him while on one of his infrequent journeys. Allanon had refused to say more on the subject after that one declaration. He had finished his dinner in silence, concluding that further talk should wait until the next morning, and he became once again the forbidding figure he had first appeared when Shea entered the inn that evening. His meal completed, he had asked to be shown to his room so that he might sleep, and then excused himself. Neither Shea nor Flick could get him to say one word further about the trip to Shady Vale and his interest in Shea. The two brothers had talked alone later that night, and Flick had related the story of his encounter with Allanon and the incident with the terrifying shadow.

Shea's thoughts drifted back to his initial question—how could Allanon have known him? Mentally he retraced the events of his life. His early years were a vague memory. He did not know where he had been born, although sometime after the Ohmsfords had adopted him, he had been told that his place of birth was a small Westland community. His father had died before he was old enough to form a lasting impression, and now he could recall almost nothing of him. For a time his mother had kept him, and he could recall bits and pieces of his years with her, playing with Elven children, surrounded by great trees and deep green solitude. He was five when she became suddenly ill and decided to return to her own people in the hamlet of Shady Vale. She must have known then that she was dying, but her first concern was for her son. The journey south was the finish for her, and she died shortly after they reached the valley.

The relatives his mother had left when she married were gone, all but the Ohmsfords, who were no more than distant cousins. Curzad Ohmsford had lost his wife less than a year earlier, and was raising his son Flick while he managed the inn. Shea became a part of their family, and the two boys had grown up as brothers, both bearing the name Ohmsford. Shea had never been told his true name, nor did he care to ask. The Ohmsfords were the only family that meant anything to him, and they had accepted him as their own. There were times that being a half-blood bothered him, but Flick had stoutly insisted that it was a distinct advantage because it gave him the instincts and character of two races to build upon.

Yet nowhere could he remember an encounter with Allanon. It was as if the event had never really occurred. Perhaps it never had. He shifted around in the chair and gazed absently into the fire. There was something about the grim wanderer that frightened him. Perhaps it was his imagination, but he could not shake off the feeling that the man could somehow read his thoughts, could see right through him whenever he chose to do so. It seemed ridiculous, but the thought had lingered with the Valeman since the meeting in the lobby of the inn. Flick had remarked on it too. And he had gone further than that, whispering in the darkness of their sleeping room to his brother, fearful that he might in some way be overheard, that he felt Allanon was dangerous.

Shea stretched himself and sighed deeply. Already it was becoming light outside. He rose to add some more wood to the fire, and heard the sound of his father's voice in the hallway, grumbling loudly about matters in general. Sighing in resignation, Shea put aside his thoughts and hastened to the kitchen to help with the morning preparations.

It was almost noon before Shea saw any sign of Allanon, who had evidently kept to his room for the duration of the morning. He appeared quite suddenly from around one corner of the inn as Shea relaxed beneath a huge shade tree at the rear of the building, absently munching on a quick luncheon he had prepared for himself. His father was occupied within, and Flick was off somewhere on an errand. The dark stranger of the previous night seemed no less forbidding in the noon sun, still a shadowed figure of tremendous height, though he appeared to have changed his cloak from black to a light gray. The lean face was slightly bowed to the path before him as he walked toward Shea and seated himself on the grass next to the Valeman, gazing absently at the hilltops to the east which appeared above the trees of the hamlet. Both men were silent for several long minutes, until at last Shea could stand it no longer.

"Why did you come to the vale, Allanon? Why were you looking for me?"

The dark face turned toward him and a slight smile played across the lean features.

"A question, my young friend, that cannot be as easily answered as you would like. Perhaps the best way in which to answer you is first to question you. Have you read anything of the history of the Northland?"

He paused.

"Do you know of the Skull Kingdom?"

Shea stiffened at the mention of the name—a name that was synonymous with all the terrible things in life, real and imagined, a name used to frighten little children who had been bad or to send shivers down the spines of grown men when stories were told before the dying coals of a late evening fire. It was a name that hinted of ghosts and goblins, of the sly forest Gnomes of the east and the great Rock Trolls of the far north. Shea looked at the grim visage before him and nodded slowly. Again Allanon paused before continuing.

"I am a historian, Shea, among other things—perhaps the most widely traveled historian alive today, since few besides myself have entered the Northland in over five hundred years. I know much about the race of Man that none now suspect. The past has become a blurred memory, and just as well perhaps; for the history of Man has not been particularly glorious in the last two thousand years. Men today have forgotten the past; they know little of the present and less of the future. The race of Man lives almost solely in the confines of the Southland. It knows nothing at all of the Northland and its peoples, and little of the Eastland and Westland. A pity that Men have developed into such a shortsighted people, for once they were the most visionary of the races. But now they are quite content to live apart from the other races, isolated from the problems of the rest of the world. They remain content, mind you, because those problems have not as yet touched them and because a fear of the past has persuaded them not to look too closely at the future."

Shea felt slightly irritated by these sweeping accusations, and his reply was sharp.

"You make it sound like a terrible thing to want to be left alone. I know enough history—no, I know enough life—to realize that Man's only hope for survival is to remain apart from the races, to rebuild everything he has lost over the last two thousand years. Then perhaps he will be smart enough not to lose it a second time. He almost destroyed himself entirely in the Great Wars by his persistent intervention in the affairs of others and his ill-conceived rejection of an isolation policy."

Allanon's dark face turned hard.

"I am well aware of the catastrophic consequences brought about by those wars—the products of power and greed that the race of Man brought down on its own head through a combination of carelessness and remarkable shortsightedness. That was long ago—and what has changed? You think that Man can start again, do you, Shea? Well, you might be quite surprised to learn that some things never change, and the dangers of power are always present, even to a race that almost completely obliterated itself. The Great Wars of the past may be gone—the wars of the races, of politics and nationalism, and the final ones of sheer energy, of ultimate power. But we face new dangers today, and these are more of a threat to the existence of the races than were any of the old! If you think Man is free to build a new life while the rest of the world drifts by, then you do not know anything of history!"

He paused suddenly, his grim features lined with anger. Shea stared back defiantly, though within he felt small and frightened.

"Enough of this," Allanon began again, his face softening as one strong hand reached up to grip Shea's shoulder in friendship. "The past is behind us, and it is with the future that we must concern ourselves. Let me refresh your memory for a moment on the history of the Northland and the legend of the Skull Kingdom. As you know, I'm sure, the Great Wars brought an end to an age where Man alone was the dominant race. Man was almost completely destroyed and even the geography he had known was completely altered, completely restructured. Countries, nations, and governments all ceased to exist as the last members of the human race fled south to survive. It was nearly a thousand years before Man had once again raised himself above the standard of the animals he hunted for food and established a progressive civilization. It was primitive, to be sure, but there was order and a semblance of government. Then Man began to discover there were other races besides himself inhabiting the world—creatures who had survived the Great Wars and developed their own races. In the mountains were the huge Trolls, powerful and ferocious, but quite content with what they had. In the hills and forests were the small and cunning creatures we now call Gnomes. Many a battle was fought between Men and Gnomes for the rights to land during the years following the Great Wars, and the battles hurt both races. But they fought to survive, and reason has no place in the mind of a creature fighting for its life.

"Man also discovered that there was another race—a race of men who had fled beneath the earth to survive the effects of the Great Wars. Years of living in the huge caverns beneath the earth's crust away from the sunlight altered their appearance. They became short and stocky, powerful in the arms and chest, with strong, thick legs for climbing and scrambling underground. Their sight in the dark became superior to that of other creatures, yet in the sunlight they could see little. They lived beneath the earth for many hundreds of years, until at last they began to emerge to live again on the face of the land. Their eyes were very bad at first, and they made their homes in the darkest forests of the Eastland. They developed their own language, though they later reverted to the language of Man. When Man first discovered remnants of this lost race, they called them Dwarfs, after a fictional race of the old days."

His voice trailed off and he remained silent for a few minutes staring out at the tips of the hills showing brilliant green in the sunlight. Shea considered the historian's comments. He had never seen a Troll, and only one or two Gnomes and Dwarfs, and those he did not remember very well.

"What about the Elves?" he asked finally.

Allanon looked back thoughtfully and bowed his head a little more.

"Ah, yes, I had not forgotten. A remarkable race of creatures, the Elves. Perhaps the greatest people of all, though no one has ever fully realized it. But the tale of the Elven people must wait for another time; suffice to say that they were always there in the great forests of the Westland, though the other races seldom encountered them at this stage of history.

"Now we shall see how much you know of the history of the Northland, my young friend. Today, it

is a land inhabited by almost no one other than the
Trolls, a barren and forbidding country where few
people of any race care to travel, let alone settle. The
Trolls, of course, are bred to survive there. Today,
Men live in the warmth and comfort of the Southland's
mild climate and green lands. They have forgotten
that once the Northland, too, was settled by creatures
of all the races, not only the Trolls in the mountain
regions, but Men, Dwarfs, and Gnomes· in the
lowlands and forests. This was in the years when all
the races were just beginning to rebuild a new
civilization with new ideas, new laws, and many new
cultures. It was a very promising future, but Men
today have forgotten that those times ever existed—
forgotten that they are more than a beaten race trying
to live apart from those who defeated them and
crippled their pride. There was no division of
countries then. It was an earth reborn, where each race
was being given a second chance at building a world.
Of course, they did not realize the significance of the
opportunity. They were too concerned with holding
what they considered theirs and building their own
private little worlds. Each race was certain that it was
destined to be the dominant power in the years
ahead—gathered together like a pack of angry rats
guarding a stale, sorry piece of cheese. And Man, oh,
yes, in all his glory, was groveling and snapping at the
chance just like the others. Did you know that, Shea?"

The Valeman shook his head slowly, unable to
believe that what he was hearing could be the truth.
He had been told that Man had been a persecuted
people ever since the Great Wars, fighting to keep
alive his dignity and honor, to protect the little land
that was his in the face of complete savagery on the
part of the other races. Man had never been the
oppressor in these battles; always he was the oppres-
sed. Allanon smiled grimly, his lips curling with
mocking satisfaction as he saw the effect of his words.

"You didn't realize that it was this way, I see. No matter—it will be the least of the surprises I have in store for you. Man has never been the great people he has fancied himself. In those days Men fought like the rest, although I will concede that perhaps they had a higher sense of honor and a clearer purpose to rebuild than some of the others, and they were slightly more civilized." He twisted the word meaningfully as he spoke it, lacing it with undisguised sarcasm. "But all this commentary has little to do with the main point of our discussion, which I hope to make clear to you shortly.

"It was about this same time, when the races had discovered one another and were fighting for dominance, that the Druid Council first opened the halls of Paranor in the lower Northland. History is rather vague about the origins and purposes of the Druids, though it is believed they were a group of highly knowledgeable men from all the races, skilled in many of the lost arts of the old world. They were philosophers and visionaries, students of the arts and science all at once, but more than this, they were the teachers of the races. They were the givers of power—the power of new knowledge in the ways of life. They were led by a man named Galaphile, a historian and philosopher like myself, who called the greatest men of the land together to form a council to establish peace and order. He relied on their learning to hold sway over the races, their ability to give knowledge to gain the people's confidence.

"The Druids were a very powerful force during those years and the plan of Galaphile seemed to be working as anticipated. But as time passed, it became apparent that some of the members of the Council had powers far surpassing those of the others, powers that had lain dormant and gathered strength in a few phenomenal, genius minds. It would be difficult to describe those powers to you without taking quite some time—more time than we have available to us. What is important for our purposes is to recognize that some among the Council who possessed the very greatest minds became convinced that they were destined to shape the future of the races. In the end, they broke from the Council to form their own group and for some time disappeared and were forgotten.

"About one hundred and fifty years later, there occurred a terrible civil war within the race of Man, which eventually widened into the First War of the Races, as the historians named it. Its cause was uncertain even then, and has now almost been forgotten. In simple terms, a small sector of the race of Man revolted against the teachings of the Council and formed a very powerful and highly trained army. The proclaimed purpose of the uprising was the subjugation of the rest of Man under a central rule for the betterment of the race and the furthering of its pride as a people. Eventually, almost all segments of the race rallied to the new cause and war was begun upon the other races, ostensibly to accomplish this new goal. The central figure behind the war was a man called Brona—an archaic Gnome term for 'Master.' It was said that he was the leader of the Druids of the first Council who had broken away and disappeared into the Northland. No reliable source ever reported seeing him or talking with him, and in the end it was concluded that Brona was merely a name, a fictitious character. The revolt, if you care to call it such, was finally crushed by the combined power of the Druids and the other allied races. Did you know of this, Shea?"

The Valeman nodded and smiled slightly.

"I have heard of the Druid Council, of its purposes and work—all ancient history since the Council died out long ago. I have heard of the First War of the Races, though not in the same way as you tell it. Prejudiced, I believe you would call my version. The war was a bitter lesson for Man."

Allanon waited patiently and did not speak as Shea paused to reflect on his own knowledge of the past before continuing.

"I know that the survivors of our race fled south after the war was over and have remained there ever since, rebuilding again the homes and cities lost, trying to create life rather than destroy it. You seem to think of it as an isolation born of fear. But I believe it was and still is the best way to live. Central governments have always been the greatest danger to mankind. Now there are none—small communities are the new rule of life. Some things are better left alone by everyone."

The tall man laughed, a deep mirthless chuckle that made Shea feel suddenly foolish.

"You know so little, though what you say is true enough. Truisms, my young friend, are the useless children of hindsight. Well, I don't propose to argue with you now on the fine points of social reform, let alone political activism. That will have to wait until another time. Tell me what you know of the creature called Brona. Perhaps . . . no, wait a moment. Someone is coming."

The words were scarcely out of his mouth before the stocky figure of Flick appeared around the corner of the inn. The Valeman stopped abruptly as he saw Allanon and hesitated until Shea waved to him. He came over slowly and remained standing, his eyes on the dark face as the big man smiled slowly down at him, the familiar enigmatic twist at the corners of his mouth.

"I was just wondering where you had gone," Flick began, speaking to his brother, "and didn't mean to interrupt . . ."

"You are not interrupting anything," Shea replied quickly. But Allanon seemed to disagree.

"This conversation was for your ears alone," he declared flatly. "If your brother chooses to stay, he will have decided his own fate in the days to come. I would strongly suggest that he not remain to hear the rest of our discussion, but forget that we ever talked. Still, it is his own choice."

The brothers looked at each other, unable to believe that the tall man was serious. But his grim face indicated that he was not joking, and for a moment both men hesitated, reluctant to say anything. Finally Flick spoke.

"I have no idea what you're talking about, but Shea and I are brothers and what happens to one must happen to both. If he's in any trouble, I should share it with him—it's my own choice, I'm sure."

Shea stared at him in amazement. He had never heard Flick sound more positive about anything in his entire life. He felt proud of his brother and smiled up at him gratefully. Flick winked back quickly and sat down, not looking at Allanon. The tall traveler stroked his small, dark beard with a lean hand and smiled quite unexpectedly.

"Indeed, the choice is your own, and you have proven yourself a brother by your words. But it is deeds that make the difference. You may regret the choice in the days to come. . . ."

He trailed off, lost in thought as he studied the bowed head of Flick for several long moments before turning to Shea.

"Well, I cannot begin my story again just for your brother. He will have to follow as best he can. Now tell me what you know of Brona."

Shea thought silently for a few minutes and then shrugged.

"I really don't know much of anything about him. He was a myth, as you said, the fictional leader of the uprising in the First War of the Races. He was supposed to have been a Druid who left the Council and used his own evil power to master the minds of his followers. Historically, he was never seen, never captured, or killed in the final battle. He never existed."

"Historically accurate, I'm sure," muttered Allanon. "What do you know of him in connection with the Second War of the Races?"

Shea smiled briefly at the question.

"Well, legend has it that he was the central force behind that war also, but it turned out to be just another myth. He was supposed to be the same creature who had organized the armies of Man in the first war, except in this one he was called the Warlock Lord—the evil counterpart to the Druid Bremen. I believe Bremen was supposed to have killed him in the second war, however. But all that was only fantasy."

Flick hastened to nod his agreement, but Allanon said nothing. Shea waited for some form of confirmation, openly amused by the whole subject.

"Where is all this talk taking us anyway?" he asked after a moment.

Allanon glanced down at him sharply, cocking one dark eyebrow in wonder.

"Your patience is remarkably limited, Shea. After all, we have just covered in a matter of minutes the history of a thousand years. However, if you think you can restrain yourself for a few moments longer, I believe I can promise you that your question will be answered."

Shea nodded, feeling no little mortification at the reprimand. It was not the words themselves that hurt; it was the way Allanon said them—with that mocking smile and ill-concealed sarcasm. The Valeman regained his composure quickly, though, and shrugged his willingness to allow the historian to continue at his own pace.

"Very well," the other acknowledged. "I shall try to complete our discussion quickly. What we have spoken of up to this point has been background history to what I will tell you now—the reason why I came to find you. I recall to your memory the events of the Second War of the Races—the most recent war in the new history of Man, fought less than five hundred years ago in the Northland. Man had no part in this war; Man was the defeated race of the first, living deep in the heart of the Southland, a few small communities trying hard to survive the threat of total extinction. This was a war of the great races—the Elven people and the Dwarfs fighting against the power of the savage Rock Trolls and the cunning Gnomes.

"After the completion of the First War of the Races, the known world partitioned into the existing four lands, and the races were at peace for quite a long time. During this period, the power and influence of the Druid Council diminished greatly as the apparent need for its assistance seemed to have ceased. It is only fair to add that the Druids had grown lax in their attention to the races, and over a period of years the new members lost sight of the Council's purposes and turned away from the peoples' problems to more personal concerns, leading a more isolated existence of study and meditation. The Elven people were the most powerful race, but confined themselves to their isolated homeland deep in the west where they were content to remain in relative isolation—a mistake they were to regret deeply. The other peoples scattered and developed into smaller, less unified societies, primarily in the Eastland, though some groups did settle in parts of the Westland and Northland in the border countries.

"The Second War of the Races began when a huge army of Trolls came down out of the Charnal Mountains and seized all of the Northland, including the Druid fortress at Paranor. The Druids had been betrayed from within by several of their own people who had been won over by promises and offers from the enemy commander, who at this time was unknown. The remaining Druids, except for a very few who escaped or were away, were captured and thrown into the dungeons of the Keep and never seen again. Those who had escaped the fate of their brothers scattered about the four lands and went into hiding. The Troll army immediately moved against the Dwarf people in the Eastland with the obvious intent of crushing all resistance as quickly as possible. But the Dwarfs gathered deep within the huge forests of the Anar, which only they know well enough to survive in for any length of time, and there held firm against the advances of the Troll armies despite the aid being given by a few of the Gnome tribes who had joined the invasion force. The Dwarf King, Raybur, recorded in his own peoples' history whom he had discovered the real enemy to be—the rebel Druid, Brona."

"How could the Dwarf King believe this?" Shea interjected quickly. "If it were true, the Warlock Lord would be over five hundred years old! At any rate, I should think that some ambitious mystic must have suggested the idea to the king with the thought of reviving an old, outdated myth—perhaps to better his own position in the court or something."

"That is a possibility," Allanon conceded. "But let me continue the story. After long months of fighting, the Trolls were evidently led to believe that the Dwarfs had been beaten, so they turned their war legions to the west and began to march against the powerful Elven kingdom. But during the months the Trolls had battled the Dwarf people, the few Druids who had escaped from Paranor had been assembled by the famous mystic Bremen, an old and highly esteemed elder of the Council. He led them to the Elven kingdom in the Westland to warn the people there of this new threat and to prepare for the almost certain invasion of the Northlanders. The Elven King in that year was Jerle Shannara—the greatest of all the Elven kings, perhaps, with the exception of Eventine. Bremen warned the King of the probable assault on his lands, and the Elven ruler quickly prepared his armies before the advancing Troll hordes had reached their borders. I'm sure that you know your history well enough to remember what happened when the battle was fought, Shea, but I want you to pay attention to the particulars of what I tell you next.''

Both Shea and an excited Flick nodded.

''The Druid Bremen gave to Jerle Shannara a special sword for the battle against the Trolls. Whoever held the sword was supposed to be invincible—even against the awesome power of the Warlock Lord. When the Troll legions entered the Valley of Rhenn in the borderlands of the Elven kingdom, they were attacked and trapped by the armies of the Elven people fighting from higher ground and were badly beaten in a two-day, pitched battle. The Elves were led by the Druids and Jerle Shannara, who carried the great sword given him by Bremen. They fought together against the Troll armies, who were said to have had the added might of beings from the spirit world under the domination of the Warlock Lord. But the courage of the Elven King and the power of the fabulous sword overwhelmed the spirit creatures and destroyed them. When the remainder of the Troll army attempted to escape back to the safety of the Northland across the Plains of Streleheim, it was caught between the pursuing army of Elves and an army of Dwarfs approaching from the Eastland. There was a terrible battle fought in which the Troll army was destroyed almost to the last man. During the battle, Bremen disappeared while in combat at the side of the Elven King, facing the Warlock Lord himself. It was recorded that both Druid and Warlock were lost in the fighting and neither was ever seen again. Not even the bodies were found.

''Jerle Shannara carried the famous sword given him until his death some years later. His son gave the weapon to the Druid Council at Paranor, where the blade was set in a huge block of Tre-Stone and placed in a vault in the Druid's Keep. I'm sure you are quite familiar with the legend of the sword and what it

stands for, what it means to all the races. The great sword rests today at Paranor just as it has for five hundred years. Have I been sufficiently lucid in my narration, Valemen?''

Flick nodded in dumbfounded wonder, still caught up in the excitement of the history. But Shea suddenly decided that he had heard enough. Nothing that Allanon had told them of the history of the races was fact—not if he was to believe what he had been taught by his own people since he was a child. The big man had simply related to them a childhood fantasy that had been passed down through the ages from parents to small children. He had listened patiently to everything Allanon had falsely represented to be the truth about the races, humoring him out of respect for his reputation. But the entire tale of the sword was ridiculous, and Shea was through being played for a fool.

''What has all this got to do with your coming to Shady Vale?'' he persisted, a faint smile betraying his disgust. ''We've heard all about a battle that took place some five hundred years ago—a battle that did not even concern Man, but Trolls and Elves and Dwarfs and goodness knows what else, as you tell it. Did you say there were spirits or something? I'm sorry if I sound incredulous, but I find this whole tale a little hard to swallow. The story of the Sword of Jerle Shannara is well known to all the races, but it's only fiction, not fact—a glorified story of heroism created to stir up a sense of loyalty and duty in the races that have a part in its history. But the legend of Shannara is a tale for children that adults must outgrow as they accept the responsibilities of manhood. Why did you waste time relating this fairy tale when all I want is a simple answer to a simple question? Why are you looking for . . . me?''

Shea stopped short as he saw Allanon's dark features tighten and grow black with anger, the great brows knitting over sudden pinpoints of light in the deep shadows that hid the eyes. The tall man seemed to be fighting to contain some terrible fury within, and for a moment it appeared to Shea that he was about to be strangled by the huge hands that locked before his face as the man glared in open rage. Flick moved back hastily and tripped over his own feet in the process, fear welling up inside.

"Fool . . . you fool," rasped the giant in barely controlled fury. "You know so little . . . children! What does the race of Man know of truth—where has Man been but hiding, creeping in terror under piteous shelters in the deepest regions of the Southland like frightened rabbits? You dare to tell me that I speak of fairy tales—you, who have never known strife, safe here in your precious Vale! I came to find the bloodline of kings, but I have found a little boy who hides himself in falsehoods. You are nothing but a child!"

Flick was fervently wishing he could sink into the ground beneath his feet or perhaps simply vanish, when to his utter astonishment he saw Shea leap to his feet before the tall man, his lean features flushed in fury and his hands knotted into fists as he braced himself. The Valeman was so overcome with anger that he could not speak, and stood before his accuser, shaking with rage and humiliation. But Allanon was not impressed and his deep voice sounded again.

"Hold, Shea. Do not be a greater fool! Pay attention to what I tell you now. All that I told you has come down through the ages as legend and was so told to the race of Man. But the time for fairy tales is ended. What I have told you is not legend; it is the truth. The sword is real; it rests today at Paranor. But most important of all, the Warlock Lord is real. He lives today and the Skull Kingdom is his domain!"

Shea started, suddenly realizing that the man was not deliberately lying after all—that he did not believe this to be a fairy tale. He relaxed and sat down slowly, his gaze still riveted on the dark face. Abruptly he recalled the historian's words.

"You said king . . . you were looking for a king . . .?"

"What is the legend of the Sword of Shannara, Shea? What does the inscription carved into the block of Tre-Stone read?"

Shea was dumbfounded, unable to recall any legend at all.

"I don't know . . . I can't remember what it said. Something about the next time . . ."

"A son!" spoke up Flick suddenly from the other side. "When the Warlock Lord appeared again in the Northland, a son of the House of Shannara would come forth to take up the Sword against him. That was the legend!"

Shea looked over at his brother, remembering then what the inscription was supposed to read. He looked back at Allanon, who was watching him intently.

"How does this concern me?" he asked quickly. "I'm not a son of the House of Shannara—I'm not even Elven. I'm a half-blood, not an Elf, not a king. Eventine is the heir to the House of Shannara. Are you telling me that I'm a lost son—a missing heir? I don't believe it!"

He looked quickly to Flick for support, but his brother appeared to be completely lost, staring in bewilderment at the face of Allanon. The dark man spoke quietly.

"You do have Elven blood in you, Shea, and you are not the true son of Curzad Ohmsford. That you must know. And Eventine is not directly of the blood of Shannara."

"I have always known that I was an adopted son," the Valeman admitted, "but surely I could not have come from . . . Flick, tell him!"

But his brother just stared at him in astonishment, unable to frame an answer to the question. Shea stopped speaking abruptly, shaking his head in disbelief. Allanon nodded.

"You are a son of the House of Shannara—a half son only, however, and far removed from the direct line of descent that can be traced down through the last five hundred years. I knew you as a child, Shea, before you were taken into the Ohmsford household as their own son. Your father was Elven—a very fine man. Your mother was of the race of Man. They both died when you were still very young, and you were given to Curzad Ohmsford to raise as his own son. But you are a son of Jerle Shannara, albeit a distant son and not of pure Elven blood."

Shea nodded absently at the tall man's explanation, confused and still suspicious. Flick was looking at his brother as if he had never seen him before.

"What does all this mean?" he asked Allanon eagerly.

"What I have told you is known also to the Lord of Darkness, though he does not yet know where you live or who you are. But his emissaries will find you sooner or later, and when they do, you will be destroyed."

Shea's head jerked up, and he looked at Flick fearfully, remembering the tale of the huge shadow seen near the lip of the Vale. His brother, too, felt a sudden chill, recalling that awful feeling of terror.

"But why?" asked Shea quickly. "What have I done to deserve that?"

"You must understand many things, Shea, before you can understand the answer to that question," replied Allanon, "and I have not the time to explain them all now. You must believe me when I tell you that you are descended from Jerle Shannara, that you are of Elven blood, and that the Ohmsfords are a foster family to you. You were not the only son of the House of Shannara, but you are the only son who survives today. The others were Elven, and they were easily found and destroyed. That is what prevented the Dark Lord from finding you for so long—he was unaware that there was a half son alive in the Southland. The Elven kin he knew of from the first.

"But know this, Shea. The power of the Sword is unlimited—it is the one great fear with which Brona lives, the one power he may not withstand. The legend of the Sword is a powerful amulet in the hands of the races, and Brona means to put an end to the legend. He will do this by destroying the entire house of Shannara, so that no son will come forth to draw the Sword against him."

"But I did not even know of the Sword," protested Shea. "I did not even know who I was, or anything about the Northland or about . . ."

"It does not matter!" cut in Allanon sharply. "If you are dead, there can be no doubt about you."

His voice died away in a weary murmur, and he turned to look again at the distant mountaintops beyond the fringe of tall elms. Shea lay back slowly on the soft grass, staring at the pale blue of the late winter sky laced with small, soft wisps of white cloud that drifted from the tall hills. For a few pleasant moments the presence of Allanon and the threat of death were submerged in the sleepy warmth of the afternoon sun and the fresh smell of the lofty trees towering over him. He closed his eyes and thought of his life in the Vale, of the plans that he had made with Flick, of their hopes for the future. They would all go up in smoke if what he had been told were true. He lay quietly considering these things, and finally sat up, his arms braced behind him.

"I'm not sure what to think," he began slowly. "There are so many questions I have to ask you. I feel confused by the whole idea of being someone other than an Ohmsford—someone threatened with death at the hands of a . . . a myth. What do you suggest that I do?"

Allanon smiled warmly for the first time.

"For the moment, do nothing. There is no immediate danger to you. Think about what I have told you and we will speak further of the implications another time. I shall be glad to answer all your questions then. But do not talk about this to anyone else, not even your father. Act as if this conversation had never taken place until we have a chance to work out the problems further."

The young men looked at each other and nodded in agreement, though it would be difficult to pretend that nothing had happened. Allanon rose silently, stretching his tall frame to relieve cramped muscles. The brothers rose with him and stood quietly as he looked down at them.

"Legends and myths that did not exist in yesterday's world will exist in tomorrow's. Things of evil, ruthless and cunning, after lying dormant for centuries, will now awaken. The shadow of the Warlock Lord begins to fall across the four lands."

He trailed off abruptly.

"I did not mean to be harsh with you," he smiled gently, quite unexpectedly, "but if this is the worst thing that happens in the days to come, you should be glad indeed. You are faced with a very real threat, not a fairy tale that can be laughed away. Nothing about any of this will be fair to you. You will learn much about life that you will not like."

He paused, a tall gray shadow against the green of the distant hills, his robes gathered carefully about his gaunt frame. One great hand reached over to grip firmly Shea's lean shoulder, and for an instant bound them together as one person. Then he turned away and was gone.

III

Allanon's plan for further discussions at the inn did not work out. He left the brothers sitting in hushed conversation behind the inn and returned to his room. Shea and Flick finally went back to their chores and shortly thereafter were dispatched on an errand by their father that took them out of the Vale to the north end of the valley. It was dark by the time they returned, and they hastened to the dining room, hoping to question the historian further, but he did not appear. They ate dinner hurriedly, unable to speak to each other about the afternoon while their father was present. After eating, they waited almost an hour, but still he did not appear and eventually, long after their father had departed for the kitchen, they decided to go to Allanon's room. Flick was reluctant to go looking for the dark stranger, especially after his meeting with him on the Vale road the previous night. But Shea was so insistent that at last his brother agreed to go along, hoping that there might be safety in numbers.

When they reached his room, they found the door unlocked and the tall wanderer gone. The room looked as if no one had even used it recently. They made a hasty search of the inn and the surrounding premises, but Allanon was not to be found. At last they were forced to conclude that for some unknown reason he had departed from Shady Vale. Shea was openly angered that Allanon had left without even a parting word, yet at the same time he began to experience a growing apprehension that he was no longer under the historian's protective wing. Flick, on the other hand, was just as happy that the man was gone. As he sat with Shea in the tall, hard-backed chairs before the fire in the big lounge room of the inn, he tried to assure his brother that everything was working out for the best. He had never completely believed the historian's wild tale of the Northland wars and the Sword of Shannara, he argued, and even if some of it were true, certainly the part about Shea's lineage and the threat from Brona was completely exaggerated—a ridiculous fairy tale.

Shea listened in silence to Flick's muddled rationalization of the possibilities, offering only an occasional nod of acquiescence, his own thoughts concentrated on deciding what he should do next. He had serious doubts about the credibility of Allanon's tale. After all, what purpose did the historian have in coming to him in the first place? He had appeared conveniently, it seemed, to tell Shea about his strange background, and to warn him that he was in danger, then had disappeared without a word about his own interest in this business. How could Shea be sure that Allanon had not come on some hidden purpose of his own, hoping to use the Valeman as his cat's-paw? There were too many questions that he didn't have the answers to.

Eventually, Flick grew tired of offering advice to the silent Shea and finally ceased to speak of the matter, slumping down in his chair and gazing resignedly into the crackling fire. Shea continued to ponder the details of Allanon's story, trying to decide what he should do now. But after an hour of quiet deliberation, he threw up his hands in disgust, feeling as confused as before. Stalking out of the lounge, he headed for his own room, the faithful Flick close behind. Neither felt inclined to discuss it further. Upon reaching their small bedroom in the east wing, Shea dropped into a chair in moody silence. Flick collapsed heavily on the bed and stared disinterestedly at the ceiling.

The twin candles on the small bedside table cast a dim glow over the large room, and Flick soon found himself on the verge of drifting off to sleep. He hastily jerked awake and, stretching his hands above his head, encountered a long piece of folded paper which had partially slipped down between the mattress and headboard. Curiously, he brought it around in front of his eyes and saw that it was addressed to Shea.

"What's this?" he muttered and tossed it across to his prostrate brother.

Shea ripped open the sealed paper and hurriedly scanned it. He had scarcely begun before he let out a low whistle and leaped to his feet. Flick sat up quickly, realizing who must have left the note.

"It's from Allanon," Shea confirmed his brother's suspicion. "Listen to this, Flick:

I have no time to find you and explain matters further. Something of the greatest importance has occurred, and I must leave immediately—perhaps even now I am too late. You must trust me and believe what I told you, even though I will not be able to return to the valley.

You will not long be safe in Shady Vale, and you must be prepared to flee quickly. Should your safety be threatened, you will find shelter at Culhaven in the forests of the Anar. I will send a friend to guide you. Place your trust in Balinor.

Speak with no one of our meeting. The danger to you is extreme. In the pocket of your maroon travel cloak, I have placed a small pouch which contains three Elfstones. They will provide you with guidance and protection when nothing else can. Be cautioned—they are for Shea alone and to be used only when all else fails.

The sign of the Skull will be your warning to flee. May luck be with you, my young friend, until we meet again.

Shea looked excitedly at his brother, but the suspicious Flick shook his head in disbelief and frowned deeply.

"I don't trust him. Whatever is he talking about anyway—Skulls and Elfstones? I never even heard of a place called Culhaven, and the Anar forests are miles from here—days and days. I don't like it."

"The stones!" Shea exclaimed, and leaped for the traveling cloak which hung in the long corner closet. He rummaged through his clothes for several minutes while Flick watched anxiously, then carefully stepped back with a small leather pouch balanced gently in his right hand. He held it up and tested its weight, displaying it to his brother, and then hurried back to the bed and sat down. A moment later he had the drawstrings open and was emptying the contents of the pouch into his open palm. Three dark blue stones tumbled out, each the size of an average pebble, finely cut and glowing brightly in the faint candlelight. The brothers peered curiously at the stones, half expecting that they would immediately do something wondrous. But nothing happened. They lay motionless in Shea's palm, shimmering like small blue stars snatched from the night, so clear that it was almost possible to see through them, as if they were merely tinted glass. Finally, after Flick had summoned enough courage to touch one, Shea dropped them back into the pouch and stuffed it into his shirt pocket.

"Well, he was right about the stones," ventured Shea a moment later.

"Maybe yes, maybe no—maybe they're not Elfstones," suggested Flick suspiciously. "How do you know—ever see one? What about the rest of the letter? I never heard of anyone named Balinor and I never heard of Culhaven. We ought to forget the whole business—especially that we ever saw Allanon."

Shea nodded doubtfully, unable to answer his brother's questions.

"Why should we worry now? All we have to do is to keep our eyes open for the sign of the Skull, whatever that may be, or for Allanon's friend to appear. Maybe nothing will happen after all."

Flick continued to voice his distrust of the letter and its author for several minutes more before losing interest. Both brothers were weary and decided to call it a night. As the candles were extinguished, Shea's last act was to place the pouch carefully beneath his pillow where he could feel its small bulk pressing against the side of his face. No matter what Flick might think, he had resolved to keep the stones close at hand in the days ahead.

The next day, it began to rain. Huge, towering black clouds rolled in from the north quite suddenly and settled over the entire valley, blotting out all traces of sun and sky as they released torrents of shattering rain which swept through the tiny hamlet with unbeliev- able ferocity. All work in the fields came to an abrupt halt and travel to and from the valley ceased entirely—first for one, then two, and finally three complete days. The downpour was a tremendous spectacle of blinding streaks of lightning lacing the darkly clouded sky and deeply rolling thunder breaking over the valley with earthshaking blasts that followed one after the other and died into slower, more ominous distant rumblings from somewhere beyond the blackness to the north. For the entire three days it rained, and the Vale people began to grow fearful that flash floods from the hills all about them would wash down with devastating effect on their small homes and unprotected fields. The men gathered daily in the Ohmsford inn and chatted worriedly over their mugs of beer, casting apprehen- sive glances at the sheets of rain falling steadily beyond the dripping windows. The Ohmsford brothers watched in silence, listening to the conversation and scanning the worried faces of the anxious Valemen huddled together in small groups about the crowded lounge. At first they held out hope that the storm would pass over, but after three days there was still little sign of clearing in the weather.

Near midday on the fourth day, the rain lessened from a steady downpour to a muggy drizzle mixed with heavy fog and a sticky, humid heat that left everyone thoroughly disgruntled and uncomfortable. The crowd at the inn began to thin out as the men left to return to their jobs, and soon Shea and Flick were occupied with repairs and general cleaning chores. The storm had smashed shutters and torn the wooden shingles from the roof, scattering them all about the surrounding premises. Large leaks had developed in the roof and walls of the inn wings, and the small tool shed in the rear of the Ohmsford property had been all but flattened by a falling elm, uprooted by the force of the storm. The young men spent several days patching up leaks, repairing the roof, and replacing lost or broken shingles and shutters. It was tedious work, and time dragged by slowly.

After ten days, the rains ceased altogether, the huge clouds rolled on, and the dark sky cleared and brightened into a friendly light blue streaked with trailing white clouds. The expected floods did not come, and as the Valemen returned to their fields, the warm sun reappeared and the land of the valley began to dry from soggy mud to solid earth, spattered here and there by small puddles of murky water that sat defiantly upon an always thirsty land. Eventually even the puddles disappeared and the valley was as it had been—the fury of the passing storm only a dim memory.

Shea and Flick, in the process of rebuilding the smashed tool shed, their other repair work on the inn complete, heard snatches of conversation from Vale-

men and inn guests about the heavy rain. No one
could ever remember a storm of such ferocity at that
particular time of the year in the Vale. It was
equivalent to a winter windstorm, the kind that caught
unsuspecting travelers in the great mountains to the
north and swept them from the passes and the cliff
trails, never to be seen again. Its sudden appearance
caused everyone in the hamlet to pause and reflect
once again on the continuing rumors of strange
happenings far to the North.

The brothers paid close attention to such talks, but
they learned nothing of interest. Often they spoke
quietly together about Allanon and the strange tale he
had told them of Shea's heritage. A pragmatic Flick
had long since dismissed the whole business as either
foolishness or a bad joke. Shea listened tolerantly,
though he was less willing than his brother to shrug
the matter off. Yet while he was unwilling to dismiss
the tale, he was at the same time unable to accept it. He
felt there was too much still hidden from him, too
much about Allanon that neither Flick nor he knew.
Until he had all the facts, he was content to let the
matter lie. He kept the pouch containing the Elfstones
close to him at all times. While Flick mumbled on,
usually several times a day, about his foolishness in
carrying the stones and believing that anything
Allanon had told them was true, Shea carefully
watched all strangers passing through the Vale,
eagerly perusing their belongings for any sign of a
Skull marking. But as time passed, he observed
nothing and eventually felt obliged to scratch the
whole matter off as an experience in the fine art of
gullibility.

Nothing occurred to change Shea's mind on the
matter until one afternoon more than three weeks
after Allanon's abrupt departure. The brothers had
been out all day cutting shingles for the inn roof, and it
was almost evening by the time they returned. Their

father was sitting in his favorite seat at the long kitchen counter when they entered, his broad face bent over a steaming plate of food. He greeted his sons with a wave of his hand.

"A letter came for you while you were gone, Shea," he informed them, holding out a long, white folded sheet of paper. "It's marked Leah."

Shea let out an exclamation of surprise and reached eagerly for the letter. Flick groaned audibly.

"I knew it, I knew it; it was too good to be true," he muttered. "The biggest wastrel in the entire Southland has decided it's time we suffered some more. Tear up the letter, Shea."

But Shea had already opened the sealed sheet of paper and was scanning its contents, totally disregarding Flick's comments. The latter shrugged in disgust and collapsed on a stool next to his father, who had returned to his evening meal.

"He wants to know where we've been hiding," laughed Shea. "He wants us to come see him as soon as we can."

"Oh, sure," muttered Flick. "He's probably in trouble and needs someone to blame it on. Why don't we just jump off the nearest cliff? You remember what happened the last time Menion Leah invited us to visit? We were lost in the Black Oaks for days and nearly devoured by wolves! I'll never forget that little adventure. The Shades will get me before I accept another invitation from him!"

His brother laughed and clapped an arm around Flick's broad shoulders.

"You are envious because Menion is the son of kings and able to live any way he chooses."

"A kingdom the size of a puddle," was the quick retort. "And royal blood is cheap stuff these days. Look at your own . . ."

He caught himself and clamped his mouth shut quickly. Both shot hurried glances at their father, but he apparently hadn't heard and was still absorbed in eating. Flick shrugged apologetically, and Shea smiled at his brother encouragingly.

"There's a man in the inn looking for you, Shea," Curzad Ohmsford announced suddenly, looking up at him. "He mentioned that tall stranger that was here several weeks back when he asked for you. Never seen him before in the Vale. He's out in the main lounge now."

Flick stood up slowly, fear gripping at him. Shea was momentarily caught off balance by the message, but motioned hurriedly to his brother, who was about to speak. If this new stranger were an enemy, he had to find out quickly. He clutched at his shirt pocket, reassuring himself that the Elfstones were still there.

"What does the man look like?" he asked quickly, unable to think of any other way of finding out about the Skull mark.

"Can't really say, son," was the muffled reply as his father continued to chew on his dinner, face bent to the plate. "He's wrapped in a long green forest cloak. Just rode in this afternoon—beautiful horse. He was very anxious to find you. Better go see what he wants right away."

"Did you see any markings?" asked the exasperated Flick.

His father stopped chewing and looked up with a puzzled frown.

"What are you talking about? Would you be satisfied if I presented you with a chalk drawing? What's wrong with you anyway?"

"It's nothing, really," interjected Shea quickly. "Flick was just wondering if . . . if the man looked anything like Allanon . . . You remember?"

"Oh, yes," his father smiled knowingly, as Flick suppressed a swallow of relief. "No, I didn't notice any real similarity, though this man is big, too. I did see a long scar running down the right cheek— probably from a knife cut."

Shea nodded his thanks and quickly pulled Flick after him as he moved out to the hallway and started for the main lounge. They hurried to the wide double doors and halted breathlessly. Cautiously, Shea pushed one door open a crack and peered into the crowded lounge area. For a moment he saw nothing but the ordinary faces of the usual customers and average Vale travelers, but a moment later he started back, and let the door swing shut as he faced the anxious Flick.

"He's out there, near the front corner by the fireplace. I can't tell who he is or what he looks like from here; he's wrapped in the green cloak, just as Father said. We've got to get closer."

"Out there?" gasped Flick. "Have you lost your mind? He would spot you in a second if he knows who he's looking for."

"Then you go," Shea ordered firmly. "Make some pretense of putting logs on the fire and get a quick look at him. See if he bears the markings of a Skull."

Flick's eyes went wide, and he turned to escape, but Shea caught his arm and pulled him back, forcibly shoving him through the doors into the lounge and quickly ducking back out of sight. A moment later he opened one door a crack and peeped out to see what was happening. He saw Flick move uncertainly across the room to the fireplace and begin to poke the glowing embers idly, finally adding another log from the woodbox. The Valeman was taking his time, apparently trying to get in a position where he could catch a glimpse of the man wrapped in the green cloak. The stranger was seated at a table several feet away from the fireplace, his back to Flick but turned slightly toward the door behind which Shea had concealed himself.

Suddenly, just as it appeared that Flick was ready to return, the stranger moved slightly in his seat and made a quick comment and Flick went stiff. Shea saw his brother turn toward the stranger and reply,

glancing hurriedly toward Shea's place of concealment. Shea slipped back further into the shadows of
the hall and let the door swing shut. Somehow, they
had given themselves away. As he pondered whether
to flee, Flick abruptly pushed through the double
doors, his face white with fear.

"He saw you at the door. The man has the eyes of a
hawk! He told me to bring you out."

Shea thought a moment and finally nodded
hopelessly. After all, where could they run to that they
wouldn't be found in a matter of minutes?

"Maybe he doesn't know everything," he
suggested hopefully. "Maybe he thinks we know
where Allanon has gone. Be careful what you tell him,
Flick."

He led the way through the wide, swinging doors
and across the lounge to the table where the stranger
sat. They stopped just behind him and waited, but
without turning, he beckoned them to seats around
the table with a sweep of his hand. They reluctantly
obeyed the unspoken command and the three sat in
silence for a few moments looking at one another. The
stranger was a big man with a broad frame, though he
did not have Allanon's height. The cloak covered all of
his body, and only his head was visible to them. His
features were rugged and strong, pleasant to the eye
except for the dark scar that ran from the outside tip of
the right eyebrow down across the cheek just above
the mouth. The eyes seemed curiously mild to Shea as
they studied the young Valemen, a hazel color that
hinted at a gentleness beneath the hard exterior. The
blond hair was cut short and lay scattered loosely
about the broad forehead and around the small ears.
As Shea viewed the stranger, he found it hard to
believe that this man could be the enemy Allanon had
warned might come to the valley. Even Flick seemed
relaxed in his presence.

"There is no time for games, Shea," the newcomer

spoke suddenly in a mild, but weary voice. "Your caution is well advised, but I am not a bearer of the Skull mark. I am a friend of Allanon. My name is Balinor. My father is Ruhl Buckhannah, the King of Callahorn."

The brothers recognized his name instantly, but Shea was not taking any chances.

"How do I know that you are who you say you are?" he demanded quickly.

The stranger smiled.

"The same way I know you, Shea. By the three Elfstones you carry in your shirt pocket—the Elfstones given you by Allanon."

The Valeman's startled nod was barely perceptible. Only someone sent by the tall historian could have known about the stones. He leaned forward cautiously.

"What has happened to Allanon?"

"I cannot be sure," the big man replied softly. "I have not seen nor heard from him in over two weeks. When I left him, he was traveling to Paranor. There was rumor of an attack against the Keep; he was afraid for the safety of the Sword. He sent me here to protect you. I would have reached you sooner, but I was delayed by the weather—and by those who sought to follow me to you."

He paused and looked directly at Shea, his hazel eyes suddenly hard as they bored into the young man.

"Allanon revealed to you your true identity and told you of the danger you would someday face. Whether you believed him or not is of no consequence now. The time has come—you must flee the valley immediately."

"Just pick up and leave?" exclaimed the astounded Shea. "I can't do that!"

"You can and you will if you wish to stay alive. The bearers of the Skull suspect you are in the valley. In a day, perhaps two, they will find you and that will be the end if you are still here. You must leave now. Travel quickly and lightly; stick with trails you know and the shelter of the forest when you can. If you are forced to travel in the open, travel only by day when their power is weaker. Allanon has told you where you are to go, but you must trust to your own resourcefulness to get you there."

The astonished Shea stared at the speaker for a moment and then turned to Flick who was speechless at this new turn of events. How could the man expect him just to pack up and run? It was ridiculous.

"I have to leave," the stranger rose suddenly, his great cloak wrapped tightly about his broad frame. "I would take you with me if I could, but I have been followed. Those who seek to destroy you will expect me to give you away eventually. I will serve you better as a decoy; perhaps they will follow me still farther, and I will be able to give you a chance to slip away without being noticed. I will ride south for a while, and then swing back toward Culhaven. We will meet again there. Remember what I said. Do not linger in the Vale—flee now, tonight! Do as Allanon has said and guard the Elfstones with care. They are a powerful weapon."

Shea and Flick rose with him and shook the extended hand, noticing for the first time that the exposed arm was covered with gleaming chain mail. Without further comment, Balinor moved swiftly across the room and disappeared through the front door into the night.

"Well, now what?" Flick asked as he collapsed back into his seat.

"How should I know?" replied Shea wearily. "I'm no fortune-teller. I don't have the vaguest idea if what he told us was the truth any more than what Allanon said! If he is right, and I have an uneasy suspicion that there is at least some truth in what he says, then for the sake of everyone concerned, I've got to get out of the valley. If someone is after me, we cannot be sure that others, like yourself and Father, won't be hurt if I stay."

He gazed despondently across the room, hopelessly entangled by the tales he had been told, unable to decide what his best move would be. Flick watched him silently, knowing he could not help, but sharing his brother's confusion and worry. Finally, he leaned across and put his hand on Shea's shoulder.

"I'm going with you," he announced softly.

Shea looked around at him, plainly startled.

"I can't have you doing that. Father would never understand. Besides, I may not be going anywhere."

"Remember what Allanon said—I'm in this with you," Flick insisted stubbornly. "Besides, you're my brother. I can't let you go alone."

Shea stared at him wonderingly, then nodded and smiled his thanks.

"We'll talk about it later. At any rate, I can't leave until I decide where I am going and what I will need—if I even go. I've got to leave some kind of note for Father—I can't just walk out, despite what Allanon and Balinor think."

They left the table and retired to the kitchen for dinner. The remainder of the evening was spent restlessly wandering about the lounge and kitchen area, with several side trips to the sleeping quarters, where Shea rifled through his personal belongings, absently noting what he owned and setting aside stray items. Flick followed him about silently, unwilling to leave him alone, inwardly afraid that his brother might decide to depart for Culhaven without telling him. He watched Shea push clothing and camping equipment into a leather pack, and when he asked his brother why he was packing, he was told that this was just a precaution in case he did have to flee suddenly. Shea assured him that he would not leave without telling him, but the reassurance did not make Flick any easier in his mind, and he watched Shea all the more closely.

It was pitch black when Shea was awakened by the hand on his arm. He had been sleeping lightly, and the cold touch woke him instantly, his heart pounding. He struggled wildly, unable to see anything in the darkness, and his free hand reached out to clutch his unseen attacker. A quick hiss reached his ears, and abruptly he recognized Flick's broad features vaguely outlined in the dim light of the cloud-masked stars and a small crescent moon that shone through the curtained window. The fear eased, replaced by sudden relief at the familiar sight of his brother.

"Flick! You scared . . ."

His relief was cut short as Flick's strong hand clamped over his open mouth and the warning hush sounded again. In the gloom, Shea could see deep lines of fear in his brother's face, the pale skin drawn tightly with the cold of the night air. He started up, but the strong arms holding him grasped him tighter and drew his face near tightly clenched lips.

"Don't speak," the whisper sounded in his ears, the voice trembling with terror. "The window—quietly!"

The hands loosened their grip and gently, hastily pulled him from the bed and down along the floor until both brothers were crouched breathlessly on the hard wooden planks deep within the shadows of the room. Then Shea crawled with Flick toward the partly open window, still crouching, not daring even to breathe. When they reached the wall, Flick pulled Shea to one side of the window with hands that were now shaking.

"Shea, by the building—look!"

Frightened beyond description, he raised his head to the windowsill and carefully peered over the wooden frame into the blackness beyond. He saw the creature almost immediately—a huge, terrible black shape, stooped in a half-crouch as it crawled, dragging itself slowly through the shadows of the buildings across from the inn, its humped back covered by a cloak that rose and billowed softly as something beneath pushed and beat against it. The hideous rasping sound of its breathing was plainly audible even from that distance, and its feet emitted a curious scraping sound as it moved across the dark earth. Shea clutched the sill tightly, his eyes locked on the approaching creature, and in the instant before he ducked below the open window, he caught a clear glimpse of a silver pendant fashioned in the shape of a gleaming Skull.

IV

Shea collapsed wordlessly next to the dark form of his brother, and they sat huddled together in the blackness. They could hear the creature moving, the scraping sound growing louder as the seconds passed, and they were certain they had heeded Balinor's warning too late. They waited, not daring to speak, even to breathe as they listened. Shea wanted to run, torn by the knowledge that the thing outside would kill him if it found him now, but afraid that if he moved he would be heard and caught on the spot. Flick sat rigid beside him, shaking in the cool of the blowing night wind that whipped the curtains about the window frame.

Suddenly they heard the sharp bark of a dog sound again and again, then shift to a hoarse growl of mingled fear and hatred. Cautiously, the brothers raised their heads above the windowsill and looked out, squinting in the dim light. The creature bearing the Skull mark was crouched against the wall of the building directly across from their window. Some ten feet away was a huge wolf dog, a hunter for one of the Valemen, its white fangs bared and gleaming as it watched the intruder. The two shapes faced each other in the night shadows, the creature breathing in the same slow, rasping wheeze, and the dog growling low and snapping the air before it, inching forward in a half crouch. Then, with a snarl of rage, the big wolf dog sprang at the intruder, its jaws open and reaching for the blackened head. But the dog was caught suddenly in midair by a clawlike limb that whipped out from beneath the billowing cloak and jerked at the throat of the hapless animal, smashing him lifeless to the ground. It happened in an instant, and the brothers were so astonished that they almost forgot to duck down again to avoid being seen. A moment later, they heard the strange scraping sound as the creature began to drag itself along the wall of the adjacent building—but the sound grew fainter and appeared to be moving away from the inn.

Long moments passed as the brothers waited breathlessly in the shadows of the room, shivering uncontrollably. The night grew quiet around them, and they strained their ears for some indication of the creature's position. Eventually Shea worked up enough courage to peer once more over the edge of the windowsill into the darkness beyond. By the time he ducked down again, the frightened Flick was ready to scramble for the nearest exit, but a hurried shake of Shea's head assured him that the creature was gone. He hastened back from the window to the warmth of his bed, but caught himself halfway under the covers as he saw Shea begin to dress hurriedly in the darkness. He tried to speak, but Shea raised a finger to his lips. Immediately, Flick began pulling on his own clothes. Whatever Shea had in mind, wherever he was going, Flick was determined to follow. When they were both dressed, Shea pulled his brother close and whispered softly in his ear.

"Everyone in the Vale will be in danger as long as we remain. We must get out tonight—now! Are you determined to go with me?"

Flick nodded emphatically and Shea continued.

"We'll go to the kitchen and pack some food to take with us—just enough to get by on for a few days. I'll leave a note for Father there."

Without another word, Shea picked up his small bundle of clothing from inside the closet and disappeared noiselessly into the pitch-black hallway that led to the kitchen. Flick hurriedly followed, groping his way from the bedroom behind his brother. It was impossible to see anything in the hallway, and it took them several minutes to feel their way along the walls and around the corners to the broad kitchen door. Once inside the kitchen, Shea lit a candle and motioned Flick over to the foodstuffs while he scratched out a note for his father on a small sheet of paper and stuck it under a beer mug. Flick finished his job in a few minutes and came back to his brother, who quickly extinguished the small candle and moved to the rear door where he stopped and turned.

"Once we're outside, don't speak at all. Just follow me closely."

Flick nodded doubtfully, more than a little concerned about what might be waiting for them beyond the closed door—waiting to rip out their throats as it had the wolf dog's a few minutes before. But there was no time for hesitation now, and Shea swung open the wooden door carefully and peered out into a brightly moonlit yard bordered by heavy clumps of trees. A moment later, he motioned to Flick, and they stepped cautiously from the building into the cool night air, closing the door carefully behind them. It was brighter outside the building in the soft light of the moon and stars, and a quick glance revealed that no one was around. There was only an hour or two until dawn, when the hamlet would begin to awaken. The brothers paused next to the building as they listened for any sound that would warn of danger. Hearing nothing, Shea led the way across the yard, and they disappeared into the shadows of an adjacent hedgerow, Flick casting a last, wistful glance back at the home he might never see again.

Shea silently picked his way through the buildings

of the hamlet. The Valeman knew that the Skull Bearer was uncertain who he was or it would have caught them at the inn. But it was a good bet that the creature suspected he lived within the valley and so had come into the sleeping town of Shady Vale on an exploratory search for the missing half son of the house of Shannara. Shea ran back over the plan of travel he had hastily formed at the inn. If the enemy had discovered where he was, as Balinor had warned, then all the possible escape routes would be watched. Moreover, once they discovered he was missing, they would lose no time in tracking him down. He had to assume that there was more than one of these frightening creatures, and that they were probably watching the whole valley. Flick and he would have to seize the advantage of stealth and secrecy to get out of the valley and the country immediately surrounding it within the next day or so. That meant a forced march with very few hours' sleep. This would be tough enough, but the real problem was where they would flee. They had to have supplies within a few days, and a trip to the Anar would take weeks. The country beyond the Vale was unfamiliar to both brothers, except for a few well-traveled roads and hamlets that the Skull Bearers would certainly be watching. Given their present situation, it would be impossible to do much more than choose a general direction. But which way should they run? Which direction would the prowling creatures least expect them to go?

Shea considered the alternatives carefully, though he had already made up his mind. West of the Vale was open country except for a few villages, and if they went that way, they would be moving away from the Anar. If they traveled south, they would eventually reach the comparative safety of the larger Southland cities of Pia and Zolomach where there were friends and relatives. But this was the logical route for them to take to escape the Skull Bearers, and the creatures would be carefully watching roads south of the Vale. Moreover, the country beyond the Duln forests was broad and open, offering little cover for the fugitives and promising a long journey to the cities, during which they could be easily caught and killed. North of the Vale and beyond the Duln was a broad sweep of land encompassing the Rappahalladran River and the huge Rainbow Lake and miles of wild, unsettled land that led eventually to the kingdom of Callahorn. The Skull Bearers would have passed through it on their journey from the Northland. They would in all likelihood know it far better than the brothers and would be watching it closely if they suspected that Balinor had come to the Vale from Tyrsis.

The Anar lay northeast of the Vale, through miles and miles of the roughest, most treacherous country in all of the vast Southland. This direct route was the most dangerous one, but the one in which the enemy searchers would least expect him to run. It wound through murky forests, treacherous lowlands, hidden swamps and any number of unknown dangers that claimed the lives of unwary travelers every year. But there was something else that lay east of the Duln forests that even the Skull Bearers could not know about—the safety of the highlands of Leah. There the brothers could seek the aid of Menion Leah, Shea's close friend and, despite Flick's fears, the one person who might be able to show them a way through the dangerous lands that led to the Anar. For Shea, this seemed the only reasonable alternative.

The brothers reached the southeast edge of town and halted breathlessly beside an old woodshed, their backs to the coarse boarding. Shea looked cautiously ahead. He had no idea where the prowling Skull creature might be by this time. Everything was still hazy in the clouded moonglow of the dying night. Somewhere off to their left, several dogs barked furiously, and scattered lights appeared in the windows of nearby houses as sleepy owners peered out curiously into the blackness. Dawn was only a little over an hour away, and Shea knew they would have to chance discovery and run for the lip of the valley and the concealment of the Duln forests. If they were still in the valley when it became light, the creature searching for them would see them climbing the slopes of the open hills, and they would be caught trying to escape.

Shea clapped Flick on the back and nodded, breaking into a slow jog as he moved away from the shelter of the Vale homes into the heavy clumps of trees and brush that dotted the valley floor. The night was silent around them except for the muffled sound of their feet padding on the long grass that was wet with early-morning dew. Leafy branches whipped at them as they ran, slapping their unprotected hands and faces in small, stinging swipes that left the dew clinging to their skin. They ran hurriedly for the gentle, brush-covered eastern slope of the Vale, dodging in and out of the heavy oaks and hickories, bounding over loose nut shells and fallen twigs that were scattered beneath the wide limbs ribbing the deep sky overhead. They reached the slope and scampered up the open grassland as quickly as their legs would carry them, not pausing to look back or even down in the darkness, but only ahead to the ground that rushed by them in sudden bounds and disappeared into the Vale behind. Slipping frequently on the damp grass, they reached the lip of the Vale, where their eyes were greeted with a clear view of the great valley walls to the east, studded with shapeless boulders and sparse shrubbery, looming like a great barrier to the world beyond.

Shea was in excellent physical condition, and his light form flew across the uneven ground, moving agilely among the clumps of brush and small boulders that blocked his path. Flick followed doggedly, the stout muscles of his legs working tirelessly to keep his heavier frame even with the fleet figure ahead. Only once did he risk a quick glance back, and his eyes recorded only a blurred image of mingled treetops that rose above the now hidden town and were outlined in the glow of the fading night stars and clouded moon. He watched Shea run ahead of him, bounding lightly over small rises and scattered rocks, apparently intent on reaching the small wooded area near the base of the eastern slope of the valley about a mile ahead. Flick's legs were beginning to tire, but his fear of the creature somewhere behind them kept him from lagging. He wondered what would happen to them now, fugitives from the only home they had known, pursued by an incredibly vicious enemy that would snuff out their lives like a small candle's flame if they were caught. Where could they go that they wouldn't be found? For the first time since Allanon had departed, Flick wished fervently that the mysterious wanderer would reappear.

The minutes passed quickly and the small woods ahead grew closer as the brothers ran on wearily, silently through the chill night. No sound reached their ears; nothing moved in the land ahead. It was as if they were the only living creatures in a vast arena, alone except for the watchful stars winking solemnly overhead in quiet contentment. The sky was growing lighter as the night came to a wistful close, and the vast audience above slowly disappeared one by one into the morning light. The brothers ran on, oblivious to everything but the need to run faster—to escape being caught in the revealing light of a sunrise only minutes away.

When the runners finally reached the wooded area, they collapsed breathlessly on the twig-covered ground beneath a stand of tall hickories, their ears and hearts pounding wildly from the strain of running. They lay motionless for several minutes, breathing heavily in the stillness. Then Shea dragged himself to his feet and looked back in the direction of the Vale. Nothing was moving either on the ground or in the air, and it appeared the brothers had gotten this far without being spotted. But they were still not out of the valley. Shea reached over and forcibly dragged Flick to his feet, pulling him along as he moved through the trees and began to ascend the steep valley slope. Flick followed wordlessly, no longer even thinking, but concentrating his ebbing willpower on putting one foot before the other.

The eastern slope was rugged and treacherous, its surface a mass of boulders, fallen trees, prickly shrubbery, and uneven ground that made the climb a long and difficult one. Shea set the pace, moving over the large obstacles as fast as he could, while Flick followed in his footsteps. The young men scrambled and clawed their way up the slope. The sky began to grow lighter and the stars disappeared altogether. Ahead of them, above the lip of the valley, the sun was sending its first faint glow into the night sky with tinges of orange and yellow that reflected vaguely the outline of the distant horizon. Shea was beginning to tire, his breath coming in short gulps, as he stumbled on. Behind him, Flick forced himself to crawl, dragging his exhausted body after his lighter brother, his hands and forearms scratched and cut by the sharp brush and rocks. The climb seemed endless. They moved at a snail's pace over the rugged terrain, the fear of discovery alone forcing their tired legs to continue moving. If they were caught here, in the open, after all this effort . . .

Suddenly, as they reached the three-quarter mark of their climb, Flick cried out sharply in warning and fell gasping against the slope. Shea whirled around fearfully, his eyes instantly catching sight of the huge black object that rose slowly from the distant Vale—climbing like a great bird into the dimness of the morning sunrise in widening spirals. The Valeman dropped flat amid the rocks and brush, motioning his fallen brother to crawl quickly from sight and praying the creature had not seen them. They lay unmoving on the mountainside as the awesome Bearer of the Skull rose higher, its circle of flight growing wider, its path carrying it closer to where the brothers lay. A sudden chilling cry burst from the creature, draining from the two young men the last faint hope that they might escape. They were gripped by the same unexplainable feeling of horror that had immobilized Flick, hidden in the brush with Allanon beneath the huge black shadow. Only this time there was no place to hide. Their terror grew rapidly into the beginning stages of hysteria as the creature soared directly toward them, and in that fleeting moment they knew they were going to die. But in the next instant, the black hunter wheeled in flight and glided north in an unaltering line, receding steadily into the horizon until it was lost from their sight.

The Valemen lay petrified, buried in the scant brush and loose rock for endless minutes, afraid the creature would come winging back to destroy them the minute they tried to move. But when the terrible, unreasoning fear had ebbed away, they climbed shakenly to their feet and in exhausted silence resumed the weary climb to the summit of the valley. It was a short distance to the lip of the rugged slope, and they hurried across the small, open field beyond to the concealment of the Duln forest. Within minutes they were lost in the great trees, and the rising morning sun in its first glow found the land that stretched back to the Vale country silent and empty.

The young men slowed their pace as they entered the Duln, and finally Flick, who still had no idea where they were going, called ahead to Shea.

"Why are we going this way?" he demanded. His own voice sounded strange after the long silence. "Where are we going anyway?"

"Where Allanon told us—to the Anar. Our best chance is to go the way the Skull Bearers least expect us to take. So we'll go east to the Black Oaks and from there travel northward and hope we can find help along the way."

"Wait a minute!" exclaimed Flick in sudden understanding. "What you mean is we're going east through Leah and hope Menion can help us. Are you completely out of your mind? Why don't we just give ourselves up to that creature? It would be quicker that way!"

Shea threw up his hands and turned wearily to face his brother.

"We do not have any other choice! Menion Leah is the only one we can turn to for help. He's familiar with the country beyond Leah. He may know a way through the Black Oaks."

"Oh, sure," nodded Flick gloomily. "Are you forgetting that he got us lost there last time? I wouldn't trust him any farther than I could throw him, and I doubt I can even lift him!"

"We have no choice," repeated Shea. "You didn't have to come on this trip, you know."

He trailed off suddenly and turned away.

"Sorry I lost my temper. But we have to do this thing my way, Flick."

He started walking again in dejected silence, and Flick followed glumly, shaking his head in disapproval. The whole idea of running away was a bad one to begin with, even though they knew that monstrous creature was prowling the valley. But the idea of going to Menion Leah was worse still. That cocky idler would lead them right into a trap if he didn't get them lost first. Menion was only interested in Menion, the great adventurer, off on another wild expedition. The whole idea of asking him for help was ridiculous.

Flick was admittedly biased. He disapproved of Menion Leah and everything he represented—he had done so from the time they met five years earlier. The only son of a family that for centuries had governed the little highland kingdom, Menion had spent his entire life involving himself in one wild escapade after another. He had never worked for a living and, as far as Flick could tell, he had never done anything worthwhile. He spent most of his time hunting or fighting, pursuits that hardworking Valemen would consider idle recreation. His attitude was equally disturbing. Nothing about his life, his family, his homeland, or his country seemed to be of very great importance to him. The highlander seemed to float through life very much the same as a cloud in an empty sky, touching nothing, leaving no trace of his passing. It was this careless approach to life that had nearly got them killed a year ago in the Black Oaks. Yet Shea was drawn to him; and in his flippant way, the highlander seemed to respond with genuine affection. But Flick had never been convinced that it was a friendship he could depend upon, and now his brother proposed to entrust their lives to the care of a man who did not know the first thing about responsibility.

He mulled the situation over in his mind, wondering what could be done to prevent the inevitable. Finally he concluded that his best chance would be to watch Menion carefully and warn Shea as tactfully as possible when he suspected they were doing the wrong thing. If he alienated his brother now, he would have no chance later of contradicting the bad advice of the Prince of Leah.

It was late afternoon when the travelers finally reached the banks of the great Rappahalladran. Shea led the way down the riverbank for about a mile until they reached a place where the far bank cut toward them and the channel began to narrow considerably. Here they stopped and gazed across at the forests beyond. The sun would be down in another hour or so, and Shea did not want to be caught on the near bank that night. He would feel safer with the water between him and any pursuers. He explained to Flick, who agreed, and they set about making a small raft, using their hand axes and hunting knives. The raft was necessarily a small one, its only purpose to carry their packs and clothing. There was no time to construct a raft large enough to carry them, and they would have to swim the river, towing their belongings. They completed the job in short order and, stripping off their packs and clothes, tied them down in the middle of the raft and slipped into the chilling waters of the Rappahalladran. The current was swift, but not dangerous at this time of the year, the spring thaws having already passed. The only problem was finding a suitable landing place along the high banks of the other shore after their swim was over. As it happened, the current swept them along for almost half a mile as they struggled to tow the cumbersome raft, and when the crossing had finally been completed, they found they were close to a narrow inlet in the far bank that offered an easy landing. They scrambled out of the cold water, shivering in the early evening air, and after dragging the raft out after them, quickly dried off and dressed again. The entire operation had taken a little over an hour, and the sun was now lost from sight beneath the tall trees, leaving only a dull reddish glow to light the afternoon sky in the minutes that remained before darkness.

The brothers were not ready to quit for the day, but Shea suggested they sleep for several hours to regain their strength and then resume their journey during the night to avoid any chance of being seen. The sheltered inlet seemed safe, so they curled up in their blankets beneath a great elm and were quickly asleep. It was not until midnight that Shea woke Flick with a light shake, and they quickly packed their gear and prepared to resume their hike through the Duln. At one point, Shea thought he heard something prowling about on the far shore and hurriedly warned Flick. They listened in silence for long minutes, but could detect nothing moving in the blackness of the massive trees and finally concluded that Shea must have been mistaken. Flick was quick to point out that nothing could be heard anyway above the sound of the surging river, and the Skull creature was probably still looking for them in the Vale. His confidence had been bolstered considerably by the mistaken belief that they had momentarily outsmarted any pursuers.

They walked until sunrise, trying to move in an easterly direction, but unable to see much from their low vantage point. Any clear view of the stars was masked by a confusing network of heavy branches and rustling leaves interlocked above them. When they finally stopped, they were still not clear of the Duln, and had no idea how much farther they had to walk before reaching the borders of Leah. Shea was relieved at the appearance of the sun rising directly before them; they were still heading in the right direction. Finding a clearing nestled in a cluster of great elms sheltered on three sides by thick brush, the young men tossed down their packs and quickly fell asleep, totally exhausted from the strenuous flight. It was late afternoon before they awoke and began preparations for the night walk. Unwilling to start a fire that might attract attention, they contented themselves with munching on dried beef and raw vegetables, completing the meal with some fruit and a little water. As they ate, Flick again brought up the question of their destination.

"Shea," he began cautiously, "I don't want to dwell on the matter, but are you sure this is the best way to go? I mean, even if Menion wants to help, we could easily get lost in the swamps and hills that lie beyond the Black Oaks and never get out."

Shea nodded slowly and then shrugged.

"It's that or go farther north where there is less cover and the country would be unfamiliar even to Menion. Do you think we have a better choice?"

"I suppose not," Flick responded unhappily. "But I keep thinking about what Allanon told us—you remember, about not telling anyone and being careful about trusting anyone. He was very definite about that."

"Let's not start that again," Shea flared up. "Allanon isn't here and the decision is mine. I don't see how we can hope to reach the Anar forests without the help of Menion. Besides, he's always been a good friend, and he's one of the finest swordsmen I have ever seen. We'll need his experience if we're forced to stand and fight."

"Which we are certain to have to do with him along," Flick finished pointedly. "Besides, what chance do we have against something like that Skull creature? Why, it would tear us to bits!"

"Don't be so gloomy," Shea laughed, "we aren't dead yet. Don't forget—we have the protection of the Elfstones."

Flick was not particularly convinced by this argument, but felt that the whole matter was best left alone for the present. He had to admit that Menion Leah would be a good man to have around in a fight, but at the same time he was not sure whose side the unpredictable fellow would decide to take. Shea trusted Menion because of the instinctive liking he had developed for the flashy adventurer during trips to Leah with his father over the past few years. But Flick did not feel that his brother was entirely rational in his analysis of the Prince of Leah. Leah was one of the few remaining monarchies in the Southland, and Shea was an outspoken advocate of decentralized government, an opponent of absolute power. Nevertheless, he claimed friendship with the heir to a monarch's throne—facts which in Flick's opinion seemed entirely inconsistent. Either you believed in something or you didn't—you couldn't have it both ways and be honest with yourself.

The meal was finished in silence as the first shadows of evening began to appear. The sun had long since disappeared from view and its soft golden rays had changed slowly to a deep red mingling with the green boughs of the giant trees. The brothers quickly packed their few belongings and began the slow, steady march eastward, their backs to the fading daylight. The woods were unusually still, even for early evening, and the wary Valemen walked in uneasy silence through the shrouded gloom of the forest night, the moon a distant beacon that appeared only at brief intervals through the dark boughs overhead. Flick was particularly disturbed by the unnatural silence of the Duln, a silence strange to this huge forest—but uncomfortably familiar to the stocky Valeman. Occasionally, they would pause in the darkness, listening to the deep stillness; then, hearing nothing, they would quickly resume the tiring march, searching for a break in the forest ahead that would open onto the highlands beyond. Flick hated the oppressive silence and once began whistling softly to himself, but was quickly stilled by a warning motion from Shea.

Sometime during the early hours of the morning, the brothers reached the edge of the Duln and broke through into the shrub-covered grasslands that stretched beyond for miles to the highlands of Leah. The morning sun was still several hours away, so the travelers continued their journey eastward. Both felt immensely relieved to be free of the Duln, away from the stifling closeness of its monstrous trees and from the unpleasant silence. They may have been safer within the concealing shadows of the forest, but they felt considerably better equipped to deal with any danger that threatened them on the open grasslands. They even began to speak again in low voices as they walked. About an hour before daybreak, they reached a small, brush-covered vale where they stopped to eat and rest. They were already able to see the dimly lighted highlands of Leah to the east, a journey of yet another day. Shea estimated that if they started walking again at sundown they could easily reach their destination before another sunrise. Then everything would depend on Menion Leah. With this unspoken thought in mind, he quickly fell asleep.

Only minutes passed and they were awake again. It was not something moving that caused them to rise in sudden apprehension, but a deathly quiet that settled ominously over the grasslands. Immediately they sensed the unmistakable presence of another being. The feeling struck them at the same instant and both came to their feet with a start, without a word, their drawn daggers gleaming in the faint light as they looked cautiously about their small cover. Nothing moved. Shea motioned his brother to follow as he crawled up the shrub-covered slope of the little vale to where they could view the land beyond. They lay motionless in the brush, peering into the early-morning gloom, eyes straining to detect what lurked beyond. They did not question the fact that something was out there. There was no need—both had known the feeling before the window of their bedroom. Now they waited, scarcely daring to breathe, wondering if the creature had found them at last, praying they had been careful enough to conceal their movements. It seemed impossible that they could be found now after their hard struggle to escape, wrong that death should come when the safety of Leah was only a few hours away.

Then with a sudden rush of wind and leaves, the black shape of the Skull Bearer rose soundlessly from a long line of scrub trees far to their left. Its dim bulk seemed to rise and hang heavily above the earth for several long moments, as if unable to move, silhouet-

ted against the faint light of an approaching dawn. The
brothers lay flat against the edge of the rise, as silent as
the brush about them, waiting for the creature to
move. How it had tracked them this far—if indeed it
had—they could only guess. Perhaps it was only blind
luck that had brought them all together in this single,
empty piece of grassland, but the fact remained that
the Valemen were hunted creatures and their death
had become a very real possibility. The creature hung
motionless against the sky a moment longer, then
slowly, sluggishly, the great wings reaching outward,
it began to move toward their place of concealment.
Flick gave an audible gasp of dismay and sank farther
back into the surrounding brush, his face ashen in the
gray light, his hand gripping Shea's slim arm. But
before reaching them, while still several hundred feet
away, the creature dropped into a small grove of trees
and was momentarily lost from sight. The brothers
peered desperately in the hazy light, unable to see
their pursuer.

"Now," Shea's determined voice whispered ur-
gently in his brother's ear, "while the creature can't
see us. Make for that line of brush ahead!"

Flick did not need to be told twice. Once the black
monster finished with the trees that now occupied its
attention, the next stop would be their hiding place.
The Valeman scampered fearfully from his place of
concealment, half running, half crawling along the
wet morning grass, his touseled head jerking in quick
glimpses over his shoulder, expecting the Skull Bearer
to rise any moment from the grove and spy him.
Behind him ran Shea, his lithe body bent close to the
ground as he darted across the open grassland,
zigzagging his way silently behind his brother's stocky
figure. They reached the brush without mishap, and
then Shea remembered they had forgotten their
packs—the packs that now lay at the bottom of the
vale they had just left. The creature could not miss

seeing them and, when it did, the chase would be over and there would be no more guessing which way they had gone. Shea felt his stomach sink. How could they have been so stupid? He grabbed Flick's shoulder in desperation, but his brother had also realized their error and slumped heavily to the ground. Shea knew he had to go back for the telltale packs, even if he were seen—there was no other choice. But even as he rose hesitantly, the black shape of the hunter appeared, hanging motionless in the brightening sky. The chance was gone.

Once again they were saved by the coming of dawn. As the Skull Bearer poised silently above the grasslands, the golden rim of the morning sun broke from its resting place in the eastern hills and sent its first emissaries of the approaching day shooting forth to light the land and sky in their warm glow. The sunlight broke over the dark bulk of the night creature, and seeing that its time was gone, it rose abruptly into the sky, wheeling about the land in great, widening circles. It screamed its deathlike cry with chilling hatred, freezing for one quick moment all the gentle sounds of morning; then turning north, it flew swiftly from sight. A moment later it was gone, and two grateful, unbelieving Valemen were left staring mutely into the distant, empty morning sky.

V

By late afternoon of that same day, the Valemen had reached the highland city of Leah. The stone and mortar walls that bounded the city were a welcome haven to the weary travelers, even though the bright afternoon sun made their hot, dull-gray mass appear as unfriendly as low-heated iron. The very size and bulk of the walls were repugnant to the Valemen, who preferred the freedom of the more pregnable forest lands surrounding their own home, but exhaustion quickly pushed any dislikes aside and they passed without hesitating through the west gates and into the narrow streets of the city. It was a busy hour, with people pushing and shoving their way past the small shops and markets that lined the entryway to the walled city and ran inward toward Menion's home, a stately old mansion screened by trees and hedges that bordered carefully manicured lawns and fragrant gardens. Leah appeared to be a great metropolis to the men of Shady Vale, though it was in fact comparatively small when one considered the size of the great cities of the deep Southland or even the border city of Tyrsis. Leah was a city set apart from the rest of the world, and travelers passed through its gates only infrequently. It was self-contained, existing primarily to serve the needs of its own people. The monarchy that governed the land was the oldest in the Southland. It was the only law that its subjects knew—perhaps the only one they needed. Shea had never been convinced of this, though the highland people for the most part were content with the government and the way of life it provided.

As the Valemen maneuvered their way through the crowds, Shea found himself reflecting on his improbable friendship with Menion Leah. It would have to be termed improbable, he mused, because on the surface they seemed to have so little in common. Valeman and highlander, with backgrounds so completely dissimilar as to defy any meaningful comparison. Shea, the adopted son of an innkeeper, hard-headed, pragmatic, and raised in the tradition of the workingman. Menion, the only son of the royal house of Leah and heir to the throne, born into a life filled with responsibilities he pointedly ignored, possessed of a brash self-confidence that he tried to conceal with only moderate success, and blessed with an uncanny hunter's instinct that merited grudging respect even from so severe a critic as Flick. Their political philosophies were as unlike as their backgrounds. Shea was staunchly conservative, an advocate of the old ways, while Menion was convinced that the old ways had proved ineffective in dealing with the problems of the races.

Yet for all their differences, they had formed a friendship that evidenced mutual respect. Menion found his small friend to be anachronistic in his thinking at times, but he admired his conviction and determination. The Valeman, contrary to Flick's oft-expressed opinion, was not blinded to Menion's shortcomings, but he saw in the Prince of Leah something others were inclined to overlook—a strong, compelling sense of right and wrong.

At the present time, Menion Leah was pursuing life without any particular concern for the future. He traveled a good deal, he hunted the highland forests, but for the most part he seemed to spend his time finding new ways to get into trouble. His hard-earned expertise with the long bow and as a tracker achieved no useful purpose. On the contrary, it merely served to aggravate his father, who had repeatedly but unsuccessfully attempted to interest his son and only heir in the problems of governing his kingdom. One day, Menion would be a king, but Shea doubted that his lighthearted friend ever gave the possibility more than a passing thought. This was foolish, if somewhat expected. Menion's mother had died several years ago, shortly after Shea had first visited the highlands. Menion's father was not an old man, but the death of a king did not always come with age, and many former rulers of Leah had died suddenly and unexpectedly. If something unforeseen should befall his father, Menion would become king whether he was prepared or not. There would be some lessons learned then, Shea thought and smiled in spite of himself.

The Leah ancestral home was a wide, two-story stone building nestled peacefully amid a cluster of spreading hickories and small gardens. The grounds were screened away from the surrounding city by high shrubbery. A broad park lay directly across from a small walkway fronting the home, and as the Valemen crossed wearily to the front gates, children splashed playfully through a small pond at the hub of the park's several paths. The day was still warm, and people hurried past the travelers on their way to meet friends or to reach their homes and families. In the west, the late afternoon sky was deepening into a soft golden haze.

The tall iron gates were ajar, and the Valemen walked quickly toward the front door of the home, winding through the long stone walkway's high shrubbery and garden borders. They were still approaching the stone threshold at the front of the home, when the heavy oak door opened from within, and there, unexpectedly, was Menion Leah. Dressed in a multicolored cloak and vest of green and pale yellow, his lean, whiplike frame moved with the graceful ease of a cat. He was not a big man, though several inches taller than the Valemen, but he was broad through the shoulders and his long arms gave him a rangy look. He was on his way down a side path, but when he caught sight of the two ragged, dusty figures approaching along the main walk, he stopped short. A moment later his eyes went wide with surprise.

"Shea!" he exclaimed sharply. "What in the name of all . . . what happened to you?"

He rushed over quickly to his friend and gripped the slim hand warmly.

"Good to see you, Menion," Shea said with a smile.

The highlander stepped back a pace, and his gray eyes studied them shrewdly.

"I never expected that my letter would get results this quickly. . . ." He trailed off and studied the other's weary face. "It hasn't, has it? But don't tell me—I don't want to hear it. I'd rather assume for the sake of our friendship that you came just to visit me. And brought distrustful old Flick, too, I see. This is a surprise."

He grinned quickly past Shea at the scowling Flick, who nodded curtly.

"This wasn't my idea, you may be sure."

"I wish that our friendship alone were the reason for this visit." Shea sighed heavily. "I wish I didn't have to involve you in any of this, but I'm afraid that we're in serious trouble and you are the one person who might be able to help us."

Menion started to smile, then changed his mind quickly as he caught the mood reflected in the other's drawn face and nodded soberly.

"Nothing funny about this, is there? Well, a hot bath and some dinner are the first order of business. We can

discuss what brought you here later. Come on in. My
father's engaged on the border, but I'm at your
disposal."

Once inside, Menion directed the servants to take
charge of the Valemen, and they were led off to a
welcome bath and a change of clothes. An hour later,
the three friends gathered in the great hall for a dinner
that would ordinarily have fed twice their number, but
on this night barely satisfied them. As they ate, Shea
related to Menion the strange tale behind their flight
from Shady Vale. He described Flick's meeting with
the mysterious wanderer Allanon and the involved
story behind the Sword of Shannara. It was necessary,
despite Allanon's order of secrecy, if he must ask
Menion's help. He told of the coming of Balinor with
his terse warning, of their narrow escape from the
black Skull creature, and finally of their flight to the
highlands. Shea did all the talking. Flick was unwilling to enter into the conversation, resisting the
temptation he felt to elaborate on his own part in the
events of the past few weeks. He chose to keep quiet
because he was determined not to trust Menion. He
was convinced that it would be better for the Valemen
if at least one of them kept his guard up and his mouth
closed.

Menion Leah listened quietly to the long tale,
evincing no visible surprise until the part about Shea's
background, with which he appeared immeasurably
pleased. His lean brown face remained for the most
part an inscrutable mask, broken only by that
perpetual half smile and the small wrinkles at the
corners of the sharp gray eyes. He recognized quickly
enough why the Valemen had come to him. They
could never expect to make it from Leah through the
lowlands of Clete and from there through the Black
Oaks without assistance from someone who knew the
country—someone they could trust. Correction, Menion thought, smiling inwardly—someone Shea could

trust. He knew that Flick would never have agreed to come to Leah unless his brother had insisted. There had never been much of a friendship between Flick and himself. Still, they were both here, both willing to seek his help, whatever the reason, and he would never be able to refuse anything to Shea, even where there was risk to his own life.

Shea finished his story and waited patiently for Menion's response. The highlander seemed lost in thought, his eyes fixed on the half-filled glass of wine at his elbow. When he spoke, his voice was distant.

"The Sword of Shannara. I haven't heard that story in years—never really believed it was true. Now out of complete obscurity it reappears with my old friend Shea Ohmsford as the heir apparent. Or are you?" His eyes snapped up suddenly. "You could be a red herring, a decoy for these Northland creatures to chase and destroy. How can we be sure about Allanon? From the tale you've told me, he seems almost as dangerous as the things hunting you—perhaps even one of them."

Flick started noticeably at this suggestion, but Shea shook his head firmly.

"I can't bring myself to believe that. It doesn't make any sense."

"Maybe not," continued Menion slowly, inwardly musing over the prospect. "Could be I'm getting old and suspicious. Frankly, this whole story is pretty improbable. If it's true, you are fortunate to have gotten this far on your own. There are a great many tales of the Northland, of the evil that dwells in the wilderness above the Streleheim Plains—power, they say, beyond the understanding of any mortal being. . . ."

He trailed off for a moment, then sipped gingerly at his wine.

"The Sword of Shannara . . . just the possibility that the legend might be true is enough to . . ." He shook his head and grinned openly. "How can I deny myself the chance to find out? You'll need a guide to get you to the Anar, and I'm your man."

"I knew you would be." Shea reached over and gripped his hand in thanks. Flick groaned softly, but managed a feeble smile.

"Now then, let's see where we stand." Menion took charge quickly, and Flick went back to drinking wine. "What about these Elfstones? Let's have a look at them."

Shea quickly produced the small leather pouch and emptied the contents into his open palm. The three stones sparkled brightly in the torchlight, their blue glow deep and rich. Menion touched one gently and then picked it up.

"They are indeed beautiful," he acknowledged approvingly. "I don't know when I've seen their like. But how can they help us?"

"I don't know that yet," admitted the Valeman reluctantly. "I only know what Allanon told us—that the stones were only to be used in emergencies, and that they were very powerful."

"Well, I hope that he was right," snorted the other. "I would hate to discover the hard way that he was mistaken. But I suppose we'll have to live with that possibility."

He paused for a moment and watched as Shea placed the stones back in the pouch and tucked the leather container into his tunic front. When the Valeman looked up again, he was staring blankly into his wineglass.

"I do know something of the man called Balinor, Shea. He is a fine soldier—I doubt we could find his equal in the whole of the Southland. We might be better off to seek the aid of his father. You would be better protected by the soldiers of Callahorn than by the forest-dwelling Dwarfs of the Anar. I know the roads to Tyrsis, all of them safe. But almost any path to

the Anar will run directly through the Black Oaks—
not the safest place in the Southland, as you know."

"Allanon told us to go to the Anar," persisted Shea.
"He must have had a reason, and until I find him
again, I'm not taking any chances. Besides, Balinor
himself advised us to follow his instructions."

Menion shrugged.

"That's unfortunate, because even if we manage to
get through the Black Oaks, I really don't know much
about the land beyond. I'm told that it's relatively
unsettled country all the way to the Anar forests. The
inhabitants are mostly Southlanders and Dwarfs, who
should not prove dangerous to us. Culhaven is a small
Dwarf village on the Silver River in the lower Anar—I
don't think we'll have much trouble finding it, if we
get that far. First, we have to navigate the Lowlands of
Clete, which will be especially bad with the spring
thaws, and then the Black Oaks. That will be the most
dangerous part of the trip."

"Can't we find a way around . . .?" Shea asked
hopefully.

Menion poured himself another glass of wine and
passed the decanter to Flick who accepted it without
blinking.

"It would take weeks. North of Leah is the Rainbow
Lake. If we go that way, we have to circle the entire
lake to the north through the Runne Mountains. The
Black Oaks stretch south from the lake for a hundred
miles. If we try to go south and come north again on
the other side, it will take us at least two weeks—and
that's open country all the way. No cover at all. We
have to go east through the lowlands, then cut
through the oaks."

Flick frowned, recalling how on their last visit to
Leah, Menion had succeeded in losing them for
several days in the dreaded forest, where they were
menaced by wolves and ravaged by hunger. They had
barely escaped with their lives.

"Old Flick remembers the Black Oaks," laughed Menion as he caught the other's dark expression. "Well, Flick, this time we shall be better prepared. It's treacherous country, but no one knows it better than I do. And we aren't likely to be followed there. Still, we'll tell no one where we're going. Simply say that we are off for an extended hunting trip. My father has his own problems anyway—he won't even miss me. He's used to having me gone, even for weeks at a time."

He paused for a moment and looked to Shea to see if he had forgotten anything. The Valeman grinned at the highlander's undisguised enthusiasm.

"Menion, I knew we could count on you. It will be good to have you along."

Flick looked openly disgusted; and Menion, catching the look, could not allow the opportunity for a little fun at the other's expense to pass.

"I think we ought to talk for a minute about what's in this for me," he declared suddenly. "I mean, what do I get out of all this if I do guide you safely to Culhaven?"

"What do you get?" exclaimed Flick without thinking. "Why should you . . ."

"It's all right," the other interrupted quickly. "I had forgotten you, old Flick, but you don't need to worry; I don't intend to take anything from your share."

"What are you talking about, sly one?" raged Flick. "I did not mean ever to take anything . . ."

"That's enough!" Shea leaned forward, his face flushed. "This cannot continue if we are to travel together. Menion, you must cease your attempts to bait my brother into anger; and you, Flick, must put aside, once and for all, your pointless suspicions of Menion. We must have some faith in one another—and we must be friends!"

Menion looked down sheepishly, and Flick was biting his lip in disgust. Shea sat back quietly as the anger drained out of him.

"Well spoken," acknowledged Menion after a moment. "Flick, here is my hand on it. Let us make a temporary truce, at least—for Shea."

Flick looked at the extended hand and then slowly accepted it.

"Words come easily for you, Menion. I hope you mean them this time."

The highlander accepted the rebuke with a smile.

"A truce, Flick."

He released the Valeman's hand and drained his wineglass. He knew he had convinced Flick of nothing.

It was growing late now, and all three were eager to complete their plans and retire for the night. They quickly decided that they would leave early the following morning. Menion arranged to have them outfitted with light camping gear, including backpacks, hunting cloaks, provisions, and weapons. He produced a map of the country east of Leah, but it was poorly detailed because the lands were so little known. The Lowlands of Clete, which spread from the highlands eastward to the Black Oaks, was a dismal, treacherous moor—yet on the map, it was no more than a blank white area with the name written in. The Black Oaks stood out prominently, a dense mass of forest land running from the Rainbow Lake southward, standing like a great wall between Leah and the Anar. Menion discussed briefly with the Valemen his knowledge of the terrain and weather conditions at this time of the year. But like the map, his information was sketchy. Most of what the travelers would find could not be accurately anticipated, and the unexpected could be most dangerous.

By midnight, the three were in bed, their preparations for the journey to the Anar complete. In the room he was sharing with Flick, Shea lay back wearily in the softness of the bedding and studied for a moment the darkness beyond his open window. The night had clouded over, the sky a mass of heavy, rolling

blackness that settled ominously about the misty
highlands. Gone was the heat of the day, blown east
by the cooling night breezes, and throughout the
sleeping city there was a peaceful solitude. In the bed
next to him, Flick was already asleep, his breathing
heavy and regular. Shea watched him thoughtfully.
His own head was heavy and his body weary from the
struggle to reach Leah, yet he remained awake. He
was beginning to realize for the first time the truth
about his predicament. The flight to reach Menion was
only the first step in a journey that might very possibly
go on for years. Even if they managed to reach the
Anar safely, Shea knew that eventually they would be
forced to run again. The search to find them would
continue until the Warlock Lord was destroyed—or
Shea was dead. Until then, there would be no going
back to the Vale, to the home and father he had left,
and wherever they were, their safety would last only
until the winged hunters found them once again.

The truth was terrifying. In the silent darkness,
Shea Ohmsford was alone with his fear, and deep
within himself, he fought back against a rising knot of
terror. He took a long time finally to fall asleep.

It was a dull, sunless day that followed, a day damp
and chilling to human flesh and bone. Shea and his
two companions found it devoid of any warmth and
comfort as they journeyed eastward through the
misty highlands of Leah and began a slow descent
toward the cheerless climate of the lowlands beyond.
There was no talking among them as they hiked in
single file down the narrow footpaths which wound
tediously about gray, hulking boulders and clumps of
dying, formless brush. Menion led, his keen eyes
carefully picking out the often obscure traces of a trail,
his stride long and relaxed as he moved almost
gracefully over the gradually roughening terrain.
Across his lean back he carried a small pack to which

he had attached a great ash bow and arrows. In addition, beneath the pack and fastened to his body by a long leather strap was the ancient sword which his father had given him when he had reached the age of manhood—the sword which was the birthright of the Prince of Leah. Its cold, gray iron glimmered faintly in the dim light; and Shea, who followed several paces back, found himself wondering if it was at all like the fabled Sword of Shannara. His Elven eyebrows lifted quizzically as he tried to peer into the endless gloom of the land ahead. Nothing seemed alive. It was a dead land for dead things, and the living were trespassers here. Not a very stimulating idea; he grinned faintly to himself as he forced his mind to turn to other matters. Flick brought up the rear, his sturdy back bearing the bulk of the provisions that would have to sustain them until they were through the Lowlands of Clete and the forbidding Black Oaks. Once they had gotten that far—if they got that far—they would be forced to buy or trade for food from the few scattered inhabitants of the country beyond, or as a last resort, seek nourishment from the land itself, a prospect that Flick did not particularly relish. Although he felt somewhat more secure in his mind now that Menion was genuinely interested in helping them on this journey, he was nevertheless still unconvinced of the highlander's ability to do so. The events of their last trip were still fresh in his mind, and he wanted no part of another hair-raising experience like that one.

The first day wore on quickly as the three traveled past the boundaries of the kingdom of Leah and by nightfall had reached the fringes of the dismal Lowlands of Clete. They found shelter for the night in a small vale under the negligible protection of a few scruffy trees and some heavy brush. The dampness of the mist had soaked their clothing completely through, and the chill of the descending night left them shivering with cold. A brief attempt was made to start a fire in an effort to gain some small warmth and dryness, but the wood in the area was so thoroughly saturated with moisture that it was impossible to get it to burn. Eventually, they gave up on the fire and settled for some cold rations while wrapped in blankets which had carefully been waterproofed at the start of the journey. Little was said because no one felt much like talking beyond mumbling curses upon the general weather conditions. There was no sound from the darkness beyond where they sat huddled within the brush; it was a penetrating stillness that prodded the mind with sudden, unexpected apprehension, forcing it to listen in a frightened effort to catch some faint, reassuring rustle of life. But there was only the silence and the blackness, and not even the wisp of a brief wind touched their chilled faces as they lay quietly in the blankets. Eventually the weariness of the day's march stole over them, and one by one they dropped uneasily off to sleep.

The second and third day were unimaginably worse than the first. It rained the entire time—a slow, chilling drizzle that soaked first the clothing, then penetrated into the skin and bone, and finally reached the very nerve centers, so that the only feeling the weary body would permit was one of thorough, discomforting wetness. The air was damp and cold in the day, dropping off to a near freeze at night. Everything around the three travelers seemed totally beaten down by this lingering coldness; what little brush and small foliage could be seen was twisted and dying, formless clumps of wood and withered leaves that silently waited to crumble and disappear altogether. No human or animal lived here—even the smallest rodent would have been swallowed up and consumed by the clutching softness of an earth seeped through with the chilling dampness of long, sunless, lifeless days and nights. Nothing moved, nothing stirred as the three walked eastward through shapeless country where there was no trail, no hint that anyone or anything had ever passed that way before, or would ever do so again. The sun never appeared during their march, no faint trace of its direct rays flickering downward to show that somewhere beyond this dead, forgotten land was a world of life. Whether it was the perpetual mist or the heavy clouds or a combination of both that so completely blotted out the sky remained an unanswered question. Their only world was that cheerless, hateful gray land through which they walked.

By the fourth day, they began to despair. Even though there had been no further sign of the winged hunters of the Warlock Lord and it appeared that any pursuit had been abandoned, the possibility offered little solace as the hours dragged by and the silence grew deeper, the land more sullen. Even Menion's great spirit began to waver and doubt wormed its stealthy way into his usually confident mind. He began to wonder if they had lost the direction, if perhaps they had even traveled in a circle. He knew the land would never tell them, that once lost in this bleak country, they were lost forever. Shea and Flick felt the fear even more deeply. They knew nothing of the lowlands and lacked the hunter's skill and instinct that Menion possessed. They relied completely on him, but sensed that something was wrong even though the highlander had purposely kept silent about his own doubts so as not to worry them. The hours passed, and the cold and the wet and the hateful deadness of the land remained unchanged. They felt their last shred of confidence in one another and in themselves begin to slip slowly, agonizingly away. Finally, as the fifth day of the journey drew to a close and still the lowland bleakness stretched on with no visible sign of the desperately-sought-after Black Oaks, Shea wearily called a halt to the endless march and dropped heavily to the ground, his questioning eyes on the Prince of Leah.

Menion shrugged and looked absently at the misty

lowlands about them, his handsome face drawn with the chill of the air.

"I won't lie to you," he murmured. "I can't be sure that we have kept our sense of direction. We may have traveled in a circle; we may even be hopelessly lost."

Flick dropped his pack disgustedly and looked at his brother with his own special "I told you so" look. Shea glanced at him and turned hurriedly back to Menion.

"I can't believe we're completely lost! Isn't there any way we can get our bearings?"

"I'm open to suggestions." His friend smiled humorlessly, stretching as he, too, dropped his pack to the rough ground and sat down beside the brooding Flick. "What's the trouble, old Flick? Have I gotten you into it again?"

Flick glanced over at him angrily; but looking into the gray eyes, he quickly reconsidered his dislike of the man. There was genuine concern there, and even a trace of sadness at the thought that he had failed them. With rare affection, Flick reached over and placed a comforting hand on the other's shoulder, nodding silently. Suddenly, Shea leaped up and flung off his own pack, hastily rummaging through its contents.

"The stones can help us," he cried.

For a moment the other two looked blankly at him and then in sudden understanding rose expectantly to their feet. A moment later, Shea produced the small leather pouch with its precious contents. They all stared at the worn container in mute anticipation that the Elfstones would at last prove their value, that they would somehow aid them in escaping the wasteland of Clete. Eagerly Shea opened the drawstrings and carefully dropped the three small, blue stones into his upturned palm. They lay there twinkling dimly as the three watched and waited.

"Hold them up, Shea," urged Menion after a moment. "Perhaps they need the light."

The Valeman did as he was told, watching the blue

stones anxiously. Nothing happened. He waited a moment longer before lowering his hand. Allanon had cautioned him against use of the Elfstones except in the gravest of emergencies. Perhaps the stones would only come to his aid in special situations. He began to despair. Whatever the case, he was faced with the hard fact that he had no idea how the stones were to be used. He looked desperately at his friends.

"Well, try something else!" exclaimed Menion heatedly.

Shea took the stones between his hands and rubbed them together sharply, then shook them and cast them like dice. Still nothing happened. Slowly he retrieved them from the damp earth and carefully wiped them clean. Their deep blue color seemed to draw him to them, and he peered closely into their clear, glasslike core as if somehow the answer might be found there.

"Maybe you should talk to them or something . . ." Flick's voice trailed off hopefully.

A mental picture of Allanon's dark face, bowed and locked in deep concentration, flashed sharply in Shea's mind. Perhaps the secret of the Elfstones could be unlocked in a different way, he thought suddenly. Holding them out in his open palm, the little Valeman closed his eyes and concentrated his thoughts on reaching into the deep blueness, searching for the power that they so desperately needed. Silently, he urged the Elfstones to help them. Long moments passed, seemingly hours. He opened his eyes and the three friends watched and waited while the stones rested in Shea's palm, their blue gleam dull in the darkness and damp of the mist.

Then, with ferocious suddenness, they flared up in a blinding blue glare that caused the travelers to reel back from the brightness, shielding their unprotected eyes. So powerful was the aura that Shea nearly dropped the small gems in astonishment. The sharp glow became steadily brighter, lighting up the dead land about them as the sun had never been able to do. The brightness intensified from the deep blue to a bright blue so dazzling that the awestruck watchers were actually hypnotized. It grew, steadied, and abruptly shot forward like a huge beacon, traveling to their left, cutting effortlessly through the mist-covered grayness to rest at last, some hundreds, perhaps thousands of yards ahead upon the great gnarled boles of the ancient Black Oaks. The light held for one brief moment, and then it was gone. The gray mist returned with its chill dampness and the three small blue stones gleamed quietly as they had before.

Menion recovered quickly, clapping Shea sharply on the back and grinning broadly. In one quick motion, he had his pack back in place and was ready to travel, his eyes already scanning the now-invisible spot through which the vision of the Black Oaks had appeared. Shea hastily returned the Elfstones to the pouch, and the Valemen strapped on their packs. Not a word was spoken as they walked rapidly in the direction the beacon had flashed, each watching eagerly for the long-expected forest. Gone was the chill of the gray darkness and slow drizzle of the past five days. Gone was the despair they had felt so strongly only minutes before. There was only the conviction that escape from these dreaded lowlands was at last at hand. They did not question, did not doubt the vision the stones had revealed to them. The Black Oaks was the most dangerous forest in the Southland, but at this particular moment, it seemed a haven of hope compared to the land of Clete.

The time seemed endless as they pushed ahead. It could have been hours or perhaps only minutes later when suddenly the graying mist grudgingly gave way to huge, moss-covered trunks which rose hulkingly into the air to be lost in the haze above. The exhausted trio halted together, their tired eyes gazing joyfully on the cheerless monsters that stood evenly, endlessly before them, their great mass an impenetrable wall of damp, scarred bark on wide, deep-rooted bases that had stood there for countless ages of man and would very likely be there until the destruction of the land itself. It was an awesome sight, even in the dim light of the misty lowlands, and the watchers felt the undeniable presence of a life-force in those woods so incredibly ancient that it almost commanded a deep, grudging respect for its years. It was as if they had stepped into another age, another world, and all that stood so silently before them had the magic of an enticingly dangerous fairy tale.

"The stones were right," murmured Shea softly, a slow smile spreading over his tired, but happy face. He breathed deeply with relief and flashed a quick grin.

"The Black Oaks," pronounced Menion in admiration.

"Here we go again," sighed Flick.

VI

They spent that night camped within the protective fringes of the Black Oaks in a small clearing, sheltered by the great trees and dense shrubbery which blotted out the dreariness of the lowlands of Clete less than fifty yards to the west. The heavy mist dissipated within the forest, and it was possible to look skyward to the magnificent canopy of interlocking boughs and leaves several hundred feet above them. Where there had been no sign of life in the deathly lowlands, within the giant oaks the mingled sounds of insect and animal life whispered through the night. It was pleasant to hear living things again, and the three weary travelers felt at ease for the first time in days. But lingering in the back of their minds was the memory of their prior journey to this deceptively peaceful haven, when they had been lost for several long days and nearly devoured by the ravenous wolves that prowled deep within its confines. Moreover, the tales of unfortunate travelers who had attempted to pass through this same forest were too numerous to be disregarded.

However, the young Southlanders felt reasonably secure at the edge of the Black Oaks and gratefully made preparations to start a fire. Wood was plentiful and dry. They stripped to the skin and hung their soggy garments on a line near the small blaze. A meal was quickly prepared—the first hot one in five days—and devoured in minutes. The floor of the forest was soft and smooth, a comfortable bed compared to the dampened earth of the lowlands. As they lay quietly on their backs gazing skyward at the gently swaying treetops, the bright light of the fire seemed to shoot upward in faint streaks of orange that gave the impression of an altar burning in some great sanctuary. The light danced and glittered against the rough bark and the soft, green moss that clung in dark patches to the massive trees. The forest insects maintained their steady hum in contentment. Occasionally one would fly into the flames of the fire and extinguish its brief life with a dazzling flash. Once or twice they heard the rustle of some small animal outside the light of the fire, watching from the protective blackness.

After a while, Menion rolled over on his side and looked curiously at Shea.

"What is the source of the power of those stones, Shea? Can they grant any wish? I'm still not sure . . ."

His voice trailed off and he shook his head vaguely. Shea continued to lie motionless on his back, staring upward for a few moments as he thought back on the events of that afternoon. He realized that none of them had spoken of the Elfstones since the mysterious vision of the Black Oaks in that awesome display of incomprehensible power. He glanced over at Flick, who was watching him closely.

"I don't think that I have that much control over them," he announced abruptly. "It was almost as if *they* made the decision . . ." He paused, and then added absently, "I don't think I can control them."

Menion nodded thoughtfully and lay back again. Flick cleared his throat.

"What's the difference? They got us out of that dismal swamp, didn't they?"

Menion glanced sharply at Flick and shrugged.

"It might be helpful to know when we can count on

that kind of support, don't you think?" He breathed deeply and clasped his hands behind his head, his keen gaze shifting to the fire at his feet. Flick stirred uneasily across from him, glancing from Menion to his brother and back again. Shea said nothing, his gaze focused on some imaginary point overhead.

Long moments passed before the highlander spoke again.

"Well, at least we've made it this far," he declared cheerfully. "Now for the next leg of the trip!"

He sat up and began to sketch a quick map of the area in the dry earth. Shea and Flick sat up with him and watched quietly.

"Here we are," Menion pointed to a spot on the dirt map representing the fringe of the Black Oaks. "At least that's where I think we are," he added quickly. "To the north is the Mist Marsh and farther north of that the Rainbow Lake, out of which runs the Silver River east to the Anar Forests. Our best bet is to travel north tomorrow until we reach the edge of the Mist Marsh. Then we'll skirt the edge of the swamp," he traced a long line, "and come out on the other side of the Black Oaks. From there, we can travel due north until we run into the Silver River, and that should get us safely to the Anar."

He paused and looked over at the other two. Neither seemed to be happy with the plan.

"What's the matter?" he asked in bewilderment. "The plan is designed to get us past the Black Oaks without forcing us to go directly through them, which was the cause of all the trouble the last time we were here. Don't forget those wolves are still in there somewhere!"

Shea nodded slowly and frowned.

"It's not the general plan," he began hesitantly, "but we've heard tales of the Mist Marsh . . ."

Menion clapped his hand to his forehead in amazement.

"Oh, no! Not the old wives' tale about a Mist Wraith that lurks on the edges of the marsh waiting to devour stray travelers? Don't tell me you believe that!"

"That's fine, coming from you," Flick blazed up angrily. "I suppose you've forgotten who it was that told us how safe the Black Oaks were just before that last trip!"

"All right," soothed the lean hunter. "I'm not saying that this is a safe part of the country and that some very strange creatures don't inhabit these woods. But no one has ever seen this so-called creature of the marsh, and we have seen the wolves. Which do you choose?"

"I suppose that your plan is the best one," interjected Shea hastily. "But I would prefer it if we could cut as far east as possible while traveling through the forest to avoid as much of the Mist Marsh as possible."

"Agreed!" exclaimed Menion. "But it may prove to be a bit difficult when we haven't seen the sun in three days and can't really be sure which way is east."

"Climb a tree," Flick suggested casually.

"Climb a . . ." stuttered the other in unabashed amazement. "Why, of course! Why didn't I think of that? I'll just climb two hundred feet of slick, damp, moss-covered tree bark with my bare hands and feet!" He shook his head in mock wonderment. "Sometimes you appall me."

He glanced wearily over at Shea for understanding, but the Valeman had bounded excitedly to his brother's side.

"You brought the climbing equipment?" he demanded in astonishment; when the other nodded, he clapped him heartily on his broad back.

"Special boots and gloves and rope," he explained quickly to a bewildered Prince of Leah. "Flick is the best climber in the Vale, and if anyone can make it up one of these monsters, he can."

Menion shook his head uncomprehendingly.

"The boots and gloves are coated with a special substance just before use that makes the surface rough enough to grip even damp, mossy bark. He'll be able to climb one of these oaks tomorrow and check the position of the sun."

Flick grinned smugly and nodded.

"Yes, indeed, wonder of wonders." Menion shook his head and looked over at the stocky Valeman. "Even the slow-witted are starting to think. My friends, we may make it yet."

When they awoke the following morning, the forest was still dark, with only faint traces of daylight filtering through at the tops of the great oaks. A thin mist had drifted in off the lowlands which, when glimpsed from the edges of the forest, appeared as sunless and dismal as ever. It was cold in the woods—not the damp, penetrating chill of the lowland country, but rather the brisk, crisp cool of a forest's early morn. They ate a quick breakfast, and then Flick prepared to climb one of the towering oaks. He pulled on the heavy, flexible boots and gloves, which Shea then coated with a thick pasty substance from a small container. Menion looked on quizzically, but his curiosity changed to astonishment as the stocky Valeman grasped the base of the great tree and, with a dexterity that belied both his bulky size and the difficulty of the task, proceeded to climb rapidly toward the summit. His strong limbs carried him upward through the tangle of heavy branches and the climbing became slower and more difficult. He was briefly lost from sight upon reaching the topmost branches, then reappeared, hastening down the smooth trunk to rejoin his friends.

Quickly the climbing gear was packed and the group proceeded in a northeasterly direction. Based on Flick's report of the sun's present position, their chosen route should bring them out at a point along the east edge of the Mist Marsh. Menion believed that the forest trek could be completed in one day. It was now early morning, and they were determined to be through the Black Oaks before darkness fell. So they marched steadily, at times rapidly, in single file. The keen-eyed Menion led, picking out the best path, relying heavily on his sense of direction in the semidarkness. Shea followed close behind him, and Flick brought up the rear, glancing occasionally over his shoulder into the still forests. They stopped only three times to rest and once more for a brief lunch, each time quickly resuming their march. They spoke infrequently, but the talk was lighthearted and cheerful. The day wore quickly away, and soon the first signs of nightfall were visible. Still the forest stretched on before them with no indication of a break in the great trees. Worse than this, a heavy graying mistiness was once again seeping into view in gradually thickening amounts. But this was a new kind of mist. It lacked the inconsistency of the lowland mist; this was an almost smokelike substance that one could actually feel clinging to the body and clothes, gripping in its own peculiarly distasteful fashion. It felt strangely like the clutching of hundreds of small, clammy, chilled hands seeking to pull the body down, and the three travelers felt an unmistakable revulsion at its insistent touch. Menion indicated that the heavy, foglike substance was from the Mist Marsh, and they were very close to the end of the forest.

Eventually, the mist grew so heavy that it was impossible for the three to see more than a few feet. Menion slowed his pace to a crawl because of the increasingly poor visibility, and they remained close to each other to avoid separation. By this time, the day was so far gone that even without the mist the forest would have appeared almost black; but with the added dimness caused by the swirling wall of heavy moisture, it was nearly impossible to pick out any sort of path. It was almost as if the three were suspended in a limbo world, where only the solidity of the invisible ground on which they trod offered any evidence of reality. It finally became so difficult to see that Menion instructed the other two to bind themselves together and to him by a length of rope to prevent separation. This was quickly done and the slow march resumed. Menion knew that they had to be very near the Mist Marsh and carefully peered into the grayness ahead in an effort to catch a glimpse of a breakthrough.

Even so, when at last he did reach the edge of the marshland bordering the north fringes of the Black Oaks, he did not realize what had happened until he had already stepped knee-deep into the thick green waters. The chill, deathlike clutching of the mud beneath, coupled with his surprise, caused him to slip farther down, and only his quick warning saved Shea and Flick from a similar fate. Responding to his cry, they hauled in on the rope that bound them together and hastily pulled their comrade from the bog and certain death. The sullen, slime-covered waters of the great swamp covered only thinly the bottomless mud beneath, which lacked the rapid suction of quicksand, but accomplished the same result in a slightly longer time span. Anything or anyone caught in its grip was doomed to a slow death by suffocation in an immeasurable abyss. For untold ages its silent surface had fooled unwary creatures into attempting to cross, or to skirt, or perhaps only to test its mirrorless waters, and the decayed remains of all lay buried together somewhere beneath its placid face. The three travelers stood silently on its banks, looking at it and experiencing inwardly the horror of its dark secret. Even Menion Leah shuddered as he remembered its brief, clutching invitation to him to share the fate of so many others. For one spellbound second, the dead paraded as shadows before them and were gone.

"What happened?" exclaimed Shea suddenly, his

voice breaking the silence with deafening sharpness. "We should have avoided this swamp!"

Menion looked upward and about for a few seconds and shook his head.

"We've come out too far to the west. We'll have to follow the edge of the bog around to the east until we can break free from this mist and the Black Oaks."

He paused and considered the time of day.

"I'm not spending the night in this place," Flick declared vehemently, anticipating the other's query. "I'd rather walk all night and most of tomorrow—and probably the next day!"

Their quick decision was to continue along the edge of the Mist Marsh until they reached open land to the east and then stop for the night. Shea was still concerned about being caught in open country by the Skull Bearers, but his growing dread of the swamp overshadowed even this fear, and his foremost thought was to get as far away as possible. The trio tightened the rope about their waists and in single file began to move along the uneven shoreline of the marsh, their eyes glued to the faint path ahead. Menion guided them cautiously, avoiding the tangle of treacherous roots and weeds that grew in abundance along the swamp's edge, their twisted, knotted forms seemingly alive in the eerie half-light of the rolling gray mist. At times the ground became soft mud, dangerously like that of the marsh itself, and had to be skirted. At other times huge trees blocked the path, their great trunks leaning heavily toward the dull, lifeless surface of the swamp's waters, their branches drooping sadly, motionless as they waited for the death that lay only inches below. If the Lowlands of Clete had been a dying land, then this marsh was the death that waited—an infinite, ageless death that gave no sign, no warning, no movement as it crouched, concealed within the very land it had so brutally destroyed. The chilling dampness of the lowlands was here, but coupled with it was the unexplainable feeling that the heavy, stagnant slime of the swamp waters permeated the mist as well, clutching eagerly at the weary travelers. The mist about them swirled slowly, but there was no sign of wind, no sound of a breeze rustling the tall swamp grass or dying oaks. All was still, a silence of permanent death that knew well who was master.

They had walked for perhaps an hour when Shea first sensed that something was wrong. There was no reason for the feeling; it stole over him gradually until every sense was keyed, trying to find where the trouble lay. Walking silently between the other two, he listened intently, peering first into the great oaks, then out over the swamp. Finally, he concluded with chilling certainty that they were not alone—that something else was out there in the invisible beyond, lost in the mist to their poor vision, but able to see them. For one brief moment the young Valeman was so terrified by the thought that he was unable to speak or even to gesture. He could only walk ahead, his mind frozen, waiting for the unspeakable to happen. But then, with a supreme effort he calmed his scattered thoughts and brought the other two men to an abrupt halt.

Menion looked around quizzically and started to speak, but Shea silenced him with a finger to his own lips and a gesture toward the swamp. Flick was already looking cautiously in that direction, his own sixth sense having warned him of his brother's fear. For long moments they stood motionless at the edge of the marsh, their eyes and ears concentrated on the impenetrable mist moving sluggishly above the surface of the dead water. The silence was oppressive.

"I think you were mistaken," Menion whispered finally as he relaxed his vigil. "Sometimes when you are this tired, it is easy to imagine things."

Shea shook his head negatively and looked at Flick.

"I don't know," the other conceded. "I thought I sensed something. . . ."

"A Mist Wraith?" chided Menion grinning.

"Maybe you're right," Shea interceded quickly. "I am pretty tired and could imagine anything at this point. Let's keep moving and get out of this place."

They hastily resumed the dreary trek, but for the next few minutes remained alert for anything unusual. When nothing happened, they began to let their thoughts drift to other matters. Shea had just succeeded in convincing himself that he had been mistaken and the victim of an overactive imagination brought about by lack of sleep, when Flick cried out.

Immediately Shea felt the rope that bound them together jerk sharply and begin to drag him in the direction of the deadly swamp. He lost his balance and fell, unable to distinguish anything in the mist. For one fleeting moment he thought he glimpsed his brother's body suspended several feet in the air over the swamp, the rope still tied to his waist. In the next second, Shea felt the chill of the swamp grapple at his legs.

They might have all been lost had it not been for the quick reflexes of the Prince of Leah. At the first sharp jerk of the rope, he had instinctively grasped at the only thing near enough to keep him on his feet. It was a huge, sinking oak, its trunk embedded so far into the soft ground that its upper branches were within reach, and Menion rapidly hooked one arm about the nearest bough and with the other grasped the rope about his waist and tried to pull back. Shea, now up to his knees in the swamp mud, felt the rope go taut on Menion's end and tried to brace himself to aid. Flick was crying out sharply in the darkness above the swamp, and both Menion and Shea shouted encouragement. Suddenly, the rope between Flick and Shea went slack, and out of the gray mistiness emerged the stout, struggling form of Flick Ohmsford, still suspended above the water's surface, his waist gripped by what appeared to be a sort of greenish, weed-coated tentacle. His right hand held the long, silver dagger, which gleamed menacingly as it slashed in repeated cuts at the thing which held him. Shea yanked hard on the rope which bound them, trying to aid his brother in breaking free, and a moment later he succeeded as the tentacle whipped back into the mist, releasing the still-struggling Flick, who promptly fell into the marsh below.

Shea had barely pulled his exhausted brother from the clutches of the swamp, freed him from the rope, and helped him to his feet before several more of the greenish arms shot out of the misty darkness. They knocked the shaken Flick sprawling and one closed about the left arm of an astonished Shea before he could think to dodge. He felt himself drawn toward the swamp and drew his own dagger to strike fiercely at the slime-covered tentacle. As he fought, he caught sight of something huge out in the marsh, its bulk covered by the night and the swamp. To one side, Flick again became entangled in the grip of two more tentacles, and his stocky form was dragged relentlessly toward the water's edge. Valiantly, Shea broke free from the tentacle that held his arm, slashing through the repulsive limb with one great cut; struggling to reach his brother, he felt another tentacle grasp his leg, knocking his feet out from under him. As he fell, his head struck an oak root, and he lost consciousness.

Again they were saved by Menion, his lithe form leaping out of the darkness behind, the great sword flashing dully in a wide arc as it severed in one powerful swing the tentacle which held the unconscious Shea. A second later, the highlander was at Flick's side, cutting and chopping his way past the arms which suddenly reached for him out of the darkness, and with a series of quick, well-placed blows freed the other Valeman. For a moment the tentacles disappeared back into the mist of the swamp, and Flick and Menion hastened to pull the unconscious Shea back from the unprotected edge of the water. But before any of them could reach the safety of the great oaks, the greenish arms again shot out of the darkness. Without hesitation, Menion and Flick placed themselves in front of their motionless friend and struck out at the encircling arms. The fight was silent, save for the labored breathing of the men as they struck again and again, chopping off bits and pieces and sometimes whole ends of the grasping tentacles. But any damage they caused did not seem to affect the monster in the swamp, which attacked with renewed fury at each stroke. Menion cursed himself for not remembering to drag the great ash bow within reach so that he might have taken a shot at whatever it was that lay beyond the mist.

"Shea!" he yelled desperately. "Shea, wake up, or for the love of heaven, we're done for!"

The silent form behind him stirred slightly.

"Get up, Shea!" pleaded Flick hoarsely, his own arms exhausted from the great strain of fighting off the tentacles.

"The stones!" yelled Menion. "Get the Elfstones!"

Shea struggled to a kneeling position, but he was knocked flat again by the force of the battle in front of him. He heard Menion shouting, and dazedly felt for his pack, realizing almost immediately that he had dropped it while helping Flick. He saw it now, several yards to the right, the tentacles waving menacingly over it. Menion seemed to realize this at the same moment and charged forward with a wild cry, his long sword cutting a path for the others. Flick was at his side, the small dagger still in his hand. With a final surge of his fading strength, Shea leaped to his feet and launched himself toward the pack containing the precious Elfstones. His slim form slipped between

several of the grasping arms, and he threw himself on
the pack. His hand was inside, groping for the pouch,
when the first tentacle reached his unprotected legs.
Kicking and struggling, he fought to keep his freedom
for the few seconds he needed to find the stones. For a
moment he thought he had lost them again. Then his
hand closed over the small pouch, and he yanked it
from his fallen pack. A sudden blow from the writhing
tentacles almost caused him to drop it, and he clutched
it tightly to his chest as he loosened the drawstrings
with numbing slowness. Flick had been forced back so
far that he stumbled against Shea's outstretched body
and fell over backward, the tentacles coming down on
top of them both. Now only the lean form of Menion
stood between them and the giant attacker, both
hands gripping tightly the great sword of Leah.

Almost without realizing it, Shea found the three
blue stones in his hand, free from the pouch at last.
Scrambling backward, struggling to his feet, the
young Valeman let out a wild cry of triumph and held
forth the faintly glowing Elfstones. The power locked
within flared up immediately, flooding the darkness
with dazzling blue light. Flick and Menion leaped
back, shielding their eyes from the glare. The tentacles
drew back hesitantly, uncertainly, and as the three
men risked a second quick glance, they saw the
brilliant light of the Elfstones streak outward into the
mist above the swamp, cutting through its vapor with
the keenness of a knife. They saw it strike with
shattering impact the huge, unspeakable bulk that had
attacked them as it was sinking sluggishly beneath the
slime-covered waters. At that same instant the glare
above the disappearing monster reached the intensity
of a small sun and the water steamed with blue flames
that seared upward into the shrouded sky. One
moment the burning glare and the flames were there
and the next they were gone. The mist and the night
returned, and the three companions were alone again
in the blackness of the marshland.

They quickly sheathed their weapons, picked up the fallen packs and dropped back among the huge black oaks. The swamp remained as silent as it had been before the unexpected attack, its dull waters disturbingly placid beneath the gray haze. For several moments, no one spoke as they collapsed silently against the trunks of the great trees and breathed deeply, grateful to be alive. The whole battle had happened quickly, like the passing of a brief, horrible instant in an all-too-real nightmare. Flick was completely drenched by the swamp waters, and Shea was soaked from the waist down. Both shivered in the chill night air; after only a few seconds of rest, they began moving slowly about in an effort to ward off the numbing cold.

Realizing that they had to get free of the marshland quickly, Menion swung his tired body away from its resting place against the rough, bark-covered oak trunk and in one smooth motion swung his pack into place over his shoulders. Shea and Flick were quick to follow, though somewhat less eager. They conferred briefly to decide what direction it would be best to take now. The choice was simple: proceed through the Black Oaks and risk becoming lost and being set upon by the wandering wolf packs or follow the edge of the swamp and chance a second encounter with the Mist Wraith. Neither choice held much appeal, but the battle with the creature from the Mist Marsh was too recent to permit any of them to risk a repeat performance. So the decision was made to stick to the woods, to try to follow a course parallel to the shoreline of the swamp and hopefully gain the open country beyond within a few hours. They now had reached the point where the long hours of traveling with the keen anticipation of danger had chipped and worn away the clear reasoning of the morning. They were tired and frightened by the strange world into which they had journeyed, and the one clear thought left in their numbed minds was to break through this stifling forest that they might find a few hours of welcome sleep. With that dominating their thoughts and overriding the caution that was so desperately needed, they forgot to tie themselves together again.

The journey continued as before, with Menion in the lead, Shea a few paces back and Flick trailing, all walking silently and steadily, their minds fixed on the reassuring thought that ahead lay the sunlit, open grasslands that would take them to the Anar. The mist seemed to have dissipated slightly, and while Menion's form was only a shadow, Shea could make him out well enough to follow. Yet at times both Shea and Flick would lose sight of the person immediately in front and would find their eyes straining wearily to keep to the path Menion was making for them. The minutes passed with agonizing slowness and the sharpness of each man's eyesight began to lessen with the increasing need for sleep. Minutes lengthened into long, endless hours and still they plodded slowly onward through the misty haze of the great Black Oaks. They found it impossible to tell how far they had traveled or how much time had passed. Soon it failed to matter at all. They became sleepwalkers in a world of half-dreams and rambling thoughts with no break in the wearing march or the never-ending, silent black trunks that came and passed in countless thousands. The only change was a gradual building of the wind from somewhere in the shrouded night, whispering its first faint cry, then growing to a numbing crescendo of sound that gripped the tired minds of the three travelers with spellbinding magic. It called to them, reminding them of the briefness of the days behind and those ahead, warning them that they were mortal creatures of no consequence in that land, crying to them to lie down in the peacefulness of sleep. They heard and fought against the tempting plea with the last of their strength, concentrating mindlessly on putting one foot before the other in an endless succession of footsteps. One minute they were all there in a ragged line; the next, Shea looked ahead and Menion was gone.

At first, he could not accept the fact, his normally keen mind hazy with lack of sleep, and he continued to walk slowly ahead, looking vainly for the shadowy form of the tall highlander. Then, abruptly he stopped as he realized with stabbing fear that they had somehow become separated. He clutched wildly for Flick and grabbed his brother's loose tunic as the fatigued Valeman stumbled into him, dead on his feet. Flick looked unthinkingly at him, not knowing, not even caring why they had stopped, his only hope that he could collapse at last and sleep. The wind in the darkness of the forest seemed to howl in wild glee, and Shea called desperately for the highland prince and heard only the echoes of his own futile cry. He called again and again, his voice rising to a near scream of desperation and fear, but nothing came back except the sound of his own voice, muffled and distorted by the wild whistling of the wind through the great oaks, whisking and wrapping about the silent trunks and limbs, and filtering out among the rustling leaves. Once he thought he heard his own name called; answering eagerly, he dragged himself and the exhausted Flick through the maze of trees toward the sound of the cry. But there was nothing. Dropping to the forest floor, he called until his voice gave out, but only the wind replied in mocking laughter to tell him that he had lost the Prince of Leah.

VII

hen Shea awoke the following day, it was noon. The bright sunlight streamed into his half-open eyes with burning sharpness as he lay on his back in the tall grass. At first he could remember nothing of the previous night except that he and Flick had become separated from Menion in the Black Oaks. Half awake, he raised himself on one elbow, looked about sleepily, and discovered that he was in an open field. Behind him rose the forbidding Black Oaks, and he knew that somehow, after losing Menion, he had managed to find his way through the dread forest before collapsing in exhaustion. Everything was hazy in his mind after their separation. He could not imagine how he had summoned the strength to finish the march. He could not even recall breaking free of the endless forest to find the grass-covered lowlands he now surveyed. The whole experience seemed strangely distant as he rubbed his eyes and sighed contentedly in the warm sunlight and fresh air. For the first time in days, the Anar forests seemed to be within reach.

Suddenly, he remembered Flick, and looked anxiously about for his brother. A moment later he spotted the stocky form collapsed in sleep several yards away. Shea climbed slowly to his feet and stretched leisurely, taking time to locate his pack. He bent down and rummaged through its contents until he located the pouch containing the Elfstones, reassuring himself that they were still safely within his possession. Then picking up the pack, he trudged over to his sleeping brother and gently shook him. Flick stirred grudgingly, clearly unhappy that anyone would disturb his slumber. Shea was forced to shake him several times before he at last reluctantly opened his eyes and squinted up sourly. Upon seeing Shea, he raised himself to a sitting position and looked slowly about.

"Hey, we made it!" he exclaimed. "But I don't know how. I don't remember anything after losing Menion except walking and walking until I thought that my legs would drop off."

Shea grinned in agreement and clapped his brother on the back. He felt a measure of gratitude when he thought of all they had been through together. So many hardships and dangers, and still Flick could laugh about it. He felt a sudden, keen sense of love for Flick, a brother who, while not related by blood, was even closer for his deep friendship.

"We made it all right," he smiled, "and we'll make it the rest of the way, too, if I can get you off the ground."

"The meanness in some people is unbelievable." Flick shook his head in mock disbelief and then climbed heavily to his feet. He looked questioningly over at Shea. "Menion . . ?"

"Lost . . . I don't know where . . ."

Flick looked away, sensing his brother's bitter disappointment, but unwilling to admit to himself that they were not better off without the highland prince. He instinctively distrusted Menion, yet the highlander had saved his life back in the forest and that was not something Flick would forget easily. He thought about it a minute or so longer, then clapped his brother lightly on the shoulder.

"Don't worry about that rogue. He'll turn up—probably at the wrong time."

Shea nodded quietly, and the conversation quickly turned to the task at hand. They agreed that the best plan was to journey northward until they reached the Silver River which flowed into the Rainbow Lake, and follow it upstream to the Anar. With any luck, Menion would also follow the river and catch up to them within a few days. His skill as a woodsman should enable him to escape the Black Oaks and at some point beyond find their trail and follow it to wherever they were. Shea was reluctant to leave his friend, but was wise enough to realize that any attempt at a search for him in the Black Oaks could only result in their own entanglement. Moreover, the danger they faced if discovered by the searching Skull Bearers far outweighed any risks Menion might encounter, even in that forest. There was nothing for them to do but to continue on.

The pair walked rapidly through the green, quiet lowlands, hoping to reach the Silver River by nightfall. It was already midafternoon, and they had no way of knowing how far they might be from the river. With the sun to serve as a guide, they felt more confident of their position than they had in the misty confines of the Black Oaks, where they had been forced to depend on their own unreliable sense of direction. They talked freely, brightened by the sunlight that had been absent for so many days and by an unspoken feeling of gratitide that they were still alive following the harrowing experiences of the Mist Marsh. As they walked, small animals and high-flying birds scattered at their appearance. Once, in the fading light of the afternoon sun, Shea thought he caught sight of the small, hunched-over form of an old man some distance to the east, moving slowly away from them. But in that light and at that distance he could not be certain and an instant later found he could see no one after all. Flick had seen nothing and the incident was forgotten.

By dusk they sighted a long, ribbon-thin stream of

water to the north which they quickly identified as the fabled Silver River, the source of the wondrous Rainbow Lake to the west and of a thousand firelight tales of adventure. It was said that there was a legendary King of the Silver River, whose wealth and power was beyond description, but whose only concern was in keeping the waters of the great river running free and clean for man and animal alike. He was seldom seen by travelers, the stories related, but he was always there to offer aid, should any require it, or to deal out punishment for violation of his domain. On sighting the river, Shea and Flick could only tell that it appeared very beautiful in the fading light, the sort of faint silver color that the name implied. When they finally reached its edge, the evening had become too dark to permit them to see how clear the waters really were, but upon tasting it they found it clean enough to drink.

They found a small, grass-covered clearing on the south bank of the river, beneath the spreading shelter of two broad, old maple trees that offered an ideal campsite for the night. Even the short journey of that afternoon had tired them, and they preferred not to risk moving about in the dark in this open country. They had just about exhausted their supplies, and after this evening's meal they would have to hunt for food. This was a particularly disheartening thought when they recalled that the only weapons they had between them for killing game were the short and highly ineffectual hunting knives. Menion carried the only long bow. They ate the last of their supplies in silence without the use of a cooking fire, which might have called attention to their presence. The moon was half full and the night cloudless, so that the thousands of stars in the limitless galaxy shone in dazzling white, lighting up the river and the land beyond in an eerie deep-green brightness. After their meal was completed, Shea turned to his brother.

"Have you thought about this trip, about this whole

business of running away?" he queried. "I mean, what are we really doing?"

"You're a funny one to ask that!" exclaimed the other shortly.

Shea smiled and nodded.

"I suppose I am. But I have to justify it all to myself and that's not an easy task. I can understand most of what Allanon told us, about the danger to the heirs of the Sword. But what good will it do for us to hide out in the Anar? This creature Brona must be after something besides the Sword of Shannara to go to all this trouble to search for the heirs of the Elven House. What is it he wants . . . what could it be . . .?"

Flick shrugged and tossed a pebble into the swift current of the lapping river, his own mind muddled, unable to offer any sensible answer.

"Maybe he wants to take over," he suggested vaguely. "Doesn't everyone who gets a little power, sooner or later?"

"No doubt," agreed Shea uncertainly, thinking that this special form of greed had brought the races to where they were today, following the long, bitter wars that had nearly destroyed all life. But it had been years since the last war and the appearance of separate and disassociated communities seemed to have provided a partial answer to the long quest for peace. He turned back to a watchful Flick.

"What are we going to do once we get to where we're going?"

"Allanon will tell us," his brother answered hesitantly.

"Allanon can't tell us what to do forever," replied Shea quickly. "Besides, I'm still not convinced that he has told us the truth about himself."

Flick nodded his agreement, thinking back to that first chilling encounter with the dark giant who had tossed him about like a rag doll. His behavior had always struck Flick as that of a man who was used to having his way and having it when and how he chose. He shivered involuntarily, recalling his first near discovery by the shadowy Skull Bearer, and found himself confronted with the fact that it was Allanon who had saved him.

"I'm not sure I want to know the truth about any of this. I'm not sure I would understand," Flick murmured softly.

Shea was startled by the comment and turned back to the moonlit waters of the river.

"We may be only little people to Allanon," he acknowledged, "but from now on, I don't move without a reason!"

"Maybe so," his brother's voice drifted up to him. "But maybe . . ."

His voice trailed off ominously into the quiet sounds of the night and the river, and Shea chose not to pursue the matter. Both lay back and were quickly asleep, their tired thoughts flowing sluggishly into the bright, colorful dreams of the momentary world of sleep. In that secure, drifting dimension of fantasy, their weary minds could relax, releasing the hidden fears of tomorrow to emerge in whatever form they wished, and there, in that most distant sanctuary for the human soul, be faced privately and overcome. But even with the reassuring sounds of life all about them and the peaceful rushing of the gleaming Silver River to soothe their cares, an inescapable, gnawing specter of apprehension wormed its stealthy way into their dream world and there, in full view of the mind's eye, it perched and waited, smiling dully, hatefully— knowing well the limits of their endurance. Both sleepers tossed fitfully, unable to shake the presence of this frightening apparition entrenched deep within them, more thought than form.

Perhaps it was that same shadow of warning, radiating its special scent of fear, that locked simultaneously in the restless minds of the Valemen and caused both to waken in the same startled instant, the sleep gone from their eyes and the air filled with stark, chilling madness that gripped them tightly and began to squeeze. They recognized it instantly, and panic shone dully in their eyes as they sat motionless, listening to the soundless night. Moments passed and nothing happened. Still they remained immobile, their senses straining for the sounds they knew must come. Then they heard the dreaded flapping of the great wings and together looked to the open river to see the hulking, silent form of the Skull Bearer swoop almost gracefully from out of the lowlands across the river to the north and settle into a long glide, bearing directly toward their place of concealment. The Valemen were frozen with terror, unable even to think, let alone move, as they watched the creature begin to close the distance between them. It did not matter that it had not yet seen them, perhaps did not even know that they were there. It would know in the next few seconds, and for the brothers there was no time to run, no place to hide, no chance to escape. Shea felt the dryness of his mouth and somewhere within his scattered thoughts remembered the Elfstones, but his mind had gone numb. He sat paralyzed with his brother and waited for the end.

Miraculously, it did not come. Just when it seemed that the servant of the Warlock Lord must surely find them, a flash of light from the other bank caught its attention. Swiftly, it winged away toward the light and then there was another a bit farther down and then another—or was it mistaken? It flew swiftly now, searching eagerly, its cunning mind telling it that the search was at an end, the long hunt over at last. Yet it could not find the source of the light. Suddenly the light flashed again, only to disappear in the swiftness of a blinking eye. The maddened creature swooped toward it, knowing it was deeper in the blackness across the river, lost somewhere in the thousands of small gullies and dales of the lowlands. The mysterious light flashed again and then again, each time moving farther inland, taunting, daring the angered beast to follow. On the other bank, the petrified figures of the two Valemen remained concealed in the darkness as their frightened eyes watched the flying shadow move ever more swiftly away from them until it could no longer be seen.

They remained immobile after the departure of the Skull Bearer. Once again they had come close to death and managed to elude its fatal touch. They sat quietly and listened as the mingled sounds of insect and animal returned to the night. Minutes passed and they began to breathe more easily, their stiff poses relaxing into more comfortable slumps as they looked at each other in amazed relief, knowing the creature had gone, but unable to comprehend how it had happened. Then, before they had any chance at all to speak of the matter, the mysterious light that had flashed from across the river reappeared suddenly on a rise several hundred yards in back of them, disappeared for an instant and then flashed again, closer than before. Shea and Flick watched in wonderment as it moved toward them, weaving slightly.

Moments later the figure of an old, old man stood before them, bent with age and clothed in woodsman's garb, his hair silver in the starlight, his face framed by a long, white beard neatly trimmed and combed. The strange light in his hand appeared fiercely bright at this close distance, and there was no hint of a flame in its center. Suddenly it disappeared and in its place was a cylindrical object gripped in the old man's gnarled hand. He looked at them and smiled a greeting. Shea looked quietly at his ancient face, sensing that the strange old man deserved his respect.

"The light," Shea spoke finally, "how . . .?"

"A toy of people long since dead and gone." The

voice rolled out in a steady whisper that drifted on the cool air. "Gone like the evil creature out there . . ." The words trailed off and he pointed in the direction of the departed Skull Bearer with a thin, wrinkled arm that seemed to hang in the night like some brittle stick of dead wood. Shea looked doubtfully at him, unsure of what should be done next.

"We are traveling eastward . . ." Flick volunteered abruptly.

"To the Anar." The gentle voice cut him short, the elderly head nodding in understanding, the wrinkled eyes sharp in the soft moonlight as they looked from one brother to the other. Suddenly he moved past them to the edge of the swift river and then turned back to them and motioned for them to sit. Shea and Flick did so without hesitation, unable to doubt the old man's intentions. As they sat they felt a great weariness steal over their bodies, their eyes suddenly unable to remain open.

"Sleep, young travelers, that your journey may be shortened." The voice became stronger in their minds, more commanding. They could not resist the feeling of weariness, so pleasant and welcome, and they stretched out on the soft grassy bank in obedience. The figure before them began to change slowly into something new, and through vague, blurred eyes and half-closed eyelids, it appeared that the old man was growing younger and his clothes were not the same. Shea began to mutter slightly, trying to stay awake, to understand, but a moment later both Valemen were asleep.

As they slept they drifted cloudlike through forgotten days of sunlight and happiness in the peaceful woodland home they had left so many days ago. Once again they roamed the friendly confines of the Duln Forest and swam in the cool waters of the mighty Rappahalladran River, the fears and cares of a lifetime swept away in an instant. They moved through the wooded hills and vales of the countryside with freedom unlike anything they had ever experienced. In their sleep they touched, as if for the first time, each plant and animal, bird and insect with new understanding of its importance as a living thing, however small and insignificant. They floated and drifted like the wind, able to smell the freshness of the land, able to see the beauty of the life nature had placed there. Everything was a kaleidoscope of color and smell, with only gentle sounds reaching their tired minds— sounds of the open air and the quiet countryside. Forgotten were the long, hard days of travel through the mist-covered Lowlands of Clete, the sunless days where life was a lost soul wandering hopelessly in a dying land. Forgotten was the darkness of the Black Oaks, the madness of the endless, giant trees hiding them from the sun and sky. Gone was the memory of the Mist Wraith and the pursuing Skull Bearer, constant, relentless in its search. The young Valemen moved in a world without the fears and cares of the real world and for those hours, time dissipated into peace with the momentary beauty of a rainbow at the end of a sudden, violent storm.

They did not know how long it was that they were lost to the world of dreams nor did they know what it was that had happened to them in that time. They only knew, as they stirred into gentle wakefulness, that they were no longer at the edge of the Silver River. They knew as well that the time was new and somehow different; the feeling was exciting but very secure.

As his vision slowly returned, Shea was aware that there were people all around him, watching and waiting. He raised himself slowly up on one elbow, his hazy vision disclosing groups of small figures standing about, bending over in an anxious manner. From out of the vague background emerged a tall, commanding figure in loose-fitting clothes, leaning down to him, a broad hand on his slim shoulder.

"Flick?" he cried apprehensively, rubbing his

sleep-filled eyes with one hand as he squinted to make out the features of the shrouded figure.

"You're safe now, Shea." The deep voice seemed to roll out of the shadowy figure. "This is the Anar."

Shea blinked quickly, struggling to rise as the broad hand held him gently down. His eyes began to clear, and he saw in a glimpse the half-raised figure of his brother next to him, just waking from his deep slumber. Around them were the squat, heavyset figures of men Shea instantly knew to be Dwarfs. Shea's eyes caught the strong face of the figure at his side, and at the moment they came to rest on the gleaming chain mail encasing the hand and forearm stretched out to grasp his shoulder lightly, he knew the journey to the Anar was ended. They had found Culhaven and Balinor.

Menion Leah had not found the last leg of the journey to the Anar quite so simple. When he first realized he had become separated from the two Valemen, panic set in. He was not afraid for himself, but he feared the very worst for the Ohmsfords if left alone to find their way out of the mist-shrouded Black Oaks. He, too, had called hopelessly, futilely, stumbling blindly about in the blackness until his voice was cracked. But in the end he was forced to admit to himself that the search was useless under such conditions. Exhausted, he pushed on through the woods in what he believed to be the general direction of the lowlands, consoling himself slightly with the promise that he would find the others in the daylight. He was in the forest a longer time than he had anticipated, breaking free near dawn and collapsing at the edge of the grasslands. Though he did not know it then, he had emerged at a point south of the sleeping brothers. By this time his endurance had been pushed to the limit and sleep came over him so quickly that he could not remember anything after the slow, featherlight feeling of falling as he collapsed in the tall lowland grass. It seemed to him that he slept a very long time, but in fact he awakened only several hours after Shea and Flick had begun their journey toward the Silver River. Believing that he was a considerable distance south of the point the group had been making for while in the Black Oaks, Menion quickly chose to travel north and try to cut across the trail of his companions before reaching the river. If he failed to find them by that time, he knew he would be confronted with the unpleasant probability that they were still lost in the entanglement of the woods.

Hurriedly, the highlander strapped on his light pack, shouldered the great ash bow and the sword of Leah and began to march rapidly northward. The few hours of afternoon daylight remaining disappeared quickly as he walked, his sharp eyes searching carefully for any sign of human passage. It was almost dusk when he finally picked up the signs of someone traveling in the direction of the Silver River. He found the trail to be several hours old, and he could be reasonably certain that there was more than one person. But there was no way to tell who the travelers were, so Menion pushed on hurriedly in the half-light of dusk, hoping to catch them when they stopped for the night. He knew that the Skull Bearers would also be searching for them, but brushed his fears aside, remembering that there was no reason to connect him with the Valemen. In any event, it was a calculated risk he had to take if he expected to be of any service to his friends.

Shortly thereafter, just before the sun dropped behind the horizon completely, Menion caught sight of a figure to the east of him traveling in the opposite direction. Menion quickly called out to the other, who seemed startled by the highlander's sudden appearance and tried to move away from him. Menion quickly took up the chase, running after the frightened traveler and calling to him that he meant no harm. After several minutes he caught the man, who turned out to be a peddler selling cooking ware to outlying villages and families in these lowlands. The peddler, a bent, timid individual who had been frightened badly by the unexpected pursuit, was now thoroughly terrified by the sight of the tall, sword-bearing highlander facing him at nightfall in the middle of nowhere. Menion hastily explained that he meant no harm, but was looking for two friends from whom he had become separated while traveling through the Black Oaks. This proved to be the worst thing he could have told the little man, who was now thoroughly convinced the stranger was insane. Menion considered telling him that he was the Prince of Leah, but quickly discarded that idea. In the end, the peddler revealed to him that he had seen two travelers fitting the general description of the Valemen from a distance earlier in the afternoon. Menion could not tell if the man had told him that much for fear of his life or to humor him, but he accepted the tale and bade good evening to the little man, who was obviously delighted to be let off so easily, and made a hasty escape southward into the sheltering darkness of evening.

Menion was forced to admit to himself that it was now too dark to attempt to follow the trail of his friends, so he cast about for a likely campsite. He found a pair of large pines that appeared to be the best shelter available and he moved into them, glancing anxiously at the clear night sky. There was sufficient light to enable a prowling Northland creature to find any camped travelers with relative ease, and he inwardly prayed that his friends had sense enough to pick a carefully hidden spot to spend the night. He tossed down his own pack and weapons beneath one of the spreading pines and crawled under the shelter of its low-hanging branches. Famished from the past two days' journey, he devoured the last of his supplies, thinking as he did so that the Valemen would be faced with the same food shortage in the days ahead. Grumbling aloud at the bad luck that had separated them, he reluctantly wrapped himself in his light blanket and was quickly asleep, the great sword of Leah unsheathed at his side, gleaming dully in the moonlight.

Unaware of the events that had transpired that night while he slept soundly several miles south of the Silver River, Menion Leah rose the next day with a new plan in mind. If he could cut across country, traveling northeast, he could catch up with the Valemen much more easily. He was certain that they would be following the edge of the Silver River as it wound its way eastward into the Anar Forests, so their paths had to cross farther up river. Abandoning the faint traces of the trail left the previous day, Menion began to journey across the lowlands in an easterly direction, thinking to himself that if he did not come across some sign of them upriver when he reached the water's edge, he could double back downstream. He also entertained hopes of sighting some small game that would provide meat for the evening meal. He whistled and sang to himself as he walked, his lean face relaxed and cheerful at the prospect of a reunion with his lost comrades. He could even picture the stolid disbelief on old Flick's stern face at the sight of his return. He walked easily with long, loping strides that covered the ground quickly and evenly, the swinging, measured step of the experienced woodsman and hunter.

As he traveled, his thoughts drifted back to the events of the past several days, and he pondered the significance of all that had transpired. He knew little about the history of the Great Wars and the reign of the Druid Council, the mysterious appearance of the so-called Warlock Lord and his defeat by the combined might of three nations. Most disturbing of all was his almost total lack of knowledge of the legend behind the Sword of Shannara, the fabled weapon that for so many years had been a watchword symbolic of freedom through courage. Now it was the birthright of an unknown orphan, half man, half elf. The thought was so preposterous that he still found it impossible to conceive of Shea in that role. He knew instinctively that something was missing from the picture—something so basic to the whole puzzle of the great Sword that, without knowing what it was, the three friends were so many windblown leaves.

Menion also knew that he was not a part of this adventure for the sake of friendship alone. Flick had been right about that. Even now he was unsure exactly why he had been persuaded to undertake this journey. He knew he was less than a Prince of Leah should be. He knew that his interest in people had not been deep enough, and he had never really wanted to know them. He had never tried to understand the important problems of governing justly in a society where the monarch's word was the only law. Yet he felt that in his own way he was as good as any man alive. Shea believed he was a man to be looked up to. Perhaps so, he thought idly, but his life to date appeared to consist of one long line of harrowing experiences and wild escapades that had served little or no constructive purpose.

The smooth, grass-covered lowlands changed to rough, barren ground, rising abruptly in small hills and dropping sharply into steep, trenchlike valleys that made travel slow and almost hazardous in places. Menion looked anxiously ahead for some indication of more level terrain, but it was impossible to see very far, even from the top of the steep rises. He plodded on, deliberately and steadily, ignoring the roughness of the ground and silently berating his decision to come that way. His mind wandered briefly, then suddenly snapped back as he caught the sound of a human voice. He listened intently for several seconds, but could hear nothing further and dismissed it as the wind or his imagination. A moment later he heard it again, only this time it was the clear sound of a woman's voice, singing softly somewhere ahead of him, faint and low. He walked more quickly, wondering if his ears were playing tricks on him, but all the time hearing the woman's mellow voice grow louder. Soon the mesmeric sound of her singing filled the air in a gay, almost wild abandon that reached into the innermost depths of the highlander's mind, bidding him to follow, to be as free as the song itself. Almost in a trance he walked steadily on, smiling broadly at the images the happy song conjured up to him. Vaguely, he wondered what a woman would be doing in these bleak lowlands, miles from any kind of civilization, but the song seemed to dispel all his doubts in its warm assurance that it came from the heart.

At the peak of a particularly bleak rise, somewhat higher than the surrounding hillocks, Menion found her sitting beneath a small twisted tree with long, gnarled branches that reminded him of willow roots. She was a young girl, very beautiful and obviously very much at home in these lands as she sang brightly, seemingly oblivious to anyone who might be attracted by the sound of her voice. He did not conceal his approach, but moved straight to her side, smiling gently at her freshness and youth. She smiled back at him, but made no effort to rise nor to greet him, continuing the gay strains of the tune she had been singing all this time. The Prince of Leah came to a halt several feet away from her, but she quickly beckoned him to come closer and sit next to her beneath the odd-shaped tree. It was then that from somewhere deep within him a small warning nerve twinged, some sixth sense not yet entranced by her vibrant song tugged at him and demanded to know why this young girl should ask a complete stranger to sit with her.

There was no reason for his hesitation other than perhaps the innate distrust the hunter has for all things out of place and time in nature; but whatever the reason, it caused the highlander to pause. In that instant the girl and the song disappeared into vapor, leaving Menion to face the strange-looking tree on the barren rise.

For one second Menion hesitated, unable to believe what had just occurred, and then hastily moved to withdraw. But the loose ground about his feet opened even as he paused, releasing a heavy cluster of thick-gnarled roots which wound themselves tightly about the young man's ankles, holding him fast. Menion stumbled over backward trying to break free. For a moment he found his predicament to be ludicrous. But try as he might, he could not work free of those clinging roots. The strangeness of the situation increased almost immediately as he glanced up to see the strange root-limbed tree, previously immobile, approaching in a slow, stretching motion, its limbs extended toward him, their tips containing small but deadly-looking needles. Thoroughly aroused now, Menion dropped his pack and bow in one motion and unsheathed the great sword, realizing that the girl and the song had been an illusion to draw him within reach of this ominous tree. He cut briefly at the roots which bound him, severing them in places, but the work was slow because they were wound so tightly about his ankles that he could not risk broad strokes. Sudden panic set in as he realized he could not get free in time, but he forced the feeling down and shouted his defiance at the plant, which by now was almost on top of him. Swinging in fury as it came within reach, he quickly severed a number of the clutching limbs and it withdrew slightly, its whole frame shuddering in pain. Menion knew that with its next approach he had to strike its nerve center if he expected to destroy it. But the strange tree had other ideas; coiling its limbs into itself, it thrust them toward the imprisoned traveler one at a time, showering him with the tiny needles that flew off the ends. Many of them missed altogether and some bounced harmlessly off his heavy tunic and boots. But others struck the exposed skin of his hands and head and embedded themselves with small stinging sensations. Menion tried to brush them off, while protecting himself from further assault, but the little needles broke off, leaving their tips embedded in his skin. He felt a kind of slow drowsiness begin to steal over him and portions of his nervous system begin to go numb. He realized at once that the needles contained some sort of drug that was designed to put the plant's victim to sleep, to render it helpless for easy disposition. Wildly, he fought the feeling seeping through his system, but soon dropped helplessly to his knees, unable to fight it, knowing that the tree had won.

But amazingly, the deadly tree appeared to hesitate and then to inch slightly backward, coiling again in attack. Slow, heavy footsteps sounded behind the fallen prince, approaching cautiously. He could not turn his head to see who it was, and a deep bass voice warned him abruptly to remain motionless. The tree coiled expectantly to strike, but an instant before it released its deadly needles, it was struck with shattering impact by a huge mace that flew over the shoulder of the fallen Menion. The strange tree was completely toppled by the blow. Obviously injured, it struggled to raise itself and fight back. Behind him, Menion heard the sharp release of a bow-string and a long black arrow embedded itself deep within the plant's thick trunk. Immediately the roots about his feet released their grip and sank into the earth and the main portion of the tree shuddered violently, limbs thrashing the air and showering needles in all direc-tions. A moment later, it drooped slowly to the earth. With a final spasm, it lay motionless.

Still heavily drugged from the needles, Menion felt the strong hands of his rescuer grip his shoulders roughly and force him into a prone position while a broad hunting knife severed the few remaining strands binding his feet. The figure before him was a powerfully built Dwarf, dressed in the green and brown woodsman's clothing worn by most of that race. He was tall for a Dwarf, a little over five feet, and carried a small arsenal of weapons bound about his broad waist. He looked down at the drugged Menion and shook his head dubiously.

"You must be a stranger to do a dumb thing like that," he reprimanded the other in his deep bass voice. "Nobody with any sense plays around with the Sirens."

"I am from Leah . . . to the west," Menion managed to gasp out, his voice thick and strange to his own ears.

"A highlander—I might have known." The Dwarf laughed heartily to himself. "You'd have to be, I suppose. Well, don't worry, you'll be fine in a few days. That drug won't kill you if we get it treated, but you'll be out for a while."

He laughed again and turned to retrieve his mace. Menion, with his final ounce of strength, grasped him by the tunic.

"I must reach . . . the Anar . . . Culhaven," he gasped sharply. "Take me to Balinor . . ."

The Dwarf looked back at him sharply, but Menion had lapsed into unconsciousness. Muttering to himself, the Dwarf picked up his own weapons and those of the fallen highlander. Then with surprising strength, he heaved the limp form of Menion over his broad shoulders, testing the load for balance. Satisfied at last that all was in place, he began trudging steadily, muttering all the while, moving toward the forests of the Anar.

VIII

Flick Ohmsford sat quietly on a long stone bench in one of the upper levels of the lavishly beautiful Meade Gardens in the Dwarf community known as Culhaven. He had a perfect view of the amazing gardens stretching down the rocky hillside in systematic levels that tapered off about the edges in carefully laid pieces of cut stone, reminiscent of a long waterfall flowing down a gentle slope. The creation of the gardens on this once barren hillside was a truly marvelous accomplishment. Special soils had been háuled from more fertile regions to be placed on the garden site, enabling thousands of beautiful flowers and plants to flourish year round in the mild climate of the lower Anar. The color was indescribable. To compare the myriad hues of the flowers to the colors of the rainbow would have been a great injustice. Flick attempted briefly to count the various shades, a task he soon found to be impossible. He gave up quickly and turned his attention to the large clearing at the foot of the gardens where members of the Dwarf community were passing on their way to or from whatever work they were engaged in. They were a curious people, it seemed to Flick, so dedicated to hard work and a well-guarded order of life. Everything they did was always carefully planned in advance, meticulously thought out to a point where even the cautious Flick was nettled by the time spent in preparation. But the people were friendly and eager to be of service, a kindness not lost on either of the visiting Valemen, who felt more than a bit out of place in this strange land.

They had been in Culhaven for two days now, and still they had not been able to learn what had happened to them, why they were there, or how long their stay would be. Balinor had told them nothing, advising them that he knew very little himself and that all would be revealed in due time, a comment Flick found to be not only melodramatic but aggravating. There was no sign of Allanon, no word of his whereabouts. Worst of all, there was no news of the absent Menion, and the brothers had been forbidden to leave the safety of the Dwarf village for any reason. Flick glanced to the floor of the gardens again to see if his personal bodyguard was still there, and quickly spied him off to one side, his tireless gaze fixed on the Valeman. Shea had been infuriated by this treatment, but Balinor was quick to point out that someone should be with them at all times in case of an attempt on their lives by one of the roving Northland creatures. Flick had acquiesced readily, remembering all too well the close calls he had already had with the Skull Bearers. He put aside his idle thoughts at the approach of Shea on the winding garden path.

"Anything?" Flick asked anxiously as the other reached his side and sat down quietly next to him.

"Not one word," came the short reply.

Shea felt vaguely exhausted all over again, even though he had had two days to recover from the strange odyssey that had brought them from their home in Shady Vale to the Forests of Anar. Their treatment had been decent if sometimes a bit overdone, and the people seemed genuinely concerned for their welfare. But there had been no word given out as to what was to happen next. Everyone, including Balinor, seemed to be waiting for something, perhaps the arrival of the long-absent Allanon. Balinor had been unable to explain to them how they had reached the Anar. Responding to a mysterious flashing light, he had found them lying on a low riverbank just outside of Culhaven two days ago, and had brought them to the village. He knew nothing of the old man nor of how they had traveled that long distance upstream. When Shea mentioned the legends concerning a King of the Silver River, Balinor shrugged and nonchalantly agreed that anything was possible.

"No news of Menion . . .?" Flick asked hesitantly.

"Only that the Dwarfs are still out looking for him, and it may take some time," Shea answered quietly. "I don't know what to do next."

Flick inwardly conceded that this last admission had proved to be the story of the entire outing. He glanced downward to the foot of the Meade Gardens where a small cluster of heavily armed Dwarfs were congregating around the commanding figure of Balinor, who had suddenly appeared from the woods beyond. Even from their vantage point atop the gardens, the Valemen could tell that he still wore the chain mail beneath the long hunting cloak they had come to recognize so well. He spoke earnestly with the Dwarfs for a few minutes, his face lined in thought. Shea and Flick knew very little about the Prince of Callahorn, but the people of Culhaven seemed to have the highest regard for him. Menion, too, had spoken well of Balinor. His homeland was the northernmost kingdom of the sprawling Southland. Commonly referred to as the borderlands, it served as a buffer zone fronting the southern boundaries of the Northland. The citizens of Callahorn were predominantly Men, but unlike the majority of the people of their race, they mingled freely with the other races and did not pursue a policy of isolationism. The highly regarded Border Legion was quartered in that distant country, a professional army commanded by Ruhl

Buckhannah, King of Callahorn and the father of Balinor. Historically, the entire Southland had relied on Callahorn and the Legion to blunt the initial thrust of an invading army, giving the rest of the land a chance to prepare for battle. In the five hundred years since its formation, the Border Legion had never been defeated.

Balinor had begun a slow ascent to the stone bench where the Valemen sat patiently waiting. He smiled a greeting as he came up to them, aware of the discomfort they felt in not knowing what was to happen to them and of the anxiety they were experiencing for the safety of their missing friend. He sat down next to them and was silent for a few minutes before speaking.

"I know how difficult this must be for you," he began patiently. "I have every available Dwarf warrior out looking for your lost friend. If anyone can find him in this region, they will—and they won't give up, I promise you."

The brothers nodded their understanding of Balinor's efforts to help them in any way possible.

"This is a very dangerous time for these people, though I suppose Allanon did not speak of it. They are facing the threat of an invasion through the upper Anar by Gnomes. There have already been skirmishes all along the border and signs of a huge army massing somewhere above the Streleheim Plains. You may have guessed that all of this is tied in with the Warlock Lord."

"Does this mean that the Southland is in danger, too?" asked an anxious Flick.

"Undoubtedly." Balinor nodded. "That's one reason why I'm here—to arrange a coordinated defensive strategy with the Dwarf nation in case of an all-out assault."

"But where is Allanon then?" asked Shea quickly. "Is he going to get here soon enough to help us? What has the Sword of Shannara got to do with all this?"

Balinor looked at the puzzled faces and shook his head slowly.

"I must honestly confess that I cannot give you the answers to any of those questions. Allanon is a very mysterious figure, but a wise man who has been a dependable ally whenever we have needed him in the past. When I saw him last, several weeks before I spoke to you in Shady Vale, we set a date to meet in the Anar. He is already three days overdue."

He paused in quiet speculation, looking down at the gardens and beyond to the great trees of the Anar Forests, listening to the sounds of the woods and the low voices of the Dwarfs moving about in the clearing below. Then abruptly a shout went up from a cluster of Dwarfs at the foot of the gardens, joined almost immediately by the shouts and cries of others mingled in with a huge clamor swelling from the woods beyond the village of Culhaven. The men on the stone bench rose uncertainly, looking quickly about for some sign of danger. Balinor's strong hand came to rest on the pommel of his broadsword, strapped tightly at his side beneath the hunting cloak. A moment later one of the Dwarfs below came rushing up the path, shouting wildly as he ran.

"They found him, they found him!" he yelled excitedly, almost stumbling in his haste to reach them.

Shea and Flick exchanged startled looks. The runner came to a breathless stop before them, and Balinor gripped his shoulder excitedly.

"Have they found Menion Leah?" he demanded quickly.

The Dwarf nodded happily, his short, stocky frame heaving with the exertion of the dash to reach them with the good news. Without a word, Balinor bounded down the path toward the shouting, Shea and Flick behind him. They reached the clearing below in a matter of seconds and ran along the main path through the woods leading to the village of Culhaven several hundred yards beyond. Ahead of them they could hear the excited shouting of the Dwarf population congratulating whomever it was who had found the lost highlander. They reached the village and, pushing through the throngs of Dwarfs blocking the way, made straight for the center of all the excitement. A ring of guards parted to let them into a small courtyard formed by buildings on the right and left and a high stone wall in the rear. On a long wooden table lay the motionless body of Menion Leah, his face pale and seemingly lifeless. A team of Dwarf doctors bent dutifully over the inert form, apparently treating him for some injury. Shea gave a sharp cry and tried to rush forward, but Balinor's strong arm held him back as the warrior called out to one of the nearby Dwarfs.

"Pahn, what's happened here?"

The solid-looking Dwarf, dressed in armor and apparently one of the returning search party, hastened to their side.

"He'll be all right after he's treated. He was found entangled in one of the Sirens out in the middle of the Battlemound lowlands below the Silver River. Our search party didn't find him. It was Hendel, returning from the cities south of Anar."

Balinor nodded and looked about for some sign of the rescuer.

"He left for the assembly hall to make his report," the Dwarf responded to the unasked question.

Motioning the two Valemen to follow him, Balinor made his way out of the courtyard through the crowd and across the main street to the large assembly hall. Inside were the offices of the governing officials of the village and the assembly room, in which they found the Dwarf Hendel sitting on one of the long benches, eating ravenously while a scribe took down his report. Hendel looked up as they approached, glanced

curiously at the Valemen and nodded briefly to Balinor, continuing to devour his meal without interruption. Balinor dismissed the scribe, and the three men sat down across from the disinterested Dwarf, who appeared both exhausted and starved.

"What an idiot, tackling one of those Sirens with a sword," he muttered. "Got spunk though. How is he?"

"He'll be fine after he's treated," replied Balinor grinning reassuringly at the uneasy Valemen. "How did you find him?"

"Heard him yelling." The other continued to eat without pausing. "I had to carry him almost seven miles before I ran into Pahn and the search party along the Silver River."

He paused and looked again at the two Valemen, who were listening intently. The Dwarf appraised them curiously and looked back at Balinor, eyebrows raised.

"Friends of the highlander—and of Allanon," responded the borderman, cocking his head meaningfully. Hendel merely nodded to them curtly.

"I'd never have known who he was if he hadn't mentioned your name," Hendel informed them shortly, indicating the tall borderman. "It might help matters if now and then someone would tell me what was going on—before it's happened, not after."

He declined to comment further, and an amused Balinor smiled over to the puzzled brothers, shrugging slightly to indicate the Dwarf was irascible by nature. Shea and Flick were a bit uncertain about the fellow's temperament and had purposely kept silent while the other two conversed, though both Valemen were eager to hear the full story behind Menion's rescue.

"What's your report on Sterne and Wayford?" Balinor asked finally, referring to the large Southland cities immediately south and west of the Anar.

Hendel ceased eating and laughed abruptly.

"The officials of those two fine communities will consider the matter and send along a report. Typical bungling officials, elected by the disinterested people to juggle the ball until it can be passed on to some other fool. I could tell five minutes after I opened my mouth that they thought I was crazy. They don't see the danger until the sword is at their own throats—then they scream for assistance from those of us who knew it all along." He paused and resumed his meal, obviously disgusted with the whole subject.

"I should have expected that, I suppose." Balinor sounded worried. "How can we convince them of the danger? There hasn't been a war in so many years that no one wants to believe it could happen now."

"That's not the real problem, as you well know," interjected the irate Hendel. "They simply don't feel they should be involved in the matter. After all, the frontiers are protected by Dwarfs, not to mention the cities of Callahorn and the Border Legion. We've been doing it up to now—why can't we keep doing it? Those poor fools . . ."

He trailed off slowly, finished with his statement and his meal, feeling tired from the long trip home. He had been on the road for almost three weeks, traveling to the cities of the Southland, and it all seemed to have been for nothing. He felt keenly discouraged.

"I don't understand what's happened," Shea announced quietly.

"Well, that's two of us," Hendel replied sullenly. "I'm going to bed for about two weeks. See you then."

He stood up abruptly and walked out of the assembly room without even a short farewell, his broad shoulders stooped wearily. The three men watched him go without speaking, their eyes fixed on his departing silhouette until it was lost from sight. Then Shea turned questioningly to Balinor.

"It's the age-old tale of complacency, Shea." The tall

warrior sighed deeply and stretched as he rose. "We may be standing on the brink of the greatest war in a thousand years, but no one wants to accept the fact. Everyone gets in the same rut—let a few take care of the gates to the city while the rest forget and go back to their homes. It becomes a habit—depending on a few to protect the rest. And then one day . . . the few are not enough, and the enemy is within the city—right through the open gates . . ."

"Is there really going to be a war?" Flick asked, almost fearfully.

"That is the question exactly," Balinor responded slowly. "The only man who can give us the answer is absent . . . and overdue."

In the excitement of finding Menion alive and well, the Valemen had temporarily forgotten Allanon, the man who was the reason for their being in the Anar in the first place. The by-now familiar questions again flashed through their minds with new persistency, but the Valemen had learned to live with them over the past few weeks and all doubts were reluctantly shoved aside once more. Balinor caught their attention as he moved toward the open door, and they quickly followed.

"You mustn't mind Hendel, you know," he reassured them as they walked. "He's gruff like that with everyone, but he's one of the finest friends you could ask for. He has fought and outwitted the Gnomes along the upper Anar for years, protecting his people and the complacent citizens of the Southland who so quickly forget the crucial role the Dwarfs play as guardians of these borders. The Gnomes would like to get their hands on him, I can tell you."

Shea and Flick said nothing, ashamed of the fact that the people of their own race could be so selfish, yet realizing that they, too, had been ignorant of the situation in the Anar before hearing of it from Balinor. They were bothered by the thought of renewed hostilities between the races, recalling their history lessons on the old race wars and the terrible hatred of those bitter years. The possibility of a third war of the races was chilling.

"Why don't you two go on back to the gardens," advised the Prince of Callahorn. "I'll have a message sent as soon as I hear of any change in Menion's condition."

The brothers reluctantly agreed, knowing they had no other choice in the matter anyway. Before turning in that night, they stopped by the room where Menion was being kept, only to be told by the Dwarf sentry that their friend was asleep and should not be disturbed.

But by the following afternoon, the highlander was awake and being visited by the anxious Valemen. Even Flick was grudgingly relieved to see the other alive and well, though he solemnly intoned that he had correctly predicted their misfortune many days in advance when they first decided to journey through the Black Oaks. Menion and Shea both laughed at Flick's eternal pessimism, but did not argue the point. Shea explained how Menion had been brought to Culhaven by the Dwarf Hendel, and then went on to relate the mysterious way in which he and Flick had been found near the Silver River. Menion was as mystified as they over their strange journey and could offer no logical explanation. Shea carefully refrained from mentioning the legend of a King of the Silver River, knowing full well what the highlander's response would be to any speculation that involved an old folktale.

That same day, in the early hours of the evening, word reached them that Allanon had returned. Shea and Flick were about to leave their rooms to visit Menion when they heard the excited shouts of Dwarfs rushing past their open windows toward the assembly hall where some sort of meeting was about to begin.

The anxious Valemen had not taken two steps beyond their doorway when they were surrounded by a team of four Dwarf guards and hustled quickly through the pushing crowds, past the open doors of the large assembly into a small adjoining room, where they were told to remain. The Dwarfs closed the door wordlessly as they exited, slid the lock bolts into place, and assumed positions immediately outside. The room was brightly lit and furnished with several long tables and benches, at which the bewildered Valemen silently seated themselves. The windows to the room were closed and even without checking, Shea knew they would be barred like the door. From the assembly hall they could hear the deep voice of a single speaker.

Several minutes later the door to the chamber opened and Menion, looking flushed but otherwise quite well, was briskly ushered in by two Dwarf guards. When they were left alone, the highlander explained that they had come for him the same as for the Valemen. From snatches of conversation he had heard on the way over, it appeared that the Dwarfs in Culhaven and probably all of the Anar were preparing for war. Whatever news Allanon had brought back with him had thrown matters into a state of confusion in the Dwarf community. He thought he had caught a quick glimpse of Balinor through the open doors of the assembly hall, standing on the platform at the front of the building, but the guards had rushed him past and he couldn't be sure.

The voices from the congregation next door rose in a thunderous roar, and all three paused expectantly. Seconds passed as the shouting continued to roll through the large hall, spreading to the open grounds outside where it was taken up by the Dwarfs there. At the deafening peak of the shouting, the door to their room suddenly burst open to admit the dark, commanding figure of Allanon.

He walked over to the Valemen quickly, shook their

hands, and congratulated them on their successful journey to Culhaven. He was dressed as he had been when Flick had first encountered him, his lean face half hidden in the long cowl, his whole appearance dark and foreboding. He greeted Menion courteously and moved to the head of the nearest table, motioning the others to be seated. He had been followed into the room by Balinor and a number of Dwarfs who were apparently leaders in the community, among them the irascible Hendel. Bringing up the rear of this procession were two slim, almost shadowy figures in curious, loose-fitting woodsman garb, who quietly took seats near Allanon at the head of the table. Shea could see them clearly from his position at the other end, and concluded after a quick observation that they were Elves from the distant Westland. Their keen features, from the sharply raised eyebrows to the strange pointed ears, marked them distinctively. Shea turned back and saw that both Flick and Menion were looking at him curiously, obviously appraising his own strong resemblance to the strangers. None of them had ever seen an Elf, and while they knew that Shea was half Elf and had heard descriptions given of the Elven people, none had ever had a chance to compare the Valeman to one.

"My friends." The deep voice of Allanon boomed out in the slight stir of voices as he rose commandingly to his full height of seven feet. The room was instantly silent as all faces turned in his direction. "My friends, I must now tell you what I have as yet told no one else. We have suffered a tragic loss."

He paused and looked at the anxious faces in turn.

"Paranor has fallen. A division of Gnome hunters under the command of the Warlock Lord has seized the Sword of Shannara!"

There was dead silence for about two seconds before the Dwarfs were on their feet, shouting in anger. Balinor rose quickly in an effort to quiet them. Shea and Flick looked at each other in disbelief. Only Menion seemed unsurprised by the announcement, his lean face carefully scrutinizing the dark figure at the head of the table.

"Paranor was taken from within," Allanon continued after some semblance of order had been restored. "There is little question as to the fate of those who guarded the fortress and the Sword. I am told that all were executed. No one knows exactly how it happened."

"Have you been there?" Shea asked suddenly, feeling almost immediately that it was a stupid question.

"I left your home in the Vale so suddenly because I received word that an attempt would be made to secure Paranor. I arrived too late to help those within and barely escaped detection myself. That is one of the reasons I am so late in reaching Culhaven."

"But if Paranor has fallen and the Sword been taken . . .?" Flick's whispered question trailed off ominously.

"Then what can we do now?" Allanon finished harshly. "This is the problem facing us, the one we must provide an immediate answer for—the reason for this council."

Allanon suddenly left his position at the head of the long table and moved around until he was standing directly behind Shea. He placed one great hand on the slim shoulder and faced his attentive audience.

"The Sword of Shannara is useless in the hands of the Warlock Lord. It can only be raised by a son of the House of Jerle Shannara—this alone prevents the evil one from striking now. Instead, he has systematically hunted down and destroyed all members of that House, one at a time, one after another, even those I tried to protect—all whom I could find. Now they are all dead—all save one, and that one is young Shea. Shea is only half Elf, but he is a direct descendant of the King who carried the great Sword so many years before. Now he must raise it once again."

Shea would have bolted for the door if it had not been for the strong hand gripping his shoulder. He looked desperately at Flick and saw the fear in his own eyes mirrored in those of his brother's. Menion had not moved, but appeared visibly impressed by this grim declaration. What Allanon seemed to expect from Shea was more than any man had the right to ask.

᠂ "Well, I think we have shaken our young friend a bit." Allanon laughed shortly. "Do not despair, Shea. Things are not as bad as they may seem to you right now." He turned abruptly, walked back to the head of the table and faced the others.

"We must recover the Sword at all costs. There is no other choice left to us. If we fail to do this, the whole of the land will be plunged into the greatest war the races have seen since the near destruction of life two thousand years ago. The Sword is the key. Without it, we must fall back on our mortal strength, our fighting prowess—a battle with iron and muscle that can only result in uncountable thousands dying on both sides. The evil is the Warlock Lord, and he cannot be destroyed without the aid of the Sword—and the courage of a few men, not the least of whom must be those of us in this room."

Again he paused to measure the force of his words. There was absolute silence as he looked doubtfully at the silent gallery of grim faces staring back. Suddenly Menion Leah rose at the far end of the table and faced the giant speaker.

"What you are suggesting is that we go after the Sword—to Paranor."

Allanon nodded slowly, a half smile playing over his thin lips as he waited for a reaction from the startled listeners. His deep-set eyes twinkled blackly beneath the great brow, watching carefully the faces about him. Menion sat down slowly, total disbelief showing plainly on his handsome features, as Allanon continued.

"The Sword is still at Paranor; there is an excellent possibility that it will remain there. Neither Brona nor the Bearers of the Skull can personally remove the talisman—its mere physical presence is an anathema to their continued existence in the mortal world. Any form of exposure for more than several minutes would cause excruciating pain. This means that any attempt to transport the Sword north to the Skull Kingdom must be accomplished by use of the Gnomes that hold Paranor.

"Eventine and his Elven warriors were given the task of securing the Druid stronghold and the Sword. While Paranor has been lost to us, the Elves still hold the southern stretch of the Streleheim north of the fortress, and any attempt to travel north to the Dark Lord would require breaking through their patrols. Apparently Eventine was not at Paranor when it was taken, and I have no reason to believe that he will not endeavor to regain the Sword or, at the very least, thwart any attempt to remove it. The Warlock Lord will be aware of this, and I do not think he will risk losing the weapon by having the Gnomes carry it out. Instead, he will entrench at Paranor until his army moves south.

"There is a possibility that the Warlock Lord does not expect us to attempt to regain the Sword. He may believe that the House of Shannara has been exterminated. He may expect us to concentrate on strengthening our defenses against his forthcoming assault. If we act immediately, a small party may be able to slip into the Keep undetected and retrieve the Sword. Such an undertaking would be dangerous, but if there is even the remotest chance of success, the risk is worth it."

Balinor had risen and indicated he wished to speak

to those assembled. Allanon nodded and sat down.

"I do not understand the power of the Sword over the Warlock Lord—that much I freely admit," the tall warrior began. "But I do know the threat that we all face if Brona's army invades the Southland and the Anar as our reports indicate it is preparing to do. My homeland will be the first to face this threat, and if I can prevent it in any way, then I cannot do otherwise. I will go with Allanon."

The Dwarfs leaped up again at this point and enthusiastically shouted their support. Allanon stood up and raised his long arm in a plea for silence.

"These two young Elves at my side are cousins of Eventine. They will accompany me, for their stake in this matter is at least as great as your own. Balinor will go as well, and I will take one of the Dwarf chieftains—no more. This must be a small, highly skilled party of hunters if we are to succeed. Pick the best man among you and let him come with us."

He looked to the end of the table, where Shea and Flick sat watching in a mixed state of shock and confusion. Menion Leah pondered quietly, looking at no one in particular. Allanon glanced expectantly at Shea, his grim face suddenly softening as he saw the frightened eyes of the young Valeman who had come so far, through so many dangers to this apparent haven of safety, only to be told that he was expected to leave it for an even more perilous trip northward. But there had been no time to break the news to the Valeman in a gentle way. He shook his head doubtfully and waited.

"I think I had better go." The abrupt declaration came from Menion, who had again risen to his feet to face the others. "I came with Shea this far to be certain he reached the safety of Culhaven, which he has done. My duty to him is finished, but I owe it to my homeland and to my people to protect them in any way I can."

"What can you offer then?" asked Allanon abruptly, astonished that the highlander would volunteer without first speaking to his friends. Shea and Flick were clearly dumbfounded by this unexpected announcement.

"I'm the best bowman in the Southland," Menion answered smoothly. "Probably the best tracker as well."

Allanon seemed to hesitate for a moment, then looked to Balinor, who quietly shrugged. For a brief moment Menion and Allanon locked gazes, as if to judge each other's intentions. Menion smiled coldly at the grim historian.

"Why should I answer to you?" he queried shortly.

The dark figure at the other end of the table stared at him almost curiously and a deathly silence settled over the company. Even Balinor stepped back one short pace in shock. Shea knew instantly that Menion was asking for trouble and that everyone at the table except the three companions knew something about the foreboding Allanon they did not. The frightened Valeman shot a quick look at Flick, whose flushed face had gone pale at the thought of a confrontation between the two men. Desperate to avoid any trouble, Shea stood up suddenly and cleared his throat. Everyone looked in his direction, and his mind went blank.

"You have something to say?" demanded Allanon blackly. Shea nodded and his mind raced desperately, knowing what was expected. He looked again to Flick, who managed a barely perceptible nod indicating that he would go along with whatever his brother decided. Shea cleared his throat a second time.

"My special skill appears to be that I was born in the wrong family, but I had better see this matter through. Flick and I—Menion, too—will go to Paranor."

Allanon nodded his approval and even managed a slight smile, inwardly pleased with the young Valeman. Shea, more than any of the others, had to be strong. He was the last son of the house of Shannara, and the fate of so many would depend on that single, small chance of birth.

At the other end of the table, Menion Leah relaxed quietly in his seat, a barely audible sigh of relief escaping his lips as he silently congratulated himself. He had deliberately provoked Allanon, and in so doing had forced Shea to come to his rescue by agreeing to go to Paranor. It had been a desperate gamble to induce the little Valeman to make up his mind that he was going with them. The highlander had come close to what might have been a fatal confrontation with Allanon. He had been lucky. He wondered if luck would smile on all of them during the journey ahead.

IX

Shea stood quietly in the darkness outside the assembly hall and let the night air wash over his hot face in cool waves. Flick was immediately to his right, the broad face grim in the shadowed moonlight. Menion leaned idly against a tall oak some yards off to their left. The meeting had concluded, and Allanon had asked them to wait for him. The tall wanderer was still inside making preparations with the Dwarf elders to counter the expected invasion from the upper Anar. Balinor was with them, coordinating the defense of the famed Border Legion in distant Callahorn with that of the Dwarf army of the Eastland. Shea was relieved to be out of the stuffy little room—out in the open night where he could consider more clearly his hasty decision to go with the company to Paranor. He knew—and he guessed Flick must have known as well—that they could not expect to stay out of the inevitable conflict centering around the Sword of Shannara. They could have stayed in Culhaven, living almost like prisoners, hoping that the Dwarf people would protect them from the searching Skull Bearers. They could have stayed in this strange land, apart from all who knew them, perhaps forgotten in time by everyone except the Dwarfs. But to alienate themselves that way would have been worse than any imaginable fate at the hands of the enemy. For the first time Shea realized that he must accept the fact, finally and forever, that he was no longer merely the adopted son of Curzad Ohmsford. He was a son of the Elven House of Shannara, the son of kings and the heir to the fabled Sword, and though he would have wished it otherwise, he must accept what chance had decreed for him.

He looked quietly at his brother, who stood lost in thought, staring at the darkened earth, and he felt a keen pang of sorrow at the remembrance of the other's loyalty. Flick was courageous and loved him, but he had not bargained for this unexpected turn of events that would take them into the heart of the enemy's country. Shea did not want Flick to be involved in this matter—it was not his responsibility. He knew that the stocky Valeman would never desert him so long as he felt he could help, but perhaps now Flick could be persuaded to remain behind, even to return to Shady Vale to explain to their father what had befallen them. But even as he toyed with the idea, he discarded it, knowing that Flick would never turn back. Whatever else happened, he would see this matter through.

"There was a time," Flick's quiet voice broke into his thoughts, "when I would have sworn that I would live out my life in uneventful solitude in Shady Vale. Now it appears that I will be a part of an effort to save mankind."

"Do you think I should have chosen otherwise?" Shea asked after a moment's silent thought.

"No, I don't think so." Flick shook his head. "But remember what we talked about on the trip here—about things being beyond our control, even our understanding? You see how little control we now have over what's to become of us."

He paused and looked squarely over to his brother. "I think you made the right choice, and whatever happens, I'll be with you."

Shea smiled broadly and placed a hand on the other's shoulder, thinking to himself that this was exactly what he had predicted Flick would say. It was a small gesture perhaps, but one that meant more to him than any other could have. He was aware of the sudden approach of Menion from the other side and turned to face the highlander.

"I suppose you think me some sort of fool after what happened in there tonight," Menion stated abruptly. "But this fool stands along with old Flick. Whatever happens, we'll face it together, be it mortal or spirit."

"You caused that scene in there to get Shea to agree to go, didn't you?" an irate Flick demanded. "That's the lowest trick I have ever witnessed!"

"Never mind, Flick," Shea cut him short. "Menion knew what he was doing, and he did the right thing. I would have decided to go anyway—at least I'd like to believe I would. Now we've got to forget the past, forget our differences, and stand together for our own preservation."

"As long as I stand where I can see him," retorted his brother bitterly.

The door to the conference room opened suddenly and the broad figure of Balinor was silhouetted in the torchlight from within. He surveyed the three men standing just beyond him in the darkness, then closed the door and walked over to them, smiling slightly as he approached.

"I'm glad you decided to come with us, all of you," he stated simply. "I must add, Shea, that without you, the trip would have been pointless. Without the heir of Jerle Shannara, the Sword is only so much metal."

"What can you tell us about this magic weapon?" Menion asked quickly.

"I'll leave that to Allanon," replied Balinor. "He plans to speak with you here in just a few minutes."

Menion nodded, inwardly disturbed at the prospect of encountering the tall man again that evening, but curious to hear more about the power of the Sword. Shea and Flick exchanged quick glances. At last they would learn the full story behind what was happening in the Northland.

"Why are you here, Balinor?" Flick asked cautiously, not wishing to pry into the borderman's personal affairs.

"It's a rather long story—you would not be interested," replied the other almost sharply, immediately causing Flick to believe he had overstepped his bounds. Balinor saw his chagrined look, and smiled reassuringly. "My family and I have not been on very good terms lately. My younger brother and I had a . . . disagreement, and I wanted to leave the city for a while. Allanon asked me to accompany him to the Anar. Hendel and others were old friends, so I agreed."

"Sounds like a familiar tale," commented Menion dryly. "I've had some problems like that myself from time to time."

Balinor nodded and managed a half smile, but Shea could tell from his eyes that he did not consider this a laughing matter. Whatever had caused him to leave Callahorn was more serious than anything Menion had ever encountered in Leah. Shea quickly changed the subject.

"What can you tell us about Allanon? We seem to be placing an unusual amount of trust in him, and we still know absolutely nothing about the man. Who is he?"

Balinor arched his eyebrows and smiled, amused by the question and at the same time uncertain as to how it should be answered. He walked away from them a little, thinking to himself, and then turned back abruptly and motioned vaguely toward the assembly hall.

"I really don't know much about Allanon myself," he admitted frankly. "He travels a great deal, exploring the country, recording in his notes the changes and growth of the land and its people. He's well known in all the nations—I think he has been everywhere. The extent of his knowledge of this world is extraordinary—most of it isn't in any book. He is very remarkable. . . ."

"But who is he?" Shea persisted eagerly, feeling that he must learn the true origin of the historian.

"I can't say for certain, because he has never confided completely even in me, and I am almost like a son to him," Balinor stated very quietly, so softly in fact that they all moved a bit closer to be certain they missed nothing of what was to follow. "The elders of the Dwarfs and of my own kingdom say that he is the greatest of the Druids, that almost forgotten Council that governed men over a thousand years ago. They say that he is a direct descendant of the Druid Bremen—perhaps even of Galaphile himself. I think there is more than a little truth in that statement, because he went to Paranor often and stayed for long periods, recording his findings in the great record books stored there."

He paused for a moment and his three listeners glanced at each other, wondering if the grim historian could actually be a direct descendant of the Druids, thinking in awe of the centuries of history behind the man. Shea had suspected before that Allanon was one of the ancient philosopher-teachers known as Druids, and it seemed apparent that the man possessed a greater knowledge of the races and the origins of the threat facing them than did anyone else. He turned back to Balinor, who was speaking again.

"I can't explain it, but I don't believe we could be in better company for any peril, even were we to come face to face with the Warlock Lord himself. Though I haven't one shred of concrete evidence nor even an example to cite you, I'm certain that Allanon's power is beyond anything we have ever seen. He would be a very, very dangerous enemy."

"Of that, I haven't the slightest doubt," Flick muttered dryly.

Only minutes later, the door of the conference room opened and Allanon stepped quietly into view. In the half-light of the moon, he was huge and forbidding, almost a replica of the dreaded Skull Bearers they feared so much, the dark cape billowing slightly as he moved toward them, his lean face hidden in the depths of the long cowl about his head. They were silent as he approached, wondering what he would tell them, what it would mean for them in the days ahead. Perhaps he knew their thoughts instinctively as he walked up to them, but their eyes could not pierce the mask of inscrutability that cloaked his grim features and sheltered the man buried within. They could only see the sudden glint of his eyes as he stopped before them and looked slowly from one face to the next. A deep silence settled ominously over the little group.

"The time has come for you to learn the full story behind the Sword of Shannara, to learn the history of the races as only I know it to be." His voice reached out and drew them commandingly to him. "It is essential that Shea should understand, and since the rest of you share the risks involved, you should also know the truth. What you will learn tonight must be kept in confidence until I tell you it no longer matters. This will be hard, but you must do it."

He motioned for them to follow him and moved away from the clearing, drawing them deeper into the darkness of the trees beyond. When they were several hundred feet into the forest, he turned into a small, almost hidden clearing. He seated himself on the worn stub of an ancient trunk and motioned the others to find a place. They did so quickly and waited in silence as the famous historian gathered his thoughts and prepared to speak.

"A very long time ago," he began finally, still considering his explanation as he spoke, "before the Great Wars, before the existence of the races as we know them today, the land was—or was thought to

be—populated only by Man. Civilization had developed even before then for many thousands of
years—years of hard toil and learning that brought
Man to a point where he was on the verge of mastering
the secrets of life itself. It was a fabulous, exciting time
to live in, so expansive that much of it would be totally
beyond your comprehension were I empowered to
draw you the most perfect picture. But while Man
worked all those years to discover the secrets of life, he
never managed to escape his overpowering fascination for death. It was a constant alternative, even in the
most civilized of the nations. Strangely enough, the
catalyst of each new discovery was the same endless
pursuit—the study of science. Not the science the
races know today—not the study of animal life, plant
life, the earth and the simple arts. This was a science of
machines and power, one that divided itself into
infinite fields of exploration, all of which worked
toward the same two ends—discovering better ways
to live or quicker ways to kill."

He paused and laughed grimly to himself, cocking
his head in the direction of the attentive Balinor.

"Very strange indeed, when you think about
it—that Man should spend so much time working
toward two such obviously different goals. Even now
nothing has changed—even after all these years. . . ."

His voice trailed off for a moment and Shea risked a
brief look at the others, but their eyes were fixed on the
speaker.

"Sciences of physical power!" Allanon's sudden
exclamation brought Shea's head around with a snap.
"These were the means to all the ends of that era. Two
thousand years ago the achievements of the human
race were unparalleled in earth's history. Man's
age-old enemy, Death, could now claim only those
who had lived out their natural lifetime. Sickness was
virtually eliminated and, given a bit more time, Man
would even have found a way to prolong life. Some

philosophers claimed that the secrets of life were forbidden to mortals. No one had ever proved otherwise. They might have done so, but their time ran out and the same elements of power that had made life free from sickness and infirmity nearly destroyed it altogether. The Great Wars began, building gradually from smaller disputes between a few peoples and spreading steadily, despite the realization of what was happening—spreading from little matters into basic hatreds: race, nationality, boundaries, creeds . . . in the end, everything. Then suddenly, so suddenly that few knew what happened, the entire world was enveloped in a series of retaliatory attacks by the different countries, all very scientifically planned and executed. In a matter of minutes, the science of thousands of years, the learning of centuries, culminated in an almost total destruction of life.

"The Great Wars." The deep voice was grim, the glint of the dark eyes watching carefully the faces of his listeners. "Very apt name. The power expended in those few minutes of battle not only succeeded in wiping out those thousands of years of human growth, but it also began a series of explosions and upheavals that completely altered the surface of the land. The initial force did most of the damage, killing every living thing over ninety percent of the face of the earth, but the aftereffects carried on the alteration and extinction, breaking the continents apart, drying up oceans, making lands and seas uninhabitable for several hundred years. It should have been the end of all life, perhaps the end of the world itself. Only a miracle prevented that end."

"I can't believe it." The words slipped out before Shea could catch himself, and Allanon looked toward him, the familiar mocking smile spreading over his lips.

"That's your history of civilized man, Shea," he murmured darkly. "But what happened thereafter concerns us more directly. Remnants of the race of Man managed to survive during the terrible period following the holocaust, living in isolated sectors of the globe, fighting the elements for survival. This was the beginning of the development of the races as they are today—Men, Dwarfs, Gnomes, Trolls, and some say the Elves—but they were always there and that's another story for another time."

Allanon had made exactly the same comment concerning the Elven people to the Ohmsford brothers in Shady Vale. Shea wanted badly to stop the narration at that point to ask about the race of Elves and about his own origin. But he knew better than to irritate the tall historian by breaking in as he had several times during their first meeting.

"A few men remembered the secrets of the sciences that had shaped their way of life prior to the destruction of the old world. Only a few remembered. Most were little more than primitive creatures, and the few could recollect only bits and pieces of knowledge. But they had kept their books of learning intact and these could tell them most of the secrets of the old sciences. They kept them hidden and secure during that first several hundred years, unable to put the words to practical use, waiting for the time when they might. They read their precious texts instead and then, as the books themselves began to crumble with age and there was no way to preserve them or copy them, those few men who possessed the books began to memorize the information. The years passed and the knowledge was passed down carefully from father to son, each generation keeping the knowledge safely within the family, guarding it from those who didn't use it wisely, who might create a world in which the Great Wars could happen a second time. In the end, even after it once again became possible to record the information in those irreplaceable books, the men who had memorized them declined to do so. They were still afraid of the consequences, afraid of each other and even themselves. So they decided, individually for the most part, to wait for the right time to offer their knowledge to the growing new races.

"The years passed in this way as the new races slowly began to develop beyond the stage of primitive life. They began to unify into communities, trying to build a new life out of the dust of the old—but as you have already been told, they did not prove equal to the task. They quarreled violently over land, petty disputes which soon turned to armed conflict between the races. It was then, when the sons of those who had first kept the secrets of the old life, the old sciences, saw that matters were steadily regressing toward the very thing that had destroyed the old world, that they decided to act. The man called Galaphile saw what was happening and realized that if nothing were done, the races would surely be at war. So he called together a select group of men, all he could find who possessed any knowledge of the old books, to a council at Paranor."

"So that was the first Druid Council," murmured Menion Leah in wonder. "A council of all the knowledgeable men of that era, pooling their learning to save the races."

"A very praiseworthy effort at explaining a desperate attempt to prevent extermination of life," laughed Allanon shortly. "The Druid Council was formed with the best intentions on the part of most, perhaps all at first. They exerted a tremendous influence over the races because they were capable of offering so much to make life considerably better for everyone. They operated strictly as a group, each man contributing his knowledge for the benefit of all. Although they succeeded in preventing an outbreak of total war, and kept peace between the races at first, they encountered unexpected problems. The knowledge that each possessed had become unavoidably altered in small

ways in the telling from generation to generation, so
that many of the key understandings were different
than they had been.

"Complicating the situation was an understandable
inability to coordinate the different materials, the
knowledge of the different sciences. For many of the
council members, the learning passed down to them
by their ancestors lacked meaning in practical terms
and much of it appeared to be so many jumbled
words. So while the Druids, as they called themselves
after an ancient group who sought understanding,
were able to aid the races in many ways, they found
themselves unable to piece together enough out of the
texts they had memorized to master readily any of the
important concepts of the great sciences, the concepts
they felt certain would help the country to grow and
prosper."

"Then the Druids wanted the old world rebuilt on
their terms," spoke up Shea quickly. "They wanted to
prevent the wars that had destroyed them the first
time, yet re-create the benefits of all the old sciences."

Flick shook his head in bewilderment, unable to see
what all this had to do with the Warlock Lord and the
Sword.

"Correct," Allanon noted. "But the Druid Council,
for all its vast knowledge and good intentions,
overlooked a basic concept of human existence.
Whenever an intelligent creature possesses an innate
desire to improve its conditions, to unlock the secrets
of progress, it will find the means to do so—if not by
one method, then by another. The Druids secluded
themselves at Paranor, away from the races of the
land, while they worked alone or in small groups to
master the secrets of the old sciences. Most relied on
the material at hand, the knowledge of individual
members related to that of the entire Council to try to
rebuild and reconstruct the old means of harnessing
power. But some were not content with this approach.

A few felt that, instead of trying to understand the words and thoughts of the ancient recollections better, such knowledge as could be immediately grasped should be acted upon and developed in connection with new ideas, new rationalizations.

"So it was that a few members of the council, acting under the leadership of one called Brona, began to delve into the ancient mysteries without waiting for a full understanding of the old sciences. They had phenomenal minds, genius in a few instances, and they were eager to succeed, impatient to master the power that would be so useful to the races. But by a strange quirk of fate, their discoveries and their developments led them further and further from the studies of the Council. The old sciences were puzzles without answers for them, and so they deviated into other fields of thought, slowly and relentlessly intertwining themselves in a realm of study that none had ever mastered and none called science. What they began to unveil was the infinite power of the mystic—sorcery! They mastered a few of the secrets of the mystic before they were discovered by the Council and commanded to abandon their work. There was a violent disagreement and the followers of Brona left the Council in anger, determined to continue their own approach. They disappeared and were not seen again."

He paused for a moment, considering his explanation. His listeners waited impatiently.

"We know now what happened in the years that followed. During his prolonged studies, Brona uncovered the deepest secrets of sorcery and mastered them. But in the process he lost his own identity, eventually even his own soul to the powers he had sought so eagerly. Forgotten were the old sciences and their purpose in the world of man. Forgotten was the Druid Council and its goal of a better world. Forgotten was everything but the driving urge to learn more of the mystic arts, the secrets of the mind's power to reach into other worlds. Brona was obsessed with the need to extend his power—to dominate men and the world they inhabited through mastery of this terrible force. The result of this ambition was the infamous First War of the Races, when he gained domination over the weak and confused minds of the race of Man, causing that hapless people to make war on the other races, subjecting them to the will of the man who was no longer a man, who was no longer even the master of himself."

"And his followers . . .?" asked Menion slowly.

"Victims of the same. They became servants to their leader, all slaves of the strange power of sorcery. . . ." Allanon trailed off hesitantly, as if to add something but uncertain of its effect on his listeners. Thinking better of it, he continued. "The fact that these unfortunate Druids stumbled onto the very opposite of what they were seeking is in itself a lesson to Man. Perhaps with patience, they might have pieced together the missing links to the old sciences rather than uncovering the terrible power of the spirit world that fed eagerly on their unprotected minds until they were devoured. Human minds are not equipped to face the realities of nonmaterial existence on this sphere. It is too much for any mortal to bear for long."

Again he trailed off into ominous silence. The listeners now understood the nature of the enemy they were trying to outwit. They were up against a man who was no longer a human, but the projection of some great force beyond their own comprehension, a force so powerful that Allanon feared it could affect the human mind.

"The rest you already know," Allanon began again rather sharply. "The creature called Brona, who no longer resembled anything human, was the directing force behind both of the Race Wars. The Skull Bearers are the followers of their old master Brona, those Druids once human in form, once a part of the Council at Paranor. They cannot escape their fate any more than he can. The very forms they take are an embodiment of the evil they represent. But more important for our purposes, they represent a new age for mankind, for all the people of the four lands. While the old sciences have disappeared into our history, forgotten now as completely as the years when machines were the godsend of an easy life, the enchantment of sorcery has replaced them—a more powerful, more dangerous threat to human life than any before it. Do not doubt me, my friends. We live in the age of the sorcerer and his power threatens to consume us all!"

There was a moment of silence. A deep stillness hung oppressively in the forest night as Allanon's final words seemed to echo back with ringing sharpness. Then Shea spoke softly.

"What is the secret of the Sword of Shannara?"

"In the First War of the Races," Allanon replied in almost a whisper, "the power of the Druid Brona was limited. As a result, the combined might of the other races, coupled with the knowledge of the Druid Council, defeated his army of Men and drove him into hiding. He might have ceased to be and the whole incident been written off as merely another chapter in history—another war between mortals—except that he managed to unlock the secret of perpetuating his spiritual essence long after his mortal remains should have decomposed and turned to dust. Somehow he preserved his own spirit, feeding it on the power of the mystic forces he now possessed, giving it a life apart from materiality, apart from mortality. He now was able to bridge the two worlds—the world we live in and the spirit world beyond, where he summoned the black wraiths that had for centuries lain dormant, and waited for his time to strike back. As he waited, he

watched the races drift apart as he knew they must in
time, and the power of the Druid Council wane as their
interest in the races grew lax. As with all things evil, he
waited until the balance of hatred, envy, greed—the
human failings common to all the races—outweighed
the goodness and kindness, and then he struck.
Gaining easy control of the primitive, warlike Rock
Trolls of the Charnal Mountains, he reinforced their
numbers with creatures of the spirit world he now
served, and his army marched on the divided races.

"As you know, they crushed the Druid Council and
destroyed it—all save a few who fled to safety. One of
those who escaped was an aged mystic named
Bremen, who had foreseen the danger and in vain
attempted to warn the others. As a Druid, he was
originally a historian and in that capacity had studied
the First War of the Races and learned of Brona and his
followers. Intrigued by what they had attempted to
do, and suspicious that perhaps the mysterious Druid
had acquired powers that no one had known about nor
could have hoped to combat, Bremen began his own
study of the mystic arts, but with greater care and
respect for the possible power he felt he might unlock.
After several years of this pursuit, he became convinced that Brona was indeed still existent and that the
next war upon the human race would be started and
eventually decided by the powers of sorcery and black
magic. You can imagine the response he received to
this theory—he was practically thrown from the
confines of Paranor. As a result, he began to master
the mystic arts on his own and so was not present
when the castle at Paranor fell to the Troll army. When
he learned that the Council had been taken, he knew
that if he did not act, the races would be left
defenseless against the enchantment Brona had
mastered, power that mortals knew nothing about.
But he was faced with the problem of how to defeat a
creature who could not be touched by any mortal

weapon, one who had survived for over five hundred years. He went to the greatest nation of his time—the Elven people under the command of a courageous young King named Jerle Shannara—and offered his assistance. The Elven people had always respected Bremen, because they understood him better than even his fellow Druids. He had lived among them for years prior to the fall of Paranor, while studying the science of the mystic.''

"There is something I don't understand." Balinor spoke up suddenly. "If Bremen was a master of the mystic arts, why could he not himself challenge the power of the Warlock Lord?"

Allanon's response was somehow evasive. "He did confront Brona in the end on the Plains of Streleheim, though it was not a battle that was visible to mortal eyes, and both disappeared. It was presumed that Bremen had defeated the Spirit King, but time has proven otherwise, and now . . .'' He hesitated only an instant before quickly returning to his narrative, but the emphasis on the pause was not lost on any of his listeners.

"In any event, Bremen realized that what was needed was a talisman to serve as a shield against the possible return of one such as Brona at another time when there was no one familiar with the mystic arts to offer assistance to the peoples of the four lands. So he conceived the idea of the Sword, a weapon which would contain the power to defeat the Warlock Lord. Bremen forged the Sword of Shannara with the aid of his own mystic prowess, shaping it with more than the mere metal of our own world, giving it that special protective characteristic of all talismans against the unknown. The Sword was to draw its strength from the minds of the mortals for whom it acted as a shield—the power of the Sword was their own desire to remain free, to give up even their lives to preserve that freedom. This was the power which enabled Jerle

Shannara to destroy the spirit-dominated Northland army then; it is the same power that must now be used to send the Warlock Lord back into the limbo world to which he belongs, to imprison him there for all eternity, to cut off entirely his passage back to this world. But as long as he has the Sword, then he has a chance to prevent its power from being used to destroy him forever, and that, my friends, is the one thing that must not be."

"But then why is it that only a son of the House of Shannara . . .?" The question formed on Shea's fumbling lips, his own mind reeling confusedly.

"That is the greatest irony of all!" exclaimed Allanon before the question was even completed. "If you have followed all that I have related about the change of life following the Great Wars, the giving way of the old materialistic sciences to the science of the present age, the science of the mystic, then you will understand what I am about to explain—the strangest phenomenon of all. While the sciences of old operated on practical theories built around things that could be seen and touched and felt, the sorcery of our own time operates on an entirely different principle. Its power is potent only when it is believed, for it is power over the mind which can neither be touched nor seen through human senses. If the mind does not truly find some basis for belief in its existence, then it can have no real effect. The Warlock Lord realizes this, and the mind's fear of and belief in the unknown—the worlds, the creatures, all the occurrences that cannot be understood by men's limited senses—offer him more than enough basis upon which to practice the mystic arts. He has been relying on this premise for over five hundred years. In the same way, the Sword of Shannara cannot be an effective weapon unless the one holding it believes in his power to use it. When Bremen gave the sword to Jerle Shannara, he made the mistake of giving it directly to a king and to the house of a king—he did not give it to the people of the lands.

As a result, through human misunderstanding and historical misconception, the universal belief grew that the Sword was the weapon of the Elven King alone and that only those descended of his blood could take up the Sword against the Warlock Lord. So now, unless it is held by a son of the House of Shannara, that person can never fully believe in his right to use it. The ancient tradition that only such a one can wield it will make all others doubt—and there must be no doubt, or it will not operate. Instead, it will become merely another piece of metal. Only the blood and belief of a descendant of Shannara can invoke the latent power of the great Sword."

He concluded. The silence that followed was hollow. There was nothing left to tell the four that could be told. Allanon reconsidered briefly what he had promised himself. He had not told them every-thing, purposely holding back the little more that would have proved the final terror for them. He inwardly felt torn between the desire to have it all out and the gnawing realization that it would destroy any chance of success; their success was of paramount importance—only he knew the full truth of that fact. So he sat in silence, bitter in his private knowledge and angered by the self-imposed limits he had set for himself—the limits that forbade a complete revelation to those who had come to depend upon him so very heavily.

"Then only Shea can use the Sword if . . ." Balinor broke the silence abruptly.

"Only Shea has the birthright. Only Shea."

It was so quiet that even the night life of the forest seemed to have stilled its incessant chatter in sober contemplation of the grim historian's reply. The future came down to each as a simple declaration of existence—succeed or be destroyed.

"Leave me now," commanded Allanon suddenly. "Sleep while you can. We leave this haven at sunrise for the halls of Paranor."

X

The morning came quickly for the small company, and the golden half-light of dawn found them preparing to begin their long journey with sleep-filled eyes. Balinor, Menion, and the Valemen waited for the appearance of Allanon and the cousins of Eventine. No one spoke, partly because each was still half asleep and had very little to recommend him in the way of good humor, and partly because each was inwardly thinking about the hazardous trip that lay ahead. Shea and Flick sat quietly on a small stone bench, not looking at each other as they considered the tale Allanon had related to them the previous night, wondering what possible chance they had of recovering the Sword of Shannara, using it against the Warlock Lord to destroy him, and still returning alive to their homeland. Shea, particularly, had passed the point where his chief emotion was fear; now he felt only a sense of numbness that dulled his mind into self-imposed surrender, a robot-like acceptance of the fact that he was being led to the proverbial slaughter. Yet in spite of this resigned attitude toward the journey to Paranor, somewhere in the back of his confused mind was the lingering belief that he could work out all of these seemingly insurmountable obstacles. He could feel it lurking there, waiting for a more opportune moment to arise and demand satisfaction. But for the moment he allowed himself to lapse dutifully into numbed acquiescence.

The Valemen were dressed in woodsman garb provided by the Dwarf people, including warm half-cloaks in which they now wrapped themselves to ward off the chill of the early morning. In addition, they carried the short hunting knives they had brought with them from the Vale, tucked in their leather belts. Their packs were necessarily compact, in accord with the Valemen's small size. The country they would pass through offered some of the best hunting in all the Southland, and there were several small communities friendly to Allanon and the Dwarfs. But it was also the home of the Gnome people, the longtime, bitter enemies of the Dwarfs. There was some hope the little band would be able to maintain an advantage of stealth and secrecy in their travel and avoid any confrontation with Gnome hunters. Shea had carefully packed away the Elfstones in their leather pouch, showing them to no one. Allanon had not mentioned them since he had arrived in Culhaven. Whether this was an oversight or not, Shea was not about to give up the one really potent weapon that he possessed and kept the pouch hidden within his tunic.

Menion Leah stood several yards away from the brothers, pacing idly. He wore particularly non-descript hunting clothes, loose-fitting and colored to blend with the land to make his task as tracker and huntsman as uncomplicated as possible. His shoes were soft leather, toughened by certain oils to enable him to stalk anything without being heard and still travel the toughest ground without injuring the soles of his feet. Strapped to his lean back was the great sword, sheathed now, its strong hilt glinting dully in the early light as he shifted restlessly about. Across his shoulder he carried the long ash bow and its arrows, his favorite weapon on hunting trips.

Balinor wore the familiar long hunting cloak wrapped closely about his tall, broad frame, the cowl

pulled up around his head. Beneath the cloak was the
chain mail which could be seen glinting sharply ever
so often as his arms emerged in brief gestures from
beneath the shielding of the garment. He carried in his
belt a long hunting knife and the most enormous
sword that the Valemen had ever seen. It was so huge
that it appeared to them that one sweep of its great
blade would cut through a man completely. It was
hidden beneath the cloak at the moment, but the
brothers had seen him strap it to his side as he came
out to them earlier that morning.

Their waiting finally came to an end as Allanon
approached from the assembly hall, accompanied by
the lithe figures of the two Elves. Without stopping, he
bade them all good morning and directed them to fall
into line for the trip, warning sharply that once they
crossed the Silver River several miles ahead, they
would be in country traveled by Gnomes and that
conversation must be kept to a minimum. Their route
would take them from the river directly north through
the Anar Forests into the mountains that lay beyond.
There was less chance that they would be detected
traveling through this rough country than across the
plains that lay farther west, where the terrain was
admittedly more even and accessible. Secrecy was the
key to their success. If the purpose of their journey
became known to the Warlock Lord, they were
finished. Travel would be restricted to the daylight
hours while they were camouflaged by the forests and
mountains, and they would resort to night travel and
risk detection by the searching Skull Bearers only
when they were forced to cross the plains many miles
to the north.

As their representative on the expedition, the Dwarf
chieftain had chosen Hendel, the closemouthed Fellow
who had saved Menion from the Siren. Hendel led the
company out of Culhaven, since he was most
familiar with this part of the country. At his side

walked Menion, talking only occasionally, concentrating mostly on staying out of the sullen Dwarf's way
and trying to avoid drawing attention to his presence,
something the Dwarf felt was totally unnecessary.
Several paces back from them were the two Elves,
their slim figures like brief shadows as they moved
gracefully, effortlessly, speaking with each other in
quiet musical voices that Shea found reassuring. Both
carried long ash bows similar to Menion's. They wore
no cloaks—only the strange, close-fitting outfits they
had worn at the council the night before. Shea and
Flick followed them, and behind the Valemen walked
the silent leader of the company, his long strides
covering the ground with ease, his dark face lowered
to the trail. Balinor brought up the rear. Both Shea and
Flick were quick to realize that their position in the
center of the company was to assure their maximum
protection. Shea knew how valuable the others felt he
was to the success of the mission, but he was also
painfully aware that they considered him incapable of
defending himself in case of any real danger.

The company reached the Silver River and crossed
at a narrow spot where the winding thread of
gleaming water was spanned by a sturdy wooden
bridge. All talking ceased once they had passed over,
and all eyes went to the dense forest about them,
watching uneasily. The going was still relatively
smooth; the ground was level as the path wound
sharply through the great forest, leading them steadily
northward. The light of the morning sun shone in long
streamers through cracks in the heavy branches,
occasionally cutting across their path and catching
their faces as they walked, warming them briefly in the
cool air of the forest. Beneath their feet, the fallen
leaves and twigs were soaked with a heavy dew,
making a cushion that masked the sound of their
footsteps and helped to preserve the quiet of the day.
All about them they could hear sounds of life, though

they saw only multicolored birds and a few squirrels that scampered eagerly about their treetop domains, sometimes raining the travelers below with torrents of nuts and twigs as they leaped from branch to branch. The trees prevented the members of the company from seeing much of anything, their great girth ranging from three to ten feet in diameter, and their huge roots stretching out from the trunks like mammoth fingers, digging their way relentlessly into the earth of the forest floor. The view from every direction was masked, and the company had to content itself with relying on Hendel's familiarity with the country and the pathfinding knowledge of Menion Leah to guide them through the maze of vegetation.

The first day passed without incident, and they spent the night beneath the giant trees, somewhere north of the Silver River and Culhaven. Hendel was apparently the only one who knew exactly where they were, though Allanon conversed briefly with the taciturn Dwarf concerning their whereabouts and the route they were taking. The company ate its dinner cold, fearing that a fire might attract attention. But the general mood was light and the conversation was enjoyable. Shea took this opportunity to speak with the two Elves. They were cousins of Eventine, chosen to accompany Allanon as representatives of the Elven kingdom and to aid him in his search for the Sword of Shannara. They were brothers, the elder called Durin, a slim, quiet Westlander who gave the instant impression to Shea and the ever-present Flick that he was a man to be trusted. The younger brother was Dayel, a shy, extremely likable fellow who was several years the junior of Shea. His boyish charm was strangely appealing to the elder members of the company, particularly Balinor and Hendel, battle-hardened veterans of so many years of protecting the frontiers of their homelands, who found his youth and fresh outlook on life almost like a second chance for them to regain something that had passed them by years before. Durin informed Shea that his brother had left their Elven home several days prior to his marriage to one of the most beautiful girls in that country. Shea would not have believed Dayel old enough to marry, and found it difficult to understand why anyone would leave on the eve of his marriage. Durin assured him that it had been his brother's own choice, but Shea told Flick later that he believed that his relationship to the king had much to do with that decision. So now as the members of the company sat quietly and spoke in low tones to one another, all save the silent, aloof Hendel, Shea wondered how much the young Elf regretted his decision to leave his bride-to-be to come on this hazardous journey to Paranor. He found himself wishing inwardly that Dayel had not chosen to be a member of their party, but had remained safe within the protective confines of his own homeland.

Later that evening, Shea approached Balinor and asked him why Dayel had been allowed to come on such an expedition. The Prince of Callahorn smiled at the Valeman's concern, thinking to himself that the difference in ages between the two was hardly noticeable to him. He told Shea that in a time when the homelands of so many people were threatened, no one stopped to question why another was there to aid them—it was merely accepted. Dayel had chosen to come because his King had asked it and because he would have felt less of a man in his own mind had he declined. Balinor explained that Hendel had been waging a constant battle with the Gnomes for years to protect his homeland. The responsibility was delegated to him because he was one of the most experienced and knowledgeable bordermen in the Eastland. He had a wife and family at home that he had seen once in the past eight weeks and could not expect to see again for many more. Everyone on the journey had a great deal to lose, he concluded, perhaps even more than Shea realized. Without explaining his final remark, the tall borderman moved off to speak with Allanon on other matters. Somewhat discontented by the abrupt finish to their conversation, Shea moved back to join Flick and the Elven brothers.

"What kind of person is Eventine?" Flick was asking as Shea joined the group. "I've always heard that he is considered the greatest of the Elven kings, respected by everyone. What is he really like?"

Durin smiled broadly and Dayel laughed merrily at the question, finding it somehow amusing and unexpected.

"What can we say about our own cousin?"

"He is a great King," responded Durin seriously after a few moments. "Very young for a king, the other monarchs and leaders would say. But he has foresight, and most important of all, he gets things done before the time for doing them has passed. He holds the love and esteem of all the Elven people. They would follow him anywhere, do anything he asked, which is fortunate for all of us. The elders of our council would prefer to ignore the other lands, to try to remain isolated. Sheer foolishness, but they're afraid of another war. Only Eventine stands against them and that policy. He knows that the only way to avoid the war they all fear is to strike first and cut off the head of the army which threatens. That is one reason why this mission is so important—to see that this invasion is checked before it has time to develop into a full-scale war."

Menion had sauntered over from the other side of the small campsite and seated himself with them just in time to hear the last comment.

"What do you know of the Sword of Shannara?" he asked curiously.

"Very little actually," admitted Dayel, "although for

us it's a matter of history rather than legend. The Sword has always represented a promise to the Elven people that they need never again fear the creatures from the spirit world. It was always assumed that the threat was finished with the conclusion of the Second War of the Races, so no one really concerned himself with the fact that the entire House of Shannara died out over the years, except for a few such as Shea whom no one knew about. Eventine's family, our family, became rulers almost a hundred years ago—the Elessedils. The Sword remained at Paranor, forgotten by nearly everyone until now."

"What is the power of the Sword?" persisted Menion, a little too eagerly to suit Flick, who shot Shea a warning glance.

"I don't know the answer to that question," Dayel admitted and looked to Durin who shrugged in response and shook his head. "Only Allanon seems to know that."

They all looked momentarily toward the tall figure seated in earnest conversation with Balinor across the clearing. Then Durin turned to the others.

"It is fortunate that we have Shea, a son of the House of Shannara. He will be able to unlock the secret of the Sword's power once we have it in our possession, and with that power we can strike at the Dark Lord before he can create the war that would destroy us."

"If we get the Sword, you mean," corrected Shea quickly. Durin acknowledged this comment with a short laugh of agreement and a reassuring nod.

"There's still something about all this that doesn't set right," Menion declared quietly, rising abruptly and moving off to find a place to sleep. Shea watched him go and found himself in agreement with the highlander, but was unable to see what they could hope to do about their dissatisfaction. Right now he felt that there was so little hope of their succeeding in their quest to regain the sword that for the moment he would concentrate on simply completing the journey to Paranor. For now, he did not even want to think about what might happen after that.

The company was awake and back on the winding path with the breaking of the dawn, led by a watchful Hendel. The Dwarf moved them along at a rapid pace through the mass of great trees and heavy foliage that had grown increasingly dense as they penetrated deeper into the Anar. The trail was beginning to slope upward, an indication that they were approaching the mountains that ran the length of the central Anar. At some point farther north they would be forced to cross these broad peaks in order to reach the plains to the west that lay between them and the halls of Paranor. Tension began to mount as they moved more deeply into the domain of the Gnome people. They began to experience the unpleasant sensation that someone was constantly watching them, hidden in the denseness of the forest, waiting for the right moment to strike. Only Hendel seemed unconcerned as he led them, his own fears apparently eased by his familiarity with the terrain. No one spoke as they marched, all eyes searching the silent forest about them.

About midday, the path turned sharply upward and the company began to climb. The trees now grew farther apart and the scrub foliage was less congested. The sky became clearly visible through the trees, a deep blue unbroken by even the faintest trace of a cloud wisp. The sun was warm and bright, shining bravely through the scattered trees to light the whole of the forest. Rocks began to appear in small clusters and they could see the land ahead rise in tall peaks and jutting ridges that signaled the beginning of the southern sector of the mountains in the central Anar. The air became steadily cooler as they climbed and breathing became more difficult. After several hours, the company reached the edge of a very dense forest of dead pines, clustered so closely that it was impossible to see for more than twenty or thirty feet ahead at any one place. On both sides of their path, tall, slab-rock cliffs rose hundreds of feet into the air and peaked against the blueness of the afternoon sky. The forest stretched several hundred yards in either direction, ending at the cliff walls. At the edge of the pines, Hendel called a brief halt and spoke for several minutes with Menion, pointing to the forest and then the cliffs, apparently questioning something. Allanon joined them, then motioned the remainder of the company to gather around in a close circle.

"The mountains we are about to cross into are the Wolfsktaag, a no-man's-land for both Dwarf and Gnome," Hendel explained quietly. "We chose this way because there was less chance of meeting up with a Gnome hunting patrol, something that would certainly result in a pitched battle. The Wolfsktaag Mountains are said to be inhabited by creatures from another world—a good joke, isn't it?"

"Get to the point," Allanon broke in.

"The point is," Hendel continued, seemingly oblivious of the dark historian, "we were spotted about fifteen minutes back by one or possibly two Gnome scouts. There may be more around, we can't be certain—the highlander says he saw signs of a large party. In any event, the scouts will report us and bring back help in a hurry, so we'll have to move fast."

"Worse than that!" declared Menion quickly. "Those signs said there are Gnomes ahead of us somewhere—through those trees or in them."

"Maybe so, maybe not, highlander," Hendel cut back in sharply. "These trees run like this for almost a mile and the cliffs continue on both sides, but narrow sharply beyond the forest to form the Pass of Noose, the entrance to the Wolfsktaag. That is the way we have to go. To try any other route would cost us two more days, and we would be risking an almost certain run-in with Gnomes."

"Enough debate," Allanon said fiercely. "Let's

move out quickly. Once we reach the other side of the pass, we'll be in the mountains. The Gnomes will not follow us there."

"Encouraging, I'm sure," muttered Flick under his breath.

The company moved into the thickly clustered trees of the pine forest, following one another in single file, weaving among the rough, disjointed trunks. Dead needles lay in heaps over the whole of the earthen forest floor, creating a soft matting on which the passing of feet made no sound. The white-bark trees rose tall and lean, touching near their skeletal tops like some intricate spider web, lacing the blueness of the clear sky in fascinating designs. The party wound steadily forward through the maze of trunks and limbs behind Hendel, who chose their route quickly and without hesitation. They had not gone more than several hundred yards when Durin brought them up sharply and motioned for silence, looking question-ingly about, apparently searching the air for some-thing.

"Smoke!" he exclaimed suddenly. "They've set fire to the forest!"

"I don't smell any smoke," declared Menion, sniffing the air tentatively.

"You don't have the sharpened senses of an Elf either," Allanon stated flatly. He turned to Durin. "Can you tell where they've fired it?"

"I smell smoke, too," declared Shea absently, amazed that his own senses were as sharp as those of the Elves.

Durin cast about for a minute, trying to catch the scent of smoke from one particular direction.

"Can't tell, but it appears that they've fired it in more than one place. If they have, the forest will go up in a matter of minutes!"

Allanon hesitated for one brief second, then motioned for them to continue toward the Pass of

Noose. The pace picked up considerably as they hastened to reach the other side of the firetrap in which they were encased. A blaze in those dry woods would quickly cut off any chance of escape once it spread through the treetops. The long strides of Allanon and the borderman forced Shea and Flick to run to keep from falling behind. Allanon shouted something to Balinor at one point in the race, and the broad figure dropped back into the trees and was lost from sight. Ahead of them, Menion and Hendel had disappeared, and there were only fleeting glimpses of the Elven brothers dashing smoothly between the leaning pines. Only Allanon stayed clearly in view, a few paces behind, calling to them to run faster. Thick clouds of heavy white smoke were beginning to seep between the closely bunched trunks like a heavy fog, obscuring the path ahead and making it steadily more difficult to breathe. There was still no sign of the actual fire. It had not yet grown strong enough to spread through the intertwining boughs and cut them off. The smoke was everywhere in a matter of minutes, and both Shea and Flick coughed heavily with every breath, their eyes beginning to sting from the heat and irritation. Suddenly Allanon called to them to halt. Reluctantly they stopped and waited for the order to continue, but Allanon appeared to be looking back for something, his lean, dark face strangely ashen in the thick white smoke. Soon the broad figure of Balinor reappeared from the forest behind them, wrapped tightly in the long hunting cloak.

"You were right, they're behind us," he informed the historian, gasping out the words as he fought for breath. "They've fired the forest all along our backs. It looks like a trap to drive us into the Pass of Noose."

"Stay with them," Allanon ordered quickly, pointing to the frightened Valemen. "I've got to catch the others before they reach the pass!"

With incredible speed for a man so big, the tall

leader leaped away and dashed into the trees ahead, disappearing almost immediately. Balinor motioned for the Valemen to follow him, and they proceeded at a rapid pace in the same direction, fighting to see and to breathe in the choking smoke. Then, with frightening suddenness, they heard the sharp crackle of burning wood and the smoke began to billow past them in huge, blinding clouds of white heat. The fire was overtaking them. In a few minutes it would reach them and they would be burned alive! Coughing furiously, the three crashed heedlessly through the pines, desperate to escape the inferno in which they had been caught. Shea shot a quick glance skyward, and to his horror saw the flames leaping madly from the tops of the tall pines above and beyond them, burning their glowing way steadily down the long trunks.

Then abruptly, the impenetrable stone wall of the cliffs appeared through the smoke and the trees, and Balinor motioned them in that direction. Minutes later, as they groped their way along the cliff face, they saw the remainder of the company crouched in a clearing beyond the fringe of the burning trees. Ahead lay an open trail that wound upward into the rocks between the cliffs and disappeared into the Pass of Noose. The three quickly joined the others as the entire forest was enveloped in flames.

"They're trying to force us to choose between roasting in that pine forest or trying to get through the pass," shouted Allanon over the crackle of burning wood, looking anxiously toward the trail ahead. "They know we have only two ways to go, but they're facing the same choice and that's where they lose the advantage. Durin, go on ahead into the pass a little way and see if the Gnomes have set an ambush."

The Elf darted away without a sound, crouching low and keeping close to the cliff wall. They watched him until he had disappeared farther up the trail into the rocks. Shea huddled with the others, wishing that there was something he could do to help.

"The Gnomes are not fools." Allanon's voice cut into his thoughts abruptly. "Those in the pass know that they are cut off from those who fired the forest unless they can get by us first. They wouldn't risk having to retreat back through the Wolfsktaag Mountains for any reason. Either there is a large force of Gnomes in the pass ahead, which Durin should be able to tell us, or they've got something else in mind."

"Whatever it is, they'll probably try it in the section called the Knot," Hendel informed them. "At that point the trail narrows so that only one man at a time can get through the path formed by the converging cliff sides." He paused and appeared to be considering something further.

"I don't understand how they plan to stop us," Balinor cut in quickly. "These cliffs are almost vertical—no one could scale them without a long and hazardous climb. The Gnomes haven't had time to get up there since they spotted us!"

Allanon nodded thoughtfully, obviously in agreement with the borderman and unable to see what the Gnomes had in store for them. Menion Leah spoke quietly to Balinor, then abruptly left the group and moved ahead to the entrance of the pass where the cliff walls began to narrow sharply, scanning the ground intently. The heat of the burning woods had become so intense that they were forced to move farther into the mouth of the pass. Everything was still obscured by the clouds of white smoke which rolled out of the dying woods like a wall and dispersed sluggishly into the air. Long moments passed while the six awaited the return of Menion and Durin. They could still see the lean highlander studying the ground at the entrance to the pass, his tall form shadowy in the smoke-filled air. Finally, he stood up and moved back

to them, joined almost immediately by the returning
Elf.

"There were footprints, but no other sign of life in
the pass ahead," Durin reported. "Everything is
apparently undisturbed up to the narrowest point. I
didn't go beyond."

"There is something else," Menion cut in quickly.
"At the entrance to the pass, I found two clear sets of
footprints leading in and two sets out—Gnome feet."

"They must have slipped in ahead of us and then
out again by staying close to the cliff walls while we
blundered up the middle," Balinor said angrily. "But if
they were in there ahead of us, what . . .?"

"We won't find out by sitting here and discussing
it!" Allanon concluded in disgust. "We would only be
guessing. Hendel, take the lead with the highlander
and watch yourself. The rest stay in formation as
before."

The stocky Dwarf moved out with Menion at his
side, their sharp eyes keyed in on every boulder that
lined the winding path as it narrowed into the Pass of
Noose. The others followed several paces back,
casting apprehensive glances at the rugged terrain
surrounding them. Shea risked one quick look behind
him and noticed that, while Allanon was close on his
heels, Balinor was nowhere in sight. Apparently,
Allanon had again left the borderman to act as a rear
guard at the edge of the burning pine forest, to watch
for the inevitable approach of the Gnome hunters
lurking somewhere beyond. Shea knew instinctively
that they were caught in a trap carefully arranged for
them by the furtive Gnomes, and all that remained
was to discover what form it would take.

The path ahead rose sharply for the first hundred
yards or so, then tapered off gradually and narrowed
to such an extent that there was only enough room for
one person to pass between the cliff sides. The pass
was no more than a deep niche in the face of the cliff,

the sides slanting inward and almost closing far above them. Only a thin ribbon of light from the blue sky streamed downward to reach them, faintly lighting the winding, boulder-laden path ahead. Their progress slowed perceptibly as the lead men searched for traps left by the Gnomes. Shea had no idea how far Durin had gone in his scouting mission, but apparently he had not ventured into what Hendel had referred to as the Knot. He could guess where the name had originated. The narrowness of the passage left the sharp impression of being drawn through the knot of a hangman's noose to the same fate as that which awaited the condemned. He could hear Flick's labored breathing almost in his ear and experienced an unpleasant feeling of suffocation at the closeness of the rock walls. The group moved slowly onward, slightly bent to avoid the narrowed cliff sides and their razor-sharp stone projections.

Suddenly, the pace slowed further and the whole line crowded together. Behind him, Shea heard the deep voice of Allanon muttering angrily, demanding to know what had happened, asking excitedly to be let to the front. But in these close quarters it was impossible for anyone to give way. Shea peered ahead and noticed a sharp ray of light beyond the leaders. Apparently the path was widening at last. They were nearly free of the Pass of Noose. But then, just as Shea felt they had reached the safety of the other end, there were loud exclamations and the entire line came to a complete stop. Menion's voice cut through the semidarkness in surprise and anger, causing Allanon to mutter a low oath of fury and order the company to move ahead. For a moment nothing happened. Then slowly the company began to inch forward, moving into a wide clearing shadowed by the cliff sides as they parted abruptly into a sky of sunshine.

"I was afraid of this," Hendel was muttering to himself as Shea followed Dayel out of the niche. "I had hoped that the Gnomes had failed to explore this far into their taboo land. It appears, highlander, that they have us trapped."

Shea stepped out into the light on a level rock shelf where the others in the company stood talking in hushed tones of anger and frustration. Allanon emerged at almost the same moment, and together they surveyed the scene before them. The rock shelf on which they stood extended out from the opening of the Pass of Noose about fifteen feet to form a small ledge that dropped abruptly into a yawning chasm hundreds of feet deep. Even in the bright sunlight, it appeared to be bottomless. The cliff walls spread outward from their backs to form a half circle around the chasm and then slanted away brokenly, giving way to the heavy forests that began several hundred yards beyond. The chasm, a trick of nature by all appearances, bore the distinct shape of a jagged noose. There was no way around it. On the other side of the fissure dangled the remains of what had previously been some sort of rope and wood bridge which had served as the only means by which travelers could cross. Eight pairs of eyes scanned the sheer walls of the cliffs, seeking a means to scale their slick surfaces. But it was all too apparent that the only way to the other side was directly across the open pit before them.

"The Gnomes knew what they were doing when they destroyed the bridge!" Menion fumed to no one in particular. "They've left us trapped between them and this bottomless hole. They don't even have to come in after us. They can wait until we starve to death. How stupid . . ."

He trailed off in fury. They all knew they had been foolish in allowing themselves to be tricked into entering such a simple, but effective trap. Allanon moved to the edge of the chasm, peered intently into its depths and then scanned the terrain on the other side, searching for a means to cross.

"If it were a bit more narrow or if I had a little more running room, I might be able to jump it," volunteered Durin hopefully. Shea estimated the distance across to be easily thirty-five feet. He shook his head doubtfully. Even if Durin had been the best jumper in the world, he would have questioned such an attempt under these conditions.

"Wait a minute!" Menion cried suddenly, leaping to Allanon's side and pointing off to the north. "How about that old tree hanging off the cliff side on the left?"

Everyone looked eagerly, unable to understand what the highlander was suggesting. The tree of which he spoke grew embedded in the cliff face to the left almost a hundred and fifty yards away from them. Its gray shape hung starkly against the clear sky, its branches leafless and bare, dipping heavily downward like the tired limbs of some weary giant frozen in midstride. It was the only tree that anyone could see on the rock-strewn path that led away from the chasm and disappeared below the cliff sides into the forests beyond. Shea looked with the others but could see no help from that corner.

"If I could put an arrow into that tree with a line tied to it, someone light could go across hand over hand and secure the rope for the rest of us," the Prince of Leah suggested, gripping in his left hand the great ash bow.

"That shot is over a hundred yards," replied Allanon testily. "With the added weight of a line tied to the arrow, you would have to make the world's greatest shot just to get it there, not to mention embedding it in the tree deep enough to hold a man's weight. I don't think it can be done."

"Well, we had better come up with something or we can forget the Sword of Shannara and everything else," growled Hendel, his craggy face flushed with anger.

"I have an idea," Flick ventured suddenly, taking a

step forward as he spoke. Everyone looked at the
stocky Valeman as if they were just seeing him for the
first time and had forgotten that he was even along.

"Well, all right, don't keep it to yourself!" exclaimed
Menion impatiently. "What is it, Flick?"

"If there were an expert bowman in the group—"
Flick shot Menion a venomous look "—he might be
able to put an arrow with a line into the wood
fragments of the bridge hanging on the other side and
pull it back across to this side."

"That is an idea worth trying!" agreed Allanon
quickly. "Now who . . ."

"I can handle it," Menion said quickly, glaring at
Flick.

Allanon nodded shortly, and Hendel produced a
stout cord which Menion Leah fastened securely
about the tip of an arrow, tying the loose end to his
wide leather belt. He fitted the arrow to the great ash
bow and sighted. All eyes peered across the chasm to
the length of rope secured at the edge on the other
side. Menion followed the length of rope downward
into the darkness of the pit until he spotted a piece of
wood hanging about thirty feet below, still fastened to
the broken bridge tie. The company watched
breathlessly as he drew back the great ash bow,
sighted quickly, surely, and released the arrow with a
sharp snap. The arrow shot into the cavern and
embedded itself in the wood, the cord dangling limply
from the tip.

"Nice shooting, Menion," Durin approved at his
shoulder, and the lean highlander smiled.

Carefully, the bridge was pulled back across until
the severed rope ends were gathered in. Allanon
looked in vain for something to secure it, but the
spikes that had held it had been removed by the
Gnomes. Finally, Hendel and Allanon braced themselves at the edge of the chasm and pulled the bridge
rope taut while Dayel worked his way hand over hand

across the yawning pit, carrying a second rope at his waist. There were a few anxious moments as the black-robed giant and the silent Dwarf held firm against the strain, but in the end Dayel stood safely on the other side. Balinor reappeared and informed them that the fire was beginning to burn itself out and the Gnome hunters would soon be making their way into the Pass of Noose. Hastily, the rope that Dayel carried was thrown back across after he had finished securing his end, and its longer length was run back into the jutting rocks at the entrance of the pass and fastened in place. The remaining members of the company proceeded to cross the chasm in the same fashion as Dayel, one by one, hand over hand in succession, until all stood safely on the far side. Then the rope was cut and dropped into the pit along with the remainder of the old bridge, to make certain that they could not be followed.

Allanon ordered the company to move out quietly to avoid warning the approaching Gnomes that they had made good their escape from the carefully laid trap. Before they left, however, the tall historian approached Flick, placed a lean, dark hand on his shoulder, and smiled grimly.

"Today, my friend, you have earned the right to be a member of this company—a right above and beyond your kinship for your brother."

He turned away abruptly and signaled Hendel to take the lead. Shea looked at Flick's flushed and happy face, and clapped his brother warmly on the back. He had indeed earned the right to stand along with the others—a right that Shea had perhaps not yet acquired.

XI

The company journeyed another ten miles into the Wolfsktaag Mountains before Allanon called a halt. The Pass of Noose and the danger of attack by Gnomes had long since been left behind, and they were now deep within the forests. Their travel had been fast and unhindered up to this point, the paths wide and clear and the terrain level even though they were several miles high in the mountains. The air was crisp and cool, which made the march almost enjoyable, and the warm afternoon sun beamed down on the company with a glow that kept their spirits high. The forests were scattered in these mountains, cut apart by jutting ridges of slab rock and peaks which were barren and snowcapped. Although this was historically a forbidden country, even for the Dwarfs, no one could find an indication of anything out of the ordinary which might signal danger for them. All the normal sounds of the forest were there, from the resonant chirping of insects to the gay songs of a huge variety of multicolored birds of all shapes and sizes. It seemed that they had chosen a wise way in which to approach the still-distant halls of Paranor.

"We will stop for the night in several hours," the tall wanderer announced after he had gathered them about him. "But I will be leaving you in the early morning to scout ahead beyond the Wolfsktaag for signs of the Warlock Lord and his emissaries. Once we complete our journey through these mountains and through a short stretch of the Anar Forests, we still have to cross the plains beyond to the Dragon's Teeth, just below Paranor. If the creatures of the Northland or their allies have blocked off the entrance, I must know now so that we may quickly decide on a new route."

"Will you go alone?" asked Balinor.

"I think it safer for all of us if I do. I'm in little danger, and you may need everyone when you reach the central Anar forests again. I have little doubt that the Gnome hunting parties will be watching all the passes leading out of these mountains to be certain that you do not leave them alive. Hendel can lead you through those pitfalls as well as I could, and I will try to meet you somewhere along the way before you reach the plains."

"Which way out will you be taking?" asked the taciturn Dwarf.

"The Pass of Jade offers the best protection. I'll mark the way with bits of cloth—as we've done before. Red will mean danger. Keep with the white cloth and all will be well. Now let's continue on while we still have some daylight."

They traveled steadily through the Wolfsktaag until the sun sank beneath the rim of the mountains in the west and it was no longer possible to see the path ahead clearly. It was a moonless night, though the stars cast a dim glow over the rugged landscape. The company made camp beneath a tall, jagged cliffside that rose several hundred feet above them like some great blade cutting sharply into the dark sky. On the open edges of the campsite were tall stands of pines enclosing them against the cliffside in a half circle that provided them with good protection on all sides. They ate a cold dinner for another evening, still unwilling to risk a fire which might draw attention to their presence. Hendel arranged for the posting of a continuous guard throughout the night, a practice he

felt to be essential in unfriendly country. The members
of the group took turns, each sitting watch for several
hours while the rest of the company slept. There was
little talk after the meal, and they rolled themselves
into their blankets almost at once, tired from the long
day of marching.

Shea volunteered to sit the first watch, eager to
participate as a member of the company, still feeling
that he had contributed little while all of the others
were risking their lives for his benefit. Shea's attitude
toward the journey to Paranor had altered considerably during the past two days. He was beginning to
realize now how important it was that the Sword be
obtained, how much the people of the four lands
depended on it for protection against the Warlock
Lord. Before, he had run away from the danger of the
Skull Bearers and his heritage as a son of the house of
Shannara. Now he was running toward an even
greater threat, a confrontation with a power so
awesome that its limits had never been defined—and
with little more than the courage of seven mortal men
for protection. But even with that knowledge confronting him, Shea felt deeply that to refuse to go on,
to hold back what little he had to offer, would be a
bitter betrayal of his kinship to both Elf and Man and a
callous denial of the pride he felt in caring about the
safety and freedom of all men. He knew that if he were
told even now that he could not succeed, he would
have to try anyway.

Allanon had turned in without a word to anyone
and was asleep in a matter of seconds. Shea watched
his still form during his own two-hour watch and then
retired as Durin took over. It was not until Flick awoke
after midnight to take his turn that the tall form of their
leader stirred slightly, then rose in a single fluid
motion, wrapped ominously in the great black cape,
just as he had been when Flick had first encountered
him on the road to Shady Vale. He stood for a moment

looking at the sleeping members of the company and at Flick sitting motionless on a boulder off to one side of the clearing. Then without a word or a gesture, he turned north on the path leading away from them and disappeared in the blackness of the forest.

Allanon walked for the remainder of the night without pausing in his journey to reach the Pass of Jade, the central Anar, and beyond that, the plainlands to the west. His dark figure passed through the silent forest with the quickness of a fleeting shadow, touching the land only momentarily, then hastening on. His form seemed substanceless, passing over the lives of little beings that saw him briefly and forgot, neither changing nor yet leaving them quite the same, his indelible print fixed in their uncomprehending minds. Once more he reflected on the journey they were making to Paranor, pondering what he knew that none other could know, and he felt strangely helpless in the face of what was surely the passing of an age. The others only suspected his own role in all that had happened, in all that yet lay ahead, but he alone was forced to live with the truth behind his own destiny and theirs. He muttered half aloud at the thought, hating what was happening, but knowing that there was no other choice for him to make. His long, lean face appeared a black mask of indecision to the silent woods he passed on his lonely march, a face lined deeply with worry, but hard with an inner resolution that would sustain the soul when the heart was gone.

Daybreak found him moving through a particularly dense stretch of woods that ran for several miles over hilly terrain strewn with boulders and fallen logs. He noticed at once that this part of the forest was strangely silent, as if a special kind of death had placed its chill hand upon the earth. The trail behind was carefully marked with small strips of white cloth. He walked more slowly. There had been nothing up to this point to cause him concern, but now a sixth sense reared up within his quick mind, warning him that all was not as it should be. He reached a break in the main path that split into two branches. One, a wide, clear path that looked as if it had once been a major road, ran to the left, downward into what appeared to be a huge valley. It was difficult to tell because the forests had overgrown everything, obscuring from view the trail beyond the first several hundred yards. The second path was choked by heavy underbrush. No more than one person at a time could pass that way without cutting a wider trail. The narrow path led upward toward a high ridge which ran at an angle away from the Pass of Jade.

Suddenly the grim historian stiffened as he sensed the presence of another being, an undeniably evil life form somewhere farther down the trail leading into the invisible valley. There was no sound of movement. Whatever it was, it preferred to lie in wait for its victims along the lower trail. Allanon quickly tore off two strips of cloth, one red and one white, tying the red cloth to the wider trail leading into the valley and the white cloth along the smaller trail leading to the ridge. When he had completed this task, he paused and listened again, but while he could still sense the presence of the creature down the valley path, he could detect no movement. Its power was no match for his own, but it would be dangerous to the men following. Checking the cloth strips one final time, he silently moved upward along the narrow ridge path and disappeared into the heavy underbrush.

Almost an hour passed before the creature that lay in wait on the path leading into the valley decided to investigate. It was highly intelligent, a possibility that Allanon had not considered, and it knew that whoever it was who had passed above had sensed its presence and purposely avoided that approach. It knew as well that this same man had powers far greater than its own, so it lay noiselessly in the forest and waited for him to go away. Now it had waited long enough. Minutes later it gazed intently at the silent fork in the main trail where the two small strips of cloth fluttered brightly in the light forest breeze. How stupid such markers were, thought the creature slyly, and with ponderous footsteps moved its great, misshapen bulk forward.

Balinor had the final watch of the evening, and as the dawn began to break sharply in dazzling golden rays over the eastern mountain horizon, the tall borderman gently awakened the remainder of the company from their peaceful slumber to the chill of the early morning. They turned out hastily, gulped down a short breakfast while attempting to warm themselves in the yet cool air of the sunny day, silently packed their gear, and prepared to begin the day's march. Someone asked about Allanon, and Flick sleepily replied that the historian had departed sometime around midnight but said nothing to him. Nobody was particularly surprised that he had left so quietly, and little more was said about the matter.

Within half an hour, the company was on the path leading northward through the forests of the Wolfsktaag, moving steadily, without conversation for the most part, in the same order as before. Hendel had relinquished his spot as point man to the talented Menion Leah, who moved with the noiseless grace of a cat through the tangled boughs and brush over the leaf-strewn floor. Hendel felt a certain respect for the Prince of Leah. In time he would be unsurpassed by any woodsman. But the Dwarf knew as well that the highlander was brash and still inexperienced, and that in these lands only the cautious and the seasoned survived. Nevertheless, practice was the only way to learn, so the Dwarf grudgingly allowed the young

tracker to lead the party, contenting himself with
double-checking everything that appeared on the
path before them.

One particularly disturbing detail caught the
Dwarf's attention almost immediately, although it
completely escaped the notice of his companion. The
trail failed to reveal any sign of the man who had come
this way only hours earlier. Although he scanned the
ground meticulously, Hendel was unable to discern
even the slightest trace of a human footprint. The
strips of white cloth appeared at regular intervals, just
as Allanon had promised they would be. Yet there was
no sign of his passage. Hendel knew the tales about
the mysterious wanderer and had heard that he
possessed extraordinary powers. But he had never
dreamed that the man was such an accomplished
tracker that he could completely hide his own trail.
The Dwarf could not understand it, but decided to
keep the matter to himself.

At the rear of the procession, Balinor, too, had been
wondering about the enigmatic man from Paranor, the
historian who knew so much that no one else had even
suspected, the wanderer who seemed to have been
everywhere and yet about whom so little was known.
He had known Allanon off and on for many years
while growing up in his father's kingdom, but could
only vaguely recall him, a dark stranger who had come
and gone without warning, who had always seemed
so kind to him, yet had never offered to reveal his own
mysterious background. The wise men of all the lands
knew Allanon as a scholar and a philosopher without
equal. Others knew him only as a traveler who paid
his way with good advice and who possessed a kind of
grim common sense with which no one could find
fault. Balinor had learned from him and had come to
trust in him with what could almost be described as
blind faith. Yet he had never really understood the
historian. He pondered that thought for a while, and

then in what came as an almost casual revelation, he realized that in all the time he had spent with Allanon, he had never seen any sign of a change in his age.

The trail began to turn upward again and to narrow as the great forest trees and heavy underbrush closed in like solid walls. Menion had followed the strips of cloth dutifully and had little doubt that they were on the right path, but automatically began to double-check himself as the going became noticeably tougher than before. It was almost noon when the trail branched unexpectedly, and a surprised Menion paused.

"This is strange. A fork in the trail and no marker—I can't understand why Allanon would fail to leave a sign."

"Something must have happened to it," concluded Shea, sighing heavily. "Which route do we take?"

Hendel scanned the ground carefully. On the path leading upward toward the ridge, there were indications of someone's passage from the bent twigs and recently fallen leaves. On the lower trail, however, there were signs of footprints, though they were very faint. Instinctively he knew that something dangerous lay along one and maybe both of the trails.

"I don't like it—something's wrong here," he grumbled to no one in particular. "The signs are confused, perhaps on purpose."

"Perhaps all the talk about this being taboo land wasn't nonsense after all," suggested Flick dryly, parking himself on a fallen tree.

Balinor came forward and conferred with Hendel briefly concerning the direction of the Pass of Jade. Hendel admitted that the lower trail would be the quickest way, and it clearly appeared to be the main passage. But there was no way to tell which trail Allanon had chosen. Finally Menion threw up his hands in exasperation and demanded that a choice be made.

"We all know that Allanon would not have passed this way without leaving a sign, so the obvious conclusion is that either something happened to the signs or something happened to him. In either case, we can't sit here and expect to find the answer. He said we would meet at the Pass of Jade or beyond in the forests, so I vote we take the lower road—the quickest way!"

Hendel again voiced his confusion over the signs on the lower trail and his nagging feeling that something dangerous lay ahead, a feeling which Shea had begun to share the minute they arrived at this point without finding the strips of cloth. Balinor and the others debated heatedly for a few minutes and finally agreed with the highlander. They would follow the quickest route, but keep an especially close watch until they were out of these mysterious mountains.

The line of march reformed with Menion leading. They started rapidly down the gently sloping lower trail which appeared to be drawing them into a valley heavily camouflaged by great trees that grew limb to limb for miles in all directions. Remarkably, the road began to widen after only a short distance, the trees and scrub brush to move back, and the geography to level off into a barely perceptible downward slope. Their fears began to dissipate as travel grew easier, and it became readily apparent that in years long since gone, the road had been a major thoroughfare for the inhabitants of this land. They walked for less than an hour's time before reaching the valley floor. It was difficult to tell where they were in relation to the mountain ranges surrounding them. The trees of the forest obscured everything from view but the path immediately ahead and the cloudless blue sky above.

After a short time of traveling across the valley floor, the party caught sight of an unusual structure that rose through the trees like a huge framework. It seemed a part of the forest about it, save for the unusual straightness of its limbs, and within moments they were close enough to see that it was a series of giant girders, covered with rust and framing square portions of the open sky. The company slowed automatically, looking cautiously about to be certain that this was not some kind of trap prepared for unwary travelers. But nothing moved, so they continued their approach, intrigued by the structure that waited silently ahead.

Suddenly the road ended and the strange framework stood completely revealed, the great metal beams decaying with age, but still straight and seemingly as sturdy as they had been in ages past. They were part of what had once been a large city built so long ago that no one recalled its existence, a city forgotten like the valley and the mountains in which it rested—a final monument to a civilization of vanished beings. The metal framework was securely set in huge foundations of something like stone, now crumbling and chipped by the weather and time. In places, remnants of what had once been walls were visible. A large number of these dying buildings were clustered together, pushing out for several hundred yards beyond the travelers and ending where the wall of the forests marked the end of man's feeble invasion into an indestructible nature. Within the structures, and through the foundation and framework, grew brush and small trees in such abundance that the city appeared to be choking to death rather than crumbling with time. The party stood in mute silence at this strange testimonial to another era, the accomplishment of people like themselves, so many years before. Shea felt an undeniable sense of futility at the sight of the grim frames, rusting their weary lives away.

"What place is this?" he asked quietly.

"The remains of some city," shrugged Hendel, turning to the young Valeman. "No one has been here for centuries, I imagine."

Balinor walked over to the nearest structure and rubbed the metal girder. Huge flecks of rust and dirt came off in a shower, leaving beneath a dull steel-gray color that told of the strength still left in the building. The others of the company followed the borderman as he walked slowly about the foundation, looking carefully at the stone-like substance. A moment later he stopped at one corner and brushed away the surface dirt and grime to reveal a single date still legible in the decaying wall. They all bent closer to read it.

"Why this city was here before the Great Wars!" Shea said in amazement. "I can't believe it—it must be the oldest structure in existence!"

"I remember what Allanon told us of the men who lived then," declared Menion in a rare moment of dreamy recollection. "That was the great age, he said, and even so, this is all it has to show us. Nothing but a few metal girders."

"How about a few minutes' rest before we leave?" suggested Shea. "I'd like to take a quick look at the other buildings."

Balinor and Hendel felt somewhat uneasy about stopping, but agreed to a short rest as long as everyone kept together. Shea wandered over to the next building, accompanied by Flick. Hendel sat down and looked warily at the huge frames, disliking every moment they spent in this metal jungle so foreign to his own forest homeland. The others followed Menion to the other side of the building on which they had just found the date, discovering a portion of a name on a fallen chunk of wall. No more than a few minutes had passed when Hendel caught himself daydreaming of Culhaven and his family and jerked into immediate watchfulness. Everyone was in view, but Shea and Flick had moved farther off to the left of the dead city, still looking curiously at the decaying remnants and searching for signs of the old civilization. In the same instant he realized that except for the low voices of his companions, the surrounding forest had gone deathly quiet. Not even the wind stirred through the peaceful valley, not a bird flew over them, not a single insect's vibrant hum was audible. His own heavy breathing was hoarse in his straining ears.

"Something's wrong." The words came out as he reached instinctively for his heavy battle mace.

At that moment, Flick caught sight of something dull white on the ground off to one side of the building that Shea and he were examining, partially hidden by the foundation. Curiously, he approached the objects which appeared to be sticks of various sizes and shapes scattered aimlessly about. Shea failed to notice his brother's interest and moved away from the building, staring in fascination at the remains of another structure. Flick came closer, but still was unable to tell from even a few feet away what the white sticks were. It was not until he stood over them and saw them shining dully against the dark earth in the noonday sun that he realized with a sickening chill they were bones.

The jungle behind the stocky Valeman burst apart with a thunderous thrashing of limbs and brush. Forth from its place of concealment emerged a grayish, multilegged horror of monstrous size. A nightmare mutation of living flesh and machine, its crooked legs balanced a body formed half of metal plating, half of coarse-haired flesh. An insect-like head bobbed fitfully on a neck of metal. Tentacles tipped with stingers dipped slightly above two glowing eyes and savage jaws that snapped with hunger. Bred by the men of another time to serve the needs of its masters, it had survived the holocaust that had destroyed them, but in surviving and in preserving its centuries-old existence with bits of metal grafted to its decaying form, it had evolved into a misshapen freak—and worse, an eater of flesh.

It was upon its hapless victim before anyone could move. Shea was closest as the mammoth creature struck his brother with an outstretched leg, knocking him flat and pinning him helplessly to the ground, rasping as its jaws reached downward. Shea never stopped to think; he yelled fiercely and drew his short hunting knife, brandishing the insignificant weapon as he rushed to Flick's rescue. The creature had just grasped its unconscious victim when its attention was directed to the other human charging wildly to the attack. Hesitating at this unexpected assault, it released its deadly grip and took a cautious step backward, its huge bulk poised to strike a second time as its bulging green eyes fixed on the tiny man before it.

"Shea, don't . . .!" yelled Menion in terror as the Valeman struck futilely at one of the creature's twisted limbs. A rasp of fury came boiling out of the depths of the monster's great body, and it swiped at Shea with an extended leg to pin him to the ground. But Shea leaped to safety by scant inches and struck again from another point with his tiny weapon. Then, before the horrified eyes of the other travelers, the nightmare from the jungle rushed the unfortunate Valeman in a flurry of legs and hair. Just as Shea was about to seize Flick to drag him to safety, the creature bowled him over, and for a second everything disappeared in a cloud of dust.

It had all happened so fast that no one else had yet had time to act. Hendel had never seen a creature of this size and ferocity, a creature that apparently had lived in these mountains for untold years, lying in wait for its hapless victims. The Dwarf was the farthest from the scene of the battle, but moved quickly to aid the fallen Valemen. At the same moment, the others reacted as well. The instant the dust settled enough to reveal the hideous head, three bowstrings sounded in harmony and the arrows buried themselves deeply in the black, hair-covered bulk with audible thuds. The creature rasped in fury and raised its body upward, forelegs extended, searching out its new attackers.

The challenge did not go unanswered. Menion Leah discarded the ash bow and drew the great sword from its sheath, gripping it in both hands.

"Leah! Leah!" The battle cry of a thousand years burst forth as the Prince charged wildly across crumbling foundations and fallen walls to reach the monster. Balinor had drawn his own sword, the huge blade gleaming fiercely in the bright sunlight, and rushed to the aid of the highlander. Durin and Dayel fired volley after volley into the head of the giant beast as it rasped in fury, using its forelegs to brush at the arrows and knock them loose from its thick skin. Menion reached the abomination ahead of Balinor and with one great swing of his sword cut deeply into the closest leg, feeling the iron strike bone with jarring impact. As the monster reared back and knocked Menion aside, it received a powerful blow to the head; Hendel's war mace struck with stunning force. A second later, Balinor stood solidly before the huge creature, the hunting cloak thrown back and billowing out behind the flashing chain mail. With a series of quick, powerful cuts of the great sword, the Prince of Callahorn completely severed a second leg. The beast struck back savagely, trying unsuccessfully to pin one of its attackers to the earth to crush the life out of him. The three men sounded their battle cries and struck ferociously, desperately trying to drive the monster back from its fallen victims. They attacked with precision, striking at the unprotected flanks, and drawing the behemoth first to one side and then to the other. Durin and Dayel moved in closer and continued to rain arrows on the massive target. Many were deflected by the metal plating, but the relentless assault constantly distracted the maddened creature. At one point, Hendel received so severe a blow that he

was knocked senseless for a few seconds and the nightmare attacker quickly moved to finish him. But a determined Balinor, mustering every ounce of strength at his command, struck so savagely and relentlessly that it could not reach the fallen Dwarf before he had been pulled to his feet by Menion.

Finally the arrows of Durin and Dayel partially blinded the creature's right eye. Bleeding profusely from its stricken eye and from a dozen other major wounds, the monster knew that it had lost the battle and would probably lose its life if it did not escape at once. Making a short feint at the closest assailant, it suddenly wheeled about with surprising dexterity and made a quick rush for the safety of its forest lair. Menion gave a brief pursuit, but the creature outdistanced him and disappeared within the great trees. The five rescuers quickly turned their attention to the two fallen Valemen, who lay crumpled and unmoving in the trampled earth. Hendel examined them, having had some experience in treating battle wounds over the years. There were numerous cuts and bruises, but apparently no broken bones. It was difficult to tell if there had been any internal damage. Both had been stung by the creature, Flick on the back of the neck and Shea on the shoulder; the ugly, deep-purple marks indicated penetration of the exposed skin. Poison! The two men remained unconscious after repeated attempts to revive them, their breathing shallow and their skin pale and beginning to turn gray.

"I can't treat them for this," Hendel declared worriedly. "We've got to get them to Allanon. He knows something about these matters; he could probably help them."

"They're dying, aren't they?" Menion asked in a barely audible whisper.

Hendel nodded faintly in the hushed silence that followed. Balinor immediately took command of the situation, ordering Durin and Menion to cut poles to make stretchers, while Hendel and he prepared hammocks to hold the Valemen in place. Dayel was placed on guard in case the creature should return unexpectedly. Fifteen minutes later the stretchers were completed, the unconscious men were securely fastened in place and covered with blankets to protect them from the cold of the approaching night, and the company was ready to march. Hendel took the lead, with the other four carrying the stretchers. The party quickly crossed through the ruins of the deathly still city and after a few minutes located a trail leading out of the hidden valley. The grim faces of the Dwarf in the lead and the bearers of the unconscious forms strapped tightly to the makeshift stretchers glanced back in futile anger at the still-visible structures rising out of the forest. A bitter feeling of helplessness welled up inside them. They had come into the valley a strong, determined company, filled with confidence in themselves and belief in the mission which had brought them together. But as they left now, their bearing was that of beaten, discouraged victims of a cruel misfortune.

They moved hurriedly out of the valley, up the gentle slopes of the enclosing mountain range, up the broad, winding path shrouded by tall, silent trees, thinking only of the wounded men they carried. The familiar sounds of the forest returned, indicating that the danger of the valley was past. None of them had time to notice now save the taciturn Dwarf, whose battle-trained mind registered the changes of his forest homeland automatically. He thought back bitterly on the choice that had brought them into the valley, wondering what had happened to Allanon and to the promised markers. Almost without considering it, he knew that the tall wanderer must have placed markers before taking the high trail, and that someone or something, perhaps the creature they had encountered, had realized what the markers were for and removed them. He shook his head at his own stupidity in failing to recognize the truth at once and stamped harder on the ground passing beneath his booted feet, grinding his wrath in bits and pieces.

They reached the lip of the valley and continued on, without pausing, through the forests that stretched ahead in an unbroken mass of great trunks and heavy limbs, tangled and woven together as if to shut out the mountain sky. The path grew narrow once more, forcing them to proceed in single file with the stretchers. The afternoon sky was rapidly changing from a deep blue to a mixed bloodred and purple that marked the close of another day. Hendel calculated that they could expect no more than another hour of sunlight. He had no idea how far they were from the Pass of Jade, but he was fairly certain that it could not be far from where they were now. All of them knew that they would not stop at nightfall, could not get any sleep that night or possibly even the next day if they expected to save the lives of the Valemen. They had to find Allanon quickly and have the injuries of the brothers treated before the poison reached their hearts. No one voiced any opinion and no one felt it necessary to discuss the matter. There was only one choice and they accepted it.

As the sun dropped behind the western mountain ridges an hour later, the arms of the four bearers had reached the limit of their endurance, stiff and strained from the uninterrupted haul out of the valley. Balinor called a brief rest and the group collapsed in a heap, breathing heavily in the early evening quiet of the forest. With the coming of night, Hendel relinquished his position as leader of the company to Dayel, who was obviously the most exhausted from carrying Flick's stretcher. The Valemen were still unconscious, wrapped in the layered blankets for warmth, their drawn faces ashen in the fading light and covered with a thin layer of perspiration. Hendel felt their pulse and could barely discern a flicker of life in the limp arms. Menion stormed audibly about the rest area in an uncontrolled fury, swearing vengeance against everything that came to mind, his lean face flushed red with the heat of the past battle and the burning desire to find something further on which to vent his wrath.

The company resumed its forced march after a short ten minutes' rest. The sun had disappeared entirely, leaving them in blackness broken only by the pale light of the stars and a sliver of new moon. The absence of any real light made the traveling slow and hazardous over the winding and often uneven path. Hendel had taken up Dayel's position at the end of Flick's stretcher, while the slim Elf utilized his highly developed senses to locate the trail through the darkness. The Dwarf thought ruefully of the cloth strips Allanon had promised he would leave to guide them out of the Wolfsktaag. Now, more than any time previously, they were needed to mark the proper route—not for himself, but for the two Valemen, whose lives depended on speed. As he walked, his arms not yet feeling the strain of carrying the stretcher, his mind mulling over the situation facing them, he found himself gazing almost absently at two tall peaks which broke the smoothness of the night sky to his left. It was several minutes before he realized with a start that he was looking at the entrance to the Pass of Jade.

At the same moment, Dayel announced to the group that the trail split in three directions just ahead. Hendel quickly informed them that the pass would be reached by following the left path. Without pausing, they moved onward. The trail began to lead them downward out of the mountains in the direction of the twin peaks. Reassured that the end was in sight, they marched faster, their strength renewed with the hope that Allanon would be waiting. Shea and Flick were no longer lying motionless on the stretchers, but were beginning to twitch uncontrollably and even thrash violently beneath the tightened blankets. A battle was waging within the poisoned bodies between the tightening grip of death and a strong will to live. Hendel thought to himself that it was a good sign. Their bodies had not yet given up the struggle to survive. He turned to the others in the company and discovered that they were gazing intently at what appeared to be a light gleaming sharply against the black horizon between the twin peaks. Then their own ears caught the distant sounds of a heavy booming noise and a low hum of voices coming from the location of the light. Balinor ordered them to keep moving, but told Dayel to scout ahead and to keep his eyes open.

"What is it?" asked Menion curiously.

"I can't be sure from this distance," Durin answered. "It sounds like drums and men chanting or singing."

"Gnomes," declared Hendel ominously.

Another hour's travel brought them close enough to determine that the curious light was caused by the burning of hundreds of small fires, and the noises were indeed the booming of dozens of drums and the chanting of many, many men. The sounds had grown to deafening proportions, and the two peaks marking the entrance of the Pass of Jade loomed like huge pillars in front of them. Balinor felt certain that if the creatures ahead were Gnomes, they would not venture into their taboo land to post guards, so the company would be reasonably safe until they reached the pass. The sound of the drums and the chanting continued to vibrate through the heavy forest trees. Whoever was blocking the pass was there to stay for a while. Only moments later, the group had reached the edge of the Pass of Jade, just beyond reach of the firelight. Moving silently off the path into the shadows, the company held a brief conference.

"What is going on?" Balinor asked anxiously of Hendel, when they were all crouched in the protection of the forest.

"It's impossible to tell from back here, unless you're a mind reader!" the Dwarf growled irately. "The chanting sounds like Gnomes, but the words are blurred. I had better go ahead and check it out."

"I don't think so," Durin advised quickly. "This is a job for an Elf, not a Dwarf. I can move more quickly and quietly than you, and I'll be able to sense the presence of any guards."

"Then it had better be me," Dayel suggested. "I'm smaller, lighter, and faster than any of you. Be back in a minute."

Without waiting for an answer, he faded into the forest and had disappeared before anyone could voice an objection. Durin swore silently, fearing for his young brother's life. If there were indeed Gnomes in the Pass of Jade, they would kill any stray Elf they caught prowling about in the dark. Hendel shrugged in disgust and sat back against a tree to wait for Dayel's return. Shea had begun to moan and thrash more violently, throwing aside his blankets and nearly rolling off the stretcher. Flick was behaving in the same manner, though less forcibly, groaning in low tones, his face frighteningly drawn. Menion and Durin moved quickly to wrap the blankets back around the Valemen, this time tying them securely in place with long strips of leather. The moans continued, but the company had little fear of discovery with all the noise coming from the other side of the pass. They sat back quietly waiting for Dayel, looking anxiously at the bright horizon and listening to the drums, knowing that somehow they would have to find a way past whomever was blocking the entrance. Long minutes slipped by. Then Dayel appeared suddenly out of the darkness.

"Are they Gnomes?" asked Hendel sharply.

"Hundreds of them," the Elf replied grimly. "They're spread out all across the entrance to the Pass of Jade and there are dozens of fires. It must be some sort of ceremony from the way they're beating the drums and chanting. The worst of it is that they are all facing right into the pass. No one could possibly go in or out without being seen."

He paused and looked briefly at the pain-wracked forms of the injured Valemen before turning back to face Balinor.

"I scouted the entire entrance and both sides of the peaks. There is no way out except straight through the Gnomes. They have us trapped!"

XII

ayel's bleak report brought an immediate reaction. Menion leaped to his feet, reaching for his sword and threatening to fight his way out or die in the attempt. Balinor tried to restrain him, or at least to quiet him, but there was complete bedlam for several minutes as the others joined the shouting highlander in his vow. Hendel questioned the somewhat shaken Dayel about what he had seen at the entrance to the pass, and after a few brief questions loudly ordered everyone to be silent.

"The Gnome chieftains are out there," he informed Balinor, who had finally managed to restrain Menion long enough to listen to the Dwarf. "They have all the high priests and members of surrounding villages here for a special ceremony that takes place once each month. They come at sunset and sing praises to their gods for protecting them from the evils of the taboo land, the Wolfsktaag. It will last all night, and by morning we can forget about helping our young friends."

"Wonderful people, the Gnomes!" exploded Menion. "They fear the evils of this place, but they align themselves with the Skull Kingdom! I don't know about the rest of you, but I'm not giving up because of a few half-wit Gnomes chanting useless spells!"

"No one is giving up, Menion," Balinor said quickly. "We're getting out of these mountains tonight. Right now."

you propose to do that?'' demanded
'Walk right through half the Gnome nation?
erhaps we'll fly out?''

Wait a minute!'' Menion exclaimed suddenly and
leaned over the unconscious Shea, searching eagerly
through his clothing until he produced the small
leather pouch containing the powerful Elfstones.

"The Elfstones will get us out of here," he
announced to the others, grasping the pouch.

"Has he lost his mind?" asked Hendel, incredulous
at the sight of the highlander eagerly waving the
leather pouch.

"It won't work, Menion," declared Balinor quietly.
"The only one with the power to use the stones is
Shea. Besides, Allanon once told me they could only
be used against things whose power lies beyond
substance, dangers that confuse the mind. Those
Gnomes are mortal flesh and blood, not creatures of
the spirit world or the imagination."

"I don't know what you're talking about, but I do
know that these stones worked against that creature
from the Mist Marsh, and I saw it work . . ." Menion
trailed off despondently, reflecting on what he was
saying, and finally lowered the pouch and its precious
contents. "What's the use? You must be right. I don't
even know what I'm saying anymore."

"There has to be a way!" Durin came forward,
casting about for suggestions. "All we need is a plan to
draw attention away from us for about five minutes
and we could slip by them."

Menion perked up at the suggestion, apparently
finding some merit in the idea, but unable to think of a
way to distract the attention of several thousand
Gnomes. Balinor paced about for a few minutes, lost
in thought while the others threw out random
suggestions. Hendel suggested in bitter humor that he
walk into their midst and let himself be captured. The
Gnomes would be so overjoyed at getting their hands

on him, the man they had tried so hard to destroy all these years, that they would forget about anything else. Menion thought little of the joke and was all for allowing him to do what he suggested.

"Enough talk!" roared the Prince of Leah finally, losing his temper altogether. "What we need now is a plan, one that will get us out of here right away, before the Valemen are completely beyond help. Now what do we do?"

"How wide is the pass?" asked Balinor absently, still pacing.

"About two hundred yards at the point the Gnomes are gathered," Dayel replied, avoiding a confrontation with Menion. He thought a minute longer, and then snapped his fingers in recollection. "The right side of the pass is completely open, but on the left side there are small trees and scrub brush growing along the cliff face. They would give us some cover."

"Not enough," interrupted Hendel. "The Pass of Jade is wide enough to march an army through, but trying to get past with the little cover offered would be suicidal. I've seen it from the other side, and any Gnome looking would spot you in a minute!"

"Then they'll have to be looking somewhere else," Balinor growled as the faint glimmer of a plan began to form in his mind. He stopped suddenly, and kneeling on the forest floor drew a crude diagram of the pass entrance, looking to Dayel and Hendel for approval. Menion had stopped complaining long enough to join them.

"From the drawing, it appears that we can stay under cover and out of the light until we reach here," Balinor explained, indicating a point of ground near the line representing the left cliff face. "The slope is gentle enough to allow us to remain above the Gnomes and within the cover of the brush. Then there is an open space for about twenty-five or thirty yards until the forests begin against the steeper cliff face beyond. That is the point of diversion, the point where the light will show us clearly to anyone looking. The Gnomes will have to be turned another way when we cross that open space."

He paused and looked at the four anxious faces, wishing fervently that he had a better plan, but knowing there was no time to come up with another if they were to preserve any chance of recovering the Sword of Shannara. Whatever else was at stake now, nothing was of such paramount importance as the life of the frail-looking Valeman who was heir to the Sword's power and the one chance left to the people of the four lands to avoid a conflict that would consume them all. Their own lives could be sold comparatively cheaply to preserve that single hope.

"It will take the best bowman in the Southland," the tall borderman announced quietly. "That man will have to be Menion Leah." The highlander looked up in surprise at the unexpected declaration, unable to hide the sense of pride he felt. "There will be only one shot," continued the Prince of Callahorn. "If it is not exactly on target, we will be lost."

"What is your plan?" interrupted Durin curiously.

"When we reach the end of our cover at the open space, Menion will locate one of the Gnome chieftains to the far side of the pass. He will have one shot with the bow to kill him, and in the confusion that follows, we can slip by."

"It won't work, my friend," growled Hendel. "The minute they see their leader struck by the arrow, they'll be all over that pass entrance. You'll be found in minutes."

Balinor shook his head and smiled faintly, but unconvincingly.

"No, we won't, because they will be after someone else. The minute the Gnome chieftain falls, one of us will show himself back in the pass. The Gnomes will be so incensed and so eager to get their hands on him, that they won't take the time to search for anyone else, and we can slip by in the confusion."

Silence greeted his appraisal of the situation, and the anxious faces looked from one person to the next, the same thought in every mind.

"It sounds just fine for everyone but the man who stays behind to show himself," broke in Menion in disbelief. "Who gets that suicidal chore?"

"It was my plan," declared Balinor. "It will be my duty to stay behind and lead the Gnomes into the Wolfsktaag, until I can circle back and join you later at the edge of the Anar."

"You must be insane if you think I'm letting you stay behind and claim all the credit," Menion declared. "If I make the shot, I stay to take the bows, and if I miss . . ."

He trailed off and smiled, shrugging casually, clapping Durin on the shoulder as the other looked on incredulously. Balinor was about to object further when Hendel stepped forward shaking his broad head in disagreement.

"The plan is fine as it goes, but we all know that the man who stays behind will have several thousand Gnomes attempting to track him down, or at best, waiting for him to come out of their taboo land. The man who stays must be a man who knows the Gnomes, their methods, how to fight and survive against them. In this case, that man is a Dwarf with a lifetime of battle knowledge behind him. It must be me.

"Besides," he added grimly, "I told you how badly they want my head. They won't pass up the chance after such an affront."

"And I've already told you," insisted Menion again, "that's my . . ."

"Hendel is right," Balinor cut in sharply. The others looked at him in amazement. Only Hendel knew that the decision the borderman had made, however

distasteful, was the same one he would have made
had their positions been reversed. "The choice has
been made, and we will abide by it. Hendel will have
the best chance to survive."

He turned to the stocky Dwarf warrior and extended
a broad hand. The other gripped it tightly for a brief
moment, then turned quickly from them and disappeared up the trail at a slow trot. The others watched,
but he was gone in a matter of seconds. The booming
of the drums and the chanting of the Gnomes rolled
deeply out of the lighted sky to the west.

"Gag the Valemen so they cannot cry out," ordered
Balinor, startling the other three with the sharpness of
the sudden command. When Menion failed to move,
but remained rooted to the spot, looking silently up
the path Hendel had taken a moment before, Balinor
turned to him and placed a reassuring hand on his
shoulder. "Be certain, Prince of Leah, that your shot is
worthy of his sacrifice for us."

The still-twisting bodies of the two Valemen were
quickly secured to the makeshift stretchers and their
low cries effectively muffled by tightly bound cloth
gags. The four remaining men picked up their gear
and the stretchers and moved out of the cover of the
trees toward the mouth of the Pass of Jade. The
Gnome fires blazed up before them, lighting the night
sky in a brilliant aura of yellow and orange flame. The
drums crashed out in steady rhythm, the sound
deafening in the ears of the four as they drew closer.
The chanting grew louder until it seemed as if the
entire Gnome nation must be gathered. The overall
sensation was one of eerie unreality, as if they were
lost in that primitive world of half-dreams traversed
by mortal and spirit alike in strange rituals that have
no recognizable purpose. The walls of the towering
cliffs rose jaggedly into the night sky on either side,
distant but ominously huge intruders on the little
scene taking place at the high entrance to the Pass of

Jade. Rock walls glimmered in a shower of color—red, orange, and yellow blended into an overriding deep green that danced and flickered in the man-made firelight. The color reflected off the hardness of the rock and mirrored softly in the grim-set faces of the four stretcher bearers, touching momentarily the fear they were trying to conceal.

Finally the men stood within the corridor of the pass, just out of sight of the chanting Gnomes. The slopes rose steeply on either side, the northern incline offering little or no cover whatsoever, while the southern fairly bristled with small trees and dense scrub brush that grew so thickly it was choking on itself. Balinor silently signaled the others to make their way up the side of this slope. He took the lead himself, searching out the safest approach, moving cautiously upward toward the small trees that grew higher on the mountain. It took them quite awhile to reach the safety of the trees, and Balinor motioned them slowly ahead into the mouth of the pass. As they inched forward, Menion could look through breaks in the trees and brush to catch quick glimpses of the fires burning below, still ahead of them, their bright flames almost completely masked by the hundreds of small, gnarled figures who moved rhythmically in the light, chanting in a deep, soul-searching drone to the spirits of the Wolfsktaag. His mouth felt dry as he visualized what would happen to them if they were discovered, and he thought grimly of Hendel. He was suddenly very afraid for the Dwarf. The brush and trees began to thin out, rising higher on the slope, and the four crept upward under their cover, but slower now, more hesitantly, as Balinor kept one eye fixed on the Gnomes below. Durin and Dayel walked on cat feet, their light Elven frames moving soundlessly through dry, brittle limbs and twigs, blending into the natural terrain about them. Again Menion peered worriedly at the Gnomes, closer than before, their yellowish bodies weaving to the drums, gleaming with the sweat of hours spent calling on their gods and praying to the mountains.

Then the four reached the end of their cover. Balinor pointed ahead to the yards of open space that lay between them and the dense forests of the Anar standing darkly beyond. It was a long distance, and there was nothing between the men and the floor of the pass but the scrub brush and a few sparse blades of grass, dried from the sun. Directly below were the chanting Gnomes, swaying in the fire's glow and in a perfect position to see anyone attempting to cross the brightly lighted open spaces of the southern slope. Dayel had been correct; it would have been suicide to attempt to sneak past under those conditions. Menion looked up and quickly saw that further efforts to reach higher ground with the two wounded Valemen were effectively prevented by a sheer cliff face that rose abruptly several hundred feet into the air, banking only slightly as it continued upward to its invisible peak. He turned back to look again at the open space. It appeared farther across than before. Balinor motioned the others into a tight circle.

"Menion can move to the edge of the cover," he whispered cautiously. "After he picks his target and the Gnome is hit, Hendel will focus their rage by calling attention to himself inside the pass, high on the other slope. He should be in place by this time. When the Gnomes rush him, we move across the open space as quickly as possible. Don't stop to look—keep moving."

The other three nodded and all eyes rested on Menion, who had unstrapped the great ash bow from his back and was testing its pull. He picked out a single long, black arrow, sighting it for accuracy, and hesitated for a minute, looking downward through the veiled covering of the trees to the hundreds of Gnomes on the valley floor. Suddenly he realized what was expected of him. He was to kill a man, not in battle or in fair combat, but from ambush, with stealth, and that man would never have a chance. He knew instinctively that he could not do it, that he was not the seasoned fighter that Balinor was, that he did not have the cold determination of Hendel. He was brash and even brave at times and ready to stand against anyone in open combat, but he was not a killer. He glanced back momentarily at the others, and they saw it at once in his eyes.

"You must do it!" whispered Balinor harshly, his eyes burning with fierce determination.

Durin's face was averted slightly in the half-light, grim and frozen with uncertainty. Dayel stared directly at Menion, his Elven eyes wide, frightened by the choice the highlander faced, the youthful countenance ashen and ghostlike.

"I cannot kill a man this way," Menion shook involuntarily at his own words, "even to save their lives. . . ."

He paused and Balinor continued to stare at him, waiting for something more.

"I can do the job," Menion announced suddenly after a moment's reflection and a second look to the valley below. "But it shall be done a different way."

Without further explanation he moved forward through the clump of trees and crouched silently on the fringe, almost beyond its sparse protection. His eyes scanned hurriedly the forms of the Gnomes below, finally coming to rest on a chieftain on the far side of the pass. The Gnome stood before his subjects, his wizened yellow face uplifted, his small hands extended, holding in offering a long bowl of glowing embers. He stood motionless as he led the chanting with the other Gnome chieftains, his face turned toward the entrance to the Wolfsktaag. Menion withdrew a second arrow from the quiver and laid it in front of him. Then on one knee, he inched from the safety of the small tree he had positioned himself behind, fitted the first arrow to the bow and sighted. The other three waited grimly, breathless within the edges of the foliage, watching the bowman. For one split second everything seemed to come to a complete standstill, and then the taut bowstring was released with an audible twang and the arrow flew invisibly to its target. Almost as if a part of the same motion, Menion fitted the second arrow to the string, sighted and fired with blinding rapidity, then dropped motionless into the cover of the closest tree.

It happened so fast that no one saw it all, but each caught glimpses of the bowman's action and the scene that followed in the midst of the unsuspecting Gnomes. The first arrow struck the long bowl in the outstretched hands of the chanting Gnome chieftain and sent it spinning in an explosion of wood splinters. Gleaming red coals flew upward in a shower of sparks. In the next instant, while the astonished Gnome and his still-mystified followers were caught momentarily frozen with uncertainty, the second arrow embedded itself painfully in the half-turned and highly vulnerable posterior of the chieftain, who gave an agonizing howl that could be heard the length and breadth of the firelit Pass of Jade. The timing was absolutely perfect. It happened so quickly that even the unfortunate victim had no time, nor inclination for that matter, to decide where the embarrassing assault had come from or who the deceitful perpetrator might have been. The Gnome chieftain leaped about in terror and pain for several wild moments as his fellow Gnomes looked on in mixed bewilderment and apprehension, emotions that quickly changed. Their ceremony had been rudely interrupted and one of their chieftains had been treacherously struck from ambush. They were humiliated and dangerously angered.

Within seconds after the arrows struck their targets, before anyone had been given a chance to collect his senses, a torch appeared far away inside the pass on the upper reaches of the northern slope, touching off a giant bonfire that blazed into the night sky as if the earth itself had erupted in answer to the cries of the vengeful Gnomes. Before the rising blaze stood the broad, immobile figure of the Dwarf Hendel, his arms raised in challenge, one great hand clutching the stone-shattering mace in menacing defiance of all who looked up at him. His laugh echoed deafeningly off the cliff walls.

"Come face me, Gnomes—worms of the earth!" he roared mockingly. "Stand and fight—it's plain you won't be caught sitting for a while. Your foolish gods cannot save you from the powers of a Dwarf, let alone the spirits of the Wolfsktaag!"

The roar of fury that went up from the Gnomes was frightening. Almost to a man, they surged forward into the Pass of Jade to reach the mocking figure on the slope above them, determined to tear his heart out for the shame and humiliation inflicted upon them. To strike a Gnome chieftain was bad enough, but to insult their religion and their courage in the same breath was unforgivable. Some of the Gnomes recognized the Dwarf immediately and shouted his name to the others, crying out for his instant death. As the Gnomes charged blindly ahead into the pass, their ceremony forgotten, the fires burning untended, the four men on the slope leaped to their feet, clutching tightly the stretchers and their precious cargo, and raced in a low crouch across the open and unprotected southern slope, fully exposed by the glare of the blaze below, their shadows appearing as huge phantoms against the cliffside above their fleeing forms. No one paused to check the progress of the angered Gnomes; they charged madly ahead, eyes glued to the sheltering blackness of the Anar forest looming in the distance.

Miraculously, they made it to the safety of the

forest. There they paused, breathing heavily in the
cool shadows of the great trees, listening to the sounds
in the pass. Below them, the floor of the pass entrance
was deserted except for a small cluster of Gnomes, one
of whom was engaged in aiding the wounded
chieftain by extracting the painful arrow. Menion
chuckled inwardly at the sight, a slow smile spreading
over his lean face. It quickly vanished, however, as he
looked into the pass where the bonfire on the northern
slope still burned fiercely. The maddened Gnomes
were climbing upward from all directions, an endless
number of small yellowish bodies, the foremost of
which had almost reached the blaze. There was no
sign of Hendel, but from all appearances he was
trapped somewhere on the slope. The four watched
for only a minute, and then Balinor silently signaled
for them to move out. The Pass of Jade was left behind.

It was dark in the heavy forests once the company
had gone beyond the light of the Gnome fires. Balinor
placed the Prince of Leah in the fore with instructions
to move downward from the southern slope to find a
trail that would take them west. It did not take long to
reach such a trail, and the little band moved into the
central Anar. The forests about them shut out most of
the dim light of the distant stars, and the great trees
framed the path ahead like black walls. The Valemen
were thrashing violently on the stretchers again and
moaning painfully, even through the heavy gags. The
carriers were beginning to lose hope for their young
friends. The poison was seeping slowly through their
systems and when enough of it reached their hearts,
the end would come abruptly. There was no way the
four men could know how much time was left the
brothers, and no way to estimate how far they might
be from any sort of medical assistance. The one man
who knew the central Anar was behind them, trapped
in the Wolfsktaag and fighting for his life.

Suddenly, so quickly that the four had no time

to get off the trail to avoid detection, a group of Gnomes appeared from out of the wall of trees on the path ahead. For a moment everyone stood motionless, each group squinting through the dim light. It only took an instant for each to realize who the other was. The four men quickly put down the cumbersome stretchers and moved forward to stand in a line across the trail. The Gnomes, numbering ten or twelve in all, clustered together for a moment and then one of them disappeared back into the trees.

"They've sent for help," Balinor whispered to the others. "If we don't get by them quickly, they will have reinforcements here to finish us off."

He had barely gotten the words out of his mouth before the remaining Gnomes let out a chilling battle cry and charged toward the four, their short, wicked-looking swords gleaming dully. The silent arrows of Menion and the Elf brothers dropped three of them in midstride before the rest swarmed over them like savage wolves. Dayel was completely bowled over by the assault and for a moment was lost from sight to the rear. Balinor stood firm as his huge blade cut two of the unfortunate Gnomes in half with one great sweep. The next several minutes were filled with sharp cries and labored breathing as the fighters battled back and forth across the narrow trail, the Gnomes seeking to get under the long reach of the men before them, the four defenders maneuvering to keep themselves between the fierce attackers and their two injured companions. In the end, the Gnomes all lay dead on the bloodied trail, their bodies small heaps in the dim light of the watching stars. Dayel had received a serious slash in the ribs that had to be bound, and Menion and Durin had received a number of small wounds. Balinor was untouched, his body protected from the Gnome swords by the lightweight chain mail beneath his shredded cloak.

The four paused only long enough to bind up

Dayel's rib wound before picking up the stretchers and continuing at an even faster pace along the deserted path. They had further reason to hasten now. Gnome hunters would be quickly on their trail once they found their slain comrades. Menion tried to guess the hour from the position of the stars and by estimating their time of travel since the sun had set back in the Wolfsktaag Mountains, but could only conclude it was somewhere in the early-morning hours. The highlander felt the final signs of fatigue begin to creep through his aching arms and strained back muscles as he walked rapidly behind the broad form of Balinor, who had taken the lead. They were all close to exhaustion, their bodies worn from the day's travel and their encounters with first the monster in the Wolfsktaag and then the Gnomes. They were kept on their feet primarily because they knew what would happen to the Valemen if they stopped. Nevertheless, thirty minutes after the brief battle with the Gnome rear guard, Dayel simply collapsed in midstride from loss of blood and exhaustion. It took the others several minutes to revive him and get him back on his feet. Even then, the pace slowed noticeably.

Balinor was forced to call a second halt only minutes later to allow them all a much-needed rest. They huddled quietly at the side of the trail and listened in dismay to the growing tumult all about them. Shouting and muffled drums, still distant, had begun again since their encounter on the trail. Apparently the Gnomes were alerted sufficiently to their presence to have called out a large number of hunting parties to track them down. It sounded as if the entire Anar forest were alive with angered Gnomes, stalking the surrounding woods and hills in an effort to find the enemy that had slipped by them on the trail and killed ten or so of their number in avoiding capture. Menion glanced down wearily at the young Valemen, their faces white and covered with a heavy sheet of perspiration. He could hear them moaning through the cloth gags, see their limbs convulse as the poison seeped relentlessly through their failing systems. He looked at them and felt suddenly that he had somehow let them down when they needed him most, and that now they would pay the price for his failure. It angered him when he thought about the whole crazy idea of journeying to Paranor to retrieve a relic of another age on the offhand chance that it would save them, or save anyone for that matter, from a creature like the Warlock Lord. Yet he knew, even as he finished the thought, that it was wrong to question now something they had accepted from the first as little more than a remote possibility. He looked at Flick wearily and wondered why they couldn't have been better friends.

Durin's sudden whisper of warning sent them all scurrying off the exposed path with the cumbersome stretchers to the seclusion of the great trees, flattening themselves against the earth and waiting breathlessly. A moment later the distinct sound of heavy boots reverberated along the deserted trail and, from the direction in which they had come, a party of Gnome warriors marched out of the darkness toward their hiding place. Balinor immediately knew there were too many for them to fight and placed a restraining hand on the excited Menion to keep him from making any sudden movement. The Gnomes marched along the trail in formation, their yellow faces stony in the starlight as their wide-set eyes glanced uneasily about at the dark forest. They reached the point where the company crouched in hiding and moved on up the trail without pausing, unaware that their quarry was within a few feet. When they had disappeared from sight and there was no further sound of them, Menion turned to Balinor.

"We are finished if we don't find Allanon. We won't get another mile carrying Shea and Flick under these conditions unless we have help!"

Balinor nodded slowly, but made no comment. He

knew their situation. But he knew as well that stopping now would be worse than capture or a second encounter with the Gnomes. Nor could they leave the brothers in these woods and hope they could find them after they got help—it was clearly too great a risk. He motioned the others to their feet. Without speaking, they picked up the stretchers and resumed the wearing march along the forest path, knowing now that the Gnomes were in front of them as well as behind. Menion wondered again what had befallen the gallant Hendel. It seemed impossible that even the resourceful Dwarf with all his skill in mountain fighting could have managed to evade those enraged Gnomes for any length of time. In any event, the Dwarf could not be in much worse shape than they were, wandering about the Anar with wounded men and no help in sight. If the Gnomes did find them again before they reached safety, Menion had little doubt as to the outcome.

Again Durin's sharp ears picked up the sound of approaching feet and everyone leaped to the safety of the great trees. They had barely gotten clear of the open trail and flattened themselves amidst the brush of the forest when figures appeared through the trees ahead. Even in the faint light of the stars, Durin's sharp eyes immediately picked out the leader of the small party as a giant of a man cloaked in a long black robe wound loosely about his lean body. A moment later the others saw him as well. It was Allanon. But Durin's sudden warning gesture stifled the exclamations of relief that were forming on the lips of Balinor and Menion. They squinted through the darkness and saw that the small, white-cloaked figures accompanying the historian were unmistakably Gnome.

"He's betrayed us!" whispered Menion harshly, his hand instinctively reaching for the long hunting knife at his belt.

"No, wait a minute," ordered Balinor quickly,

motioning them all to lie flat as the party came closer to their hiding spot.

Allanon's tall figure approached slowly along the trail in no apparent hurry, the deep-set eyes turned straight ahead as he walked. His dark brow was furrowed in concentration. Menion knew instinctively that they would be found and tensed his muscles for the leap onto the trail where his first blow would destroy the traitor. He knew he would have no second chance. The white-garbed Gnomes followed their leader dutifully, not marching in any particular order as they shuffled along in apparent disinterest. Suddenly Allanon halted and looked around in startled realization, as if sensing their presence. Menion prepared to spring, but a heavy hand grasped his shoulder, holding him firmly against the earth.

"Balinor," called the tall wanderer evenly, moving neither forward nor to either side as he looked about expectantly.

"Release me!" demanded Menion furiously of the Prince of Callahorn.

"They have no weapons!" Balinor's voice cut through his anger, causing him to scan again the white-robed Gnomes at the tall man's side. There were no weapons visible.

Balinor stood up slowly and advanced into the clearing, his great sword gripped tightly in one hand. Menion was right behind him, noting the lean figure of Durin just within the trees, an arrow fitted to his bow in readiness. Allanon came forward with a sigh of relief and reached for Balinor's hand, stopping quickly as he saw the faint distrust mirrored in the border-man's eyes and the outright bitterness registered on the face of the highlander. He seemed baffled for a moment, and then looked back suddenly at the small figures standing motionless behind him.

"No, it's all right!" he exclaimed hastily. "These are

friends. They have no weapons and no hatred toward
you. They are healers, physicians."

For a moment no one moved. Then Balinor
sheathed the great sword and took Allanon's extended hand in welcome. Menion followed suit, still
distrustful of the Gnomes waiting up the trail.

"Now tell me what has happened," ordered
Allanon, once again in command of the weary
company. "Where are the others?"

Quickly Balinor recounted what had befallen them
in the Wolfsktaag, their incorrect choice of the trail at
the fork, the battle that had followed with the creature
in the city ruins, their journey to the pass and the plan
that had gotten them past the assembled Gnomes.
Upon hearing of the Valemen's injuries, Allanon
immediately spoke to the Gnomes who had accompanied him, informing the suspicious Menion that
they could treat the wounds his friends had incurred.
Balinor continued his tale while the white-robed
Gnomes hastened to the side of the injured Valemen
and hovered over them in obvious concern, applying a
liquid from some vials they carried. Menion looked on
anxiously, wondering to himself why these Gnomes
were any different from the rest. As Balinor concluded, Allanon shook his head in disgust.

"It was my fault, my miscalculation," he muttered
angrily. "I was looking too far ahead in the journey and
not watching closely enough for immediate dangers. If
those two men die, the whole trip will have been for
nothing!"

He spoke again to the scurrying Gnomes, and one of
them departed at a hasty walk up the trail toward the
Pass of Jade.

"I sent one of them back to see what he could learn
about Hendel. If anything has happened to him, I'll be
the only one to blame."

He ordered the Gnome physicians to pick up the
Valemen and the whole group moved back onto the

trail, heading westward, the stretcher bearers in the lead and the weary members of the company trailing behind. Dayel's rib wound had been attended to, and he was able to walk without assistance. As the company traveled along the deserted trail, Allanon explained to them why they would not encounter Gnome hunting parties in this region.

"We are approaching the land of the Stors, these Gnomes that came with me," he informed them. "They are healers, separate from the rest of the Gnome nations and all other races, dedicated to helping those in need of sanctuary or medical aid. They govern themselves, live apart from the petty bickerings of other nations—something most men could never manage to do. Everyone in this part of the world respects and honors them. Their land, which we will enter soon, is called Storlock. It is hallowed ground that no Gnome hunting party would dare to cross into unless invited. You may rest assured that invitations are at a premium this night."

He went on to explain that he had been a friend to these harmless people for many years, sharing their secrets, living with them for as long as several months at a time. The Stors could be counted on, he guaranteed Menion, to cure whatever might be wrong with the young Valemen. They were the foremost healers in the world, and it was no accident that they had come along with the historian when he had returned through the Anar to meet the company at the Pass of Jade. Hearing of the strange events that had taken place from a frightened Gnome runner he had encountered on the trail at the edge of Storlock, who believed the spirits of the taboo land had sallied forth to consume them all, he had asked the Stors to come with him in search of his friends, fearing that they might have sustained injuries at the pass.

"I had no idea that the creature whose presence I detected in that valley in the Wolfsktaag would have the intelligence to remove the trail markers after I had passed," he admitted angrily. "I should have suspected, though, and left other signs to be certain that you bypassed that place. Worse still, I passed right through the Pass of Jade in the early afternoon without realizing that the Gnomes would be gathering that evening for the purging of the mountain spirits. It appears I have failed you badly."

"We were all at fault," Balinor declared, although Menion, listening silently from the other side, was not so willing to believe he was right. "Had we all been more alert, none of this would have happened. What matters is curing Shea and Flick and trying to do something about Hendel before the Gnome hunting parties find him."

They walked on in silence for a while, dejected men too tired to think further on the matter, concentrating only on putting one foot in front of the next until they reached the promised safety of the Stor village. The trail seemed to wind endlessly through the trees of the Anar forest, and after a while the four lost all sense of time and place, their minds dulled into sleepless exhaustion. The night slowly passed away, and finally the first tinges of the dawn's light appeared unexpectedly on the eastern horizon; still they had not reached their destination. It was an hour later when they finally saw the light of night fires burning in the Stor village, reflecting off the trees encircling the tired travelers. All at once they were in the village, surrounded by ghostlike Stors, wrapped in the same white cloaks, looking at the men with sad, unblinking expressions as they helped the exhausted travelers into the shelter of one of the low buildings.

Once within, the members of the company collapsed wordlessly on the soft beds provided, too tired to wash or even undress. All were asleep in seconds except for Menion Leah, whose high-strung temperament fought back the clutches of a soothing sleep

long enough to allow his bleary eyes to search silently
about the room for Allanon. Upon not finding him, he
rose sluggishly from the softness of the bed and
stumbled wearily to the closed wooden door, which
he dimly recalled led to a second room beyond.
Leaning heavily against the door, his ear pressed
closely to the crack in the jamb, he listened to snatches
of conversation between the historian and the Stors.
In a daze of half-sleep, he heard a brief digression
concerning Shea and Flick. The strange little people
felt that the Valemen would recover with rest and
special medication. Then abruptly a door beyond
opened to admit several people, and their voices
blended meaninglessly in exclamations of dismay and
shock. Allanon's deep voice cut through in icy
clearness.

"What have you discovered?" he demanded. "Is it
as bad as we feared?"

"They caught somebody in the mountains," came
the timid answer. "It was impossible to tell who it was
or even what it was by the time they were finished.
They tore him to pieces!"

Hendel!

Stunned, even in his exhausted condition, the
highlander pushed himself upright and stumbled
back to his waiting bed, unable to believe he had heard
them correctly. Deep within him, a great empty space
opened. Helpless tears of anger welled up, unable to
reach his still-dry eyes, and hung poised there until
the Prince of Leah finally dropped off into comforting
sleep.

XIII

When Shea finally opened his eyes, it was midafternoon of the following day. He found himself resting comfortably in a long bed, tucked in with clean sheets and blankets, his hunting clothes replaced by a loose white gown tied about his neck. On the bed next to him lay the still-sleeping Flick, his broad face no longer drawn and pale, but alive once more with the color of life and peaceful in slumber. They were in a small, plaster-walled room with a ceiling supported by long wooden beams. Through the windows, the young Valeman could see the trees of the Anar and the shining blueness of the afternoon sky. He had no idea how long he had been unconscious or what had happened during that time to bring him to this unknown place. But he felt certain that the creature of the Wolfsktaag had nearly killed him, and that Flick and he owed their lives to the men of the company. His attention was quickly drawn to the opening door at one end of the small room and the appearance of an anxious Menion Leah.

"Well, old friend, I see that you've come back to the world of the living." The highlander smiled slowly as he came over to the bedside. "You gave us quite a scare there for a while, you know."

"We made it, didn't we?" Shea grinned happily at the familiar joking voice.

Menion nodded briefly and turned to the supine

228

figure of Flick, who had stirred slightly beneath the covers and was beginning to awake. The stocky Valeman opened his eyes slowly and looked up hesitantly, seeing the grinning face of the highlander.

"I knew it was too good to be true," he groaned painfully. "Even dead, I can't escape him. It's a curse!"

"Old Flick has fully recovered as well." Menion laughed shortly. "I hope he appreciates the work it took to carry that cumbersome body of his all this way."

"The day you do any honest work, I'll be amazed," mumbled Flick, trying to clear his sleep-fogged eyes. He looked over at a smiling Shea and grinned back with a short wave of greeting.

"Where are we anyway?" asked Shea curiously, forcing himself to sit up in bed. He was still feeling weak. "How long have I been unconscious?"

Menion sat down on the edge of the bed and repeated the entire tale of their journey after escaping the creature in the valley. He told them of the march to the Pass of Jade and the encounter with the Gnomes there, the plan to get them by, and the results. He faltered a bit retelling of Hendel's sacrifice to the company. Shocked looks registered on the Valemen's faces on hearing of the gallant Dwarf's grisly death at the hands of the enraged Gnomes. Menion quickly continued with the remainder of the story, explaining how they had wandered through the Anar until discovered by Allanon and the strange people called Stors, who had treated their wounds and brought them to this place.

"This land is called Storlock," he concluded finally. "The people here are Gnomes who have dedicated their lives to healing the sick and injured. It's really amazing what they can do. They have a salve which, when applied to an open wound, closes it up and heals it over in twelve hours. I saw it work myself on an injury Dayel received."

Shea shook his head in disbelief and was about to ask for further details when the door again opened to admit Allanon. For the first time he could remember, Shea thought the dark wanderer actually seemed happy, and detected a sincere smile of relief on the grim face. The man walked quickly over to them and nodded in satisfaction.

"I am certainly pleased that you have both recovered from your wounds. I was gravely concerned about you, but it appears the Stors have done their work well. Do you feel recovered enough to get out of bed and walk around a bit, perhaps to have some food?"

Shea looked inquiringly over at Flick, and they both nodded.

"Very well, then, go along with Menion and test your strength," the historian suggested. "It is important that you feel well enough to travel again soon."

Without further word, he left by the same door, shutting it softly behind him. They watched him go, wondering how he could continue to be so coldly formal in his attitude toward them. Menion shrugged, advising them that he would find their hunting clothes which had been taken out and cleaned. He left and quickly returned with their clothing, whereupon the Valemen rose weakly from their beds and dressed while Menion told them a little more about the Stors. He explained that he had mistrusted them at first because they were Gnomes, but his fears had rapidly vanished upon watching them care for the Valemen. The others in the company had slept well into the morning before waking and were scattered now about the village, enjoying their brief respite on the journey to Paranor.

The three left the room shortly thereafter and entered another building that served as a dining hall for the village, where they were given generous portions of hot food to appease their ravenous appetites. Even with their injuries, the Valemen found themselves able to put away several helpings of the nourishing meal. After finishing, Menion led them outside where they encountered a fully recuperated Durin and Dayel, both delighted to see the Valemen back on their feet. At Menion's suggestion, the five walked to the south end of the village to see the wondrous Blue Pond that the highlander had been told about by the Stors earlier in the day. It took only a few minutes for them to reach the small pond, and they sat at its edge beneath a huge weeping willow and gazed in silence at the placid blue surface. Menion told them that the Stors made many of their salves and balms from the waters of that pond, which were said to have special healing elements that could be found nowhere else in the world. Shea tasted the water and found it different from anything he had ever encountered, but not at all displeasing to drink. The others tried it as well and murmured their approval. The Blue Pond was such a peaceful place that for a moment they all sat back and forgot their hazardous journey, thinking about their homes and the people they had left behind.

"This pond reminds me of Beleal, my home in the Westland." Durin smiled to himself as he ran a finger through the water, tracing out some image from his mind. "There, you can find the same sort of peace we have here."

"We'll be back there before you know it," Dayel promised, and then added eagerly, almost boyishly, "And I'll be married to Lynliss and we'll have many children."

"Forget it," declared Menion abruptly. "Stay single and stay happy."

"You haven't seen her, Menion," Dayel continued brightly. "She is like no one you have seen—a gentle, kind girl, as beautiful as this pond is clear."

Menion shook his head in mock despair and

slapped the frail Elf on his shoulder lightly, smiling his understanding of the other's deep feeling for the Elven girl. No one spoke for a few minutes as they continued to gaze with mixed feelings at the blue waters of the Stor pond. Then Shea turned to them questioningly.

"Do you think we are doing the right thing? I mean going on this trip and all. Does it all seem worth it to you?"

"That seems funny coming from you, Shea," remarked Durin thoughtfully. "The way I see it, you have the most to lose by coming along. In fact, you are the whole purpose of this journey. Do you feel it's worth it?"

Shea considered for a moment while the others looked on silently.

"That's not really a fair question to ask him," defended Flick.

"Yes, it is," Shea cut in soberly. "They are all risking their lives for me, and I've been the only one expressing any doubts about what we're doing. But I can't answer my own question, even to myself, because I feel I still don't know exactly what's happening. I do not think that we have the whole picture before us."

"I know what you mean," Menion agreed. "Allanon hasn't told us everything about what we're doing on this trip. There's more to this business about the Sword of Shannara than we know."

"Has anybody ever seen the Sword?" Dayel asked suddenly. The others shook their heads negatively. "Maybe there is no Sword."

"Oh, I think that the Sword exists, all right," Durin declared quickly. "But once we get it, what do we do with it? What can Shea do against the power of the Warlock Lord, even with the Sword of Shannara?"

"I think we must trust to Allanon to answer that when the time comes," another voice said.

The new voice came from behind the five, and they turned around sharply, breathing an audible sigh of relief when it was Balinor who appeared. Even as he watched the Prince of Callahorn stroll over to them, Shea wondered to himself why it was that they all still felt an unspoken fear of Allanon. The borderman smiled a greeting to Shea and Flick and seated himself with the others.

"Well, it appears that our hardships in coming through the Pass of Jade were worth it after all. I'm glad to see that you're all right."

"I'm sorry about Hendel." Shea sounded awkward to himself. "I know he was a close friend."

"It was a calculated risk that the situation demanded," replied Balinor softly. "He knew what he was doing and what the chances were. He did it for all of us."

"What happens next?" asked Flick after a moment.

"We wait for Allanon to decide on our route for the last leg of the journey," replied Balinor. "Incidentally, I meant what I said about trusting him. He is a great man, a good man, though it may appear otherwise at times. He tells us what he feels we ought to know, but believe me, he does the worrying for us all. Do not be too quick to judge him."

"You know that he hasn't told us everything," Menion stated simply.

"I am certain he has told us only part of the tale." Balinor nodded. "But he is the only one who realized the threat to the four lands in the first place. We owe him a great deal, and the very least of that is a little trust."

The others nodded slowly in agreement, more for the reason that they all respected the borderman than because they felt convinced by his reassurances. This was especially true of Menion, who recognized that Balinor was a man of great courage, the kind of man whom Menion looked to as a leader. They spoke no more on the matter, but turned to a further discussion of the Stors, their history as a branch of the Gnome nations and their long, abiding friendship with Allanon. The sun was setting when the tall historian appeared unexpectedly and joined them by the Blue Pond.

"After I am finished with you I want the Valemen back in bed for a few hours' rest. It probably wouldn't hurt the rest of you to get some sleep as well. We will leave this place some time around midnight."

"Isn't this a little sudden after the wounds Shea and Flick received?" Menion asked cautiously.

"That cannot be helped, highlander." The grim face seemed black even in the fading sunlight. "We are all running out of time. If word of our mission, or even our presence in this part of the Anar, reaches the Warlock Lord, he will try to move the Sword immediately, and without it this journey is pointless."

"Flick and I can make it," Shea declared resolutely.

"What will be the route?" Balinor asked.

"We will cross the Rabb Plains tonight, a march of about four hours. If we are lucky, we will not be caught out in the open, although I am quite sure the Skull Bearers will still be searching for both Shea and myself. We can only hope they haven't managed to trace us into the Anar. I hadn't told you before, because you had enough to concern you, but any use of the Elfstones pinpoints our position to Brona and his hunters. The mystical power of the stones can be detected by any creature of the spirit world, warning him that sorcery similar to his own is being used."

"Then, when we used the Elfstones in the Mist Marsh . . ." Flick began in horror.

"You told the Skull Bearers exactly where you were," Allanon finished with that infuriating smile. "If you hadn't lost yourselves in the mist and the Black Oaks, they might have had you right there."

Shea felt a sudden chill sweep over him as he

recalled how close they had felt to death at the time, little realizing how much danger they were really in from the creatures they feared the most.

"If you knew that use of the stones would attract the spirit creatures, then why didn't you tell us?" demanded Shea angrily. "Why did you give them to us to use for protection when you knew what would happen?"

"You were cautioned, my young friend," came the slow, growling response that always indicated Allanon's temper was shortening. "Without them, you would have been at the mercy of other equally dangerous elements. Besides, they are protection enough in themselves against the winged ones."

He waved off further questions, indicating that the subject was closed, causing Shea to become even more suspicious and angered. A watchful Durin saw all the signs and placed a restraining hand on the young Valeman's shoulder, shaking his head in warning.

"If we may return to the matter at hand," Allanon continued on a more even tone, "let me explain further the chosen route for the next few days— without interruption. The journey across the Rabb Plains will put us at the foot of the Dragon's Teeth at daybreak. Those mountains offer all the protection we need from anyone searching for us. But the real problem is getting over them and down the other side to the forests surrounding Paranor. All the known passes through the Dragon's Teeth will be closely guarded by the allies of the Warlock Lord, and any attempt to scale those peaks without using one of the passes would get half of us killed. So we'll go through the mountains by a different route, one that they won't be guarding."

"Wait a minute!" exclaimed Balinor in astonishment. "You don't plan to take us through the Tomb of the Kings!"

"There is no other alternative open to us if we wish

to avoid being discovered. We can enter the Hall of
Kings at sunrise and be completely through the
mountains and outside Paranor by sundown without
the guards at the passes being any the wiser."

"But the stories say no one has ever gotten through
those caverns alive!" insisted Durin, coming quickly to
Balinor's aid in discounting the suggested plan.
"None of us is afraid of the living, but the spirits of the
dead inhabit those caves and only the dead may pass
through unharmed. No living person has ever done
it!"

Balinor nodded his head slowly in agreement, while
the others looked on anxiously. Menion and the
Valemen had never even heard of the place of which
the others seemed so deathly afraid. Allanon was
actually grinning strangely at Durin's last comment,
his eyes dark beneath the heavy brows, his white teeth
showing in menacing fashion.

"You are not entirely correct, Durin," he replied
after a minute. "I have been through the Hall of Kings,
and I tell you that it can be done. It is not a journey to
be made without risk. The caverns are indeed
inhabited by the spirits of the dead, and it is on this
that Brona relies to prevent the entry of humans. But
my power should be sufficient to protect us."

Menion Leah had no idea what it was about the
caverns that could cause even a man like Balinor to
have second thoughts, but whatever it was, he felt
there was a good reason to fear it. Moreover, he was
through questioning what he had called old wives'
tales and foolish legends, since the encounters in the
Mist Marsh and the Wolfsktaag. What really concerned him now was what sort of powers the man who
proposed to lead them through the caves of the
Dragon's Teeth might possess that could protect them
from spirits.

"The entire journey has been a calculated risk."
Allanon was speaking once again. "We all knew what

the dangers were before we began it. Are you ready to turn back at this point, or do we see the matter through to the end?"

"We will follow you," Balinor declared after only a moment's hesitation. "You knew we would. The risk is worth it if we can lay our hands on the Sword."

Allanon smiled slightly, his deep-set eyes traveling over the faces of the others, meeting each gaze piercingly, coming to rest at last on Shea. The Valeman stared back unfalteringly, though his heart felt twinges of fear and uncertainty as those eyes bored into his innermost thoughts, seemingly aware of every secret doubt the Valeman had tried to conceal.

"Very well." Allanon nodded darkly. "Go now and rest."

He turned abruptly and walked back toward the Stor village. Balinor hastened after the departing figure, apparently wishing to ask something further. The others watched both until they were out of sight. Then, for the first time, Shea realized it was almost dark, the sun sinking slowly beneath the horizon and the twilight a soft white light in the deepening purple sky. For a moment no one moved, and then silently they climbed to their feet and retired to the peaceful village to sleep until the appointed hour of midnight.

It seemed to Shea that he had just fallen asleep when he felt the rough grip of a strong hand shaking him awake. A moment later, the sharp glare of a burning torch flickered through the darkened room, causing him to squint protectively while his sleep-filled eyes adjusted to this new light. Through a mist of sleep, he saw the determined face of Menion Leah, the anxious eyes telling him that the hour had come for them to depart. He rose unsteadily in the cold night air and, after a moment's hesitation, hastened to dress. Flick was already awake and half dressed, the stolid face a welcome sight in the eerie silence of midnight. Shea felt strong once again, strong enough to make the long march across the Rabb Plains to the Dragon's Teeth and beyond if necessary—anything to reach the end of the journey.

Minutes later, the three companions were making their way through the sleeping Stor village to meet the other members of the company. The darkened houses were black, squarish bulks in the dim light of a night sky which was moonless and screened by a heavy blanket of clouds that moved sluggishly toward some undetermined destination. It was a good night to travel in the open, and Shea felt reassured by the idea that any searching emissaries of the Warlock Lord would have a very difficult time spotting them. As they walked, he found that he could barely detect the tread of their light hunting boots on the damp earth. Everything seemed to be working in their favor.

When they reached the western boundary of Storlock, they found the others waiting, except for Allanon. Durin and Dayel appeared like empty forms in the blackness, their slight figures only shadows as they paced wordlessly, listening to the sounds of the night. Passing close to them at one point, Shea was struck by the distinctive Elven features, the strange pointed ears and the pencil-thin eyebrows arching upward onto the forehead. He wondered if other humans looked at him the way he now looked at the Elven brothers. Were they truly different creatures? He wondered again about the history behind the Elf people, the history that Allanon had referred to once as remarkable, but had never described further. Their history was his own; he knew now what he had always suspected. It was something he wanted to know more about, perhaps if only better to understand his own heritage and the tale of the Sword of Shannara.

He looked over to the tall, broad figure of Balinor standing like a statue to one side, his face featureless in the dark. Balinor was unquestionably the most reassuring thing about the whole expedition. There was something very durable about the borderman, a quality of indestructibility that lent itself freely to all of the members of the company and gave them courage. Even Allanon did not inspire them in quite this way, although Shea felt that he was easily the more powerful of the two. Perhaps Allanon, in his seemingly infinite awareness of all matters, knew what Balinor did for other men and had brought him along for precisely that reason.

"Quite so, Shea." The soft voice was so close to his ear that the Valeman leaped violently in surprise as the black-cloaked wanderer strolled past him and motioned the others to his side. "The journey must be made while we have the cover of the night. Stay together and keep your eyes on the men ahead. There will be no talking."

Without further greeting, the dark giant led them into the Anar Forests along a narrow trail that ran directly west out of Storlock. Shea fell into step behind Menion, his heart still in his throat from the fright he had received, his mind racing madly back over the past encounters with the strange man, wondering if what he had suspected all along were true after all. In any event, he would keep his thoughts to himself any time Allanon was close, however difficult that task might prove to be.

The company reached the western edges of the Anar Forests and the beginning of the Rabb Plains sooner than Shea had expected. Despite the blackness of the night sky, the Valemen could sense the presence of the Dragon's Teeth looming in the distance; without speaking, they looked at one another briefly, then turned back to peer anxiously into the darkness. Allanon led them across the empty plainland without pausing and without slackening the pace. The Plains were completely flat, totally free of natural obstructions and visibly lifeless. The only things growing were small scrub trees and bits of scattered brush that were bare and skeletonlike in appearance. The floor of the plain was hard-packed earth, so dry in parts that it split apart in long, jagged crevices. Nothing moved about the travelers as they marched in silence, their eyes and ears alert to anything out of the ordinary. At one point, when they were almost three hours into the Rabb Plains, Dayel brought them up with a quick gesture, indicating that he had heard something behind them, far back in the blackness. They crouched soundless and immobile for several long minutes, but nothing happened. At last Allanon shrugged and motioned them back into line, and they resumed their march.

They reached the Dragon's Teeth just before daybreak, the night sky still black and clouded as they halted at the foot of the forbidding mountains that spread upward across their path like monstrous spikes on an iron gate. Both Shea and Flick felt strong, even after the long march, and quickly indicated to the others that they were ready to continue without a rest. Allanon seemed eager to move on immediately, almost as if he were determined to keep an appointment. He took them straight into the treacherous-looking mountains along a pebble-strewn trail that wound gently upward into what appeared to be a pocket in the face of the cliffs. Flick found himself looking up at the peaks on either side of the trail as he walked, craning his stout neck at right angles to catch occasional glimpses of the jagged tips. The Dragon's Teeth seemed an appropriate name.

The mountains on either side began to fold about them as they worked their way toward the cliff pocket. Beyond that shallow pass, they could glimpse other mountains, higher than these and clearly insurmountable by anything that could not fly. Shea paused momentarily at one point, picked up a piece of the loose rock from beneath his feet, and examined it curiously as he resumed walking. To his surprise, it was smooth on its flat surfaces, almost glassy in appearance, and its color was a deep, mirroring black that reminded the Valeman of the coal he had seen burned as fuel in some of the Southland communities. Yet this appeared to be more durable than coal, as if it had been pressed and polished to reach its present state. He handed it to Flick, who glanced at it, shrugged disinterestedly and tossed it aside.

The trail began to twist through huge clusters of fallen boulders, causing the travelers momentarily to lose all sight of the surrounding mountains. They wound about in the tangle of rock for a long time, still climbing toward the pocket, their dark leader apparently oblivious to the fact that no one had any idea where they were going. Finally they reached a clearing in the rocks where they could see enough of the high cliffs about them to tell that they were at the opening to the pocket and evidently close to the summit of the trail, which would then either have to turn downward or level off into the mountains. It was here that Balinor broke the silence with a low whistle, bringing the company to a halt. He spoke momentarily with Durin, who had fallen back with the borderman at the foot of the mountains, then quickly turned to Allanon and the others with a startled look on his face.

"Durin is certain he heard someone following us on the trail up!" he informed them tensely. "There's no question about it this time—someone is back there."

Allanon glanced up hurriedly at the night sky. His dark brow furrowed in concern, the lean face revealing that he was deeply worried by this report. He looked at Durin uncertainly.

"I'm sure there is someone back there," Durin affirmed.

"I cannot stop here to deal with this myself. I have to be in the valley ahead before the break of day," Allanon declared abruptly. "Whatever is back there must be delayed until I have finished—it is essential!"

Shea had never heard the man sound so determined about anything, and he caught the looks of consternation on both Flick's and Menion's faces as they glanced quickly at one another. Whatever it was Allanon had to do in the valley, it was critical to him that he not be interrupted until he had finished.

"I'll stay behind," Balinor volunteered, drawing his great sword. "Wait for me in the valley."

"Not alone, you won't," Menion spoke up quickly. "I'm staying, too, just in case."

Balinor smiled briefly and nodded his approval to the highlander. Allanon looked at him for a moment as if to object, then nodded curtly and motioned the others to follow him. The Elven brothers hastened up the trail behind the tall leader, but Shea and Flick hung back uncertainly until Menion motioned for them to get going. Shea waved briefly, reluctant to desert his friend, but realizing that he would be of little help in staying. He glanced back only once and saw the two men positioning themselves among the rocks on either side of the narrow trail, their swords gleaming dully in the faint starlight, their dark hunting cloaks blending with the shadows of the rocks.

Allanon led the remaining four members of the company ahead through the jumbled mass of boulders where the cliff face split apart, climbing steadily upward toward what appeared to be the rim of the mysterious valley. It was only a few short minutes before they stood quietly at its edge, gazing wonderingly at what lay before them. The valley was a barbaric wilderness of crushed rock and boulders strewn about the sides and floor, black and glistening like the rock Shea had examined on the trail; the place was completely covered with them. Nothing else was visible except for a small lake with murky waters that glistened a dull greenish-black and moved in small sluggish swirls as if possessing a life of its own. Shea was immediately struck with the strange movement of the water. There was no wind which might cause the slow rippling. He looked at the silent Allanon and was shocked to see a strange glow radiating from his dark, forbidding face. The tall wanderer seemed momentarily lost in his thoughts as he gazed downward at the lake, and the Valeman could sense a peculiar wistfulness about the man's unbroken study of the slowly churning waters.

"This is the Valley of Shale, the doorstep to the Hall of Kings and the home of the spirits of the ages." The deep voice rolled suddenly out of the depths of the great chest. "The lake is the Hadeshorn—its waters are death to mortals. Walk with me to the floor of the valley, and then I must go on alone."

Without waiting for a response, he started slowly down the slope of the valley, stepping surefootedly through the loose rock, his gaze fixed on the lake beyond. The others followed in mystified silence, sensing that this was going to be an important moment for them all, that here more than anywhere else in all the lands, Allanon was king. Without being able to explain why, Shea knew that the historian, the wanderer, the philosopher, and the mystic, the man who had brought them through countless dangers on a wild gamble that only he fully understood, the mysterious man they knew as Allanon, had at last come home. Moments later, when they stood together on the floor of the Valley of Shale, he turned to them again.

"You will wait for me here. No matter what happens next, you will not follow me. You will not move from this spot until I have finished. Where I go, there is only death."

They stood rooted in place as he moved away from them across the rocky floor toward the mysterious lake. They watched his tall, black form walk steadily ahead without variation in either speed or direction,

the great cloak billowing slightly. Shea shot a quick
glance at Flick, whose tense face revealed his fear of
what would happen next. For a split second Shea
considered getting out of there, but realized immediately what a foolhardy decision that would be.
Instinctively he clutched his tunic, feeling the reassuring bulk of the small pouch that contained the
Elfstones. Their presence made him feel safer, even
though he doubted that they would be of much use
against anything that Allanon could not handle. He
glanced anxiously at the others as they watched the
diminishing figure, then turning back, saw that
Allanon had reached the edge of the Hadeshorn,
where he was apparently awaiting something. A
deathly silence seemed to grip the entire valley. The
four waited, their eyes locked on the dark figure who
stood motionless at the water's edge.

Slowly, the tall wanderer raised his black-caped
arms to the sky and the amazed men saw the lake
begin to stir rapidly and then churn in deep dissatisfaction. The valley shuddered heavily, as if some form
of hidden, sleeping life had been awakened. The
terrified mortals looked about in disbelief, fearing they
were about to be swallowed by the rock-strewn maw
of some nightmare disguised as the valley. Allanon
stood firm at the shoreline as the water began to boil
fiercely at its center, a spray mist rising toward the
darkened heavens with a sharp hiss of relief at its
newfound freedom from the depths. From out of the
night air came the sound of low moaning, the cries of
imprisoned souls, their sleep disturbed by the man at
the edge of the Hadeshorn. The voices, less than
human and chill with death, cut through the raw edge
of sanity of the four who shivered and watched at the
valley's edge, straining their frightened minds and
twisting with unmerciful cruelty until it seemed the
little courage that remained must surely be wrested
from them, leaving them stripped completely of all

defenses. Unable to move, to speak, even to think, they stood frozen in terror as the sounds of the spirit world reached up to them and passed through their minds, warning of the things that lay beyond this life and their understanding.

In the midst of the chilling cries, with a low rumble that sounded from the heart of the earth, the Hadeshorn opened at its center in the manner of a thrashing whirlpool and from out of its murky waters rose the shroud of an old man, bowed with age. The figure rose to full height and appeared to stand on the waters themselves, the tall, thin body a transparent gray of ghostlike hue that shimmered like the lake beneath it. Flick turned completely white. The appearance of this final horror only confirmed his belief that their last moments on earth were at hand. Allanon stood motionless at the edge of the lake, his lean arms lowered now, the black cloak wrapped closely about his statuesque figure, his face turned toward the shade which stood before him. They appeared to be conversing, but the four onlookers could hear nothing beyond the continual, maddening sound of the inhuman cries that rose piercingly out of the night each time the figure from the Hadeshorn gestured. The conversation, whatever its nature, lasted no more than a few brief minutes, ending when the wraith turned toward them suddenly, raised its tattered skeletal arm, and pointed. Shea felt a chill slice through his unprotected body that seemed to cut to the bones, and he knew that for a brief second he had been touched by death. Then the shade turned away and, with a final gesture of farewell to Allanon, sank slowly back into the dark waters of the Hadeshorn and was gone. As he disappeared from view, the waters again churned sluggishly, and the moans and cries reached a new pitch before dying out in a low wail of anguish. Then the lake was smooth and calm and the men were alone.

As sunrise broke on the eastern horizon, the tall, black figure on the lake's edge seemed to sway slightly and then crumple to the ground. For a second the four men watching hesitated, then dashed across the valley floor toward their fallen leader, slipping and stumbling on the loose rock. They reached him in a matter of seconds and bent cautiously over him, uncertain what they should do. Finally, Durin reached down and shook the still form gingerly, calling his name. Shea rubbed the great hands, finding the skin ice-cold to his touch and alarmingly pale. But their fears were relieved when after a few minutes Allanon stirred slightly and the deep-set eyes opened once more. He stared at them for a few seconds, and then sat up slowly as they crouched anxiously next to him.

"The strain must have been too great," he muttered to himself, rubbing his forehead. "Blacked out after I lost contact. I'll be fine in a moment."

"Who was that creature?" Flick asked quickly, afraid that it might reappear at any moment.

Allanon seemed to reflect on his question, staring into space as his dark face twisted in anguish and then relaxed softly.

"A lost soul, a being forgotten by this world and its people," he declared sadly. "He has doomed himself to an existence of half-life that may not end for all eternity."

"I don't understand," Shea said.

"It's not important right now." Allanon brushed the question aside abruptly. "That sad figure to whom I just spoke is the Shade of Bremen, the Druid who once fought against the Warlock Lord. I spoke to him of the Sword of Shannara, of our trip to Paranor, and of the destiny of this company. I could learn little from him, an indication that our fortunes are not to be decided in the very near future, but that the fate of us all will be decided in days still far away—that is, all but one."

"What do you mean?" Shea demanded hesitantly.

Allanon climbed wearily to his feet, gazed about the valley silently as if to assure himself that the encounter with the ghost of Bremen was ended, and then turned back to the anxious faces waiting on him.

"There is no easy way to say this, but you've come this far, almost to the end of the quest. You have earned the right to know. The Shade of Bremen made two prophesies on the destiny of this company when I called him up from the limbo world to which he is confined. He promised that within two dawns we would behold the Sword of Shannara. But he also foresaw that one member of our company would not reach the far side of the Dragon's Teeth. Yet he will be the first to lay hands upon the sacred blade."

"I still don't understand," Shea admitted after a moment's thought. "We've already lost Hendel. He must have been speaking of him in some way."

"No, you are wrong, my young friend." Allanon sighed softly. "Upon making the last part of the prophesy, the shade pointed to the four of you standing at the edge of the valley. One of you will not reach Paranor!"

Menion Leah crouched silently in the cover of the boulders along the path leading upward to the Valley of Shale, waiting expectantly for the mysterious being who had been trailing them into the Dragon's Teeth. Across from him, hidden in the blackness of the shadows, was the Prince of Callahorn, his great sword balanced blade downward in the rocks, one big hand resting lightly on the pommel. Menion gripped his own weapon and peered into the darkness. Nothing was moving. He could see for only about fifteen yards before an abrupt twist in the trail concealed the remainder of the pathway behind a cluster of massive boulders. They had been waiting for at least half an hour and still nothing had appeared, despite Durin's assurance that something was following. Menion

wondered for a moment if perhaps the creature who
had been trailing them was one of the emissaries of the
Warlock Lord. A Skull Bearer could take to the air and
get behind them to reach the others. The idea startled
him, and he was about to signal Balinor when a
sudden noise on the trail below caught his attention.
He immediately flattened himself against the rocks.

The sound of someone picking his way up the
twisting pathway, threading slowly among the great
boulders in the dim light of the approaching dawn,
was clearly audible. Whoever or whatever it was, he
apparently did not suspect they were hidden above, or
worse, did not care, because he was making no effort
to mask his approach. Scant seconds later, a dim form
appeared on the pathway just below their hiding
place. Menion risked a quick glance and for one brief
second the squat shape and shuffling gait of the figure
approaching reminded him of Hendel. He gripped the
sword of Leah in anticipation and waited. The plan of
attack was simple. He would leap in front of the
intruder, barring his path forward. In the same
moment, Balinor would cut off his retreat.

With a lightning-quick spring, the highlander shot
out of the rocks to stand face to face with the
mysterious intruder, his sword held poised as he gave
a sharp command to halt. The figure before him went
into a low crouch and one powerful arm came up
slightly to reveal a huge, iron-headed mace, glinting
dully. One second later, as the eyes of the combatants
came to rest on one another, the arms dropped in
shocked recognition, and a cry of surprise burst from
the lips of the Prince of Leah.

"Hendel!"

Balinor came out of the shadows to the rear of the
newcomer in time to see an elated Menion leap into
the air with a wild shout and charge down to embrace
the smaller, stockier figure with unrestrained joy. The
Prince of Callahorn sheathed the great sword in relief,

smiling and shaking his head in wonder at the sight of the ecstatic highlander and the struggling, muttering Dwarf they had presumed dead. For the first time since they had escaped through the Pass of Jade from the Wolfsktaag, he felt that success was within their grasp and that the company would surely stand together at Paranor before the Sword of Shannara.

XIV

Dawn hung above the sweeping ridges and peaks of the Dragon's Teeth with a cold, gray determination that was neither cheerful nor welcome. The warmth and brightness of the rising sun was entirely screened away by low cloud banks and heavy mist that settled into the ominous heights and did not stir. The winds blew with vicious force over the barren rocks, whipping through canyons and craggy drops, across slopes and ridges, cutting into the scant vegetation and bending it close to the point of breaking, yet slipping through the mixture of clouds and mist with elusive quickness, leaving it unexplainably and strangely motionless. The sound of the wind was like the deep roar of the ocean breaking on an open beach, heavy and rolling, blanketing the empty peaks in a peculiar drone that, when one had been enveloped for a while, created its own level of silence. Birds rose and fell with the wind, their cries scattered and muffled. There were few animals at this height— isolated herds of a particularly tough breed of mountain goat and small, furry mice that inhabited the innermost recesses of the rocks. The air was more than chill; it was bitterly cold. Snow covered the upper reaches of the Dragon's Teeth, and changes in the seasons had little effect at this altitude on a temperature that seldom reached thirty degrees.

These were treacherous mountains, vast, towering

and incredibly massive. On this morning they seemed shrouded with a strange expectancy, and the eight men who comprised the little company from Culhaven could not ignore the feeling of uneasiness that preoccupied their thoughts as they trudged deeper into the cold and the gray. It was more than the disturbing prophecy of Bremen or even the knowledge that they would soon attempt to pass through the forbidden Hall of Kings. Something was waiting for them, something that had patience and cunning, a life force that lay hidden in the barren, rocky terrain they were passing through, filled with vindictive hatred of them, watching as they struggled deeper into the giant mountains that shut away the ancient kingdom of Paranor. They trudged northward in a ragged line, strung out against the misty skyline, their bodies wrapped tightly in woolen cloaks for protection against the cold, their faces bent before the wind. The slopes and canyons were covered with loose rock and split by hidden crevices that made the footing extremely hazardous. More than once, a member of the little band went down in a shower of loose rock and dirt. But still the thing concealed in the land chose not to show itself, content merely to let its presence be known and to wait for the effect of that knowledge to wear away at the resistance of the eight men. The hunters would then become the hunted.

It did not take long. Doubts began to gnaw quietly, persistently at their tired minds—doubts that rose phantomlike from the fears and secrets the men concealed deep within. Locked away from each other by the cold and the roar of the rising wind, each man was cut off from his companions, and the inability to communicate only heightened the growing feeling of uneasiness. Only Hendel was immune. His taciturn, solitary nature had hardened him against self-doubt, and his harrowing escape from the maddened Gnomes in the Pass of Jade had drained him at least temporarily of any fear of death. He had come close to dying, so close that in the end only instinct had saved him. The Gnomes had come at him from every direction, swarming up the slope in reckless disregard, enraged to the point where only bloodshed would quiet their hatred. He had been quick, slipping back into the fringes of the Wolfsktaag, motionless in the brush, coolly letting the Gnomes overextend themselves until one had come within reach. It had taken only seconds to stun the unsuspecting hunter, to cloak his captive in his own distinctive Dwarf habit, and then yell for assistance. In the darkness, flushed with the excitement of the hunt, the Gnomes were unable to recognize anything except the cloak. They tore their own brother to pieces without realizing it. Hendel had stayed hidden and slipped through the pass the following day. He had survived once again.

The Valemen and the Elves did not possess Hendel's strong sense of self-reliance. The prophecy of the Shade of Bremen had left them stunned. The words seemed to repeat themselves over and over in the howl of the mountain winds. One of them was going to die. Oh, the words of the prophecy had phrased it differently than that, but the implication was unmistakable. It was a bitter prospect to face, and none of them could really accept it. Somehow they would find a way to prove the prediction wrong.

Far in the lead, his great frame bent against the driving force of the mountain winds, Allanon was mulling over the events that had transpired in the Valley of Shale. He considered for the hundredth time his strange confrontation with the Shade of Bremen, the aged Druid doomed to wander in limbo until the Warlock Lord was finally destroyed. Yet it was not the appearance of the driven wraith that so disturbed him now. It was the terrible knowledge which he carried, buried deep among his blackest truths. His foot struck a projecting rock, causing him to stumble slightly, and he fought to keep his balance. A wheeling hawk screamed shrilly in the grayness and shot down out of the sky over a distant ridge. The Druid turned slightly as the thin line following struggled to keep pace. He had learned more from the Shade than the words of the prophecy. But he had not told the others, those who had trusted him, the whole truth, just as he had not told them the whole story behind the legendary Sword of Shannara. His deep-set eyes blazed with inner fury at the predicament in which he had placed himself in not telling them everything, and for a moment he even considered doing so. They had given so much of themselves, and the giving had only begun. . . . But a moment later, he wrenched the idea from his thoughts. Necessity was a higher god than truth.

The grayness of dawn passed slowly into the grayness of midday, and the march into the Dragon's Teeth wore on. The ridges and slopes appeared and faded with a dreary sameness that created the impression in the minds of the laboring travelers that no progress was being made. Ahead, a vast, towering line of peaks rose bleakly against the misty northern horizon, and it appeared that they were moving directly into a wall of impenetrable stone. Then they entered a broad canyon which wound sharply downward into a narrow, twisting path that broke between two huge cliffs and faded into the heavy mist. Allanon led them into the swirling grayness as the horizon disappeared and the wind died into stillness. The silence was abrupt and unexpected, sounding almost like a soft whisper through the towering mass of rock, speaking in hushed, cautious words in the ears of the groping travelers. Then the pass widened slightly and the mist cleared to a faint haze, revealing a high, cavernous opening in the cliff face where the winding passage ended.

The entrance to the Hall of Kings.

It was awesome, majestic, frightening. On either side of the rectangular black entryway stood two monstrous stone statues carved into the rock and rising well over a hundred feet against the dark cliff face. The stone sentries had been fashioned in the shape of armor-clad warriors, standing watchfully in the deep gloom, hands gripping the pommels of huge swords which rested blade downward at their feet. Their weathered, bearded faces were scarred by time and the wind, yet the eyes seemed almost alive, fixed carefully on the eight mortals who stood at the threshold of the ancient hall they guarded. Above the great entryway, scrolled into the rock, three words of a language centuries old and long forgotten served as a warning to those who would enter that this was the tomb of the dead. Beyond the vast opening, all was blackness and silence.

Allanon gathered them closely around him.

"Years ago, before the First War of the Races, a cult of men whose origins have been lost in time, served as priests for the gods of death. Within these caverns, they buried the monarchs of the four lands along with their families, servants, favorite possessions and much of their wealth. The legend grew that only the dead could survive within these chambers, and only the priests were permitted to see that the dead rulers were interred. All others who entered were never seen again. In time, the cult died out, but the evil instilled in the Hall of Kings continued to exist, blindly to serve the priests whose bones had years before returned to the earth. Few men have ever passed . . ."

He caught himself, seeing in the eyes of his listeners the unasked question.

"I have been through the Hall of Kings—I alone from this age, and now you. I am a Druid, the last to walk this earth. Like Bremen, like Brona before him, I have studied the black arts, and I am a sorcerer. I do not possess the power of the Dark Lord—but I can get us safely through these caverns to the other side of the Dragon's Teeth.''

''And then?'' Balinor's question came softly out of the mist.

''A narrow cliff-trail men call the Dragon's Crease leads downward out of the mountains. Once there, we will be within sight of Paranor.''

There was a long, awkward silence. Allanon knew what they were thinking; disregarding it, he continued.

''Beyond this entrance, there are a number of passages and chambers, a maze to one who does not know the way. Some of these are dangerous, some are not. Soon after we enter, we will reach the tunnel of the Sphinxes, giant statues like these sentries, but carved as half man, half beast. If you look into their eyes, you will be turned to stone instantly. So you must be blindfolded. In addition you will be roped to one another. You must concentrate on me, think only of me, for their will, their mental command, is strong enough to force you to tear off the blindfolds and gaze into their eyes.''

The seven men looked at one another doubtfully. Already they were beginning to question the soundness of this whole approach.

''Once past the Sphinxes, there are several harmless passages leading to the Corridor of the Winds, a tunnel inhabited by invisible beings called Banshees after the legendary astral spirits. They are no more than voices, but those voices will drive mortal men insane. Your ears will be bound for protection, but again the important thing for you to do is to concentrate on me, let my mind blanket yours to prevent it from receiving the full force of those voices. You must relax; do not fight me. Do you understand?''

He counted seven barely perceptible nods.

''Once beyond the Corridor of the Winds, we will be

in the Tomb of the Kings. Then there will be only one
more obstacle . . .''

He stopped talking, his eyes turned warily to the
cavern entrance. For a moment it seemed he might
finish the sentence, but instead he motioned them
toward the dark entryway. They stood uneasily
between the stone giants, the graying mist clouding
the high cliff walls surrounding them, the black,
yawning opening before them waiting like the open
maw of some great beast of prey. Allanon produced a
number of wide cloth strips and gave one to each man.
Utilizing a heavy length of climbing rope, the little
group bound themselves to one another, the
surefooted Durin taking the lead position, the Prince
of Callahorn again assuming his post as rear guard.
The blindfolds were securely fastened in place and
hands were joined to form a chain. A moment later,
the line moved cautiously through the entrance to the
Hall of Kings.

There was a deep, hushed stillness in the caverns,
magnified by the sudden dying of the winds and the
echoing of their footfalls along the rocky passageway.
The tunnel floor was strangely smooth and level, but
the cold that had settled into the aged stone from
centuries of constant temperatures seeped quickly
through their tensed bodies and left them chill and
shaking. No one spoke, each man trying to relax as
Allanon led them carefully through a series of gently
winding turns. In the middle of the groping line, Shea
felt Flick's hand grip his own tightly in the blackness
that surrounded them. They had drawn closer to each
other since their flight from the Vale, bound now by
ties of experiences shared more than by kinship.
Whatever happened to them, Shea felt they would
never lose that closeness. Nor would he forget what
Menion had done for him. He thought about the
Prince of Leah for a moment and found himself
smiling. The highlander had changed so much during

the past few days that he was almost a different person. The old Menion was still in evidence, but there was a new dimension to him that Shea found difficult to define. But then all of them, Menion, Flick and himself, had changed in little ways that could not be readily detected until each man was considered as a whole. He wondered if Allanon had seen the changes in him—Allanon, who had always treated him somehow as less than a man, more a boy.

They came to an unsteady halt, and in the deep silence that followed the commanding voice of the Druid leader whispered soundlessly in the mind of each man: *Remember my warning, let your thoughts turn to me, concentrate only on me.* Then the line moved forward, the booted feet echoing hollowly on the cavern floor. Immediately the blindfolded men could sense the presence of something waiting ahead of them, watching silently, patiently. The seconds flitted away as the company moved deeper into the cavern. The men became aware of huge, still forms rising up on either side—images carved of stone with faces that were human, but attached to the crouched bodies of indescribable beasts. The Sphinxes. In their minds the men could see those eyes, burning past the fading image of Allanon, and they began to feel the strain of trying to concentrate on the giant Druid. The insistent will of the stone monsters pushed into their brains, weaving and tangling into their scattered thoughts, working tenaciously toward the moment when human eyes would meet their own lifeless gaze. Each man began to feel a rapidly growing urge to rip away the restraining cloth which shackled his sight, to strip away the darkness and gaze freely on the wondrous creatures staring silently down on him.

But just when it seemed that the probing whisper of the Sphinxes must at last break through the waning resolve of the beleaguered men and draw their thoughts completely away from the fading image of

Allanon, his iron thought cut through to them with the sharpness of a knife, soundlessly calling to them. *Think only of me*. Their minds obeyed instinctively, wrenching free of the almost overpowering urge to gaze upward into the watching stone faces. The strange battle wore on without respite as the line of men, sweating and breathing harshly in the stillness, groped its way through the tangled maze of unseen images, bound together by the rope about their waists, the chain of tightly clenched hands, and the commanding voice of Allanon. No one lost his grip. The Druid led them steadily down the row of Sphinxes, his own eyes locked onto the cavern floor, his indomitable will fighting to hold the minds of his sightless charges. Then at last the faces of the stone creatures began to fade and fall away, leaving the mortals alone in the silence and darkness.

They kept moving, winding through a long series of twisting passages. Then once again the line stopped, and Allanon's low voice cut through the blackness, ordering them to remove the blindfolds. They did so hesitantly and found themselves in a narrow tunnel where the rough stone gave off a peculiar greenish light. Their drawn faces bathed in the strange glow, the men glanced quickly at one another to reassure themselves that they were all present. The dark figure of the Druid passed noiselessly down the line, testing the rope that bound their waists and warning them that the Corridor of the Winds still lay ahead. Stuffing bits of cloth in their ears and binding them with the loosened blindfolds to mask the sounds of the invisible beings Allanon had named Banshees, the men joined hands once more.

The line wound slowly through the faint green light of the narrow tunnel, their footsteps barely perceptible to their tightly covered ears. This section of the caverns ran for more than a mile, then faded abruptly as the passage widened and grew into a towering corridor that was totally black. The rock walls drew away and the ceiling rose until both had disappeared altogether, leaving the company alone in a strange limbo of darkness where only the smooth cavern floor offered any reassurance that the earth had not dissolved entirely. Allanon led them into the blackness, showing no signs of hesitancy.

Then abruptly, the sound began. Its incredible fury caught them completely unprepared, and for a moment there was panic. The initial shock grew to an enormous roar like the sound of a thousand winds combined in fury and biting force. But beneath this was the horrifying cry of souls screaming in anguish, voices scraping and twisting their tortured way through all the imaginable horrors of inhumanity in utter despair of any hope for salvation. The roar climbed to a shriek, reaching a pitch so far beyond the comprehension of the mortals' stunned minds that their sanity began to break apart. The terrible sounds washed over them, mirroring their own growing despair, driving relentlessly inward and stripping away the tattered nerve ends like layers of skin until the very bone was laid bare.

It had taken only an instant. In another instant, they would have been lost. But for the second time the hopelessly numbed humans were saved, this time from complete madness, as the powerful will of Allanon broke through the crazed sound to cloak them with protective reassurance. The screams and the roar seemed to lessen and fade into a strange buzzing as the grim, dark face projected itself into the seven feverish minds and the iron thoughts spoke soothingly, commandingly: *Let your minds relax—think only of me.* The men stumbled mechanically through the heavy darkness of the tunnel, their minds groping at the safety line of coherence and calm that the Druid held out to them. The walls of the corridor reverberated with the still-audible shrieks, and the massive stone of the cavern rumbled frighteningly. One final time the voices of the Banshees rose in feverish pitch, screeching violently in a desperate effort to break through the subconscious wall erected by the Druid's powerful mind, but the wall would not yield and the power of the voices spent itself and faded into a deathly whisper. A moment later, the passageway narrowed once more, and the company was clear of the Corridor of the Winds.

Visibly shaken, their faces streaked with sweat, the men stood dumbly as Allanon brought the line to a halt. Shaking their scattered thoughts into some semblance of order, they removed the rope about their waists and the cloth binding their ears. They were in a small cave, facing toward two huge stone doors laced by iron bindings. The rock walls around them emitted the same peculiar greenish light. Allanon waited patiently until everyone had fully recovered, then beckoned them forward. He paused before the stone portals. With only a slight shove from the lean hand, the massive doors swung silently open. The Druid's deep voice was only a whisper in the stillness.

"The Hall of Kings."

For over a thousand years, none but Allanon had entered the forbidden tomb. All that time it had remained otherwise undisturbed—a mammoth, circular cavern, the great walls smooth and polished, the ceiling shimmering in a green glow similar to that reflected by the tunnels they had already passed through. Along the circular wall of the giant rotunda, standing with the same proud defiance they presumably had exhibited in life, were stone statues of the dead rulers, each facing toward the center of the chamber and the strange altar that rose upward in the shape of a coiled serpent. Before each statue was piled the wealth of the dead, casks and trunks of precious metals and jewels, furs, weapons, all the favorite possessions of the deceased. In the walls immediately behind each statue were the sealed, rectangular openings in which rested the remains of the dead—kings, their families, their servants. Inscriptions above the sealed crypts gave the history of the rulers interred there, frequently in languages unfamiliar to any of the wondering members of the company. The entire chamber was bathed in the deep green light. The metal and stone seemed to absorb the color. Dust covered everything, a deep rock powder that had settled over the centuries and now rose in small clouds as the footsteps of the men disturbed its long rest. For over a thousand years, no one had violated the peace of this ancient chamber. No one had tampered with its secrets nor attempted to unlock the doors that guarded the dead and their possessions. No one but Allanon. And now . . .

Shea shivered violently, unexplainably. He shouldn't be here; he could feel a small, distant voice telling him he shouldn't be here. It wasn't that the Hall of Kings was sacred or forbidden. But it was a tomb—it was a tomb for the ancient dead. It was no place for the living. Something gripped him, and with a start he realized it was Allanon's hand touching his shoulder. The Druid frowned darkly at him, then called softly to the others. They huddled silently in the greenish light as he addressed them in hushed tones.

"Through those doors at the far end of the Hall is the Assembly." He directed their gaze to the other end of the rotunda where a second set of huge stone doors stood closed. "A wide set of stone stairs leads downward to a long pool fed by a spring somewhere deep beneath the mountain. At the foot of the stairs, directly before the pool, stands the Pyre of the Dead, where the monarchs buried here lay in state for a certain number of days, depending on their rank and wealth, presumably so that their souls could escape to the life beyond. We must pass through that chamber in order to reach the passageway that will take us to the Dragon's Crease on the other side of the mountains."

He paused and breathed deeply.

"When I traveled through these caverns before, I was able to hide myself from the eyes of the creatures put here to destroy intruders. I cannot do this for you. There is something in the Assembly, something whose power may prove to be greater than my own. Though it could not sense my presence, I was conscious of it hidden beneath the deep waters of the pool. Below the stairs, to either side of the pool, are narrow walkways leading to the other end of the chamber and the opening to the passages beyond. These walkways are the only way past the pool. Whatever it is that guards the Pyre of the Dead will strike at us there. When we get into the room, Balinor, Menion, and I will move onto the walkway to the left. That should draw the creature out from his hiding place. When we are attacked, Hendel will take the rest of you along the right walkway through the opening at the far end. Don't stop until you reach the Dragon's Crease. Do you understand?"

They nodded slowly. Shea felt strangely trapped, but there was nothing to be gained by talking about it now. Allanon straightened to his full seven-foot height and grinned menacingly, his strong teeth gleaming. The little Valeman felt a chill run through him that made him glad ten times over he was not the enemy of the mystic. In one effortless motion, Balinor drew forth his great sword, the metal blade ringing sharply as it cleared the sheath. Hendel was already moving across the Hall, the heavy mace held tightly in one hand. Menion started to follow, then hesitated, gazing doubtfully on the stores of treasure heaped about the tombs. Would it hurt to take a few? The Valemen and Elves were moving after Hendel and Balinor. Allanon stood watching the highlander, his long arms folded into the black cloak. Menion turned and looked questioningly at the mystic.

"I wouldn't if I were you," the other warned shortly. "It's all coated with a substance poisonous to the skin of living things. Touch it and you will be dead in less than a minute."

Menion stared at him incredulously for a moment, shot a quick glance back at the treasure, then shook his head resignedly. He was halfway across the chamber when, on sudden inspiration, he whipped out two long black arrows and walked over to an open chest of gold pieces. Carefully, he rubbed the metal tips in the precious metal, making certain that his hands did not touch anything but the feathered ends. Grinning with perverse satisfaction, he rejoined the others across the room. Whatever waited beyond the stone doors was going to be given the opportunity to test its resistance to this poison that would supposedly kill any living creature. In a tight cluster, the company gathered around Allanon, their metal weapons glinting coldly. A stillness settled over the great room, broken only by the expectant breathing of the eight men huddled about the closed doors. Shea glanced back for just a moment at the Hall of Kings. The tomb seemed undisturbed save for the ragged trail of footprints in the dust leading across the chamber. A deep haze of this dust hung swirling in the greenish light, stirred by the intruders' footsteps, but settling slowly back to the ancient cavern floor. In time, all evidence of their passing would be erased as the tracks were covered over entirely.

At Allanon's touch, the stone portals swung open and the company moved noiselessly into the Assembly. They were on a high platform that ran forward into a wide alcove and then descended in a series of broad stairs. The cavern beyond was enormous, a vast, towering cave that still exhibited the full, unaltered splendor of its rough, natural creation by nature's careful hands. From the high ceiling hung jagged stalactites, stone icicles formed by water and mineral deposits over thousands of years. Beneath these sculptured stone spears lay a long, rectangular pool of deep green water, the surface smooth and glasslike. When a single drop of water fell heavily from an overhanging stone projection, the placid surface rippled outward once and was still. The wary men moved forward to the edge of the platform and looked down on the high stone altar set at the foot of the stairs before the pool, its ancient surface scarred and pocked and in places almost crumbling. The cavern was dimly lit by streaks of phosphorescence that ran brokenly through its rocky walls, giving an eerie, fluorescent glow to the ancient chamber.

Slowly the men moved down the stairway, their eyes picking out a single word inscribed in the stone surface of the altar. A few knew its meaning. *Valg*—a word taken from the ancient Gnome tongue. It meant Death. Their footsteps reverberated in muffled echoes through the vast cavern. Nothing moved. Everything was shrouded in age and silence. On reaching the foot of the long stairway, they hesitated for a second, eyes fastened on the silent pool. Impatiently, Allanon motioned Hendel and his charges to the right; then with Menion and Balinor following, he moved quickly onto the left walkway. A misstep now would prove fatal. From across the pool, Shea watched the three figures edge their way silently along the rough stone wall, keeping well to the rear of the open walkway. There was no movement in the placid waters. They were about midway now, and Shea breathed for the first time.

Then the still surface of the dark pool surged upward and from out of the depths emerged a nightmare. Serpentine in appearance, the loathsome monster seemed to fill the cavern, its slime-covered bulk raising skyward, shattering the ancient stalactites. Its shriek of fury boomed through the Assembly. The massive body twisted and flexed as it reared out of the water. Long front legs tipped with deadly hooked claws clutched the empty air, and the great jaws clashed sharply, grinding together the blackened, pointed teeth that lined the edges. The wide, staring eyes burned red amid a cluster of bumps and stunted horns that covered the misshapen head. The entire bulk of the creature was covered with a reptilian skin that dripped with scum and waste that must have been carried from the nether world's blackest pits. The mouth oozed venom that fell into the water and rose with faint traces of steam. The monstrous thing glared at the three humans on the walkway and hissed with unbridled hatred. Jaws wide, screeching in anticipation of the kill, it attacked.

Everyone reacted instantly. Menion Leah's great ash bow sounded in staccato pings as the poisoned arrows flew with deadly accuracy, burying themselves deeply within the unprotected inner flesh of the serpent's gaping mouth. The creature reared back in pain, and Balinor quickly seized the initiative. Moving to the edge of the walkway, the giant borderman struck powerfully at the exposed forearm of the monster. But to his shock, the great sword only barely scratched the scaly hide, glancing off the heavy coating of slime. The second forearm made a quick swipe at the attacker, missing by inches as the intended victim dove to one side. On the opposite walkway, Hendel made a rush for the open passage at the far end of the pool, shoving the Valemen and the Elven brothers before him. But one of them triggered a hidden release, and a heavy stone slab collapsed in the opening, sealing off the escape route. In desperation, Hendel threw his powerful body against the stone barricade, but it refused to budge.

The serpent had been attracted by the sound of the falling stone. Turning away from its battle with Menion and Balinor, it moved eagerly toward these smaller foes. That would have been the finish if not for the quick reactions of the battle-hardened Dwarf.

Forgetting the stone slab and disregarding his own safety entirely, Hendel charged at the huge monster bearing down on him and drove the heavy iron mace directly into the closest burning eye. The weapon struck with such force that it smashed the glowing orb. The serpent reared upward in excruciating pain, crashing heavily into the jagged stalactites as it whipped its bulk from side to side. Deadly rock fragments showered the entire chamber. Flick went down with a sharp blow to the head. At the edge of the pool, Hendel was buried under a cascade of crumbling stone and lay motionless. The other three fell back against the blocked entryway as the massive attacker loomed above them.

At last Allanon joined the unequal battle. Raising both arms, he extended his lean hands, and his fingers seemed to light up like small glowing balls. Streaks of blinding, blue flame shot out of the tips and struck the head of the raging creature. The force of this new attack completely stunned the unprepared serpent, who thrashed wildly above the boiling water of the pool, shrieking in pain and fury. Moving quickly ahead on the walkway, the Druid struck a second time, the blue flames flashing against the head of the enraged beast, twisting it completely around. This second strike threw the great scaled body backward against the cavern wall where, thrashing in an uncontrollable frenzy, it jarred loose the stone slab that blocked the passageway out. Shea and the Elven brothers had barely managed to drag the unconscious Flick out of the way in time to avoid being crushed by the massive body. They heard the stone slab drop forward with an audible thud and, spying the open passage, yelled wildly to the other fighters. Balinor had reattacked the writhing monster as it again came within reach, striking vainly for the head as it swung down at him, still stunned by the force of Allanon's bolts. Allanon had his eyes fixed on the serpent, and only Menion saw what the others were yelling about and waved them madly toward the opening. Dayel and Shea picked up the fallen Flick and carried him into the tunnel beyond. Durin started to follow, but then hesitated as he caught sight of the unconscious Hendel, still buried beneath the shattered stone rubble. Turning back, he rushed to the pool's edge, grasped the Dwarf's limp arm and vainly attempted to pull him clear of the debris.

"Get out!" roared Allanon, who had suddenly spotted the Elf near the opening.

Choosing this moment of distraction, the serpent struck back. With one mighty sweep of its clawed arm it brushed Balinor aside, knocking him with crushing force against the chamber wall. Menion leaped in front of the monster, but its sudden rush bowled the Prince of Leah over, and he was knocked from sight. The serpent, still in great pain from its multiple wounds, could think only of reaching the tall figure in the black robes and crushing the life out of him. The beast had one more weapon in its arsenal, and it used it now. The venom-tipped jaws gaped wide at the sight of the intended victim, standing alone and unprotected, and great sheets of flame shot forth, completely encasing the Druid. Durin, who was in position to see everything happening on the walkway, gave an audible gasp of dismay. Shea and Dayel, standing just beyond the entrance to the tunnel leading from the Assembly, watched in mute horror as the flames covered the tall mystic. But a second later the fire died, and Allanon stood untouched before the astonished onlookers. His hands raised and the blue streaks of flame shot out of his extended fingers, striking the head of the serpent with terrific force, sending the scaled body reeling back once again. Steam rose in great clouds from the thrashing waters of the pool, mingling in a heavy mist with the dust and smoke stirred by the battle until everything was obscured from view.

Then, from out of the haze, Balinor appeared at

Durin's side, his cloak torn and shredded, the shining
chain mail chipped and battered, the familiar face
streaked with sweat and blood. Together they pulled
Hendel from beneath the rocks. With one great arm,
the Prince of Callahorn lifted the silent form over his
shoulder and motioned Durin ahead of him into the
passage where Dayel and Shea still lingered with the
unconscious Flick. The giant borderman ordered them
to pick up the fallen Valeman, and without waiting to
see if they obeyed, disappeared down the darkened
corridor, Hendel over one shoulder, the great broad
sword held tightly in his free hand. The Elven brothers
quickly did as they were told, but Shea hesitated,
searching worriedly for some sign of Menion. The
Assembly was a shambles, the long rows of stalactites
smashed, the walkways a mass of rubble, the walls
cracked and shattered, and everything obscured by
dust and steam from the boiling pool. To one side of
the cavern, the massive form of the serpent was still
visible, thrashing in agony against the broken wall, its
great bulk a writhing mass of scales and blood. Neither
Menion nor Allanon was in view. But a moment later
both appeared from out of the thick haze, Menion
limping slightly, but still clutching the ash bow and
the sword of Leah, Allanon's dark form tattered and
layered with dust and ash. Without speaking, the
Druid waved the Valeman ahead of them, and
together the three stumbled through the partially
blocked opening.

What happened after was vague in everyone's
mind. Numbly, the battered group hurried along the
tunnel, carrying the two wounded and unconscious
men. Time dragged agonizingly away, then abruptly
they were outside, blinking in the bright light of the
afternoon sun, standing at the edge of a dangerously
steep cliff face. To their right, the Dragon's Crease
wound its way downward to the open hill country
below. Suddenly the whole mountain began to

rumble menacingly, shaking in short tremors beneath their feet. With a sharp command, Allanon ordered them down the narrow trail. Balinor led the way, carrying the still form of Hendel, Menion Leah a couple of steps behind. Durin and Dayel followed, carrying Flick. Behind them came Shea and finally Allanon. The sinister rumbling continued somewhere deep within the mountain. Slowly the little group moved along the narrow pathway. The trail wound unevenly amid jagged overhangs and sudden drops, and the men were forced to flatten themselves against the cliff face at regular intervals to avoid losing their balance and falling to the rocks hundreds of feet below. The Dragon's Crease was well named. The continual twists and turns in the path required concentrated skill and caution to navigate successfully, and the recurring tremors made the task doubly hazardous.

They had progressed only a short distance along the treacherous pathway when a new sound became audible, a deep roar that quickly drowned out the rumblings in the mountain. Shea, last in line with Allanon, was unable to define the source of the roar until he was almost on top of its origin. Rounding a sharp cut in the side of the mountain, which brought him onto a ledge facing northward, he discovered an enormous waterfall directly across from their position on the mountainside. Tons of cascading water crashed with a deafening roar into a great river hundreds of feet below that swept between the mountain ranges and poured into a series of rapids than ran eastward to the Rabb Plains. The mighty river swept directly below the ledge on which he stood and the narrow trail ahead, its white waters churning and slapping against the confining sides of the two peaks that hemmed it in. Shea looked at it for a moment, and then hastened on down the trail at Allanon's command. The rest of the company had gone a good distance ahead of them and for a moment were lost from view in the rocks.

Shea had gone about a hundred feet past the ledge when a sudden tremor, more violent than the others, shook the mountain to its core. Without warning the section of the trail on which he was standing broke away and slid steadily down the mountainside, carrying the hapless Valeman with it. He gave a cry of dismay, fighting to break his fall as he saw himself sliding toward a steep overhang which dropped off sharply into a long, long fall to the raging river on the valley floor. Allanon rushed forward as the Valeman slid wildly in a cloud of dust and rock toward the waiting overhang.

"Grab something!" roared the Druid. "Catch yourself!"

Shea clutched vainly, clawing at the sheer face of the cliff, and just at the edge of the drop-off caught himself on a projecting rock. He lay flat against the nearly vertical surface, not daring to try to climb back up, his arms nearly breaking from the exertion.

"Hold on, Shea!" Allanon encouraged him. "I'll get a rope. Don't move an inch!"

Allanon called down the trail for the others, but whether they could have helped, Shea never discovered. As the Druid shouted for assistance, a second tremor shook the mountain and jarred loose the unfortunate Valeman from his precarious perch, sending him sliding out beyond the overhang before he could even think to catch himself. Arms and legs flying madly, he fell headlong into the swiftly flowing waters of the river below. Allanon watched helplessly as the Valeman struck with crushing force, bobbed to the surface, and was swept away eastward toward the plains beyond, tossing and turning in the boiling river like a small cork until he was lost from sight.

XV

Flick Ohmsford stood quietly at the foot of the Dragon's Teeth and stared into space. The fading rays of the late afternoon sun crossed his stocky frame in faint glimmers, casting his shadow onto the cooling rocks of the giant mountain at his back. He listened for a moment to the sounds about him, the muffled voices of somebody from the company off to his left, the chirping cries of the birds in the forest ahead. In his own mind he heard Shea's determined voice for an instant, and he recalled his brother's great courage in the face of the countless dangers they had encountered together. Now Shea was gone, probably dead, washed out by that unknown river to the plains on the other side of the mountains they had battled so hard to cross through. He rubbed his head gently, feeling the bump and the dull pain from the blow of the rock fragment that had knocked him senseless, preventing him from being able to help when his brother had needed him the most. They had been ready to face death at the hands of the Skull Bearers, ready to perish by the swords of the roving Gnomes, and even ready to succumb to the terrors of the Hall of Kings. But for it all to be ended by a fluke of nature on a narrow cliff ledge, when they were so close to escaping, was too much for anyone to accept. Flick felt such biting hurt inside that he wanted to cry out his bitterness. But even now, he could not.

His insides knotted at the anger he could not manage, and he felt instead only a great sense of waste.

Menion Leah seemed in marked contrast as he paced in furious desperation several yards away from the Valeman, his lean figure bent in what could only be described as a wounded crouch. His own thoughts burned deep with anger, the kind of futile rage that a caged beast displays when there is no hope of escape, and only its pride and its hatred of what has happened to it remain. There was nothing he could have done to help Shea, he knew. But that did little to ease the sense of guilt he felt at not having been there when the cliff ledge gave way and the Valeman was thrown to the churning waters of the rapids below. Something might have been done to prevent it had he not left Shea alone with the Druid. Yet he knew it was not Allanon's fault; he had done everything possible to protect Shea. Menion moved with long, angry strides, digging into the ground with the sharp heels of his boots. He refused to admit that the quest was ended, that they would be forced to admit defeat when the Sword of Shannara was so nearly within their grasp. He paused and considered for a moment the object of their search. It still didn't make any sense to the highlander. Even if they got the Sword, what could a man, not yet more than a grown boy, hope to do against the power of a creature like the Warlock Lord? Now they would never know, for Shea was probably dead; even if he wasn't dead, he was lost to them. Nothing seemed to make much sense anymore, and Menion Leah realized suddenly how very much that casual, relaxed friendship between them had meant. They had never spoken of it, never really openly acknowledged it, but it had been there all the same, and it had been dear to him. Now it was ended. Menion bit down on his lip in helpless anger and continued to pace.

The others in the company were gathered near the foot of the Dragon's Crease, which ended just yards behind them. Durin and Dayel spoke to each other in hushed tones, their fine Elven features wrinkled with concern, their eyes lowered, looking at each other only occasionally. Close at hand, his solid frame propped against a massive boulder, rested Hendel, who, while always closemouthed, was now moody and unapproachable. His shoulder and leg were bandaged, his stolid face scarred and bruised from the battle with the serpent. He thought briefly of his homeland, his waiting family, and for an instant wished he could see the green of Culhaven once more before the end. He knew that without the Sword of Shannara, and without Shea to wield it, his land would be overrun by the Northland armies. Hendel was not alone in his thoughts. Balinor was thinking much the same thing, his eyes on the solitary giant standing motionless in a small grove of trees some distance away from the others. He knew that they now faced an impossible decision. Either they must give up the quest and turn back in an effort to reach their homelands and perhaps locate Shea, or they must continue on to Paranor and seize the Sword of Shannara without the courageous Valeman. It was a difficult choice to make, and no one would be very pleased either way. He shook his head sadly as the memory of the bitter quarrel between his brother and himself passed momentarily through his mind. He had his own decision to make when he returned to the city of Tyrsis—and it would not be pleasant. He had not spoken to the others about it, and at the moment, his personal problems were of secondary importance.

Suddenly the Druid wheeled about and started back to them, his own mind evidently decided. They watched him approach, the black robe flowing gently as he came, the fierce dark face resolute even in this moment of bitter defeat. Menion had frozen in his tracks, his heart beating madly as he awaited the confrontation he knew must come between them, for the highlander had chosen his own course of action, and he suspected it would not be that of Allanon. Flick caught the hint of fear in the face of the Prince of Leah, but saw there, too, a strange courage as the man braced himself. All of them rose hesitantly and came together as the dark form drew closer, their tired, discouraged minds suddenly regenerated with a fierce determination not to admit defeat. They could not know what Allanon would command, but they knew they had come too far and sacrificed too much to give up now.

He stood before them, the deep eyes burning with mixed feelings, the shadowed face a granite wall of strength, worn and scarred. When he spoke, the words were frosted and sharp in the silence.

"It may be that we are beaten, but to turn back would be to dishonor ourselves in our own eyes as much as in the eyes of those who depend on us. If we are to be defeated by the evil in the Northland, by things born of the spirit world, then we must turn and face it. We cannot back away and hope for some elusive miracle to stand between us and what most surely moves even now to enslave and destroy us. If death comes, it should find us with weapons drawn and the Sword of Shannara in our hands!"

He bit off the last sentence with such icy determination that even Balinor felt a slight shiver of excitement course through him. All stood in mute admiration of the Druid's unflagging strength, and they felt a sudden pride in being with him, being a part of the little group he had chosen for this dangerous and costly quest.

"What about Shea?" Menion spoke out suddenly, perhaps a bit sharply, as the Druid's penetrating eyes turned on him. "What has become of Shea, who was the reason for this expedition in the first place?"

Allanon shook his head slowly, considering once again the Valeman's fate.

"I cannot guess any better than you. He was washed out to the plains by that mountain river. Perhaps he lives, perhaps not, but we can do nothing for him now."

"What you are proposing is that we forget him and go after the Sword—a useless piece of metal without the rightful bearer!" Menion shouted in anger, his pent-up frustration coming to the fore at last. "Well, I go no farther until I know what has happened to Shea, even if it means giving up the quest and searching until I find him. I will not desert my friend!"

"Watch yourself, highlander," warned the slow, mocking voice of the mystic. "Do not be foolish. To blame me for the loss of Shea is pointless, for I most of all would wish him no harm. What you suggest lacks any resemblance to reason."

"Enough wise words, Druid!" stormed Menion, stepping forward in absolute disregard for what might happen next, his hot temper driven to the brink by the tall wanderer's impassive acceptance of the loss of the Valeman. "We have followed you for weeks, through a hundred lands and perils without once questioning what you ordered. But this is too much for me. I am a Prince of Leah, not some beggar who does what he is told without question, caring for no one but himself! My friendship with Shea was nothing to you, but it was more to me than a hundred Swords of Shannara. Now stand aside! I will go my own way!"

"Fool, you are less a prince and more a clown to speak like this!" Allanon raged, his face tightening into a mask of anger, the great hands balling into fists and clenching before him. The others paled as the two opponents lashed verbally at each other in unbridled fury. Then sensing the physical combat that was about to ensue, they stepped between them, talking quickly, trying to calm them with reason, fearful that a split in the company now would mark the end of any chance for success. Flick alone had made no move, his own thoughts still on his brother, disgusted by the helplessness he felt at being powerless to do anything but feel inadequate. The minute Menion had spoken, he knew that the highlander had expressed his own feelings, and he would not leave here without knowing what had befallen Shea. But it always seemed that Allanon knew so much more than the rest of them, that his decisions were always the right ones. To disregard the Druid's words completely now seemed somehow wrong. He struggled within his own mind for a moment, trying to think what Shea would do in this situation, what he might suggest to the others. Then almost without realizing it, he knew the answer.

"Allanon, there is a way," he declared abruptly, shouting to be heard above the noise. They all looked over at him at once, surprised by the determined look on the stocky Valeman's face. Allanon nodded to indicate he was listening.

"You have the power to speak to the dead. We saw you do it back in the valley. Can you not tell if Shea lives? Your power is great enough to seek out the living if you can raise the dead. You can tell where he is, can't you?"

Everyone looked back at the Druid, waiting to see what he would do. Allanon sighed heavily and looked downward, his anger for Menion forgotten as he pondered the Valeman's question.

"I could do this," he responded to everyone's amazement and general relief, "but I will not. If I use my power to find out where Shea is, whether he is dead or alive, I will most certainly reveal our presence to the Warlock Lord and to the Skull Bearers. They would be alerted and waiting for us at Paranor."

"If we go to Paranor," Menion cut in darkly, whereupon Allanon wheeled on him in fury, his lagging anger revived. Again everyone leaped to separate them.

"Stop it, stop it!" Flick ordered angrily. "This is helping no one, least of all Shea. Allanon, I have asked for nothing during this entire trip. I had no right to ask; I came by my own choice. But I have the right now because Shea is my brother, perhaps not by blood or race, but by stronger bonds still. If you will not use your power to find out where he is and what has happened to him, then I will go with Menion and search until Shea is found."

"He is right, Allanon." Balinor nodded slowly, one great hand coming to rest lightly on the little Valeman's shoulder. "Whatever befalls us, these two have a right to know whether there is any chance for Shea. I know what it means if we are discovered, but I say we must take that chance."

Durin and Dayel nodded vigorously in agreement. The Druid mystic looked aside to Hendel for his opinion, but the taciturn Dwarf made no movement, staring into the other's black eyes. Allanon looked at them one by one, perhaps assessing their true feelings as he thought of the risk involved, weighing the worth of the Sword against the loss of two of the company. He stared absently at the fading sun as the twilight of early evening settled into the mountains with slow ripples of darkness blending into the red and purple of the passing day. It had been a long, hard trip, and they had nothing to show for it—only the loss of the man for whom the whole journey had been made. It seemed so wrong, and he could appreciate their reluctance to continue now. He nodded to himself in understanding, then looked back at the others and saw their eyes turn suddenly bright, believing him to be nodding his agreement to Flick's demand. Without even a small smile of acquiescence, the tall wanderer shook his head firmly.

"The choice is yours. I will do as you ask. Stand back and do not speak to me or approach me until I tell you."

The members of the company backed away while he remained quietly in place, head bent in concentration, the long arms clasped before him with the great hands buried in the long cloak. Only the distant sounds of evening were audible in the deepening gloom. Then the Druid stiffened and a white glow spread out from his tensed body, a blinding aura of light that caused the others to squint, then shield their eyes protectively. One moment the glow was everywhere and the dark form of Allanon was lost from sight, and in the next it flashed brilliantly and was gone. Allanon stood as he had before, motionless against the darkness, then slowly slumped to the ground, one lean hand pressed tightly to his forehead. The others hesitated for only a moment, then disregarded his earlier command and rushed forward, afraid that he had been injured. Allanon looked up in disapproval, angered that they had disobeyed him. Then he saw in the bent faces their deep concern. He stared in disbelief and with sudden understanding as they gathered about in silence. He was deeply touched, a strange warmth spreading through him as he realized the loyalty these six men of different races, different lands, different lives felt for him, even after all that had happened. For the first time since the loss of Shea, Allanon felt a sense of relief. He climbed shakily to his feet, leaning slightly on the strong arm of Balinor, still weak from the strain of seeking Shea. He stood quietly for a moment and then smiled faintly.

"Our young friend is indeed alive, though it's a miracle I cannot explain. I located his life-force on the other side of these mountains, probably somewhere near the river that carried him out to the east plains. There were others with him, but I could not determine what their purpose was without an extensive mind probe. That would surely give our position away and weaken me to the point of uselessness."

"But he is alive, you're certain?" Flick demanded eagerly.

Allanon nodded his assurance. The entire group broke into broad smiles of relief. Menion slapped the elated Flick on his broad back and did a small dance step and leap.

"Then the problem has resolved itself," the Prince of Leah exulted. "We have to go back over the Dragon's Teeth and find him, then continue the trip to Paranor to get the Sword."

His smiling face fell abruptly and the slow burn of anger replaced it as Allanon shook his head negatively. The others stared in astonishment, certain that this was what the Druid himself would have suggested.

"Shea is in the hands of a Gnome patrol," the mystic stated pointedly. "He is being taken northward, more than likely to Paranor. We could not reach him without fighting our way back through the guarded passes of the Dragon's Teeth and trailing him over those Gnome-infested plains. We would be diverted for days, perhaps longer, and our presence would be detected in no time."

"There's no guarantee they don't already know about us," Menion shouted irately. "You said that yourself. What good will we be to Shea if he falls into the hands of the Warlock Lord? What good will the Sword do us without the bearer?"

"We cannot desert him," pleaded Flick, stepping forward once more.

The others said nothing, but stood mutely, waiting to hear Allanon's explanation. Darkness had completely enfolded the high mountain country, and the men could barely make out one another's faces in the dim light; the moon was hidden from view by the monstrous peaks that rose behind them.

"You have forgotten the prophecy," admonished Allanon patiently. "The last part promised that one of us would not see the other side of the Dragon's Teeth, but that he would be first to place hands on the Sword of Shannara. That one we now know to be Shea. Furthermore, the prophecy said that we who reached the other side of the mountains would view the Sword before the passing of two nights. It would seem that fate will bring us all together."

"That may be good enough for you, but not for me," stated Menion flatly, with Flick nodding in vigorous agreement. "How can we place our trust in some crazy promise made by a ghost? You're asking us to risk Shea's life!"

Allanon seemed to smolder in fury for a moment, fighting to control his quick temper, then calmly he looked at the two and shook his head in disappointment.

"Have you not believed in a legend from the very start?" he asked quietly. "Have you not yourself seen the foothold that the spirit world has secured in your world of flesh and blood, earth and stone? Have we not from the beginning been fighting against beings born of this other existence, beings who possess powers that surely do not belong to mortal men? You have witnessed the potency of the Elfstones. Why would you now turn your back on all that, in favor of what your common sense tells you—a reasoning process that relies on fact and stimuli accumulated in this world, your material world, unable to transpose itself to an existence where even your most basic understandings have no meaning."

They stared at him wordlessly, realizing that he was right, but unwilling to abandon their plan to find Shea. The whole journey had been premised on half dreams and old legends, not on common sense, and suddenly to decide it was time to be practical once again was indeed a ludicrous idea. Flick had given up being practical the day he had first run in fear from Shady Vale.

"I would not be concerned, my young friends," Allanon soothed, suddenly next to them, a lean hand on each shoulder, strangely comforting even now. "Shea still carries the Elfstones, and their power will give him great protection. They may also guide him toward the Sword, since they are attuned to it. With luck, we will find him when we find the Sword at Paranor. All roads now lead to the Druid's Keep, and we must be certain we are there to give what aid we can to Shea."

The other members of the company had gathered up their weapons and small packs and stood ready, their silhouettes shadowlike in the dim starlight, finely etched pencil lines against the blackness of the mountains. Flick gazed northward to the dark forest that blanketed the low country beyond the Dragon's Teeth. In its midst, rising upward like an obelisk, were the cliffs of Paranor, and there at the apex, the Druid's Keep and the Sword of Shannara. The end of the quest. Flick looked quietly for a few moments at the solitary pinnacle, then turned to Menion. The highlander nodded reluctantly.

"We'll go with you." Flick's voice was a hushed whisper in the stillness.

The swirling waters of the rushing river dashed madly against the confining walls of their mountain channel, beating and raging their way eastward, dragging with them stray debris and driftwood that had fallen into their restless grasp. They rushed down out of the mountains in heavy rapids that churned fiercely around smooth-surfaced rocks and sudden bends, winding slowly toward the calm of the quiet rivers that branched into the hilly lowlands above the Rabb Plains. It was in one of these small, quiet tributaries that the man, still bound to the splintered log by his leather belt, finally washed up on a mud riverbank, unconscious and nearly drowned. The clothes he wore were ripped and shredded, the leather boots lost, the damp face ashen and bloodied from the beating sustained when he had been swept through the series of rapids down the river that had carried him

to this place. He awakened, realizing that he had at
last reached land. Feebly untying himself from the
beached log, he dragged himself on hands and knees
farther onto the shore and into the deep grass of a low
hill. As if by reflex, his battered hands felt for the small
leather pouch at his waist, and to his relief it was still
there, securely bound by the leather thongs. A
moment later, the last of his remaining strength
exhausted, he fell into a deep, welcome sleep.

He slept soundly in the warmth and quiet of the day
until late afternoon, when the cooling grass whipping
against his face in a building breeze caused him to stir
slightly. There was something else as well, something
in his now-rested mind that warned him suddenly
that he was in danger. But he could barely rouse his
sluggish body to a half-sitting position as a group of
ten or twelve figures appeared at the crest of the hill
above him, paused in astonishment as they saw his
raised figure, then hastened down the hill to reach
him. Instead of carefully turning his battered body to
check for injuries, they flung him flat once again,
gripping his helpless arms behind his back and tying
them securely with leather thongs that bit into the
unprotected skin. His feet were bound as well, and at
last he was turned faceup where he could finally focus
on his captors. His worst fears were immediately
confirmed. The gnarled yellow frames, clothed in
forest garb and armed with short swords, were easily
recognizable after Menion's description of the incident
that had taken place only days before in the Pass of
Jade. He looked fearfully into the sharp Gnome eyes
as they gazed with some amazement at his half-man,
half-Elf features and at the remnants of his unusual
Southland garb. Finally, the leader reached down and
began to search him thoroughly. Shea struggled, but
was slapped hard several times and at last lay motionless as the Gnome removed the small leather pouch
containing the precious Elfstones.

The Gnomes gathered around curiously as the three blue stones, shining brightly in the warm sunlight, were emptied into the hand of the leader. There was a brief discussion, none of which the captive was able to follow, concerning what he was doing with the stones and where he could have found them. At last it was decided that both the captive and the stones should be taken to the main encampment at Paranor where higher authorities could be consulted. The Gnomes dragged their captive to his feet, cutting the thongs that bound his legs, and proceeded to march him northward, pushing him from time to time when he slowed from exhaustion. They were still moving northward at sunset when, on the other side of the mountain barrier known as the Dragon's Teeth, the Druid leader of a small band of determined seekers struggled within his own mind to pinpoint the missing Shea Ohmsford.

It was in the early-morning hours, wrapped with the blanket silence of darkness and hidden by the shadows of the heavy forests that so completely shut out the reassuring light of the moon and stars, that the company stood at last before the cliffs of Paranor. It was a moment that would last forever in their minds, as expectant eyes traveled upward over the steep rock walls, unbroken by trail or ledge, upward past the dwarfed height of the tall pines and oaks, which ended abruptly as the cliffs began, upward still farther to the man-made structure at its apex—the Druid's Keep. The Keep was castlelike, age-old walls of blocked stone rising to peaked turrets and spiraled towers that cut the sky in proud defiance. It was unmistakably a fortress built to withstand assault by the strongest army, the ancient home and protectorate of the all but extinguished race of men called Druids. Within the heart of this stronghold of stone and iron had long rested the memorial of Man's triumph over the forces of the spirit world, the symbol of the courage and hope of the races in times long past, forgotten over the years as generations passed away and old legends died—the wondrous Sword of Shannara.

As the seven men stood there surveying the Druid's Keep, Flick's mind traveled back over the events that had taken place since the company had departed the Dragon's Teeth at sunset. They had traveled quickly over the open grasslands separating them from the forest surrounding Paranor, reaching the seclusion of its dark perimeter without incident in only a few short hours. At that time, Allanon briefed them on what to expect next. The forest, he said, was impenetrable unless one knew how to avoid the dangerous obstacles that the Warlock Lord had created to discourage any attempt to reach the Druid's Keep. Wolves prowled the entire woodland, huge, gray beasts that could catch anything on two or four feet and tear it to pieces within seconds. Beyond the wolves, surrounding the base of the cliffs beneath the Keep, was an impregnable barrier of thorns, coated with a poison for which there was no known cure. But the resourceful Druid was prepared. They moved quickly into the black forest, not bothering to choose any approach but the direct one, their path taking them straight for the fortress. Allanon warned them to stay close to him, but the warning was quite unnecessary. Only Menion seemed eager to forge ahead of the group, and the highlander rejoined them instantly at the first sound of the marauding wolves. The great, gray beasts attacked within minutes after the men entered the forest, their eyes bloodred in the darkness, their huge jaws snapping in blind hatred. But before they could reach the alarmed group, Allanon placed a strange whistle to his lips and blew softly. A sound so high pitched as to be indistinguishable to the men was emitted and the snarling wolves scattered

brokenly, wheeling about and scurrying off with loud cries of dismay, their frightened whimpers still audible long after they were lost from sight.

The wolves appeared twice more during the remainder of the trek through the forest, although it was impossible to tell if it was the same pack or a different one. Flick was inclined to believe they were different packs after observing the effect of the strange whistle. Each time the wolves cringed in terror, leaving the travelers untouched. The company reached the thorn barrier without difficulty. But the bristling mass of poisonous spikes that confronted them seemed truly impenetrable, even by the redoubtable Allanon. Once again he reminded them that this was the homeland of the Druids, not the Warlock Lord. Leading them to the right, he skirted the edge of the barrier until he reached a point that seemed to satisfy him. Quickly pacing off a distance from a nearby oak that looked for all the world to Flick like any other oak, the Druid marked a spot on the ground before the thorny obstruction, nodding to the others that this was to be the spot of entry. Then to their amazement, the grim mystic simply walked up to the razor-sharp spikes and disappeared into the vegetation, only to reappear a moment later unharmed. In hushed tones he explained to them that at this point the barrier was fake and quite harmless, a secret passage to the fortress. There were others as well, all indistinguishable to any human eye unaware of what to look for. And so the company passed through the barrier, discovering that the spikes were indeed harmless, and stood at last before the walls of Paranor.

It seemed impossible somehow to Flick that they should be here at all. The journey had been an endless one while they were making it, the dangers encountered by them never conquered, only evaded and ultimately substituted, one for another. Yet here they were. All that remained was to scale the cliffs and seize the Sword, no simple task, but nevertheless no more difficult than the others they had faced and successfully completed. He gazed upward to the castle battlements, studying briefly the spaced torches that lit the ramparts, knowing that the enemy guarded those walls and the Sword within. He wondered who the enemy was, what it was. Not the Gnomes or the Trolls, but the real enemy—the creature that belonged in another world, but that had invaded this one in some inexplicable way to enslave the humans who inhabited it. He wondered vaguely if he would ever know the reason behind all that had happened to them, the reason why they stood here now, hunters for the legendary Sword of Shannara, of which none of them save the Druid mystic knew anything. He sensed that there was a lesson somewhere to be learned, but at the moment it eluded him. He only wanted to get the matter over with and get out of there alive.

His thoughts ended abruptly as Allanon motioned them forward along the steep walls of the cliff. Again, the Druid seemed to be searching for something. A few minutes later he halted before a smooth portion of the cliff face, touched something in the rock, and a concealed door swung open to reveal a hidden passageway. Allanon stepped inside for a moment and returned with unlit torches, giving one to each of the company and indicating that they were to follow him. They moved silently inside, halting momentarily in the small entryway as the stone door closed noiselessly behind them. Squinting in the near blackness, they saw a vague outline of stone steps leading upward into the rock, barely visible in the dim light of a lone torch flickering just ahead in the passage. They climbed carefully to that torch and each man lit his own to provide the necessary light for the ascent to the castle. Putting a single finger to his lips to indicate that he expected absolute silence, the dark figure of their leader turned and began to climb the damp stone steps, his black cloak billowing slightly as he walked, filling the entire passageway ahead with its shadow. The others followed without a word. The assault of the Druid's Keep had begun.

The staircase rose in a continual spiral, winding and twisting until at last no one knew how far they had come. The air in the passage became gradually warmer and more comfortable to breathe, and the dampness of the walls and steps diminished until it was entirely gone. Their heavy leather hunting boots scraped faintly against the stone, echoing through the deep silence of the caverns. Hundreds of steps and many minutes later, the company reached the end of the tunnel. A massive wooden door, bound with iron and fastened into the rock, blocked their passage. Allanon again proved that he knew the way well. A single touch on the binding and the door swung silently open to admit the men into a large chamber with numerous passages leading out of it, all of them well lit by burning torches. A quick look around revealed no one in sight, so Allanon brought the company around him once again.

"We are directly below the castle proper," he explained in a barely audible whisper as the others crowded close. "If we can reach the room where the Sword of Shannara rests without being seen, then we may be able to escape without a fight."

"Something's wrong," Balinor cautioned shortly. "Where are the guards?"

Allanon shook his head to indicate he couldn't answer, but the others saw the concern in his eyes. Something was amiss.

"The passage we will take runs to the main heating ducts and a back stairway that leads to the central hall. Say nothing more until we are there, but keep your eyes open!"

Without waiting for any response, he turned and

moved quickly toward one of the open tunnels, and the others followed hastily. The passage led upward, twisting tightly around after a short distance until it seemed they must be cutting back on themselves. Balinor had discarded his torch and drawn his broadsword after only a few steps, then the rest of the company was quick to follow his lead. The flickering light from the torches, fastened in iron racks to the bedrock of the cavern, cast their crouched shadows against the stone walls, their reflected images moving like furtive creatures seeking to escape the light. They crept warily through those ancient tunnels—the Druid, the two Princes, the Valeman, the Elven brothers and the Dwarf—all watching expectantly, caught up in the guarded excitement that comes with the end of a long hunt. Apart from one another, spread out along the walls of the passage, weapons held ready, eyes and ears straining for any hint of danger, they moved steadily forward, farther upward, deeper into the core of the Druid's Keep. Then the silence slowly faded, and there was a muffled sound like heavy breathing and the heat became more intense. Ahead, the passageway ended and a stone door with an iron handle came into view, its edges outlined sharply by a piercing light from the chamber just beyond. The mysterious sound increased in volume and became identifiable. It was the throbbing hum of machinery lodged in the rock beneath them, pumping with steady rhythm. Apprehensively, the members of the company approached the closed door on Allanon's silent command.

As the giant Druid opened the heavy stone barrier, the unsuspecting men were struck by a blast of hot air that surged violently through their lungs to lodge in the pits of their stomachs. Gasping for air, they momentarily hesitated, then moved reluctantly into the room. The door swung shut behind them. They knew where they were in an instant. The room was

actually little more than a circular catwalk above a
huge pit that dropped off into the rock for well over a
hundred feet. At the bottom burned a fierce blaze, fed
by some unknown source, its red-orange flames
leaping into the air toward the top of the deep well.
The pit cut away the greater portion of the chamber,
leaving only the small walkway several feet wide with
a short iron guard rail that rimmed its inner edge.
From the ceiling and walls ran various heating ducts
which carried the hot air to other parts of the structure.
A concealed pumping system controlled the amount
of heat generated by the open furnace. Because it was
night, the pumping system had been shut down, and
the temperature level along the catwalk was still
tolerable, despite the intense heat of the pit fire below.
When the bellows were in full operation, any human
passing through the chamber would be fried in a
matter of seconds.

Menion, Flick and the Elven brothers paused by the
railing to get a closer look at the system. Hendel hung
back, uncomfortable in this confining rock structure,
comparing it unfavorably to the open woodlands with
which he was familiar. Allanon moved to Balinor's
side and conversed with him for a few moments,
glancing uneasily at the several closed doors leading
into the chamber and pointing to the open spiral
staircase that led to the upper halls of the castle.
Finally, the two seemed to settle on something,
nodding in agreement, and signaled the others to
catch up. Hendel was only too glad to comply. Menion
and the Elven brothers moved away from the railing to
join him. Only Flick lingered a second, strangely
attracted by the fascinating blaze below. This slight
delay produced an unexpected result. As he lifted his
eyes with a parting glance to the other side of the
chamber, he saw the dark figure of a Skull Bearer
appear out of nowhere.

Flick froze instantly. The creature remained in a

half-crouch directly across the pit from him, its body a black mass even in the light of the pit fires, the caped wings billowing out slightly behind it. Its legs were crooked, the feet ending in cruel-looking claws that seemed capable of rending the stone itself. Hunched low between the massive shoulders, the head and face bore a vague resemblance to scarred coal. The wicked eyes fastened on the speechless Valeman, their depths drawing him closer to the reddish glow that burned within, an open invitation to death. With slow, dragging steps, it began to make its way around the chamber, its breath rasping with every labored step as it drew closer and closer to the spellbound Flick. He wanted to cry out, run away, do anything but stay where he was, yet the strange eyes held him motionless. He knew he was finished.

But the others had noticed his immobile form; following his frightened gaze across the chamber, they had discovered the black Skull Bearer creeping noiselessly around the rim of the pit. In a flash, Allanon leaped in front of Flick, yanking him around to break the spell of the creature's terrible eyes. Dazed, Flick stumbled backward into the waiting arms of Menion, who had rushed to his assistance. The others stood just behind the Druid, their weapons held ready. The creature stopped several yards from Allanon, still in a half-crouch, hiding the hideous face from the fire's glow with one raised wing and clawed hand. Its breath sounded in slow, steady rasps as its cruel eyes rested on the tall figure that stood between it and the little Valeman.

"Druid, you are a fool to oppose me." The voice hissed from somewhere deep within the creature's formless face. "You are all doomed. You were doomed from the moment you chose to come after the Sword. The Master knew you would come, Druid! He *knew*."

"Get away while you can, hateful one!" Allanon commanded in the most menacing tone any of the

members of the company had ever heard him use.
"You frighten no one here. We will take the Sword,
and you will not stand in our way. Step aside, lackey,
and let your Master show himself!"

The words burned into the air, cutting through to
the Skull Bearer like knives. The creature hissed its
fury, the rasping breath coming in quick gasps as it
took another step, crouching lower, its eyes frightful
to look into as they blazed with new hatred.

"I will destroy you, Allanon. Then no one will be left
to oppose the Master! You have been our pawn from
the start, though you could not have guessed. Now we
have you within our reach, along with your most
valuable allies. And look what you have brought us,
Druid—the last heir of Shannara!"

To the shock of everyone, the clawlike hand pointed
to an astonished Flick. The creature did not seem to
realize that Flick was not the heir or that Shea had been
lost to them on the Dragon's Teeth. For a moment no
one spoke. The fire roared in the pit below, billowing
up suddenly with a gust of boiling air that singed the
unprotected faces of the mortals. The claws of the
black spirit creature seemed to reach toward them.

"Now, fools," the hate-filled voice rasped at them,
"you shall receive the kind of death your species
deserves!"

XVI

As the final words of the black creature hissed away in the flame-lit air, everything seemed to happen at once. With a dramatic sweep of one lean arm and a command so sharp it jarred them all into instant action, the giant Druid sent the tensed members of his little company charging toward the open staircase that led to the main hall of the Druid's Keep. As the six men broke in a mad dash for the winding stairway behind them, the Skull Bearer lunged for Allanon. The thudding impact of their collision could be heard even by the fleeing men, who were already starting up the staircase—save for one. Flick hesitated, torn by the desire to escape, but held spellbound by the titanic struggle between the two powerful beings locked in combat only inches from the rising flames of the great open furnace. He stood at the bottom of the staircase, hearing the disappearing footfalls of his companions as they raced for the upper hall. A moment later the footsteps were gone, leaving him the sole witness to the incredible struggle between Druid and Skull Bearer.

The black-garbed figures were immobile at the edge of the furnace, statues frozen in place with the great strain of their battle, dark faces only inches apart, the lean arms of the giant Druid holding firm the claw-tipped limbs of the deadly spirit creature. The Skull Bearer was attempting to bring his razor-sharp hands close enough to the mystic's unprotected throat to rip the life out of him and end the battle quickly. The black wings heaved with the exertion, flapping in fury to add momentum to the assault, the unmistakable rasp of its breathing cutting the heated air with ragged desperation. Then suddenly the Northland creature's wiry leg shot out, tripping the Druid so that he fell backward onto the stone floor at the edge of the pit. Like a shot, the attacker was upon him, one clawed hand sweeping downward for the kill. But the victim was too quick, rolling deftly away from the deadly talons and free from the creature's grasp. Nevertheless, Flick saw the blow catch a portion of the shoulder and heard the distinct rending of cloth as first blood was drawn. Flick gave a gasp of dismay, but a moment later the Druid was on his feet, showing no sign of injury. Twin bolts of blue flame shot out of the extended fingers of his hands, striking the rising Skull Bearer with shattering force, throwing the infuriated creature back against the railing. But while the mystic bolts had visibly hurt the serpent during the battle in the Hall of Kings, they did little more than slow the Northland creature for a few brief seconds. Roaring in fury, it counterattacked. Blazing red bolts shot from its burning eyes. Allanon brought his cloak up in a sweeping movement, and the bolts appeared to deflect into the stone walls of the chamber. For a moment, the creature hesitated, and the two opponents circled each other warily in the manner of two beasts of the forest, locked in a life-and-death struggle which only one could survive.

For the first time, Flick noticed that the temperature was rising. With the approach of dawn, the furnace tenders had risen to care for the heating needs of the awakening castle. Unaware of the battle taking place in the walkway overhead, they had activated the dormant bellows machinery at the bottom of the pit, stoking the fire to build it up to an intensity which would enable heated air to warm all the chambers of the Druid's Keep. As a result, flames were now visible above the edge of the pit and the temperature of the chamber was rising steadily. Flick felt the sweat pouring down over his face, soaking through his warm hunting outfit. But still he would not leave. He sensed that if Allanon were defeated, they would all be doomed, and he was determined to know the outcome. The Sword of Shannara would mean nothing to them if the man who had brought them to this final battleground were destroyed. With rapt fascination clouding his stocky face, Flick Ohmsford watched what might be the fate of the races and the lands being decided by the two seemingly indestructible protagonists of mortal man and Spirit Lord.

Allanon had attacked again with the flashing blue bolts, striking at the circling Skull Bearer in brief, biting blows, trying to force it into a hasty move, trying to cause it to slip, to make a single fatal mistake. The spirit creature was no fool, but an evil spawned of a hundred hunts in which it alone had been the victor and the victims all lay forgotten beyond the world of mortal men. It dodged and twisted with frightening ease, always coming back to the same tense crouch, watching and waiting for its own moment to strike. Then, in a totally unexpected move, the black wings spread wide and it circled into the air in a sweep that carried it soaring around the flames of the furnace and down again with vicious speed onto the tall figure of Allanon. The clawed hands raked downward, and for a moment Flick thought all was surely lost. Miraculously, the floored Druid escaped the deadly hands, throwing the Skull Bearer completely over him with one mighty heave of his powerful arms. The hapless creature flew wildly through the air and crashed with an audible thud into the stone wall beyond. It struggled to its feet in an instant, but the force of the blow had shaken it, slowing it down just enough, and before it could escape, the giant Druid was upon it. The two black figures thrashed about against the wall as if inextricably joined, their limbs locked onto each other like twisted branches. When they reared to full height, Flick could see that Allanon was behind the struggling Skull Bearer, his mighty arms locked viselike about the head of the creature, the straining muscles slowly crushing the life away. The victim's wings beat madly, its hooked arms clutching vainly for something to break the hold that was destroying it. The fire-red eyes burned with the fury of the furnace pit itself, shooting forth bolts of fire that tore into the stone walls, leaving gaping, blackened holes. The combatants lurched away from the wall and rocked wildly toward the blazing pit at the center of the heated chamber until they were against the low iron railing. For a moment it appeared to the wide-eyed Valeman that both would lose their balance and plunge into the flames below. But abruptly Allanon straightened with a mighty effort, dragging his captive back from the railing a few scant feet. It was this sudden movement that brought the entangled spirit creature about, its hate-filled eyes coming to rest directly on the partially hidden Valeman. Grasping at any opportunity to divert the clinging Druid for the instant that would permit it a chance to break free of those crushing arms, the Skull Bearer struck at the unprepared Flick. Twin bolts of flame shot out of the burning eyes, shattering the stone blocks of the staircase into deadly fragments which flew in all directions like little knives. Flick acted instinctively, diving out of the staircase onto the walkway, his hands and face cut by the stone, but his life saved by his quickness. As he leaped clear, the entire entryway shuddered abruptly and collapsed in a cascade of broken stone blocks that completely shut off the passage upward, the dust billowing out of the rubble in heavy clouds.

In that same instant, as Flick lay frightened and shaken but still conscious on the stone floor of the furnace chamber, with the flames from the roaring pit rising higher to meet the clouds of dust from the blocked passage, Allanon's grip relaxed just enough to permit the crafty spirit creature to break loose. Whirling about with a cry of hatred, it struck the distracted Druid a crushing blow on the head, knocking the tall wanderer to his knees. The North-lander moved in for the kill, but somehow the dazed mystic was on his feet again, the blue bolts from the lean hands flashing fiercely as they struck the unprotected head of the attacker. Powerful fists rained resounding blows on both sides of the creature's black head, turning the battered figure about once again as the great arms wound with crushing force about its chest, pinning the wings and claw-tipped hands back against the writhing body. Holding the creature thus, the steel-eyed Druid gritted his gleaming teeth in fury and squeezed. Flick, still lying on the floor as the two combatants loomed above him several yards away, heard a horrible crunching sound as something snapped inside the Skull Bearer. Then with a lurch the two figures were again next to the low iron railing, every straining feature clearly revealed in the flames, the thunder of the burning pit matched in its power and its fury by the wail of agony from the shattered victim as the black, hooked body shuddered once. From some deep well of strength and hatred buried within, the Skull Bearer summoned one last desperate surge of power, throwing itself over the iron railing, its clutching fingers embedded in the black-cloaked attacker as it fell, dragging its hated enemy with it, and both figures were lost in the glow of the hungry flames.

The fallen Flick climbed dazedly to his feet, shock slowly spreading over his battered face. He tottered unsteadily toward the edge of the furnace pit, but the heat was so intense that he was forced back. He tried once more without success, the sweat pouring down from his forehead into his eyes and mouth, mingling slowly with tears of helpless anger. The flames from the pit soared above the low iron railing, licking hungrily at the stone and crackling with new life as if to acknowledge the addition of the two black-garbed creatures to the fuel it greedily consumed. Through the mist that coated his burning eyes, the Valeman gazed fixedly toward the bottomless pit. There was nothing beyond the red glow of the flames and the unbearable heat. Hopelessly, he called out the Druid's name over and over in futile desperation, each call sending the echoes bouncing off the stone walls and dying in the heat of the fire. But the Valeman found himself alone with the roar of the flames, and he knew at last that the Druid was gone.

He panicked then. In a mad dash, he scrambled back from the fiery pit. He reached the rubble of the stairway before he remembered that it had been blocked, and he collapsed for a moment amid the broken rock. Shaking his head to clear his muddled brain, he felt the full intensity of the fire. He knew instinctively that if he did not escape the chamber in a matter of minutes, the heat would bake him alive. He bounded up and ran to the closest stone door, pushing and pulling on it in desperation. But the door did not move, and at last he stopped, his hands bloody from the effort. He looked down the wall, his eyes finding a second door. He stumbled on to this one, but it, too, was secured from the other side. He felt his hopes dim into nothingness, certain now that he was trapped. Woodenly, he forced himself to move on to the third. It was with the last of his fading strength, as he pushed and pulled frantically on the stubborn barricade, that he touched something hidden in the rock and triggered the mechanism that permitted it to open. With a cry of relief, the battered Valeman fell through the opening into the passageway beyond, kicking the stone door shut as he lay in the semidarkness, locking himself away from the heat and the death that remained behind.

For many long minutes he lay exhausted in the darkness of the corridor, his burning body soaking up the cool of the stone floor and the soothing air. He didn't try to think, didn't care to remember, but wished only to lose himself in the peace and quiet of the tunnel rock. At last he forced himself wearily to his knees, then to his feet in a final effort, leaning dazedly against the cold stone of the passage wall as he waited for his strength to return. He realized for the first time that his clothing was torn and burned almost beyond recognition, his hands and face singed and blackened from the heat. He looked around slowly, his stocky frame straightening itself as he pushed away from the wall. The dim light of the torch on the wall ahead indicated the direction in which the winding corridor ran, and he stumbled forward until he was able to grasp the burning piece of wood from its rack. He shuffled along slowly, the torch extended to light his way. Somewhere ahead he heard shouting, and instinctively his free hand went to the handle of his short hunting knife, drawing the weapon from its sheath. After several minutes, the noise seemed to move farther away and at last die out altogether, and still the Valeman had seen nothing. The corridor wound through the rock in curious fashion, taking Flick past several doors, all of which were closed and barred, but never leading upward and never branching off into other passageways. Ever so often the darkness ahead was broken by the dim light of a burning torch securely fastened to the stone, its yellow light casting his shadow against the far wall like a misshapen wraith fleeing into the darkness.

Then abruptly the passage widened and the light ahead grew stronger. Flick hesitated a moment, grasping his weapon tightly, his face streaked with lines of smoke and sweat, but grimly determined in the flickering glow. There was no sound as he inched his way forward. He knew that somewhere there had to be a stairway leading to the main hall of the Druid's Keep. So far, it had been a long and futile search, and he was becoming exhausted. He wished belatedly that he hadn't been so eager to remain behind, allowing himself to be cut off from the main party. Now he was trapped in these unfathomable corridors at the center of Paranor. Anything could have happened to the others by this time, he thought dismally, and he might never find them wandering through this maze. He edged his way a little farther around a bend in the rock, his muscles tensed, peering carefully into the light. To his surprise he found himself at the entrance to a round chamber with numerous other passages leading into it. A dozen or so torches burned cheerfully from the circular wall. He breathed a sigh of relief when he saw that the rotunda was deserted. Then he realized that he was no better off than he had been before. The other passages looked exactly like the one he had come through. There were no doors leading to other rooms, no stairways leading to the upper level, and no indication as to which way he should go. He looked around in bewilderment, desperately trying to identify one passage from another, his hope fading with each passing second and each repeated survey. At last he shook his head in confusion. Moving to one of the walls, he sat down wearily, closing his eyes as he forced himself to accept the bitter fact that he was hopelessly lost.

On Allanon's command, the remainder of the company had broken for the stairway. Durin and Dayel were closest to the stone passage and, being the fastest in the group, found themselves halfway up the steps before the others had even begun the short climb. Their lithe Elven limbs carried them up the flight of stairs in gliding, bounding leaps, barely touching the stone as they ran. Hendel, Menion, and Balinor came in a rush behind, their progress partially impeded by their heavy weapons and greater weight, and partially by each other as they tried to avoid stumbling over one another in the narrow, winding staircase. It was a wild, disorganized charge to the upper hall, each man scrambling to reach the object of the long quest and to escape the terrifying spirit creature. In their haste to accomplish both ends, the hapless Flick was not even missed.

Durin was first through the stairway entrance of the Druid's Keep, nearly stumbling into the great hall as he broke clear, the smaller form of his brother close behind. The hall was lavishly impressive, a huge, high-ceilinged corridor whose great walls were solid wood, polished until they shone with burnished magnificence in the mixed yellow light of burning torches and the reddish tinges of the dawn seeping through high, slanted windows. The panels were adorned with paintings, carved figures of stone and wood on mosaic display stands and long, handwoven tapestries that hung in folds to the polished marble floor that ran the length of the corridor. At various intervals, there were great statues of iron and fine stone, sculptures of another age preserved through the long centuries by the shelter of this timeless refuge. They seemed to be guarding the heavy, carved wooden doors that were beautifully or-namented with handles of copper-colored brass held fast by iron studs. A few of these stood open, and in the chambers that lay beyond could be seen the same carefully designed splendor, glowing radiantly as tall, open glass windows let in the sunshine in long streams of lingering color, fresh with the new day.

The Elven brothers had little time to admire the ageless beauty of Paranor. An instant after they were through the open staircase, they were set upon by Gnome guards, who seemed to come from everywhere at once, the gnarled, yellow bodies sliding from concealment behind doors, statues, the walls themselves. Durin met the rush with his long hunting knife and withstood the assault only a moment before they were on him. Dayel came to his brother's rescue, swinging his long bow as a weapon, knocking the attackers aside until the sturdy ash broke with an audible snap. For a moment it seemed they would be torn to pieces before their stronger comrades could come to their aid, until Durin broke free and snatched a long, wicked-looking pike from an iron warrior of another age and scattered the scrambling Gnomes with sweeping cuts, knocking them away from his struggling brother. But they were reinforced in an instant and quickly reassembled for a second charge. The Elven brothers had moved back to the wall, panting with the strain and covered with slashes and the blood of their attackers. The Gnomes gathered together in a yellow group, their deadly short swords held before them, intent on breaking past Durin's swinging pike and hacking both Elves to pieces. With a wild piercing cry, they charged in for the kill.

Unfortunately for the Gnomes, they had forgotten to watch the open stairway against the possible chance that the Elves were not alone. At the instant they rushed Durin and Dayel, the other three members of the company burst through the doorway and fell upon the unprepared attackers. The Gnomes had never in their lives encountered men such as these. In the center came the huge borderman from Callahorn, his gleaming sword cutting a path through the shorter swords with such ferocity that the Gnomes fell over each other trying to escape. On one side they ran headlong into the bludgeoning mace of the powerful Dwarf, while on the other they faced the quick blade of the swift, agile highlander. For a moment they stood and fought against the five madmen, then wavered slightly as the attack pressed ahead, and finally broke

and ran, all thoughts of winning abandoned. Without a word, the five battered warriors charged down the magnificent hall, leaping over the wounded and dead, their hunting boots ringing on the polished marble. The few Gnomes who stood against them as they came soon went down before the rush, to lie in silent, unmoving heaps. After all that they had suffered and lost, the five who remained from the little company would not be denied any longer the victory they had sought so desperately.

Near the end of the ancient corridor, now littered with dead and wounded Gnomes, the tapestries and paintings torn and scattered from the sharp battle, a last desperate band of guards crowded together in tight formation before a set of tall, carved wooden doors that stood closed and barred. Their short hunting swords held before them like a wall of spikes, the determined Gnomes prepared to make a final stand. The attackers made a short rush at the deadly wall, trying to break through at the center behind the long swords of Balinor and Menion, but the battle-hardened guards repulsed the assault after several minutes of bitter fighting. The five withdrew in exhaustion, panting and sweating freely with the exertion, their bodies cut and battered. Durin dropped heavily to one knee, both an arm and a leg badly slashed by Gnome swords. Menion had been clipped along one side of his head by a pike edge, and the blood rose to the wound in a vivid red streak. The highlander seemed unaware of the injury. Again the five attacked and again, after long minutes of bitter hand-to-hand combat, they were repulsed. The number of Gnomes had diminished by almost half, but time was running out for the men of the company. There was no sign of Allanon, and the Gnomes would have reinforcements on the way to protect the Sword of Shannara, if indeed it did stand within the chamber they now so desperately sought to hold.

Then, in an amazing display of raw strength, the towering Balinor rushed to the other side of the hall and with one mighty heave overturned a huge stone pillar, at the top of which was affixed a metal urn. Pillar and urn struck the stone floor with a crash that jarred everyone to the bone, the echoes reverberating through the bloodied hall. Stone should have shattered, but the pillar remained whole. With the aid of Hendel, the giant borderman began to roll the rounded battering ram sideways toward the wedge of Gnomes and the closed doors to the chamber beyond, the monstrous roller gathering speed and power with each revolution as it thundered toward the hapless guards. For an instant the wiry yellow creatures hesitated, their short swords held ready as the crushing weight of the stone pillar bore down on them. Then they broke, bolting for safety, their spirit gone, the battle lost. Even so, several were not fast enough to escape the makeshift ram and were caught beneath its great bulk as it crashed amid a shower of stone and wood splinters into the barred doors. The doors shuddered and buckled with the blow, the wood cracking and the iron fastenings snapping like the crack of a whip, yet somehow they withstood the force of the ram. But an instant later they flew off their hinges with a resounding crash as the weight of the Prince of Callahorn struck them, and the five men rushed into the chamber beyond to claim the Sword of Shannara.

To their amazement, the room stood empty. There were tall windows and long, flowing curtains, masterful paintings that lined the walls, and even several small pieces of ornate furniture placed carefully about the large chamber. But nowhere was there any trace of the coveted Sword. In shocked disbelief, the five gazed slowly about the closed room. Durin dropped heavily to his knees, weak from loss of blood and close to passing out. Dayel came quickly to his aid, tearing up strips of cloth to bind the open wounds, then helping his brother to one of the chairs, where he collapsed in exhaustion. Menion looked from one wall to the next, searching for another exit to the room. Then Balinor, who had been pacing the floor of the chamber in slow scrutiny of its marble finish, gave a low exclamation. A portion of the floor at the very center of the room was scarred and discolored beneath a poor attempt to conceal the fact that something large and square had stood there for many years.

"The block of Tre-Stone!" exclaimed Menion quickly.

"But if it has been moved, it must have been recently," Balinor speculated, his breathing labored, his voice weary as he tried to think. "So why did the Gnomes try to keep us out . . .?"

"Maybe they didn't know it had been moved," suggested Menion desperately.

"Perhaps a decoy . . .?" ventured Hendel abruptly. "But why waste time with a decoy unless . . .?"

"They wanted to keep us busy here, because the Sword was still in the castle and they hadn't gotten it out!" finished Balinor excitedly. "They haven't had time to get it out, so they tried to decoy us! But where is the Sword now—who has it?"

For a moment all three were at a loss. Had the Warlock Lord known that the company was coming all along, just as the Skull Bearer in the furnace had seemed to indicate? If their attack had caught everyone by surprise, what could have happened to the Sword since Allanon had last seen it in this chamber?

"Wait!" exclaimed Durin weakly from across the room, rising slowly to his feet. "When I came through the staircase, there was something happening on another set of stairs down the hall—men moving up those stairs."

"The tower!" shouted Hendel, racing for the open

doorway. "They've got the Sword locked in the tower!"

Balinor and Menion hurried after the disappearing Dwarf, the weariness gone. The Sword of Shannara was still within reach. Durin and Dayel followed at a slower pace, the former still weak and leaning heavily on his younger brother for support, but their eyes bright with hope. A moment later, the chamber stood empty.

Flick climbed despondently to his feet after a few minutes' rest and decided that the only course of action left to him was to choose one of the passageways and follow it to the end, hoping that it would take him to a stairway leading upward to the fortress. He thought briefly of the others, somewhere in the corridors above, perhaps already in possession of the Sword. They could not know of Allanon's fall nor of his own fate, lost in these impossible tunnels. He hoped they would search for him, but realized at the same time that, if they did get the Sword, there would be no time to waste looking for him. They would have to make their escape before the Warlock Lord could send the Skull Bearers to retrieve the coveted blade. He wondered what had become of Shea, if he had been found alive, if he had been rescued. Somehow he knew that Shea would never leave Paranor while Flick was alive; but then there was no way for his brother to know that he had not perished in the furnace chamber. He had to admit that his own situation looked pretty hopeless.

At that instant there was a loud clamor from one of the tunnels, the sound of boots thudding on the stone floor, of men rushing directly toward the rotunda. In a flash, the Valeman crossed the room and hastened into concealment down a different tunnel, keeping flat against the rock in the protective shadows. He paused just within sight of the lighted rotunda and drew his short hunting knife. A few moments later a swarm of fleeing Gnome guards charged into the connecting room and disappeared down another of the passage-ways without pausing. The sounds of their flight were soon lost in the bends and turns of the rock. Flick had no idea what they were running from or perhaps running to, but wherever they had been was where he wanted to be. It was a good bet that they had come from the upper chambers of the Druids' Keep, and that was the place the Valeman had to reach. He moved cautiously back into the lighted chamber and crossed to the tunnel from which the Gnomes had come. Backtracking their path of flight, he entered the now-deserted corridor and disappeared into the darkness beyond. He held his knife before him, groping his way along the dimly lit walls toward the first torch rack. Freeing the burning wood from its clasp, he proceeded deeper into the passage, his eager eyes scanning the rough walls for signs of a door or an open stairway. He had only gone about a hundred yards when without warning a portion of the rock slid open almost at his elbow, and a single Gnome stepped into view.

It was disputable as to which of the two was more surprised at the appearance of the other. The Gnome guard was a straggler from the larger group fleeing the battle in the halls above, and the sight of another of the invaders here in the tunnels momentarily startled him. Although smaller than the Valeman, the Gnome was wiry and armed with a short sword. He attacked immediately. Flick dodged instinctively as the sweep-ing blade went wide of the mark. The Valeman leaped onto the Gnome before he could recover and wrestled him to the stone floor, trying vainly to take the sword away from his agile opponent, his own knife lost in the scuffle. Flick was not trained in hand-to-hand combat, but the Gnome was, and this gave the little yellow man a distinct advantage. He had killed before and

would do so again without a second thought, while
Flick sought only to disarm his attacker and escape.
They rolled and fought across the floor for several long
minutes before the Gnome again broke free and took a
vicious cut at his adversary, barely missing the
exposed head. Flick threw himself back, desperately
looking for his knife. The little guard charged at him
just as his groping fingers closed over the heavy wood
of the torch he had dropped at the first assault. The
short sword came down, glancing off Flick's shoulder
and cutting into the exposed flesh of his arm painfully.
At the same moment, the stunned Valeman brought
the torch up with a powerful swing and felt it strike the
Gnome's raised head with jarring impact. The guard
sprawled forward with the force of the blow and did
not move again. Flick slowly regained his footing and
recovered his knife after a moment's search. His arm
throbbed painfully and the blood had soaked into his
hunting tunic, running down his arm and into his
hand where he could clearly see it. Afraid that he was
bleeding to death, he quickly tore up strips of cloth
from the fallen Gnome's short cloak and bound them
about the injured limb until the bleeding had stopped.
Picking up the other's sword, he moved over to the
still partially open rock slab to see where it led.

To his relief, he found a winding staircase beyond
the doorway that spiraled upward. He slipped into the
passage, closing the rock slab behind him with several
pulls of his good arm. The stairs were dimly outlined
by the familiar torchlight, and he proceeded to climb
with slow, cautious steps. All was quiet in the passage
as he moved steadily upward, the long torches in iron
racks giving him enough light to pick out his footing
on the rough stone. He reached a closed door at the top
of the stairway and paused there to listen, his ear
placed next to the cracks between the iron bindings.
There was only silence beyond. Cautiously, he pushed
the door open a bit and peered through into the

ancient halls of Paranor. He had reached his goal. He opened the door a bit farther and stepped watchfully into the silent corridor.

Then the steel grip of a lean dark hand came down on his extended sword arm and yanked him into the open.

Hendel paused hesitantly at the bottom of the stairway that led to the tower of the Druids' Keep, peering upward into the gloom. The others stood quietly at his back, following his gaze intently. The stairway consisted of little more than a set of open stone steps, narrow and treacherous-looking, that wound upward in a spiral along the walls of the rounded turret. The entire tower was shrouded in gloomy darkness, unlighted by torches or openings in the dark stone. From their poor vantage point, the members of the company could see little beyond the first few turns in the staircase. The open stairwell dropped away from where they stood into a blackened pit. Menion crossed to the edge of the landing and peered downward, mindful of the absence of any guard rail either here or along the stairs. He dropped a small pebble into the black abyss and waited for it to hit bottom. No sound came back to him. He glanced again at the open stairs and the gloom above, then turned to the others.

"Looks like an open invitation to a trap," he declared pointedly.

"Very likely," Balinor agreed, stepping forward for a closer look. "But we have to get up there."

Menion nodded, then shrugged casually, moving toward the stairway. The others followed without a word, Hendel right at the highlander's heels, Balinor next and the Elven brothers bringing up the rear. They moved cautiously up the narrow stone steps, alert for any sign of a trap, their shoulders close to the wall, away from the dangerous open edge of the stairwell.

They wound their way steadily through the musty gloom. Menion studied each step as he went, his keen eyes searching the seams of the stone-block wall for hidden devices. From time to time, he tossed stones onto the steps ahead of them, testing for traps that might be released by any sudden weight on the steps. But nothing happened. The abyss below was a silent black hole cut into the heavy gloom of the tower air, no sound penetrating its dark serenity save the soft scraping of hunting boots ascending the worn steps. At last, the faint light of burning torches cut through the darkness far above them, the small fires flickering briskly with the gusting of an unknown source of wind from the turret peak. A small landing came into view at the summit of the staircase, and beyond, the dim shape of a huge stone door, bound with iron and standing closed. The top of the Druids' Keep.

Then Menion sprang the first hidden trap. A series of long, barbed spikes shot out of the stone wall, triggered by the pressure of Menion's foot on the stone stairway. Had Menion still been on the step, they would have cut into his unprotected legs, crippling him and forcing him over the edge of the open stairwell into the black abyss below. But Hendel had heard the click of the released spring an instant before the trap opened. With a quick pull he yanked the astonished highlander backward to the others, almost knocking them all off the narrow steps. They staggered wildly in the heavy gloom, inches from the sharpened steel spikes. Regaining their footing, the five remained flattened against the wall for several long minutes, breathing audibly in the still darkness. Then the taciturn Dwarf smashed the spikes before them with several well-placed blows of his great mace, opening the route once more. Now he led the way in alert silence, while the shaken Menion dropped back behind Balinor. Quickly Hendel found a second trap of the same type and triggered it, breaking the spikes and moving on.

They were almost to the landing now, and it appeared they would reach it without further difficulty when Dayel called out sharply. His keen Elven hearing had caught something that the others had missed, a small click that signaled the triggering of still another trap. For a moment everyone froze in position as alert eyes searched the walls and steps. But they found nothing, and at last Hendel ventured a single step farther on the stairs. Surprisingly, nothing happened, and the cautious Dwarf proceeded to the top of the stairway while the others remained in position. Once he had safely reached the landing, the others hastened after him until at last all five stood together at the top, looking anxiously down the winding staircase into the black pit. How they had managed to escape the third trap they could not imagine. Balinor was of the opinion that it had failed to function properly due to long years of neglect, but Hendel was not so easily persuaded. He could not shake the feeling that somehow they had overlooked the obvious.

The tower hung like a huge shadow over the open stairwell, its dark stone chill and wet to the touch, a mass of giant blocks that had been assembled ages ago and had stubbornly withstood the ravages of time with the endurance of the earth itself. The huge door at the landing appeared to be immovable, its surface scarred, the iron bindings as sturdy as the day they had been imbedded in the rock. Great iron spikes, hammered into the stone, held the hinges and lock in place, and it appeared to the five who stood before it that nothing less than an earthquake could force the monstrous slab of stone open even an inch. Balinor approached the formidable barrier cautiously and ran his hands along the seams and lock, trying to find some hidden device that might release it. Gingerly, he turned the iron handle and pushed forward. To the astonishment of all, the stone slab slid partially open with a shudder and a grinding of rusted iron. A moment later, the mystery of the tower was revealed as the door swung open all the way, striking the inner walls with a sharp crash.

In the exact center of the rounded chamber, set in the polished black surface of the giant Tre-Stone block, blade downward so that it rose before them like a gleaming cross of silver and gold, they beheld the legendary Sword of Shannara. Its long blade flashed brightly in the light of the sun streaming through the high, iron-barred windows of the tower, reflecting sharply off the mirror finish of the square stone. None of the five had ever seen the fabulous Sword, but they were instantly sure this was it. For a moment they remained framed in the doorway, gazing in astonishment, unable to believe that at last, after all their effort, the endless marches, the miserable days and nights of hiding, there before them stood the ancient talisman they had risked everything to find. The Sword of Shannara was theirs! They had outwitted the Warlock Lord. Slowly they filed into the stone chamber, smiles on their faces, the weariness gone, their wounds forgotten. They stood for long moments staring at it, silent, wondering, grateful. They could not bring themselves to step forward and take the treasure from the stone. It seemed too sacred for mortal hands. But Allanon was missing, and Shea was lost as well, and where . . .

"Where is Flick?" Dayel voiced the question suddenly. For the first time they realized that he was missing. They glanced about the chamber, looking blankly at one another for an explanation. Then Menion, who had turned apprehensively back to the gleaming Sword, watched the impossible happen. The great block of Tre-Stone and its precious display began to shimmer and dissolve before his astonished eyes. It took only seconds for the entire image to fade into smoke, then into a heavy haze, and at last into the air itself, until the five men stood alone in an empty room staring into space.

"A trap! The third trap!" roared Menion, recovering from the initial shock.

But behind him, he could already hear the huge rock slab swing shut on their inescapable prison, creaking and groaning sharply as the rusted hinges gave way under the monstrous weight of the stone. The highlander launched himself across the room, crashing into the door just as it closed on them, the sharp snap of its locks clicking firmly into place. He collapsed slowly to the worn stone floor, his heart beating violently in rage and frustration. The others had not moved, but stood in silent despair as they watched the slim figure at the door bury his face in his hands. The faint but unmistakable sound of muffled laughter echoed brokenly off the chill walls in long peals, mocking their foolishness and their bitter, inevitable defeat.

XVII

The cheerless cold of the Northland sky hung in thin strips of gray fog against the dull edges that formed the peaks of the solitary mountain of pitted blackness that was the castle of the Warlock Lord. Above and below the surrounding plain of the Skull Kingdom, standing like rusted sawteeth, were the blunted tips of the Razor Mountains and the Knife Edge, an impenetrable barrier to mortal life. Between them stood the dying mountain of the Spirit Lord, forgotten by nature, spurned by the seasons as it wasted slowly away. The shroud of death that claimed its tall peaks, clinging with pitiless certainty to its shattered faces, spread its evil aura across the entire land with unmistakable hatred toward the few vestiges of life and beauty that had somehow managed to survive. A doomed era waited quietly in the Northland kingdom of the Warlock Lord. Now was the hour of death, the last signs of life slowly fading back into the ground as only the shell of nature's touch, once bright and magnificent, remained.

Within the skull of the lone mountain ran hundreds of timeless caverns, their enduring rock walls sunless in the never-changing grayness of the sky beyond. They wound about with the ruthless coiling of a cornered snake, twisting violently through the core of the rock. All was silence and death in the gray mist of the spirit kingdom, a permeating somber air that

marked the total extinction of hope, the complete
burial of gaiety and lightness. There was movement
even here, however, but it was life unlike anything
known to mortal man. Its source was the single, black
chamber at the peak of the mountain, a monstrous
room with its north face open to the dim light of the
cheerless sky beyond and the endless stretch of
forbidding mountains that formed the north gate to
the kingdom. In this cavernous room, its walls wet
with the cold that cut knifelike through the rock,
scurried the inky minions of the Warlock Lord. Their
small, black forms crawled about the floor of the silent
chamber, their spineless frames bent and shattered
with the terrible, wrenching power their Master
wielded over them. Even walking would have been
redemption in their existence. They were mindless
wraiths, kept only to serve the one who held them
enslaved. They muttered as they hustled about, small
cries and weepings that sounded of unforgettable
agony. In the center of the room rose a large pedestal
that held a basin of water, its murky surface placid and
deathly. From time to time, one of the little crawling
creatures would hasten to its edge and peer cautiously
into the cold water, eyes darting furtively about,
waiting, watching expectantly. A moment later, with a
small whimper, it would scurry away to blend back in
the shadows of the cavern. "Where is the Master,
where is the Master?" the sounds would cry like
whispers in the grayness as the little beings moved
about uneasily. "He will come, he will come, he will
come," the answer echoed back hatefully.

Then the air stirred violently as if wrenching free of
the space that held it, and the mist seemed to come
together in a huge black shadow that tightened slowly
into material form at the edge of the basin. The mist
gathered and swirled and became the Spirit Lord, a
huge, cloaked figure of black that seemed to hang in
the air. The sleeves rose, but there were no arms
within, and the folds of the trailing robes covered

nothing but the floor. "The Master, the Master," the terrified creatures' voices sounded in unison, and their bent shapes groveled obediently before him. The faceless cowl turned to them and looked down, and they could see within the blackness the tiny glints of flame that burned with satisfied hatred, flashing sparklike in a hazy green mist that hung all about the inner recesses of the shroud. Then the Warlock Lord turned from them, and they were forgotten as he gazed steadily into the waters of the strange basin, waiting for the commanded mental picture to appear. Seconds later the darkness was gone and in its place was the furnace room at Paranor where the company of Allanon again stood face to face with the dreaded Skull Bearer. The fiery eyes in the green mist stared first at the Valeman, then watched the battle between the two dark figures until both tumbled over the edge of the pit and were lost in the flames below. At that moment a sudden noise behind him caused the Spirit Lord to pause and turn slightly. Two of his Skull Bearers entered the room from one of the dark tunnels of the mountain to stand silently, awaiting his attention. He was not ready for them, and so returned to the waters of the basin. Again they cleared, forming a picture of the tower, where the astonished members of the company stood frozen in excited relief before the Sword of Shannara. He waited a few seconds, toying with them, enjoying his mastery of the situation as they moved closer to the Sword like mice to the baited trap of cheese. Seconds later, the trap was sprung as he dissolved his illusion before their startled eyes and watched the tower door fly shut, trapping them in the keep for eternity. Behind him, the two winged servants could sense the chilling laugh that rolled through his substanceless frame into the cavern air.

Without turning to face them, the Warlock Lord gestured abruptly toward the open wall facing north, and the Skull Bearers moved off without hesitation. They knew without asking what was expected of them. They would fly to Paranor and destroy the captured son of Shannara, the sole heir to the hated Sword. With the last member of the House of Shannara dead and the Sword itself within their grasp, they no longer need fear a mystical power greater than their own. Even now, the precious Sword was en route from the halls of Paranor to the Northland kingdom where it would be buried and forgotten in the endless caverns of the Skull Mountain. The Warlock Lord turned slightly to watch his two servants shuffle awkwardly across the dark chamber until they reached the open wall, where they rose heavily into the gray sky and wheeled southward. To be sure, the Elf king, Eventine, would attempt to intercept the Sword, to regain it for his own people. But the attempt would fail, and Eventine would be taken—the last great leader of the free lands, the last hope of the races. With Eventine his prisoner, the Sword in his possession, the last heir to the House of Shannara dead, and the most hated enemy of all, the Druid Allanon, destroyed in the furnace at Paranor, the battle was ended before it had begun. There would be no defeat in the Third War of the Races. He had won.

A wave of his cloak sleeve and the water again turned murky, the picture of the Druids' Keep and the trapped mortals gone. Then the air rushed violently about the black spirit and his form began to dissolve back into the mist of the chamber, fading gradually until there was nothing left but the basin and the empty room. Long moments passed in silence until at last the groveling minions of the Warlock Lord were certain the Master had again gone from them, and they came forth from the shadows, their small, black shapes creeping eagerly to the basin edge where they peered curiously, crying and whimpering their misery to the placid waters.

In the high tower of Paranor, in the remote and now

inaccessible room of the Druids' Keep, four silent, tired members of the little company from Culhaven paced dejectedly about their prison. Only Durin sat quietly against one wall of the tower, his wound so painful that he could no longer move about. Balinor rocked slightly on his heels as he stood close to a high, barred window of the Keep, watching the faint rays of the sun filter down in long streamers of floating dust to light the otherwise gloomy chamber with small squares of sunlight that fell carelessly across the stone slabs of the floor. They had been there for over an hour now, hopelessly imprisoned behind the mammoth, ironbound door. The Sword was lost to them and with it their hopes of any victory. At first they had waited patiently in the belief that Allanon would soon reach them, smashing through the great stone barrier that barred the way to freedom. They had even called his name, hoping he could hear them and follow their voices to the tower. Menion had reminded them that Flick was still missing, possibly wandering about the halls of Paranor searching for them. But before very long their faith faltered and at last faded entirely, as each forced himself to admit inwardly, though none would speak the words, that there would be no rescue, that the courageous Druid and the little Valeman had fallen prey to the deadly Skull Bearer, that the Warlock Lord had won.

Menion was thinking once again of Shea, wondering what had befallen his friend. The company had done all it could, but it had not even been enough to save the life of one small human being, and now no one could guess what end he had come to, left alone in the wilds of the Eastland border plains to fend for himself. Shea was gone, probably dead. Allanon had believed they would find Shea when they found the Sword, but the Sword had been lost and there was no sign of the missing heir. Now Allanon was gone as well, killed in the furnace room of the Druids' Council, his ancestral home—or if not killed, then taken prisoner, chained and shackled in some dungeon just as they were locked in this tower. They would be left to rot, or worse, and it had all been for nothing. He smiled grimly as he considered their fate, wishing he could have had at least one opportunity to confront the real enemy, to take one swift cut at the all-powerful Warlock Lord.

Suddenly a short hush of warning from the ever-alert Dayel caused the others to freeze where they were, eyes fixed on the great door, listening guardedly to the sound of faint footfalls on the stone steps beyond. Menion dropped his hand to the sword of Leah resting in the leather sheath on the floor and noiselessly pulled it free. The giant borderman at his elbow already held his drawn broadsword. All moved in short, hurried steps to encircle the entrance. Even the wounded Durin staggered to his feet, limping painfully over to stand with his companions. The footsteps reached the landing and stopped. There was a moment of ominous silence.

Then the great stone door suddenly opened, swinging ponderously inward, its iron hinges groaning only slightly as they took the full weight of the rock slab. From out of the darkness beyond appeared the frightened features of Flick Ohmsford, his eyes darting wildly as he beheld his imprisoned friends armed and ready to strike. Swords and maces lowered slowly as if the astonished men holding them were mechanical toys. The little Valeman moved reluctantly into the dim light of the tower, partially shadowed by the tall black figure following.

It was Allanon.

They stared at him wordlessly. Streaked with sweat, his dark form coated with several layers of ash and soot, he moved silently into their midst, one great hand resting gently on Flick's small shoulder. He smiled at their reaction.

"I'm all right," he assured them.

Flick was still shaking his head in disbelief at having been found by Allanon.

"I saw him fall . . . " he tried to explain to the others.

"Flick, I'm all right." Allanon patted the little Valeman's shoulder.

Balinor came a step closer, as if to convince himself that this was indeed Allanon and not another apparition.

"We thought you were . . . lost," he managed.

The familiar mocking grin appeared on the lean face.

"The blame for that lies in part at least with our young friend here. He saw me tumble into the furnace pit with the Skull Bearer and presumed me dead. What he did not realize is that the furnace is equipped with a series of iron rungs, which allow workmen to descend into the pit for the purpose of making repairs. Since Paranor has for centuries been the ancestral home of the Druids, I knew of the existence of the rungs. When I felt the evil one pull me over the railing, I reached for them and caught myself several feet below the rim. Flick, of course, could see none of this, and the roar of the fire drowned out my voice as I called out to him."

He paused to brush some of the dirt from his robe.

"Flick was fortunate enough to escape the chamber, but then he lost his way in the tunnels. The battle with the Skull Bearer left me weakened, and even though I enjoy special protection from fire, it took me quite some time to pull myself out of the pit. I went looking for Flick, lost in that maze of underground corridors, found him at last and frightened him half to death when I pulled him into the light. Then we came after the rest of you. But now we must leave— quickly."

"The Sword . . .?" Hendel asked sharply.

"Gone—removed sometime earlier. We can speak

of that later. It is dangerous for us to remain here any longer. The Gnomes will send reinforcements to secure Paranor and the Warlock Lord will dispatch others of his winged bearers to be certain you cause him no further trouble. With the Sword of Shannara still in his possession and believing you trapped in the Druids' Keep, he will quickly turn his attention to his plans for an invasion of the four lands. If he can seize Callahorn and the border countries quickly enough, the rest of the Southland will fall without a struggle."

"Then we're too late—we've lost!" exclaimed Menion bitterly.

Allanon shook his head emphatically.

"We have only been outmaneuvered, not defeated, Prince of Leah. The Warlock Lord rests easy in the belief that he has won, that we are destroyed and no longer a threat. Perhaps we can use that against him. We must not despair. Now come with me."

He led them quickly through the open doorway. A moment later, the tower chamber stood empty.

XVIII

he little band of Gnomes marched Shea northward until sunset. The Valeman was exhausted
when the march began and by the time the
group finally halted for the night, he immediately
collapsed and was asleep before the Gnomes had even
finished binding his legs. The long trek took them
from the banks of the unknown river northward into
hill country west of the upper Anar Forest bordering
on the Northland. Travel became considerably
rougher, the terrain changing from the flat grasslands
of the Rabb Plains into choppy, rolling hillocks. After a
time, the band found itself doing more climbing than
walking, with constant changes of direction made to
avoid the bigger hills. It was beautiful country,
grasslands patched with small forests of aged shade
trees, their bending limbs graceful in the light spring
winds. But its beauty was lost on the exhausted
Valeman, who could only concentrate on putting one
foot ahead of the other as his disinterested captors
pushed him along without rest. By nightfall, the group
was deep into the hill country, and had Shea been able
to consult a map of the region, he would have
discovered that they were camped directly east of
Paranor. As it was, sleep came to him so fast that he
could only remember dropping wearily to the grassy
earth and then nothing more.

The industrious Gnomes finished tying him and

then prepared a fire for their meager dinner. One Gnome was placed on sentry duty, mostly out of habit, since they felt there was little to fear this far into their own homeland, and a second was ordered to keep a close watch over the sleeping captive. The Gnome leader still did not realize who Shea was, nor did he realize the importance of the Elfstones, though he was intelligent enough to conclude that they must be worth something. His plan was to take the Valeman to Paranor where he could consult with his superiors concerning the fate of both the youth and the stones. Perhaps they would know the significance of these matters. The Gnome's only concern was doing the right thing in accordance with his orders to patrol this region, and beyond that duty, he did not care to know anything.

The fire was completed in short order, and the Gnomes ate a hastily prepared meal of bread and stripped meat. When the meal was finished, they gathered eagerly about the warm blaze and contemplated curiously the three small Elfstones which the leader had produced for inspection at his followers' urging. The wizened yellow faces bent closer to the fire and to the outstretched hand of the leader where the stones twinkled brightly in the glowing light. One eager follower tried to touch one, but a stinging blow from his superior sent him sprawling back into the shadows. The Gnome leader touched the stones curiously and rolled them about in his open palm as the others watched in fascination. Finally, the Gnomes tired of the sport, and the stones were put back in the small leather pouch and returned to the leader's tunic. A bottle of ale was broken out to ward off the chill in the night air as well as to aid the weary Gnomes in forgetting their immediate troubles. The bottle was passed around freely, and the little yellow soldiers laughed and joked far into the night, keeping the fire blazing for warmth. Even the lone sentry wandered in, knowing that his guard duty was unnecessary. At last the ale was gone, and the weary hunters turned in, pulling up their blankets in a tight circle about the fire. The sentry even had presence of mind enough to throw a blanket over the sleeping captive, concluding that it would do no good to bring him into Paranor suffering from a fever. Moments later, the campsite was silent, all asleep save the sentry who stood drowsily in the shadows just beyond the light of the small campfire that was dying slowly into coals.

Shea slept fitfully, his slumber disturbed by recurring nightmares of his harrowing flight with Flick and Menion to reach Culhaven, and from there, the ill-fated journey to reach Paranor. He relived in his dreams the battle with the Mist Wraith, feeling its cold, slimy grip about his body, experiencing terror at the touch of the deadly swamp waters lapping about his legs. He felt desperation creeping all through him as the three again became separated in the Black Oaks, only this time he was alone in the great forest, and he knew there was no way out. He would wander until he died there. He could hear the cries of the hunting wolves closing in about him as he struggled to run, dodging madly through the endless maze of giant trees. A moment later the scene changed, and the company stood in the ruins of the city in the middle of the Wolfsktaag Mountains. They were looking curiously at the metal girders, unaware of the danger lurking silently in the jungle beyond. Only Shea knew what was about to happen, but when he tried to warn the others, he found he could not speak. Then he saw the giant creature creeping forth from its concealment to strike the unsuspecting men, and he could not move to warn them. They seemed unaware of what was about to happen, and the creature attacked, a mass of black hair and teeth. Then Shea was in the river, tossing and turning madly as he sought futilely to keep his head above the swift waters, to breathe the life-giving air. But he was being pulled down, and he knew he was suffocating. Desperately he sought to fight it, thrashing wildly as he was pulled farther and farther down.

Then suddenly he was awake and staring into the first faint tinges of light from the approaching dawn, his hands and feet cold and numb from the biting leather thongs that bound him. He looked anxiously about the clearing at the dying coals of the fire and the motionless Gnome bodies huddled in deep slumber. The hills were silent in the semidarkness, so quiet that the Valeman could hear his own breathing, rasping heavily in the stillness. To one side of the campsite was the lone figure of the sentry, his small form a dim shadow on the far edges of the clearing, near some heavy brush. His figure was so vague in the mistiness of the dying night that for several seconds Shea was not really sure he was not a part of the brush. Shea glanced about the silent camp a second time, twisting himself up on one elbow and wiping the sleep from his eyes as he peered cautiously about. Briefly, he tried to work on the thongs that bound him, hoping vaguely that he might be able to work himself loose and make a dash for freedom before the sleeping Gnomes could catch him. But after long minutes of trying to free himself, he was forced to give up the idea. The bonds were too well tied to be worked loose, and he did not have the strength to break them. For a moment he stared helplessly at the ground in front of him, convinced that he had reached the end of the line, that once the Gnomes reached Paranor, he would be turned over to the Skull Bearers and disposed of quickly.

Then he heard something. It was only a faint rustle from somewhere in the darkness beyond the clearing, but it caused him to look up alertly, listening for something further. His Elven eyes traveled quickly over the campsite and the Gnomes, but nothing seemed out of place. It took him several moments to relocate the lone guard at the edge of the brush, but the man had not moved from his position. Then a huge black shadow detached itself from the brush, and the sentry was enveloped and suddenly gone. Shea blinked in disbelief, but there was no mistake. Where the figure of the sentry had stood a moment before, there was nothing. Long moments passed as Shea waited for something further to happen. It was sunrise now. The last traces of the night faded rapidly, and the edge of the golden morning sun appeared on the tips of the distant eastern hills.

There was a soft sound off to his left, and the Valeman twisted about sharply. From behind the cover of a small grove of trees emerged one of the strangest sights that the youth had ever seen. It was a man clad all in scarlet, the like of which no one in Shady Vale had ever encountered. At first the Valeman thought it might be Menion, recalling an outlandish red hunting outfit he had once seen the highlander wearing. But it became apparent almost immediately that this stranger was not Menion, nor in any way like him. The size, the stance, the manner of approach were all different. It was impossible to make out his features in the dim light. In one hand he carried a short hunting knife and in the other was a strange pointed object. The scarlet figure crept slowly over to his side and moved in back of him before he could get a good look at his face. The hunting knife went through the leather bonds silently and easily, freeing the captive Valeman. Then the other hand came around in front of his face, and Shea's eyes went wide in shock as he saw that the man's left hand was missing and in its place a deadly looking iron pike protruded.

"Not a word," the leather-edged voice sounded in his ear. "Don't look, don't think, just move out for the trees to the left and wait there. Now move!"

Shea did not stop to ask questions, but quickly did as he was told. Even without seeing the face of the rescuer, he could guess from the rough voice and the severed limb that it would be wise to do as he was told. He scurried silently from the camp, running in a low crouch until he had reached the cover of the trees. He stopped there and turned back to wait for the other, but to his astonishment the scarlet figure was prowling noiselessly through the midst of the sleeping Gnomes, apparently searching for something. The sun had risen into full view in the east now, and its light framed the stranger as he bent over the huddled form of the sleeping Gnome leader. One gloved hand reached cautiously into the Gnome's tunic, fumbled about for a moment, and came forth holding the small leather pouch with the precious Elfstones. As the hand with the pouch remained poised for an instant, the Gnome awakened, one hand coming up to seize the stranger's wrist as the other whipped a short sword around to finish the thief with one blow. But Shea's rescuer was too quick to be caught off guard. The long iron pike blocked the blow in a sharp clash of metal, and then came back in a long swipe across the Gnome's exposed throat. As the stranger rose to his feet and bounded away from the lifeless body, the entire camp came awake with the sound of the struggle. The Gnomes were on their feet in an instant, swords in hand, charging after the intruder before he could make a complete escape. The scarlet rescuer was forced to turn and fight, the short knife held in one hand as he faced a dozen attackers.

Shea was certain that this was the end for the man, and he prepared to leap from the cover of the trees to try to aid him. But the amazing stranger shrugged off the first onslaught of Gnome hunters as if they were mice, cutting through their disorganized assault and leaving two writhing on the earth with fatal wounds. Then he gave a sharp cry as the second wave of attackers moved in, and from out of the shadows on the other side of the camp charged a massive black figure bearing a huge club. Without slowing once, the black shape tore into the surprised Gnomes with indescribable fury, scattering them with great blows of the mace as if they were no more than fragile leaves. In less than a minute all the Gnomes lay motionless on the ground. Shea watched in astonishment at the edge of the trees as the huge figure approached Shea's rescuer, somewhat in the manner of a faithful dog seeking its master's approval. The stranger spoke softly to the giant for several moments, and then sauntered over to Shea while his companion remained to look after the Gnomes.

"I think that's about all of it," the voice rolled out as the scarlet figure came up to the Valeman, hefting the leather pouch in his good hand.

Shea took a moment to study the man's face, still uncertain as to who his benefactor might be. The way the man swaggered, there was no question in Shea's mind but that he was an arrogant fellow whose unshakable confidence in himself was probably matched only by his undeniable efficiency as a fighter. The tanned, worn face was clean-shaven except for a small mustache cut evenly above the upper lip. He had one of those faces that defied age; he looked neither old nor young, but somewhere in between. Yet his manner was youthful, and only the leathery skin and deep eyes revealed that he would never see forty years again. The dark hair seemed flecked slightly with bits of gray, though in the misty dawn light it was difficult to be certain. The face was broad and his features prominent, particularly the wide, friendly mouth. It was a handsome, beguiling type of face, but one that Shea instinctively felt was a carefully worn mask that hid the true nature of the man. The stranger stood easily before the uncertain Valeman, smiling and waiting for some indication of his attitude toward his rescuers, apparently unsure of what it might be.

"I want to thank you," Shea quickly sputtered. "It would have been all over for me if you hadn't . . ."

"Quite all right, quite all right. Rescuing people is not exactly our business, but those devils would cut you up for sport. I'm from the Southland myself, you know. Haven't been back in quite awhile, but it's my home nevertheless. You're from there, I can tell. One of the hill communities, maybe? Of course, you have Elven blood in you, too. . . ."

He trailed off abruptly, and for an instant Shea was certain that the man not only knew who he was, but what he was, and that he had stepped from the frying pan into the fire. A quick look back at the huge creature by the fallen Gnomes was necessary to reassure the youth that this was not a Skull Bearer.

"Who are you, friend, and where are you from?" the stranger demanded suddenly.

Shea gave him his name and explained that he was from Shady Vale. He told him that he had been exploring on a river to the south when his boat overturned, and he had been washed downstream and left unconscious on a bank where the band of Gnomes had found him. The fabricated tale was close enough to the truth so that the man might believe him, and Shea was not yet ready to trust strangers with the whole truth until he knew more than he knew about these two. He concluded his story by stating that the Gnomes had found him and decided to take him prisoner. The man looked at him for a long moment, an amused smile crossing his lips as he played idly with the leather pouch.

"Well, I doubt that you have told me the whole truth." He laughed shortly. "But I can't blame you. If I were in your place, I wouldn't tell me everything either. There will be time enough for the truth later. My name is Panamon Creel."

He extended his one broad hand which Shea

accepted and shook heartily. The stranger had a grip like iron and the Valeman winced involuntarily at the strong handshake. The man smiled faintly and released his grip, pointing to the dark giant behind them.

"My companion, Keltset. We've been together for almost two years now and I never had a better friend, although I could have wished for a more talkative one, perhaps. Keltset is a mute."

"What is he?" asked Shea curiously, watching the great figure lumber slowly about the little clearing.

"You certainly are a stranger to this part of the world." The other laughed in amusement. "Keltset is a Rock Troll. His home was in the Charnal Mountains until his people made an outcast of him. We're both outcasts in this thankless world, but life deals a different hand to each, I suppose. We have no choice in the matter."

"A Rock Troll," Shea repeated wonderingly. "I've never seen a Rock Troll before. I thought they were all savage creatures, almost like animals. How could you . . .?"

"Watch your tongue, friend," the stranger warned sharply. "Keltset doesn't like that kind of talk, and he is just sensitive enough to step on you for using it. Your problem is that you look at him and see a monster, a misshapen creature unlike you or me, and you wonder if he's dangerous. Then I tell you that he's a Rock Troll, and you're twice as certain he's more animal than man. Part of your limited education and lack of practical experience, I warrant. You should have traveled with me during the last few years—ha, you would have learned that even a friendly smile shows the teeth behind!"

Shea looked closely at the giant Rock Troll as Keltset bent idly over the fallen Gnomes, glancing about for anything he might have missed in his extensive search of their garments and packs. Keltset was basically

man-shaped, dressed in knee-length pants and a tunic
belted with a green cord. About the neck and wrists he
wore protective metal collars. His really different
feature was the strange, almost barklike skin that
covered the entire body, coloring it something on
the order of meat well done, but not yet charred.
The dark face was small featured, blunt and nondescript, with a heavy brow and deep-set eyes. The
extremities were the same as a man's except for
the hands. There was no little finger on either hand—
only a thumb and three stout, powerful fingers
nearly as large as the Valeman's small wrists.

"He doesn't look very tame to me," Shea declared
quietly.

"There you are! The perfect example of a hasty
opinion totally without foundation. Just because
Keltset doesn't look civilized and doesn't appear an
intelligent creature on the face of things, you label him
an animal. Shea, my boy, you may believe me when I
say that Keltset is a sensitive man with the same
feelings as you or I. Being a Troll in the Northland is
every bit as normal as being an Elf in the Westland and
so on! You and I are the strangers in this part of the
world."

Shea looked carefully at the broad, reassuring face,
the easy smile that seemed to come so naturally, and
he instinctively distrusted the man. These two were
more than travelers passing through this country who
had seen his plight and had come to his aid out of love
for their fellowman. They had stalked that Gnome
encampment with skill and cunning, and when
discovered, destroyed the entire Gnome patrol with
ruthless efficiency. As dangerous as the Rock Troll
appeared, Shea was certain that Panamon Creel was
twice as deadly.

"You are most certainly better informed on the
matter than I," admitted Shea, choosing his words
carefully. "Being from the Southland, and having

traveled little outside of its borders, I am unfamiliar
with all life in this region of the world. I owe you both
my life, and my thanks go to Keltset as well."

The dashing stranger smiled happily at the expression of gratitude, obviously pleased at the unexpected compliment.

"No thanks are necessary; I told you that," he
replied. "Come over here and sit with me for a
moment while we wait for Keltset to finish his task.
We must talk more about what brought you to this part
of the country. It's very dangerous in these parts, you
know, especially traveling alone."

He led the way over to the nearest tree where he sat
down wearily, resting his back against the slender
trunk. He still held the pouch with the Elfstones in his
one good hand, and Shea did not feel that he should
bring that subject up just yet. Hopefully, the stranger
would ask if they belonged to him, and he could
recover them and be on his way to Paranor. The others
in the company would be looking for him by now,
either along the eastern edge of the Dragon's Teeth or
farther up near Paranor.

"Why is Keltset searching those Gnomes?" the
youth asked after a moment's silence.

"Well, there might be some indication of where they
are from, where they were going. They might have
some food, which we could use right now. Who
knows, they might even have something valuable . . .?"

He trailed off sharply and looked questioningly at
Shea, one hand balancing the leather pouch with the
Elfstones before the Valeman's eyes, holding it like
bait before the hunted animal. Shea swallowed hard
and hesitated, realizing suddenly the man had sensed
all along that the stones belonged to him. He had to do
something quickly, or he would give himself away.

"They belong to me. The pouch and the stones are
mine."

"Are they now?" Panamon Creel grinned wolfishly at the youth. "I don't see your name on the pouch. How did you come by them?"

"They were given to me by my father," Shea lied quickly. "I've had them for years. I carry them everywhere—a sort of good-luck piece. When the Gnomes captured me, they searched me and took the pouch and the stones away. But they are mine."

The scarlet-clad rescuer smiled faintly and opened the pouch, pouring the stones into his open palm, holding the pouch with the wicked-looking pike. He hefted them and held them up to the light, admiring their brilliant blue glow. Then he turned back to Shea, raising his eyebrows quizzically.

"What you say may be true, but it may be that you stole them. They look rather valuable to be carrying around as a good-luck charm. I think I should keep them until I am satisfied that you are the true owner."

"But I have to go— I have to meet my friends," Shea sputtered desperately. "I can't stay with you until you're certain I own the stones!"

Panamon Creel rose slowly to his feet and smiled down, tucking the pouch and its contents into his tunic.

"That should pose no problem. Just tell me where I can reach you, and I'll bring the stones to you there after I've checked out your story. I'll be down in the Southland in several months or so."

Shea was absolutely beside himself with anger, and he leaped to his feet in a rage.

"Why, you're nothing but a thief, a common highwayman!" he stormed, bracing the other defiantly.

Panamon Creel erupted suddenly into a fit of uncontrollable laughter, holding his sides in mirth. He finally regained control of himself, shaking his head in disbelief as the tears rolled down his broad face. Shea looked on in astonishment, unable to see what was so humorous about the accusation. Even the huge Rock Troll had stopped momentarily and turned to look at them, his placid face dark and expressionless.

"Shea, I have to admire a man who speaks his mind," exclaimed the stranger, still chuckling in delight. "No one could accuse you of being unperceptive!"

The irate Valeman started to make a hasty retort and then caught himself quickly as the facts of the situation recalled themselves sharply in his puzzled mind. What were these two strange companions doing in this part of the Northland? Why had they bothered to rescue him in the first place? How had they even known he was a prisoner of the small band of Gnomes? He realized the truth in an instant; it had been so obvious that he had overlooked it.

"Panamon Creel, the kind rescuer!" he mocked bitterly. "No wonder you found my remark so amusing. You and your friend are exactly what I called you. You are thieves, robbers, highwaymen! It was the stones you were after all along! How low can you be . . .?"

"Watch your tongue, youngster!" The scarlet stranger leaped in front of him, brandishing the iron pike. The broad face was distorted in sudden hate, the constant smile suddenly villainous beneath the small mustache as anger flashed sharply in the dark eyes. "What you may think of us had best be kept to yourself. I've come a long way in this world, and no one has ever given me anything! Since this is so, I let no man take anything away!"

Shea backed away guardedly, terrified that he had foolishly overstepped his bounds with the unpredictable pair. Undoubtedly, his own rescue had been almost an afterthought on their part, their primary concern having been the theft of the Elfstones from the Gnome raiders. Panamon Creel was no one to fool around with, and a reckless tongue at this stage of the game could cost the Valeman his life. The tall thief stared balefully at his frightened captive a moment longer and then stepped back slowly, the angered features relaxing and a faint hint of his former good-naturedness returning in a quick smile.

"Why should we deny it, Keltset and I?" He swaggered backward and around a few paces, wheeling abruptly on Shea again. "We are wayfarers of fortune, he and I. Men who live by their wits and by their cunning—yet we are no different than other men, save in our methods. And perhaps our disdain for hypocrisy! All men are thieves in one way or another; we are simply the old-fashioned type, the honest type who are not ashamed of what they are."

"How did you happen on this camp?" Shea asked hesitantly, fearful of aggravating the temperamental man further.

"We came across their fire last night, just after sunset," the other replied easily, all traces of hostility gone. "I came down to the edge of the clearing for a closer look and saw my little yellow friends playing with those three blue gems. I saw you as well, all trussed up for delivery. So I decided to bring Keltset down and kill two birds with one stone—ah, ha, you see, I wasn't lying when I told you that I did not like to see a fellow Southlander in the hands of those devils!"

Shea nodded, happy to be free, but unsure whether he was better off now than when he had been a prisoner of the Gnomes.

"Quit worrying, friend." Panamon Creel recognized the unspoken fear. "We don't mean you any harm. We only want the stones—they'll bring a good price, and we can use the money. You're free to go back to where you came from anytime."

He turned away abruptly and walked over to the waiting Keltset, who was standing obediently next to a small pile of arms, clothing, and assorted articles of value that he had collected from the fallen Gnomes.

The huge frame of the Troll dwarfed the normally large figure of his companion; the dark, barklike skin made him appear somewhat like a gnarled tree casting its shadow over the scarlet-clad human. The two conversed briefly, Panamon speaking in low tones to his giant friend while the other replied with sign language and nods of his broad head. They turned to the pile of goods, which the man shuffled through quickly, casting most of the effects aside as useless junk. Shea watched momentarily, uncertain what he should do next. He had lost the stones, and without them he was virtually defenseless in this savage land. He had lost his companions in the Dragon's Teeth, the only ones who would stand with him, the only ones who could really help him recover the stones. He had come so far that it was unthinkable to turn back now, even if he thought he could do so safely. The others in the company depended on him, and he would never desert Flick and Menion whatever the dangers involved.

Panamon Creel cast a short glance over his shoulder to see if the Valeman had made any move to leave, and a faint trace of surprise registered on his handsome face when he saw the youth still standing where he had left him.

"What are you waiting for?"

Shea shook his head slowly, indicating that he wasn't quite sure. The tall thief watched him a moment longer, and then waved him over with a short smile.

"Come on and have a bite to eat, Shea," he invited. "The least we can do is feed you before you start back for the Southland."

Fifteen minutes later the three were seated around a small campfire, watching strips of dried beef warm enticingly in the smoking heat. The mute Keltset sat silently next to the little Valeman, the deep eyes fixed on the smoking meat, the huge hands clasped childlike as he squatted before the small fire. Shea had an uncontrollable urge to reach out and touch the strange creature, to feel the rough, barklike skin. The features of the Troll were indescribably bland even from this close distance. The Troll never moved while the meat was cooking, but sat absolutely still like some immobile rock that time and the ages had passed by without changing. Panamon Creel glanced over once and noticed Shea casting a watchful eye on the huge creature. He smiled broadly, one hand coming across to clap the startled Valeman on the shoulder.

"He won't bite—long as he gets fed! I keep telling you the same thing, but you don't listen. That's youth for you—wild and fancy free and no time for the old folks. Keltset is just like you and me, only bigger and quieter, which is what I like in a partner in this line of work. He does his job better than any man I've ever worked with, and I've worked with quite a few, I can tell you."

"He does what you tell him, I suppose?" Shea asked shortly.

"Sure he does, sure he does," came the quick answer; then the scarlet figure bent closer to the other's pale face, the iron pike coming up sharply in emphasis. "But don't get me wrong, boy, because I don't mean to say he's any kind of animal. He can think for himself when it's needed. But I was his friend when no one else would even look his way—no one! He's the strongest living thing I've ever seen. He could crush me without half thinking about it. But do you know what? I beat him, and now he follows me!"

He paused to judge the other's reaction, eyes wide with delight at the Valeman's startled look of disbelief. He laughed merrily and slapped his knee with exaggerated humor at the reaction he had drawn.

"I beat him with friendship, not strength! I respected him as a man, treated him as an equal, and for that cheap price, I won his loyalty. Hah, surprised you!"

Still chuckling at his thin attempt at humor, the thief lifted the strips of beef from the fire and held out the stick on which they rested to the silent Troll, who removed several and began munching hungrily. Shea helped himself slowly when offered and suddenly realized that he was starving. He couldn't even remember when he had eaten last, and gnawed ravenously at the tasty beef. Panamon Creel shook his head in amusement and offered the Valeman a second piece before taking one himself. The three ate in silence for several minutes before Shea ventured a further inquiry concerning his companions.

"What made you decide to become . . . robbers?" he asked guardedly.

Panamon Creel shot a quick look at him, arching his eyebrows in surprise.

"What do you care what the reasons were? Plan on writing our life story?" He paused and caught himself suddenly, smiling quickly at his own irritability. "There's no secret to it, Shea. I've never been much at making an honest living, never very good at common work. I was a wild kid, loved adventure, loved the outdoors—hated work. Then I lost my hand in an accident, and it became even harder to find work that would make me a comfortable living, get me what I wanted. I was deep in the Southland then, living in Talhan. I got in a little trouble and then a lot more. The next thing I knew I was roaming the four lands robbing for a living. The funny thing was I found myself so good at it that I couldn't quit. And I enjoyed it—all of it! So here I am, maybe not rich, but happy in the prime of my youth—or at least, my manhood."

"Don't you ever think about going back?" Shea persisted, unable to believe the man was being honest with himself. "Don't you ever think about a home and . . .?"

"Please, let's not be maudlin, lad!" The other roared in laughter. "Keep this up and you'll have me in tears, begging for forgiveness on my tired old knees!"

He broke into such an uncontrollable fit of raucous guffaws that even the silent Troll glanced over in quiet contemplation for a moment before returning to his meal. Shea felt a fierce flush of indignation spreading over his face and turned slowly back to his food, chewing the beef with grinding bites of anger and embarrassment. After several moments the laughter died into small chuckles, the thief shaking his head in amusement as he tried to swallow a little food. Then without further prompting, he continued his narration in a quieter tone of voice.

"Keltset has a different story than mine, I want to make that clear. I had no reason to take up this kind of life, but he had every reason. He was a mute since birth, and the Trolls don't like deformed people. Kind of a joke on them, I guess. So they made life pretty rough for him, kicked him around and beat him when they were mad at anything that they couldn't take their anger out on directly. He was the butt of every joke, but he never fought back because those people were all he had. Then he became big, so big and strong that the others were frightened of him. One night some of the young ones tried to hurt him, really hurt him so he might go away, even die. But it didn't work out quite as they expected. They pushed him too far, and he fought back and killed three of them. As a result he was driven from the village, and an outcast Troll has no home once outside his own tribe or whatever they are. So he wandered around on his own until I found him."

He smiled faintly and looked over at the massive, placid face bent intently over the last several strips of beef, eating hungrily.

"He knows what we're doing, though, and I guess he knows that it's not honest work. But he's like a child who's been so badly mistreated that he has no respect for other people because they never did him any good. Besides, we stay in this part of the country where there's only Gnomes and Dwarfs—a Troll's natural enemies. We steer away from the deep Northland and seldom get south very far. We do all right."

He returned to his piece of beef, munching absently as he stared into the dying embers of the fire, poking them with the toe of his leather boot, the sparks rising in small showers and fading into dust. Shea finished his own food without further comment, wondering what he could possibly do to regain the Elfstones, wishing that he knew where the other members of the company were now. Moments later the meal was ended, and the scarlet-clad thief rose abruptly, scattering the embers of the fire with a swift kick of his boot. The massive Rock Troll rose with him and stood quietly waiting for his friend to make the next move, his great bulk towering over Shea. The Valeman stood at last and watched Panamon Creel gather up several small trinkets and a few weapons to place in a sack which he handed to Keltset to carry. Then he turned to his small captive and nodded shortly.

"It's been interesting knowing you, Shea, and I wish you good luck. When I think of the little gems in this pouch, I shall think of you. Too bad it couldn't work out so that you could save them, but at least you saved your life—or rather, I saved it. Think of the stones as a gift for services rendered. It may make losing them easier. Now you'd better be moving along if you plan to reach the safety of the Southland in the next several days. The city of Varfleet lies just to the south and west, and you'll find help there. Just stick to the open country."

He turned to leave, motioning Keltset to follow and had taken several long strides before he glanced back over his shoulder. The Valeman had not moved, but was looking after the departing men as if in a trance. Panamon Creel shook his head in disgust and walked a bit farther, then stopped in annoyance and wheeled about, knowing the other was still standing immobile where he had left him.

"What's the matter with you?" he demanded

angrily. "Now don't tell me that you have any foolish ideas about trailing us and trying to get the gems back? That would spoil a very nice relationship because I'd have to cut your ears off—maybe worse! Now get going, get out of here!"

"You don't understand what those stones mean!" Shea shouted desperately.

"I think I do," came the quick reply. "They mean that for a while Keltset and I will be more than merely poverty-stricken thieves. It means we won't have to steal or beg for a handout for quite some time. It means money, Shea."

Desperately, Shea dashed after the two robbers, unable to think of anything but recovering the precious Elfstones. Panamon Creel watched him approach in astonishment, certain that the Valeman was crazed to the point of daring to attack them to regain possession of the three blue gems. Never had he encountered such a persistent fellow in all his days. He had spared the lad's life and graciously given him his freedom, but still it didn't seem to be enough to satisfy him. Shea came to a panting halt several yards away from the two tall figures, and the thought flashed through his mind that he had reached the end of his rope. Their patience was exhausted and now they would dispose of him without further consideration.

"I didn't tell you the truth before," he gasped finally. "I couldn't . . . I don't know it all myself. But the stones are very important—not only to me, but to everyone in all the lands. Even to you, Panamon."

The scarlet robber looked at him with a mixture of surprise and distrust, the smile gone, but the dark eyes still free of anger. He said nothing, but stood motionless waiting for the exasperated Valeman to speak further.

"You've got to believe me!" Shea exclaimed vehemently. "There's more to this than you realize."

"You certainly seem to believe so," admitted the

other flatly. He looked over at the huge Keltset, who stood at his elbow, and shrugged his incredulity at Shea's strange behavior. The Rock Troll made a quick move toward Shea, and the Valeman shrank back in terror; but Panamon Creel stopped his massive companion with a raised hand.

"Look, just grant me one favor," Shea pleaded desperately, grasping at any chance to gain a little time to think. "Take me north with you to Paranor."

"You must be mad!" cried the thief, aghast at the suggestion. "What possible reason could you have for going to that black fortress? It's extremely unfriendly country. You wouldn't last five minutes! Go home, boy. Go home to the Southland and leave me in peace."

"I've got to get to Paranor," the other insisted quickly. "That was where I was going when the Gnomes captured me. I have friends there—friends who will be searching for me. I have to join them at Paranor!"

"Paranor is an evil place, a spawning ground for Northland creatures even I would be afraid to run into!" Panamon said heatedly. "Besides, if you do have friends there, you probably plan to lead Keltset and me into some sort of trap so you can get your hands on the stones. That's your plan, isn't it? Forget it right now. Take my advice and turn south while you still can!"

"You're afraid, aren't you?" Shea sputtered angrily. "You're afraid of Paranor and afraid of my friends. You haven't the courage . . ."

He trailed off sharply as the deep fires of anger kindled explosively in the scarlet thief, the broad face flushing heatedly at the accusation. For a moment Panamon Creel stood motionless, his entire frame quivering with rage as he glared at the small Valeman. Shea stood his ground, gambling everything on this final plea.

"If you won't take me with you—just to Paranor—

then I'll go alone and take my chances," he promised. He watched their reaction for a moment and then continued: "All I'm asking is to be taken just to the borders of Paranor. I won't ask you to go beyond; I won't lead you into a trap."

Panamon Creel shook his head once again in disbelief, the anger gone from his eyes and a faint smile playing over his tightened lips as he turned from the Valeman to look at the giant Rock Troll. He shrugged shortly and nodded.

"Why should we be worried?" he mused mockingly. "It's your neck on the block. Come on along, Shea."

XIX

The three strange companions journeyed northward through the rough hill country until midday, when they paused for a quick meal and a few welcome minutes of rest. The terrain of the country had remained changeless during the morning's march, a consistently rugged series of elevations and depressions that made traveling extremely difficult. Even the powerful Keltset was forced to climb and scramble with the two men, unable to find sure footing or level ground that would permit him to walk upright. The land was not only humped and misshapen, but also rather barren and unfriendly in appearance. The hills were grass-covered and dotted with brush and small trees, but they conveyed a lonely and wild emptiness to the travelers that caused them to feel uneasy and moody. The grass was a tall, whiplike weed so strong that it slapped at the men's pants legs with stinging swipes. When crushed down by their heavy boots, it lay matted only seconds before springing back into place. Upon looking back in the direction from which they had come, Shea could not tell from the appearance of the land that anyone had passed that way. The scattered trees were gnarled and bent, filled with small leaves, but giving the overall impression that they were nature's stepchildren, stunted at birth and left to survive in this lonely country as best they could. There was no sign at all of any animal or bird life, and since dawn, the three men had neither seen nor heard another living creature.

Conversation was not lacking, however. In fact, there were several times when Shea wished that Panamon Creel would tire of his own voice for a few minutes. The tall thief carried on a steady conversation with his companions, with himself, and on occasion with no one in particular, for the entire morning. He talked about everything imaginable, including a good many things about which he seemed to know nothing. The one topic of conversation he scrupulously avoided was Shea. He acted as if the Valeman were merely a comrade in arms, a fellow thief with whom he could freely speak about his own wild experiences without fear of reprimand. But he meticulously avoided mentioning Shea's background, the Elfstones, or the purpose of this journey. Apparently he had concluded that the best way to handle the matter was to get the bothersome Valeman to Paranor as quickly as possible, reunite him with his friends, and without further delay continue on. Shea had no idea where the two had intended to travel before encountering him. Perhaps even they had been uncertain of their destination. He listened attentively while the thief rambled on, interjecting comments of his own when he thought it appropriate or the other seemed interested in his opinion. But for the most part, he concentrated on the journey and tried to decide the best way to go about recovering the stones. The situation was somewhat untenable no matter how he went about it; both the thieves and he knew that he was going to try to get the stones away from them. The only question remaining was the method he would try. Shea was convinced that the clever Panamon Creel would merely toy with him, give him enough rope to find out how he planned to get the stones, and then gaily haul in the noose about the Valeman's neck.

Occasionally while they walked and conversed,

Shea glanced at the silent Rock Troll, wondering what sort of person lay beneath the expressionless exterior. Panamon had said the Troll was a misfit, a creature spurned by his own people, a companion to the flashy thief because the man had proved to be his friend. This could be true, as trite as the tale seemed on first appraisal, but there was something about the Troll's bearing that caused the Valeman to question that he was an exile driven out by his own people. The Troll carried himself with undeniable dignity, head erect, the massive frame ramrod straight. He never spoke, apparently because he really was mute. Yet there was an intelligence in the deep-set eyes that led Shea to believe Keltset was far more complex than his companion had indicated. Just as with Allanon, Shea felt that Panamon Creel had not told him the whole truth. But unlike the Druid, the clever thief was probably a liar, and the youth felt that he should not believe anything he had been told. He was certain that he did not know the whole story behind Keltset, whether because Panamon had lied or because the man simply didn't know it. He was equally sure that the scarlet-clad adventurer, who had in one instant saved his life and in the next calmly stolen the precious Elfstones, was more than an ordinary road agent.

They finished the midday meal quickly. As Keltset packed up their cooking implements, Panamon explained to Shea that they were not far from the Jannisson Pass at the northern borders of the hill country. Once through this pass, they would cross the Plains of Streleheim to the west to reach Paranor. There they would part ways, the thief declared pointedly, and Shea could meet with his friends or go to the Druids' Keep as he saw fit. The Valeman nodded his understanding, catching the hint of eagerness in the other's voice, knowing that they expected him to make his move to recover the stones soon. He said nothing, however, and gave no indication that he suspected they were baiting him, but picked up what little gear he still had, to continue the journey. The three men wound their way slowly through the foothills toward the low mountains that had appeared ahead. Shea was certain the distant mountains on his left were an extension of the formidable Dragon's Teeth, but this new set of mountains appeared to be a completely different range, and it was between the two chains that the Jannisson Pass must lie. They were very near the Northland now, and for the Valeman there was no turning back.

Panamon Creel had launched into another in the seemingly never-ending series of tales about his adventures. Strangely, he seldom mentioned Keltset, another indication to Shea that the thief knew less about the Rock Troll than he professed. It was beginning to appear to Shea that the giant Troll was as much a mystery to his companion as he was to the Valeman. If they had lived together as thieves for two years, as Panamon had claimed, then some of the tales certainly ought to include Keltset. Moreover, while at first it had seemed to Shea that the Troll was a doglike follower of the crimson thief, it was beginning to appear on closer observation that he traveled with the man for entirely different reasons. It was not a conclusion Shea arrived at so much by listening to Panamon as from observing the mute conduct of the Troll. Shea was mystified by his proud bearing and detached attitude. Keltset had been swift and deadly in his extermination of the Gnome hunting party, but in retrospect it seemed almost as if he had done it because it had to be done—not to please his companion or to gain possession of the stones. Shea found it difficult to surmise who Keltset might be, but he was certain that he was not a downtrodden, shunned misfit who had been driven from his people as a hated outcast.

It was a particularly warm day, and Shea was beginning to perspire freely. The terrain had failed to level off at all, and traversing the stubborn, winding hills was laborious and slow. Panamon Creel talked on all the while, laughing and joking with Shea as if they were old friends, companions on the road to high adventure. He told him about the four lands; he had traveled them all, seen their people, studied their ways of life. Shea thought he seemed a bit vague about the Westland, and seriously doubted that the thief had learned much about the Elven people, but decided it would be unwise to pursue the matter. He listened dutifully to the tales of the women Panamon had met in his travels, including a standard narration about a beautiful king's daughter whom he had saved and fallen in love with, only to lose her when her father stepped between them and spirited her away to distant lands. The Valeman sighed with exaggerated pity, inwardly chuckling at the tale, as the anguished thief ended by confiding that to this day he continued his search for her. Shea remarked that he hoped Panamon would find her and she might persuade him to give up this way of life. The man looked at him sharply, studying the serious face, and for a few moments he was silent as he mulled the prospect over.

They reached the Jannisson Pass about two hours later. The pass was formed by a break at the meeting of the two mountain chains, a wide, easily accessible passage leading to the broad plainland beyond. The great mountain range coming up from the south was an extension of the towering Dragon's Teeth, but the northern range was unfamiliar to Shea. He knew that the Charnal Mountains, the home of the huge Rock Trolls, lay somewhere to the north of them, and this second range could be a southerly extension. Those desolate and relatively unexplored peaks had for centuries remained a vast wilderness inhabited solely by the ferocious and warlike Troll colonies. While the

Rock Trolls were the largest of that breed, there were several other types of Trolls living in that sector of the Northland. If Keltset were any example of the Rock Trolls, then Shea imagined they must be a more intelligent people than Southlanders believed. It seemed somehow strange that his own countrymen should be so misinformed about another race inhabiting the same world. Even the textbooks he had studied when he was younger had described the Troll nations as ignorant and uncivilized.

Panamon called a sudden halt at the entrance to the wide pass and walked ahead several yards, peering cautiously up into the high slopes to either side, obviously wary of what might be waiting there. After several minutes' perusal, he ordered the stolid Keltset to investigate the pass to be certain it was safe for them to proceed. Quickly the giant Troll lumbered forward and was soon lost between the hills and rocks. Panamon suggested Shea sit down to wait, smiling that unforgivably smug smile that indicated the thief thought he was incredibly clever to take this added precaution to avoid any traps that friends of Shea might have arranged for him. While he felt safe enough keeping Shea with him, being reasonably certain that Shea posed no threat by himself, he was concerned that the Valeman might have friends powerful enough to cause trouble if they found the opportunity. While waiting for his companion to return, the garrulous adventurer decided to launch into still another wild tale of his hair-raising life as a road agent. Shea found this one, like the others, incredible and obviously exaggerated. Panamon seemed to enjoy telling these stories far more than anyone could possibly enjoy listening, as if each were the very first and not the five hundredth. Shea endured the tale in stoic silence, trying to look interested as he thought about what lay ahead. They had to be quite close to the borders of Paranor now, and once they reached that point, he would be left on his own. He would have to find his friends quickly if he expected to stay alive in this region of the country. The Warlock Lord and his hunters would be searching tirelessly for any trace of him, and if they reached him before he gained the protection of Allanon and the company, his death was certain. Still, it was possible that by this time they had taken possession of the Druid's Keep and seized the precious Sword of Shannara. Perhaps the victory was already won.

Keltset appeared suddenly in the pass and signaled for them to come forward. They hastened to his side and together the three proceeded. There was little cover in the Jannisson Pass that would hide an ambush party, and it was apparent that there would be no trouble at this point. There were a few stray clumps of boulders and a few narrow hillocks, but none of these was big enough to hide more than one or two men. The pass was quite long, and it took the three travelers almost an hour to reach the other end. But it was a pleasant walk and the time passed quickly. When they reached the northern entrance, they could see plains stretching northward and beyond these still another mountain range which appeared to run toward the west. The travelers marched out of the pass onto the smooth floor of the plains which were set in a pocket, surrounded on three sides in horseshoe fashion by mountains and forests and opening out to the west. The plains were sparsely covered with a thin, pale green grass which grew in shaggy tufts over the dry earthen land. There were small bushes, all only knee-high on Shea, and these were bent and gaunt in appearance. Apparently, even in the spring, these plains were never very green, and little life existed in the lonely expanse of country beyond Paranor.

Shea knew they were nearing their destination when Panamon turned the little group westward,

keeping their line of march several hundred yards
north of the forest and mountain bordering to their
left, careful to protect against any surprise assaults.
When the Valeman asked the scarlet-clad leader
where they were in relation to Paranor, the thief only
smiled slyly and assured him they were getting closer
all the time. Further questioning was pointless, and
the youth resigned himself to being kept in the dark as
to where they were until the other decided he was
ready to let his uninvited guest go on alone. Instead,
Shea turned his attention to the plains ahead, their
barren vastness awesome and fascinating to the
Southlander. It was an entirely new world for him,
and while he was understandably afraid for his life, he
was determined that he would miss nothing. This was
the fabulous odyssey Flick and he had always
dreamed they would someday make, and while its
end might find them both dead and forgotten, the
quest a failure and the Sword lost, still he would see it
all in the time remaining to him.

By midafternoon, the three were sweating and
tempers were growing short in the steady heat of the
open plainlands. Keltset walked slightly apart from
the other two, his pace steady and unwavering, his
rough face expressionless, his eyes dark and unfriendly in the hot, white sunlight. Panamon had
stopped talking and was interested only in completing
the day's march and being rid of Shea, whom he had
begun to regard as an unnecessary burden. Shea was
tired and sore, his limited stamina greatly sapped by
the two long days of constant travel. The three were
walking right into the face of the burning sun,
unprotected and unshaded on the open plains, their
eyes squinting sharply in the piercing light. It became
increasingly harder to distinguish the land ahead as
the sun moved closer toward the western horizon, and
after a while Shea gave up trying, relying on
Panamon's skill to get them to Paranor. The travelers

were drawing closer to the end of the mountain range northward on their right, and it appeared that where the mountain peaks ceased the plains opened into an endless expanse. It was so vast that Shea could see the lateral line of the horizon where the sky dropped to the parched earth. When he asked at last if these were the Streleheim Plains, Panamon gave no immediate answer, but after a few moments' consideration nodded shortly.

Nothing further was said about their present location or Panamon Creel's unspoken plans for Shea. They passed out of the horseshoe valley onto the eastern borders of the Streleheim Plains, a wide, flat expanse extending north and west. The land immediately before them, running parallel to the cliff face and forest land on their left, was surprisingly hilly. It was not a change in terrain that could be distinguished by one still in the valley, but became distinct only when one was nearly on top of it. There were even groves of small trees and dense stretches of brush farther on, and . . . something else, something foreign to the land. All three travelers spotted it at the same moment, and Panamon signaled a sharp halt, peering suspiciously into the distance. Shea squinted into the strong light of the afternoon sun, shading his eyes with one hand. He saw a series of strange poles set in the earth, and scattered about for several hundred yards in every direction were heaps of colored cloth and bits of shining metal or glass. He could just barely make out the movement of a number of small, black objects amid the cloth and debris. Finally Panamon called out loudly to whomever might be up ahead of them. To their shock, there was a flurried rushing of raven-black wings, accompanied by a frightful shrieking of disrupted scavengers as the black objects turned suddenly into great vultures rising slowly and reluctantly as they scattered into the brilliant sunlight. Panamon and Shea stood rooted in

mute astonishment as the giant Keltset moved several
yards closer and peered carefully ahead. A moment
later, he wheeled about and motioned sharply to his
watchful comrade. The scarlet thief nodded soberly.

"There's been a battle of some sort," he announced
curtly. "Those are dead men up there!"

The three moved forward toward the grisly scene of
battle. Shea hung back slightly, suddenly afraid that
the still, tattered forms might be his friends. The
strange poles became distinct after the men had gone
only several yards; they were lances and standards of
battle. The bright bits of light were the blades of
swords and knives, some discarded by fleeing men,
others still clenched by the dead hands of their fallen
owners. The cloth heaps became men, their still, blood-
soaked forms sprawled in death, baking slowly in the
white heat of the sun. Shea choked as the smell of
death struck his nostrils for the first time and his ears
caught the sound of flies buzzing busily about the
human carcasses. Panamon looked back and smiled
grimly. He knew that the Valeman had never before
seen death at close range, and it would be a lesson he
would not forget.

Shea fought the sickening feeling creeping through
his stomach and forced himself to move with the other
two onto the battleground. Several hundred bodies
lay on the little stretch of rolling land, sprawled
carelessly in death. There was no movement anywhere; they were all dead. From the random scattering of the bodies and the lack of any single concentration of men, Panamon quickly concluded in his own
mind that it had been a long, bitter struggle to the
death—no quarter asked and none given. He recognized the Gnome standards immediately, and the
gnarled yellow bodies were easily distinguishable. But
it was not until he had looked closely at several
huddled forms that he realized that the opposing force
had been composed of Elven warriors.

Finally Panamon halted in the middle of the slain men, uncertain what he should do next. Shea could only stare in horror at the carnage, his shocked gaze moving robotlike from one dead face to the next, from Gnome to Elf, from the raw, open wounds to the bloodied ground. At that moment, he knew what death really meant and he was afraid. There was no adventure in it, no sense of purpose or choice, nothing but a sickening disgust and shock. All those men had died for some senseless reason, died perhaps without ever knowing exactly what they had fought to accomplish. Nothing was worth such terrible slaughter—nothing.

A sudden movement by Keltset snapped his attention back to his companions, and he saw the Troll pick up a fallen standard, its pennant torn and bloodied, the pole broken in half. The insignia on the pennant was a crown seated over a spreading tree surrounded by a wreath of boughs. Keltset seemed very excited and gestured vigorously to Panamon. The other frowned sharply and hurriedly made a quick study of the faces of the nearby bodies, working his way outward from his companions in a widening circle. Keltset looked around anxiously, suddenly stopping as his deep-set eyes came to rest on Shea, apparently fascinated by something he saw in the little Valeman's face. A moment later Panamon was back at his side, an unusually worried expression clouding his broad features.

"We've got real trouble here, friend Shea," he announced solemnly, resting his hands determinedly on his hips and planting his feet. "That standard is the banner of the royal Elven house of Elessedil—the personal staff of Eventine. I can't find his body among the dead, but that doesn't make me feel any easier. If anything has happened to the Elven king, it could start a war of unbelievable proportions. The whole country will go up in smoke!"

"Eventine!" exclaimed Shea fearfully. "He was guarding the northern borders of Paranor in case . . ."

He caught himself abruptly, afraid that he had given himself away, but Panamon Creel was still talking and apparently hadn't heard.

"It doesn't make any sense—Gnomes and Elves fighting out here in the middle of nowhere. What would bring Eventine this far away from his own land? They must have been fighting for something. I can't under . . ." He paused with the thought left hanging, unspoken in the silence. Suddenly he stared at Shea.

"What did you just say? What was that about Eventine?"

"Nothing," the Valeman stammered fearfully. "I didn't say . . ."

The tall thief snatched the hapless Valeman by his tunic front, dragging him close and raising him bodily off the ground, until their faces were only inches away.

"Don't try to be clever, little man!" The flushed, angered face seemed gigantic and the fierce eyes were narrowed with suspicion. "You know something about all of this—now talk. All along I've suspected you knew a lot more than you were telling about those stones and the reason those Gnomes bothered to take you prisoner. Now your time for fooling around is over. Out with it!"

But Shea would never know what his response would have been. As he hung in midair, struggling violently in the powerful thief's ironhanded grip, a huge black shadow suddenly fell over them and then passed on in a great rustling of wings as a monstrous shape descended from the late afternoon skies. Its giant, black bulk swooped slowly, gracefully to the battlefield only yards away from them, and in horror Shea felt the familiar chilling fear surge through him at the sight of its deathlike form. Panamon Creel, still angered, but now bewildered by the sudden appearance of this creature, lowered Shea to the earth abruptly and turned to face the strange newcomer. Shea stood on shaking legs, his blood turned to ice, his senses raw and distorted with terror, the last vestiges of his courage gone. The creature was one of the dreaded Skull Bearers of the Warlock Lord! There was no time left to run; they had found him at last.

The cruel red eyes of the creature passed quickly over the giant Troll, who had remained motionless to one side, stopped for a moment on the scarlet thief, then passed on to the little Valeman, burning into him, probing his scattered thoughts. Panamon Creel, while still bewildered at the sight of this winged monster, was nevertheless not in the least panicked. He turned fully about to face the evil being, the broad, devilish grin spreading slowly over his flushed countenance as he raised one arm and pointed in warning.

"Whatever manner of creature you might be, keep your distance," he warned sharply. "My concern is with this man alone, and not . . ."

The burning eyes fastened hatefully on him, and suddenly he was unable to continue. He stared at the black creature in shock and surprise.

"Where is the Sword, mortal?" the voice rasped menacingly. "I can sense its presence. Give it to me!"

Panamon Creel stared uncomprehendingly at the dark speaker for a long moment, then shot a sharp look at the frightened face of Shea. For the first time, he realized that for some unknown reason this terrible creature was the Valeman's enemy. It was a dangerous moment.

"It is useless to deny you have it!" The grating voice pierced the distressed mind of the thief. "I know it is here among you, and I must have it. It is useless to fight me. The battle is over for you. The last heir to the Sword has long since been taken and destroyed. You must give me the Sword!"

For once, Panamon Creel was speechless. He had

no idea what the huge black creature was talking about, but he realized that there was no point in trying to tell him that. The winged monster was determined to finish them all anyway, and the time for any explanations was past. The tall thief raised his left hand and stroked the tips of his small mustache with the deadly pike. He smiled bravely, looking aside fleetingly at the motionless form of his giant companion. They both knew instinctively that this would be a battle to the death.

"Do not be foolish, mortals!" The command rang out in a sharp hiss. "I care nothing for you—only the Sword. I can destroy you easily—even in daylight."

Suddenly Shea saw a glimmer of hope. Allanon had once said that the power of the Skull Bearers faded with the light of day. Perhaps they were not invincible while the sun shone. Perhaps the two battle-hardened thieves would have a chance. But how could they expect to destroy something that was not mortal, but only the spirit of a dead soul, a wraith of deathless existence embodied in physical form? For a few moments no one moved, and then abruptly the creature took a step forward. Immediately Panamon Creel's good right hand unsheathed the broadsword at his side in a lightninglike motion and the thief crouched for the attack. The great form of Keltset moved forward a few paces at the same instant, changing from a motionless statue into an iron-muscled fighting machine, the heavy mace in one hand, the thick legs braced for the assault. The Skull Bearer hesitated and his burning eyes fastened momentarily on the face of the approaching Rock Troll, studying the huge being closely for the first time. Then the crimson eyes went wide in astonishment.

"Keltset!"

Only an instant remained to ponder how the Bearer could have known the mute giant—a split second of astonished disbelief in the creature's eyes, mirroring similar incomprehension in the eyes of Panamon Creel, and then the huge Troll attacked with blinding speed. The mace hurtled through the air, powered by Keltset's massive right arm, striking the black Skull creature directly in the chest with a sickening crunch. Panamon was already leaping forward, pike and sword blade sweeping downward toward the Bearer's chest and neck. But the deadly Northland creature was not to be so easily finished. Recovering from the blow dealt by the mace, it parried Panamon's weapons with one clawed hand, knocking the man sprawling. In the next instant the burning eyes began to smolder, and bolts of searing red light shot out at the dazed thief. He lunged quickly to one side, and the bolts caught him only a glancing blow, singeing his scarlet tunic and knocking him down again. Before the attacker could find his target for a second assault, the huge form of Keltset was upon him, bearing him heavily to the earth. Even the comparatively large size of the winged monster was dwarfed in comparison to the massive Rock Troll as the two rolled and battled over the bloodied ground. Panamon was still on his knees, shaking his dazed head, trying to regain his senses. Realizing that he had to do something, Shea rushed to the fallen thief and grabbed one arm in desperation.

"The stones!" he begged wildly. "Give me the stones, and I can help!"

The battered face turned up to him for a moment, and then the familiar look of anger crept into his eyes, and he shoved the Valeman rudely away.

"Shut up and keep out of this," he roared, climbing unsteadily to his feet. "No tricks now, friend. Just stay put!"

Retrieving his fallen sword, he rushed to the aid of his giant companion, trying vainly to strike a solid blow at the caped Skull Bearer. For long minutes the

three struggled fiercely back and forth across the
rolling battleground, thrashing madly over the still
bodies of the fallen Gnomes and Elves. Panamon was
not nearly as strong as the other two, but he was quick
and extremely durable, bouncing away from the blows
struck at him, dancing nimbly aside when the
Northlander sent the reddish bolts flashing his way.
The incredible strength of Keltset was proving to be a
match for even the spirit powers of the Skull creature,
and the evil being was becoming desperate. The rough
Troll skin was singed and burned in a dozen places
from the fire that struck it, but the giant merely
shrugged the powerful jolts aside and fought on. Shea
desperately wanted to help, but he was dwarfed by
their power and size, and his weapons were ridicu-
lously inadequate. If only he could get the stones . . .

At last the two mortals began to tire in the face of the
repeated, inexhaustible assaults from the spirit creature. Their blows were not having any lasting effect
and they began slowly to realize that human strength
alone could not destroy the attacker. They were losing
the battle. Suddenly the valiant Keltset stumbled and
fell to one knee. Instantly the Skull creature lashed out
with one clawed limb, slashing the unprotected Troll
from neck to waist, knocking him backward to the
earth. Panamon cried out in fury and struck wildly at
the spirit creature, but his blows were parried, and in
his haste he dropped his guard and left himself
momentarily vulnerable. The emissary of the Warlock
Lord struck viciously, one arm knocking aside the
thief's piked hand as the narrowed eyes sent their fiery
blasts directly into the man's chest. The deadly bolts
seared the hapless Panamon Creel about the face and
arms, and burned right through the chest covering
with such force that he was knocked unconscious. The
Skull Bearer would have finished him then had not
Shea, disregarding his own fears at the other's grave
peril, thrown a piece of a lance at the attacker's

unprotected head, striking it full in the evil face. The clawed hands came up too late to ward off the painful blow, and they gripped the blackened visage in fury, trying angrily to recover. Panamon was still lying motionless on the ground, but the durable Keltset was back on his feet, seizing the Skull creature in an agonizing headlock, desperately trying to crush the life out of it.

There were only seconds left to act before the deadly monster was free again. Shea rushed to Panamon Creel's side, shouting at him to get up. The battered figure responded with inhuman courage, but fell back a moment later, blinded and exhausted. Shea pleaded with him, shaking him into consciousness, begging him to give him the stones. Only the stones could help now, the Valeman cried desperately! They were the only chance for survival! He glanced back at the two dark combatants, and to his horror he saw that Keltset was slowly losing his hold on the spirit creature. In seconds the evil being would be free, and they would all be finished. Then abruptly the little leather pouch was thrust into his hand by the bloodied fist of Panamon, and he had the precious stones once more.

Leaping clear of the fallen thief, the little Valeman tore open the drawstrings to the leather pouch and emptied the three blue stones into his open hand. At that moment the Skull Bearer broke free from Keltset's powerful grip and turned to finish the battle. Shea yelled wildly, holding the stones stretched forth toward the attacker, praying for their strange power to aid him now. The blinding blue glow spread outward just as the creature turned. Too late the Skull Bearer saw the heir to Shannara bring the power of the Elfstones to life. Too late he focused his burning eyes on the Valeman, the red bolts of searing fire flashing menacingly. The great blue light blocked and shattered the attack, slicing through in a powerful, blazing surge of energy to reach the crouched black figure beyond. The light struck the immobile Skull creature with a sharp crackle, holding him fast and draining the dark spirit from the mortal shell as the creature writhed in agony and screamed its loathing of the power destroying it. Keltset came to his feet in a bound, picked up a fallen lance, reared back his giant frame, the arms extended high, and with a lunge shoved the spear completely through the creature's caped back. The Northlander shuddered horribly, twisting almost completely about with one final shriek, and then slid slowly to the earth, the black body crumbling into dust as it sank. In another second it was gone, and only a small pile of black ashes remained. Shea stood motionless, the stones extended, their piercing blue light still concentrated on the dust. Then the dust stirred in still another shudder and from its midst rose a whipish black cloud that shot upward like a thin stream of smoke and disappeared into the air. The blue light abruptly ceased and the battle was ended, the three mortals positioned like statues in the silence and emptiness of the bloodied ground.

For long seconds no one moved, still stunned by the sudden finality of the violent combat. Shea and Keltset stood staring at the small pile of black ashes as if waiting for it to come back to life. Panamon Creel lay wearily on the earth to one side, propped up on one elbow, his singed eyes trying vainly to grasp what had just transpired. Finally Keltset stepped forward gingerly and prodded the ashes of the Skull Bearer with one foot, stirring them about to see if anything had been missed. Shea watched quietly, mechanically replacing the three Elfstones in the leather pouch and dropping it back into the front of his tunic. Remembering Panamon, he turned quickly to check on the injured thief, but the durable Southlander was already struggling to a sitting position, his deep brown eyes fixed wonderingly on the Valeman. Keltset hastened over and gently raised his companion to his feet. The man was burned and cut, his face and bared chest blackened and raw in places, but nothing seemed to be broken. He stared at Keltset as well for a moment, then shrugged off the other's strong arm and tottered over to a waiting Shea.

"I was right about you after all," he growled, breathing heavily and shaking his broad head. "You did know a lot more than you were telling—especially about those stones. Why didn't you tell me the truth from the start?"

"You wouldn't listen," Shea alibied shortly. "Besides, you didn't tell me the truth about yourself—or Keltset either." He paused to glance sharply at the massive Troll. "I don't think you know very much about him."

The battered face stared at the Valeman incredulously, then the broad smile slowly spread over his handsome features. It was as if the scarlet thief suddenly saw new humor in the whole situation, but Shea thought he caught a hint of grudging respect in the dark eyes for his candid evaluation.

"You may be right. I'm beginning to think I don't know anything about him." The smile turned into a hearty laugh, and the thief looked sharply at the rough, expressionless face of the great Rock Troll. Then he looked back to Shea.

"You saved our lives, Shea, and that's a debt we can never repay. But I'll start by saying that the stones are yours to keep. I'll never argue that point again. More than that, you have my promise that should the need ever arise, my sword and my skill, such as it is, shall be in your service at a word."

He paused wearily to catch his breath, still shaken badly from the blows he had received. Shea stepped hurriedly forward to offer his aid, but the tall thief held him away, shaking his head negatively.

"I assume that we shall be great friends, Shea," he murmured seriously. "Still, we cannot be friends when we hide things from each other. I think you owe me some sort of explanation about those stones, about that creature that nearly put an end to my illustrious career, and about this confounded sword I've never seen. In return, I shall enlighten you on a few, ah, misunderstandings concerning Keltset and myself. Do you agree?"

Shea frowned at him suspiciously, trying to read behind the battered visage into the man himself. Finally he nodded affirmatively and even managed a short smile.

"Good for you, Shea," Panamon commended heartily, clapping the Valeman on his slender shoulder. A second later, the tall thief had collapsed, weakened by loss of blood and dizzy from trying to move about too quickly. The other two rushed to his side, and despite protestations that he was quite all right, forced him to remain in a supine position while the giant Keltset cleaned his face with a wetted cloth like any mother would a small, injured child. Shea was amazed at the Troll's quick change from a nearly indestructible fighting machine to a gentle, concerned nurse. There was something very extraordinary about him, and Shea was certain that in some strange way Keltset was connected with the Warlock Lord and the quest for the Sword of Shannara. It had been no accident that the Skull Bearer had known the Rock Troll. The two had encountered each other before—and had not parted as friends.

Panamon was not unconscious, but it was clear that he was not yet in any condition to travel very far on his own legs. He tried vainly to rise several times, but the watchful Keltset gently pushed him back. The irascible thief swore vehemently and demanded to be let to his feet, all to no avail. Finally, he realized that he was getting nowhere and asked that he be taken out of the sun to rest for a while. Shea looked around the barren plainland and quickly concluded they would find no shelter there. The only shade within reasonable walking distance was to the south—the forests surrounding the Druids' Keep within the borders of Paranor. Panamon had previously indicated that he would not go anywhere near Paranor, but the decision was no longer entirely his to make. Shea pointed to the forests to the south, less than a mile's walk, and Keltset nodded his agreement. The injured man saw what Shea was suggesting and cried out furiously that he would not be carried into those forests even if it meant he would die where he lay. Shea tried to reason with him, assuring him that they would face no danger from his companions if by chance they managed to find them, but the thief seemed more disturbed by the strange rumors he had heard concerning Paranor. Shea had to laugh at this, recalling Panamon's boasts of all the past hair-raising perils he had survived. While the two men conversed, Keltset had risen slowly to his feet and was scanning the land about them, apparently in idle speculation. The two were still talking when he bent down to them and gave a sharp signal to Panamon. The thief started, the color drained from his face as he nodded shortly. Shea started to rise in apprehension, but the thief's strong hand held him down.

"Keltset has just spotted something moving in the brush to the south of us. He can't tell from here what it is; it's just on the fringes of this battlefield, about halfway between us and the forest."

Shea immediately turned ashen.

"Get your stones ready in case we need them," the other ordered quietly, an unmistakable indication that he thought it might be a second Skull Bearer lurking in the cover of the brush, waiting for sundown and a chance to catch them off guard.

"What are we going to do?" Shea asked fearfully, clutching the little pouch.

"Get him before he gets us—what other choice do

we have?" Panamon declared irritably, motioning to Keltset to pick him up.

The obedient giant bent down and carefully lifted Panamon in the cradle of his two massive arms. Shea retrieved the wounded thief's fallen broadsword and followed the slowly departing form of Keltset, who proceeded southward with relaxed, easy strides. Panamon talked steadily as they walked, calling on Shea to hurry, chiding Keltset on being too rough in his duty as bearer of the wounded. Shea could not bring himself to be quite so relaxed, and was content with bringing up the rear, glancing uneasily from side to side as they moved southward, searching vainly for some sign of movement that might indicate where the danger lay. In his right hand he clutched tightly the leather pouch with the invaluable Elfstones, their only weapon against the power of the Warlock Lord. They were about a hundred yards from the scene of their battle with the Skull Bearer when Panamon called a sudden halt, complaining bitterly of an injured shoulder. Gently, Keltset lowered his burden to the ground and stood up.

"My shoulder is never going to stand such wanton disregard of its tissues and bones," growled Panamon Creel irritably, and looked meaningfully at Shea.

Instantly the Valeman knew that this was the place, and his hands shook as he loosened the strings on the pouch and withdrew the Elfstones. A moment later Keltset stood leisurely beside the still-muttering thief, the great mace held loosely in one hand. Shea glanced around hastily, his eyes coming to rest directly on the huge clump of brush immediately to the left of the other two. His heart jumped to his throat as one section of the brush moved ever so slightly.

Then Keltset made his move. With a sharp lunge he whirled about, leaped into the center of the brush, and was lost from view.

XX

hat followed was complete pandemonium. A terrible high-pitched shriek sounded from the bushes and the entire mass of shrubbery shook violently. Panamon struggled wildly to his knees, calling to Shea to throw him the great broadsword which the fear-struck Valeman still clutched tightly in his left hand. Shea stood frozen in place, his other hand clasping the powerful Elfstones in readiness, waiting in terror for the assault that surely would come from the unknown creature in the brush. Panamon finally fell back in hopeless exhaustion, unable to get Shea's attention and incapable of walking over to where he stood. There were a few more cries from the heavy bushes, some vague thrashing within, and then silence. A moment later the durable Keltset emerged, the heavy mace still held in one lowered hand. In the other was the squirming, twisting body of a Gnome, his neck held fast in the iron grip of the Troll. The gnarled yellow body appeared childlike next to the huge frame of its captor, the arms and legs moving all at once in different directions like snakes caught by their tails. The Gnome was one of the familiar hunters, clothed in a leather tunic, hunting boots, and sword belt. The sword was missing, and Shea correctly surmised that the struggle in the bushes involved the disarming of the little fellow. Keltset came over to Panamon, who had managed to raise himself back up to a sitting position, and dutifully held forth the struggling captive for inspection.

"Let me go, let me go, curse you!" the thrashing Gnome cried venomously. "You have no right! I have done nothing—I'm not even armed, I tell you. Let me go!"

Panamon Creel looked at the little creature humorously, shaking his head in relief. Finally, as the Gnome continued to plead, the thief burst out laughing.

"What a terrible foe, Keltset! Why, he might have destroyed us all had you not captured him. That must have been a fearful struggle! Ha, ha, I can't believe it. And we were afraid of another of those winged black monsters!"

Shea was not quite so inclined to be amused by the incident, recalling clearly the close calls the company had already had with the little yellow creatures while traveling through the Anar. They were dangerous and crafty—a foe whom he did not regard as harmless. Panamon looked over and, upon spying the serious countenance, ceased his chiding of the captive and turned his attention to Shea.

"Do not be angry, Shea. It's more habit than stupidity when I laugh at these things. I laugh at them to stay a sane man. But enough of all this. What do we do with our little friend, eh?"

The Gnome stared fearfully at the no longer laughing man, the large eyes wide as the insistent voice died away to a low whine.

"Please, let me go," he begged subserviently. "I will go away and say nothing to anyone about you. I will do whatever you say, good friends. Just let me go."

Keltset still held the hapless Gnome by the scruff of his neck about a foot off the ground in front of Shea and Panamon, and the little fellow was beginning to choke violently from the tight clasp. Seeing the prisoner's plight, Panamon at last motioned for the

Rock Troll to lower his victim to the ground and release his grip. Pausing for a moment's serious contemplation of the Gnome's eager plea, the thief looked over at Shea and winked quickly, turning back to the captive sharply and snapping the pike at the end of his left arm up to the yellow throat.

"I can see no reason for permitting you to live, let alone go free, Gnome," he announced menacingly. "I think it would be best for all concerned if I just cut your throat right here and now. Then none of us would have to worry about you further."

Shea did not believe the thief was serious, but his voice sounded as if he were in deadly earnest. The terrified Gnome gulped and held forth his hands in a final desperate cry for mercy. He whined and cried so that Shea finally became almost embarrassed for him. Panamon made no move, but only sat there staring into the unfortunate fellow's horror-stricken face.

"No, no, I beg you, don't kill me," the frantic Gnome pleaded, his wide green eyes shifting from one face to the next. "Please, please let me live—I can be of use to you—I can help! I can tell you about the Sword of Shannara! I can even get it for you."

Shea started involuntarily at the unexpected mention of the Sword, and he placed a restraining hand on Panamon's wide shoulder.

"So you can tell us about the Sword, can you?" The icy voice of the thief sounded only slightly interested, and he ignored Shea completely. "What can you tell us?"

The wiry yellow frame relaxed slightly, and the eyes returned to normal size, shifting about eagerly, seizing on any chance to stay alive. Yet Shea saw something else there, something he could not quite define. It was almost a fervid cunning, revealed as the Gnome momentarily relaxed his carefully masked feelings. A second later it was gone, replaced by a look of total subjugation and helplessness.

"I can lead you to the Sword if you wish," he whispered harshly as if he were afraid someone would hear. "I can take you to where it is—if you let me live!"

Panamon moved the sharp iron tip of his piked hand back from the throat of the cringing Gnome, leaving just a small trace of blood on the yellow neck. Keltset had not moved and gave no indication that he had any interest in what was happening. Shea wanted to warn Panamon how important that Gnome might be if there was even the slightest chance of finding the Sword of Shannara, but he realized the thief preferred to keep the captive Gnome guessing. The Valeman could not be sure how much Panamon Creel knew about the legend; so far, he had shown little concern with the races generally and had not indicated he knew anything about the history of the Sword of Shannara. The grim features of the thief relaxed briefly and a faint smile crossed his lips as he eyed the still quivering captive.

"Is this Sword valuable, Gnome?" he queried easily, almost slyly. "Can I sell it for gold?"

"It is priceless to the right people," the other promised, nodding eagerly. "There are those who would pay anything, give anything to get possession of it. In the Northland . . ."

He ceased talking abruptly, afraid that he had already said too much. Panamon smiled wolfishly and nodded to Shea.

"This Gnome says it could be worth money to us," he mocked quietly, "and the Gnome wouldn't lie, would you, Gnome?" The yellow head shook vehemently. "Well, then, perhaps we should let you live long enough to prove you have something of value to barter for your worthless hide. I wouldn't want to throw away a chance to make money simply to satisfy my inborn desire to cut the throat of a Gnome when I get one within my grasp. What do you think, Gnome?"

"You understand perfectly, you know my value,"

whined the little fellow, fawning at the knees of the smiling thief. "I can help; I can make you rich. You can count on me."

Panamon was smiling broadly now, his big frame relaxed and his good hand on the Gnome's small shoulder as if they were old friends. He patted the stooped shoulder a few times, as if to put the captive at ease, and nodded reassuringly, looking from the Gnome to Keltset to Shea and back again for several long seconds.

"Tell us what you're doing way out here by yourself, Gnome," Panamon urged a moment later. "By the way, what are you called?"

"I am Orl Fane, a warrior of the Pelle tribe of the upper Anar," he answered eagerly. "I . . . I was on a courier mission from Paranor when I came upon this battlefield. They were all dead, all of them, and there was nothing I could do. Then I heard you and I hid. I was afraid you were . . . Elves."

He paused and looked fearfully at Shea, noting the youth's Elven features with dismay. Shea made no move, but waited to see what Panamon would do. Panamon just looked understandingly at the Gnome and smiled in friendly fashion.

"Orl Fane—of the Pelle tribe," the tall thief repeated slowly. "A great tribe of hunters, brave men." He shook his head as if deeply regretting something and turned again to the mystified Gnome. "Orl Fane, if we are going to be of any service to one another, we must have mutual trust. Lies can only hinder the purpose binding our new partnership. There was a Pelle standard on the battlefield—the standard of your tribe in the Gnome nation. You must have been with them when they fought."

The Gnome stood speechless, a mixture of fear and doubt creeping slowly back into his shifting green eyes. Panamon continued to smile easily at him.

"Just look at yourself Orl Fane—covered with specks of blood and a bad cut on your forehead at the hairline. Why hide the truth from us? You had to be here, isn't that right?'' The persuasive voice coaxed a quick nod out of the other, and Panamon laughed almost merrily. ''Of course you were here, Orl Fane. And when you were set upon by the Elf people, you fought until you were wounded, perhaps knocked unconscious, eh, and you lay here until just before we came along. That's the truth of the matter, isn't it?''

''Yes, that's the truth,'' the Gnome agreed eagerly now.

''No, that's not the truth!''

There was a moment of stunned silence. Panamon was still smiling, and Orl Fane was caught between emotions, a trace of doubt still in his eyes, a half-smile forming on his lips. Shea looked at both curiously, unable to follow exactly what was happening.

''Listen to me, you lying little rodent.'' The smile was gone from Panamon's face, the features hardened as he spoke, the voice cold and menacing once more. ''You have lied from the beginning! A member of the Pelle would wear their insignia—you wear none. You weren't wounded in battle; that little scratch on your forehead is nothing! You are a scavenger—a deserter, aren't you? Aren't you?''

The thief had seized the terrified Gnome by the front of his hunting tunic and was shaking him so hard that Shea could hear his teeth rattle with the force. The wiry captive was struggling to catch his breath, gasping in disbelief at this sudden turn of events.

''Yes, yes!'' The admission was throttled out of him at last, and Panamon released him with a quick thrust backward into the grip of the watchful Keltset.

''A deserter from your own people.'' Panamon spat the words out in distaste. ''The lowest form of life that walks or crawls is a deserter. You've been scavenging this battlefield for valuables from the dead. Where are they, Orl Fane? Shea, check in those bushes where he was hiding.''

As Shea moved toward the brush, the struggling Gnome let out the most frightful shriek of dismay imaginable, causing the youth to believe Keltset had twisted his neck off. But Panamon just smiled and nodded for the Valeman to proceed, certain now that the Gnome had indeed hidden something in the bushes. Shea pushed his way past the thick branches into the center of the clump, searching carefully for any sign of a cache. The ground and the limbs in the center were badly torn up from the struggle between Keltset and the Gnome, and there was nothing immediately visible. He hunted about unsuccessfully for several minutes. He was just about to give up, when his eye caught a glimpse of something half buried at the far end of the bushes beneath leaves, branches, and dirt. Using his short hunting knife and his hands, he quickly uncovered a long sack containing metal objects that rattled against one another as he worked. He called out to Panamon that he had discovered something, which immediately set off another series of whining cries from the distraught captive. When the sack was uncovered, he pulled it out of the brush into the fading afternoon sunlight and dropped it before the others. Orl Fane was in a frenzy by this time, and Keltset was forced to use both hands just to hold him.

"Whatever's in here is certainly important to our little friend." Panamon grinned at Shea and reached for the sack.

Shea moved to his side and peered over the broad shoulders as Panamon untied the leather thong binding the top and reached eagerly into the dark interior. Changing his mind suddenly, the scarlet thief removed his hand and, grabbing the other end of the sack, turned it upside down and poured the contents onto the open earth. The others stared at the cache, looking from item to item curiously.

"Junk," growled Panamon Creel after a moment's

consideration. "Just junk. The Gnome is too stupid even to bother with valuable things."

Shea looked at the contents of the sack without answering. Nothing but assorted daggers, knives, and swords in the collection, some still in their leather sheaths. A few pieces of cheap jewelry sparkled in the sunlight, and there were one or two Gnome coins, practically worthless to anyone but a Gnome. It certainly appeared to be useless junk, but the whining Orl Fane had evidently considered it worth something to him. Shea shook his head in pity for the little Gnome. He had lost everything when he turned deserter, and all he had to show for it were these few worthless pieces of metal and cheap jewelry. Now it seemed certain that he would lose his life as well for having dared to lie to the volatile Panamon Creel.

"Hardly worth dying for, Gnome," Panamon growled, nodding shortly to Keltset, who raised the heavy mace to finish the hapless fellow.

"No, no, wait, wait a minute, please," the Gnome cried, his voice edged with a harsh note of desperation. It was the end for him; this was his final plea. "I didn't lie about the Sword—I swear I didn't! I can get it for you. Don't you realize what the Sword of Shannara is worth to the Dark Lord?"

Without thinking, Shea put out a hand to grasp Keltset's massive arm. The giant Troll seemed to understand. Slowly he lowered the mace and looked curiously at Shea. Panamon Creel opened his mouth angrily and then hesitated. He wanted to learn the truth behind Shea's presence in the Northland, and the secret of this Sword evidently had much to do with it. He stared momentarily at the Valeman, then turned back to Keltset and shrugged disinterestedly.

"We can always kill you later, Orl Fane, if this is another deception. Put a rope around his worthless neck and bring him along, Keltset. Shea, if you would give me a hand up and an arm to lean on, I think I can make it to the woods. Keltset will keep a close watch over our clever little deserter.''

Shea helped the injured Panamon to his feet and tried to support him as he took a few careful test steps. Keltset tied Orl Fane and placed a length of rope about his neck so that he could be led. The Gnome allowed himself to be bound without complaining, though he was visibly distraught about something. Shea imagined that the fellow was still lying when he said he knew where the Sword could be found and was desperately trying to figure out how he would get free from his captors before they discovered his treachery and killed him. While Shea would not himself kill the Gnome, nor even agree to have it done, nevertheless he felt little compassion for the deceitful creature. Orl Fane was a coward, a deserter, a scavenger—a man without a people or a country. Shea was certain now that the whining, groveling attitude the Gnome had displayed earlier was a carefully studied shield for the crafty, desperate creature that lay hidden beneath. Orl Fane would cut their throats without the slightest compunction if he thought there would be no danger to himself. Shea almost wished that Keltset had ended their worries a few minutes earlier by finishing the fellow. Shea would have felt easier in his own mind.

Panamon signaled that he was ready to proceed toward the woodland, but before they had taken two steps, the whining pleas of Orl Fane had stopped them. The unhappy Gnome refused to go farther if he were not allowed to keep his sack and its treasures. He set up such a stubborn howl of protest that Panamon was again on the verge of bashing in the hateful yellow head.

''What does it matter, Panamon?'' Shea finally asked in exasperation. ''Let him have his trinkets if it will make him happy. We can get rid of them later after he quiets down.''

Panamon shook his handsome face in dismay,

finally nodding his reluctant acquiescence. He was fed up with Orl Fane already.

"Very well, I'll give in just this once," the thief agreed. Orl Fane immediately quieted down. "However, if he opens his mouth like that once more, I'll cut out his tongue. Keltset, you keep him away from that sack. I don't want him getting hold of one of those weapons long enough to cut himself free and do us in! Worthless blades probably wouldn't do a neat job of it anyway, and I'd die of blood poisoning."

Shea had to laugh in spite of himself. They were poor-looking weapons, though he rather fancied the slim broadsword with the extended arm and burning torch cut into the hilt. Even that one was rather gaudy, the cheap gold paint chipped and flecked about the hilt. Like several of the others, it rested in a worn leather sheath so it was difficult to tell what condition the blade might be in. At any rate, it could prove dangerous in the hands of the wily Orl Fane. Keltset hoisted the sack and its contents over one shoulder, and the party continued on its way toward the woodland.

It was a comparatively short hike, but by the time they reached the perimeter of the forest Shea was exhausted from supporting the weight of the injured Panamon. The little group stopped on the thief's command; as an afterthought, he sent Keltset back to cover their trail and to create a number of false trails that would confuse anyone following. Shea did not object, for although he hoped that Allanon and the others were searching for him, there was a dangerous possibility that patrolling Gnome hunters or, worse still, another Skull Bearer might come across their tracks instead.

After tying the captive Orl Fane to a tree, the Rock Troll backtracked onto the battlefield to erase any sign of their passage in this direction. Panamon collapsed wearily against a broad maple, and the tired Valeman took up a position opposite him, lying peacefully back on a small, grassy knoll, staring absently into the treetops and breathing deeply the forest air. The sun was fading rapidly now with the close of the afternoon and the faint beginnings of evening crept into the western sky in streaks of purple and deep blue. Less than an hour of sunlight remained, and the night would help to hide them from their enemies. Shea fervently wished now for the aid of the company, for the strong, wise leadership and fantastic mystical prowess of Allanon, for the courage of the others—Balinor, Hendel, Durin, Dayel, and the fiery Menion Leah. Most of all he wished Flick were with him—Flick, with his unwavering, unquestioning loyalty and trust. Panamon Creel was a good man to have on his side, but there were no real ties between them. The thief had lived too long by his wits and cunning to understand basic honesty and truth. And what about Keltset—an enigma, even to Panamon?

"Panamon, you said back there you would explain about Keltset," Shea remarked quietly. "About how the Skull Bearer knew him."

For a moment there was no answer, and Shea raised up to see if the man had heard him. Panamon was staring quietly at him.

"Skull Bearer? You seem to know a great deal more about this whole matter than I. You tell me about my giant companion, Shea."

"That wasn't the truth you told me when you saved me from those Gnomes, was it?" Shea asked him. "He wasn't a freak driven from his village by his own people. He didn't kill them for attacking him, did he?"

Panamon laughed merrily, the pike coming up to scratch the small mustache.

"Maybe it was the truth. Maybe those things did happen to him. I don't know. It always seemed to me that something of the sort must have happened to him to make him take up with someone like myself. He's

no thief; I don't know what he is. But he is my
friend—he is that. I didn't lie to you when I said that."

"Where did he come from?" Shea asked after a
moment's silence.

"I found him north of here about two months ago.
He wandered down out of the Charnal Mountains,
battered, beaten, just barely alive. I don't know what
happened to him; he never volunteered the information, and I didn't ask. He was entitled to keep his past
hidden, just as I. I took care of him for several weeks. I
knew a little sign language, and he understood it, so
we could communicate. I guessed his name from his
word signs. We learned a little about each other—only
a little. When he was well, I asked him to come along
and he agreed. We've had some good times, you
know. Too bad he's not really a thief."

Shea shook his head and chuckled softly at that last
remark. Panamon Creel would probably never
change. He didn't understand any other way of life
and didn't want to. The only people who made any
sense to him were those who told the world to hang by
its thumbs and took by force what they needed for
themselves. Yet friendship remained a prized com-
modity, even for a thief, and it was something that
would not be tossed aside lightly. Even Shea was
beginning to feel a strange sort of friendship for the
flamboyant Panamon Creel, a friendship that was
improbable because their characters and their values
were complete opposites. But each had an understanding of what the other felt, though not why he felt
it, and there was the experience of the battle shared
against a common enemy. Perhaps that was all that
anyone ever needed as a basis for friendship.

"How could the Skull creature have known him?"
Shea persisted.

Panamon shrugged casually, indicating he neither
knew nor cared. The watchful Valeman felt the latter
was not the case, and Panamon would very much like

to find out the truth behind Keltset's appearance two months earlier. His hidden past had something to do with the spirit creature's unexplained recognition of the giant Troll. There had been a trace of fear in those cruel eyes, and Shea found it difficult to imagine how anything mortal could have frightened the powerful Skull Bearer. Panamon had seen it, too, and certainly he must be asking himself the same question.

By the time Keltset rejoined them, it was sundown and the faint rays of the late afternoon sun only barely lit the dark forest. The Troll had carefully erased all signs of their passing from the battlefield, leaving a number of confusing false trails for anyone who attempted to follow. Panamon was feeling well enough to maneuver on his own strength, but requested that Keltset help support him until they reached a suitable campsite because it was becoming dark too quickly for travel. Shea was given the task of leading the docile Orl Fane by the rope leash, a chore he did not relish, but which he accepted without complaint. Again, Panamon tried to leave the worn sack and its contents behind, but Orl Fane was not to be deprived of his treasures so easily. He immediately set up such a howl of anguish that the thief ordered him bound about the mouth until the only sound the hapless Gnome could make was a muffled groan. But when they tried to move into the forest, the desperate captive threw himself on the ground and refused to rise, even when kicked painfully by a thoroughly irate Panamon. Keltset could have carried the Gnome and supported Panamon, too, but that was more trouble than it was worth. Muttering dire threats at the whining Gnome, the thief at last had Keltset pick up the sack, and the four began their journey into the darkening woods.

When it became too dark to tell with any certainty where they were going, Panamon called a halt in a small clearing between giant oaks whose interlocking

boughs formed a weblike roof for shelter. Orl Fane
was tied to one of the tall oaks while the other three set
about building a fire and preparing a meal. When the
food was ready, Orl Fane was unfettered long enough
to allow him to eat. While Panamon did not know
exactly where they were, he felt safe enough to permit
a fire, relatively certain that no one would be trailing
them at night. He might have felt a little less secure
had he known of the dangers of the impenetrable
forests that surrounded the dark cliffs of Paranor. As it
happened, the four men were in an adjoining forest
east of the dangerous woodlands ringing Paranor.
The section of woods in which they were camped was
seldom traveled by the minions of the Warlock Lord,
and there was little possibility that anyone would
happen along to discover them. They ate in silence, a
hungry and tired group after the long day's travel.
Even the whines of the bothersome Orl Fane were
temporarily stilled as the little Gnome ate ravenously,
his crafty yellow face bent close to the warmth of the
small fire as the dark green eyes shifted warily from
one face to the next. Shea paid no attention,
concentrating instead on what he should tell Panamon
Creel about himself, the company, and most important of all, the Sword of Shannara. He had not made
up his mind when dinner was completed. The captive
was again bound to the nearest oak and permitted to
breathe without the gag after his solemn promise that
he would not begin whining and crying again. Then
placing himself comfortably close to the dying fire,
Panamon turned his attention to the expectant
Valeman.

"The time is here, Shea, for you to tell me what you
know about all this Sword business," he began
briskly. "No lies, no half-truths, and leave nothing
out. I promised my help, but we must have mutual
trust—and not the kind I spoke of to this pitiful
deserter. I have been fair and open with you. Do
likewise for me."

So Shea told him everything. He didn't mean to when he started. He wasn't really sure how much he should tell, but one thing led to another and before he knew it the whole tale was out in the open. He told about the coming of Allanon, and the subsequent appearance of the Skull Bearer which forced the brothers to flee from Shady Vale. He related the events surrounding the journey to Leah and the meeting with Menion, followed by the terrible flight through the Black Oaks to Culhaven, where they joined the rest of the company. He skimmed over the details of the journey to the Dragon's Teeth, a great part of which was still hazy in his own mind. He concluded by explaining how he had fallen from the Crease into the river and been washed out onto the Rabb Plain where he was captured by the Gnome hunting party. Panamon listened without interruption, his eyes wide in astonishment at the tale. Keltset sat next to him in impenetrable silence, the rough-hewn but intelligent face gazing intently at the little Valeman during the entire narration. Orl Fane shifted about uneasily, groaning and muttering unintelligibly as he listened with the other two, his eyes darting wildly about the campsite as if expecting the Warlock Lord himself at any minute.

"That is the most fantastic tale I have ever heard," Panamon announced at last. "It's so incredible that even I find it hard to believe. But I do believe you, Shea. I believe you because I've fought that black-winged monster on the plainlands and because I've seen the strange power you have over those Elfstones, as you call them. But this business about the Sword and your being the lost heir of Shannara—I don't know. Do you believe it yourself?"

"I didn't at first," Shea admitted slowly, "but now I don't know what to think. So much has happened that I can't decide who or what to believe anymore. In any case, I've got to rejoin Allanon and the others. They may even have the Sword by this time. They may have the answer to this whole riddle of my heritage and the power of the Sword."

Orl Fane suddenly doubled up laughing, his voice high-pitched and frenzied.

"No, no, they don't have the Sword," he shrieked like a fool caught up in his own madness. "No, no, only I can show you the Sword! I can lead you to it. Only I. You can search and you can search and you can search, ha, ha, ha—go ahead. But I know where it is! I know who has it! Only I!"

"I think he's losing his mind," Panamon Creel muttered humorlessly, and ordered Keltset to regag the bothersome Gnome. "We'll find out exactly what he knows in the morning. If he knows anything about the Sword of Shannara, which I seriously doubt, he'll tell us or wish he had!"

"Do you think he might know who has it?" Shea asked soberly. "That Sword could mean so much, not only to us, but to all the peoples of the four lands. We've got to try to find out what he really knows."

"You bring tears to my eyes with that plea for the people," Panamon mocked disdainfully. "They can go hang for all I care. They've never done anything for me—except travel alone, unarmed, with fat purses, and that's been all too infrequently." He looked up at Shea's disappointed face and shrugged nonchalantly. "Still, I am curious about the Sword, so I might be willing to help you. After all, I owe you a great favor, and I'm not one to forget a favor."

Keltset finished gagging the babbling Gnome once again and rejoined them next to the small fire. Orl Fane had lapsed into a series of small, shrill laughs coupled with incoherent mumblings that even the cloth gag did not completely muffle. Shea glanced uneasily at the little captive, watching the gnarled yellow body twist about as if possessed by some devil, the dark eyes wide and rolling wildly. Panamon gallantly ignored the moans for a brief time, but at last, losing all patience, leaped to his feet and drew his dagger to cut the Gnome's tongue out. Orl Fane immediately quieted down and for a while they forgot about him.

"Why do you suppose," Panamon began after a moment, "that Northland creature believed we were hiding the Sword of Shannara? It was strange he wouldn't even argue the point. He said he could sense that we had it. How do you explain that?"

Shea thought for a moment and finally shrugged uncertainly.

"It must have been the Elfstones."

"You may be right," Panamon agreed slowly, thoughtfully, his good hand rubbing his chin. "I frankly don't understand any of this. Keltset, what do you think about it."

The giant Rock Troll regarded them solemnly for a moment and then made several brief signs with his hands. Panamon watched intently, then turned to Shea with a disgusted look.

"He thinks the Sword is very important and that the Warlock Lord is a very great danger to us all." The thief laughed humorously. "He's a great help, I must say!"

"The Sword *is* very important!" Shea repeated, his voice trailing off in the darkness, and they sat quietly, lost in thought.

It was late evening now, the night around them black beyond the faint light of the fire's reddish embers. The woods were a wall of concealment, shutting them into the little clearing, surrounding them with the sharp sounds of the insect world and the occasional cry of some faraway creature. The sky above showed through the boughs of the great trees in patches of dark blue broken by one or two distant stars. Panamon talked on quietly for a few minutes more as the coals died into ashes. Then he rose, kicking the ashes and grinding them into the earth, bidding good night to his companions with a finality that discouraged further attempts at conversation. Keltset was wrapped in a blanket and sleeping before Shea had even selected a suitable patch of forest earth. The Valeman felt incredibly weary from the strain of the long day's march and the battle with the Skull Bearer. Dropping his blanket, he lay down on his back, kicked off the hunting boots and stared aimlessly at the blackness above him through which he could just barely discern the limbs of the trees and the shadows of the sky.

Shea thought about all that had happened to him, once again retracing mentally his long, endless journey from Shady Vale. So much of it was still a mystery. He had come so far, endured so much, and still he didn't know what it was all about. The secret of the Sword of Shannara, the Warlock Lord, his own heritage—it was no clearer now than before. The company was out there somewhere looking for him, led by the secretive, mystic Allanon, who seemed to be the only man with the answers to all the unanswered questions. Why had he not told Shea everything from the beginning? Why had he insisted on giving the company only a piece of the story at a time, always reserving that small bit, always holding back the key to their complete understanding of the unknown power locked in the elusive Sword of Shannara?

He rolled over on his side, peering through the darkness to the sleeping form of Panamon Creel just a few feet away. Beyond and to the other side of the clearing he could hear the heavy breathing of Keltset blending in with the sounds of the forest night. Orl Fane sat with his back straight against the tree to which he was bound, his eyes shining like a cat's in the dark, unmoving as they stared fixedly at Shea. The Valeman stared back for a moment, unnerved by the Gnome's gaze, but finally he forced himself to turn the other way and closed his eyes, dropping off to sleep in a matter of seconds. The last thing he remembered was clutching the small bulk of the Elfstones close to his chest within the tunic, wondering if their power would continue to protect him in the days ahead.

Shea was awakened abruptly to the gray light of an early forest morning by a long string of venomous oaths of dismay and frustration from a wrathful Panamon Creel. The thief was stamping about the campsite in absolute fury, shouting and cursing all at the same time. Shea could not decide what had happened right away, and it was several minutes before he had wiped the sleep from his eyes and propped himself up on one elbow, squinting wearily in the gloom. He felt as if he had slept no more than a few minutes, his muscles sore and strained, his mind hazy. Panamon continued to storm about the small clearing as Keltset knelt silently next to one of the great oaks. Then Shea realized that Orl Fane was missing. He leaped to his feet and rushed over, suddenly afraid. In a moment his worst fears were realized; the ropes that had bound the crafty Gnome lay in pieces about the base of the huge trunk. The Gnome had escaped, and Shea had lost his one chance to find the missing Sword.

"How did he get away?" Shea demanded angrily. "I thought you tied him up, away from anything that might cut his bonds!"

Panamon Creel looked at him as if he were an idiot, disgust registered all over the flushed countenance.

"Do I look like a complete fool? Of course I tied him up away from any weapons. I even tied him to the confounded tree and had him gagged as an added precaution. Where were you? The little devil didn't cut these ropes and that gag. He chewed his way through them!"

Now it was Shea's turn to be amazed.

"I'm dead serious, I assure you," Panamon continued angrily. "The ropes were chewed through by teeth. Our little rodent friend was more resourceful than I imagined."

"Or perhaps more desperate," the Valeman added thoughtfully. "I wonder why he didn't try to kill us. He had reason enough to hate us."

"Very uncharitable of you to suggest such a thing," the other declared in mock disbelief. "I'll tell you why, though, since you asked. He was terrified that he might be caught in the act. That Gnome was a deserter—a coward of the lowest order. He didn't have the courage to do anything but run! What is it, Keltset?"

The huge Rock Troll had lumbered silently over to his comrade and made several quick gestures, pointing to the north. Panamon shook his head in disgust.

"The spineless mouse has been gone since early this morning—hours ago. Worse still, the fool fled northward, and it would not be healthy for us to chase him in that country. His own people will probably find him and dispose of him for us. They won't shelter a deserter. Bah, let him go! We're better off without him, Shea. He was probably lying about the Sword of Shannara anyway."

Shea nodded doubtfully, unconvinced that the Gnome had been lying about everything he had told them. As unbalanced as the little fellow had seemed, he had nevertheless appeared certain that he knew where the Sword could be found and who had possession of it. The whole idea that he knew such a secret was unnerving to the Valeman. Suppose he had gone after the Sword? Suppose he knew where it was?

"Forget the whole matter, Shea," Panamon interjected in resignation. "That Gnome was scared to death of us; his only thought was to escape. The story of the Sword was merely a trick to keep us from killing him until he found the opportunity to escape. Look at this! He left in such a hurry, he even forgot his precious sack."

For the first time Shea noticed the sack lying partially open at the other side of the clearing. It was strange indeed that Orl Fane should abandon his treasures after going to so much trouble to persuade his captors to bring them along. That useless sack had been so important to him, and yet there it lay forgotten, its contents still visible as small bulks beneath the cloth. Shea walked over to it curiously, staring at it with visible suspicion. He emptied the contents onto the forest earth, the swords and the daggers and the jewelry clattering together as they tumbled out in a heap. Shea stared at them, aware that the giant form of Keltset was at his side, the dark, expressionless face bent next to his. They stood together, studying the Gnome's abandoned hoard as if somehow it held a mysterious secret. Their companion watched for a few seconds, then muttered in disgust and strolled over to join them, glancing down at the weapons and jewelry.

"Let's be on our way," he advised lightly. "We've got to find your friends, Shea, and perhaps with their help we can locate this elusive Sword. What are you staring at? You've already seen that worthless junk once. It hasn't changed."

Then Shea saw it.

"It's not the same," he announced slowly. "It's gone. He's taken it."

"What's gone?" snapped Panamon irritably, kicking at the pile of junk. "What are you talking about?"

"That old sword in the leather scabbard. The one with the arm and the torch."

Panamon looked quickly at the swords in the little heap, frowning curiously. Keltset straightened abruptly and looked at Shea with those deeply intelligent eyes fixed on the little Valeman. He realized the truth as well.

"So he took one sword," Panamon growled without stopping to think. "That doesn't mean he . . ." He caught himself, his jaw dropping open in dismay, his eyes rolling back in disbelief. "Oh, no! That can't be—it can't. You mean he has . . .?"

He couldn't finish the thought, but choked on his words. Shea shook his head in quiet despair.

"The Sword of Shannara!"

XXI

The same morning that found Shea and his new companions facing the awful truth about the fleeing Orl Fane and the Sword of Shannara also found Allanon and the remaining members of the company embroiled in difficulties of their own. They had escaped from the Druids' Keep under the aged mystic's sure guidance, winding downward through the maze of tunnels in the core of the mountain to the forest land below. They had encountered no initial resistance to their escape, finding only a few scattered Gnomes scurrying about the passages, remnants of the broken palace guard that had fled earlier. It was early evening by the time the little band was clear of the forbidding heights and moving northward through the forests. Allanon was certain that the Gnomes had removed the Sword of Shannara from the Keep sometime before the encounter with the Skull Bearer in the furnace room, but it was impossible to tell exactly when the removal had been accomplished. Eventine was patrolling the northern perimeter of Paranor and any attempt to move the Sword would be met with resistance from his soldiers. Perhaps the Elven king had already gained possession of the Sword. Perhaps he had even intercepted the missing Shea. Allanon was extremely worried about the little Valeman, whom he had expected to find at the Druids' Keep. There had been no mistake when he had made his mental search for the youth back at the foot of the Dragon's Teeth. Shea was in the company of others, and they were moving northward toward Paranor. Something had diverted them. Still, Shea was a resourceful fellow, and he had the power of the Elfstones to protect him from the Warlock Lord. The Druid could only hope that somehow they would find each other without further complications, and that when they did, Shea would be safe and unharmed.

Allanon had other worries, however, which demanded his immediate attention. Gnome reinforcements began to arrive in large numbers, and it did not take them long to conclude that Allanon and his little band of invaders had fled the castle and were somewhere in the dangerous Impregnable Forest surrounding Paranor. In truth, the Gnomes had no idea for whom they were searching; they only knew that the castle had been invaded, and the intruders had to be captured or destroyed. The emissaries of the Warlock Lord had not arrived, and the Skull King himself did not yet realize his prey had escaped him once again. He rested contentedly in the dark recesses of his domain, assured that the troublesome Allanon had been destroyed in the furnaces of Paranor, that the heir of Shannara and the others with him were prisoners, and that the Sword of Shannara was safely on its way to the Northland, intercepted by this time by a Skull Bearer whom he had dispatched a day earlier to be certain the precious Sword was not retaken. So the newly arrived Gnomes began to comb the forests surrounding Paranor in an effort to find the unknown intruders, believing that they would flee south and sending the majority of their hunters in that direction.

Allanon and his small band were moving steadily northward, but progress was slowed from time to time with the appearance of large Gnome search parties patrolling the woodlands. The little company would never have escaped undetected had they proceeded south, but the enemy numbers were reduced enough to the north that they managed to elude the hunting parties by hiding until they had passed and then pressing onward. It was light by the time they finally reached the fringes of the forest and could look northward over the awesome Plains of Streleheim, their pursuers momentarily behind them.

Allanon turned to them, his dark countenance worn and grim, but the eyes still bright with determination. His companions waited as he studied them one by one as if he were seeing each for the first time. Finally he spoke, the words slow and reluctant.

"We have reached the end of the road, my friends. The journey to Paranor is at an end, and it is time for the company to disband and each of us to go his own way. We have lost our chance to gain possession of the Sword—at least for the moment. Shea is still missing, and we cannot tell how long it may take to find him. But the greatest threat facing us is an invasion from the north. We must protect ourselves and the peoples of the lands south, east, and west of us from that. We have seen no sign of the Elven armies of Eventine, though they were supposed to be patrolling this region. It appears they have been withdrawn, and this would only be done if the Warlock Lord had begun to move his armies southward."

"Then the invasion has begun?" Balinor asked shortly.

Allanon nodded solemnly, and the others exchanged startled looks.

"Without the Sword we cannot defeat the Warlock Lord, so we must attempt to stop his armies. To do this, we must unite the free nations quickly. We may already be too late. Brona will use his armies to seize all of the central Southland. To do this he need only destroy the Border Legion of Callahorn. Balinor, the

Legion must hold the cities of Callahorn to give the nations enough time to unite their armies and strike back at the invader. Durin and Dayel can accompany you to Tyrsis and from there travel westward to their own land. Eventine must bring his Elven armies across the Plains of Streleheim to reinforce Tyrsis. If we lose there, the Warlock Lord will have succeeded in driving a wedge between the armies, and there will be little chance of uniting them. Worse still, the entire Southland will lie open and unprotected. Men will never be able to form their armies in time. The Border Legion of Callahorn is the only chance they have.''

Balinor nodded in agreement and turned to Hendel.

"What support can the Dwarfs give us?''

"The city of Varfleet is the key to the eastern sector of Callahorn.'' Hendel pondered the situation carefully. "My people must protect against any assault through the Anar, but we can spare enough men to help defend Varfleet as well. But you must hold the cities of Kern and Tyrsis yourself.''

"The Elven armies will help you on the west,'' Durin promised quickly.

"Wait a minute!'' exclaimed Menion incredulously. "What about Shea? You've kind of forgotten about him, haven't you?''

"Still allowing your words to precede your thinking, I see,'' Allanon said darkly. Menion turned scarlet with anger, but waited to see what the mystic had to say.

"I'm not abandoning the search for my brother,'' Flick announced quietly.

"Nor am I suggesting you should, Flick.'' Allanon smiled at the other's concern. "You and Menion and I shall continue to search for our young friend and for the missing Sword. I suspect that where we find one, we shall find the other. Remember the words spoken to me by the Shade of Bremen. Shea shall be the first to lay hands on the Sword of Shannara. Perhaps he has already done so."

"Then let's get on with the search," suggested Menion irritably, avoiding the eyes of the Druid.

"We shall leave now," Allanon announced, adding pointedly, "but you must see that you keep a closer guard over your tongue. A Prince of Leah should speak with wisdom and foresight, with patience and understanding—not with foolish anger."

Menion nodded grudgingly. The seven said their farewells with mixed emotions and parted. Balinor, Hendel, and the Elven brothers turned westward past the forest in which Shea and his companions had spent the night, hoping to circle the Impregnable Forest and pass down through the hill country north of the Dragon's Teeth and thereby reach Kern and Tyrsis within two days. Allanon and his two youthful companions moved eastward, searching for some sign of Shea. Allanon was convinced that the Valeman must have eventually come northward toward Paranor and perhaps was a prisoner in one of the Gnome camps in that region. Rescuing him would not be easy, but the Druid's greatest fear was that the Warlock Lord would learn of his capture and find out who he was, then have him immediately executed. If that happened, the Sword of Shannara would be worthless to them anyway, and they would have no choice but to rely on the strength of the divided armies of the three besieged lands. It was not a promising thought, and Allanon quickly turned his attention to the land ahead. Menion walked slightly in front as they traveled, his keen eyes picking out the trails and studying the footprints of all who had passed. His concern was the weather. If it rained, they would never find the trail. Even if the weather stayed favorable for them, the sudden wind storms that blew across the Streleheim would have the same effect as a rainfall, erasing all traces of anyone's passage. Flick, dutifully bringing up the rear, walked in abject silence, hoping against hope that they would find some sign of Shea, but fearful that he had seen the last of his brother.

By noonday, the barren plains were shimmering with the blistering heat of the white-hot sun, and the three travelers walked as close to the forest edge as possible to take advantage of small patches of shade from the great trees. Allanon alone seemed unperturbed by the fearful heat, his dark face calm and relaxed in the scorching sunlight, free from even the slightest trace of perspiration. Flick felt ready to collapse at any moment, and even the durable Menion Leah was beginning to feel ill. His sharp eyes were dry and blurred, and his senses were starting to play tricks on him. He was seeing things that weren't there, hearing and smelling images formed by his muddled brain in the seething flatlands ahead.

At last the two Southlanders could go no farther, and their tall leader called a brief halt, leading them into the cooling shade of the forest. In silence they ate a small, tasteless meal of bread and dried meats. Flick wanted to ask the Druid more about Shea's chances of surviving alone in that desolate land, but he couldn't bring himself to voice the questions. The answers were all too apparent. He felt strangely alone now that the others were gone. He had never felt close to Allanon, always plagued by nagging doubts about the Druid's strange powers. The mystic remained a giant shadowy figure, as mysterious and deadly as the Skull Bearers that pursued them so relentlessly. He remained a personification of the deathless spirit of Bremen that had risen from the nether world in the Valley of Shale. He was power and wisdom of such magnitude that he didn't seem a part of Flick's mortal world; he was more a part of the Warlock Lord's domain, that black, frightful corner of the mortal mind where fear is master and reason cannot penetrate.

Flick could not forget the terrible battle between the great mystic and the treacherous Skull creature which had resulted in a fiery climax in the flames of the furnace beneath the Druids' Keep. Yet Allanon had saved himself; he had survived what no other man could have survived. It was more than merely uncanny—it was terrifying. Balinor alone had seemed able to deal with the giant leader, but now he was gone, and Flick felt very alone and vulnerable.

Menion Leah felt even less certain of himself. He was not really afraid of the powerful Druid, but he was aware that the giant did not think much of him and had brought him along primarily because Shea had wanted him. Shea had believed in the Prince of Leah when even Flick had doubted the adventurer's motives. But Shea was gone now. Menion felt he had only to anger the Druid once more and the unpredictable mystic would dispose of him for good. So he ate quietly and said nothing, believing that for the moment discretion was the better part of valor.

When the silent meal was concluded, the Druid motioned them to their feet. Again they marched eastward along the fringes of the forest, their faces bathed in the withering heat of the sun, their tired eyes scanning the barren plains for the missing Shea. This time they walked for only fifteen minutes before they found signs of something out of the ordinary. Menion spotted the tracks almost immediately. A large number of Gnomes had passed that way several days earlier, booted and undoubtedly armed. They followed the tracks northward for about half a mile. Upon topping a small rise of ground, they found the remains of the Gnomes and Elves who had died in battle. The decaying bodies lay where they had fallen, still untouched and unburied, less than a hundred yards from the rise. The three walked slowly down into the graveyard of bleached bones and rotting flesh, the terrible stench rising to their nostrils in sickening waves. Flick could go no farther, and stopped where he was to watch the other two walk into the midst of the dead bodies.

Allanon wandered in silent contemplation through the fallen men, studying discarded weapons and standards, glancing only briefly at the dead. Menion discovered a fresh set of tracks almost immediately and began moving mechanically about the battlefield, his eyes fixed on the dusty earth. Flick could not tell exactly what was going on from his distant vantage point, but it appeared that the highlander retraced his own steps several times, casting about for traces of new trails, the thin hands shading his reddened eyes. Finally, he turned southward toward the forest and began strolling slowly back toward Flick, his head lowered thoughtfully. He stopped at a large clump of bushes and dropped to one knee, apparently observing something of interest. Momentarily forgetting his distaste for the battlefield and its corpses, the curious Valeman hastened forward. He had just reached the kneeling man's side when Allanon, standing in the center of the battlefield, let out a shout of astonishment. The two men paused and watched silently while the tall black figure peered downward for a moment as if to be certain, then turned and moved toward them in long strides. The mystic's dark face was flushed with excitement when he reached them, and they were relieved to see the familiar mocking smile slowly spread into a wide grin.

"Amazing! It's amazing indeed. Our young friend is more resourceful than I had imagined. Up there, I found a small pile of ashes—all that remains of one of the Skull Bearers. Nothing mortal destroyed that creature; it was the power of the Elfstones!"

"Then Shea has been here ahead of us!" exclaimed Flick hopefully.

"No other has the power to use the stones." Allanon nodded assuringly. "There are signs of a terrific battle, tracks that show Shea was not alone. But I cannot tell whether those who were with him were friends or enemies. Nor can I tell if the creature of the north was destroyed during or after the battle between Gnome and Elf. What have you found, highlander?"

"A lot of false trails left by a very intelligent Troll," Menion responded wryly. "It's impossible for me to tell much from all the footprints, but I am sure that a large Rock Troll was among the prior occupants of this field. He left his tracks all over it but none of them lead anywhere. There are indications that some sort of scuffle took place within these bushes, though. See the bent branches and newly fallen leaves? But more important, there are footprints of a small man. They could be Shea's."

"Do you think he was captured by the Troll?" Flick queried fearfully.

Menion smiled at his concern and shrugged.

"If he could handle one of those Skull creatures, then I doubt he would have much trouble with an ordinary Troll."

"The Elfstones are no protection against mortal creatures," Allanon pointed out chillingly. "Is there any clear indication which way this Troll went?"

Menion shook his head negatively.

"To be certain, we would have had to find the tracks right away. These tracks are at least a day old. The Troll knew what he was doing when he left. We could search forever and never be sure which way he went."

Flick felt his heart sink at this news. If Shea had been taken by this mysterious creature, then it appeared they had reached another dead end.

"I found something else," Allanon announced after a moment. "I found a broken standard from the house of Elessedil—Eventine's personal banner. He may have been present at the battle. He may have been taken prisoner or even killed. It seems possible that the slain Gnomes were attempting to escape from

Paranor with the Sword and were intercepted by the Elf King and his warriors. If so, then Eventine, Shea and the Sword may all be in the hands of the enemy."

"I'm sure of one thing," Menion declared quickly. "Those Troll footprints and this battle in the bushes took place yesterday, while the battle between the Gnomes and Elves is several days old."

"Yes . . . yes, you're right, of course," the Druid agreed thoughtfully. "There has been a sequence of events taking place that we can't piece together from the little we know. I'm afraid we won't find all the answers here."

"What do we do now?" Flick asked anxiously.

"There are tracks leading westward across the Streleheim," Allanon mused thoughtfully, gazing in that direction as he spoke. "The tracks are blurred, but they may have been made by survivors of this battle. . . ."

He looked questioningly at the silent Menion Leah for his opinion.

"Our mysterious Troll did not go that way," Menion stated worriedly. "He would not bother with a lot of false trails if he were going to leave a clear one when he left! I don't like it."

"Do we have any choice?" Allanon persisted. "The only clear set of tracks leaving this battleground leads westward. We'll have to follow them and hope for the best."

Flick thought that such optimism was unwarranted in view of the hard facts of the situation and found the comments out of character for the grim Druid. Still, it seemed they had little choice in the matter. Perhaps whoever had made those tracks could tell them something about Shea. The little Valeman turned to Menion and nodded his willingness to follow the Druid's advice, noting the look of consternation clouding the highlander's lean features. Clearly Menion was not happy with the decision, convinced that there was another trail to be found that would tell them more about the Troll and the slain Skull creature. Allanon beckoned to them, and retracing their steps they began the long march back across the Streleheim Plains to the lands west of Paranor. Flick cast one final look at the field of slain men, their carcasses rotting slowly in the boiling heat of the sun, shunned by man and nature in senseless death. He shook his broad head. Perhaps this was the way it would end for them all.

The three travelers walked steadily westward for the remainder of the day. They spoke little, lost in private thoughts, their eyes following almost carelessly the blurred trail before them as they watched the brilliant sun turn red in the horizon and die into evening. When it was too dark to continue, Allanon directed them into the bordering forests where they made camp for the night. The trio had reached a point near the northwestern sector of the dreaded Impregnable Forest and they were once again in danger of discovery by Gnome hunting parties or prowling wolf packs. The resolute Druid explained that, while they were in some danger of discovery, he believed the search for them would have been abandoned by this time in favor of more urgent matters. As a necessary precaution, they would light no fire and would keep constant watch through the night for the wolves. Flick silently prayed that the wolf packs would not venture this close to the plainland, but would keep to the dark interior of the woods, closer to the Druids' Keep. They ate a brief, tasteless meal and quickly turned in for the night. Menion offered to stand the first watch. Flick was asleep in moments, but it seemed he had slept for only an instant when the highlander awoke him for his turn as guard. About midnight, Allanon approached without a sound and ordered Flick to go back to sleep. The Valeman had been guarding for only about an hour, but he did as he was told without arguing.

When Flick and Menion awoke again, it was dawn.

In the faint red and yellow slivers of sunlight which crept slowly into the shadowed forest, they saw the giant Druid resting peacefully against a tall elm as he stared at them. The tall, dark figure seemed almost a part of the forest, sitting there motionlessly, the deep eyes black in the caverns beneath the great brow. They knew that Allanon must have stood guard over them all night without sleep. It seemed impossible that he could be rested, yet he rose without stretching, the grim face relaxed and alert. They ate a quick breakfast and marched out of the forest onto the Streleheim once more. A moment later they halted in shocked disbelief. All about them, the skies were clear and faintly blue in the new light of day, the sun rising in blinding brilliance above the mountain ranges far to the east. But to the north stood a gigantic, towering wall of darkness against the skyline, as if all the ominous thunderclouds of the earth had been massed together and piled one on top of the next to form a black wall of gloom. The wall rose into the air until it was lost in the curving atmosphere of the earth's horizon, and it stretched across all of the rugged Northland, huge, dark, and terrible—its center the kingdom of the Warlock Lord. It seemed to foreshadow the relentless, inevitable approach of an endless night.

"What do you make of that?" Menion could barely get the question out.

For a moment Allanon said nothing, his own dark face mirroring the blackness of the northern wall as he stared in silence. The muscles of his lean jaw seemed to tighten beneath the small black beard and the eyes narrowed as if deep in concentration. Menion waited quietly, and at last the Druid seemed to realize he had spoken, turning to him in recognition.

"It is the beginning of the end. Brona has signaled the start of his conquest. That terrible darkness will follow his armies as they sweep southward, then east and west, until the whole earth is blanketed. When the sun is gone in all the lands, freedom is dead, too."

"Are we beaten?" Flick asked after a moment. "Are we really beaten? Is it hopeless for us, Allanon?"

His worried voice struck a responsive chord within the giant Druid, who turned quietly to him, gazing reassuringly into the wide, frightened eyes.

"Not yet, my young friend. Not yet."

Allanon led them westward for several hours from that point, staying close to the fringes of the forest, warning Menion and Flick to keep their eyes open for any sign of the enemy. The Skull Bearers would be flying in the day as well as by night, now that the Warlock Lord had begun his conquest, no longer afraid of the sunlight, no longer trying to conceal their presence. The Master was finished with hiding in the Northland; now, he would begin to move into the other lands, sending his faithful spirits ahead of him like great birds of prey. He would give them the power they needed to withstand the sun—the power he had harnessed in the great dark wall that shadowed his kingdom and would soon begin to shadow all of the lands beyond. The days of light were drawing to a close.

About midmorning, the three travelers turned southward on the Streleheim Plains, keeping close to the western fringes of the forests surrounding Paranor. The tracks they had been following merged at this point with others coming down from the north to continue southward toward Callahorn. The trail they left was broad and open; there had been no attempt to hide either their number or their direction. From the width of the trail and the impressions left by the footprints, Menion concluded that at least several thousand men had passed this way a few days earlier. The footprints were Gnome and Troll—obviously part of the Northland hordes of the Warlock Lord. Allanon was certain now that a giant army was massing on the

plains above Callahorn to begin a sweep through the
Southland that would divide the free lands and their
armies. The trail had become so obscured by the
intermingling of constant additional parties into the
main body that it was no longer possible to tell
whether a small group might have detached itself.
Shea or the Sword could have been taken a different
way at some point, and his friends would fail to catch
it, continuing to follow the main army.

They walked southward all day with only occasional
periods of rest, intent on catching the huge column of
men ahead before nightfall. The trail of the invading
army was so apparent that Menion merely glanced out
of habit from time to time at the trampled earth. The
barren Plains of Streleheim were replaced by green
grasslands. To Flick, it almost seemed that they were
going home again, and the familiar hills of Shady Vale
might be just over the rise of the plains. The weather
was warm and humid, and the terrain was considerably more friendly. They were still some distance from
Callahorn, but it was clear that they were passing out
of the bleakness of the Northland into the warmth and
greenness of their home. The day passed quickly, and
conversation between the travelers resumed. At
Flick's urging, Allanon told them more about the
Council of the Druids. He recounted in detail the
history of Man since the Great Wars, explaining how
their race had progressed to its present state of
existence. Menion said little, content to listen to the
Druid and keep a close watch over the surrounding
countryside.

When they had begun the day's march, the sun had
been bright and warm, and the sky clear. By
midafternoon, the weather had changed abruptly and
the brightness of the sun was replaced by low-
hanging, gray rain clouds and an even more humid
atmosphere that clung uncomfortably to the exposed
skin. The air felt sticky and wet, and there was

little doubt that a storm was approaching. They were near the southernmost boundaries of the Impregnable Forest by this time, and the jagged peaks of the Dragon's Teeth were visible in the dark horizon to the south. Still there was no sign of the massive army traveling ahead of them, and Menion was beginning to wonder how far south it might have already penetrated. They were not far now from the borders of Callahorn, which lay immediately below the Dragon's Teeth. If the Northland armies had already taken Callahorn, then the end had indeed come. The gray light of the afternoon dropped off sharply and the sky closed over in sullen darkness.

It was dusk when they first heard the ominous booming rising out of the night, echoing off the giant peaks ahead of them. Menion recognized it at once—he had heard that sound before in the forests of the Anar. It was the sound of hundreds of Gnome drums, their steady rhythm throbbing through the stillness of the humid air, filling the night with a sinister tension. The earth shook with the force of the beat, and all life had gone mute in awe and fear. Menion could tell by the intensity of the drums that there were far more than they had encountered at the Pass of Jade. If the army of the Northland could be measured by the sound of those drums, then there must be thousands. As the three moved quickly ahead, the frightening sound enveloped them entirely, booming all about them in shuddering echoes. The gray clouds of late afternoon still masked the night sky, leaving the searching men shrouded in inky darkness. Menion and Flick could no longer find the way alone, and the silent Druid led them with uncanny precision into the rough lowlands below Paranor. No one spoke, each man frozen into watchful apprehension by the deathly booming of those Gnome drums. They knew that the enemy camp was just ahead.

Then the terrain changed abruptly from the low hills and scattered brush to steep slopes dotted with boulders and treacherous rock ledges. The surefooted Allanon moved steadily ahead, his tall form unmistakable even in the near blackness, and the two Southlanders followed dutifully. Menion estimated that they must have reached the smaller mountains and foothills just above the Dragon's Teeth and that Allanon had chosen to come this way to avoid any chance encounters with members of the Northland army. It was still impossible to tell where the enemy army was encamped, but from the sound of the drums, it seemed as if they were right on top of it. The three dark shapes wound their way cautiously through the night for what must have been almost an hour, at times feeling their way blindly through the boulders and brush. Their clothes were scraped and torn, their exposed limbs scratched and bruised, but the silent Druid did not slacken the pace or pause to rest. At the end of that long hour's time, he halted abruptly and turned to them, placing a warning finger over pursed lips. Then slowly, cautiously, he led them forward into a huge mass of boulders. For several minutes, the three climbed noiselessly upward. Suddenly there were lights in the distance—dim, flickering yellow lights that came from burning fires. They crawled on hands and knees to the rim of the boulders. Upon reaching a tilted shelf of rock that sloped upward to the edge of the boulder cluster, they raised their heads slowly to the rim and peered breathlessly over.

What they saw was awesome and terrifying. As far as the eye could see, stretching miles in all directions, the fires of the Northland army burned in the night. They were like thousands of blazing yellow dots in the blackness of the plains, and moving busily about in their bright light were the dim shapes of wiry, gnarled Gnomes and bulky, thick-limbed Trolls. There were thousands of them, all armed, all waiting to descend on the kingdom of Callahorn. It was inconceivable to Menion and Flick that even the legendary Border Legion could hope to stand against such a mighty force. It was as if the entire Gnome and Troll population had been gathered on the plains below. Allanon had avoided any chance encounters with scouts or guards by approaching along the edges of the Dragon's Teeth on the western borders, and now the three were perched in a crow's nest of boulders several hundred feet up from the army encamped below. From this height, the shocked Southlanders could see the entirety of the massive force assembled to invade their poorly defended homeland. The drums of the Gnomes boomed out in steady crescendo as the men stared down, their eyes traveling from one end of the sprawled camp to the other in disbelief. For the first time, they understood fully what they were up against. Before, it had been only Allanon's words describing the invasion; now they could see the enemy and judge for themselves. Now they could feel the desperate need for the mysterious Sword of Shannara—a need for the one power that could destroy the evil being who had caused this army to materialize and march against them. But now was already too late.

For several long minutes, no one said anything as they stared down at the enemy encampment. Then Menion touched Allanon on the shoulder and started to speak, but the Druid clamped his hand quickly over the surprised highlander's mouth and pointed toward the base of the slope on which they lay concealed. Menion and Flick peered cautiously downward and to their surprise they made out the vague shapes of Gnome guards patrolling near the base of their hiding place. Neither had believed the enemy would bother to place guards this far from the actual camp, but apparently they were taking no chances. Allanon motioned for the two to move back from the edge of the boulders and they quickly complied, following his lead as he inched his way down into the tall rocks. Once they had reached the bottom of the boulder cluster, safely away from the rim of the ledge, the Druid huddled together with them in earnest council.

"We have to be very quiet," he warned in a tense whisper. "The sound of our voices would have echoed off the cliff face onto the plains from up there. Those Gnome guards would have heard us!"

Menion and Flick nodded in understanding.

"The situation is more serious than I thought," Allanon continued, his voice a hushed rasp in the gloom. "It appears the entire Northland army has bunched at this one point to strike at Callahorn. Brona intends to crush any resistance from the Southland immediately, dividing the better prepared armies of the East and West so he can deal with them separately. The evil one already holds everything north of Callahorn. Balinor and the others must be warned!"

He paused a moment, then turned expectantly to Menion Leah.

"I can't leave now," Menion exclaimed heatedly. "I've got to help you find Shea!"

"We haven't the time to argue the priorities of the situation," Allanon declared almost menacingly, one finger coming up like a dagger at the highlander's face. "If Balinor is not warned about the situation, Callahorn will fall and the rest of the Southland will follow, including Leah. The time has come for you to start thinking about your own people. Shea is only one man, and right now there is nothing you can do for him. But there is something you can do for the thousands of Southlanders who face enslavement at the hands of the Warlock Lord if Callahorn should fall!"

Allanon's voice was so cold that Flick could feel the chills run up his spine. He could sense Menion tensing expectantly, fearfully, at his side, but the Prince of Leah kept silent in the face of this stinging reprimand. Druid and Prince faced one another in the darkness for several interminable minutes, their eyes locked in open anger. Then Menion looked away abruptly and nodded shortly. Flick breathed an audible sigh of relief.

"I'll go to Callahorn and warn Balinor," Menion muttered, his voice still muffled with fury, "but I'll be back to find you."

"Do as you wish when you have found the others," replied Allanon coldly. "However, any attempt to return through enemy lines would be foolhardy at best. Flick and I shall try to find out what has happened to Shea and the Sword. We will not desert him, highlander, I promise you."

Menion looked back at him sharply, almost in disbelief, but the Druid's eyes were clear and undisguised. He was not lying.

"Keep close to these smaller mountains until you get past the enemy picket lines," the giant wanderer advised quietly. "When you reach the Mermidon River above Kern, cross there and enter the city before dawn. I expect the Northland army will march on Kern first. There is little chance that the city can be successfully defended against a force of that size. The people should be evacuated and moved into Tyrsis before the invaders can cut off their retreat. Tyrsis is built on a plateau against the back of a mountain. Properly defended, it can withstand any assault for at least several days. That should be time enough for Durin and Dayel to reach their homeland and return with the Elven army. Hendel should be able to offer some help from the Eastland. Perhaps Callahorn can be held long enough to mobilize and combine the armies of the three lands to strike back at the Warlock Lord. It is the only chance we have without the Sword of Shannara!"

Menion nodded in understanding and turned to Flick, extending his hand in a gesture of farewell. Flick smiled faintly and clasped the hand warmly.

"Good luck to you, Menion Leah."

Allanon came forward and placed a strong hand on the highlander's lean shoulder.

"Remember, Prince of Leah, we depend on you. The people of Callahorn must be made aware of the danger they face. If they falter or hesitate, they are lost, and with them all of the Southland. Do not fail."

Menion turned abruptly and moved like a shadow into the rocks beyond. The giant Druid and the little Valeman stood silently as the lean figure flitted agilely between the rocks and then disappeared from sight. They stood for a few minutes without speaking after he was gone, and then Allanon turned to Flick.

"To us is left the task of finding out what has happened to Shea and the Sword." He spoke again in a lowered voice, sitting heavily down on a small rock. Flick moved closer to him. "I'm worried about Eventine as well. That broken standard we found back at the battlefield was his personal banner. He may have been taken prisoner, and if he has, the Elven army may hesitate to act until he has been rescued. They love him too dearly to take a chance with his life, even to save the Southland."

"You mean the Elven people don't care what happens to the people of the Southland?" Flick exclaimed incredulously. "Don't they know what will happen to them should the Southland fall to the Warlock Lord?"

"It's not quite as simple as it seems," Allanon stated, sighing deeply. "Those who follow Eventine understand the danger, but there are others who believe that the Elven people should stay out of the affairs of the other lands unless they are directly attacked or threatened. With Eventine absent, the choice will not be so clear, and discussion of what is right and proper may delay any move by the Elven army until it is too late for them to help."

Flick nodded slowly, thinking of another time at Culhaven when a bitter Hendel had reported much the same thing about the people of the Southland cities. It seemed incredible that people could be so undecided and confused in the face of such obvious danger. Yet Shea and he had been like that when they had first learned about Shea's birthright and the threat of the Skull Bearers. It was not until they had seen one crawling, searching for them . . .

"I've got to know what's happening in that camp." Allanon's voice cut into Flick's thoughts with a sharp rasp of determination. He paused in thought a moment, staring at the little Valeman.

"My young friend, Flick . . ." He smiled faintly in the darkness. "How would you like to be a Gnome for a little while?"

XXII

ith Shea still missing somewhere north of the Dragon's Teeth and Allanon, Flick, and Menion in search of some definite sign of his whereabouts, the remaining four members of the now divided company of friends drew within sight of the great towers of the fortress city of Tyrsis. It had taken them almost two days of constant travel, their hazardous journey through the lines of the Northland army further impeded by the formidable mountain barrier cutting off the Southland kingdom of Callahorn from the land of Paranor. The first day was long, but without incident, as the four wound southward through the forests adjoining the Gnome-patrolled Impregnable Forest to reach the lowlands beyond, which formed the doorstep to the awesome Dragon's Teeth. The mountain passes were all carefully guarded by Gnome hunters, and it seemed it would prove to be impossible to get past them without a fight. But a simple ruse lured most of the guards away from the entrance to the high, winding Kennon Pass, allowing the four an opportunity to get into the mountains. The difficult task of getting out again at the southern end was accomplished only after several Gnomes were silently dispatched at a midpoint check camp and twenty more were frightened into believing the entire Border Legion of Callahorn had seized the pass and was descending on the luckless sentries with every intention of killing them all. Hendel was laughing so hard when they finally reached the safety of the forests south of the Kennon Pass that all four were forced to pause momentarily until he could recover his composure. Durin and Dayel looked doubtfully at one another, recalling the taciturn Dwarf's grim attitude during the journey to Paranor. They had never seen him laugh at anything, and somehow it seemed out of character. They shook their lean faces in disbelief and glanced questioningly at Balinor. But the giant borderman only shrugged. He was an old friend to Hendel and the Dwarf's changeable character was well known to him. It was good to hear his laughter again.

Now in the twilight of the early evening, with the sun's fading light a hazy purple and red in the vast horizon of the western plains, the four stood within sight of their destination. Their bodies were worn and sore, their normally keen minds numbed by lack of sleep and constant travel, but their spirits rose with unspoken excitement at the sight of the majestic city of Tyrsis. They paused for an instant at the edge of the forests that ran south from the Dragon's Teeth through Callahorn. To the east was the city of Varfleet, which guarded the only sizable passage through the Mountains of Runne, a small range that lay above the fabled Rainbow Lake. The sluggish Mermidon River wound its way through the forest at their backs above Tyrsis. Westward lay the smaller island city of Kern, and the source of the river was farther west in the vast emptiness of the Streleheim Plains. The river was broad at all points, forming a natural barrier against any would-be enemy and offering reliable protection for the inhabitants on the island. While the river ran full, which it did almost the year around, the waters were deep and swift, and no enemy had ever taken the island city.

Yet while both Kern, surrounded by the waters of

the Mermidon, and Varfleet, nestled in the Mountains of Runne, seemed formidable and well defended, it was the ancient city of Tyrsis that harbored the Border Legion—the precision fighting machine that had for countless generations successfully guarded the borders of the Southland against invasion. It was the Border Legion that had always taken the brunt of any assault against the race of Man, offering the first line of defense against an enemy invader. Tyrsis had given birth to the Border Legion of Callahorn, and as a fortress it was without equal. The old city of Tyrsis had been destroyed in the First War of the Races, but had been rebuilt and then expanded over the years until now it was one of the largest cities in all the Southland and by far the strongest city standing in the northern regions. It had been designed as a fortress capable of withstanding any enemy attack—a bastion of towering walls and jagged ramparts set on a natural plateau against the face of an unscalable cliff. Each generation of its citizens had contributed in the construction of the city, each making it more formidable. Over seven hundred years ago, the great Outer Wall had been built on the edge of the plateau, extending the boundaries of Tyrsis as far as nature would permit on the bluff face. In the fertile plains below the fortress were the farms and croplands that fed the city, the dark earth nurtured and sustained by the life-giving waters of the great Mermidon which ran east and south. The people had their homes scattered throughout the surrounding countryside, relying on the city's walled protection only in the event of invasion. For hundreds of years following the First War of the Races, the cities of Callahorn had successfully repelled assaults by unfriendly neighbors. None of the three had ever been seized by an enemy. The famed Border Legion had never been defeated in battle. But Callahorn had never faced an army the size of that sent by the Warlock Lord. The real test of strength and courage lay ahead.

Balinor looked upon the distant towers of his city with mixed feelings. His father had been a great King and a good man, but he was growing old. For years he had commanded the Border Legion in its unceasing battle against persistent Gnome raiders from the Eastland. Several times he had been forced to wage long and costly campaigns against the great Northland Trolls, when scattered tribes had moved into his land, intent on seizing its cities and subjugating its people. Balinor was the elder son and the logical heir to the throne. He had studied hard under his father's careful guidance, and he was well liked by the people— people whose friendship could be won only through respect and understanding. He had worked beside them, fought beside them, and learned from them, so that now he could feel what they felt and look through their eyes. He loved the land enough to fight to hold it, as he was doing now, as he had been doing for a number of years. He commanded a regiment of the Border Legion, and they wore his personal insignia—a crouched leopard. They were the key unit of the entire fighting force. For Balinor, holding their respect and devotion was more important than anything. He had been gone from them for months now—gone, by his own choosing, to a self-imposed exile of travel with the mysterious Allanon and the company from Culhaven. His father had asked him not to go, pleaded with him to reconsider his decision. But he had already decided; he was not to be swayed, even by his father. His brow furrowed and a strange feeling of gloom settled into his mind as he looked down on his homeland. Unconsciously, he raised one gloved hand to his face, the cold chain mail tracing the line of the scar that ran down the exposed right cheek to his chin.

"Thinking about your brother again?" Hendel asked, although it was not so much a question as a statement of fact.

Balinor looked over at him, momentarily startled, then nodded slowly.

"You've got to stop thinking about that whole business, you know," the Dwarf stated flatly. "He could be a real threat to you if you persist in thinking of him as a brother and not as a person."

"It is not so easy to forget that his blood and mine make us more than sons born to the same father," the borderman declared gloomily. "I cannot ignore nor forget such strong ties."

Durin and Dayel looked at each other, unable to comprehend what the two were talking about. They knew that Balinor had a brother, but they had never seen him and had heard no mention of him since they had begun the long journey from Culhaven.

Balinor noticed the baffled looks on the faces of the two Elven brothers and shot a quick smile in their direction.

"It's not as bad as it might seem," he assured them calmly.

Hendel shook his head hopelessly and lapsed into silence for the next few minutes.

"My younger brother Palance and I are the only sons of Ruhl Buckhannah, the King of Callahorn," Balinor volunteered, his eyes wandering back toward the distant city as if looking for another time. "We were very close while growing up—as close as you two. As we got older, we developed different ideas about life . . . different personalities, as all individuals must, brothers or not. I was the elder; I was next in line to the throne. Palance always realized this, of course, but it divided us as we grew older, mainly because his ideas of ruling the land were not always the same as mine. . . . It's difficult to explain, you understand."

"It's not so difficult," Hendel snorted meaningfully.

"All right, then, it's not so difficult," Balinor conceded wearily, to which Hendel responded with a knowing nod. "Palance believes Callahorn should cease to serve as a first line of defense in case of attack on the Southland people. He wants to disband the Border Legion and isolate Callahorn from the rest of the Southland. We cannot agree at all on this point. . . ."

He trailed off in bitter silence for a moment.

"Tell them the rest, Balinor." Hendel again spoke icily.

"My distrustful friend believes my brother is no longer his own master—that he says these things without meaning them. He keeps counsel with a mystic known as Stenmin, a man Allanon feels is without honor and will guide Palance to his own destruction. Stenmin has told my father and the people that my brother should rule and not I. He has turned him against me. When I left, even Palance seemed to believe that I was not fit to rule Callahorn."

"And that scar . . .?" Durin asked quietly.

"An argument we had just before I left with Allanon," Balinor replied, shaking his head as he thought back on the matter. "I can't even remember how it started, but all at once Palance was in a rage—there was real hatred in his eyes. I turned to leave, and he grabbed a whip from the wall, striking out at me, cutting into my face with the tip. That was the reason I decided to get away from Tyrsis for a time, to give Palance a chance to regain his senses. If I had stayed after that incident, we might have . . ."

Again he trailed off ominously, and Hendel shot the Elven brothers a glance that left no doubt in their minds what would have happened if the brothers had had another altercation. Durin frowned in disbelief, wondering what sort of person would take sides against a man like Balinor. The tall borderman had repeatedly proved his courage and strength of character during their dangerous journey to Paranor, and even Allanon had relied heavily on him. Yet his brother had deliberately and vindictively turned against him. The Elf felt a deep sadness for this brave warrior, returned to a homeland where peace even in his own family was denied him.

"You must believe me when I tell you that my

brother was not always like that—nor do I believe he is
now a bad man," Balinor continued, more as if he
were explaining it to himself than to the others. "This
mystic Stenmin has some kind of hold over Palance
that provokes him into these rages, turning him
against me and what he knows to be right."

"There is more to him than that," Hendel interrupted sharply. "Palance is an idealistic fanatic—he
seeks the throne and turns against you under pretext
of upholding the interests of the people. He is choking
on his own self-righteousness."

"Perhaps you are right, Hendel," Balinor conceded
quietly. "But he is still my brother, and I love him."

"That's what makes him so dangerous," the Dwarf
declared, standing before the tall borderman, meeting
his gaze squarely. "He no longer loves you."

Balinor did not reply, but stared into the plainlands
to the west and toward the city of Tyrsis. The others
remained silent for a few minutes, leaving the
brooding Prince to his own thoughts. Finally he
turned back to them, his face relaxed and calm,
looking as if the whole matter had never come up.

"Time to be moving on. We want to reach the walls
of the city before nightfall."

"I'm going no farther with you, Balinor," Hendel
interjected quickly. "I must return to my own land and
help prepare the Dwarf armies against an invasion of
the Anar."

"Well, you can rest in Tyrsis for tonight and leave
tomorrow," Dayel replied quickly, knowing how tired
they all were and anxious for the Dwarf's safety.

Hendel smiled patiently, then shook his head.

"No, I must travel at night in these lands. If I stay the
night in Tyrsis, I lose a whole day's travel, and time is
very precious to us all. The entire Southland stands or
falls on how quickly we can assemble our armies into a
combined fighting unit to strike back at the Warlock
Lord. If Shea and the Sword of Shannara are lost to us,

then our armies are all we have left. I will travel to Varfleet and rest there. Take care my friends. Luck to you in the days ahead."

"And to you, brave Hendel." Balinor extended a great hand. Hendel clasped it warmly, then those of the Elven brothers, and disappeared into the forests with a parting wave.

Balinor and the Elven brothers waited until they could no longer see him moving through the trees and then began their walk across the plains toward Tyrsis. The sun had dropped behind the horizon, and the sky had turned from dusky red to a deep gray and blue that signaled the momentary approach of night. They were about halfway when the sky turned completely black, revealing the first of the night's stars shining in a clear, cloudless sky. As they neared the fabled city, its vast bulk sprawling and dark against the night horizon, the Prince of Callahorn described in detail to the Elven brothers the history behind the building of Tyrsis.

A series of natural defenses protected the man-made fortress. The city had been built on a high plateau which ran back against a line of small, but treacherous cliffs. The cliffs bounded the plateau entirely on the south and partially on the west and east. While they were not nearly so high or formidable in appearance as the Dragon's Teeth or the Charnal Mountains of the far Northland, they were incredibly steep. That portion of the cliffs that faced north onto the plateau rose almost straight up, and no one had ever successfully scaled it. Thus, the city was well protected from the rear, and it had never been necessary to construct any defenses to the south. The plateau on which the city was built was a little over three miles across at its widest point, dropping off sharply onto the plainlands which ran unbroken and open all the way north and west to the Mermidon River and east to the forests of Callahorn. The swift

Mermidon actually formed the first line of defense against invasion, and few armies had ever gotten beyond that point to reach the plateau and the city walls. The enemy who did manage to cross the Mermidon onto the plainlands immediately found itself confronted by the steep wall of the plateau, which could be defended from above. The main route of access to this bluff was a huge iron and stone rampway, which was rigged to collapse by knocking out pins in the major supports.

But even if the enemy managed to reach the top of the plateau and thereby gain a foothold, the third defense waited—the defense that no army had ever broken through. Standing a scant two hundred yards from the edge of the plateau and ringing the entire city in a semicircle, the ends reaching back to the cliff sides protecting the southern approach, was the monstrous Outer Wall. Constructed from great blocks of stone welded together with mortar, the surface had been smoothed down to make scaling by hand virtually impossible. It rose nearly a hundred feet into the air, massive, towering, impregnable. At the top of the wall, ramparts had been built for the men fighting within the city, with sections cut away to allow concealed bowmen room to shoot down on the unprotected attackers. It was ancient in styling, crude and rough-hewn, but it had repelled invaders for almost a thousand years. No enemy army had penetrated into the inner city since its construction following the First War of the Races.

Just within the great Outer Wall, the Border Legion was quartered in a series of long, sloping barracks interspersed by buildings used for storage of supplies and weapons. Approximately one-third of this great fighting force was kept on duty at any given time, while the other two-thirds remained at home with their families, pursuing their secondary occupations as laborers, craftsmen, or shopkeepers in the city. The barracks were equipped to house the entire army if the need should ever arise, as indeed it had already done on more than one occasion, but at present they were only partially filled. Set back from the barracks, supply housing, and parade grounds was a second wall of stone blocks separating the soldiers' quarters from the city proper. Within this second wall, lining the neat, winding city streets, were the homes and businesses of the urban population of Tyrsis, all carefully constructed and meticulously cared for buildings. The city sprawled over most of the plateau's elevation, running from this second stone wall almost to the cliffs bordering the south approach. At this innermost point of the city, a low third wall had been built which marked the entrance to the government buildings and the royal palace of the King, complete with public forum and landscaped grounds. The tree-shaded parks surrounding the palace provided the only sylvan setting on the otherwise open and sparse flatland of the plateau. The third wall had not been built for defensive purposes, but as a line of demarcation, signifying government-owned property that had been reserved for the King's use and, in the case of the parks, for all the people. Balinor deviated from his description of the city's construction long enough to point out to the Elven brothers that the Kingdom of Callahorn was one of the few remaining enlightened monarchies in the world. While it was technically a monarchy ruled by a King, the government also consisted of a parliamentary body composed of representatives chosen by the people of Callahorn, who helped the ruler hammer out the laws that governed the land. The people took great pride in their government and in the Border Legion in which most either had served at one time or were serving now. It was a country in which they could be free men, and this was something worth fighting for.

Callahorn was a land that reflected both the past and

the future. On the one hand its cities had been built primarily as fortresses to withstand the frequent assaults by warlike neighbors. The Border Legion was a carry-over from earlier times when the newly formed nations were constantly at war, when an almost fanatical pride in national sovereignty resulted in a long struggle over jealously guarded land boundaries, when brotherhood between the peoples of the four lands was still only a distant possibility. The rustic, old-fashioned decor and architecture could be found nowhere else in the quickly growing cities of the deep Southland—cities where more enlightened cultures and less warlike policies were beginning to prevail. Yet it was Tyrsis, with her barbaric walls of stone and warrior men of iron, that had shielded the lower Southland and given it that chance to expand in new directions. There were signs of what was to come in this picturesque land as well, signs that told of another age and time not too far distant. There was a unity of expression in the people that spoke of tolerance and understanding of all races and peoples. In Callahorn, as in no other country in all the sheltered Southland, a man was accepted for what he was and treated accordingly.

Tyrsis was the crossroads of the four lands, and through its walls and lands passed members of all the nations, giving its people an opportunity to see and understand that the differences in face and body that distinguished the races outwardly were negligible. It was the inner person the people had learned to judge. A giant Rock Troll would not be stared at and shunned because of his grotesque appearance by the people of Callahorn; Trolls were common in that land. Gnomes, Elves, and Dwarfs of all types and species made regular passages through that country, and if they were friends, they were welcomed. Balinor smiled as he spoke of this new, growing phenomenon that had begun at last to spread to all the lands, and he felt proud that his people were among the first to turn from the old prejudices to look for common grounds of understanding and friendship. Durin and Dayel listened in silent agreement. The Elven people knew what it was like to be alone in a world of people who couldn't see beyond their own limits.

Balinor had finished, and the three comrades swung from the tall grass of the plainland onto a broad roadway. The road wound ahead into the darkness toward the low, squat plateau looming blackly against the horizon. They were close enough now to make out the lights of the sprawling city and the movement of people on the stone ramp. The entrance through the towering Outer Wall was sharply outlined by torchlight, the giant gates standing open on oiled hinges, guarded by a number of dark-garbed sentries. From the courtyard within shone the lights of the barracks, but there was an absence of men's laughter and joking that Balinor found peculiar. The voices that were audible were hushed, even muffled, as if no one wished to be heard. The tall borderman peered ahead watchfully, suddenly concerned that something was amiss, but he could detect nothing out of the ordinary, aside from the unusual silence. He dismissed the matter from his mind.

The Elven brothers followed wordlessly as the determined Balinor mounted the causeway leading to the darkened bluff. Several people passed them as they climbed, and those who looked carefully turned to stare in open shock at the Prince of Callahorn. Balinor failed to acknowledge these strange looks, intent upon the city ahead, but the brothers missed nothing and looked at each other in silent warning. Something was seriously wrong. Moments later, as the three reached the plateau, Balinor, too, stopped in sudden concern. He peered intently toward the gates of the city, then looked about him at the shadowed faces of the people passing, who scattered quickly and wordlessly into the night upon discovering his identity. For a moment the three stood rooted in silence, watching the few remaining passers-by disappear into the darkness, leaving them alone.

"What is it, Balinor?" Durin asked at last.

"I'm not certain," the Prince replied anxiously. "Look at the insignia of those guards at the gate. None of them bear the crest of the leopard—the standard of my Border Legion. Instead they wear the sign of a falcon, a mark I do not recognize. The people, too—did you notice their looks?"

The slim Elven faces nodded as one, the keen slanted eyes casting about in undisguised apprehension.

"No matter," the borderman declared shortly. "This is still my father's city, and these are my people. We'll get to the bottom of this when we reach the palace."

Again he started toward the mammoth gates of the Outer Wall, the Elves a step or two behind him. The tall Prince made no effort to hide his face as he approached the four armed guards, and their reaction was the same as that of the astonished passers-by. They made no move to stop the Prince and no words passed between them, yet one hurriedly abandoned his post and disappeared quickly through the gates of the Inner Wall into the streets of the city beyond. Balinor and the Elves passed beneath the shadow of the giant gateway, which seemed to hang in the darkness above them like a monstrous stone arm. They moved past the open gates and the watchful guards into the courtyard beyond, where they could see the low, Spartanlike barracks that housed the famed Border Legion. There were few lights burning, and the barracks appeared to be nearly deserted. A few men scattered about the courtyard wore tunics bearing the insignia of the leopard, but they wore no armor and carried no weapons. One stared momentarily as the three paused in the center of the courtyard, then started in disbelief and cried out sharply to his fellow soldiers. A door burst open from one of the barracks and a grizzled veteran appeared, staring with the others at Balinor and the Elven brothers. He gave a short command, and the soldiers reluctantly turned back to whatever they had been doing, while he hastened over to the three newcomers.

"My Lord Balinor, you've come at last," the soldier exclaimed in greeting, his head bowing briefly as he came to attention before his commander.

"Captain Sheelon, it's good to see you." Balinor clasped the veteran's gnarled hand in his own. "What's going on in the city? Why do the guards wear the sign of a falcon and not that of our fighting leopard?"

"My Lord, the Border Legion has been ordered to disband! Only a handful of us still remain on duty; the rest are returned to their homes!"

They stared at the man as if he were insane. The Border Legion had been disbanded in the midst of the greatest invasion ever to threaten the Southland? Almost as one they recalled the words of Allanon telling them that the Border Legion was the only hope left to the people of the threatened lands, that the Border Legion must at least temporarily delay the awesome force assembled by the Warlock Lord. Now the army of Callahorn had been mysteriously scattered . . .

"By whose order . . .?" Balinor asked in slow fury.

"It was your brother," the grizzled Sheelon declared quickly. "He ordered his own guardsmen to assume our duties and commanded the Legion to disband until further notice. The Lords Acton and Messaline went to the palace to beg the King to reconsider, but they did not return. There was nothing more any of us could do but obey. . . ."

"Has everyone gone mad?" the infuriated borderman demanded, clasping the soldier's tunic. "What of my father, the King? Does he not still rule this land and command the Border Legion? What does he say of this fool's play?"

Sheelon looked away, groping for the words to the answer he was afraid to speak. Balinor jerked him around violently.

"I—I do not know, my Lord," the man muttered, still trying to turn away. "We heard the King was ill, and then there was nothing more. Your brother declared himself temporary ruler in the King's absence from the throne. That was three weeks ago."

Balinor released the man in shocked silence and stared absently at the lights of the distant palace—the home he had come back to with such great hopes. He had left Callahorn because of an intolerable rift between his brother and himself, yet his going had only made matters worse. Now he must face the unpredictable Palance on terms not of his own choosing—face him and persuade him somehow of the folly of his action in disbanding the desperately needed Border Legion.

"We must go at once to the palace and speak with your brother." The eager, impatient voice of Dayel cut into his thoughts. He looked at the youthful Elf for a moment, reminded suddenly of his own brother's young age. It was going to be so hard to reason with Palance.

"Yes, you're right, of course," he agreed almost absently. "We must go to him."

"No, you mustn't go in there!" The sharp cry of Sheelon held them rooted in place. "The others who went did not come out again. There are rumors that your brother has declared you a traitor—found you to be in league with the evil Allanon, the black wanderer who serves the dark powers. It has been said that you shall be imprisoned and put to death!"

"That is ridiculous!" exclaimed the tall borderman

quickly. "I am no traitor and even my brother knows this to be true. As for Allanon, he is the best friend and ally the Southland will ever find. I must go to Palance and speak with him. We may disagree, but he would not imprison his own brother. The power is not his!"

"Unless, perhaps, your father is dead, my friend," Durin cautioned from one side. "The time to be prudent is now, before we have entered the palace grounds. Hendel believes your brother to be under the influence of the mystic Stenmin, and if he is, you may be in greater danger than you realize."

Balinor paused, then nodded his agreement. Quickly he explained to Sheelon the threat to Callahorn of an impending Northland invasion, emphasizing his belief that the Border Legion would be vital to the defense of their homeland. Then he gripped the aged soldier's shoulder tightly and bent close to him.

"You will wait four hours for my return or for my personal messenger. If I have not come out or sent word in that time, you will seek out the Lords Ginnisson and Fandwick; the Border Legion is to be reassembled immediately! Then go to the people and demand an open trial of our cause from my brother. He cannot refuse this. You will also send word west and east to the Elf and Dwarf nations, informing them that we are thus held, both I and the cousins of Eventine. Can you remember all I have said to you?"

"Yes, my Lord." The soldier nodded eagerly. "It shall be done as you command. May fortune go with you, Prince of Callahorn."

He turned and disappeared back into the barracks, while an impatient and angry Balinor moved toward the inner city. Once again, Durin whispered to his younger brother, urging him to remain outside the city walls until he knew what would happen to Balinor and himself, but Dayel stubbornly refused to be left behind. Durin knew it was pointless to argue the matter further, and at last conceded Dayel's right to go along. The slim Elf had not yet reached his twentieth year, and for him life was just beginning. All of the members of the little company that had come from Culhaven had felt a special kind of affection for Dayel, the protective love that close friends always feel for the youngest. His fresh candor and ready friendship were rare qualities in a time when most men lived lives hemmed in by suspicion and distrust. Durin was afraid for him, for he had the most to look ahead to and the fewest years behind. If the boy were harmed in any way, he realized that an irreplaceable part of himself would be lost. Durin watched his brother in silence as the lights of Tyrsis burned through the darkness ahead.

In moments, the three crossed the courtyard and passed through the gates of the Inner Wall to the streets of the city beyond. Once more the guards stared in open amazement, but again they did not move to stop the travelers from entering. Balinor seemed to grow in size as the three proceeded down the Tyrsian Way, the main city thoroughfare, his dark form wrapped ominously in the hunting cloak, the chain mail glinting from exposed fists and neck. He stood taller than before, no longer the weary traveler at his journey's end, but the Prince of Callahorn come home. The people knew him at once, at first stopping and staring like those at the outer gates, then gathering heart from his proud bearing and rushing after him, eager to welcome him home. The crowd swelled from a few dozen to several hundred as the favorite son of Callahorn strode boldly through the city, smiling to those who followed, but hastening to reach the palace. The shouts and cries of the people rose deafeningly, changing from scattered voices to a single rising chant calling the tall borderman's name. A few of the crowd managed to get next to the determined man, whispering ominous warnings. But the Prince would not listen to cautious voices any longer; shaking his head after each warning, he continued on.

The growing crowd passed through the heart of Tyrsis, milling under the giant archways and crosswalks that ran overhead, pushing through the narrow portions of the Tyrsian Way past tall, white-walled buildings and smaller single-family residences to the Bridge of Sendic which spanned the lower levels of the people's parks. At the other end stood the gates of the palace, darkened and closed. At the peak of the bridge's wide arch, the Prince of Callahorn turned abruptly to face the throng still faithfully following him and threw up his hands in a command to halt. They came to an obedient stop, their voices lowering into silence as the tall figure addressed them.

"My friends—my countrymen." The proud voice rang out in the near darkness, its thundering echoes rolling back. "I have missed this land and its brave citizens, but I have come home—and I will not leave again! There is no need for fear. This land shall stand eternal! If there be trouble within the monarchy, then it is for me to face it. You must go back now to your homes and wait for morning to show you in a better light that all is well. Please, go now to your homes and I shall go to mine!"

Without waiting to judge the crowd's reaction, Balinor wheeled about and proceeded on across the bridge toward the gates of the palace, the Elven brothers still close at his heels. The voice of the people rose again to call after them, but the crowd did not follow, though many might have wished to do so. Obedient to his command, they turned slowly about, some still shouting his name in defiance at the silent, darkened castle, though others mumbled grim prophecies of what awaited the tall borderman and his two friends within the walls of the imperial home. The three travelers quickly lost sight of the people as they

started down the slope of the bridge's high arch in
quick, determined strides. In minutes they reached
the tall, metal-bound gates of the palace of the
Buckhannahs. Balinor never paused, but reached for
the huge iron ring fastened to the wood and brought it
crashing down against the shuttered gate in thundering knocks. For a moment there was no other sound,
as the men stood in the darkness without, listening
with mixed feelings of anger and apprehension. Then
a low voice from within called for identification.
Balinor gave his name and a sharp command to those
within to open the gates immediately. In an instant,
the heavy bars were drawn back and the gates swung
inward to admit the three. Balinor moved into the
garden courtyard without a backward glance at the
silent guards, his eyes on the magnificent columned
building beyond. Its high windows were dark except
for those on the ground floor in the left wing. Durin
motioned Dayel ahead of him, taking the opportunity
to peer into the shadows about them where he quickly
discovered a dozen well-armed guards close at hand.
All bore the insignia of the falcon.

The watchful Elf knew instantly that they were
walking into a trap, just as he had silently anticipated
when they had entered the city. His first inclination
was to stop Balinor and warn him of what he had seen.
But he instinctively knew that the borderman was far
too seasoned a fighter not to know what he was
getting into. Durin wished once more that his brother
had stayed outside the palace walls, but it was too late
now. The three crossed the garden walks to the doors
of the palace. There were no guards and the doors
opened without resistance to Balinor's hurried shove.
The halls of the aged building glowed brightly in the
torchlight, the flames catching the splendor of the
colorful wall murals and paintings that decorated the
Buckhannah family home. The wood trimming was
old and rich, polished with care and partially covered

by fine tapestries and metal plaques of family crests from generations of the famed rulers of the land. As the Elven brothers followed the tall Prince down these silent halls, they recalled darkly another time and place in the recent past—the ancient fortress of Paranor. There, too, a trap had awaited them amid the historic splendor of another age.

They turned left into another hallway, Balinor still in the lead by several strides, his big form filling the high corridor, the long hunting cloak billowing out behind him as he walked. For an instant, he reminded Durin of Allanon, huge, angered, dangerous when he moved catlike as the Prince of Callahorn did now. Durin glanced anxiously at Dayel, but the younger Elf did not seem to notice; his face was flushed with excitement. Durin felt for the handle of his dagger, the cold metal reassuring to his hot palm. If they were to be trapped again, it would not be without a fight.

Then the giant borderman stopped suddenly before an open doorway. The Elven brothers hastened to his side, peering past his broad frame into the lighted room beyond. There was a man standing near the back of the elegantly furnished chamber—a big man, blond and bearded, his broad figure cloaked in a long purple robe with a falcon marking. He was several years younger than Balinor, but held his tall frame erect in the same manner, the hands clasped loosely behind his back. The Elves knew immediately that he was Palance Buckhannah. Balinor moved several steps into the chamber, saying nothing, his eyes riveted on his brother's face. The Elves followed the borderman, looking cautiously about. There were too many doors, too many heavy drapes that could be concealing armed guards. A moment later there was a movement in the hall behind them just out of sight. Dayel turned slightly to face the open doorway. Durin moved a little apart from the others, his long hunting knife drawn, his lean frame bent slightly in a half-crouch.

Balinor made no move, but stood silently before his brother, staring at the familiar face, amazed that the eyes were filled with a strange hatred. He had known it would be a trap, known that his brother would be prepared for them. Yet he had believed all along that they would at least be able to talk as brothers, converse with one another in a frank and reasonable manner despite their differences. But as he looked into those eyes and caught the undisguised glint of burning fury, he realized that his brother was beyond reason, perhaps beyond sanity.

"Where is my father . . .?"

Balinor's abrupt query was cut short by a sudden swishing sound as hidden cords released a large leather and rope net that had hung unnoticed above the intruders, dropping it instantly over all three. The attached weights brought all of them crashing to the floor in staggered dismay, their weapons useless against the toughened cords. Doors flew open from all sides and the heavy drapes whipped back as several dozen armed guards rushed over to subdue the struggling captives. There was never any chance to escape the carefully prepared trap, never even a momentary opportunity to fight back. The captives were relieved of their weapons, their hands bound unceremoniously behind their backs and their eyes blindfolded. They were lifted roughly to their feet and firmly held in place by a dozen unseen hands. There was momentary silence as someone approached and stood before them.

"You were a fool to come back, Balinor," a chilling voice sounded out of the blackness. "You knew what would happen to you if I found you again. You are thrice over a traitor and a coward for what you have done—to the people, to my father, and now even to me. What have you done with Shirl? What have you done with her? You will die for this, Balinor, I swear it! Take them below!"

The hands spun them about, shoving and dragging them down the hallway, through one door, down a long flight of stairs to a landing and another hall that wound about in a maze of twists and turns. Their feet thudded heavily on dank stones in a black, unbroken silence. Suddenly they were going down yet another set of stairs and into another passageway. They could smell the stale, chill air and feel the dampness ooze from the stone walls and floor. A set of heavy bolts was drawn slowly back with a screech of aged iron against iron, and the door they held in place ponderously opened. The hands turned them sharply, releasing them without warning as they fell dazed and battered to the stone floor, still bound and blindfolded. The door closed and the bolts slid heavily into place. The three companions listened wordlessly. They heard the sound of footsteps retreating rapidly into the distance until they had faded away altogether. They heard the sounds of clanging metal as doors were barred and shuttered, each farther away than the last, until finally there was only the sound of their own breathing in the deep silence of their prison. Balinor had come home.

XXIII

t was nearing midnight by the time Allanon had finished disguising the reluctant Flick to his satisfaction. Using a strange lotion produced from a pouch he carried at his waist, the Druid rubbed the skin of the Valeman's face and hands until it was a dark yellow. A piece of soft coal altered the lines in the face and the appearance of the eyes. It was a makeshift job at best, but in the dark he could pass for a large, heavyset Gnome, if not closely examined. It would have been a perilous undertaking even for a seasoned hunter, and for an untrained man to attempt to pass himself off as a Gnome appeared to be suicide. But there was no alternative left. Someone had to get into that giant encampment and attempt to discover what had happened to Eventine, Shea, and the elusive Sword. It was out of the question for Allanon to go down there; he would have been recognized in an instant, even in the best disguise. So the task fell to the frightened Flick, disguised as a Gnome, under cover of darkness, to work his way down the slopes, past the watching guards, into the camp occupied by thousands of Gnomes and Trolls, and there find out if his brother or the missing Elven King were prisoners, in addition to trying to learn something of the whereabouts of the Sword. To complicate matters, the Valeman had to get clear of the enemy camp before daybreak. If he failed to do this, someone would most

certainly see through his disguise in the daylight and
he would be caught.

Allanon asked Flick to remove his hunting cloak and
worked on the material for several minutes, altering
the cut slightly and lengthening the hood covering to
conceal its wearer better. When he was done, Flick
covered himself and found that with the cloak pulled
closely about his body, nothing was visible aside from
his hands and a shadowed portion of his face. If he
stayed away from any true Gnomes and kept moving
until dawn, there was an outside chance that he might
learn something important and still escape to tell
Allanon. He checked to be certain the short hunting
dagger was securely fastened to his waist. It was a
poor substitute for a weapon, should he have need of
one once he was within the encampment, but it gave
him a little reassurance that he was not totally without
protection. He stood up slowly, his short, heavyset
frame wrapped in the cloak as Allanon looked him
over carefully and then nodded.

The weather had become threatening during the
past hour, the sky a solid bank of rolling, blackened
clouds that completely blotted out the moon and stars,
leaving the earth in almost complete darkness. The
only visible light in any direction came from the
blazing fires of the encamped enemy, the flames
rushing higher with the sudden appearance of a
strong north wind that howled fiercely through the
Dragon's Teeth to sweep in rising gusts onto the
unprotected plainlands below. A storm was on the
way, and it would very likely reach them before
morning. The silent Druid was hopeful that the winds
and darkness would offer the disguised Valeman a
little added cover from the eyes of the sleeping army.

In brief, clipped sentences, the giant mystic offered
Flick a few parting words of caution. He explained the
manner in which the camp would be arranged, noting
the pattern in which guards would be posted about the

perimeter of the main army. He told him to look for the standards of the Gnome chieftains and the Maturens, the Troll leaders, which would undoubtedly lie somewhere near the center of the fires. At all costs, he was to avoid speaking to anyone, for the tone of his voice would instantly betray him as a Southlander. Flick listened attentively, his heart pounding wildly as he waited to go, his own mind already made up that he had no chance of escaping detection; but his loyalty to his brother was too great to permit the interference of common sense when Shea's safety was threatened. Allanon closed his brief explanation by promising to see that the youth got safely past the first guard line that had been posted at the base of these slopes. He signaled for complete silence, then motioned for the other to follow.

They moved down out of the rocky shelter of the high boulders, winding their way through the darkness toward the open plain. It was so black that Flick could see almost nothing and had to be led by the hand in order to stay with the surefooted Druid. It seemed to take an interminable length of time for the two to reach an exit point from the twisting maze of boulders, but at last they were able to see once more the fires of the enemy camp burning in the darkness ahead. Flick was bruised and battered from his climb down out of the mountain heights, his limbs aching from the strain, his cloak torn in several places. The darkness of the plain seemed to stand like an unbroken wall between the fires and themselves, and Flick could neither see nor hear the guard lines he knew were there. Allanon said nothing, but crouched back in the shelter of the rocks, his head cocked slightly as he listened. The two remained motionless for long minutes, then suddenly Allanon rose, motioning Flick to remain where he was, and silently disappeared in the night.

When he was gone, the little Valeman looked about anxiously, alone and frightened because he had no idea what was happening. Leaning his heated face against the cool surface of the rock, he went over in his mind what he would do once he reached the encampment. He didn't have much of a plan to rely on. He would avoid speaking with anyone, and if possible, avoid passing close to anyone. He would stay clear of the illuminating firelight which might betray his poor disguise. The prisoners, if in the camp at all, would be held in a guarded tent near the center of the fires, so his first objective would be to find that tent. Once he found it, he would try to get a look inside to see who was there. Then, assuming he got that far, which seemed highly unlikely, he would make his way back to the slopes, where Allanon would be waiting and they would decide their next move.

Flick shook his head in frustration. He knew he would never be able to get away with this disguise—he was neither talented nor clever enough to fool anyone. But ever since losing Shea over the side of the Dragon's Crease days earlier, his attitude had completely altered and the old pessimism and hard-nosed practicality had been replaced by a strange sense of futile desperation. His familiar world had altered so drastically in the past few weeks that he no longer seemed capable of identifying with his old values and sensible practices. Time had become almost meaningless in the punishing, endless days of running and hiding, of fighting creatures that belonged to another world. The years spent living and growing in the peace and solitude of Shady Vale were distant, forgotten days of an early youth. The only constant forces in his upended life of the past weeks had been his companions, particularly his brother. Now they, too, had been scattered one by one until at last Flick stood alone, on the verge of exhaustion and mental collapse, his world a mad, impossible puzzle of nightmares and spirits that chased and haunted him to the brink of despair.

The hulking presence of Allanon had given him little comfort. The giant Druid had remained from their first meeting both an impenetrable wall of secrecy and a mystical force with powers that defied explanation. Despite the growing camaraderie of the company on the journey to Paranor and beyond, the Druid had remained aloof and secretive. Even what he had told them about his own origin and purposes did little to lighten the dark veil of mystery in which he had wrapped himself.

When the company had been together, the mystic's domination of them had not seemed so overpowering, even though he had remained the undisputed force behind their hazardous search for the Sword of Shannara. But now, with the others gone, leaving the frightened Valeman alone with this unpredictable giant, Flick found himself unable to escape that terrible awesomeness that formed the essence of this strange man. He thought back again on the mysterious tale of the history of the fabled Sword, and again he remembered Allanon's refusal to tell the members of the little company the whole story behind its power. They had risked everything for that elusive talisman, and still no one but Allanon knew how the weapon could be used to defeat the Warlock Lord. Why was it that Allanon knew so much about it?

A sudden noise in the darkness behind him brought the terrified Valeman about in a flash, the short hunting knife drawn and extended in self-defense. There was a sharp whisper and the huge form of Allanon moved silently to Flick's side. A powerful hand gripped his shoulder, guiding him back into the shelter of the rock-covered slope, where the two crouched cautiously in the blackness. Allanon studied the Valeman's face for an instant as if judging his courage, reading his mind to see the nature of his thoughts. Flick could just barely force himself to meet the penetrating gaze, his heart pounding in mingled fear and excitement.

"The guards are disposed of—the way is clear." The deep voice seemed to rise up out of the depths of the earth. "Go now, my young friend, and keep your courage and your good sense close at hand."

Flick nodded shortly and rose, his cloak-shrouded form gliding quickly and stealthily out of the cover of the boulders onto the blackness of the empty plains. His mind ceased to reason, ceased to wonder, as his body took command and his instincts probed the darkness for hidden danger. He moved swiftly toward the distant firelight, running in a half-crouch, pausing occasionally to check his position and listen for the sounds of human movement. The night was an impenetrable shroud all about him, the sky still heavily overcast and wrapped in a huge cloud blanket that shut out even the dim whiteness of the moon and stars. The only light came from the campfires ahead. The plainland was smooth and open, its surface a grassy blanket that muffled the Valeman's footfalls as he raced silently forward. There were few bushes to break the pattern, and it was left to one or two thin, twisted trees to fill the vast emptiness. There was no sign of life anywhere in the darkness and the only sounds were the muffled howl of the rising wind and his own heavy breathing. The campfires that had formerly seemed a low haze of orange light from the base of the mountains spread apart into individual fires as the Valeman drew closer, some burning brightly, their flames well fed on new wood, while others had dimmed and nearly died into coals as the men who tended them slept undisturbed. Flick was close enough now to hear the faint sound of voices in the sleeping camp, but they were not distinct enough to enable him to make out the words.

Almost half an hour passed before Flick reached the outer perimeter of the enemy fires. He paused in a crouch just beyond the light to study the lay of the camp ahead. The cool night wind blowing out of the north fanned the crackling flames of the large wood fires, sending thin clouds of smoke swirling across the open plains toward the Valeman. There was a second ring of sentries encircling the encampment, but it was only a secondary guard line loosely set at wide intervals. The Northlanders felt there was little need for caution this close to the campsite. The sentries were primarily Gnome hunters, although Flick could distinguish the larger bulks of Troll men scattered about as well.

He paused momentarily to study the strange, unfamiliar features of the Trolls. They were of different sizes, all thick-limbed and covered with a dark, wood-like skin that appeared rough and highly protective. The sentries and the few members of the army that were not asleep, but standing idly about or crouched near the low-burning fires for warmth, had wrapped themselves in heavy cloaks that masked most of their bodies and faces. Flick nodded to himself in satisfaction. It would be easier for him to slip into the camp undetected if everyone remained wrapped in their cloaks, and judging from the increasing coolness of the wind, the temperature would continue to drop until sunrise. It was difficult to see much beyond the outer fires, due to the clouded darkness and the smoke given off by the quick-burning wood.

Somehow the camp seemed smaller from this viewpoint than it had from the heights of the Dragon's Teeth. Flick could not get the same sense of depth from his present position, but he did not try to fool himself. Despite what it appeared to be from where he crouched, he knew that it stretched for over a mile in all directions. Once past the inner sentry line, he would have to pick his way through thousands of sleeping Gnomes and Trolls, past hundreds of fires bright enough to reveal his identity, and all the way avoid contact with the enemy soldiers who were still awake. The first miscalculation the Valeman made would give him away. Even if he managed to avoid discovery, he still had to locate the prisoners and the Sword. He shook his head in doubt and moved forward slowly.

The natural curiosity of the Valeman prompted him to linger near the fringes of the firelight to study further the Gnomes and Trolls still awake, but he resisted the impulse, reminding himself that he didn't have much time as it was. Though he had lived all his life on the same earth with these two foreign races, they were like species from another world to the little Southlander. During his journey to Paranor, he had fought the cunning, savage Gnomes several times, once hand to hand in the labyrinth passages of the Druids' Keep. But he still knew little about them; they were simply an enemy who had tried to kill him. He had learned nothing of the giant Trolls, a habitually reclusive people dwelling principally in the northern mountains and their hidden valleys. In any event, Flick knew that the army was under the leadership of the Warlock Lord, and there was no question as to what *his* goals were!

He waited until the wind carried the smoke from the burning fires between the closest sentry and himself in a series of billowing gusts, then rose and strolled in a casual manner toward the encampment. He had carefully selected an entry point where the soldiers were all sleeping. The smoke and the night masked his bulky form as he moved out of the shadows and into the circle of fires nearest to him. A moment later he stood in the midst of the soundly sleeping forms. The sentry continued to stare blankly into the darkness behind him, unaware of the hurried passage.

Flick wrapped the cloak and head covering closely about his body, making certain that only his hands were immediately visible to anyone passing by. His face was a dim shadow beneath the hood. He glanced about quickly, but there was no movement by anyone close at hand; he had made it this far unnoticed. He breathed deeply of the cool night air to steady himself, then tried to gauge his position in relation to the center of the encampment. He chose a direction which he believed would take him directly toward the hub of the burning fires, glanced about once more to reassure himself, then moved forward with steady, measured steps. Now there could be no turning back.

What he saw, what he heard, what he experienced deep within his mind that night left an indelible print in his memory that would stay with him forever. It was like a strange, somehow elusive nightmare of sights and sounds, creatures and shapes from another time and place—things that never were in and could never belong to his own world, and yet had been cast onto it like so much driftwood from an endless sea. Perhaps it was the night and the wafting smoke from the hundreds of dying fires that clouded his normal senses and created this dreamlike experience. Perhaps, too, it was the aftereffect of a tired, frightened mind that had never conceived of the existence of such creatures, nor imagined their number could be so vast.

The night passed in slow minutes and endless hours as the little Valeman wound his way through the giant encampment, shielding his face from the light of the fires as he moved steadily forward, his eyes searching, studying and always looking further. Cautiously, he picked his tortured way over thousands of sleeping bodies huddled close to the flames, often blocking his progress entirely, each another chance that he might be discovered and killed. There were times when he was certain that he had been discovered, times when his hand moved swiftly, silently to the small hunting knife, his heart dying within him as he prepared to fight for his freedom at the cost of his life. Again and again, men came toward him as if they knew he was an impostor, as if they would stop him and expose him to everyone. But each time they passed by without pausing, without speaking, and Flick would be left alone once again, a forgotten figure in a gathering of thousands.

Several times he passed close to groups of men talking and joking in low tones as they huddled around the fires, rubbing their hands and drawing from the crackling flames what little heat there was to protect them against the growing cold of the night. Twice, perhaps three times, they nodded or waved as he pushed past them, his face lowered, the cloak held close about his body, and he would make some feeble gesture in acknowledgment. Time and again he was afraid he had made a wrong move, failed to speak when he should, walked where he was not permitted—but each time the terrible moment of doubt vanished as he hurried on, and he found himself alone once more.

He wandered through the immense camp for hours without finding any clue to the whereabouts of Shea, Eventine, or the Sword of Shannara. As morning drew near, he began to despair of finding anything. He had passed countless fires, burning low and dying with the close of night, gazed on a sea of sleeping bodies, some with faces turned skyward, some with blankets all around them, all unknown. There had been tents everywhere, marked by the standards of the enemy leaders, both Gnome and Troll, but there had been no guards stationed before them to distinguish them in importance. A few he had checked closely on a chance that he might stumble onto something, but he had found nothing.

He listened to snatches of conversation between the Gnomes and Trolls who were not sleeping, trying to remain inconspicuous and at the same time come close enough to hear what was being said. But the Troll tongue was completely foreign, and what little he understood of the garbled Gnome speech consisted of useless information. It was as if no one knew anything of the two missing men and the Sword—as if they had never been brought to this camp at all. Flick began to wonder if Allanon had been completely mistaken about the trail signs they had followed these past few days.

He glanced apprehensively at the clouded night sky. He could not be certain of the time, but he knew there could be no more than several hours of darkness remaining. For a moment he panicked, abruptly realizing that he might not even have enough time to find his way back to where Allanon was concealed. But shaking off his fear, he quickly reasoned that in the confusion of breaking camp at dawn he would be able to slip quickly back through the sleepy hunters and make the short dash for the slopes of the Dragon's Teeth before the sun found him.

There was a sudden movement in the darkness off to his right, and into the firelight trudged four massive Troll warriors, all fully armed, muttering in low tones among themselves as they moved past the startled Valeman. On impulse more than reason, Flick fell in several yards behind them, curious as to where they might be going dressed in full battle array while it was still night. They were moving at right angles to the course the disguised Flick had chosen to follow into the encampment, and he stayed just behind them in the shadows as they trudged steadily through the sleeping army. Several times they passed darkened tents that Flick believed might be their destination, but they continued on without pausing.

The little Valeman noticed that the style of the encampment was changing rapidly in this particular area. There were more tents than before, some with high, lighted canopies that silhouetted men moving within. There were fewer common soldiers sleeping on the chill earth, but more sentries patrolling between the well-fed fires that lighted the open spaces between tents. Flick found it harder to remain hidden in this new light; to avoid questions and to protect against an increased risk of discovery, he moved right up behind the marching Trolls as if he were one of them. They passed numerous sentries that offered short greetings and watched as they passed, but no one attempted to question the heavily cloaked Gnome who scampered along at the rear of the small procession.

Then abruptly the Trolls turned left and automatically Flick turned with them—only to find himself almost on top of a long, low tent guarded by more armed Trolls. There was no time to turn back or avoid being seen, so when the procession came to a halt before the tent, the fearful Valeman kept right on walking, moving past them as if he were oblivious to what was taking place. The guards evidently failed to think there was anything out of the ordinary, all glancing briefly his way as he shuffled past, the cloak pulled closely about him, and in an instant he was beyond them, alone in the blackness of the shadows.

He halted sharply, sweat running down his body beneath the heavy clothing, his breathing short and labored. There had only been a second to glance through the open front of the lighted tent, between the towering Troll sentries holding the long, iron pikes— only a second to see the crouched, black-winged monster that stood within, surrounded by the lesser forms of both Trolls and Gnomes. But there was no mistaking one of those deadly creatures that had hunted them across the four lands. There was no mistaking the chill feeling of terror that ran through the Valeman's body as he stood breathlessly in the shadows to still his pounding heart.

Something vitally important was taking place inside that heavily guarded tent. Perhaps the missing men and the Sword were there, held by the servants of the Warlock Lord. It was a chilling thought and Flick knew that he had to get a look inside. His time was up, his luck run out. The guards alone were deterrent

enough to anyone trying to pass through the open
flaps, and the added presence of the Skull Bearer
made the idea suicidal. Flick sat back on his heels in
the darkness between the tents and shook his head
hopelessly. The enormity of the task utterly discouraged any hope for success, yet what other course lay
open? If he returned to Allanon now, they would
know nothing more than they had known previously
and his arduous night of creeping about the enemy
encampment would have been for nothing.

He gazed expectantly at the night sky, as if it might
hold some clue to the answer to his problem. The
cloud bank remained solidly in position overhead,
hanging ominously between the light of the moon and
stars and the blackness of the sleeping earth. The night
was almost over. Flick rose and pulled the cloak
closely about his chilled body once again. Fate may
have decided that he should come all these torturous
miles only to be killed in a foolish gamble, but Shea
depended on him—perhaps Allanon and the others as
well. He had to know what was in that tent. Slowly,
cautiously, he began to inch his way forward.

The dawn came quickly, a sullen gray lightening of
the eastern sky, heavy with mist and silence. The
weather had not improved below the Streleheim,
south of the persistent wall of darkness that marked
the advance of the Warlock Lord. Huge thunderclouds remained locked overhead like an ominous
shroud covering its earthen corpse. Near the base of
the western Dragon's Teeth, the enemy sentries had
abandoned their night watch to return to the awakening encampment of the Northland army. Allanon sat
quietly in the shelter of the boulder-strewn slope, the
long, black cloak that was wrapped loosely around his
lean, reedlike body offering little protection against
either the chill dawn air or the faint drizzle that was
rapidly turning into a heavy downpour. He had been

there all night, his eyes watching, searching for some sign of Flick, his hopes slowly fading as the sky lightened in the east and the enemy came to life. Still he waited, hoping against the odds that the little Valeman had somehow managed to conceal his identity, somehow managed to slip through the camp undetected and find his missing brother, the Elven King, and the Sword, then somehow managed to work his way clear of the pickets before daylight to reach freedom.

The encampment was breaking up, the tents disassembled and packed as the huge army fell into columns that covered the vast plain like giant black squares. Finally the fighting machine of the Warlock Lord began to march southward in the direction of Kern, and the giant Druid came down out of the rocks where he could be seen by the missing Valeman if he were anywhere close at hand. There was no movement, no sound but the wind blowing softly across the grasslands, and the tall dark figure stood silently. Only the eyes betrayed the keen bitterness he felt.

At last, the Druid turned southward, choosing a course parallel to that of the army marching ahead. Giant strides quickly ate up the distance between them as the rain began to fall in heavy sheets and the vast emptiness of the plains was left behind.

Menion Leah reached the winding Mermidon River immediately north of the island city of Kern only minutes before dawn. Allanon had not been wrong when he had warned the Prince that he would have a difficult time slipping through the enemy lines undetected. The sentry outposts extended beyond the perimeter of the sprawling plain encampment, running west above the Mermidon from the southern edge of the Dragon's Teeth. Everything north of that line belonged to the Warlock Lord. Enemy patrols roamed unchallenged along the southern boundaries of the towering Dragon's Teeth, guarding the few passages that cut through these formidable peaks. Balinor, Hendel, and the Elven brothers had managed to break the security of one of these enemy patrols in the high Kennon Pass. Menion did not have the protective shelter of the mountains in which to conceal himself from the Northlanders. Once he had left Allanon and Flick, he was forced to proceed directly across the flat, open grasslands that stretched south to the Mermidon. But the highlander had two things in his favor. The night remained clouded and completely, impenetrably black, making it nearly impossible to see more than several yards ahead. More important than this, Menion was a tracker and hunter without equal in the Southland. He could move through this shroudlike blackness with speed and stealth, undetected by any but the most sensitive ears.

So it happened that he moved silently from the side of his two companions, still angered that Allanon had forced him to give up the search for Shea in order that he might warn Balinor and the people of Callahorn of the impending invasion. He felt strangely uneasy about leaving Flick alone with the mysterious and unpredictable Druid. He had never completely trusted the giant mystic, knowing that the man was keeping the truth about the Sword of Shannara hidden from them, knowing that there was more to Allanon than he had chosen to tell them. They had done everything the Druid had commanded of them in blind faith, trusting him implicitly each time a crisis had arisen. Each time he had been right—but still they had failed to gain possession of the Sword, and they had lost Shea. Now on top of everything else, it appeared the Northland army would successfully invade the Southland. Only the border kingdom of Callahorn stood ready to resist the assault. Having seen the awesome size of the invader, Menion did not see how even the legendary Border Legion could hope to withstand such a mighty force. His own common sense told him that the only hope was to stall the advancing enemy long enough to unite the Elven and Dwarf armies with the Border Legion and then strike back. He felt certain the missing Sword was lost to them, and that even when they relocated Shea, there would be no further opportunity to search for the strange weapon.

He uttered a low oath as his exposed knee jammed painfully against the sharp edge of a jutting boulder, and he turned his attention to the matter at hand, all further speculation about the future put aside for the time being. Like a lean, black lizard, he skimmed noiselessly down the low slopes of the Dragon's Teeth, winding his torturous way through the maze of knife-edged boulders and rocks that covered the mountainside, the sword of Leah and the long ash bow strapped securely to his back. He reached the base of the slope without encountering anyone, and he peered into the darkness. There was no sign of life. He moved cautiously onto the grass-covered plainlands, inching forward a few yards at a time, pausing periodically to listen. He knew the sentry lines had to be posted close to this point to be effective, but it was impossible to see anyone.

At last he rose to his feet, as silent as the shadows all about him; hearing nothing, he began to walk slowly southward through the wall of darkness, his hunting knife held loosely in one hand. He walked for long minutes without incident and had just begun to relax in the belief that he had somehow slipped through the enemy lines without either of them knowing it, when he heard a small noise. He froze in midstride, trying to locate the source, and then it came again, a low cough from someone in the darkness directly in front of him. A sentry had given himself away just in time to save the highlander from stumbling into him. One cry would have brought others in an instant.

Menion dropped into a crouch on his hands and

knees, the dagger clutched tightly. He began to creep forward toward the source of the cough, his movement soundless. At last his eyes were able to discern the dim outline of someone standing silently before him. From his small size, the sentry was clearly a Gnome. Menion waited a few minutes longer to be certain that the Gnome had his back turned to him, then he crept still closer until he was within several feet. In one fluid motion he rose to tower over the unsuspecting sentry, one steellike arm gripping the fellow's throat, cutting off the cry of warning before it could escape. The butt end of the knife came down sharply on the exposed head, just back of the ear, and the unconscious Gnome crumpled to the earth. The highlander did not pause, but slipped ahead into the darkness, knowing there would be others close at hand, and eager to move beyond their range of hearing. He held the dagger ready, anticipating that there might be still another sentry line. The chill wind blew steadily and the long minutes of the night crawled on.

Finally he was at the Mermidon, just above the island city of Kern, its lights faint in the distant south. He paused at the top of a small rise which dropped off gradually and sloped downward to form the north bank of the swift river. He remained in a half-crouch, his long hunting cloak wrapped about his lean frame to protect himself from the growing chill of the dawn wind. He was surprised and relieved that he had reached the river without running into still other enemy pickets. He suspected that his earlier assumption had been correct, and that he had passed through at least one other sentry line without realizing it.

Gazing carefully around, the Prince of Leah assured himself that no one else was about, then rose and stretched wearily. He knew he had to cross the Mermidon farther downriver if he wished to avoid a chilling swim in the icy waters. Once he reached a point directly across from the island, he was certain he would find a boat or ferry service to the city. Hitching his weapons higher on his back and smiling grimly against the cold, he began to walk southward along the river rise.

He had not gone very far, perhaps no more than a thousand yards, when the rushing of the dawn wind faded for an instant, and in the sudden stillness he heard an unfamiliar murmur from somewhere ahead. Instantly he dropped to the ground, his dark form flat against the small rise. The wind rushed back into his straining ears as he listened in the blackness. The gusting breeze died a second time and again he heard the low murmur, but this time he was certain of its origin. It was the muffled sound of human voices carried out of the darkness ahead near the bank of the river. The highlander crawled hurriedly back over the rise to where the terrain again shielded him from the faint lights of the distant city. Then he rose and moved forward in a half crouch, running parallel to the river, his passing noiseless and swift. The voices grew louder and more distinct and at last seemed to come from directly behind the grassy rise. He listened a minute longer, but found it impossible to decipher what was being said. Cautiously, he crawled on his stomach to the top of the rise where he was able to make out a group of dark figures huddled next to the Mermidon.

The first thing that caught his eye was the boat pulled up onto the riverbank and tied to a low bush. There was his transportation if he could get to it, but he discarded the idea almost instantly. Standing in a tight circle next to the moored boat were four very large, armed Trolls, their huge black bulks unmistakable even in this poor light. They were speaking with a fifth figure, smaller and slighter in build, his robes clearly marking him as a Southlander.

Menion studied them a moment with great care, trying to make out their faces, but the dim light gave him only brief glimpses of the man and he didn't appear to be anyone Menion had ever encountered previously. A small, dark beard covered the thin, shallow face of the stranger, and he had a peculiar habit of stroking the little beard in short, nervous pats while he talked.

Then the Prince of Leah saw something else. To one side of the circle of men was a large bundle covered with a heavy cloak and securely tied. Menion studied it dubiously, unable to tell what it was in the darkness. Then to his astonishment, the bundle moved slightly—enough to convince the highlander that there was something alive beneath the heavy coverings. Desperately he tried to think of a way he might move closer to the small party, but already he was too late. The four Trolls and the stranger were parting company. One of the Trolls moved over to the mysterious bundle and, in one effortless heave, threw it over his broad, bulky shoulder. The stranger was returning to the boat, loosening the fastenings and climbing in, the oars lowered to the choppy waters. There were several parting words exchanged, and Menion caught snatches of the brief conversation, including something about having the situation well in hand. The final comment as the boat moved out into the swift waters was a warning from the stranger to wait for further word from him on the Prince.

Menion inched back a bit on the damp grass of the little rise, watching the man and the small boat disappear into the misty darkness of the Mermidon. Dawn was breaking at last, but it came in the form of a dim, hazy grayness that hampered visibility almost as effectively as the night. The sky was still overcast by low-hanging cumulous clouds that threatened to drop to the earth itself should they swell further. A heavy rain would fall before much longer and already the air was coated with a damp, penetrating mist that soaked the highlander's clothing and chilled the exposed skin. The huge Northland army would be on the march toward the island city of Kern within the hour, probably reaching it by midday. There was little time remaining for him to warn its citizens of the impending assault—an onslaught of men and weapons against which the city could not hope to defend itself for long. The people had to be evacuated immediately and taken to Tyrsis or farther south for protection. Balinor had to be warned that time had run out, that the Border Legion must assemble and fight a delaying action until reinforced by the Dwarf and Elven armies.

The Prince of Leah knew there was no time to ponder further the mysterious meeting he had just accidentally witnessed, but he lingered a moment longer as the four Trolls turned from the riverbank, carrying the struggling bundle, and moved toward the rise to his right. Menion was certain that someone had been taken prisoner by the stranger in the boat and turned over to these soldiers of the Northland army. This night meeting had been prearranged by both parties and the exchange made for reasons known only to them. If they had gone to all that trouble, the prisoner must be someone very important to them— and therefore important to the Warlock Lord.

Menion watched the Trolls move away from him into the heavy morning mist, still undecided as to whether he should intervene. Allanon had given him a task to complete—a vital task that might save thousands of lives. There was no time for wild forays in enemy country just to satisfy personal curiosity, even if it meant saving . . . Shea! Suppose it was Shea they had taken prisoner? The thought flashed through the impetuous mind, and instantly the decision had been made. Shea was the key to everything—if there was any chance that he was the captive wrapped in that bundle, Menion had to try to rescue him.

He leaped to his feet and began running swiftly northward, back in the direction from which he had

just come, trying to stay on a course parallel to that
taken by the Trolls. In the heavy mist, it was difficult to
keep his sense of direction, but Menion had no time to
be concerned with that. It was going to be extremely
difficult to take that prisoner away from four armed
Trolls, especially when any one of them was easily a
match physically for the slight highlander. There was
the added danger that they might at any point pass
back through the sentry lines of the Northland outposts. If he failed to stop them before then, he was
finished. Any chance of rescue depended on keeping
open an escape route to the Mermidon. Menion felt
the first rains of the coming storm strike his face as he
ran, and the thunder rumbled ominously overhead as
the wind began to grow in force. Desperately he
searched through the rolling clouds of mist and fog for
some sign of his quarry, but there was nothing to be
seen. Certain that he had been too slow and had
missed them, he raced at breakneck speed across the
grasslands, charging like a wild black shadow through
the mist, dodging the small trees and clumps of brush,
his eyes searching the empty flatlands. The rain beat
against his face and ran into his eyes, blinding him,
forcing him to slow down momentarily to wipe away
the warm haze of mingled rain and perspiration. He
shook his head in anger. They had to be somewhere
close! He couldn't have lost them!

Abruptly the four Trolls appeared out of the fog
behind him and off to the left. Menion had misjudged
and completely overtaken and passed them. He
dropped into a crouch behind a small clump of bushes
and watched a moment as the four moved closer. If
they stayed on their present course, they would pass
almost next to a large clump of scrub brush farther
ahead—still beyond their vision, but within Menion's.
The highlander bounded from cover and raced back
into the mist until he could no longer see the Trolls. If
they had seen him make that quick dash into the fog,

he was through. They would be expecting him when they reached the scrub brush. But if not, he would spring his ambush there and make a break for the river. He cut back across the plains to his left until he reached the seclusion of the brush where, panting heavily, he dropped to all fours and peered cautiously through the branches.

For a moment there was nothing but the fog and the rain, and then four bulky figures appeared out of the gray mist, moving steadily toward his place of concealment. He threw off the cumbersome hunting cloak, already soaked through by the morning rains. He would need speed to elude the massive Trolls once he managed to get the prisoner away from them, and the cloak would only slow him down. He removed the heavy hunting boots as well. At his side he placed the sword of Leah, its bright blade drawn clear of the leather sheath. Hurriedly, he fitted the loosened string to the great ash bow and withdrew two long, black arrows from their casing. The Trolls were closing quickly on his cover now, their dark forms visible through the leafy branches of the brush. They walked in pairs, one of the foremost carrying the limp form of the bound prisoner. They came carelessly toward the hidden man, obviously at ease in territory they believed entirely under the control of their own forces. Menion rose slowly to one knee, a black arrow fitted to the long bow, and waited silently.

The unsuspecting Trolls were almost on top of the scrub brush when the first arrow flew from out of nowhere with a sharp hum, striking the fleshy calf muscle of the bulky Northlander carrying the prisoner. In a roar of mingled rage and pain, the Troll dropped his burden and fell, clutching the injured leg with both hands. In that instant of shock and confusion, Menion fired the second arrow, scoring a solid hit to the exposed shoulder of the second member of the front pair, spinning the massive form entirely about so that he stumbled wildly into the two behind him.

Without pausing, the agile highlander sprang free of the scrub brush and rushed the amazed Trolls, yelling and swinging the sword of Leah. The Trolls had dropped back a step or two from the momentarily forgotten prisoner, and the quick attacker swept the limp form up onto one shoulder with his free arm before the astonished Northlanders could act. In another instant, he had swept past them, his sword cutting into the forearm of the nearest Troll, who made a vain effort to stop the fleet form. The path to the Mermidon lay open!

Two Trolls, one uninjured and the other slightly wounded, gave immediate chase, lumbering heavily across the rain-covered grasslands in determined silence. Their cumbersome armor and large frames slowed them down considerably, but they moved faster than Menion had expected, and they were refreshed and strong while he was already tiring. Even without the hunting cloak and boots, the lean highlander could not run very fast while carrying the still-bound prisoner. The rain had begun to fall in increasingly heavier sheets, windswept and stinging against his skin as he forced his aching body to run faster still. In leaps and bounds he streaked across the grasslands, twisting past small trees, dodging scrub brush and water-soaked potholes. Even in bare feet, his footing on the wet, slippery grass was unsure. Several times he stumbled and fell to his knees, only to bound immediately to his feet to run again.

There were hidden rocks and thorn-tipped plants scattered through the soft grasses, and soon his feet were cut and bleeding freely. But he didn't feel the pain and he raced onward. The vast plains alone were witness to the strange race between the huge, lumbering hunters and the shadowlike quarry as they labored southward through the driving rains and the

chilling wind. They ran without hearing, without
seeing, without feeling through the panoramic emptiness, and there was nothing to break the terrible
silence but the rush of the gusting wind in the runners'
ears. It became a lonely, fearful ordeal of survival—a
trial of spirit and stamina that demanded from the
youthful Prince of Leah his final, complete reserve of
strength.

Time ceased to exist for the fleeing highlander as he
forced his legs to move when the muscles had long
since passed the normal end of endurance—and still
there was no river. He no longer looked back to see if
the Trolls were closing. He could sense their presence,
hear their labored breathing in his mind; they must be
closing the distance rapidly. He had to run faster! He
had to reach the river and free Shea. . . .

In his near exhaustion, he unconsciously referred to
the person wrapped in the bundle as his friend. He
had known immediately upon grasping the mysterious prisoner that he was small and slight of build.
There was no reason to believe it might not be the
missing Valeman. The bundled captive was awake
and moving awkwardly as the highlander ran,
speaking in muffled phrases to which Menion replied
in short, gasping assurances that they were close to
safety.

The rain suddenly intensified in force until it was
impossible to see more than a few feet in any direction,
and the sodden plains turned quickly into a grass-
tipped marsh. Then Menion fell over a water-covered
root and tumbled headlong into the muddied grass,
his precious burden falling in a struggling heap beside
him. Bruised and exhausted, the highlander raised
himself to his hands and knees, the great sword held
ready, and looked back for his pursuers. To his relief,
they were nowhere in sight. In the heavy rain and fog,
they had momentarily lost him. But even the limited
visibility would only slow them down for a few

minutes and then . . . Menion shook his head sharply
to clear the haze of rain and weariness from his eyes,
then crawled quickly to the water-logged heap of
clothing that bound the struggling prisoner. Whoever
was in that hunting cloak was in good enough shape to
run beside him, and Menion's strength was nearly
gone. He knew he could carry the added weight no
farther.

Awkwardly, hardly aware of what he was doing,
the highlander sawed at the tough bonds with his
sword. It had to be Shea, his mind told him over and
over, it had to be Shea. The Trolls and that stranger
had gone to so much trouble not to be seen, had been
so secretive . . . The bonds snapped as the sword
finally severed them. It had to be Shea! The ropes
unwound and the cloak flew back as the person within
struggled into the open air.

An astonished Menion Leah wiped the rain from his
blinking eyes and stared. He had rescued a woman!

XXIV

woman! Why would the Northlanders kidnap a woman? Menion stared through the pouring rain into the clear blue eyes that blinked back at him uncertainly. She was no ordinary woman in any case. She was strikingly beautiful—deeply browned skin covering the finely formed features of the rounded face, a slim graceful figure clothed in a silky material, and her hair . . .! He had never seen anything like it. Even wetted and plastered against her face by the driving rain, falling shoulder length and lower in long, wistful strands, the strange color showed through the grayness of the morning in a deep reddish hue. For a moment he gazed at her in a half-conscious trance, then the throbbing pain from his cut and bleeding feet recalled him to his present situation and the grave danger still facing them.

Quickly he climbed back to his feet, wincing with the pressure on his exposed soles, the weariness flooding through him until he thought he would collapse in total exhaustion. His mind battled fiercely for several long moments as he swayed almost drunkenly, bracing himself on the great sword. The frightened face of the girl—yes, she could still be called a girl, he thought suddenly—peered up at him out of a gray haze. Then she was on her feet next to him, holding him up, talking to him in low, distant tones. He shook his head and nodded stupidly.

"It's all right now, I'm all right." The words sounded garbled as he spoke. "Run for the river—we have to reach Kern."

They began moving again through the mist and the rain, walking rapidly, at times staggering on the uncertain footing of the marshy grasslands. Menion felt his head begin to clear and his strength return as they walked, the girl next to him, her hands locked onto his arm, half holding onto him for her own support, half helping to support him. His keen eyes searched the gloom about them for some sign of the prowling Trolls, certain that they were not too far away. Then abruptly his ears picked up a new sound, the pounding, rushing throb of the Mermidon, its rain-filled waters overflowing the lowland banks as it swept southward toward Kern. The girl heard it, too, and gripped his arm tightly in encouragement.

Moments later they stood on the crest of the small rise that ran parallel with the north bank. The swift river had long since flooded its low banks and was continuing to rise. Menion had no idea where they stood in relation to Kern, but he realized that if they crossed at the wrong point, they would miss the island entirely. The girl seemed to recognize the problem; taking his arm, she began moving downstream along the low rise, peering across the river into the gloom. Menion let her lead him without question, his own eyes casting about anxiously for some sign of the pursuing Trolls. The rain had begun to slacken and the mist was beginning to clear. It would not be long before the storm would end and visibility return, leaving the two revealed to the persistent hunters. They had to chance a crossing quickly.

Menion did not know how long the young woman led him along the river's edge, but at last she halted and indicated in hurried gestures a small skiff drawn up against the grassy embankment. Quickly the highlander strapped the sword of Leah to his back,

and together the two pushed off into the swift waters of the Mermidon. The river was icy and the shock of the extreme cold from the spray of the foam-tipped waves jarred Menion to the bone. He rowed fiercely across the swift current as it swept them downriver with terrific force, frequently turning them about completely as they fought to reach the other side. It was a wild, careening battle between river and man that seemed to go on endlessly, and at last everything became hazy and numb in Menion's mind.

What happened in the end was never clear to him. He was vaguely aware of hands reaching to pull him from the skiff to a grassy bank where he collapsed in a breathless stupor. He heard the girl's soft voice speaking to him, and then there was blackness and numbness all about him as he lapsed into unconsciousness. He drifted in and out of darkness and sleep, plagued by an uneasy sense of danger that prodded at his tired mind and demanded that he rise and stand ready. But his body could not respond, and finally he dropped off into a deep slumber.

When he awoke, it was still light out and the rain was falling in a slow, steady drizzle through deep, gray skies. He lay in the warmth and comfort of a bed, dry and rested, his torn feet cleaned and bandaged, and the terrible race to escape the Northlanders behind him. The slow rain beat peacefully on the paned glass windows that let in the daylight through the wood and stone walls. He glanced idly around the finely furnished chamber, realizing quickly that this was not the home of an average citizen, but of royalty. There were insignia and crests on the woodwork that Menion knew to belong to the kings of Callahorn. For a moment the highlander lay quietly and studied the room in silent leisure, allowing the sleep to disperse and his rested mind to awaken fully. He saw a dry set of clothes lying on a chair near the bed, and was just about to rise to dress when the door opened and an elderly serving woman appeared, carrying a tray of steaming food. Nodding politely and smiling, she hastened to the bed with the tray and deposited it on the highlander's lap, propping him up with pillows and urging him to eat it all while it was still hot. Strangely, she reminded Menion of his own mother, a kind, fussy woman who had died when he was twelve. The serving lady lingered until he had taken the first bite, then turned away and went out again, closing the door quietly behind her.

Menion ate slowly, savoring the excellent food, feeling the strength return to his body. It occurred to him only after he had finished almost half the meal that he had not eaten for over twenty-four hours—or perhaps it had been longer. He glanced again through the window to the rain beyond, unable to tell if it was even the same day. It might be the following day. . . .

In a flash he recalled his original purpose in coming to Kern—to warn them of the impending invasion by the Northland army. He might already be too late! He was still frozen with the thought, a fork raised halfway to his mouth, when the door opened a second time. It was the young woman he had rescued, refreshed and dry now, dressed in a flowing gown of warm, mixed colors, her long red tresses combed and shining even in the gray light of the rain-clouded day. She was easily the most stunning woman the Prince of Leah had ever encountered. Remembering suddenly the half-raised fork, he lowered it to the tray and smiled in greeting. She closed the door behind her and moved gracefully to his bedside. She was incredibly beautiful, he thought again. Why had she been kidnapped? What would Balinor know about her—what answers could he supply? She stood next to the bedside, looking down at him, studying him with those clear, deep eyes for a moment.

"You look very well, Prince of Leah," she smiled. "The rest and the food have made you whole again."

"How did you know who . . .?"

"Your sword bears the markings of the King of Leah; that much I know. Who else but his son would carry such a weapon? But I don't know you by name."

"Menion," the highlander responded, somewhat surprised at the girl's knowledge of his little homeland, a kingdom unfamiliar to most outlanders.

The young woman stretched forth a slim bronzed hand to grasp his own in warm greeting and nodded happily.

"I am Shirl Ravenlock, and this is my home, Menion—the island city of Kern. If not for your courage, I should never have seen it again. For that I shall remain eternally grateful and your friend always. Now finish your meal while we talk."

She seated herself on the bed next to him and motioned for Menion to continue eating. Again he began to raise his fork; then remembering the invasion, he dropped it to the tray with a noisy clatter.

"You've got to get word to Tyrsis, to Balinor—the invasion from the Northland has begun! There is an army camped just above Kern waiting to . . ."

"I know, it's all right," Shirl responded quickly, raising her hand to stop him from continuing. "Even in your sleep, you spoke of the danger—you warned us before you passed out entirely. Word has been sent to Tyrsis. Palance Buckhannah rules in his brother's absence; the King is still very ill. The city of Kern is mobilizing its defenses, but for the moment there is no real danger. The rains have flooded the Mermidon and made any crossing by a large force impossible. We will be safe until help arrives."

"Balinor should have been in Tyrsis several days ago," Menion announced with alarm. "What about the Border Legion? Is it fully mobilized?"

The girl looked at him blankly, indicating that she had no idea what the situation was with regard to either the Legion or Balinor. Abruptly, Menion shoved the tray aside and climbed out of bed, an astonished Shirl rising with him, still trying to calm the excited highlander.

"Shirl, you may think that you're safe on this island, but I can guarantee that time is running out for all of us!" Menion exclaimed, reaching for his clothes. "I've seen the size of that army, and no amount of flooding is going to slow it down for long—and you can forget about any help short of a miracle."

He paused at the second button of his nightshirt, suddenly remembering the young woman with him. He pointed meaningfully to the door, but she shook her head negatively and turned away so she couldn't see him changing.

"What about your kidnapping?" Menion asked, dressing himself quickly as he studied her slim back across the room. "Do you have any idea why you would be so important to the Northlanders—other than the fact that you're a beautiful woman?"

He smiled roguishly, a little of the brashness that Flick distrusted returning. Although he could not see her face, the highlander was certain she was blushing furiously. She was silent a moment before speaking.

"I don't remember exactly what happened," the answer came at last. "I was asleep. I was awakened by a noise in the room, then someone grabbed me and I blacked out—I think I was struck or . . . No, I remember now—it was a cloth soaked in some foul liquid that prevented me from breathing. I blacked out and the next thing I remember was lying on the sand near the river—I gather it was the Mermidon. You know how I was tied in that blanket. I couldn't see anything and could hear only a little—but nothing that I could understand. Did you see anything?"

Menion shook his head and shrugged. "No, nothing much," he added, remembering that the girl was not looking at him. "One man brought you across in a boat, then turned you over to four Trolls. I couldn't see the man distinctly, but I might recognize him if I saw him again. How about answering my first question—why would anyone kidnap you? Turn around. I'm dressed now."

The young woman turned obediently and came over next to him, watching curiously as he pulled on the high hunting boots.

"I'm of royal blood, Menion," she responded quietly. Menion stopped quickly and looked up at her. He had suspected she was no ordinary citizen of Kern when she had recognized the crest of Leah on his sword. Now perhaps he would discover the reason behind her abduction from the city.

"My ancestors were kings of Kern—and for a while of all Callahorn, before the Buckhannahs came to power about one hundred years ago. I am a . . . well, I guess you could say I'm a princess—in absentia." She laughed at the foolishness of the idea, and Menion smiled back. "My father is an elder of the council that governs the internal affairs of Kern. The King is the ruler of Callahorn, but this is an enlightened monarchy, as the saying goes, and the King seldom interferes with the governmental workings of this city. His son Palance has been attracted to me for some time, and it is no secret that he plans to marry me. I . . . I believe that, to get to him, an enemy might try to harm me."

Menion nodded soberly, a sudden premonition springing into his alert mind. Palance was not in line for the throne of Callahorn unless something happened to Balinor. Why would anyone waste time trying to put pressure on the younger son unless they were certain that Balinor would not be around? Again he recalled Shirl's lack of knowledge of the arrival of the Prince of Callahorn, an event that should have taken place days ago and one that all the citizens of the land should have known about.

"Shirl, how long have I been asleep?" he asked apprehensively.

"Nearly an entire day," she answered. "You were exhausted when they pulled us from the Mermidon yesterday morning, and I thought you should sleep. You gave us your warning . . ."

"Twenty-four hours lost!" Menion exclaimed angrily. "If not for the rain, the city would have already fallen! We've got to act now, but what . . . Shirl, your father and the council! I must speak with them!" He grasped her arms with urgency when she hesitated. "Don't ask questions now, just do what I say. Where are the council chambers? Quick, take me to them!"

Without waiting for the girl to lead him, Menion took her arm and propelled her through the door to a long hallway beyond. Together they hurried through the empty home and out the front doorway onto a wide, tree-shaded lawn, running to escape the persistent drizzle of the morning rain. The walkways of the buildings beyond were partially sheltered from the rain, and they were spared a second soaking. As they proceeded toward the council hall, Shirl asked him how he happened to be in this part of the country, but Menion responded evasively, still unwilling to tell anyone about Allanon and the Sword of Shannara. He felt he could trust this girl, but Allanon's warning that none of those who journeyed to Paranor should reveal the story behind the missing Sword prevented him from confiding even in her. Instead, he explained that he had come to aid Balinor at his request upon hearing of an impending Northland invasion. She accepted his story without question, and he felt a little guilty for lying to her. Yet Allanon had never told him the complete truth, so perhaps he knew less than he imagined anyway.

They had reached the council hall, its ancient chambers housed within a tall, stone structure surrounded by weathered columns and arched windows laced with metal latticework. The guards that stood leisurely next to the entryway did not question them and they hurried inside, moving down the long, high corridors and up the winding stairways as the walls echoed with the rap of their boots on the worn stone flooring. The council met in chambers situated on the fourth floor of the great building. When at last they were outside its wooden doors, Shirl advised Menion that she would inform her father and the other members of his wish to address them. Reluctantly, the highlander agreed to wait. He stood quietly in the corridor after she had gone inside, listening to the hushed murmur of voices as the seconds ticked slowly away, and the rain continued to beat in a soft, steady rhythm on the glass of the windows that lined the silent hall.

Losing himself for a moment in the peace and solitude of the ancient building, the highlander recalled in brief flashes the faces of the divided company of friends, wondering sadly what had befallen them since Paranor. Perhaps they would never again be together as they had been during those fearful days on the road to the Druids' Keep, but he would never forget their courage and sacrifice and the pride he felt now in recalling the dangers they had faced and overcome. Even the reluctant Flick had displayed a bravery and steadfastness that Menion would not have expected from him.

And what of Shea, his oldest friend? He shook his head as he thought about his missing companion. He missed the Valeman's peculiar mixture of hardheaded practicality and antiquated beliefs. Somehow Shea could not seem to see the change in times even when the sun moved from east to west in the sky above. He did not seem to realize that the land and the people were growing, expanding once more—that the wars of the past were slowly being forgotten. Shea believed that one could turn his back on the past and build a new world with the future, never understanding that the future was inextricably tied to the past, an interwoven tapestry of events and ideas that would never be entirely severed. In his own small way, the little Valeman was a part of the passing age, his convictions a reminder of yesterday rather than a promise of tomorrow. How strange, how incredibly strange it all seemed, Menion thought suddenly, standing in the center of the hall, motionless, his gaze lost in the depths of the weathered stone wall. Shea and the Sword of Shannara—things of an age slowly dying; yet they were the hope of the hour to come. They were the key to life.

The heavy wooden doors to the council hall opened behind the highlander, and his thoughts faded with Shirl's soft voice. She seemed small and vulnerable as she waited beneath the massive beams of the high entryway, her face beautiful and anxious. No wonder Palance Buckhannah wanted this woman for his wife. Menion moved toward her, taking her warm hand in his own, and they entered the council chamber. He noted the ancient austerity of the massive chamber as he moved into the gray light that seemed to slide in tired streaks through the high, iron-webbed windows. The council hall was old and proud, a cornerstone of the island city. Twenty men were seated around a long, burnished wood table, their faces strangely similar as they waited for the highlander to speak—all aged, wise perhaps, and determined. The eyes betrayed the unspoken fear that lingered beneath the calm exteriors—a fear for their city and their people. They knew what the Northland army would do when the rains ceased and the waters of the Mermidon receded in the heat of the open sun. He stopped before them, the girl still next to him, his footfalls dying away into the expectant silence.

He chose his words carefully, describing the massive enemy force that had been assembled under the leadership of the Warlock Lord. He related in part the story of his long journey to Callahorn, speaking of Balinor and the men of the company formed at

Culhaven who were now scattered throughout the four lands. He did not tell them about the Sword or about Shea's mysterious origin or even about Allanon. There was no reason for the elders of this council to know anything beyond the fact that the city of Kern stood in danger of being overrun. As he finished, calling upon them to save their people while there was still time, to evacuate the city immediately before all hope of retreat was cut off, he felt a strange sense of satisfaction. He had risked a great deal more than his own life to warn these people. If he had failed to reach them, they might all have perished without ever having had a chance to flee to safety. It was important, really important, to the Prince of Leah that he had carried out his task responsibly.

The questions from the members of the council came with cries of alarm when the highlander had finished, some angry, some frightened. Menion answered quickly, trying to stay calm as he assured them that the size of the Northland army was as awesome as he had described and the threat of attack certain. Eventually the initial furor died away into a more rational deliberation of the possibilities. A few of the elders believed that the city should be defended until Palance Buckhannah could come up from Tyrsis with the Border Legion, but most were of the opinion that once the rains subsided, as they were certain to do within a few days, the invading army would easily gain the shores of the island and the city would stand defenseless. Menion listened silently while the council deliberated the matter, weighing in his own mind the courses of action open to them. Finally, the flushed, gray-haired man, whom Shirl had introduced as her father, turned to Menion, drawing him aside in private conference as the council continued its debate.

"Have you seen Balinor, young man? Do you know where he can be found?"

"He should have been in Tyrsis days ago," Menion

responded worriedly. "He was going there to mobilize the Border Legion in preparation for this invasion. He was in the company of two cousins of Eventine Elessedil."

The older man frowned and shook his head, consternation registering in his lined face.

"Prince of Leah, I must tell you that the situation is more desperate than it appears. The King of Callahorn, Ruhl Buckhannah, became seriously ill several weeks earlier and his condition does not seem to be improving. Balinor was absent from the city at the time, and so the King's younger son assumed his father's duties. While he has always been a rather unsteady personality, he has of late seemed highly erratic. One of his first acts was to disband the Border Legion, reducing it to a fraction of its former size."

"Disbanded!" Menion exclaimed in disbelief. "Why in the name . . .?"

"He found them unnecessary," the other continued quickly, "so he replaced them with a small company of his own men. The fact of the matter is that he has always felt overshadowed by his brother, and the Border Legion was under the direct command of Balinor by the King's own order. It's highly probable that Palance felt they would remain loyal to the firstborn son of the King in preference to himself, and he has no intention of returning the throne to Balinor should the King die. He has already made this quite apparent. The commanders of the Border Legion and several close associates of Balinor were seized and imprisoned—all very quietly so that the people would not be outraged by this senseless action. Our new King has taken as his only confidant and adviser a man named Stenmin, a viperous mystic and trickster whose only concern is for his own ambitions, not for the welfare of the people or even Palance Buckhannah. I do not see how we can hope to face this invasion with our own leadership so badly divided and undermined. I'm not even sure we can convince the Prince that the danger exists until the enemy is standing at the open gates!"

"Then Balinor is in grave danger," Menion said darkly. "He has gone to Tyrsis, not realizing that his father is ill and that his brother has taken command. We've got to get word to him at once!"

The council members had suddenly risen to their feet, shouting heatedly, still arguing over what should be done to save the doomed city of Kern. Shirl's father hastened to their midst, but it took several minutes for the few rational members of the distraught council to quiet the others enough to permit the discussion to continue on an orderly basis. Menion listened for a little while, then allowed his attention to drift momentarily to the high, arched windows and the solemn sky beyond. It was not as dark as before, and the rain had begun to slacken further. Unquestionably, it would end by tomorrow, and the enemy force camped beyond the flooded Mermidon would attempt a crossing. Eventual success in attaining a landing was assured, even if the vastly outnumbered soldiers stationed or living in Kern tried to defend the island. Without a large, well-organized army to protect the city, the people would be quickly slain and Kern would fall. He thought back quickly to his parting with Allanon, wondering suddenly what the resourceful Druid would do if he were there. The situation was not promising. Tyrsis was ruled by an irrational, ambitious usurper. Kern was leaderless, its councilmen divided and unsure, debating a course of action that should already have been executed. Menion felt his temper slipping. It was madness to ponder the alternatives further!

"Councilmen! Hear me!" His own voice rose in fury, reverberating back from the ancient stone walls as the voices of the elders of Kern died into whispering silence. "Not only Callahorn, but all of the Southland, my home and yours, faces certain destruction if we do not act now! By tomorrow night, Kern will be ashes and its people enslaved. Our one chance for survival is escape to Tyrsis; our one hope for victory over this mighty Northland army is the Border Legion, reassembled under Balinor. The Elven armies stand ready to fight with us. Eventine will lead them. The Dwarf people, engaged for years in fighting the Gnomes, have promised to aid us. But we must stand fast separately until all are united against this monstrous threat to our existence!"

"Your plea is well spoken, Prince of Leah," Shirl's father responded quickly as the flushed highlander paused. "But give us a solution to our immediate problem so that our people can reach Tyrsis. The enemy is camped directly across the Mermidon, and we stand virtually defenseless. We must evacuate almost forty thousand people from this island and then guide them safely to Tyrsis, which is miles to the south. Undoubtedly the enemy has already posted sentries all around our shores to prevent any attempt to cross the Mermidon before the assault on Kern. How can we overcome such obstacles?"

A fleeting smile crossed Menion's lips.

"We'll attack," he stated simply.

For a moment there was shocked silence as they all stared in utter disbelief at the deceptively passive face. The words of astonished reply were still forming on their lips as he held up one hand.

"An attack is exactly what they will not be expecting—particularly if it comes in the night. A quick strike against a flank position of their main encampment, if executed properly, will confuse them, cause them to think that it's an assault by a heavily armed force. The darkness and the confusion will hide our true size. Such an attack is certain to draw in their outlying sentry lines around the island. A small command can make a great amount of noise, set a few fires, and pin them down for at least an hour—perhaps longer. While that's going on—evacuate the city!"

One of the elders shook his head negatively.

"Even an hour would not be sufficient time, though your plan may be daring enough to catch the Northlanders off guard, young man. Even if we managed to ferry all forty thousand people from the island to the southern shore, it would still be necessary to march them southward to Tyrsis—almost fifty miles. The women and children would require days to travel that distance under normal conditions, and once the enemy finds Kern has been abandoned, they'll follow its people southward. We cannot hope to outrun them. Why should we even attempt it?"

"You will not have to outrun them," Menion declared quickly. "You won't be taking these people south by land—you will take them down the Mermidon! Put them in small boats, rafts, anything that you now have or can build by tonight that will float. The Mermidon flows southward deep into Callahorn, within ten miles of Tyrsis. Disembark at that point, and all can easily reach the safety of the city by daybreak, long before the cumbersome Northland army can mobilize and follow!"

The council rose to its feet, shouting their approval, caught up in the fire and determination of the highlander's spirit. If there was any way that the people of Kern could be saved, even though the island city itself must fall to the enemy hordes, it must be tried. The council adjourned after a short discussion to mobilize the working people of the city. Between this time and sunset, every citizen who was able to assist would be expected to aid in the construction of large wooden rafts capable of transporting several hundred people. There were already hundreds of small boats scattered about the island which individual citizens used to navigate the river in order to reach the mainland. In addition, there were a number of larger ferries for mass transportation which could be pressed into service. Menion suggested that the council order all armed soldiers in the city to begin a vigilant patrol of the coastline, permitting no one to leave the island. All details of the planned escape would be carefully concealed from everyone but the council members for as long as possible. The highlander's greatest concern was that someone might betray them to the enemy, cutting off their escape route before they had a chance to act. Someone had seized Shirl in her own home, whisked her out of the heavily populated city, and ferried her across into the hands of the Trolls—a chore that could not have been accomplished by anyone unfamiliar with the island. Whoever he was, he remained free and hidden, perhaps still safe within the city. If he learned the exact details of the evacuation plan, he would undoubtedly attempt to warn the Northlanders. Secrecy was absolutely necessary if this dangerous venture was to be successful.

The remainder of the day passed quickly for Menion. Forgotten for the moment were Shea and his companions of the past few weeks. For the first time since Shea had come to him in the highlands, the Prince of Leah was faced with a problem that he fully understood, requiring skills he knew how to employ. The enemy was no longer the Skull King or the spirit creatures that served him. The enemy was flesh and blood—creatures that lived and died according to the same rules as other men, and their threat was one the highlander could appreciate and analyze. Time was the greatest single factor in his plan to outwit the waiting army, and so he threw himself into the most important undertaking of his life, the saving of an entire city.

Together with the members of the council, he directed the building of the giant wooden rafts which would be utilized to convey the majority of the besieged citizens of Kern down the still-flooded

Mermidon to the safety of Tyrsis. The point of embarkation was to be the southwest coastline immediately below the city proper. There was a broad but well-concealed inlet from which the rafts and smaller boats would be launched under cover of darkness. Directly across the river from the inlet stood a series of low bluffs that ran to the edge of the embankment. Menion thought that a handful of men could ford the river when the main attack on the enemy encampment began later that night; once across, they could subdue the small guard post that would be keeping watch. After the sentries were dispatched, the boats and rafts would be launched, flowing downriver with the current, following the south branch of the Mermidon to Tyrsis. There was nothing to assure them that the vessels would not be spotted instantly, but it was the only possible course of action. Menion believed that if the sky remained clouded, the sentry commands were withdrawn upriver to defend against the fake assault on the main encampment, and the people of the city kept silent on the rafts, then the evacuation might be successful.

But toward late afternoon, the rain started to slacken off altogether and the clouds began to thin out, permitting small strips of blue to seep through the rolling grayness. The storm was drawing to an end, and it appeared the night sky would be cloudless and the land exposed to the revealing light of the new moon and a thousand winking stars. Menion was seated in one of the smaller rooms of the council hall when he saw these first signs of a clearing, his attention momentarily diverted from the huge map spread out on the table before him. At his side were two members of the disbanded Border Legion, Janus Senpre, a lieutenant commander of the Legion and the highest ranking officer on the island, and a grizzled veteran named Fandrez. The latter knew the country around Kern better than anyone and had been called in to advise the attack squad in its strike against the giant Northland army. Senpre, his superior, was surprisingly young for his rank, but a sharp and determined soldier with a dozen years of field duty already behind him. He was a devoted follower of Balinor, and like Menion, he was considerably upset to learn that nothing had been heard from Tyrsis concerning the Prince's arrival. Earlier that afternoon, he had selected two hundred seasoned soldiers from the disbanded Border Legion to form the strike force that would be directed against the enemy camp.

Menion had offered his aid and it had been eagerly accepted. The highlander was still cut and bruised about the feet and lower legs from his arduous flight after rescuing Shirl Ravenlock, but he refused to stay behind with the evacuation party when the feint by the small attack squad had been his idea. Flick would have written off his insistence as a foolish mixture of stubbornness and pride, but Menion Leah would not be left in comparative safety on the island while a battle was being fought across the river. It had taken him years to find something worthwhile to fight for, something more than personal satisfaction and the irresistible lure of one more adventure. He was not about to be a passive spectator while the most awesome threat in centuries decimated the race of Man.

"This point—over here by the Spinn Barr—that's the landing point to take," the slow, grating voice of Fandrez cut into his thoughts, drawing his attention back to the carefully detailed map. Janus Senpre agreed, looking at Menion to be certain he was taking careful note. The highlander nodded quickly.

"They will have sentries posted all along that grassland just above the bar," he said in reply. "If we don't dispose of them immediately, they could cut off any retreat."

"Your job will be to keep them out of there—

keep the way open," the Legion commander stated.

Menion opened his mouth in objection, but was cut short.

"I appreciate your desire to come with us, Menion, but we still have to move much faster than the enemy, and your feet are in poor condition for any prolonged running. You know that as well as I. So the shore patrol is yours. Keep our path to the boats open, and you will be doing us a much greater service than by coming with us."

Menion quietly nodded his agreement, though he was keenly disappointed. He had wanted to be in the forefront of the assault. Deep in the back of his mind, he still maintained hope of finding Shea a prisoner in the enemy camp. His thoughts drifted to Allanon and Flick. Perhaps they had found the missing Valeman, as the Druid had promised they would try to do. He shook his head sadly. Shea, Shea, why did it have to happen to someone like you—someone who just wanted to be left alone? There was a madness in the scheme of life that men were forced to accept either with resigned fury or blunt indifference. There could be no final resolution—except, perhaps, in death.

The meeting ended shortly thereafter, and a despondent and bitter Menion Leah wandered aimlessly out of the council chamber still lost in thought. Almost without realizing it, he walked down the stone stairway of the huge building to the street and from there made his way back toward Shirl's home, keeping close to the covered walks and building walls. Where was it all leading? The threat of the Warlock Lord loomed before them like a towering, unscalable wall. How could they possibly hope to defeat a creature that had no soul—a creature that lived according to laws of nature completely foreign to the world into which they had been born? Why should a simple young man from an obscure hamlet be the only mortal entity with the ability to destroy such an indescribably powerful being? Menion desperately needed to understand something of what was happening to him and to his absent friends—even if it was only one small piece in a thousand comprising the puzzle of the Warlock Lord and the Sword of Shannara.

Suddenly he found himself in front of the Ravenlock home, the heavy doors standing closed, their metal latches looking cold and frosted in the graying mist that hung in wisps with the cooling of the late afternoon air. He turned quickly from the entryway, not wishing to go in or to be with people for the moment, but preferring the solitude of the empty veranda. Slowly he moved along its stone path into the little garden at the side of the house, the leaves and flowers dripping softly with the rain of several days, the grounds beyond damp and green. He stood quietly, his own thoughts as hazy and wistful as the setting in which he paused, giving way for one brief moment to the sinking despair that seized him when he thought of how much he had lost. He had never felt alone like this before, even in the dark emptiness of the highlands of Leah when he had hunted far from his own home and friends. Something deep within hinted with dread persistence that he would never go back to what had been, that he would never go back to his friends, his home, his old life. Somewhere in the days behind, he had lost it all. He shook his head, the unwanted tears building on the edge of his lids as the dampness closed in about him and the chill of the rain slipped deep into his chest.

There were sudden footsteps on the stone behind him and a small, lithe form came to a silent halt at his elbow, the rust-red locks shadowing wide eyes that looked up at him momentarily and then strayed to the garden beyond. The two stood without speaking for a long time, the rest of the world shut away. In the sky above, heavy clouds were rolling in, covering the last faint traces of blue as the darkness of early twilight began to deepen. Rain was falling again in steady sheets on the besieged land of Callahorn, and Menion noted with absent relief that it would be a black and moonless night on the island of Kern.

It was well after midnight, the rain still falling in a soggy drizzle, the night sky still impenetrably black and ominous, when an exhausted Menion Leah stumbled heavily onto a small, crudely constructed raft moored in a peaceful inlet on the southwestern coast of the island. Two slim arms reached out to catch him as he collapsed, and he stared wonderingly into the dark eyes of Shirl Ravenlock. She had waited for him as she said she would, even though he had begged her to go with the others when the mass evacuation began. Cut and bruised, his clothing torn and his skin wet from the rain and his own blood, he let her wrap him in a cloak still somehow dry and warm and pull him against her shoulder as they crouched in the night shadows and waited.

There had been some who had returned with Menion, and a few more who boarded now, all battle weary, but fiercely proud of the courage and sacrifice they had displayed that night on the plains north of Kern. Never had the Prince of Leah seen such bravery in the face of such impossible odds. Those few men of the fabled Border Legion had so utterly disrupted the enemy camp that even now, some four hours after the initial strike, the confusion was still continuing. The enemy numbers had been unbelievable—thousands after thousands milling about, striking out at anyone within reach, inflicting injury and death upon even their own companions. They had been driven by more than mortal fear or hatred. They had been driven by the inhuman power of the Warlock Lord, his incredible fury thrusting them into battle like crazed beings with no purpose but to destroy. Yet the men of the

Legion had held them at bay, repeatedly thrown back only to regroup and strike once more. Many had died. Menion did not know what had preserved his own meager life, but it bordered on a miracle.

The mooring ropes were loosened, and he felt the raft begin to drift away from the shore, the current catching it and pulling it into the center of the flooded Mermidon. Moments later they were in the main channel, moving silently downriver toward the walled city of Tyrsis, where the people of Kern had fled several hours earlier in a perfectly executed mass evacuation. Forty thousand people, huddled on giant rafts, small boats, even two-man dinghies, had slipped undetected from the besieged city as the enemy sentry posts guarding the western bank of the Mermidon hastily returned to the main encampment, where it appeared a full-scale attack by the armies of Callahorn was in progress. The beating of the rain, the rushing of the river, and the cries of the distant camp had blotted out the muffled sounds of the people on the rafts and boats, crowded and jammed together in a desperate, fearful bid for freedom. The darkness of the clouded sky had hidden them well, and their collective courage had sustained them. For the time being at least, they had eluded the Warlock Lord.

Menion dozed off for a time, aware of nothing but a gentle rocking sensation as the river bore the raft steadily southward. Strange dreams flashed through his restless mind as time drifted away in long moments of peaceful silence. Then voices reached through to him, jostling his subconscious, forcing him to wake abruptly, and his eyes were seared by a vast red glare that filled the damp air about him. Squinting sharply, he raised himself from Shirl's arms, uncertainty registering on his lean face as he saw the northern sky filled with a reddish glow that matched the brightness of the dawn's gold. Shirl was speaking softly in his ear, the words faint and poignant.

"They have burned the city, Menion. They have burned my home!"

Menion lowered his eyes and gripped the girl's slim arm with one hand. Though its people had been able to escape, the city of Kern had seen the end of its days and, with terrible grandness, was passing into ashes.

XXV

he hours slipped silently away in the entombed blackness of the little cell. Even after the eyes of the captives had grown used to the impenetrable dark, there remained a solitude that numbed the senses and destroyed their ability to discern the passage of time. Beyond the empty darkness of the room and their own muffled breathing, the three captives could hear nothing save the infrequent scurrying of a small rodent and the steady drip of icy water on worn stone. Finally their own ears began to lie to them, to hear sounds where there was only silence. Their own movement was meaningless, because they could expect it, identify it, and dismiss it as insignificant and hopeless. An interminable length of time lingered and faded, and still no one came.

Somewhere in the light and air above, amid the sounds of the people and the city, Palance Buckhannah was deciding their fate and indirectly the fate of the Southland. Time was running out for the land of Callahorn; the Warlock Lord moved closer with each passing hour. But here, in the silent blackness of this small prison, in a world shut away from the pulse beat of the human world, time had no meaning and tomorrow would be the same as today. Eventually they would be discovered, but would they emerge again into the sun's friendly light, or would it be a transfer from one darkness into yet another? Would they find only the terrible gloom of the Skull King, his power extended not only into Callahorn, but into the farthest reaches of all the provinces of the Southland?

Balinor and the Elven brothers had freed themselves within a short time after their captors had departed. The ropes binding them had not been secured with the intention of preventing any chance of escape once they were safely locked within that dungeon room, and the three had lost no time in working the knots loose. Huddled together in the darkness, the ropes and blindfolds cast aside, they discussed what would become of them. The dank, rotting smell of the ancient cellar almost stifled their breathing as they crouched close to one another, and the air was chill and biting even through their heavy cloaks. The floor was earthen, the walls stone and iron, the room barren and empty.

Balinor was familiar with the cellar beneath the palace but he did not recognize the room in which they had been imprisoned. The cellar was used primarily for storage, and while there had always been a number of walled rooms in which wine barrels had been placed to age, this was not one of them. Then, with chilling certainty, he realized that they had been imprisoned in the ancient dungeon constructed centuries ago beneath the cellar and later sealed off and forgotten. Palance must have discovered its existence and reopened the cells for his own use. Quite probably, he had imprisoned Balinor's friends somewhere in this maze when they had come to the palace to object to the disbanding of the Border Legion. It was a well-concealed prison, and Balinor doubted that anyone searching for them would ever find it.

The discussion was completed quickly. There was little to say. Balinor had left his instructions with Captain Sheelon. Should they fail to return, he was to seek out Ginnisson and Fandwick, two of Balinor's most dependable commanders, and order them to reassemble the Border Legion to defend against any assault by the Warlock Lord and his invading army. Sheelon had also been told to send word to the Elf and Dwarf nations, warning them of the situation and calling for their immediate support. Eventine would not permit his cousins to remain the prisoners of Callahorn for very long, and Allanon would come as soon as he heard of their misfortune. Four hours must have passed long ago, he thought, so it should only be a matter of time. But time was precious, and with Palance determined to gain the throne of Callahorn, their own lives were in grave danger. The borderman began to wish silently that he had listened to Durin's advice and avoided a confrontation with his brother until he had been certain of the outcome.

He had never imagined that matters would go this far awry. Palance had been like a wild man, his hatred so consuming that he had not even waited to hear what Balinor would say. Yet there was little mystery to this irrational behavior. It was more than personal differences between the two brothers that had prompted the youth's savage action. It was more than the illness of his father, an illness Palance somehow believed his brother was responsible for. It had something to do with Shirl Ravenlock, the alluring woman Palance had fallen in love with months before and had vowed to marry despite her own reticence toward the match. Something had happened to the young Kern girl, and Balinor had received the blame. Palance would do anything to get her back safely, if she was indeed missing, as his brother's few words immediately before they had been brought to this dungeon had indicated.

The borderman explained the situation to the Elven brothers. He felt certain Palance would come to them soon and demand information concerning the young woman. But he would not believe them when they said they knew nothing. . . .

More than twenty-four hours passed, and still no one came. There was nothing to eat. Even after their eyes gradually grew accustomed to the blackness, there was nothing to view but their own shadowy forms and the walls about them. They took turns sleeping, trying to conserve their strength for whatever lay ahead, but the abnormal silence prevented any real sleep, and they resigned themselves to a light, restless slumber that did little to refresh their bodies or their spirits. At first they attempted to find a weak spot on the hinges of the bulky iron door, but it was securely fastened in place. Without tools of any sort, they found it impossible to dig very far into the chill, iron-hard surface of the dirt flooring. The stone walls were aged, but still firm and solid, without any sign of a weak or crumbling layer in the mortar. Eventually they abandoned their attempts to escape and sat back in silence.

Finally, after endless hours of waiting in the chill darkness, they heard the distant sound of clanging metal as an ancient iron door somewhere above swung ponderously open. There were voices, muffled and soft, and then footsteps on stone as someone began to descend the worn stairs to the lower dungeon where the three were imprisoned. Quickly they rose to their feet and crowded close to the cell door, listening expectantly as the footsteps and the voices drew closer. Balinor could distinguish the voice of his brother above the rest, strangely hesitant and broken. Then the heavy latches were drawn back, the sudden grating of metal piercing to the ears of the three captives, who had become accustomed now to the deathlike silence of their prison, and they moved back from the massive cell door as it swung slowly inward. Blazing streaks of torchlight flashed into the darkened room, forcing the prisoners to shield their weakened eyes. As they slowly adjusted to this new light, several figures entered the room and came to a halt just within the entryway.

The younger son of the ailing King of Callahorn stood foremost of four figures, his broad face relaxed and his lips pursed. His eyes alone betrayed the hatred that burned within, and there was a maddened, almost desperate way that they moved from one captive to the next as he clenched his hands tightly behind him. He was clearly Balinor's brother, possessing the same facial construction, the same wide mouth and prominent nose, and the same big, rugged build. Next to him stood a man that even the Elven brothers recognized instantly, though they had never met him. He was the mystic Stenmin, a gaunt, slightly stooped figure, lean and sharp in his features, and clothed in reddish robes and trappings. His eyes were strangely shadowed, reflecting an undisguisable evil in the man who had gained the complete confidence of the new, self-proclaimed King. His hands moved over his body nervously, raising almost mechanically from time to time to stroke the small, pointed black beard that shaded the angular face. Behind him stood two armed guards, dressed in black and bearing the insignia of the falcon. Beyond them, just outside the doorway, stood two more. All held wicked-looking pikes. For a moment no one spoke; no one even moved as the two parties scrutinized each other in the torchlit gloom of the little cell. Then Palance made a quick motion toward the open door.

"I will speak with my brother alone. Take these other two out."

The guards silently complied, leading the reluctant Elven brothers from the room. The tall Prince waited until they had left, then turned questioningly to the scarlet-robed figure still at his side.

"I thought that perhaps you might have need of me . . .?" The lean, calculating face stared steadily at the impassive Balinor.

"Leave us, Stenmin. I will speak with my brother alone."

His tone of voice bordered on anger, and the mystic

nodded obediently, quickly backing out of the cell.
The heavy door closed with an ominous thud, leaving
the two brothers alone in a silence broken only by the
hissing of the torch flame as it consumed the dry wood
and flashed into gleaming sparks. Balinor did not
move, but stood waiting expectantly, his eyes trying to
probe his brother's young face, trying to reach the old
feelings of love and friendship they had shared as
children. But they were missing, or at least carefully
submerged in some dark corner of the heart, and in
their place was a strange, restless anger that seemed to
rise as much from dissatisfaction with the situation as
from dislike of the captive brother. An instant later the
fury and the contempt were gone, replaced by a calm
detachment that Balinor found both irrational and
false, as if Palance were playing a role without any real
understanding of the character.

"Why did you come back, Balinor?" The words
came out slowly, sadly. "Why did you do it?"

The tall borderman did not reply, unable to
comprehend this sudden change of mood. Before, his
brother had been willing to have him torn to pieces in
order to learn the whereabouts of the beautiful Shirl
Ravenlock, yet now he seemed to have completely
dismissed the matter from his mind.

"No matter, no matter I suppose." The reply came
before Balinor had recovered from his astonishment at
the abrupt change. "You could have stayed away
after . . . after all the . . . after your treachery. I
hoped you would, you know, because we were so
close as children and you are, after all, my only
brother. I will be King of Callahorn . . . I should have
been firstborn anyway. . . ."

He trailed off into a whisper, his mind suddenly lost
in some unspoken thought. He had gone mad, Balinor
thought in desperation, and could no longer be
reached!

"Palance, listen to me—just listen to me. I have
done nothing to you or to Shirl. I've been in Paranor

since I left here weeks before, and I returned only to warn our people that the Skull King has assembled an army of such awesome proportions that it will sweep through the entire Southland unchallenged unless we stop it here! For the sake of all these people, please listen to me. . . ."

His brother's voice pierced the air in shrill command. "I will hear no more of this foolish talk of invasion! My scouts have checked the country's borders and report no enemy armies anywhere. Besides, no enemy would dare to attack Callahorn—to attack me. . . . Our people are safe here. What do I care for the rest of the Southland? What do I owe them? They have always left us to fight alone, to guard these borderlands alone. I owe them nothing!"

He took a step toward Balinor and pointed menacingly at him, the strange hatred flaming anew as the young face contorted savagely.

"You turned against me, brother, when you knew that I was to be king. You tried to poison me as you poisoned my father—you wanted me as sick and helpless as he is now . . . dying alone, forgotten, alone. You thought you had found an ally that could gain the throne for you when you left with that traitor Allanon. How I hate that man—no, not a man, but an evil thing! He must be destroyed! But *you* will remain in this cell, alone and forgotten, Balinor, until you die—the fate you had planned for me!"

He turned away suddenly, breaking his tirade off with a sharp laugh as he paced to the closed door. Balinor thought he was about to open it, when the hulking youth paused and looked back at him. Slowly he came around, the eyes sad again.

"You could have stayed away from this land and been safe," he muttered as if confused by this fact. "Stenmin said you would come back even when I assured him you would not. He was right again. He is always right. Why did you come back?"

Balinor thought quickly. He had to keep his

brother's attention long enough to find out what had happened to his father and his friends.

"I . . . I discovered I had been mistaken—that I was wrong," he answered slowly. "I came home to see our father and to see you, Palance."

"Father." The word came out like an unfamiliar name as the Prince moved a step closer. "He is beyond our help, lying like one already dead in that room in the south wing. Stenmin looks after him, as I do, but nothing can be done. He does not seem to want to live. . . ."

"But what is wrong with him?" Balinor's impatience burst free, and he moved toward the other threateningly.

"Keep your distance, Balinor." Palance backed away hastily, drawing a long dagger and holding it protectively before him. Balinor hesitated a moment. It would be easy to seize the dagger, hold the Prince captive until he was released. Yet something restrained him, something deep inside that warned against such a move. Quickly he stopped, holding up his hands and backing away to the far wall.

"You must remember you are my prisoner." Palance nodded in satisfaction, his voice unsteady. "You poisoned the King and you tried to poison me. I could have you put to death. Stenmin advised me to have you executed immediately, but I am not the coward that he is. I was a commander in the Border Legion, too, before . . . But they're gone now— disbanded and sent home to their families. My reign shall be a time of peace. You don't understand that, Balinor, do you?"

The borderman shook his head negatively, desperately trying to hold his brother's attention for a few minutes longer. Palance had apparently gone mad, whether from a latent congenital defect of the mind or from the strain of whatever it was that had been happening since Balinor had left Tyrsis with Allanon;

it was impossible to tell. In any event, he was no longer the brother that Balinor had grown to manhood with and had loved as he had loved no one else. It was a stranger living in the physical shell that was his brother's body—a stranger obsessed with the need to be King of Callahorn. Stenmin was behind this; Balinor knew it. The mystic had somehow twisted the mind of his maddened brother, bending it to his own uses, filling it with promises of his destiny as King. Palance had always wanted to rule Callahorn. Even when Balinor had left the city, he knew Palance felt certain he would one day be King. Stenmin had been there all the time, counseling and advising in the manner of a close friend, poisoning his mind against his brother. But Palance had been strong-willed and independent, a sane and healthy man who would not be broken easily. Yet he was changed. Hendel had been wrong about Palance, but apparently Balinor had been wrong as well. Neither could have foreseen this, and now it was too late.

"Shirl—what of Shirl?" the tall borderman asked quickly.

Again the anger faded from his brother's darting eyes and a slow smile crept over his lips, relaxing the anguished face for an instant.

"She is so beautiful . . . so beautiful." He sighed foolishly, the dagger falling harmlessly to the cell floor as the Prince opened his hands to emphasize the feeling. "You took her from me, Balinor—tried to keep her from me. But she is safe now. She was saved by a Southlander, a Prince like myself. No, I am King of Tyrsis now, and he is only a Prince. It's just a little kingdom; I had never heard of it myself. He and I will be good friends, Balinor, the way you and I once were. But Stenmin . . . says I can trust no one. I even had to lock away Messaline and Acton. They came to me when the Border Legion was sent home, trying to persuade me to . . . well, I guess to give up my plans for peace. They didn't understand . . . why . . ."

He stopped suddenly, his lowered eyes falling on the momentarily forgotten dagger. He picked it up quickly, placing it back in its belted sheath with a sly smile at his brother, looking strikingly like a clever child that has just avoided a scolding. There was no longer any doubt in Balinor's mind that his brother was totally incapable of making rational decisions. He was suddenly struck with his earlier premonition that while he could easily seize the dagger and hold his brother prisoner, it would be a serious mistake. Now he knew why that innate sense of warning had been generated. Stenmin fully realized Palance's condition and had purposely left the brothers alone in that cell. If Balinor had attempted to disarm Palance and to escape while holding him prisoner, the evil mystic could have accomplished his obvious goal in one bold stroke by killing both brothers. Who would question him when he explained that Palance had met his death by accident while his brother was attempting to flee his prison confinement? With both brothers dead and their father incapable of governing, the mystic might be able to seize control of the government of Callahorn. Then he alone would determine the fate of the Southland.

"Palance, listen to me, I beg of you," Balinor pleaded quietly. "We were so close once. We were more than just brothers by bloodline. We were friends, companions. We trusted each other, loved each other, and we could always work our problems out by understanding each other. You can't have forgotten all that. Listen to me! Even a king must try to understand his people—even when they don't agree on the way things are to be handled. You agree with that, don't you?"

Palance nodded soberly, the eyes vacant and detached as he tried to fight the haze that blocked his thought processes. There was a glimmer of understanding, and Balinor was determined to reach the memory that lay locked somewhere deep within.

"Stenmin is using you—he is an evil man." His brother started abruptly, taking a step backward as if to avoid hearing more. "You've got to understand, Palance. I am not your enemy, nor am I the enemy of this country. I did not poison our father. I did not harm Shirl in any way. I only want to help . . ."

His plea was suddenly cut short as the ponderous cell door swung open with a sharp rasp, and the angular features of the wily Stenmin appeared. Bowing condescendingly, he entered the cell, his cruel eyes fastened intently on Balinor.

"I thought I heard you call me, my King," he smiled quickly. "You've been in here alone so long, I thought something might have happened . . ."

Palance stared at him uncomprehendingly for a moment, then shook his head negatively and turned to leave. In that instant Balinor considered leaping upon the evil mystic and crushing the life from him before the absent guards could act. But he hesitated for that single brief moment, uncertain that even this would save him or aid his brother, and so the opportunity was lost. The guards came back into the cell, leading the Elven brothers, who looked about dubiously, then rejoined their comrade on the far side of the little room. Suddenly Balinor recalled something Palance had said when he was talking about Shirl. He had mentioned a Prince from a tiny Southland kingdom—a Prince who had rescued the young girl. Menion Leah! But how could he be in Callahorn . . .?

The guards were turning to leave now and with them the silent Palance and his evil consort, a red-clad arm guiding the mindless Prince from the room. Then abruptly, the lean figure turned to look once more on the three captives, a thin smile spreading over the pursed lips as the bowed head cocked carefully to one side.

"In the event my King should have failed to mention

it, Balinor . . ." The words sounded with a slow, burning hatred. "The guards at the Outer Wall saw you speaking with a certain Captain Sheelon, formerly of the Border Legion. He was trying to speak with others about your . . . predicament, when he was seized and imprisoned. I don't believe he will have much chance to cause us any further trouble. The matter is quite ended now, and within time even you will be forgotten."

Balinor's heart sank suddenly at this final piece of news. If Sheelon had been seized and confined before he had been able to reach Ginnisson and Fandwick, then there would be no one to assemble the Border Legion and no one to appeal to the people on his behalf. His absent companions would not know of his imprisonment upon reaching Tyrsis, and even if they suspected what had happened, what hope would they have of ever finding out what had become of him? This lower level of the ancient palace was unknown to all but a very few, and its entrance was well concealed. The three despondent captives watched in bitter silence as the guards placed a small tray of bread and a jug of water just inside the open door, then moved back into the hallway, carrying with them all of the burning torches but one. The grimly smiling Stenmin held this last light as he waited for the stooped form of Palance to follow the burly guards. But Palance paused uncertainly, unable to take his eyes from his brother's proud, resigned face; the faint torchlight illuminated the broad features in reddish streaks and the long, deep-rutted scar emerged dark and cruel in the half shadow. The brothers faced each other in silence for several long moments, and then Palance started back toward Balinor with slow, measured steps, shaking off Stenmin's hand as it tried to restrain him. He came to a halt only inches away from his brother, the dazed, searching eyes still fastened on that granite-hewn countenance as if trying to absorb from it the determination mirrored there. An uncertain hand raised itself quickly, pausing for an instant, then resting firmly on Balinor's shoulder, the fingers gripping tightly.

"I want to . . . know." The words were a whisper in the near darkness. "I want to understand . . . You must help me. . . ."

Balinor nodded silently, his own great hand reaching up to take his brother's in a brief clasp of love. For a moment they remained locked together, as if the friendship and love of childhood had never faded. Then Palance turned away and moved quickly out of the cell, hastily followed by a disturbed Stenmin. The heavy door closed with the grating of iron fastenings and metal clasps, shutting in the three friends and the impenetrable darkness once more. The departing footsteps died slowly into silence. The waiting began anew, but any real hope of rescue seemed irretrievably lost.

A shadowy form detached itself from the blackness of the night-shrouded trees in the deserted park beneath the high span of the Sendic Bridge and darted silently toward the palace of the Buckhannahs. In quick, surefooted leaps, the powerful, compact form cleared the low hedges and shrubs, weaving between the stately elms, a pair of watchful eyes studying the wall enclosing the royal grounds, searching carefully for any sign of the night watch. Near the iron-wrought gates above the park, where the bridge opened onto the high ground, several guards patrolled, the falcon insignia visible in the torchlight of the gate entrance. Slowly the dark form climbed the gently sloping embankment toward the moss- and ivy-covered walls above; upon gaining the higher ground, it melted instantly into the shadows of the stone.

For long moments, it remained completely invisible as it moved steadily away from the main gate and the feeble torchlight. Then the intruder was visible once more, a dark blur against the faintly moonlit west wall as strong arms clung tenaciously to the sturdy vines, pulling the bulky form silently to the rim of the stone. There the head raised itself cautiously, and the keen eyes peered down into the empty palace gardens, making certain there were no guards close at hand. With a mighty heave of the powerful shoulders, the intruder gained the lip of the wall and, springing lightly over, landed with a soft thud amid the garden flowers.

Running in a half-crouch, the mysterious figure sprinted for the shadowy cover of a huge spreading willow. Pausing breathlessly within the giant tree's protective limbs, the intruder heard the approaching sound of voices. Listening carefully for a few moments, he concluded it was nothing more than the idle conversation of several palace guards making their appointed rounds. He waited confidently, his compact frame blending so closely with the squat trunk of the tree that he was totally invisible from more than a few feet away. The guards appeared seconds later, still conversing in relaxed voices as they passed through the silent gardens and were gone. Resting furtively for a few minutes longer, the stranger studied the dark bulk that occupied the center of these tree-shaded gardens—the tall, ancient palace of the Kings of Callahorn. A few lighted windows broke the misty blackness of the massive stone structure, casting bright streamers into the deserted gardens. There were faint, distant voices within, but their owners remained anonymous.

In a quick dash, the intruder crossed to the shadows of the building, pausing briefly beneath a small, darkened window in a recessed alcove. His strong hands worked frantically at the ancient catch, pushing at it and loosening the fastening. At last, with an audible snap that seemed to penetrate the entire palace grounds, the catch broke and the window swung silently inward. Without waiting to see if the patrolling guards had heard the sounds of his forced entry, the intruder slipped hastily through the small opening. As the window closed behind him, the faint light of a clouded moon caught for just an instant the broad, determined face of the redoubtable Hendel.

Stenmin had made one serious miscalculation when he had imprisoned Balinor and the cousins of Eventine. His original plan had been a simple one. The aged Sheelon had been secured almost the moment after he left Balinor's side, preventing him from carrying out the Prince's instructions for warning his friends of his own imprisonment. With Balinor and the Elven brothers, his only companions when he had entered the city of Tyrsis, safely locked away beneath the palace, and with the Prince's close friends, Acton and Messaline, imprisoned as well, it seemed safe to assume that no one else in the city would cause any real difficulty. The word had already been spread that Balinor had come for a brief visit and gone on his way, returning to the company of the mystic Allanon, the man whom Stenmin had convinced Palance Buck-hannah and most of the people of Tyrsis was an enemy and a threat to the land of Callahorn. Should any other friends of Balinor's appear and question the story of the borderman's abrupt departure, they would come first to the palace to speak with his brother, now the King, and it would be a simple matter to have them quietly disposed of. Undoubtedly this would have been exactly the situation with just about anyone except Hendel. But the taciturn Dwarf was already familiar with Stenmin's treacherous ways and suspected that he had gained an unshakable hold over the disturbed Palance. Hendel knew better than to reveal his presence before finding out what had actually happened to his missing companions.

It was a peculiar turn of events that brought him

back to Tyrsis. When he left Balinor and the Elven brothers near the woodlands north of the fortress, he fully intended to travel straight to the western city of Varfleet and from there proceed back to Culhaven. Once in his own land, he would assist in mobilizing the Dwarf armies to defend the southern territories of the Anar against the expected invasion of the Warlock Lord. He traveled all night through the forests north of Varfleet and by morning entered the city, where he immediately called on old friends and, after a brief greeting, went directly to sleep. It was afternoon by the time he was awakened, and after washing and eating, he prepared to depart for his homeland. He had not yet reached the gates of the city when a ragged band of Dwarfs staggered through the streets and demanded to be taken before the council. Hendel hurried along with them, questioning one he recognized as they were escorted to the council chambers. To his dismay he learned that a massive force of Trolls and Gnomes was marching directly for the city of Varfleet from out of the Dragon's Teeth and would strike within the next day or two. The Dwarfs were part of a patrol that had spotted the huge army and tried to slip past it to warn the Southlanders. Unfortunately they were seen and most were killed in a pitched battle. Only this small handful had managed to reach the unsuspecting city.

Hendel knew that if an armed force were moving toward Varfleet, there was in all probability a second, much larger force moving against Tyrsis. He was certain that the Spirit Lord planned to destroy the cities of Callahorn quickly and thoroughly, leaving the gateway to all the Southland open and undefended. His first duty was to warn his own people, but it was a long, two-day march to Culhaven and two more days back again.

He quickly discovered that Balinor had been mistaken in his belief that his father was still the King.

If Balinor were killed or imprisoned by his insanely jealous brother or the treacherous mystic Stenmin before he could secure the throne and gain command of the Border Legion, then Callahorn was doomed. Someone had to reach the borderman before it was too late. There was nobody available for the job but Hendel. Allanon was still searching the Northland for the missing Shea, accompanied by Flick and Menion Leah. He made his decision quickly, ordering one of the battered Dwarfs in the ragged patrol to leave that very night for Culhaven. Whatever else happened, word would have to be brought to the Dwarf elders that the invasion of the Southland had begun through Callahorn and that the Dwarf armies must march to the aid of Varfleet. The cities of Callahorn must not fall or the lands would be divided and the very thing Allanon feared most would come to pass. With the Southland conquered, the Dwarf armies and the Elven armies would be divided and the Warlock Lord would be assured his eventual victory over all the lands. The ragged Dwarf gave his solemn promise to Hendel that he would not fail—that they would all leave at once for the Anar.

It took Hendel many hours to get back to Tyrsis, since this time travel was slow and dangerous. The forests had been penetrated by Gnome hunters whose mission it was to prevent any communication between the cities of Callahorn. More than once Hendel was forced to hide himself until a large patrol had passed, and time and again he was compelled to go far out of his way to avoid crossing heavily guarded sentry lines. The network of sentry posts was far tighter than it had been in the Dragon's Teeth, an indication to the seasoned border fighter that the attack was close at hand. If the Northlanders planned to strike Varfleet within the next day or so, then Tyrsis would be assaulted at the same time. The smaller island city of Kern might have already fallen. It was daylight when

the Dwarf succeeded in penetrating the last of the
sentry lines and was approaching the plains above
Tyrsis, the danger of detection by the Gnomes behind
and the threat of discovery by the evil Stenmin and the
misguided Palance just ahead. He had met Palance
several times, but it was unlikely the prince would
remember him, and he had encountered Stenmin only
once. Nevertheless, it would be wise to avoid
attracting anyone's attention.

He entered the waking city of Tyrsis, concealed in
the midst of dozens of traders and travelers. Once
within the great Outer Wall, he wandered for several
hours through the nearly deserted barracks of the
Border Legion, speaking with the soldiers there and
searching for some clue concerning his friends. Finally
he was able to learn that they had arrived in the city at
sunset two days ago and gone directly to the palace.
They had not been seen again, but there was good
reason to believe that Balinor had visited briefly with
his father and then left. Hendel knew what this meant,
and for the remainder of the daylight hours he posted
himself close to the palace grounds, watching for any
sign of his missing friends.

He noticed that the palace was well-guarded by
soldiers wearing the crest of a falcon, a sign he didn't
recognize. There were soldiers stationed at the main
gates and throughout the city, all bearing the same
insignia, and these were apparently the only activated
units in all of Tyrsis. Even if he found Balinor alive and
managed to free him, it would not be a simple task to
regain control of the city and reactivate the Border
Legion. The Dwarf heard no mention of the invasion
from the north, and it appeared the people were
totally ignorant of the danger facing them. It was
incredible to Hendel that even someone as disturbed
and misguided as Palance Buckhannah would refuse
to prepare the city against a threat as awesome as that
posed by the Warlock Lord. If Tyrsis fell, the younger

son of Ruhl Buckhannah would have no throne left him. Hendel silently studied the terrain composing the People's Park that stretched beneath the wide span of the Bridge of Sendic. When it was dark, he began his assault on the guarded palace.

Now he paused momentarily within the darkened room, closing the window tightly behind him. He was in a small study, the walls lined with shelves of books carefully marked and labeled. It was the personal library of the Buckhannah family, a luxury in these times when so few books were written and dissemination was considerably limited. The Great Wars had nearly obliterated literature from the face of the earth, and little had been written in the embattled, desperate years since. To have a private library and to be able to sit and read any of several hundred books at leisure were privileges shared by very few, even in the most enlightened societies of the four lands.

But Hendel scarcely gave the room more than a passing thought as he moved on catlike feet for the door at the far end, his keen eyes detecting a dim light along the crack near the floor. Cautiously the Dwarf peered into the lighted hallway. There was no one in sight, but he suddenly realized that he had not yet decided what his next step would be. Balinor and the Elven brothers could be anywhere in the palace. After rapid consideration of the alternatives, he concluded that they would be imprisoned in the cellar beneath the palace if they were alive. He would search there first. Listening for a long moment to the silence, the Dwarf took a deep breath and stepped calmly into the hallway.

Hendel was familiar with the palace, having visited Balinor on more than one occasion. He did not recall whcιe specific rooms were situated, but he knew the halls and stairways, and he had been taken to the cellar where the wines and food were stored. At the end of the hall, he turned left at the cross passage, certain the cellar stairs were just ahead. He reached the massive door that shut out the chill of the lower passages when he heard voices in the hall behind him. Hastily he tugged at the door, but to his dismay it would not open. He pulled again with his powerful shoulders hunched down and knotted, and still the door did not move. The voices were almost on top of him now, and in desperation he moved to reach another place of concealment. At that instant his eyes fell on a safety catch close to the floor which he had missed. With the voices just beyond the corner of the hall and the footsteps of several men echoing on the polished stone flooring, the Dwarf coolly drew back this second latch, swung open the heavy door, and darted inside. The door closed behind him just as three sentries rounded the corner on their way to relieve the guards stationed at the south gate.

Hendel did not wait to find out whether he had been seen, but darted down the stone-hewn stairs into the blackness of the deserted storage cellar. Pausing at the bottom of the stairway, the Dwarf groped along the cold stone of the wall for an iron torch rack. After several long minutes he found it, wresting the torch quickly from its setting and lighting it with the aid of flint and iron.

Then, with slow, painstaking care he searched the entire cellar, room by room, corner to corner. Time passed quickly, and still he found nothing. At last he had searched everywhere without any success, and it began to appear his friends were not being held captive in that part of the palace. Reluctantly Hendel forced himself to admit that they might have been imprisoned in one of the upper rooms. It seemed strange that either Palance or his evil adviser would risk having the captives seen by people visiting. Still, Hendel considered, perhaps Balinor had indeed left the city of Tyrsis and gone in search of Allanon. But he knew that guess was wrong even before the thought was completed. Balinor was not the kind of man who would seek anyone's help with this kind of problem—he would face his brother, not run. Desperately, Hendel tried to imagine where the borderman and the brothers might have been secured, where in the ancient building prisoners could be safely concealed from everyone. The logical place was beneath the palace in the dark, windowless depths he had just . . .

Suddenly Hendel remembered that there were ancient dungeons that lay beneath even this cellar. Balinor had mentioned them in passing, remarking briefly on their history, noting that they had been abandoned and the entry sealed over. Excitedly, the Dwarf peered around the shadowed chamber, trying to recall where the ancient passage had been built. He was certain that this was where his friends had been taken—it was the one place a man could be hidden and never found. Almost no one knew of its existence outside of the royal family and their close associates. It had been sealed over and forgotten for so many years that even the eldest citizens of Tyrsis might not recall its existence.

Ignoring the small adjoining rooms and passages, the determined Hendel carefully studied the walls and flooring of the central chamber, certain that it had been here he had viewed the sealed opening. If it had indeed been reopened, it should not be difficult to find. Yet he could see it nowhere. The walls appeared solid and the molding unbroken as he probed and tapped along the base. Once again his search proved fruitless, and once again he felt that he might have been mistaken. Despondently, he collapsed against one of the wine casings resting in the center of the floor, his eyes scouring the walls desperately as he tried to remember. Time was running out for Hendel. If he did not escape before daylight, he would probably join his friends in captivity. He knew he was missing something, overlooking something that was so obvious it had managed to escape him. Cursing silently, he rose from the wine barrel and walked slowly about the large chamber, thinking, trying to recall. It was something about the walls . . . something about the walls . . .

Then he had it. The passageway was not through the walls, but through the center of the floor! Suppressing a wild shout of glee, the Dwarf rushed over to the wine casings against which he had twice that evening so casually rested. Straining his powerful muscles to almost superhuman limits, he managed to roll aside several of the unwieldy barrels so that the stone slab which covered the hidden entryway was revealed. Grasping an iron ring hinged at one end of the slab, the sweating Dwarf pulled upward with an audible groan. Slowly, the stone grating in protest, the giant slab swung upward and fell back heavily on the flooring. Hendel peered cautiously into the black hole before him, extending the feeble torchlight into the musty depths. There was an ancient stone stairway, wet and covered with a greenish moss, that disappeared into the blackness. Holding the light before him, the little man descended into the forgotten dungeon, silently praying that he was not making another mistake.

Almost immediately he felt the biting chill of the stale, imprisoned air cutting through his clothing to cling maliciously to the warm skin beneath. The musty, barely breathable atmosphere caused him to wrinkle his nose in distaste and move down the steps more quickly. Such confining, tomblike holes frightened him more than anything, and he began to question his wisdom in deciding to venture into the ancient prison. But if Balinor were truly a captive in this terrible place, the risk was worth taking. Hendel would not abandon his friends. He reached the bottom of the stairs and could see a single corridor leading directly ahead. As he moved slowly forward, trying to peer through the damp gloom that defied even the light of the slow-burning torch, he could make out iron doors cut into the solid stone of either wall at regular intervals. These ancient, rusted slabs of iron were windowless and fastened securely in place by huge metal clasps. This was a dungeon that would terrify any human being—a windowless, lightless row of cubicles where lives could be shuttered away and forgotten as surely as the dead.

For untold years the Dwarfs had lived like this following the devastating Great Wars in order to stay alive and had emerged half-blind into a nearly forgotten world of light. That terrible memory had imbedded itself in generations of Dwarfs, leaving them with an instinctive fear of unlighted, confined places that they would never completely overcome. Hendel felt it now, as nagging and hateful as the clammy chill of the earth's depths into which this ancient grave had been carved.

Forcing down the rising knot of terror that hung in his throat, the determined hunter studied the first several doors. The bolts were still rusted in place and the metal covered with layers of dust and unbroken cobwebs. As he passed slowly down the line of grim iron portals, he could see that none of them had been opened in many years. He lost count of the number of doors he checked and the dim corridor seemed to continue on endlessly into the blackness. He was tempted to call out, but the sound might carry back through the open entryway to the chambers above. Glancing apprehensively behind him, he realized that he could no longer see the opening or the stairs. The darkness looked exactly the same behind as it did ahead. Gritting his teeth and muttering softly to himself to bolster his waning confidence, he moved forward, carefully scrutinizing each door he passed for signs of recent use. Then, to his astonishment, he heard the vague whisper of human voices through the heavy silence.

Freezing into a motionless statue, he listened intently, afraid that his senses were deceiving him. Yet there they were again, faint, but clearly human. Moving ahead quickly, the Dwarf tried to follow the sound. But as suddenly as they had appeared, the voices were gone. Desperately, Hendel glanced at the doors to either side. One was rusted shut, but the other bore fresh scratches in the metal, and the dust and cobwebs had been brushed away. The latch was oiled and had been recently used! With one quick tug, the Dwarf pulled back the metal fastening and yanked open the massive door, thrusting the torch before him, the light falling sharply on three astonished, half-blinded figures who rose hesitantly to face this new intruder.

There were warm cries of recognition, a rushing together with outstretched hands, and the four friends were reunited. The rough visage of Balinor, towering above the drawn faces of the smiling Elven brothers, appeared relaxed and confident, and only the blue eyes betrayed the borderman's deep sense of relief. Once again, the resourceful Dwarf had saved their lives. But this was no time for words or feelings, and Hendel quickly motioned them back down the darkened passage toward the stairway leading up from this frightening dungeon. If daybreak found them still wandering beneath the palace, the chance of discovery and recapture would be a near certainty. They had to escape immediately into the city. In hurried steps they moved down the corridor, the dying torchlight held before them like the probing cane of a blind man seeking the way.

Then came the sudden grating of stone on stone and a heavy thudding noise as if a tomb had closed. Horrified, Hendel charged ahead, reaching the damp stone steps and stopping short. Above, the huge stone slab had been closed, the fastenings secured, and the exit to freedom barred. The Dwarf stood helplessly beside his three friends, shaking his head in stunned disbelief. His attempt to save them had failed; he had only succeeded in becoming a captive himself. The torch in his gnarled hand was almost burned out. Soon, they would be left in total blackness, and the waiting would begin again.

XXVI

Junk, nothing but junk!" roared Panamon Creel in frustration, kicking once more the pile of worthless metal blades and jewelry that lay on the ground before him. "How could I have been such a fool? I should have seen it right away!"

Shea walked silently to the north end of the clearing, his eyes staring at the faint trail in the forest earth that the crafty Orl Fane had left in his flight northward. He had been so close. He had held the precious Sword in his own hands—only to lose it through an unforgivable failure to recognize the truth. The massive form of Keltset loomed silently beside him, the great bulk bending close to the damp, leaf-strewn ground, the inscrutable face almost next to his own as the strangely gentle eyes studied and searched. Shea turned quietly back to the raging Panamon.

"It wasn't your fault—you had no reason to suspect the truth," he muttered dejectedly. "I should have listened to his raving with a little more wisdom and a little less . . . whatever. I knew the signs to look for and I forgot to keep my eyes open when it counted."

Panamon nodded and shrugged, stroking the carefully trimmed mustaches with the point of his piked hand. With a last kick at the discarded implements, he called once to Keltset, and without further discussion the two began quickly to break camp, strapping together the gear and weapons that had been deposited for the night. Shea watched them for a moment, still unable to accept his failure to gain possession of the Sword. Panamon called gruffly to him to lend a hand, and he silently obeyed. He could not face the inevitable aftermath of this most recent setback. Panamon Creel had obviously been pushed as far as he would stand it, chaperoning a foolish and amazingly stupid little Valeman around in the dangerous borderlands of Paranor, searching for some people who might very well turn out to be enemies and for a Sword that only Shea knew anything about, but couldn't recognize when he had it in his own hands. The scarlet highwayman and his giant companion had nearly lost their lives once already over this mysterious Sword and undoubtedly once was more than enough. The Valeman had no choice now except to try to locate his friends. But when he did find them, he would have to confront Allanon and tell him how he had failed—failed them all. He shuddered at the prospect of facing the grim Druid, of feeling those remorseless eyes peer into his most carefully hidden thoughts for the whole truth. It was not going to be pleasant.

He recalled suddenly the strange prophecy related to them in the Valley of Shale on that dark, misted dawn over a week ago. It was the Shade of Bremen who had forewarned of the danger in the forbidding Dragon's Teeth—how one would not see Paranor, how one would not reach the other side of the mountain, yet would be first to lay hands on the Sword of Shannara. It had all been foretold, but Shea had forgotten it in the stress and excitement of the past few days.

The weary Valeman closed his eyes against the world for a few moments and wondered how on earth he could possibly be a part of this incredible puzzle that centered around a war of power with the spirit world and a legendary Sword. He felt so small and helpless that it seemed that the easiest path for him to choose now was to bury himself and pray for a quick end to life. So much depended on him, if Allanon were to be believed, and from the beginning he had been completely inadequate to the task. He had been unable to do anything for himself, depending on the strength of other men to get him this far. How much had they all sacrificed for him so that he might lay hands on the magic Sword. Yet when he had it in his grasp . . .

"I've decided. We're going after him."

Panamon Creel's deep voice cut through the quiet of the little clearing like the sharp crack of an iron blade through dry wood. Shea stared at the broad, unsmiling face in astonishment.

"You mean . . . into the Northland?"

The scarlet thief shot him one of those angry looks that dismissed the Valeman as an idiot incapable of understanding sane men.

"He made a fool out of me. I'd rather cut my own throat than let the little rat get away from me now. When I get my hands on him this time, I'll leave him for the worms to chew on."

The handsome face was emotionless, but there was undisguisable hatred in the menacing tone of voice that cut through to the bone. This was the other side of Panamon—the cold professional who had ruthlessly destroyed an entire encampment of Gnomes and later stood in battle against the incomparable power of the Skull Bearer. He wasn't doing this for Shea or even to gain possession of the Sword of Shannara. This was strictly a matter of his injured pride and desire for revenge on the unfortunate creature who had dared to bruise it. Shea glanced quickly at the motionless Keltset, but the giant Rock Troll gave no indication of either approval or disapproval; the barklike face was blank, the deep-set eyes expressionless. Panamon laughed sharply, taking a few quick strides toward the hesitant Valeman.

"Think on this, Shea. Our Gnome friend has made matters so much more simple by revealing the exact location of the Sword you have been searching so long to find. Now you don't have to search for it—we know where it is."

Shea nodded in silent agreement, still wary of the adventurer's true motives. "Do we have a chance of catching up with him?"

"That's more like it—that's the spirit we need." Panamon grinned at him, his face a mask of confidence. "Of course we can catch up with him—it's merely a matter of time. The difficulty will be if someone else catches up with him first. Keltset knows the Northland as well as anyone alive. The Gnome will not be able to hide from us. He will have to run, run, and keep running, because he has no one to turn to, not even his own people. It's impossible to know exactly how he stumbled onto the Sword, or even how he surmised its value, but I do know I was not mistaken about his being a deserter and a scavenger."

"He could have been a member of the band of Gnomes transporting the Sword to the Warlock Lord—or perhaps even a prisoner?" Shea suggested thoughtfully.

"More probably the latter," the other agreed, hesitating as if trying to recall something, staring northward into the gray mistiness of the forest morning. The sun had already cleared the horizon of the eastern edge of the world, its fresh light bright and warm, seeping slowly into the darkened corners of the forestland. But the mist of early morning had not yet cleared, leaving the three companions shrouded in a hazy mixture of sunlight and dying night. The sky to the north appeared unaccountably dark and forbidding even for early morning, causing the normally verbose Panamon to stare wordlessly at this curious

blackness for several long minutes. Finally he turned
back to them, his face clouded with doubt.

"Something strange is going on to the north.
Keltset, let's move out now—find that Gnome before
he has a chance to stumble onto a patrol of hunters. I
don't want to share his final moments in this world
with anyone!"

The giant Rock Troll moved into the lead in quick,
easy strides, his head lowered slightly as he searched
the ground before him, picking out the signs left by the
fleeing Orl Fane. Panamon and Shea followed close
behind in silent concentration. The trail of their quarry
was readily apparent to the keen eyes of Keltset. He
turned back to them and made a short signal with one
hand, which Panamon translated for the curious Shea
to mean that the Gnome was running hard and fast,
not bothering to hide his footsteps, and had evidently
decided on his eventual destination.

Shea began to speculate in his own mind where the
wily little fellow would run. With the Sword in his
possession, he might be able to redeem himself in the
eyes of his own people by turning it over to them for
presentation to the Warlock Lord. But Orl Fane had
appeared highly irrational in his behavior while he
was their prisoner, and Shea felt certain that the
Gnome had not been faking. He had rambled on as if
the victim of a madness he could only partially control,
speaking in garbled sentences that had in a jumbled
fashion revealed the truth concerning the whereabouts of the Sword. If Shea had thought the matter
through a little more carefully, he would have seen
it—he would have known that Orl Fane had the
coveted talisman with him. No, the Gnome had
crossed the mental barrier between sanity and madness, and his actions would not be entirely predictable. He would run from them, but to whom would he
run?

"I remember now." Panamon broke into his

thoughts as they continued to make their way back toward the Plains of Streleheim. "That winged creature insisted that we had possession of the Sword when it confronted us yesterday. It kept telling us that it could sense the presence of the Sword—and so it could, because Orl Fane was concealed in the brush with the weapon hidden in his sack."

Shea nodded quietly, recalling the incident bitterly. The Skull Bearer had unwittingly tipped them off that the precious Sword was in the area, but they had failed to notice this important clue in the heat and fury of their battle to survive. Panamon continued to ramble on in barely concealed fury, threatening to dispose of Orl Fane when they caught up with him in a number of extremely unpleasant ways. Then abruptly the fringes of the forest broke away, opening into the vast expanse of the Plains of Streleheim.

In astonishment, the three halted together, their disbelieving eyes fixed on the awesome spectacle that loomed directly to the north—a huge, unbroken wall of blackness, towering skyward until it vanished into the infinity of space, stretching along the horizon to encircle the entire Northland. It was as if the Skull King had bound the ancient land in the shroud of darkness that lay upon the spirit world. It was more than the blackness of a clouded night. It was a heavy mistiness that rolled and swirled in deepening shades of gray as it ran northward toward the heart of the Skull Kingdom. It was the most terrifying sight that Shea had ever witnessed. His initial fear was heightened twice over by a sudden, unexplainable certainty in his mind that this huge wall was crawling slowly southward, blanketing the entire world. It meant that the Warlock Lord was coming. . . .

"What in heaven's name is that . . .?" Panamon trailed off into stunned silence.

Shea shook his head absently. There could be no answer to that question. This was something beyond the understanding of mortal man. The three stood looking at the massive wall for several long moments, as if waiting for something more to happen. Finally, Keltset stooped to peer carefully at the hard grassland before them, moving forward several yards at a time until he was some distance away. Then he rose and pointed directly into the center of the ominous black haze. Panamon started, his face frozen.

"The Gnome is running directly into that stuff," he muttered angrily. "If we do not catch him before he reaches it, the darkness will hide his trail completely. We will have lost him."

Several miles ahead, on the graying fringes of the blackened wall of mist and haze, the small, bent form of Orl Fane hesitated momentarily in its exhausting flight as the greenish eyes peered fearfully, uncomprehendingly into the swirling darkness. The Gnome had been moving northward since his escape from the three strangers during the early hours of the morning, running while his strength held out, then pushing forward in a shuffling trot, always with one eye straying back, waiting for the inevitable pursuit. His mind no longer functioned in a rational manner; for several weeks he had lived on instinct and luck, preying off the dead, avoiding the living. He could not force himself to think of anything beyond survival, a gut instinct to live another day among those who did not want him, would not accept him as one of their own. Even his own people had turned him away, scorning him as a creature lower than the insects that crawled the earth at their feet. It was a savage land that surrounded him—a land in which one could not survive alone for very long. Yet he was alone, and the mind that had once been sane had slowly turned inward on itself, shutting away the fears that were imbedded there until madness began to take hold and all reason began to die.

Yet the inevitable death did not come easily, as fate intervened with twisted humor and favored the outcast with a final glimmer of false hope, placing in his hands the means by which to regain the seemingly unattainable warmth of human companionship once more. While still a scavenger, still fighting a losing battle to stay alive, the desperate Gnome had learned of the presence of the legendary Sword of Shannara, its awesome secret gasped in faint warning from the rigid lips of one dying on the Streleheim Plains, the blinded eyes failing as the life thread snapped. Then the Sword was in his grasp—the key to power over mortal men in the hands of Orl Fane.

But the madness lingered, the fears and doubts wrenching ceaselessly at his failing reason as he pondered a course of action. This fatal hesitation resulted in the Gnome's capture and the loss of the coveted Sword—the lifeline back to his own kind. Reason gave way to despair and raving, and the already badly unbalanced mind collapsed. There was room now for only one burning, haunting thought— the Sword must be his or his life was over. He boasted irrationally to his unsuspecting captors that the Sword was his, that only he knew where it could be found, unwittingly betraying his last chance to keep possession. But the strangers failed to read between the lines, dismissing him too hastily as merely crazed. Then came the escape, the seizure of the Sword, and the flight northward.

He paused now, staring blankly at the mysterious wall of blackness that barred his way northward. Yes, northward, northward, he mused, smiling crookedly, the eyes widening madly. There lay safety and redemption for an outcast. Deep within, he could feel an almost uncanny desire to run back the way he had come. But the thought remained locked inescapably in his mind that his salvation lay in the Northland alone. It was there that he would find . . . the Master. The

Warlock Lord. His gaze dropped momentarily to the ancient blade strapped tightly to his waist, its length dragging clumsily in the dirt behind him. The gnarled yellow hands strayed briefly down over the carved handle, touching the engraved hand raised high with burning torch, the gilt paint already flecking off in chips to reveal the burnished hilt beneath. He clutched the handle tightly, as if trying to draw his own strength from its sturdy grip. Fools! Fools all, that had not treated him with the respect he should command. For he was the bearer of the Sword, the keeper of the greatest legend their world had ever known, and it would be he who would . . . He shut out the thought hastily, fearful that even the void about him could read his mind, peer into his secret thoughts and steal them away.

Ahead, the frightening darkness waited for him to enter. Orl Fane was afraid of this, as he was of everything else, but there was no other way to go. Dimly he recalled those who followed—the giant Troll, the man with one hand, whose hatred he instinctively sensed, and the youth who was half man, half Elf. There was something the Gnome could not explain about the latter, something that nagged with unshakable persistence at his already beleaguered mind.

Shaking his rounded head blankly, the little man moved forward into the graying fringes of the dark wall, the air about him dead and silent. He did not look back until the blackness was all about him and the silence had disappeared in a sudden rush of wind and chilling moisture. When he did glance back briefly, he saw to his horror that there was nothing there—nothing but the same blackness that lay all about in heavy, impenetrable layers. The wind began to rush violently as he moved on, and he became aware of other creatures in the darkness. They came first as a vague awareness in his mind, then as soft cries that seemed to seep through the haze and cling inquisitively about him. At last they appeared as living bodies, touching softly with cringing fingers the flesh of his person. He laughed in maddened frenzy, knowing somehow that he was no longer in a world of living creatures, but a world of death where soulless beings wandered in hopeless search of escape from their eternal prison. He stumbled on amidst them, laughing, talking, even singing gaily, his mind no longer a part of his mortal being. All about him, the creatures of the dark world followed in cringing companionship, knowing that the maddened mortal was almost one of them. It was all a matter of time. When the mortal life was gone, he would be as they were—lost forever. Orl Fane would be with his own kind at last.

Almost two hours passed, winding away with the slow, deliberate sweep of the morning sun, and the three pursuers stood on the fringes of the wall of mist into which their quarry had disappeared. They paused as he had done, silently studying the forbidding blackness that marked the threshold to the kingdom of the Warlock Lord. The haze seemed to lie upon the deadened earth in layers, each one a little darker as the eyes peered deeper into the unseen center, each one a little less friendly as the mind envisioned the heart's undetermined fears. Panamon Creel paced back and forth in measured steps, his eyes never leaving the darkness as he attempted to muster enough confidence to push on. The massive Keltset, after a cursory study of the ground and a short motion to indicate that the Gnome had indeed gone northward, lapsed into statuelike immobility, the great arms folded and the eyes faint slits of life beneath the heavy brow.

There was no choice, Shea reasoned, his mind already determined, his hopes not yet dampened by the thought of temporarily losing the trail in the darkness. He had regained something of the old faith in providence, certain since they had begun this pursuit that Orl Fane would be found and the Sword regained. There was something pulling at him, reassuring him, confiding in him that he would not fail—something deep within his heart that gave him fresh courage. He waited impatiently for Panamon to give the word to proceed.

"There is a madness in what we're doing," the scarlet thief muttered as he passed by Shea once more. "I can feel death in the very air of this wall . . ."

He trailed off sharply, halting at last, waiting for Shea to speak.

"We must go on," Shea responded quickly, tonelessly.

Panamon looked slowly at his giant friend, but the Rock Troll made no movement. The other waited a moment longer, clearly disturbed that Keltset had ventured no opinion since they had undertaken this journey into the Northland. Before, when it was just the two of them, the giant had always indicated agreement when Panamon had looked to him for support, but of late the Troll was strangely noncommittal.

At last the adventurer nodded affirmatively, and the three plunged resolutely into the graying haze. The plains were level and barren, and for a while they moved forward without difficulty. Then, as the mists gradually deepened about them, their vision began to fail badly until they appeared to one another as little more than vague shadows. Panamon quickly called a momentary halt, extracted a length of rope from his pack, and suggested they tie themselves together to avoid becoming separated. When this was accomplished, they continued on. There was no sound save the occasional faint scrape of their boots on the hardened earth. The mist was not damp, but nevertheless seemed to cling to their exposed skin in a most unpleasant manner, recalling to Shea the unhealthy, fetid air of the Mist Marsh. It appeared to be moving faster the deeper they proceeded, yet they could feel no wind propelling its widening gusts. Finally it closed in from all directions and the three were left in total darkness.

They walked for what must have been hours, but their sense of time became confused in the soundless black haze that encased their fragile mortal beings. The rope held them back from the loneliness of death which permeated the mist, its strands reaching not so much to one another as to the world of sunlight and vision they had left behind them. This place into which they had dared to venture was a limbo world of half-life, where the senses were stifled and fears grew in an unfettered imagination. One could feel the presence of death fragmenting the darkness, a touch here, a touch there, brushing softly the mortal creature it would one day claim. The unreal became almost acceptable in this strange darkness as all the restrictions of the human senses vanished into dreamlike remembrances, and the visions of the inner mind, the subconscious, pushed quickly to the fore, searching for recognition.

For a time it was almost pleasant to be able to lapse into this indulgence of the subconscious, and then it was neither enjoyable nor disagreeable, but simply deadening. For a long time this latter feeling persisted, soothing, caressing their minds into disinterest and vague boredom, leaving both bodies and minds with the sluggish drowsiness of the ancient lotus-eaters. Time disappeared entirely and the world of mist stretched on forever.

From out of the dim recesses of the world of life came the slow sensation of burning pain, coursing through Shea's deadened body with shocking abruptness. With a sudden wrenching, his mind was torn free of the listlessness which cloaked its thoughts and the searing sensation grew sharper in his breast. Still drowsy, his body strangely weightless, he groped tiredly at his tunic, his hand coming to rest at last on the source of the irritation—a small leather pouch. Then his mind snapped into alertness as he clutched tightly the precious Elfstones, and he was awake once more.

In sudden horror, he realized that he was stretched full length upon the earth, no longer walking, no longer even aware of where he had been going. Frantically he clutched the rope about his waist and pulled violently. He was rewarded by a sluggish groan from the other end; his companions were still with him. Struggling heavily, wearily to his feet once more, he realized what had happened. This frightening limbo world of eternal sleep had almost claimed them as its victims, lulling them, soothing them, dulling their senses until they had fallen and drifted closer and closer to quiet death. Only the power of the stones had saved them.

Shea felt incredibly weak but, summoning the little strength that remained, he tugged and pulled desperately on the length of rope, dragging Keltset and Panamon Creel back from the edge of the abyss of death, back to the world of the living. He shouted wildly as he yanked on the rope, then stumbled to them, kicking at the listless bodies until the pain brought them back to consciousness. Long minutes later they were roused sufficiently to be aware of what had happened; with the awakening, the spirit of life revived the will to survive, as both forced themselves to their feet. They hung onto one another with sleep-ridden limbs closely entangled, their minds fighting to remain conscious. Then they began to walk, stumbling blindly in the unbroken darkness, one foot before the other, each step an incredible struggle of mind and body. Shea was in the lead, uncertain of his direction, but relying on the instinct sparked by the powerful Elfstones to guide him.

For a long time they pushed ahead through the endless dark, fighting to remain awake and alert as the deadening mists swirled lazily about them. The strange, sleeplike sensation of death clung to them, trying to overpower their tired minds, silently urging their exhausted bodies to accept the welcome rest that waited. But the mortals resisted with iron determination, their strength a small fragment of courage and desperation that, when all else was gone, still would not quit.

At last the deep weariness began to draw back into the dark haze. Death had failed this time to stifle the will to survive. There would be other times for these three, but for the moment they would live on a little longer in the world of men. So the sluggishness passed away and the drowsiness faded—not in the normal manner of sleep, but with quiet warnings that it would come again. The three companions were suddenly the same as before, the muscles unfettered as if there had been no sleep, the mind released rather than awakened. There was no inner desire to stretch or to yawn, but only a lingering memory that the sleep of death was a slumber without sensation, without time.

For long minutes no one spoke, though all were fully revived, each still savoring in unspoken fear and quiet desperation the taste of dying they had experienced, knowing that one day its inevitable touch would claim them forever. For several brief seconds they had stood at the edge of life and gazed into the forbidden land beyond—something no mortal was permitted to do before the end of his natural life. To have been this close was numbing, frightening, even maddening. They should not have survived.

But then the memories were gone, all but the dim knowledge that the three had narrowly escaped

dying. Regaining their composure, they continued to
search for an end to the confining blackness. Panamon
spoke once to Shea in low tones, asking whether he
knew if they were proceeding in the right direction.
The reluctant response was a curt nod. What difference did it make if he did not know, the little Valeman
wondered to himself angrily. What other direction
would they take? If his instincts were wrong, then
there was nothing left that could help them anyway.
The Elfstones had saved him once; he would trust
them again.

He wondered how Orl Fane had fared in his attempt
to pass through the strange wall of mist. Perhaps the
maddened Gnome had found his own way to escape
its deadening effects, but it seemed unlikely. And if
the little fellow had fallen by the way, then the Sword
was lost somewhere in the impenetrable blackness
and they would never regain it in time. This unpleasant prospect caused the Valeman to pause mentally for
several long moments, weighing the possibilities of
the Sword lying about in this haze, perhaps only yards
away from them, waiting for someone to discover it
once again.

Then abruptly the darkness faded into dingy gray
and the wall of mist was behind them. It happened so
quickly that they were caught completely by surprise.
One minute they were shrouded in blackness, barely
able to distinguish each other, and the next they were
standing in shocked silence beneath the leaden gray
skies of the Northland.

They took a moment to study the country into which
they had emerged. It was the most dismal land Shea
had ever seen—even more forbidding than the dreary
lowlands of Clete and the frightening Black Oaks in the
distant Southland. The terrain was barren and desolate, a gray-brown earth totally devoid of sunlight and
plant life. Not even the hardiest scrub brush had
survived—a mute warning that this was indeed the

kingdom of the Dark Lord. The earth stretched away to the north in low, uneven hills of hardened dirt, unbroken by even a wisp of grassland. Blunted, sprawling boulders thrust upright into the dim, gray horizon, and in places the lowlands were gutted by dusty gullies where rivers had long since dried away. There was no sound of life anywhere—not even the faint hum of insects to break the haunting stillness. Nothing remained in this once living land but death. Far to the north, jutting sharply into the vacant sky, rose a low series of treacherous-looking peaks. Without being told, Shea knew that this was the home of Brona, the Warlock Lord.

"What do you propose now?" Panamon Creel demanded. "We've lost the trail entirely. We don't even know if our Gnome friend got out of that stuff alive. In fact, I don't see how he could have managed it."

"We'll have to keep looking for him," Shea replied evenly.

"While those flying creatures keep looking for us," the other pointed out quickly. "The odds are becoming a little more than I bargained for, Shea. I don't mind telling you that I'm rapidly losing interest in this chase—especially when I don't know what it is I'm fighting. We almost died back there, and I couldn't even see what was killing us!"

Shea nodded understandingly, suddenly in command of the situation. For the first time in his life, Panamon Creel was worried about staying alive, even if it meant backing away with a severely wounded pride. It was up to Shea to make sure that the journey would continue now. Keltset stood apart from the two men, the soft brown eyes fixed on the Valeman as the heavy brows knitted in understanding. Again Shea was struck with the intelligence he saw, deep-rooted and unimposing in the gentle eyes of the massive creature. He still knew nothing about the giant Troll, but there was a great deal he wanted to learn. Keltset was the key to some strange, important secret that not even Panamon Creel knew, for all his boasting of their close friendship.

"The choices are limited," the little Valeman replied at last. "We can search for Orl Fane on this side of the mist and take our chances with the Skull creatures, or we can risk another journey back . . ."

He trailed off ominously, leaving the thought unspoken as he watched Panamon turn a shade paler.

"I'm not going back through that—at least not right away," the unnerved thief declared vehemently. He shook his head emphatically, the piked hand raising quickly to ward off the very air that carried such an insane suggestion. Then, almost sheepishly, the familiar broad smile returned as the old Panamon Creel reassumed command of his wits. He was too hardened an individual, too much a professional in the game of life, to allow anything to frighten him for very long. Grimly, he fought down the memories of what he had felt while stumbling blindly through the dead world within the darkness, calling on his long experience as an adventurer and border thief to rebuild his confidence. If he was destined to die in this venture, then he would meet it with the courage and determination that had carried him through so many hard years.

"Now let's think this situation through a minute," he mused, pacing away from them and back again. The old swagger and grit were returning. "If the Gnome did not make it out of the mist barrier, then the Sword will still be in there—we can get it anytime. But if he escaped, as we did, then where . . .?"

He paused in midsentence, his eyes studying the surrounding countryside as he tried to narrow the possibilities. Keltset stepped quickly to his side and pointed directly north to the jagged peaks that marked the borders of the Skull Kingdom.

"Yes, of course, you're right again," Panamon agreed with a faint smile. "He must have been heading there all along. It's the only place he could go."

"The Warlock Lord?" Shea asked quietly. "Is he taking the Sword directly to the Warlock Lord?"

The other nodded briefly. Shea paled slightly at the prospect of tracking the elusive Gnome right up to the doorstep of the Spirit King without even the comparatively strong mystical prowess of Allanon to aid them. If they were discovered, they would be entirely defenseless except for the Elfstones. While the stones might have prevailed over the Skull Bearers, it seemed highly doubtful that they would have any chance against a creature as awesome as Brona.

The first question was whether or not Orl Fane had even managed to get through the treacherous mist. They decided to follow the fringes of the rolling wall westward in an effort to cut across any tracks the fleeing Gnome might have left once he broke through into this region. If they discovered no trail in that direction, they would try going eastward for the same distance. If there was still no trace of Orl Fane, then they must assume that he had fallen in the killing haze, and they would be forced to reenter it in an effort to find the Sword. No one favored the latter alternative, but Shea gave them some reassurance by promising to chance using the power of the Elfstones to locate the missing talisman. Using the precious stones would undoubtedly alert the spirit world of their presence, but it was a gamble they would have to take if they expected to find anything in that impenetrable blackness.

Quickly now, the three began to hike northward, Keltset's keen eyes studying the barren ground for traces of the Gnome's footsteps. Heavy cloud banks blocked out the entire sky, enfolding the Northland in an unfriendly gray haze. Shea tried to estimate how

much time had lapsed since they had entered the wall
of mist, but he was unsure. It could have been a few
hours or even a few days. In any event, the grayness of
the land was deepening steadily, signaling the
approach of nightfall and a temporary end to their
search for Orl Fane.

Overhead the massing gray clouds had begun to
grow darker and were rolling heavily across the
hidden skies. The wind had picked up, gusting
sharply through the barren hills and gullies, pushing
angrily at the few clumps of boulders which barred its
progress. The temperature was dropping quickly,
turning so much colder that the three were forced to
wrap themselves tightly in their hunting cloaks as they
pushed ahead. Before long it became apparent that a
storm was building, and they realized angrily that a
heavy rain would wash away all traces of any
footprints left by the fleeing Gnome. And if they were
forced to guess whether or not he had escaped . . .

But in a rare stroke of good fortune, Keltset
discovered footprints on the barren earth—footprints
that came out of the wall of mist and continued
northward. The Rock Troll showed Panamon Creel
that the prints indicated a small person, probably a
Gnome, and that whoever it was had been weaving
and staggering badly, either from injury or exhaustion. Elated by this discovery and certain that they had
found Orl Fane once again, they followed the faint trail
northward, moving at a much faster pace than before.
Forgotten was the ordeal of that morning. Forgotten
was the threat of the omnipresent Warlock Lord,
whose kingdom lay directly in their path. Forgotten
was the exhaustion and despair they had felt since
losing the precious Sword of Shannara. Orl Fane
would not escape them again.

Overhead the skies continued to darken. Far to the
west came the deep sound of thunder, an ominous
rumble that was carried by the increasing force of the

wind across the length and breadth of the Northland. It was going to be a terrific storm, almost as if nature had decided to breathe new life into this dying land by washing it clean so that it might again be fertile ground for living things. The air was bitingly cold, and although the temperature had ceased falling, the gusting wind knifed through the garments of the three travelers. Yet they scarcely felt it, their eyes scanning anxiously the northern horizon for any sign of their quarry. The trail was growing fresher; he was somewhere just ahead.

The face of the land had begun to change noticeably. The barren countryside had retained its basic feature, an iron-hard ground studded with scattered rock and boulder clumps, but it had grown steadily more hilly and rutted, making travel increasingly difficult. The cracked, dry earth was particularly difficult to maneuver because it lacked the forms of vegetation that normally offered decent footing. As the hills and vales rose higher and dipped more sharply, the three pursuers found themselves slipping and clawing their way forward.

The rising west wind had grown in force to an earsplitting howl, at times nearly sweeping the unprotected men off their feet as it rushed across the desolate hilltops in frantic bursts. The loose topsoil flew in all directions at once in the merciless grip of the wind, striking at the skin, eyes, and mouths of the three men in stinging, choking thrusts. It soon became so bad that the entire countryside was swathed in wind and dirt, as if it were a sandstorm in a desert. It became difficult to breathe, much less to see, and eventually even the keen eyes of Keltset could no longer discern the faintest trace of the trail they were following. Quite probably there was nothing left to find, so completely had the wind cut into the unprotected earth, but the three pushed on.

The rumble of distant thunder had risen to a steady

crashing, interspersed by jagged flickers of lightning directly to the west and almost on top of them. The sky above had turned black, though with the blinding effect of the wind and the dust, they scarcely noticed this added hindrance to their vision. Bit by bit, a heavy haze moved closer from the western horizon—a haze that was clearly formed by sheet upon sheet of driving rain blown by the shrieking wind. Finally it became so bad that Panamon yelled wildly above the rush of the wind for a halt.

"It's no use! We've got to find shelter before that storm hits us!"

"We can't give up now!" Shea cried angrily, his words almost entirely drowned out by a sudden crash of thunder.

"Don't be a fool!" The tall thief struggled to his side, dropping to one knee as he peered through the blowing dust, his hands shielding his eyes from the stinging, blinding particles. To the right, he spotted a large hill dotted with clusters of overhanging boulders that appeared to offer some shelter against the force of the wind. Signaling the other two, he abandoned all attempts to proceed north and turned toward the rocks. Heavy drops of rain were beginning to fall, striking with chilling effect against the warm skin of the sweating men; the crashing of thunder had risen to deafening proportions. Shea continued to peer northward into the darkness, unwilling to accept Panamon's decision to give up the chase when he knew they were so very close.

They had almost reached the shelter of the rocks when he saw something moving. A dazzling flash of lightning outlined a small form near the crest of a tall hill far, far ahead, struggling madly to gain the summit in the face of the driving wind. Yelling frantically, the little Valeman grabbed Panamon's arm and pointed toward the distant hill, now almost totally invisible in the darkness. For a second the three remained frozen in place, searching the blackness as the storm descended on them in blinding sheets of rain, completely drenching them in seconds. Then the lightning flashed with shattering brightness a second time to reveal again the distant hill with its tiny challenger, still clawing wildly for footing near the crest. Then the vision was gone and the rain fell again.

"It's him! It's him!" yelled Shea in frenzied recognition. "I'm going after him!"

Without waiting for the other two, the excited Valeman plunged down the side of the wet embankment, determined that the Sword should not escape him again.

"Shea. No, Shea!" Panamon called after him in vain. "Keltset, get him!"

Lunging quickly down the hill, the giant Troll overtook the little Valeman in several leaps, picking him up effortlessly with one huge arm and carrying him back toward the waiting Panamon. Shea was yelling and kicking furiously, but he had no chance of breaking the Troll's iron grip. The storm had reached its peak already, the rain cutting away the unprotected landscape in huge chunks of earth and rock that washed down into the gullies to form small, wild rivers. Panamon led them into the rocks, ignoring Shea's repeated threats and pleas as he searched for shelter on the east slope of the hill, away from the force of the wind and rain. After a quick study, he chose a point high on the crest which was protected on three sides by large clusters of boulders that would offer good protection from the force of the storm if not from its wetness and chill. Scrambling wearily, fighting with the little strength left them against the incredible thrust of the wind, the three at last reached the meager shelter, where they collapsed in exhaustion. Panamon quickly signaled Keltset to release the struggling Shea. Angrily the Valeman confronted the tall adventurer, the rain running into his eyes and mouth in steady rivulets.

"Are you mad?" he exploded against the shriek of

the wind and the deep, constant rumble of the storm. "I could have caught him! I could have had him. . . ."

"Shea, listen to me!" Panamon cut in quickly as he peered through the heavy grayness to meet the other's angry gaze. There was a sudden moment of stilled voices in the roar of the Northland storm as Shea hesitated. "He was too far ahead to be caught in this kind of a storm. We would have all been blown away or injured in mud slides. It's too treacherous in these hills to travel ten feet in a heavy rainstorm—much less several miles. Relax a bit and cool your temper. We can pick up the remains of the Gnome when this gale blows over."

For a second Shea felt compelled to argue the point, but again he paused and the anger quickly subsided as his good sense returned, and he realized that Panamon was right.

The full force of the storm was tearing away at the unprotected land, stripping away its barren face and reshaping its stark features. Slowly the hills were washing down into the water-logged gullies and the ancient Streleheim Plains began to widen gradually into the vast Northland. Huddled against the cold of the massive boulders, Shea stared out into the sheets of rain as they came and passed in endless torrents, masking out the desolation of this lifeless, dying land. It seemed as if there were no one else alive but the three of them. Perhaps if the storm continued long enough, they would all be washed away and life could begin anew, he thought disconsolately.

Although the rain did not fall directly on them within the small refuge, they could not escape the chilling dampness of their water-logged clothing, and so their discomfort persisted. At first they sat in expectant silence, as if waiting for the storm to abate and the pursuit of Orl Fane to begin again, but gradually they grew weary of the lonely vigil and settled back to other pastimes, convinced the rain and the wind would claim the entire day. They ate a little food, more from common sense than hunger, and then tried to sleep as best they could in the close quarters. Panamon had managed to salvage two blankets from his pack which had been sealed in watertight wrappings, and these he passed to Shea. The grateful Valeman refused, offering them to his friends, but the giant Keltset, who seemed seldom very distraught by anything, was already asleep. So Panamon and Shea wrapped themselves in the warmth of the blankets, huddled next to each other on one side of the enclosure, and stared quietly into the falling rain.

After a time they began to talk of things past, of quiet times and distant places which they felt compelled to share in this hour of vague despondency and loneliness. As usual, Panamon carried the conversation, but the stories of his travels were not the same as before. The element of improbability and wildness had been lifted, and for the first time, Shea knew the colorful thief was talking about the real Panamon Creel. It was idle, almost carefree talk that passed between the two men—a bit like the conversation of two old friends reunited after many years.

Panamon told of his youth and the hard times the people all around him had known and lived with while he grew into manhood. There were no excuses, no regrets offered, but only the simple narrative of years long past that lingered on in memories. The little Valeman told about his boyhood with his brother Flick, recalling their wild, exciting expeditions into the Duln forests. He spoke in smiles about the unpredictable Menion Leah, who in vague ways suggested Panamon Creel as a young man. Time drifted away as they talked, shutting out the storm and drawing the two strangely close to one another for the first time since they had met. As the hours passed and darkness came, Shea grew to understand the other man, to know him as he could not have known him otherwise. Perhaps the thief understood Shea a little better as well. The Valeman wanted to believe so.

At last, when night shrouded the entire land and even the pounding rain had disappeared from view, so that nothing remained but the sound of the wind and the splash of puddles and rivers, the conversation drew itself around to the sleeping Keltset. In quiet tones, the two men speculated about the giant Rock Troll's origin, trying to understand what had brought him to them, what had made him undertake this suicidal journey into the Northland. It was his home, they knew, and perhaps he planned to return to the distant Charnal Mountains. Yet had he not been driven from there—if not by his own people, then by something equally powerful and compelling? The Skull Bearer had known him on sight—but how? Even Panamon admitted that Keltset was more than a mere thief and adventurer. There was tremendous pride and courage in his bearing, a deep intelligence in his silent determination, and somewhere in his past, a terrible secret he had chosen to share with no one. Something unspeakable had happened to him, and both men could sense that it had something to do with the Warlock Lord, if only in an indirect way. There had been fear in the Skull Bearer's eyes when he had recognized the massive Troll. The two men talked awhile longer until sleep came in the early-morning hours; then wrapped in the blankets for protection from the chill of the night and the rain, they drifted into slumber.

XXVII

ou there! Hold it a minute!"

The sharp command came out of the darkness behind Flick, cutting knifelike to the bone of his already waning courage. In slow shock, the terrified Valeman turned, lacking sufficient presence of mind even to attempt to run. He had been discovered at last. It was useless to draw the short hunting knife still grasped firmly beneath the hunting cloak, but his unresponsive fingers remained locked in place as his eyes sought out the dim form of the approaching enemy. His comprehension of the Gnome language was poor, but the tone of voice alone was enough to enable him to understand that brief command. Rigidly, he watched a bulky, cursing form emerge from out of the darkness of the tents.

"Don't just stand there," the voice shrilled angrily as the roundish form waddled closer. "Lend a hand where it's needed!"

Astonished, the Valeman peered closely at the squat figure as his discoverer moved toward him, the thick arms laden with trays and platters and on the verge of dropping everything with each hesitant step of the stubby legs. Almost without thinking, Flick sprang to the fellow's assistance, removing the upper layer of trays and cradling them in his own arms, his nose catching the savory smell of freshly cooked meat and vegetables seeping from beneath the covers to the warm platters.

"There now, that's a whole sight better." The stocky Gnome breathed a sigh of relief. "I might have spilled the whole mess if I'd had to go another step on my own. A whole army encamped here, and can I get anyone to help carry the chieftains' own dinners? Not one Gnome so much as offers. I have to do it all. It's maddening—but you're a good fellow to lend a hand. I'll see you're properly repaid with a good meal. Hah?"

Flick didn't know what the verbose fellow was saying for the most part, and it didn't really matter. What did matter was that he had not been discovered after all. Breathing his silent gratitude, Flick adjusted his armload of food while his new companion continued to ramble on merrily about nothing, the heavy trays balanced precariously in the stubby arms. From beneath the concealing darkness of the hunting cloak's wide hood, the wary Valeman nodded in pretended understanding of the other's conversation, his eyes still fastened intently on the shadows moving within the great tent before them.

The thought remained indelibly fixed in his mind—he had to get inside that tent; he had to know what was going on in there. But then, almost as if he had read Flick's mind, the little Gnome began to move toward the canvas housing with measured steps, the trays before him, the little yellow face half turned so that his unending monologue might be better heard by his newfound companion. There was no question about it now. They were delivering dinner to the people in that tent, to the chieftains of the two nations comprising this giant army and to the dreaded Skull Bearer.

This is madness, Flick thought suddenly; *I'll be spotted the instant they lay eyes on me.* But he needed that one quick look inside . . .

Then they were at the entrance, standing quietly before the two giant Troll guards who towered over them like trees over stalks of grass. Flick could not bring himself to look anywhere but downward, though he was conscious of the fact that, had he drawn himself up to full height to face the enemy, he would have found himself staring directly into an armored, barklike chest.

Even though he was totally dwarfed in size, Flick's self-appointed friend barked a sharp command for admittance, apparently convinced that his presence was earnestly desired by those within—or at least the food he bore was. Quickly, one of the sentries stepped into the brightly lit interior of the canopy to speak briefly to someone, then reappeared a moment later, silently beckoning the two men to enter. With a quick nod over his shoulder to the trembling Flick, the little Gnome pushed past the guards into the tent and the Valeman, scarcely daring to breathe, followed dutifully, praying for yet another miracle.

The interior of the large canvas structure was comparatively well lighted by slow-burning torches set on iron standards about a large, heavy wooden table that stood unoccupied at the center of the enclosure. There were Trolls of varying size moving busily within the great tent, some carrying rolled charts and maps from the table to a large, brassbound chest while the others prepared to sit down to a long-awaited evening meal. All wore the military trappings and insignia of Maturens—Troll commanders.

The rear section of the canvas enclosure was screened off by a heavy tapestry which even the bright torchlight could not penetrate. The air in the army headquarters was smoky and fetid, so heavy in fact that Flick found it almost difficult to breathe. Weapons and armor lay piled neatly about the room, and battered shields hung on iron standards like crude attempts at decoration. Flick could still sense the undeniable presence of the terrifying Skull Bearer, and he quickly

concluded that the dark monster was behind the bleak
tapestry in the other section of the tent. Such a
creature did not eat—its mortal self had long since
passed into dust, and the spirit that remained needed
only the fire of the Warlock Lord to nourish its hunger.

Then abruptly the Valeman saw something else. At
the rear of the front portion of the enclosure, close to
the tapestry and half hidden by the torch smoke and
moving Trolls, was a dim form seated in a tall wooden
chair. Flick started involuntarily, certain for an instant
that the man was the missing Shea. The eager Trolls
were moving up to him now, removing the platters of
food and placing them on the heavy table, and for a
moment they blocked the Valeman's view of the
figure. The Trolls conversed quietly among themselves as they stood over the two servers, their strange
tongue completely unintelligible to Flick, who was
attempting to shrink farther down into the shadowed
folds of his hunting cloak in the revealing torchlight.
He should have been discovered, but the unsuspecting Troll commanders were tired and hungry and
much too concerned with the invasion plans to notice
the unusual features of the rather large Gnome who
had waited on them.

The last of the trays was removed and set upon the
table as the Maturens gathered wearily about it to
begin the meal. The little Gnome who had brought
Flick into the quarters turned to leave, but the eager
Valeman paused a moment longer to study quickly the
form at the rear.

It was not Shea. The prisoner was Elven, a man of
about thirty-five, with strong, intelligent features.
More it was impossible to tell at this distance. But Flick
felt certain it was Eventine, the young Elven King who
Allanon had declared could mean the difference
between victory or defeat for the Southland. It was the
Westland, the great, secluded kingdom of the Elven
people, that housed the mightiest army of the free

world. If the Sword of Shannara were lost, then this man alone commanded the power to stop the awesome might of the Warlock Lord—this man, a prisoner, whose life could be snuffed out at a single command.

Flick felt a hand on his shoulder, and he started violently at the sudden touch.

"C'mon now, c'mon, we must leave," the hushed voice of the little Gnome cajoled him earnestly. "You can stare at him some other time. He'll still be here."

Flick hesitated again, a sudden, daring plan forming as he stood there. If he had taken time to dwell on it, the idea would have terrified him, but there was no time and he had long since passed the point of rational deliberation. It was already too late to escape the encampment and return to Allanon before daylight, and he had come to this dreadful place to do an important task—one which remained uncompleted. He would not leave yet.

"C'mon, I said, we have to . . . Hey, what're you doing . . .?" The little Gnome yelled involuntarily as Flick grasped him harshly by one arm and propelled him forward toward the Troll commanders, who had paused momentarily in their eating at the sharp cry and were staring curiously at the two small figures. Quickly Flick raised one hand and pointed questioningly at the bound prisoner. The Trolls followed his gaze mechanically. Flick waited breathlessly as one of them gave a curt command and the others shrugged and nodded.

"You're mad, you're out of your head!" the little Gnome gasped in amazement, trying vainly to hold his voice down to a whisper. "What do you care whether or not the Elf gets something to eat? What does it matter if he shrivels up and dies . . .?"

His comments were cut short. A Troll called over to them, one gnarled hand extending a plate of food. Flick hesitated momentarily, glancing quickly at his astonished companion, who was shaking his head and grumbling inaudibly at the whole proposition.

"Don't look at me!" he exclaimed shortly. "This was your idea. You feed him!"

Flick failed to pick up everything the Gnome said, but he got the gist of the exclamation, and moved quickly to take possession of the plate. At no time did he glance into anyone's face for more than an instant, and even then the shadows of the wide cowl masked his identity. He kept his cloak wrapped tightly about him as he moved cautiously toward the prisoner on the other side of the tent, inwardly cheering madly that his gamble had paid off. If he could get close enough to the bound figure of Eventine, he could let him know that Allanon was close and that some sort of attempt to rescue him would be made. Still wary, he glanced back once at the other occupants of the enclosure, but the Troll commanders had returned to their dinner and only the little Gnome chef was still staring after him. If he had tried this kind of foolish stunt anywhere but in the very teeth of the enemy forces, Flick was well aware that he would have been discovered immediately. But here, in the commanders' own headquarters, with the awesome Skull Bearer just yards away and the entire area surrounded by thousands of Northlanders, the idea of anyone even sneaking into camp, let alone into this guarded tent, was preposterous.

Quietly, Flick approached the waiting captive, his face still concealed within the dark recesses of the hood, the plate of food extended before him. Eventine was of normal height and stature for a man, although for an Elf he was big. He wore woodland garb covered by the remnants of a chain mail vest, the worn insignia of the house of Elessedil still faintly visible in the dim torchlight. His strong face was battered and cut, apparently from the battle that had ended with his capture. At first glance there appeared to be nothing distinctive about him; he was not the kind of man who would be singled out in a group. His expression was set and impassive as Flick came to a halt directly in front of him, his thoughts apparently concentrated elsewhere. Then his head moved slightly as if aware he was being studied, and the deep green eyes fastened on the small figure facing him.

When Flick saw those eyes, he froze in sudden shock. They reflected a fierce determination, a fiery strength of character and inner conviction that reminded the Valeman, rather strangely, of Allanon. They reached into him, seized his own mind in a manner of speaking, demanding his attention, his obedience. He had seen this look in no other man, not even Balinor, whom they had all felt drawn to as a natural leader. Like those of the dark Druid, the eyes of the Elven King frightened him. Looking down quickly at the plate of food in his hands, Flick paused to consider what he should do next. Mechanically, he fitted a piece of the still warm meat to the tip of the fork. His corner of the large tent was dimly lit, and the haze of smoke aided in concealing his movements from the enemy. Only the little Gnome was watching him closely, he was certain, but a single mistake would bring them all down on him.

Slowly he raised his face until the light from the torches had fully revealed his features to the watchful captive. As their eyes met, a flicker of curiosity crossed the otherwise impassive Elven face and one eyebrow lifted sharply. Quickly Flick pursed his lips, warning silence, and looked down again at the food. Eventine was unable to feed himself, so the Valeman began to hand-feed him slowly and carefully as he planned his next step. Now the captive Elven King knew he was not a Gnome, but Flick was terrified that if he spoke to the Elf, even in a faint whisper, he would be overheard. He abruptly recalled that the Skull Bearer was just on the other side of the heavy tapestry, perhaps only inches away, and if he should possess unusual hearing powers . . . But there was no other alternative; he had to communicate somehow with the prisoner before he left. There might not be another chance. Mustering the little courage he had reserved, the Valeman leaned forward a few inches farther as he lifted the fork, carefully putting himself between Eventine and the Trolls.

"Allanon."

The word was spoken in a barely audible whisper. Eventine took the proffered bite of food and responded with a faint nod, his face stony and impassive. Flick had had enough. It was time to get out of there before his luck ran out. Taking the plate of half-finished food, he slowly turned and walked back across the enclosure to the waiting Gnome chef, whose face mirrored mingled disgust and edginess. The Troll commanders were still eating as he passed them, their conversation low and earnest. They didn't even look up. Flick handed the plate to the little Gnome as he passed him, mumbling something incoherent, then quickly hastened from the tent, exiting between the two giant Troll guards before his astonished companion could think to act. As he strolled unconcernedly away from the tent, the Gnome appeared suddenly in the open entrance, yelling and grumbling in garbled phrases that the Valeman could not begin to comprehend. Turning, the Valeman waved quickly to the little figure, a faint smile of satisfaction on his broad face, and disappeared into the darkness.

At dawn, the Northland army began its march southward toward Callahorn. Flick had been unable to work his way clear of the encampment before then; so, as a bitter and gravely concerned Allanon watched from the seclusion of the Dragon's Teeth, the subject of his misgivings was forced to continue his disguise another day. The heavy morning rains had almost persuaded the Valeman to make a dash for safety, so convinced was he that the downpour would wash out the coloring Allanon had applied to his skin to give it a yellow hue. But escape in daylight was impossible, so he wrapped himself tightly in the hunting cloak and tried to remain inconspicuous. Before long, he was thoroughly drenched. To his happy astonishment, the yellow coloring on his skin did not appear to be washing out after all. There was a certain amount of fading, but in the excitement of moving the camp, no one had time to take notice of anyone else. It was the terrible weather, in fact, that saved Flick from being unmasked. Had it been a warm, dry summer day filled with sunshine and good spirits, the army would have been more concerned with exchanging pleasantries. If the sun had been shining, there would have been no need for the heavy hunting cloaks, and Flick would have attracted the attention of everyone around him by continuing to wear his. Once it had been removed, the Northlanders would have seen through his thin disguise immediately. The bright sunlight would have revealed to anyone casting so much as a passing glance in his direction that the Valeman did not even remotely resemble a Gnome in his facial bone structure and individual features. The heavy rains and wind saved Flick from all of this and permitted him to remain isolated and concealed as the huge invasion force trudged steadily across the grasslands into the Southland kingdom of Callahorn.

The bad weather persisted throughout the remainder of that day and, as it turned out, for several days thereafter. The storm clouds sullenly locked in place between the sun and the earth in great gray and black masses that churned and rolled with ferocious discontent. The rains fell unchecked, sometimes in pounding sheets driven by the unrelenting force of the west winds, sometimes in a steady melancholy drizzle that gave false hope to the belief that the storm's end was near. The air was chill and at times almost bitter, leaving an already water-drenched army shivering and disconsolate.

Flick remained on the move throughout the day's tiring, unpleasant march, soaked through by the blowing rains, but relieved that he could move about without calling attention to himself. He made it a point to avoid walking with any particular group for very long, always staying apart, always avoiding a situation which might force him to engage in conversation with anyone. The Northland invasion force was so vast that it was an easy matter to avoid ever being with the same men twice, and his deception was further facilitated by the fact that there appeared to be no overt attempts to exercise marching discipline over the great army. Either discipline was extremely lax or so thoroughly ingrained in the individual soldier that superior officers were not needed to maintain order. Flick could not conceive of the latter and concluded that fear of the omnipresent Skull Bearers and their mysterious Master kept the individual Troll or Gnome from doing anything foolish. In any event, the little Valeman remained just another member of the Northland army, biding his time until nightfall, when he planned to make his escape back to Allanon.

By midafternoon, the army had reached the swollen banks of the upper Mermidon, directly across from the island city of Kern. Again the invasion force encamped. Its commanders realized immediately that, due to the heavy rain, the Mermidon could not be crossed without tremendous hazard; even so, it would require large rafts capable of transporting vast numbers of men in order to secure the far bank. They had no rafts, so those would have to be built. That would require several days, and by that time the storms should have diminished and the waters of the Mermidon retreated sufficiently to permit an easy crossing. Across the river in the city of Kern, the Northland force had been sighted while Menion Leah still slept in the house of Shirl Ravenlock, and the people were beginning to panic as they realized the extent of their danger. The enemy invasion force could not afford to bypass Kern and proceed to Tyrsis, the main objective. Kern would have to be taken; considering the size of the city and the extent of the reduced army defending it, this would not be difficult. Only the rising river and the fortuitous storm delayed its fall.

Flick knew nothing of these matters, his own mind preoccupied with thoughts of escape. The storm could abate in a matter of hours, leaving him defenseless in the very heart of the enemy camp. Worse still, the actual invasion of the Southland was under way, and a battle with the Border Legion of Callahorn could come at any time. Suppose he was forced into battle as a Gnome hunter against his own friends?

Flick had changed considerably since his first meeting with Allanon weeks earlier in Shady Vale, developing an inner strength and maturity and a confidence in himself he had never believed himself capable of sustaining. But the past twenty-four hours had proved a supreme test of raw courage and perseverance that even a seasoned border fighter like Hendel would have found frightening. The little Valeman, unseasoned and vulnerable, could sense that he was on the verge of cracking under the extreme pressures, of giving way completely to the terrible sense of fear and doubt gripping him with every move he made.

Shea had been the reason behind his decision to make the hazardous journey to Paranor in the beginning, but more than that, he had been the one steadying influence on a pessimistic, distrustful Flick. Now Shea had been lost to them all for many days with little indication as to whether he was dead or alive, and his faithful brother, while refusing to give up hope that they would eventually find him, had never felt more alone. Not only was he in a strange land, embroiled in a mad venture against a mysterious creature not even of the mortal world, but now he was isolated in the midst of thousands of Northlanders who would kill him without a second thought the moment they discovered who he really was. The entire situation was impossible, and he was beginning to doubt that there was any real point to anything he had done.

While the vast army encamped on the banks of the Mermidon in the shadows of the late afternoon and the gray of twilight, a disconsolate, frightened Valeman moved uneasily through the camp, trying desperately to maintain a firm grip on his fading resolve. The rain continued to fall steadily, masking faces and bodies until they were merely moving shadows, drenching men and earth alike in a cold, cheerless haze. Fires were out of the question in such weather, so the evening remained dark and impenetrable and the men remained faceless. As he moved silently about the encampment, Flick mentally noted the arrangement of the commanders' quarters, the deployment of the Gnome and Troll forces, and the setting of the sentry lines, thinking that this knowledge might be of some value to Allanon in planning a rescue of the Elven King.

He relocated without difficulty the large tent that housed the Troll Maturens and their valuable prisoner, but, like the rest of the enemy camp, it was dark and cold, shrouded in mist and rain. There was no way even to be sure that Eventine was still there; he could have been moved to another tent or removed from the camp entirely during the march southward. The two giant Troll sentries remained posted at the entrance, but there was no sign of movement within. Flick studied the silent structure for several long minutes and then slipped quietly away.

As night descended, and Troll and Gnome alike retired to a chill, water-drenched slumber that more closely resembled an uneasy doze, the Valeman decided to make his escape. He had no idea where he might find Allanon; he could only presume the giant Druid had followed the invasion force as it moved southward to Callahorn. In the rain and darkness, it would be nearly impossible to locate him, and the best he could hope to do would be to hide out somewhere until daylight and then attempt to find him. He moved silently toward the eastern fringes of the encampment, treading carefully over the huddled forms of the half-sleeping men, winding his way through the baggage and armor, still wrapped protectively in the water-soaked hunting cloak.

He could very likely have walked through the camp without any disguise on this night. In addition to the darkness and the persistent drizzle, which had finally begun to taper off, a low rolling mist had moved across the grasslands, blanketing everything so completely that a man could see no more than a few feet in front of his nose. Without wanting to, Flick found himself thinking about Shea. Finding his brother had been the major reason behind his decision to slip into this camp disguised as a Gnome. He had learned nothing of Shea, though he had scarcely expected to. He had been fully prepared to be discovered and captured within minutes after he entered the vast encampment. Yet he was still free. If he could escape now and find Allanon, then they could find a way to help the imprisoned Elven King and . . .

Flick paused, his progress abruptly halted as he sank down into a crouch beside a canvas-covered pile of heavy baggage. Even if he did eventually find his way back to the Druid, what could they hope to do for Eventine? It would take time to reach Balinor in the walled city of Tyrsis, and they had little time remaining. What would become of Shea while they were trying to find a way to rescue Eventine—who was unquestionably more valuable to the Southland, since the loss of the Sword of Shannara, than Flick's brother? Suppose that Eventine knew something about Shea? Suppose he knew where Shea was—perhaps even where the powerful Sword had been carried?

Flick's tired mind began to rush quickly over the possibilities. He had to find Shea; nothing else was really important to him at this point. There was no one left to help him since Menion had gone ahead to warn the cities of Callahorn. Even Allanon seemed to have exhausted his vast resources without result. But Eventine might know Shea's whereabouts, and Flick alone was in a position to do something about that possibility.

Shivering in the chill night air, he brushed the rain from his eyes and peered in numbed disbelief into the mist. How could he even consider going back? He was virtually on the edge of panic and exhaustion now without taking any further risks. Yet the night was perfect—dark, misty, impenetrable. Such an opportunity might not come again in the short time left, and there was no one to take advantage of it but himself. Madness—madness! he thought desperately. If he went back there, if he tried to free Eventine alone . . . he would be killed.

Yet he decided suddenly that that was exactly what he was going to do. Shea was the only one he really cared about and the imprisoned Elven King appeared to be the only man who might have any idea what had happened to his missing brother. He had come this far alone, spending twenty-four torturous hours trying to stay hidden, trying to stay alive in a camp of enemies that had somehow overlooked him. He had even managed to get inside the Troll commanders' tent, to get close enough to the great King of the Elven people to pass him that brief message. Perhaps it had all been the result of blind chance, miraculous and fleeting, yet, could he flee now, with so little accomplished? He smiled faintly at his own dim sense of the heroic, an irresistible challenge he had always successfully ignored before, but which now ensnared him and would undoubtedly prove his undoing. Cold, exhausted, close to mental and physical collapse, he would nevertheless take this final gamble simply because circumstances had placed him here at this time and this place. He alone. How Menion Leah would smile to see this, he thought grimly, wishing at the same time that the wild highlander were here to lend a little of his reckless courage. But Menion was not here, and time was slipping quickly away. . . .

Then, almost before he realized it, he had retraced his steps through the sleeping men and the rolling fog, and was crouching breathlessly within yards of the long Maturen tent. The mist and his own sweat ran in small rivulets down his heated face and into his soaked garments as he stared in motionless silence at his objective. Doubts crowded remorselessly into his tired mind. The terrible creature that served the Warlock Lord had been there earlier, a black, soulless instrument of death that would destroy Flick without thinking. It was probably still within, waiting in sleepless watch for exactly this sort of foolish attempt to free Eventine. Worse still, the Elven King might have been removed, taken anywhere . . .

Flick forced the doubts aside and breathed deeply. Slowly he mustered his courage as he finished his study of the canvas enclosure, which was no more than a misty shadow in the unbroken darkness before him. He could not even make out the forms of the giant Troll guards. One hand reached into the damp tunic beneath his cloak and withdrew the short hunting knife, his only weapon. Mentally he pinpointed the position on the canvas of the silent tent where he imagined Eventine had been bound at the time he had fed him that previous night. Then slowly he crept forward.

Flick crouched next to the wet canvas of the great

tent, the chill imprint of the weave rough against his cheek as he listened for the sounds of human life that stirred uneasily within. He must have paused for fifteen long minutes, motionless in the fog and the dark as he listened intently to the muffled sound of heavy breathing and intermittent snores emitted by the sleeping Northlanders. Briefly he contemplated attempting to sneak through the front entrance of the structure, but quickly discarded that idea as he realized that once he was inside, he would have to navigate his way in the darkness over a number of sleeping Trolls in order to reach Eventine. Instead he selected the section of the tent where he imagined the heavy tapestry formed a divider—the corner in which the Elven King had been bound to the chair. Then, with agonizing slowness, he inserted the tip of his hunting knife into the rain-soaked canvas and began to cut downward, one strand at a time, just a fraction of an inch with each pressured stroke.

He would never remember how long it took him to make the three-foot incision—only the endless sawing in the silence of the night, afraid that the slightest sound of tearing would arouse the entire tent. As the long minutes passed, he began to feel as if he were entirely alone in the giant encampment, deserted by all human life in the black shroud of the mist and the rain. No one came near him, or at least he did not see anyone pass, and the sound of human voices did not reach his straining ears. He might indeed have been alone in the world for those brief, desperate minutes. . . .

Then a long, vertical slit in the glistening canvas stared back at him in slack anticipation, inviting him to enter. Cautiously he advanced, feeling his way carefully with his hands just inside the opening. There was nothing except the canvas floor, dry, but as cold as the damp earth that braced his knees and feet. Carefully he inserted his head, peering fearfully into the deep blackness of the interior that was filled with the sounds of sleeping men. He waited for his eyes to adjust to this new darkness, trying desperately to hold his breathing to a steady, noiseless whisper, feeling horribly exposed from the rear, the bulk of his body outside the tent and vulnerable to anyone who happened to pass.

It was taking his eyes much too long to adjust and he could not risk being discovered by a chance passerby at this stage, so he risked moving a few feet farther, slipping his stocky frame through the opening and into the dark shelter of the tent. The labored breathing and the snores continued undisturbed, and there was the occasional sound of a heavy body shifting position somewhere in the darkness beyond him. But no one awoke. Flick remained crouched just inside the long slit for more endless minutes, his eyes working madly to distinguish the faint shapes of men, tables, and baggage against the blackness of the night.

It seemed to take forever, but at last he was able to discern the huddled forms of sleeping men scattered about the floor of the tent, their bodies rolled tightly in the warmth of their blankets. To his astonishment, he realized that one motionless form lay slumbering only inches in front of his balanced body. Had he attempted to crawl any farther before his eyes had adjusted to this darkness, he would have stumbled onto and undoubtedly awakened the sleeper. The old sensation of fear returned sharply, and for a moment he fought back against a rising sense of panic that commanded him to turn and run. He could feel the sweat sliding down his crouched body beneath the water-soaked clothing, tracing thin, searching paths over the heated skin as his labored breathing became more ragged. At that moment, he was aware of his every feeling, his mind pushed right to the brink of collapse—yet later, he would recall nothing of these feelings. Mercifully, they would be blocked from his memory, and all that would remain would be one sharp picture etched indelibly in his brain of the sleeping Troll Maturens and the object of his search—Eventine. Flick spotted him quickly, the lean form no longer seated upright in the wooden chair at the corner of the heavy tapestry, but lying on the canvas floor only a few feet from the poised Valeman, the dark eyes open and watching. Flick had judged his point of entry correctly, and now he moved catlike to the King's side, the hunting knife severing quickly the taut ropes that bound hands and feet.

In an instant the Elf was free, and the two shadowy figures were moving quickly to reach the vertical opening in the side of the tent. Eventine paused momentarily to pick something up from the side of one of the sleeping Trolls. Flick did not wait to see what the Elf had seized, but hastened through the slit into the misty darkness beyond. Once outside, he crouched silently next to the tent, glancing anxiously about for any sign of movement. But there was only the persistent drizzle of the rain breaking the night's deep silence. Seconds later, the canvas parted again, and the Elven King passed through and hunched down beside his rescuer. He was carrying an all-weather poncho and a broadsword. As he wrapped himself in the cloak, he paused momentarily and smiled grimly at a frightened, but elated Flick, then gripped his hand in warm, unspoken gratitude. The Valeman grinned back in satisfaction and nodded.

So Eventine Elessedil was rescued, snatched from the very teeth of the sleeping enemy. It was Flick Ohmsford's finest moment. He felt now that the worst was over, that once clear of the great Maturen tent with Eventine a free man, escape from the camp could never be denied them. He had not even thought to look beyond his entry into the Troll commanders' quarters. Now the moment to look ahead was there, but as the two paused in the shadows, the moment passed and was lost.

From out of nowhere strolled three fully armed Troll sentries, who instantly spotted the two figures crouching at the side of the Maturen tent. For an instant everyone froze; then slowly Eventine rose, standing directly in front of the tear in the canvas. To Flick's astonishment, the quick-thinking Elven King waved the three over to them, speaking fluently in their own language. Hesitantly, the sentries approached, their long pikes lowered carelessly as they heard the familiar sound of their own tongue. Eventine stepped aside to reveal the gaping slit, nodding warningly to Flick as the unsuspecting Trolls now rushed forward. The terrified Valeman stepped away, his hand gripping the short hunting knife beneath his cloak. As the Trolls reached them, their eyes still momentarily fastened on the torn canvas, the Elven King struck out with the broadsword.

Two of the Trolls were silenced before they had a chance to defend themselves, their throats cut away. The final sentry got off a quick cry for help and slashed wildly at Eventine, cutting into the exposed flesh of the Elf's shoulder; then he, too, fell lifeless into the muddied earth. For a moment there was silence once more. Flick stood white-faced against the tent wall, staring in fright at the dead Trolls as the wounded Elven King tried vainly to stem the blood flow from his slashed shoulder. Then they heard the sharp sound of voices from close by.

"Which way?" Eventine whispered harshly, the bloodied sword still tightly clenched in his good hand.

In mute silence the little Valeman rushed to the Elf's side and pointed into the darkness behind him. The voices grew louder now, coming from more than one direction, and swiftly, wordlessly, the two fugitives fled from the Troll sleeping quarters. Stumbling between the fog-shrouded tents and baggage, unable to find their footing on the water-soaked grasslands and blinded by the darkness and the rolling mist, the two struggled to outdistance their pursuers. The

voices faded to either side of them and then fell
behind, only to rise sharply in alarm within seconds as
the bodies of the sentries were discovered. The two
dashed on as the deep, haunting sound of a Troll battle
horn shattered the night sleep of the Northland army,
and everywhere men awoke to the call to arms and
battle.

Flick was in the lead, frantically trying to remember
the quickest way back to the camp perimeter. He was
running blindly now, terrified beyond reason, his one
thought to gain the safety of the silent darkness
beyond this hateful camp. Struggling painfully to
keep up with the Valeman, his shoulder bleeding
freely from the pike wound, Eventine realized what
had happened to his young rescuer and called vainly
after him, trying to warn him to be careful.

Too late. The words had just left his mouth when
they ran headlong into a band of still-groggy Northlanders who had been abruptly awakened by the
battle horn's blast. Everyone went down in a tangle of
arms and legs, both parties completely caught by
surprise and unable to avoid the collision. Flick felt the
hunting cloak ripped from his body as he was kicked
and buffeted by unseen hands and feet, and in
maddened terror he fought back, slashing wildly with
the hunting knife at anything that came within reach.
Howls of pain and fury went up from his attackers,
and for an instant the arms and legs drew back and he
was free again. He leaped to his feet, only to be borne
back a moment later by a renewed assault. He caught
the dull flash of a sweeping sword blade as it whisked
past his unprotected head and his own knife came up
to ward off the blow. For several minutes, everything
became chaotic as the Valeman rolled and thrashed his
way through the clinging hands and heavy bodies, the
fogbound night a maze of wild cries and scuffling
figures. He was cut and battered unmercifully as he
sought to fight his way clear, sometimes forced back to

the earth, but always rebounding within seconds and struggling onward, calling sharply for Eventine.

What he did not realize was that he had stumbled into a band of unarmed Northlanders who were caught completely by surprise when he charged madly into them, wielding the hunting knife. For several minutes they sought to pin him down and disarm him, but the terrified Valeman struggled so violently they were unable to contain him. Eventine rushed quickly to his aid, battling his way through the mass of attackers to reach the youth and at last they gave way entirely, scattering for the safety of the darkness. Quickly downing the last persistent Northlander, a rather large Gnome who had fastened himself bodily to the struggling Flick, the Elven King grabbed his rescuer by the tunic collar and hauled him to his feet. The Valeman continued to struggle violently for a moment more; then realizing who held him, he abruptly relaxed, his heart beating wildly. All around him the sounds of the Northland battle horns blasted in deafening tones through the camp, mingling with the rising cries of the aroused army. Vainly he tried to listen to what the other was saying, his battered head still ringing from the blows struck.

". . . find the quickest way out. Don't run—walk steadily, but unhurriedly. Running will just call attention to us. Now go!"

Eventine's words died into the darkness as his strong hand gripped Flick's shoulder and turned him about. Their eyes locked momentarily, but the Valeman could only meet the Elven King's piercing stare for an instant, feeling it burn right through to his frightened heart. Then they were moving toward the perimeter of the awakened encampment, side by side, their weapons held ready. Flick was thinking rapidly but clearly now, recalling vague landmarks within the Northland camp that indicated he was proceeding in the right direction. The fear was momentarily buried as a cold sense of determination gripped him, fostered in part by the strong presence striding quietly at his side. It might have been Allanon himself, so unshakable was the confidence that the Elven King radiated.

Dozens of the enemy rushed past them, some coming within several feet, but no one stopped them or spoke to them. Unmolested, the two men passed quietly through the chaos that had engulfed the Northlanders at the unexpected call to battle, moving steadily toward the sentry lines surrounding the encampment. The cries continued from within, although they were dropping behind the fugitives little by little. The rains had momentarily ceased altogether, but the heavy mist continued unbroken, shrouding the entire grasslands from the Streleheim to the Mermidon. Flick glanced once at his silent companion, noticing with concern that the lean figure was bent slightly in pain, the left arm hanging limp and bleeding freely. The valiant Elf was tiring rapidly, growing steadily weaker from loss of blood, his face pale and drawn from the effort to stay on his feet. Unconsciously, Flick slowed the pace, walking closer to his companion in case he should stumble.

They reached the camp perimeter within a very short time—so quickly, in fact, that the word of what had taken place at the Maturen headquarters had not yet reached the sentries. But the battle horn had put them on the alert, and they stood close to the encampment in small groups, their weapons ready. Ironically, they believed that the danger lay from an enemy outside the camp. Their eyes were fastened dutifully away from the camp, permitting Eventine and Flick to approach undetected to the very edge of their lines. The Elven King did not hesitate, moving forward between the outposts at a steady walk, trusting to the darkness, the mist, and the confusion to prevent their discovery.

Time was running out. Within a matter of minutes

the entire army would be mobilized and ready for battle, and once it was discovered that he had managed to escape, trackers would be out searching for him. He would find safety if he could reach the borders of Kern, just to the south, or alternatively, if he could reach the concealment of the Dragon's Teeth and surrounding forests to the east. It would take several hours in either case and his strength was fading. He could not pause now, even if it meant risking almost certain discovery by passing into the open unprotected.

Boldly the two strolled directly between two of the sentry parties, looking neither left nor right as they moved into the emptiness of the open grasslands beyond. They succeeded in not calling attention to themselves until they were past the perimeter of the guard lines. Suddenly several of the sentries caught sight of them at the same moment and called out. Eventine turned slightly and waved with his good arm, calling back in the Troll language, all the while maintaining a steady pace as he moved farther into the darkness. Flick followed warily, waiting expectantly as the sentries stared after them, still undecided. Then abruptly one of them called sharply and began to move after them, waving them back in excited motions. Eventine yelled to Flick to run for it, and the chase was on. As the two men raced for safety, close to twenty guards took up the pursuit, brandishing their pikes and yelling wildly.

It was an uneven contest from the beginning. Both Eventine and Flick were of lighter build and under normal circumstances could have outdistanced their pursuers. But the Elf was wounded badly and weakened from loss of blood, while the little Valeman was physically exhausted from the ordeal of the last two days. The pursuers were fresh and strong, well rested and fed. Flick knew that their only hope was to find concealment in the mist and darkness, hoping their enemies would be unable to find them. Breathing harshly, stumbling with labored strides, they pushed their failing bodies to the limits of physical endurance. Everything became a large black blur made up of rolling mist all about them and the slickness of the grasslands beneath their racing feet. They ran until they thought they could run no farther, and still there were no mountains, no forests, no place to hide.

Abruptly, from out of the darkness ahead of them, there flashed an iron-tipped pike, piercing Eventine's cloak and pinning him to the damp earth. The outer perimeter of sentries, Flick thought in horror—he had forgotten about them! A dim form shot out of the mist, hurtling itself on the fallen Elf. With the last of his waning strength, the wounded King twisted sharply to one side to avoid the sword blade that buried itself in the earth next to his head, at the same instant bringing his own weapon around and up. The rushing figure fell forward with a quick gasp, impaled on the blade.

Flick stood rooted in place, staring wildly about for other attackers. But there had only been the lone sentry. Quickly he rushed to his companion's side, wrenching the pike free and pulling the exhausted Elf to his feet with almost superhuman effort. Eventine took a few steps before collapsing to the ground once more. Fearfully, the Valeman dropped to his knees beside him, trying to shake the man awake.

"No—no, I'm finished," the hoarse reply came at last. "I can go no farther. . . ."

Behind them, the cries of the Northlanders shot out of the darkness. Their pursuers were drawing closer! Again Flick tried in vain to pull the limp form to its feet, but this time there was no response at all. Helplessly the Valeman stared into the darkness about him, the short hunting knife held ready. This was the end. In final desperation, he called wildly into the darkness and the mist.

"Allanon! Allanon!"

The call died quickly into the night. The rain had begun once more, falling in a slow drizzle onto an already oversaturated earth to form still larger puddles and mires on the quiet grasslands. Dawn was no more than an hour away, although it was impossible to tell time in such weather as this. Flick crouched silently next to the unconscious Elven King and listened to the sounds of the men closing in about him. He could tell by their voices that they were drawing nearer, though they still had not seen him. As if to further mock the futility of the situation, he realized that after risking everything to free Eventine, he had still failed to learn what had befallen the missing Shea. Sudden shouts from his left brought him about to face dim figures approaching from out of the fog. They had found him! Grimly, he rose to meet them.

An instant later the hazy darkness between them exploded in a blinding flash of fire that seemed to erupt from out of the earth, the terrific force throwing Flick to the ground, leaving him dazed and blinded. Showers of sparks and burning grass fell all about him and the thunder of a long series of explosions shook the ground violently. One instant the Northlanders were shadowy figures caught in the dazzling light and the next they disappeared altogether. Columns of crackling flame shot upward into the night like giant pillars, thrusting through the darkness and fog to reach the heavens. Squinting into the maelstrom of destruction, Flick thought it was the end of the world. For several endless minutes the wall of fire blazed skyward in unabated fury, tearing the earth into blackened chunks, scorching the night air until the heat began to burn Flick's skin. Then with a final flash of surging energy, it flared up brightly and disappeared into a hush of mingled smoke and steam, blending quickly into the mist and rain until all that remained was the intense heat of the night air, drifting slowly to rest.

Flick rose cautiously to one knee and peered into the emptiness before him, then turned sharply as he sensed rather than heard the approach of someone behind him. From out of the rolling mist and steam emerged a giant black form, cloaked in flowing robes and reaching outward as if it were the angel of death come to claim her own. Flick stared in numbed terror and then started in recognition as the awesome form passed before him. It was the dark wanderer come at last. It was Allanon.

XXVIII

Dawn had just broken with dazzling brightness against a cloudless, deep-blue sky as the last band of refugees from the island city of Kern passed through the gates of the great Outer Wall and entered Tyrsis. Gone was the damp, impenetrable mist and the vast dark ceiling of storm clouds that had blanketed the land of Callahorn for so many days. The grasslands remained soggy and sprinkled with small ponds the saturated earth could not yet manage to absorb, but the persistent rains had moved on to be replaced by a fresh sky and sun that brought a new cheerfulness to the morning. The people of Kern had been arriving in scattered groups for several hours, all weary, horrified by what had happened and frightened of what lay ahead. Their home had been completely destroyed, though some did not yet realize the Northlanders had put everything to the torch following the unexpected attack on their encampment.

The evacuation of the doomed city had been a miraculous success, and, although their homes were gone, they were still alive and, for the moment, secure. The Northlanders had failed to detect the mass escape, their attention completely occupied by the courageous band of Legion soldiers that had assaulted the central camp and drawn them away from even the most distant outposts in the mistaken belief that a

full-scale attack was under way. By the time they
realized the strike was only a feint designed to confuse
them, the island had been evacuated and its people
were far down the swift Mermidon and beyond the
reach of the maddened enemy.

Menion Leah was one of the last to enter the walled
city, his lean frame battered and exhausted. The
wounds on his feet had been reopened during the
ten-mile march from the Mermidon to Tyrsis, but he
had refused to be carried. It was with the last of his
strength that he struggled up the wide ramp leading to
the gates of the Outer Wall, supported on one side by
the faithful Shirl, who had refused to leave his side
even to sleep, and gripped firmly on the other by an
equally weary Janus Senpre.

The youthful Legion commander had survived the
fighting of that terrible night battle, escaping the
besieged island on the same small raft that had carried
Menion and Shirl. The ordeal they had been through
had brought them closer together, and on the trip
southward they had spoken frankly, though in
hushed tones, about the disbanding of the Border
Legion. They were in complete accord that if the city of
Tyrsis were to withstand an assault by a force the size
of the Northland army, the Legion would be needed.
Moreover, only the missing Balinor possessed the
battle knowledge and skill necessary to lead them. The
Prince must be found quickly and placed in command,
even though his brother would undoubtedly oppose
such a move, just as he was certain to oppose the
re-forming of the legendary fighting force he had so
foolishly demobilized.

Neither the highlander nor the Legion commander
realized at this moment how difficult their task would
be, though they suspected that Balinor had been
seized by his brother upon entering Tyrsis some days
earlier. Nevertheless, they were resolved that Tyrsis
would not be destroyed as easily as Kern. This time
they would stand and fight.

A squad of black-clad palace guards met the little group just inside the gates of the city, extending warm greetings from the King and insisting that they come to him at once. When Janus Senpre remarked that he had heard the King was deathly ill and confined to his bed, the squad captain quickly, though somewhat belatedly, added that his son Palance extended the offer in his father's place. Nothing could have pleased Menion more—he was anxious to get inside the palace walls for a look around. Forgotten was the fatigue and pain, though his companions still stood close to offer their support. The squad captain signaled to the guards near the Inner Wall, and an ornate carriage was quickly brought up to convey the privileged party to the palace. Menion and Shirl climbed into the carriage, but Janus Senpre declined to accompany them, explaining that he wished first to see to the welfare of his soldiers in the vacant Legion barracks. With disarming warmth, he promised he would join them later.

As the carriage drew away to the Inner Wall, the youthful commander waved once in sharp salute to Menion, his face impassive. Then accompanied by the grizzled Fandrez and several select officers, he strode purposefully toward the Legion barracks. In the coach, Menion smiled faintly to himself and gripped Shirl's hand.

The carriage passed through the gates of the Inner Wall and moved slowly onto the crowded Tyrsian Way. The people of the walled city had risen early that day, anxious to welcome the unfortunate fugitives from their sister city, eager to offer both food and shelter to friends and strangers alike. Everyone wanted to know more about the massive invasion force that was now advancing on their own homes. Throngs of worried and frightened people lingered uncertainly in the busy streets, talking anxiously among themselves, pausing to stare curiously as the carriage escorted by the palace guards rolled slowly past them. A few pointed or waved in astonishment as they recognized the slim girl who rode within, the dark, rust-colored hair shadowing her worn and drawn face. Menion sat close to her, suddenly aware once more of the pain stabbing in quick twinges from his battered feet. He was grateful now that it was not necessary to walk any farther.

The great city seemed to rush past him in short flashes of buildings and overpasses, all crowded with men, women, and children of all ages and descriptions, all rushing somewhere in noisy waves. The highlander breathed deeply and settled back in the cushioned seat, his hand still holding Shirl's, his eyes closing momentarily as he allowed his tired mind to drift into the gray haze that clouded his thoughts. The city and its multitudes faded quickly into a faint drone of sound that soothed him, lulled him quietly toward the comfort of sleep.

He was on the verge of slipping away entirely when a gentle shaking of his shoulder brought him quickly around, and his eyes opened to view the distant palace grounds as the carriage mounted the wide avenue of the Sendic Bridge. The youth gazed appreciatively down on the sunlit parks and gardens beneath the bridge, their tree-shaded lawns dotted with color from seemingly countless carefully tended flower beds. Everything lay in peace and warmth, as if this sector of the city were somehow an unrelated part of the turbulent human existence that had created it.

At the other end of the bridge the gates to the palace swung open in reception. Menion peered ahead in disbelief. The entire entryway was lined with soldiers of the palace guard, all immaculately dressed in their black uniforms crested by the emblem of the falcon, all standing stiffly at attention. From within the enclosure, trumpets announced the arrival of the coach and its passengers. The highlander was astonished. They were being accorded the formal welcome normally reserved for only the greatest leaders of the four lands, a policy strictly observed by the few monarchies remaining in the vast Southland. The pomp and display of a full military salute clearly indicated that Palance Buckhannah was determined to ignore not only the circumstances under which they had arrived, but the inviolate tradition of centuries.

"He must be mad—absolutely mad!" the angered Southlander stormed. "What does he think this is? We're besieged by an invading army, and he turns out the troops for a dress parade!"

"Menion, be careful what you say to him. We must be patient if we are to be of any use to Balinor." Shirl gripped his shoulder and faced him for a moment, smiling quickly in warning. "Remember as well that he loves me, misguided though he may be. He was a good man once, and he is Balinor's brother still."

Impatient and impulsive as always, Menion nevertheless realized that she was right. There was nothing to be gained by showing he was angered with the foolish pageant, and he was well advised to go along with the Prince's whims until Balinor was located and freed. He sat quietly back in the coach as it entered the palace gates, passing in slow review before the rows of expressionless soldiers that formed the elite of the King's personal guard. The fanfares continued to roll from all sides, and a small squad of cavalry wheeled in precise formation about the courtyard for the benefit of the new arrivals. Then the carriage came to a gentle halt, and the big figure of the new ruler of Callahorn appeared at the coach door, the broad face smiling in nervous delight.

"Shirl—Shirl, I thought I would never see you again!" He reached into the coach and helped the slim girl from the small enclosure, holding her close to him for a moment and stepping away to view her once more. "I . . . I really thought I had lost you."

Burning quietly, an impassive Menion helped

himself from the carriage, stepping down beside them, smiling faintly as Palance turned to greet him.

"Prince of Leah, you are indeed welcome in my kingdom," the big man greeted the lean highlander, reaching warmly for his hand. "You have done me . . . a very great service. Anything I have is yours—anything. We shall be great friends, you and I! Great friends! It has been . . . so long since . . ."

He trailed off sharply, looking intensely at the highlander, suddenly lost in thought. His speech was stilted and nervous, almost as if he weren't quite sure of what he was saying at any one point. If he weren't completely mad already, Menion thought quickly, he was certainly very ill.

"I'm very pleased to be in Tyrsis," he responded, "although I wish the circumstances could have been more pleasant for all concerned."

"You mean my brother, of course?" The question shot out as the other snapped awake again, his face flushed. Menion started momentarily in surprise.

"Palance, he means the invasion of the Northlanders, the burning of Kern," Shirl interposed quickly.

"Yes . . . Kern . . ." Again he trailed off, this time looking anxiously about as if someone were missing. Menion glanced about uneasily, realizing that the mystic Stenmin was strangely absent. According to Shirl and Janus Senpre, the Prince never went anywhere without his adviser. Quickly he caught Shirl's watchful eye.

"Is there something wrong, my Lord?" Menion used the formal address to catch the other's instant attention, smiling quickly in reassurance that he was a concerned friend prepared to help. The deception brought unexpected results.

"You can help me . . . and this kingdom, Menion Leah," Palance responded quickly. "My brother seeks to be King in my place. He would have me killed. My adviser Stenmin has saved me from this—but there are other enemies . . . all around! You and I must be friends. We must stand together against those who seek to take my throne—to bring harm to this lovely woman whom you have returned to me. I . . . I cannot talk with Stenmin . . . the way I would talk with a friend. But you, I could talk with you!"

Like a small child, he gazed eagerly at the amazed Menion Leah, awaiting his reply. A sudden feeling of pity for this son of Ruhl Buckhannah swept over the highlander, and he truly wished there was something he could do to help the unfortunate man. Smiling sadly, he nodded his agreement.

"I knew you would stand with me!" the other exclaimed excitedly, laughing in delight. "We are both men of royal blood, and that . . . binds us closely. You and I shall be great friends, Menion. But now . . . you must rest."

He seemed to recall suddenly that his palace corps were still standing stiffly at parade attention, waiting patiently for the Prince to give the order for dismissal. With a sharp wave of his hand, the new ruler of Callahorn led his two guests toward the Buckhannah home, nodding to the commander of his personal guard as they passed to signal that his soldiers could be dispersed for regular duty. The trio passed into the entryway of the ancient home, where a number of servants stood waiting to escort the guests to their rooms. Pausing briefly once more, the host turned to his guests, bending close to whisper.

"My brother is locked in the dungeons beneath us. You need not be afraid." He stared meaningfully at them for a moment, glancing quickly at the curious servants who waited respectfully in the background. "He has friends everywhere, you know."

Both Menion and Shirl nodded, because it was expected of them.

"He won't escape from the dungeons then?" Menion pursued the matter a bit further.

"He tried last night . . . with his friends." Palance smiled with satisfaction. "But we caught them and trapped them . . . trapped them in the dungeon forever. Stenmin is there now . . . you must meet him . . ."

Again he straightened up with the thought left unspoken, his attention given over to the servants, several of whom he beckoned to his side. He crisply directed them to escort his friends to their quarters where they could bathe themselves and don fresh clothing before joining him for breakfast. It was still only about an hour after dawn and the refugees from Kern had not eaten since the previous night. Menion needed medical treatment for his hastily bandaged wounds, and the house physician stood ready to change the dressings and apply fresh medicines. He needed rest, too, but that could wait. The small party started down one long hallway when suddenly a distracted voice called after Shirl, and the new ruler of Callahorn came after them, approaching the wondering girl with hesitant steps, finally stopping before her and quickly embracing her. Menion kept his face averted, but their words were clear.

"You must not go away from me again, Shirl." It was a command, not a request, though the words were softly spoken. "Your new home must be in Tyrsis—as my wife."

There was a long moment of silence.

"Palance, I think we . . ." Shirl's voice shook as she tried to interpose a quiet explanation.

"No—say nothing. No discussion is necessary now . . . not now," Palance interrupted quickly. "Later . . . when we are alone, when you are rested . . . there will be time. You know I love you . . . I always have. And you have loved me, I know."

Again the long moment of silence, and then Shirl was walking quickly past Menion, forcing the servants to dash ahead in order to lead the way to the guest quarters. The highlander quickly came up beside the beautiful girl, not daring to reach for her while his host stood silently watching them move down the hallway. Shirl's face was lowered, shaded by the long red hair, the slim, bronzed hands clasped tightly before her. Neither spoke as the servants led them down the wide corridor to their rooms in the west wing of the ancient home. They separated briefly while Menion allowed the persistent physician to treat his wounds and wrap them in fresh bandages. Clean clothing lay on the huge, four-posted bed, and a hot bath stood waiting, but a distraught Menion ignored them both. Quickly he slipped from his room into the empty hallway; he knocked softly, pushed open the door to Shirl's room, and entered. She rose slowly from the bed as he closed the heavy wooden door, then ran quickly to him, her arms encircling and holding him tightly to her.

They stood in silence for several minutes, just holding each other, feeling the warm life flow quickly through their bodies, knotting and winding in unbreakable ties. Softly Menion stroked the dark red tresses, gently pressing the beautiful face close against his chest. She depended on him; the thought flashed with relief through his numbed mind. When her own strength, her own courage had faltered, she had turned to him, and Menion realized that he loved her desperately.

It was very strange that it should happen now, when their world seemed destined to crumble about them and death stood waiting in the shadows. Yet Menion's turbulent life of the past several weeks had drawn him from one frightening struggle to the next, each a battle for survival that seemed senseless in mortal terms and found its logic solely in the strange legend of the mystic Sword of Shannara and the Warlock Lord. In those terrible days since Culhaven, life had raged around him like a battle, and he had surged directionless through its center. His deep friendship and love for Shea, and his now broken companionship with the members of the company that had journeyed to Paranor and beyond, had provided a faint sense of stability, an indication that something constant would remain while the rest of the world rushed away. Then unexpectedly, he had found Shirl Ravenlock, and the fast pace of events and dangers shared in those past few days, combined with a totally predictable meshing of personal needs, had drawn and bound them inextricably to one another. Menion closed his eyes and pressed her closer.

Palance had been helpful in at least one respect—he had told them that Balinor and probably the others with him were imprisoned in the dungeons somewhere beneath the palace. Evidently one escape had already failed, and Menion was determined that he would not make any mistakes. Quietly he conversed with Shirl, trying to decide what their next step should be. If Palance insisted on keeping Shirl close to him in order to assure her protection, her movement would be severely restricted. A worse threat was the Prince's obsession with marrying her in the false belief that she truly loved him. Palance Buckhannah seemed poised on the brink of total madness, his sanity precariously balanced. It could be tipped at any moment, and if that should happen while Balinor was his prisoner . . .

Menion paused mentally, aware that time did not permit speculation of what might happen tomorrow. By then it would make little difference because the Northland invasion force would be at the gates and it would be too late for anyone to do anything. Balinor had to be freed now. Menion had a strong ally in Janus Senpre, but the palace was secured by the special black-garbed soldiers who served only the ruler, and at the moment it appeared they served Palance Buckhannah. No one seemed to know what had become of the old King; he had not been seen for weeks. Evidently he was unable to move from his sickbed, yet there was only his son's word for that—and his son relied on the word of the strange mystic Stenmin.

Shirl had once remarked that she had never seen Palance alone for more than a few moments without his adviser close at hand, yet when they arrived from Kern, Stenmin had been nowhere in sight. This was peculiar, especially since it was common knowledge that Stenmin had made himself the real power behind the unstable Prince. Shirl's father had stated in the council chambers of Kern that the evil mystic seemed to possess some strange hold over the younger son of Ruhl Buckhannah. If only Menion could discover what that power was—for he was sure that the mystic was the key to the Prince's unbalanced behavior. But there was no time left. He would have to do the best he could with what little he knew now.

When he left Shirl and returned to his own room, ready now for that hot bath and a clean change of clothing, a plan for freeing Balinor was already forming in his mind. He was still filling in the details when the bath was finished and there was a knock on the door. Slipping into a robe his host had furnished, he crossed the room and opened the door. One of the palace servants had brought him the sword of Leah. Smiling gratefully, he thanked the man and dropped the precious weapon on the bed, recalling that he had deposited it on the seat in the carriage during his ride to the palace and forgotten to remove it. His mind wandered briefly as he dressed, remembering proudly the service that battle-worn implement had seen. He had been through so much since Shea had appeared in Leah those many weeks ago—it might have been a lifetime for any man.

Pausing momentarily, he reflected sadly on his missing friend and wondered for the thousandth time if the little Valeman were still alive. He should not be in Tyrsis, he chided himself in bitter recrimination.

Shea had depended on him for protection, but it appeared that his trust had been badly misplaced. Menion had repeatedly allowed himself to be governed by the wishes of Allanon, and each time his conscience had warned him that he was somehow failing his companion by following the Druid's council. He felt deeply angered at the thought that he had ignored his clear responsibility to the Valeman, and yet the choices that had brought him to Tyrsis had been his own. There were others besides Shea who desperately needed him. . . .

Crossing the spacious bedroom in measured steps, still lost in thought, he dropped heavily to the welcome softness of the large bed, his outstretched hand coming to rest on the cool metal of his sword. He fingered it lightly as he lay back wearily and pondered the problems facing him. Shirl's frightened face lingered in his mind, her eyes searching Menion's own. She was very important to him; he could not leave her now in order to resume the search for Shea, no matter what the consequences might be. It was a bitter choice to make, if indeed there was any real choice at all, for his duty ran beyond those two single lives to those of Balinor and his imprisoned comrades and ultimately to those of the people of Callahorn. It would be for Allanon and Flick to find and rescue the missing Valeman if he were still alive. So much depended on them all, he thought absently, his tired mind and body already drifting toward a much-needed sleep. They could only pray for success . . . pray and wait. He hovered on the brink of slumber and then softly dropped off.

A moment later his sleeping mind jerked sharply and he was instantly awake. There may have been a slight noise or perhaps only a highly keyed sixth sense, but whatever it was snapped him back from a sleep that would have ended in his death. He lay motionless on the great bed as his listening ears caught a faint scraping sound from the far wall, and through the slits of his eyelids he saw a portion of a tapestry ripple with movement. A part of the heavy stone behind the tapestry seemed to push outward and a bent, scarlet-cloaked figure slid noiselessly into view.

Menion forced himself to continue breathing in measured intervals, although his heart was beating wildly, urging him to leap from the bed and seize the mysterious intruder. The cloaked figure moved silently across the bedroom floor, the unfamiliar face glancing quickly about the room and then turning back to the highlander's sprawled form. The intruder was only several feet from the bed when a lean hand slipped beneath the scarlet cloak and emerged, gripping a long, wicked dagger.

Menion's outstretched hand rested loosely on the sword of Leah, but still he did not move. He waited a moment longer until the attacker was within about a yard of the bed, the dagger held at waist level; then with the lightning speed of a cat, he struck. The lean body whipped upward and toward the startled intruder, one hand clenching the sword still sheathed in its leather scabbard as the flat of the blade snapped sharply around at the man's unprotected face, striking it in a stinging slap. The mysterious figure reeled backward, the dagger raised defensively. The sword struck a second time, and the weapon clattered to the floor as the numbed fingers of the attacker clenched suddenly in pain. Menion did not pause, but threw himself at the scarlet figure, his own weight dragging the struggling man to the floor where he quickly pinned him, twisting one arm sharply as his fingers closed tightly about the windpipe.

"Speak up, assassin!" Menion growled menacingly.

"No, no wait, you've made a mistake . . . I'm not an enemy . . . please, I can't breathe. . . ."

The voice choked sharply and the man's breath rasped in ragged gulps as the highlander's grip remained unaltered and the cold dark eyes surveyed the face of his captive. To his knowledge, Menion had never seen the man. The face was pinched and sharp, framed by a small black beard and lined with pain. Even as he studied the teeth clenched in anger and the eyes burning with hatred, the highlander instinctively knew there had been no mistake made. Stepping quickly to one side, he jerked the intruder to his feet, one hand still firmly fastened on the scrawny neck.

"Tell me about my mistake, then. You have about a minute before I cut your tongue out and turn you over to the guards!"

He released his grip on the man's throat, his hand dropping to seize the front of the scarlet tunic. Tossing his sword on the bed, he quickly picked up the fallen dagger, holding it ready should his attacker attempt anything further.

"This was a gift, Prince of Leah . . . merely a gift from the King." The voice broke slightly as the fellow struggled to regain his composure. "The King wanted to show his gratitude, and I . . . I came through another door so as not to disturb your sleep."

He paused as if waiting for something, the sharp eyes riveted on the highlander's own. He wasn't waiting to see if his story would be believed—it was something else, almost as if he were expecting Menion to see something more. . . . The Prince of Leah jerked him sharply, snapping the lean face close to his own.

"That is unquestionably the weakest tale I have ever heard! Who are you, assassin?"

The eyes burned into his own with intense hatred.

"I am Stenmin, the King's personal adviser." He seemed to have suddenly regained his senses now. "I did not lie to you. The dagger was a present from Palance Buckhannah which I was asked to bring to you. I meant you no harm. If you do not believe me, go to the King. Ask him!"

There was a hint of confidence in the man's voice

that convinced Menion that Palance would affirm his adviser's story whether it was true or not. He had in his grasp the most dangerous man in Callahorn, the evil mystic who had become the power behind the monarchy—the one man he had to eliminate if Balinor were to be rescued. Why the man had chosen to attack him when they had never met was something he did not understand, but it was clear that if he released him now or even took him before Palance in an effort to discredit him, the highlander would lose the initiative and place his own life in danger again. Roughly he threw the mystic into a nearby chair and ordered him to remain motionless. The man sat quietly, his eyes drifting aimlessly about the room, the hands moving nervously to stroke the small pointed beard. Menion eyed him absently, his mind carefully pondering the choices open to him. It took him only a moment to decide. He could no longer bide his time, waiting for the right moment to free his friends; the decision had been taken out of his hands.

"On your feet, mystic, or whatever you prefer to call yourself!" The evil face stared menacingly at him, and in fury Menion yanked the man violently up from the chair. "I ought to dispose of you without further consideration; the people of Callahorn would be much the better for it. But for the time being, I need your services. Take me to the dungeons where Balinor and the others are imprisoned—now!"

Stenmin's eyes went wide in sudden shock at the mention of Balinor.

"How could you know of him . . . a traitor to this kingdom?" the mystic exclaimed in astonishment. "The King himself has ordered his brother imprisoned until his natural death, Prince of Leah, and even I . . ."

His sentence ended in a strangled gasp as Menion grabbed him roughly by the throat and began to squeeze. Stenmin's face turned slowly purple.

"I didn't ask for excuses or explanations. Just take me to him!"

Once more he tightened his iron grip and finally the gasping captive nodded violently his acquiescence. Menion released him with a snap of his wrist and the nearly throttled man fell dizzily to one knee. Quickly the highlander slipped out of his robe and into his clothing, strapping on the sword and shoving the dagger into his belt. For an instant he thought about arousing Shirl in the next room, but quickly discarded that idea. His plan was dangerous enough; there was no reason to risk her life as well. If he succeeded in freeing his friends, there would be time enough to come back for her. He turned to his captive, drawing the dagger from his belt and holding it up for the other to see.

"The present that you were so kind to bring me will be returned to you, assassin, if you attempt to trick or betray me in any way," he warned in his most menacing tone of voice. "So don't try to be clever. When we leave this room, you will take me down the back corridors and stairs to the prison where Balinor and his companions are held. Don't try to alarm the guards—you won't be fast enough. If you doubt anything I've told you, then understand this. I was sent to this city by Allanon!"

Stenmin seemed to go suddenly white at the mention of the giant Druid and undisguised fear shot into his widening eyes. Apparently cowed into obeying his captor, the scarlet mystic moved silently toward the bedroom door and Menion fell into step directly behind him, the dagger back in his belt with one hand gripping the hilt. Time was the all-important factor now. He had to act quickly, freeing Balinor and the other imprisoned members of the company of friends and seizing the deranged Palance before the members of the palace guard were alerted. Then a quick message to Janus Senpre would bring to their aid those still loyal to Balinor, and the power of the monarchy would be restored without a battle.

Already the massive Northland army would be mobilizing on the grasslands above the island of Kern, preparing to move on Tyrsis. If the Border Legion could be reassembled and deployed quickly enough that day, there was a chance the invader might be stopped on the north shore of the Mermidon. It would be a nearly impossible task to cross that flooded river with a defensive force holding the opposite bank, and it would take the enemy several days to manage a flanking maneuver—more than enough time for the armies of Eventine to reach them. Menion knew it would all depend on the next few minutes.

The two men stepped cautiously into the hallway beyond the room. Menion quickly glanced in both directions for any sign of the black-garbed sentries, but the hall was deserted, and the highlander motioned Stenmin ahead. The mystic reluctantly led his captor toward the inner rooms of the central palace, winding his way along the corridors that ran to the rear of the ancient building, carefully avoiding the occupied rooms. Twice they passed members of the palace guard, but each time Stenmin withheld any comment or greeting, his dark face lowered in grim determination.

Through the latticework of the castle windows, Menion could see the gardens that decorated the grounds of the Buckhannah home, the sunlight falling warmly on the brightly colored flowers. It was already midmorning, and before much longer the normal gathering of visitors and business personages would begin. There had been no sign of Palance Buckhannah, and Menion was hopeful that the Prince was preoccupied with other matters.

As the two walked slowly down the hallways, the sound of voices was distinctly audible in all directions. Servants began to appear in increasing numbers, moving busily about their assigned tasks. When they passed, they pointedly ignored Stenmin and his apparent companion, a good indication that they neither liked nor trusted the mystic. None questioned their presence and at last they approached the massive doorway that led to the castle cellars. Two armed sentries were stationed before the door, and a huge metal bar now held the latches firmly in place.

"Be careful what you say," Menion cautioned in a sharp whisper as they neared the guards.

They came to a slow halt before the massive cellar door, the watchful highlander placing one hand in a leisurely manner on the hilt of the dagger as he stood close behind Stenmin. The guards glanced curiously at him for a moment, then turned their attention to the King's adviser, who had begun to address them.

"Open the door, guards. The Prince of Leah and I will inspect the wine cellar and the dungeons."

"All persons are forbidden to enter this area by order of the King, my Lord," the guard to the right stated pointedly.

"I am here by order of the King!" Stenmin shouted angrily, causing Menion to give him a warning nudge.

"Sentry, this is the King's personal counselor—not an enemy of the Kingdom," the highlander pointed out with a deceiving smile. "We are on a tour of the palace, and since it was I who rescued the King's betrothed, it was his belief that I might recognize the lady's abductors. Now if necessary, I shall disturb the King and bring him down here . . ."

He trailed off meaningfully, praying that the guards would be sufficiently forewarned of Palance's irrational behavior to think twice about calling him down. The guards hesitated momentarily, then nodded quietly, released the latches on the door and stepped aside, swinging the massive portal open to reveal the stone stairway leading downward. Stenmin again led the way without comment. Apparently he had decided to follow Menion's instructions to the letter, but the cautious highlander knew that the mystic was no fool. If Balinor were successfully freed and restored to command of the Border Legion, then his own power over the throne of Callahorn would be finished. He would undoubtedly attempt something, but the time and the place had not yet come. The heavy door closed quietly behind them and they began their descent into the torchlit cellar.

Menion saw the trapdoor in the center of the cellar floor almost immediately. The guards had not bothered to conceal it a second time with the wine barrels, but had fastened a series of iron bars and latches across the stone slab, effectively preventing anyone imprisoned below from breaking free. Although Menion could not have known, the prisoners had not been returned to their cells following the aborted escape attempt earlier that same morning. Instead, they had been left to roam in the darkness of the dungeon corridors. Two guards were stationed next to the sealed opening, their attention now focused on the two men who had just been admitted from the palace. Menion saw a plate of cheese and bread resting half eaten on one of the wine barrels and two cups of wine placed next to a half-drained flask. They had been drinking. The highlander smiled slightly.

As the two reached the stone flooring, Menion pretended to glance about the wine cellar in great interest, beginning a jovial conversation with the silent Stenmin. The guards rose slowly and came to attention at the sight of the King's adviser, who was looking decidedly grim about something. The highlander knew they had been caught off balance by this unexpected visit and he decided to make the most of it.

"I see what you mean, my Lord." He glowered fiercely at the mystic as they drew near to the sentries. "These men have been drinking while on duty!

Suppose the prisoners should have escaped while
these men lay in a drunken stupor? The King must be
told of this as soon as we have finished our business
here."

The guards turned pale with fear at mention of the
King.

"My Lord, you are mistaken," the one pleaded
hastily. "We were only taking a little wine with our
breakfast. We have not been lax . . ."

"The King should decide that." Menion cut him off
with a wave of his hand.

"But . . . the King will not listen . . ."

Stenmin glowered in fury at the deception, but the
guards misunderstood and quickly assumed he meant
to have them punished. The mystic tried to say
something, but Menion moved quickly in front of him,
as if in an effort to restrain his advance toward the
unfortunate guards, drawing the dagger and holding
it close to the man's unprotected chest.

"Yes, of course they are probably lying," Menion
continued without changing his tone of voice. "Still
the King is a busy man and I hate to bother him with
little problems. Perhaps a word of warning to
them . . .?"

He glanced back at the guards who nodded dumbly,
grasping at any chance to avoid Stenmin's wrath. Like
everyone else in the Kingdom, they were frightened of
the power the strange mystic possessed over Palance
and were more than eager to avoid angering him.

"Very good, then, you have had your warning."
Menion sheathed the dagger and turned back to the
still-shaken sentries. "Now open the dungeon door
and bring up the prisoners."

He stood close to Stenmin, glancing at him quickly
in warning. The dark face did not seem to see him
anymore, the eyes staring vacantly at the stone slab
that barred their entry to the dungeons beneath. The
sentries had not moved, but were glancing at each
other in new desperation.

"My Lord, the King has forbidden anyone to see the prisoners . . . for any reason," the one guard gulped at last. "I cannot bring them out of the dungeon."

"So you would bar the King's adviser and his personal guest." Menion did not hesitate. He had expected this. "Then we have no choice but to call the King down here . . ."

That was all it took. There was no further deliberation as the sentries raced to the stone slab, quickly sliding back the latches and bolts. Bracing themselves, the guards pulled back on the iron ring and the trapdoor swung ponderously upward and fell back heavily against the stone flooring, leaving a gaping black hole. Holding their swords ready, the sentries called down into the darkness, commanding the prisoners to come out. There were footsteps on the ancient stone stairway as Menion waited expectantly at Stenmin's side, his own sword now drawn. His free hand held the mystic's arm tightly, and in a sharp whisper he warned the lean adviser not to speak or move. Then Balinor's broad form appeared from out of the pit, closely followed by the Elven brothers and the durable Hendel, his own attempt to rescue his friends thwarted only hours earlier. They did not see Menion at first. Quickly the highlander stepped forward, still holding the silent Stenmin.

"That's it, keep them moving, keep them together. Such men must be watched carefully. They are always dangerous."

The wearied prisoners glanced over abruptly, only thinly masking their astonishment on seeing the Prince of Leah. Menion winked quickly behind the guards' backs, and the four captives turned away, only the slow smile on Dayel's young face betraying the sudden joy they were experiencing at the sight of their old friend. They were out of the pit now and standing quietly a few feet from the guards, who stood with their backs to the highlander. But before Menion could act, the heretofore passive Stenmin wrested his whiplike form free from his captor's iron grip and sprang aside to shout a quick warning to the unsuspecting sentries.

"Traitor! Guards, it's a trick . . ."

He was never able to finish. As the distracted sentries whirled about, Menion leaped catlike at the fleeing mystic, throwing him violently to the stone floor. The soldiers realized their mistake too late. The four prisoners sprang into action, closing the short space of ground separating them from their jailers and disarming them before they could recover. Within seconds the guards were subdued, quickly bound and gagged, and dragged into a corner of the cellar where they were hidden from sight. A thoroughly beaten Stenmin was yanked unceremoniously to his feet to face his new captors. Menion glanced anxiously at the closed door at the top of the cellar stairway, but no one appeared. Apparently the shout had gone unheeded. Balinor and the others came over to him with smiles of gratitude on their tired faces, clapping him on the back and shaking his hand once again.

"Menion Leah, we owe you more than we can ever hope to give back." The giant borderman gripped his hand tightly. "I did not think we would ever see you again. Where is Allanon?"

Quickly Menion explained how he had left Allanon and Flick concealed above the camp of the Northland army and come to Callahorn to warn of the impending advance against Tyrsis. Pausing momentarily to gag Stenmin in the event the evil adviser should attempt to call out another warning to the guards posted outside the cellar door, the highlander told of rescuing Shirl Ravenlock, fleeing to Kern and subsequently to the walls of Tyrsis after the island city was besieged and destroyed. His friends listened grimly until he had finished.

"Whatever else may come out of this, highlander," Hendel declared quietly, "you have proved yourself this day and we shall never forget it."

"The Border Legion must be re-formed and sent to hold the Mermidon immediately," Balinor cut in quickly. "We must get word to the lower city. Then we must find my father . . . and my brother. But I want to secure the palace and the army without a battle. Menion, can we trust Janus Senpre to come to our aid if we call for him?"

"He is loyal to you and to the King." Menion nodded affirmatively.

"You must get a message to him while we remain here," the Prince of Callahorn continued, pacing over toward the captive Stenmin. "Once he arrives with help, we should have no trouble—my brother will be left without support. But what of my father . . .?"

Towering over the dark form of the mystic, he removed the gag from the captive's mouth and stared coldly down at him. Stenmin met his gaze briefly, his own eyes furtive and filled with hate. The mystic knew he was beaten if Palance was captured and removed as monarch of Callahorn, and he was becoming increasingly desperate as the end drew near and his plans began to break apart. Standing with the Elven brothers and Hendel as Balinor confronted the mysterious captive, Menion found himself wondering what the man had hoped to gain by encouraging Palance to take the steps he had. Certainly it was no mystery why he had supported the distraught and unstable Prince as the new King of Callahorn. His own position was assured with Balinor's brother ruling. But why had he encouraged the disbanding of the Border Legion when he knew that an invading army was threatening to overrun the little Southland kingdom and put an end to its enlightened monarchy? Why had he gone to such pains to imprison Balinor and to secrete his father in a distant wing of the palace when they could have been quietly disposed of? And why had he tried to kill Menion Leah, a man he had never met before?

"Stenmin, your rule over this land and its people

and your domination of my brother are over," Balinor
declared with cold determination. "Whether or not
you will ever see the light of another day depends on
what you do from now until the time I am again in
command of the city. What have you done with my
father?"

There was a long moment of silence as the mystic
looked desperately around, the dark face ashen with
fear.

"He . . . he is in the north wing . . . in the tower,"
the answer was a whisper.

"If he has been harmed, mystic . . ."

Balinor turned away sharply, leaving the terrified
man momentarily forgotten. Stenmin shrank away
against one wall, gazing after the tall figure of the
borderman. One hand came up nervously to stroke
the small, pointed beard. Menion watched him,
almost in pity, and then suddenly something clicked
in his mind. An image flashed sharply—a memory of a
scene he had witnessed several days earlier on the
banks of the Mermidon north of the island of Kern as
he had lain concealed on a small hillock overlooking a
windy beachhead. That same mannerism—the stroking of a small pointed beard! Now he knew exactly
what Stenmin was attempting to do! His face turned to
a mask of rage and he started forward, brushing past
Balinor as if he wasn't even there.

"You were the man on the beach—the kidnapper!"
he accused in undisguised fury. "You tried to kill me
because you thought I would recognize you as the
man who kidnapped Shirl—the man who turned her
over to the Northlanders. You traitor! You intended to
betray us all—to turn the city over to the Warlock
Lord!"

Heedless of the cries of his companions, he rushed
toward the now hysterical mystic, who somehow
managed to evade his initial lunge and break away
toward the cellar stairway. Menion was after him with

a bound, the gleaming sword of his father raised to strike. Halfway up the stone steps he caught him, one hand jerking the dark form about as the man shrieked in terror. Yet the end did not come, for as the sword drew back and Menion held the maddened Stenmin tightly against the stone wall, the massive door to the ancient cellar suddenly swung open, the thrust of the pull slamming the ironbound wood back against the wall with a jarring crash. Framed in the entryway stood the broad figure of Palance Buckhannah.

XXIX

For a moment no one moved. Even the terrified Stenmin had gone limp against the cellar wall, his dark face staring blankly at the silent form that waited statuelike at the top of the ancient stairway. The lined face of the Prince was drained of color, and the eyes reflected a curious mixture of anger and confusion. Resolutely, Menion Leah met those searching eyes, his sword arm lowering slowly, his own hatred fading with the sudden turn of events. Their lives might all be forfeited if he didn't act fast. Roughly he yanked Stenmin to his feet and threw him disdainfully toward the Prince.

"Here is your traitor, Palance—the real enemy of Callahorn. This is the man who gave Shirl Ravenlock to the Northlanders. This is the man who would give Tyrsis to the Warlock Lord. . . ."

"My Lord, you've come just in time." The mystic had recovered his wits enough to cut Menion off before any more damage could be done. He stumbled fearfully to his feet and rushed up the stairs, throwing himself at Palance's feet and pointing down at the company of friends. "I discovered them escaping—I was running to warn you! The highlander is a friend of Balinor—he came to kill you!" The words were tumbling out of the man's mouth in undisguised hatred as he groped at his benefactor's tunic and raised himself slowly to his side. "They would have

582

killed me—and then you, my Lord. Can't you see what is happening?"

Menion fought down the urge to rush up the steps and cut the evil mystic's lying tongue out, forcing himself to remain outwardly calm, his gaze riveted on that of the stunned Palance Buckhannah.

"You have been betrayed by this man, Palance," he continued evenly. "He has poisoned your heart and your mind. He has sapped you of your will to think for yourself. He cares nothing for you; he cares nothing for this land, which he has so cheaply sold to the enemy that has already destroyed Kern." Stenmin roared in fury, but Menion continued in stoney disregard. "You once said we would be friends, and friends must have trust for each other. Do not be deceived now, or your kingdom will surely be lost."

At the bottom of the stairway, Balinor and his friends watched silently, afraid that any distraction might break the strange spell Menion Leah was weaving, for Palance was still listening, his clouded mind struggling to break the wall of confusion surrounding it. Slowly he stepped forward on the landing, closing the door quietly behind him and brushing past Stenmin as if he hadn't seen him. His adviser hesitated in confusion, glancing uncertainly at the cellar door as if debating the wisdom of attempting to flee. But he was not yet prepared to accept defeat, and he whirled quickly, catching Palance by the arm and thrusting his lean face next to the man's ear.

"Are you mad? Are you as insane as some say, my King?" he whispered venomously. "Will you throw everything away now—give it all back to your brother? Was he meant to be king—or you? This is all a lie! The Prince of Leah is a friend to Allanon."

Palance turned toward him slightly, his eyes widening.

"Yes, Allanon!" Stenmin knew he had struck a nerve and was determined to pursue it. "Who do you think seized your betrothed from her home in Kern? This man who speaks of friendship was part of the kidnapping—it was all a ruse to get inside the palace and then assassinate you. You were to be killed!"

Below the stairway, Hendel took a step forward, but Balinor put out a restraining hand. Menion stood quietly, knowing that any sudden move now would only confirm Stenmin's charges. He directed a withering glance at the wily mystic, turning quickly back to Palance and shaking his head.

"He is a traitor. He belongs to the Warlock Lord."

Palance took several steps down the stairway, glancing briefly at Menion and then staring fixedly at his brother who waited patiently at the foot of the stairs. A faint smile crossed his lips as he paused confusedly.

"What do you think, brother? Am I really . . . mad? If not me, then . . . why, it must be everyone else, and I alone am . . . sane. Say something, Balinor. We should have that talk now . . . Before . . . I did want to say something . . ."

But the sentence was left unfinished as he straightened his tall frame and looked back once again at Stenmin, who had taken on the appearance of a dangerously cornered animal, crouched and waiting to attack.

"You are pathetic, Stenmin. Stand up!" The sharp command cut through the stillness and the bent figure of the mystic snapped upright. "Advise me what I should do," Palance ordered sharply. "Do I have everyone killed—will that protect me?"

In an instant Stenmin was back at his side, the sharp eyes cold with fury.

"Call your guard, my Lord. Dispose of these assassins now!"

Suddenly Palance seemed to waver, his tall frame drooping, his eyes glancing at the walls of the cellar in studied concentration of the stonework. Menion sensed that the Prince of Callahorn was again losing his grip on reality and falling back into the clouded world of madness that had impaired his once sound reason. Stenmin recognized it as well, a grim smile creeping over his dark face, his hand coming up to stroke the small pointed beard. Then abruptly, Palance spoke once more.

"No, there will be no soldiers . . . no killing. A King must be a man of judgment . . . Balinor is my brother, though he wishes to be King in my place. He and I must talk now . . . he is not to be harmed . . . not harmed." His voice trailed off and he smiled unexpectedly at Menion. "You brought Shirl back to me . . . I thought I had lost her, you know. Why . . . would you do that . . . if you were an enemy . . .?"

Stenmin screamed in fury, grasping furiously at the other's tunic, but the Prince did not seem to realize he was even there.

"It is difficult for me . . . to think clearly, Balinor," Palance continued in a low whisper, shaking his head slowly. "Nothing is clear anymore . . . I don't even feel angry toward you for wanting to be King. I have always . . . wanted to be King. I have, you know. But I have to have . . . friends . . . someone to talk to . . ."

He turned dispassionately toward Stenmin, his eyes blank and expressionless. Something his adviser saw there caused the mystic to release his grip on the other's arm and shrink limply back against the stone wall, his jaw sagging in fear. Only Menion was close enough to realize what had happened. Whatever hold the evil mystic had managed to secure over Palance Buckhannah was gone. The man's already muddled thought processes had been pushed beyond the brink of even basic comprehension of identities, and Stenmin was now no more than another face in a sea of indistinguishable beings that haunted the nightmare world of the maddened Prince of Callahorn.

"Palance, listen to me," Menion called softly to him,

reaching through the web of darkness to the man beneath for just an instant. The broad figure turned slightly. "Call Shirl down from her room. Call Shirl and she will help you."

The Prince hesitated for a moment as if trying to remember, then a small smile crossed his haggard face and a deep calm seemed to settle through his whole body. He remembered her soft voice, her gentle manner, her fragile beauty—memories that recalled peace and serenity, moments of deep affection that he had never found with any other human being. If he could just be with her for a while . . .

"Shirl," he spoke her name softly and turned back to the closed cellar door, one hand outstretched. As he brushed past Stenmin, the crouched mystic seemed suddenly to go berserk. Shrieking with rage and frustration, he threw himself at the other man, grappling wildly at his tunic front. Responding instantly, Menion Leah bounded quickly toward the high landing to part the struggling men. But he was still several steps away when Stenmin's lean hand drew back momentarily, holding high a long dagger seized from beneath his robes. The weapon raised and for one terrible second hung poised above the men, as Balinor cried out in helpless shock. Then it fell. Palance Buckhannah rose sharply to his full height, the dagger buried to the hilt in his broad chest, a terrible whiteness flooding his young face.

"I give you back your brother, fool!" shrieked the maddened Stenmin, shoving the rigid form down the stone stairway.

The stricken Prince fell heavily into Menion's outstretched arms, knocking him back roughly against the wall, causing him momentarily to lose his balance and the opportunity to reach the hated enemy. Stenmin had already turned to flee, pulling frantically on the massive cellar door. Balinor bounded up the stairway, desperately trying to stop the mystic's

escape, the Elven brothers immediately behind him, yelling for the guards. The scarlet figure had pulled the door partially open and was just slipping to freedom when Hendel, still standing at the foot of the stairs, seized a discarded mace and hurled it wildly at the fleeing man. It struck the mystic's exposed shoulder with bone-crunching force, and a scream of pain echoed off the dank walls. Yet it wasn't enough to stop him completely, and a moment later he had disappeared through the doorway. From the hallway beyond they could hear his shrill cry that the prisoners had assassinated the King.

Balinor paused only an instant in his pursuit to glance down on the still form resting quietly in the strong arms of Menion Leah, then raced for the open cellar door. Two black-clad palace guards appeared suddenly from the hallway beyond, swords drawn, to confront the unarmed borderman. They could have been statues for all the difference their unexpected appearance made to Balinor, who bowled them over with a lightning assault, seizing a fallen sword as he disappeared from view. Durin and Dayel were only steps behind. Menion knelt alone on the stairway, gazing after them and holding the stricken Palance, cradling gently the body of the self-proclaimed King of Callahorn. Silently, Hendel climbed the stone steps to stand beside him, shaking his grizzled head sadly. The Prince was still alive, the shallow breathing harsh and the eyelids twitching sporadically. Grimly the Dwarf reached down as Menion held the limp form and slowly withdrew the deadly blade, casting the weapon away with disgust. The Dwarf bent to help the highlander raise the wounded man, and abruptly the eyes opened for an instant. Palance spoke softly, a barely perceptible murmur, and then drifted into unconsciousness once more.

"He's calling for Shirl," Menion whispered, tears in his eyes as he glanced briefly at the other. "He still loves her. He still loves her."

In the hallway beyond, Balinor and the Elven brothers were struggling to catch the fleeing Stenmin. Everything was in a state of utter confusion as guards, household servants, and visitors milled through the panic-stricken palace. Shouts of terror echoed off the ancient walls, decrying the death of the King and warning of assassins bent on killing everyone. The sounds of still another battle rose from the palace gates to add to the growing chaos. Balinor and his two companions fought their way through the knots of frightened people, who seemed to go into a state of complete hysteria at the sight of drawn weapons. A few scattered guards even attempted to bar their passage, but each time the giant borderman merely flung the unfortunate men aside without pausing and raced in pursuit of the red-cloaked figure stumbling ahead. Stenmin was still in sight when the three pursuers reached the central hallway, but he had broken through the hindering throngs and was beginning to draw away. With unbelievable fury Balinor pushed ahead, heedlessly knocking everyone in his path aside, his face grim and terrible.

Then suddenly the palace doors shuddered under the weight of dozens of battling men and burst open with a crash, directly in front of the giant borderman and his Elven friends. The confusion was complete as a huge knot of fighting men rushed wildly into the entryway and the halls beyond, shouting for Balinor and waving their drawn weapons with grand flourishes. For a moment, the Prince was uncertain who they were; then he saw that they were wearing the leopard insignia of the Border Legion. The few palace guards who remained either fled or threw down their weapons and were seized. The Legion soldiers immediately spotted Balinor and rushed over to him, grasping him and raising him to their shoulders with cheers of victory. Durin and Dayel were cut off from him, and the cheering mass of men barred their pursuit of the rapidly disappearing

Stenmin. Balinor shouted and struggled furiously, desperately trying to break away, but the sheer weight of numbers prevented him from resisting the tide that suddenly surged forward, carrying him back toward the cellar.

The frustrated Elves finally broke through the mass of bodies, racing after their quarry, who had turned down a different hallway and was momentarily lost from sight. The lean Elves were very fast, however, and closed the gap between themselves and Stenmin in a matter of seconds. Rounding the corner of the hallway, they caught sight of him once again, the dark face flushed with terror, the right arm hanging limp and useless. Silently Durin cursed himself for having failed to pick up a longbow. Abruptly, the fleeing man halted and vainly tried to wrest open one of the several doors lining the left side of the passage. The latch held despite the mystic's repeated efforts to force it, and at last he turned once more and raced to open the next door down the hall. Durin and Dayel were only yards away as Stenmin succeeded in opening this one and disappeared inside, closing it with a resounding crash. The Elves were there in seconds. Finding the door secured from within, they proceeded to force the iron latch with their swords. The clasp was sturdy and it took them several endless minutes to break through. By the time they pried open the door and burst into the room with swords held ready, it was deserted.

Menion Leah stood quietly at the front gates of the Buckhannah home as Balinor conversed in low tones with the commanders of the Border Legion. Shirl was next to him, one slim arm locked in his, her young face lined with worry in the noon sunlight. Menion glanced down at her momentarily and smiled reassuringly, holding her closer to him. Beyond the great Outer Wall of the city of Tyrsis, two divisions of the reassembled Border Legion waited patiently for the command that would take them into battle against the awesome Northland army. The huge invasion force had reached the northern banks of the swollen Mermidon River, and even now was beginning to make its crossing. If the Legion could hold the southern bank, even for a few days, it might give the Elven armies a chance to mobilize and march to their aid. Time, Menion thought bitterly—all they needed was just a little more time, and so far they hadn't gotten it. The Border Legion had been reassembled as quickly as possible once the city was secured and Balinor was reinstated as commander, but by that time the advancing Northlanders had already reached the Mermidon and begun preparations for the crossing.

Balinor was now King of Callahorn, though it was anything but a cause for celebration. His brother lay in a coma, weakened and extremely close to death. The best physicians in Tyrsis had examined him with labored patience in an effort to determine the cause of his irrational behavior and after some time had concluded that he had been given a powerful drug over a long period of time to break down his resistance and reduce him, for all practical purposes, to a mindless puppet. Finally, the dosage had been increased to the point where his mind and body had been pushed beyond the point of physical and mental endurance. In the end, his madness was real.

Balinor had listened to their conclusions without comment. An hour earlier, he had found his father in a deserted room in the north tower of the Buckhannah home. The aged King had been dead for several days and a physician's report revealed that he had been systematically poisoned. Stenmin had kept everyone from that room except himself and the already unbalanced Palance, so the secret of Ruhl Buckhannah's death had been easily kept. Had the mystic succeeded in having Balinor killed, it would have been a simple matter to persuade Palance to open the gates to the armies of the Warlock Lord, and in so doing, assure the destruction of Tyrsis. He had nearly succeeded once, and he might still do so. Stenmin had managed to elude the Elven brothers and was hidden somewhere within the city.

In a very real sense, the future of the Southland rested in the hands of the Prince of Callahorn. The people of Tyrsis looked to the Buckhannah family for dependable government and strong leadership. The Border Legion functioned best as a fighting unit when Balinor was in command. Now the giant borderman was the last of his family and the man to whom everyone turned for leadership, whether openly or subconsciously. If anything were to happen to him, the Legion would lose its finest commander and the heart of its fighting strength, while the city would lose the last Buckhannah. The few who fully understood the gravity of the situation realized that Tyrsis must be held against the advancing Northland army, or the Southland would be lost and a wedge driven between the armies of the Elves and the Dwarfs. Allanon had warned them that if this should happen, the Warlock Lord had won. Tyrsis was the key to success or failure, and Balinor was the key to Tyrsis.

Janus Senpre had carried out his part in securing the city earlier that morning. After Menion left him at the gates, he sought out the Legion commanders Fandwick and Ginnisson. Secretly, they reassembled key members of the disbanded Legion and, striking quickly and quietly, seized the gates and the army barracks. Moving rapidly toward the palace, they gained strength almost without opposition until finally the entire city surrounding the Buckhannah family home and gardens was resecured. Waiting just outside the palace grounds for a signal from Menion, the three commanders and their followers heard the cries within of assassination; fearing the worst, they rushed the gates, forcing their way inside just in time to prevent Balinor from catching the fleeing Stenmin. There was almost no loss of life in the brief uprising, and the followers of Palance were either imprisoned or freed to rejoin their old units in the Legion. Already two of the five Legion divisions were reassembled, and the other three would be formed up and properly armed by sunset. But scouts from the city had reported to Balinor the progress of the Northlanders in reaching the Mermidon, and concluded that he must act immediately to prevent the crossing.

Hendel and the Elven brothers lounged restlessly off to the right on the steps of the palace, their faces reflecting mixed emotions. The Dwarf appeared as resolute as ever, his aging countenance implacable as he glanced casually over at the highlander and his beautiful charge. Durin seemed somehow older, his lean Elven features clouded by the knowledge of what lay ahead, while Dayel, though shadowed by the same uncertainty, managed a cheerful smile. Menion shifted his gaze back to Balinor and the Legion commanders. Ginnisson was heavyset with shocking red hair and powerful arms; Fandwick was aged and grizzled with a drooping white mustache and a scowl to match; Acton was a man of medium height and regular appearance, whose horsemanship was said to be matchless; Messaline was tall and broad shouldered, almost arrogant-looking as he rocked carelessly back on his heels while Balinor spoke to them; and last came Janus Senpre, recently promoted to full commander in recognition of his courageous stand at Kern and his vital role in the recapture of Tyrsis. Menion studied them carefully for long minutes as if somehow his visual appraisal could ascertain their worth. Then Balinor turned and walked over to him, motioning for Hendel and the Elves to join them.

"I'm leaving at once for the Mermidon," he informed them quietly when they were all together. Menion started to speak, but Balinor quickly cut him off. "No, Menion, I know what you are going to ask, and the answer is no. You will all remain here in the city. I would trust any one of you with my life, and since my life is of secondary importance in comparison with Tyrsis, I ask you to guard the city instead. If anything should happen to me, you will know best how to continue the battle. Janus remains with you in command of the city defenses, and I have instructed him to confer with you on all matters."

"Eventine will come," Dayel spoke quickly, trying hard to sound cheerful.

Balinor smiled and nodded in agreement.

"Allanon has never failed. He won't fail us now."

"Don't expose yourself unnecessarily," Hendel warned grimly. "This city and its people depend on you. They need you alive."

"Good-bye, old friend." Balinor gripped the Dwarf's hand tightly. "I depend on you most of all. Your experience is twice mine, and you are twice the strategist. Take care."

He turned quickly, motioning for his commanders, and entered the waiting carriage that would convey them to the city gates. Janus Senpre waved reassuringly to Menion as the palace coach drew away, the mounted escort falling into sharp formation to the rear, and the gallant procession galloped with a clashing of iron-shod hooves toward the Sendic Bridge. The four companions and Shirl Ravenlock watched until they were lost from sight and the thunder of the horses had drifted into silence. Then Hendel muttered absently about checking the palace once more for some sign of the missing Stenmin and, without waiting for a response, reentered the Buckhannah home. Durin and Dayel trailed after him, feeling strangely disconsolate. It was the first time they had been separated from Balinor for more than several hours since the long journey from Culhaven had begun many weeks earlier, and it was a disquieting experience to allow him to go on alone to the Mermidon.

Menion knew exactly how they felt, his own restless nature inwardly urging him to go after the borderman, to join him in the crucial battle against the hordes of the Warlock Lord. But he was nearly exhausted—he had not slept for almost two days. The strain of the battle above the island of Kern, the long flight down the Mermidon, and the rapid series of events which had led to the freeing of Balinor and the others had sapped even his great stamina. Almost drunkenly, he steered Shirl into the gardens at the side of the palace, dropping heavily onto a wide stone bench. The girl sat quietly next to him, watching his face as he closed his eyes and forced his mind to relax.

"I know what you must be thinking, Menion." Her soft voice drifted gently through his weariness. "You want to be with him."

The highlander smiled and nodded slowly, his thoughts hazy and jumbled.

"You must get some sleep, you know."

Again he nodded, and suddenly he thought of Shea. Where was Shea? Where had the Valeman wandered in his futile search for the elusive Sword of Shannara? Quickly he raised himself, snapping awake and turning to Shirl, almost as if he thought she might not be there. He was exhausted, but he wanted to talk—he needed to talk, because there might never be another chance. In low, somber tones he began to speak to her, telling her about himself and Shea, unfolding in bits and pieces the friendship that had so closely bound them in the years they had known one another. He spoke of the times they had spent in the highlands of Leah, drifting gradually into the full story behind the journey to Paranor and the search for the Sword. At times he rambled in vain attempts to explore in depth the rationale behind feelings they had shared and philosophies they could not. As the highlander continued, Shirl began to realize that it was not really Shea that Menion was trying to describe—it was himself. Finally she stopped him, reaching without thinking to place a slim hand over his lips.

"He was the only person you ever really got to know, wasn't he?" she asked quietly. "He was like a brother, and you feel responsible for what happened to him?"

Menion shrugged disconsolately. "I couldn't have done anything but what I did. Keeping him in Leah in the first place would have only prolonged the inevitable. But knowing all that doesn't help. I still feel a sort of . . . guilt . . ."

"If he feels as deeply for you as you do for him, then he knows in his heart the truth of what you have done, wherever he is now," she responded quickly. "No man can fault you for the courage you have shown these past five days—and I love you, Menion Leah."

Menion stared at her stupidly, the sudden declaration catching him off balance. Laughing at his confusion, the slim girl wrapped her arms around him, the reddish locks falling like a soft veil about his face as she clung to him. Menion held her close for a moment, then gripped her shoulders gently and pushed her back to study her face and eyes. She met his gaze squarely.

"I wanted to say it out loud. I wanted you to hear it, Menion. If we are going to die . . ."

She choked suddenly on the words and looked away, and the wondering Southlander saw tears slowly roll down her cheeks. He reached up and quickly brushed them away, smiling in the old way as he raised himself to his feet, drawing her up with him.

"I came a long, long way," he murmured gently. "I could have been dead a hundred times, but I survived. I've seen the evil there is in this world and in worlds that mortals only dream exist. There is nothing that can hurt us. Love supplies a kind of strength that can withstand even death. But you need a little faith. Just believe, Shirl. Believe in us."

She smiled in spite of herself.

"I believe in you, Menion Leah. Now you remember to believe in yourself."

The weary highlander smiled back at her, gripping her hands tightly. She was the most beautiful woman he had ever seen, and he loved her as much as his own life. He leaned down and kissed her warmly.

"It will be all right," he assured her quietly. "It will all work out."

They remained a few minutes longer in the solitude of the gardens, talking quietly and absently following the little paths that wound through the warm, fragrant summer flowers. But Menion was fighting to remain awake, and Shirl was quick to demand that he get some sleep while he had the opportunity. Still smiling to himself, he retired to his bedchamber in the palace, where he collapsed, still fully clothed, onto one of the wide, soft beds and immediately fell into a deep, dreamless slumber. While he slept, the hours of the afternoon drifted slowly away, the sun slipping into the western sky and finally sinking in a brilliant scarlet blaze beneath the horizon. At the coming of complete darkness, the highlander awoke, fully rested but strangely disturbed. He hastened to find Shirl, and together they walked the almost deserted corridors of the Buckhannah home, searching for Hendel and the Elven brothers. The long hallways echoed the low tapping of their boots as they hastened past statue-like sentries and darkened rooms, pausing only momentarily to observe the still, deathlike form of Palance Buckhannah, as his physicians watched over him with expressionless faces. His condition remained unchanged, his wounded body and shattered spirit struggling to survive the crushing weight of a death that was slowly, inevitably pushing down against him. When the two silent forms moved at last from his bedside, there were tears again in Shirl's dark eyes.

Convinced that his friends had gone to the city gates to await the return of the Prince of Callahorn, Menion saddled two horses and the couple rode toward the Tyrsian Way. It was a cool, cloudless night lighted by the silver shimmer of the moon and stars, and the towers of the city stood clearly outlined against the sky. As the horses swung onto the Bridge of Sendic, Menion felt the welcome coolness of a friendly night breeze blowing in soothing waves over his flushed face. It was unusually quiet along the Tyrsian Way, the streets deserted and the houses that lined the Way lighted but empty of laughter and friendly conversation. An audible hush had settled over the besieged city, a grim whispering solitude that hovered and waited for the death that came with battle. The riders rode anxiously through this eerie silence, trying to find some comfort in the beauty of the starlit sky that seemed to promise a thousand tomorrows for the races. The towering heights of the Outer Wall loomed blackly in the distance, and on the parapets burned hundreds of torches, lighting the way home to the soldiers of Tyrsis. They had been gone a long time, Menion thought to himself. But perhaps they had been more successful than anyone had dared to hope. Perhaps they had held the Mermidon against the Northland hordes. . . .

Moments later the riders were dismounting at the mammoth gates of the giant wall. The Legion barracks were alive with activity as the restless garrison worked feverishly in preparation for the battle to come. There were knots of soldiers at every turn, and it was with considerable difficulty that Menion and Shirl finally managed to reach the ramparts at the top of the broad walls, where they were greeted warmly by Janus Senpre. The youthful commander had maintained his vigilant lookout without rest since Balinor had departed, and the slim face was lined with weariness and anxiety. After a few moments, Durin and Hendel appeared out of the darkness to join them, followed somewhat later by a wandering Dayel. The little group stood in silence and stared into the darkness that ran northward to the Mermidon and the Border Legion. From far away they could hear the muffled shouts and cries of men fighting, the sounds carried tauntingly by the fresh night wind to the straining ears of those who waited.

Janus remarked absently that he had sent out half a dozen scouts in an effort to discover what was happening at the river, but none had returned—an ominous sign. He had decided several times to go himself, but a gruff Hendel had reminded him each time that he had been placed in charge of the defense of Tyrsis, and each time he had reluctantly discarded the idea. Durin had resolved in his own mind that if Balinor did not return by midnight, he was going out to search for his friend. An Elf could travel undetected through almost any opposition. But for the time being, he waited like the others in growing apprehension. Shirl spoke briefly of the unchanged condition of Palance Buckhannah, but she received only a disinterested response and quickly gave up the impossible task of trying to take their minds off the battle at the river. The little group waited one hour, then two. The sounds had grown slowly louder and more desperate, and it seemed that the fighting had moved closer to the city.

Then suddenly a vast formation of horsemen and foot soldiers appeared out of the darkness almost directly in front of the bluff, winding in staggered columns onto the wide stone rampway leading into the city. Their approach had been almost imperceptible, and their unexpected appearance from out of nowhere caused everyone atop the Outer Wall to gasp audibly. Janus Senpre sprang in alarm toward the

mechanism that secured the iron fastenings to the
giant gates, fearful that somehow the enemy had
managed to outflank Balinor. But Hendel quietly
called him back. He recognized what was happening
even before the others suspected. Leaning out over
the rim of the wall, the Dwarf called down sharply in
his own language, and received an almost instant
response. Nodding grimly to the others, Hendel
pointed to the tall rider who had moved to the point of
the long column. In the soft moonlight, the dust-
covered face of Balinor peered upward, the grim
visage confirming what they all had suspected the
moment they recognized him. The Border Legion had
failed to hold the Mermidon, and the army of the
Warlock Lord was moving against Tyrsis.

It was nearly midnight when the five who remained
together of the little band from Culhaven gathered
in a small, secluded dining room in the Buckhannah
family home for a brief evening meal. The long
afternoon and evening battle to hold the Mermidon
against the Northland army had been lost, although
the cost in lives to the enemy had been terrible. For a
while it appeared that the veteran soldiers of the
Border Legion would succeed in preventing the
floundering Northlanders from gaining the southern
bank of the swift river. But there were thousands of
the enemy, and where hundreds failed, thousands
ultimately succeeded. Acton's horsemen had swept
lightninglike along the fringes of the Legion line,
shattering every attempt by the enemy to outflank the
entrenched foot soldiers. Advances into the heart of
the Southland ranks had resulted in the death of
hundreds of Trolls and Gnomes. It was the most
dreadful slaughter Balinor had ever witnessed, and
eventually the Mermidon began to change color with
the blood of the wounded and dying. And still they
kept trying—trying as if they were mindless creatures

without feeling, without understanding, without human fear. The power of the Warlock Lord had so enslaved the collective mortal mind of the giant army that even death had no meaning. Finally a large band of ferocious Rock Trolls breached the far right tip of the Legion's line of defense; although they were slain almost to a man, the diversionary tactic forced the Tyrsians to shorten their left flank. In the end, the Northlanders were across.

By this time it was almost sunset, and Balinor quickly realized that even the finest soldiers in the world would be unable to retake and hold the southern bank once darkness set in. The Legion had suffered only mild losses during the afternoon's fighting, and so he ordered the two divisions to fall back to a small rise several hundred yards south of the Mermidon and reassemble in battle formation. He kept the cavalry busy on the left and right flanks, making short rushes at the enemy to keep them off balance and to prevent an organized counterthrust. Then he waited for darkness. The hordes of the Northland army began to cross in force as twilight fell; in mingled astonishment and fear, the men of the Border Legion watched as the hundreds that had first crossed turned to thousands and still they kept coming. It was a frightening spectacle the bordermen beheld—an army of such incredible size that it completely covered the land on both sides of the Mermidon as far as the eye could see.

But its size hampered its maneuverability, and the chain of command seemed disorganized and confused. There was no concentrated effort made to dislodge the entrenched Tyrsians from the small rise. Instead the bulk of the army milled about on the banks of the southern shore after crossing, as if waiting for someone to tell them what to do next. Several squads of heavily armed Trolls made a series of rushes at the Legion command, but they were equally matched in numbers and the veteran soldiers quickly repelled them. When darkness came at last, the enemy army suddenly began to organize into columns five deep, and Balinor knew that the first sustained rush would break the Legion to pieces.

With the skill and daring that had made him the spirit behind the fabled Border Legion and the finest field commander in the Southland, the Prince of Callahorn began to execute a most difficult tactical maneuver. Without waiting for the enemy to strike, he suddenly divided his army and attacked far to the right and left of the Northland columns. Striking sharply in short feints, and taking full advantage of the darkness, in terrain every Borderman knew well, the soldiers of the Legion drew in the flanks of the enemy to form a ragged half circle. Each time the circle grew tighter and each time the Tyrsians retreated a little farther. Balinor and Fandwick held the left flank while Acton and Messaline commanded the right.

The enraged enemy began to charge madly, stumbling awkwardly over the unfamiliar ground in the growing darkness, the retreating soldiers of the Legion always just a few steps out of reach. Slowly Balinor drew his flanks in and narrowed his lines, pulling the searching Northlanders in with him. Then, when the foot soldiers had completely fallen back in retreat, covered by the darkness and the battle behind them, the skilled cavalry drew their lines together in a final feint and slipped from between the jaws of the closing enemy trap and was gone. Suddenly the right and left flanks of the harried Northland army met, each believing that the other was the hated enemy that had eluded it for several hours. Without hesitating, they attacked.

How many Trolls and Gnomes were slain by their own people would never be known, but the fighting was still raging when Balinor and the two divisions of the Border Legion arrived safely at the gates of Tyrsis.

The horses' hooves and soldiers' feet had been muffled to cover their retreat. With the exception of a squad of horsemen who had strayed too far west and been cut off and decimated, the Legion had escaped intact. Yet the damage done to the mammoth Northland army had not stopped its advance, and the Mermidon, the first line of defense to the city of Tyrsis, had been lost.

Now the vast encampment of the enemy sprawled on the grasslands below the city, the night fires burning as far as the eye could see through the moonlit darkness. At dawn the assault on Tyrsis would begin as the combined strength of thousands of Trolls and Gnomes, obedient to the will of the Warlock Lord, hurled itself against the towering band of stone and iron that formed the Outer Wall. One would eventually shatter.

Hendel, sitting thoughtfully across from Balinor at the small dining table, recalled again the ominous sensation he had felt earlier that day while inspecting with Janus Senpre the fortifications of the great city. Unquestionably, the Outer Wall was a formidable barrier, but there was something wrong. He had been unable to put his finger on exactly what was causing his uneasiness; but even now, in the solitude of the dining room and the warm companionship of his friends, he could not shake the nagging suspicion that something vital had been overlooked in preparing for the long siege that lay ahead.

Mentally, he retraced the lines of defense protecting the sprawling city. At the edge of the bluff, the men of Tyrsis had erected a low bulwark to prevent the enemy from gaining a foothold on the plateau. If the Northlanders could not be contained on the grass-lands below the bluff, then the Border Legion would fall back into the city proper and rely on the mammoth Outer Wall to halt the enemy advance. The rear approach to Tyrsis was cut off by the sheer cliffs that rose hundreds of feet into the air directly behind the palace grounds. Balinor had assured him that the cliffs could not be scaled; they were like smooth sheets of rock, completely without the normal nooks and crannies that would permit a foothold. The defenses surrounding Tyrsis should be impenetrable, and yet Hendel remained dissatisfied.

For a moment his thoughts drifted back to his homeland—to Culhaven and to his family, whom he hadn't seen in weeks. He had never spent much time with them, his whole life expended in the ceaseless border wars in the Anar. He missed the woodlands and the green shading that came with the spring and summer months, and he suddenly wondered how he had let so much time pass without a visit home. Perhaps he would never get back. The thought swept through his mind and vanished; he had no time for regrets.

Durin and Dayel conversed soberly with Balinor, their own thoughts centered on the Westland. Dayel, like Hendel, was thinking of his home. He was frightened of the battle that lay ahead, but he accepted his fear, encouraged by the presence of the others and determined that he would do no less than they in standing firm against the army that had come to destroy them. He thought quietly of Lynliss, her shy, warm face a permanent fixture in his mind. He would be fighting for her safety as well as his own. Durin studied his brother, noting the sudden smile, and he knew without asking that the youth was thinking of the Elven girl he was to marry. Nothing was more important to Durin than the safety of Dayel; from the beginning he had made a point of staying close to his brother to protect him. Several times during the long journey to Paranor, they had nearly lost their lives. Tomorrow would bring still greater danger, and once again, Durin would be watching over his brother.

Briefly he thought of Eventine and the mighty Elven

armies, wondering if they would reach Tyrsis in time. Without their great strength to supplement the Border Legion, the hordes of the Warlock Lord would eventually break through the city's defenses. He picked up his wineglass and drank deeply, the liquid warm in his throat. His sharp eyes surveyed the faces of the others and came to rest momentarily on the troubled face of Menion Leah.

The lean highlander had devoured his dinner ravenously, having eaten nothing for almost twenty-four hours. Finishing long before his companions, he had contented himself with a fresh glass of wine, directing continual questions to Balinor about the afternoon's battle. Now, in the quiet hours of early morning, with dinner completed and the wine seeping through him like a slow drowsiness, it suddenly occurred to him that the key to everything that had happened since Culhaven, and everything that would happen in the days remaining, was Allanon. He could not bring himself to think any more of Shea and the Sword, nor even of Shirl. He could only see in the forefront of his mind the dark, forbidding figure of the mysterious Druid. Allanon held the answers to every question. He alone knew the secret of the talisman men called the Sword of Shannara. He alone knew the purpose behind the strange appearance of the shrouded wraith in the Valley of Shale—the Druid Bremen, a man over five hundred years dead. He alone, in every instance, along every step of the dangerous journey to Paranor, had known what to expect and how to deal with it. Yet the man himself had remained an enigma.

Now he was gone from them, and only Flick, if he were still alive, could ask him what was going to happen to them. They all depended on Allanon for survival—but what would the giant Druid do? What was left to him when the Sword of Shannara was lost? What was left when the young heir of Jerle Shannara was missing and probably dead? Menion bit his lip in anger as the hated thought slipped quickly through his mind and was banished. Shea had to be alive!

Menion cursed everything that had brought them all to this sorry end. They had allowed themselves to be backed into a corner. There was only one path still open to them. In the holocaust of tomorrow's battle, human beings would die, and few, if any, would know the reason. It was an unavoidable part of war, that men should die for unknown reasons—it had been happening for centuries. But this war was something beyond human comprehension, this war between a substanceless spirit being and mortals. How could evil such as the Warlock Lord be destroyed when it could not even be understood? Only Allanon seemed fully to appreciate the nature of the creature. But where was the Druid when they needed him most?

The candles burned low on the table before them, and the darkness of the secluded room deepened. On the wood and tapestry decorated walls, torches sputtered slowly in their iron racks, and the five voices dropped to low murmurs, hushed as if the night were a child in danger of being unexpectedly awakened. The city of Tyrsis slept now, and in the grasslands beyond, the Northland army. In the peace and solitude of the moonlit night, it seemed that all forms of life were at rest, and that war, with its promise of death and pain, was merely a vague, nearly forgotten memory of years past. But the five who spoke in quiet tones of better days and the friendship shared could not, even for a few moments, completely stifle the lingering realization that the horror of war was no more distant than the sunrise and as inevitable as the darkness of the Warlock Lord, reaching slowly, inexorably from out of the north to snuff out their frail lives.

XXX

n the morning of the third day of the search for Orl Fane, the torrential rains that had swept through the vastness of the barren Northland subsided, and the sun reappeared as a dim, fuzzy ball of white fire, burning through the misty darkness left with the passing of the Warlock Lord's black wall to the mud and rock-strewn terrain with the fury of an oven. The storm had left the topography of the land completely altered, the rains sweeping away almost every distinguishable landmark and leaving only four identical horizons of rocky hillocks and muddied valleys.

At first the appearance of the sun was a welcome sight. The heat from its rays penetrated the hateful gloom that had become permanently affixed to the barren surface of the earth to warm away the chill left by the now-vanished storm as the temperature rose steadily, and the character of the land began to alter once more. But in an hour's time, the temperature had risen thirty degrees and was continuing to rise unchecked. The rivers that washed through the winding gullies carved out by the force of the rain began to steam and mist in the heat, and the humidity soared, drenching everything in a new, even more uncomfortable wetness.

The little plant life born in the aftermath of the devastating storm withered and died in suffocation,

cut off from the sun's life-giving brightness and
choked by the stifling heat that permeated the graying
mist. The muddied earth lay unprotected from the
heat and soon baked into a cracked, hardened clay that
would support no life. The rivers and lakes and
puddles began to dry up quickly, and in almost no
time had disappeared altogether. The exposed surface
of the huge boulders that dotted the parched land
quickly absorbed the burning heat like iron settled in
live coals. Slowly, inexorably the land became what it
had been before the rains had swept its surface—a dry,
barren slab of earth, devoid of life, silent and
forbidding beneath a vast, cloudless sky. The only
movement came from the slow, unchanging arc of an
ageless, disinterested sun as it followed its ceaseless
path from east to west, turning days into years and
years into centuries.

Three bent figures stepped gingerly from beneath
the shelter of a rocky alcove cut in the side of one of the
countless, nondescript hillocks, their cramped bodies
straightening slowly, their eyes peering grimly into
the unbroken wall of mist. They stood for long
moments in the lifeless gloom, staring into the dying
land that seemed to stretch on forever, a dismal
graveyard of rocky mounds that covered the mortal
remains of those who had ventured into this forbidden
kingdom. There was absolute silence filtering evilly
through the misty grayness, hanging its unspoken
warning of death in the minds of the three living
creatures. They stood in apprehensive watchfulness,
staring at the wasteland surrounding them.

Shea turned to his companions. Panamon Creel was
arching his back and rubbing his limbs in an effort to
awaken the benumbed muscles. His dark hair was
shaggy and unkempt, his broad face shaded by a
three-day beard. He had a haggard look about him,
but the keen eyes burned warily as he met Shea's
inquisitive stare. The massive Keltset had moved

noiselessly to the summit of the hill and was surveying the northern horizon.

They had huddled in the sparse shelter of their rocky alcove for almost three days while the fierce northland storm had raged unchecked through the empty lands about them. Three days lost in the pursuit of Orl Fane and the Sword of Shannara—three days during which all traces of the elusive Gnome had been thoroughly obliterated. They had crouched restlessly amid the boulders, eating because it was necessary, sleeping because there was nothing else to do. Talking had given Shea and Panamon a greater understanding of one another, though Keltset still remained a complete enigma. Shea persisted in his belief that they should have ignored the storm and pursued their quarry, but Panamon had refused to discuss the idea. No one could travel far in such a storm, and Orl Fane would be forced to seek shelter or risk being caught in a mud slide or drowned in the swift gully rivers. In any event, the thief had calmly reasoned, the Gnome would have made little progress. Keltset descended from the crest of the hill, making a quick sweeping gesture with one hand. The horizon was clear.

There was no further discussion of what should be done. It was already decided. Picking up their meager possessions, they trudged briskly down the side of the steep embankment, angling northward. For once Shea and Panamon were in complete agreement. The search for the Sword of Shannara had become more than a matter of injured pride, more than a mission to seek out a mysterious talisman. It had become a dangerous, frantic hunt for the one means, however questionable, by which they might stay alive in this savage land.

The fortress of the Warlock Lord lay amid the tall, black peaks directly north. Behind them lay the deadly wall of mist that marked the outer boundaries of the Skull Kingdom. To escape this hated land, they would have to pass one way or the other. The obvious choice was to go back through the misty darkness, but while the Elfstones might show them a passage to the Southland, using them would also reveal their presence to the spirit world. Allanon had told Shea so at Culhaven, and he in turn had told Panamon. The Sword of Shannara was the one weapon that could protect them from the Warlock Lord, and if they had it in their possession, they could be assured of at least a fighting chance. The basic plan was to regain possession of the talisman and escape back through the wall of darkness as quickly as possible. It was hardly a brilliant strategy, but under the circumstances it would have to do.

Traveling was as difficult as it had been prior to the storm. The ground was hard and coated with rubble and loose topsoil that made the footing treacherous. Scrambling and clawing their way over the rough terrain, the three were quickly covered with dirt and bruised by continual falls. Because of the unevenness of the topography, it was difficult to keep their bearings and nearly impossible to calculate their progress. Landmarks were nonexistent and the country looked almost exactly the same in every direction. The minutes wore away with agonizing slowness, and still they discovered nothing. The humidity continued to rise and the garments worn by the three men were quickly soaked through with sweat. They removed their cloaks and tied them on their backs; it would be cold again when night descended.

"This is the place we last saw him."

Panamon stood motionlessly at the summit of the broad hill they had just scaled, breathing heavily. Shea reached his side and glanced about in disbelief. All the surrounding hills looked exactly the same as this one, save for small variations in size and shape. He stared dubiously at the horizon. He wasn't even sure where they had come from.

"Keltset, what do you see?" the other man demanded.

The Rock Troll strode slowly about the hilltop, scanning the ground for any trace left by the passage of the little Gnome, but the storm appeared to have erased any signs. He moved about noiselessly for several minutes more, then turned to them and shook his head negatively. Panamon's dirt-stained face burned red in sudden anger.

"He was here. We'll walk on a bit farther."

They moved ahead in silence, scrambling unceremoniously down one hill and up the next. There was no further discussion. There was nothing further to be said. If Panamon were mistaken, nobody had any better idea, except to keep looking. An hour crawled by as they labored northward. Still there was nothing. Shea began to realize the hopelessness of their task. It would be impossible to search all of the land stretching east and west; if the wily Gnome had traveled just fifty yards to either side of them, they would probably never know he had gone that way. Perhaps he had been buried in a mud slide during the storm along with the Sword and they would never find him.

Shea's muscles ached from the strenuous climbing, and he considered calling a brief halt to reassess their decision to proceed in this direction. Perhaps they should try to cut across the elusive trail. Yet a glance at Panamon's dark face quickly dissuaded the Valeman from even suggesting such an action. The tall adventurer had the same look in his face Shea had seen just before he had destroyed the Gnomes days ago. He was the hunter once more. If Panamon found him, Orl Fane was a dead man. Shea shuddered involuntarily and looked away.

Several hills later, they found a piece of what they were searching for. Keltset spotted it from atop a small hillock, his sharp eyes picking out the foreign object as it lay half buried in dust at the bottom of a small ravine.

Directing the other two, he slid quickly down the
rock-strewn hill and rushed eagerly over to the
discarded object, snatching it up and holding it out to
them. It was a large strip of cloth—cloth that had once
been the major portion of a tunic sleeve. They stared at
it quietly for a moment, and then Shea looked at
Keltset for confirmation that it was indeed Orl Fane's.
The giant Troll nodded solemnly. Panamon Creel
impaled the piece of cloth on the end of his pike,
smiling grimly.

"So we've found him again. This time he won't get
away!"

But they didn't find him that day, nor did they
discover any further signs of his passing. In the heavy
dust, the Gnome's footprints would have clearly
shown, yet there were none. Despite Panamon's
earlier opinion, Orl Fane had somehow wandered on
during the storm, escaping both mud slides and
drowning. The rain had washed away his tracks but,
with freakish perversity, had left uncovered the torn
sleeve. It could have been washed down from
anywhere, so there was no way to tell which direction
the Gnome had come from or gone. By nightfall, the
blackness shrouding the land was so heavy that it was
impossible to see more than several feet, and the
search was reluctantly abandoned for the night. With
Keltset standing the first watch, Panamon and Shea
collapsed in near exhaustion and fell asleep almost
instantly. The night air was cool, though the humidity
of the day lingered on, and all three wrapped
themselves once again in the half-dry hunting cloaks.

The morning returned all too swiftly in the familiar
graying haze. This day was not as humid as the
previous one, but it was no more cheerful; the sun was
still nearly blotted out by the leaden mist that hung
immovably overhead. The same eerie silence persisted
and the three men stared about with a feeling of
complete isolation from the living world. The vast

emptiness was beginning to have a noticeable effect on both Shea and Panamon Creel. Shea had grown edgy and nervous in these past several days and the normally cheerful and talkative Panamon had lapsed into almost total silence. Keltset alone retained his usual demeanor, his face as bland and implacable as ever.

A short breakfast was consumed without interest, and the search began again. They resumed the hunt almost with distaste; their common desire was to end this wearing trek quickly. They went ahead partly out of a sense of self-preservation and partly because they had nowhere else to go. Although neither realized it, both Panamon and Shea were beginning to wonder why Keltset continued the pursuit. He was in his own country and could probably have survived alone, had he chosen to go his own way. The two men had tried unsuccessfully to decipher Keltset's reasons for continuing on with them during the three-day rain, and now, too worn to reason the matter further, they had fallen back on suspicious acceptance of his presence and a growing determination that they would know who and what he was before this journey ended. They plodded on through the dust and the haze as the morning drifted dully into noonday.

It was totally unexpected when Panamon suddenly drew up short.

"Tracks!"

The tall thief let out a wild yell of delight and charged madly into the small draw to their left, leaving both Keltset and Shea staring after him in amazement. Moments later the trio knelt eagerly over a set of clearly defined footprints outlined in the heavy dust. There was no mistaking their origin; even Shea recognized that they were made by Gnome boots, worn and cracked about the heels. The trail they left was undisguised, leading generally northward, but weaving badly as if the destination of the man passing

were no longer certain. It almost appeared as if Orl
Fane were wandering aimlessly. They paused a
moment longer and then rose hurriedly at Panamon's
urgent command. The tracks were only hours old and,
judging from their meandering nature, the elusive Orl
Fane could be overtaken easily. Panamon could only
thinly disguise the almost vicious glee that surged
through his revitalized body as he saw the end of the
long hunt in sight. Without speaking further, the three
hitched up their cumbersome gear and moved northward in grim resolution. This was the day they would
catch Orl Fane.

The trail left by the little Gnome wound in erratically
confusing fashion through the dusty hills of the lower
Northland. At times the three found themselves
traveling almost directly eastward, and once they
were turned about entirely. The afternoon wore on
with tedious precision, and while Keltset indicated
that the footprints were growing fresher, it appeared
that they were still not gaining rapidly. If nightfall set
in before they had caught up with their quarry, they
might very well lose him once again. Twice before they
had been on the verge of catching him, and each time
an unexpected occurrence had forced them temporarily to abandon the search. They were not in the mood
to have this happen a third time, and Shea had
inwardly vowed that, if need be, he would track Orl
Fane even in total darkness.

The giant peaks of the forbidding Skull Kingdom
loomed menacingly in the distance, their black, razor
tips jutting knifelike into the horizon. There was a
sense of fear in the mind of the Valeman that he could
not shake, a fear that had grown steadily stronger as
the three men had pushed deeper into the Northland.
He had begun to feel that he was undertaking much
more than he had originally imagined, that somehow
the search for Orl Fane and the Sword of Shannara
was only a small part of a much larger scheme of

events. He was not yet panicked by what he felt, but he was prodded by an urgent need to finish this insane chase and turn back to his own land.

It was midafternoon when the hilly terrain began to level off into a rolling plainland that enabled the three men to see for greater distances and to walk upright in an almost relaxed manner for the first time since they had passed through the black wall. The country ahead spread out before them with breathtaking starkness, a bleak, empty plain of brown earth and gray rock that rolled unevenly northward toward the tall peaks that bordered the Skull Kingdom and the home of the Warlock Lord. These vast flatlands diminished the farther north the eye traveled, breaking around masses of rock and mountainous ridgeland that led in stepping-stone manner to the awesome peaks beyond. The entire expanse, naked, hot, and desolate, lay masked in the same eerie, deathly silence. Nothing moved, no creature stirred, no insect hummed, no bird flew, not even the wind brushed against the layered dust. Everywhere there was the same blasted emptiness, unmarked by life, shrouded with death. The winding tracks of Orl Fane led into this vastness and disappeared far in the distance. It was as if the land had swallowed him up.

The hunters paused for several long minutes, their faces mirroring their obvious reluctance to proceed into this unfriendly land. But there was little time for weighing the merits of the matter, and they moved ahead. The twisting path was visible for a greater distance in this rolling plainland, and the three pursuers were able to track on a more direct course. They began to make up time quickly. Less than two hours later Keltset indicated that they were no more than an hour behind their quarry. Dusk was rapidly approaching, the sun dipping behind a broken horizon far to the west. The dim twilight was masked further still by the ever-present gray haze, and the terrain was beginning to take on a peculiarly fuzzy appearance.

The trio had followed the Gnome's trail into a deep draw that was formed by a series of high ridges cropped by sharp overhangs and great, jutting rock formations. The fading sunlight was lost almost entirely in the shadows of the darkened valley, and Panamon Creel, who had eagerly taken the lead sometime earlier, was forced to squint sharply to find the outline of the footprints in the heavy dust. They slowed to a halting walk as the thief bent closer to the earth. So intent was Panamon Creel on studying the tracks immediately before him that it came as a shock when the prints abruptly ended. Shea and Keltset were at his side instantly, and it was only after a careful study of the ground ahead of them that they were able to discover that someone had methodically brushed away all further traces of the little Gnome's passing.

It was in that same instant that the huge, dark forms began to detach themselves from the shadows of the draw, lumbering ponderously forward in the deepening twilight. Shea saw them first, but believed his eyes were playing tricks on him. Panamon was quicker to realize what was happening. Springing upright, the thief drew out the great broadsword and raised his pike. He might have made a rush to break through the tightening ring, but the normally predictable Keltset did a surprising thing. Springing quickly forward, he pulled the astonished thief back. Panamon stared incredulously at his silent companion, then reluctantly lowered his weapons. There were at least a dozen forms standing guardedly all around the three men, and even in the hazy twilight a terrified Shea realized that they had been discovered by a band of giant Trolls.

The company of weary Elven riders reined in their

sweating mounts and gazed absently down the valley slopes into the broad length of the Rhenn. Two miles of empty valley stretched eastward before them, the high slopes to either side cresting in sharp ridges lined with thinning stretches of trees and scrub brush. The legendary pass had served for over a thousand years as the gateway from the lower Streleheim Plains to the great forests of the Westland, a natural door to the homeland of the Elves. It was in this famous pass that the awesome might of the armies of the Warlock Lord had been broken in defeat by the Elven legions and Jerle Shannara. It was here that Brona had faced and run from the aged Bremen and the mysterious power of the Sword of Shannara—run with his great armies back into the plainlands, only to be halted by advancing Dwarf armies, trapped, and destroyed. The Pass of Rhenn had seen the beginning of the downfall of the greatest threat the world had encountered since the devastating Great Wars, and the people of all the races looked upon this peaceful valley as a historic landmark. It was a natural monument of mankind's history that some had journeyed halfway around the world to see just so that they, too, might feel somehow a part of that terrible event.

Jon Lin Sandor gave the order to dismount, and the Elven riders climbed down gratefully. His concern was not with the history of the past but with the immediate future. Worriedly, he stared at the heavy black wall descending from the Northland across the Plains of Streleheim, its hazy shadow drawing daily nearer to the borders of the Westland and the home of the Elves. His sharp eyes peered far into the eastern horizon where the darkness had already permeated into the forests surrounding the ancient fortress of Paranor. He shook his head bitterly and cursed the day he had permitted himself to leave the side of his King and oldest friend. He had grown to manhood with Eventine, and when his friend became King he had stayed with him as his personal counselor and self-appointed watchdog. Together they had prepared for the invasion of the armies of Brona, the Spirit Lord they had once believed destroyed in the Second War of the Races. The mysterious wanderer Allanon had warned the Elven people, and while some had scoffed in misconceived disdain, Eventine had known better. Allanon had never been wrong; his ability to see into the future was uncanny, but unerringly accurate.

The Elven people had followed Eventine's advice and they had prepared for war, but the invasion did not come as expected. Then Paranor had fallen and with it the Sword of Shannara. Again Allanon had come to them, asking that they patrol the Plains of Streleheim above Paranor to guard against any attempt by the Gnomes holding the Druid fortress to move the Sword northward to the castle of the Warlock Lord. Again they had obeyed without question.

But the unexpected had happened, and it had happened while Jon Lin Sandor was away from the King. The Gnomes entrenched at Paranor had unexpectedly decided to break for the safety of the deep Northland, and three heavy patrols made a rush at the Elven lines. Eventine and Jon Lin had led separate commands to intercept two of these forces and would have destroyed the Gnomes easily had it not been for the planned intervention of a combined army of Gnomes and Trolls detached from the now advancing Northland army of the Warlock Lord. Jon Lin's command was nearly annihilated, and he barely escaped with his life. He had been unable to reach Eventine, and the Elven King had disappeared with his entire patrol. Jon Lin Sandor had been searching for him for nearly three days.

"We will find him, Jon Lin. He is not an easy one to kill. He will find a way to survive."

The grim Elf nodded with a barely perceptible shake

of his close-cropped head, his darting eyes glancing quickly at the young face of the man standing next to him.

"It's a strange thing, but I know he's alive," the other continued soberly. "I can't really explain how I know—it's just something I can sense."

Breen Elessedil was Eventine's younger brother; he was also the next King of the Westland Elves if his brother were dead. It was a position he was not yet ready for and quite honestly did not want. Since Eventine's disappearance he had done nothing to assume command of the languishing Elven armies or of the dismayed King's Council, but had joined immediately in the search for his brother. As a result, the Elven government was in a state of near chaos, and what had only two weeks earlier been a people united against the imminent threat of invasion from the north was now an unsure, divided cluster of separated groups, badly frightened because there was no one prepared to assume leadership of the government.

The Elven people would not panic altogether; they were far too disciplined to allow matters to fall apart totally. But Eventine had been an undeniably powerful personality, and the people had been united solidly behind him since his ascension to the throne. Young, but possessing unusual strength of character and an infallible common sense, he had always been there to advise them and they had always listened. The rumors of his disappearance had shaken the people badly.

But neither Breen Elessedil nor Jon Lin had time to worry about anything but finding the missing King. After skirting Gnome patrols and the main body of the Northland army while they searched, the haggard survivors of the decimated Elven patrols had returned briefly to the tiny outland village of Koos, where they had obtained fresh horses and supplies. Now they were on their way back to pick up the search once more.

Jon Lin Sandor believed he knew where Eventine

would be found, if he were still alive. The giant Northland army had moved south toward the Kingdom of Callahorn almost a week earlier, and it would pass no farther until the famed Border Legion had been destroyed. It was probable that if Eventine were a prisoner, as both Breen and he now believed must be the case, then they would find him with the commanders of Brona's invasion force as a hostage of great bargaining value. With Eventine Elessedil defeated, cities whose leaders were lesser men would be more willing to consider surrender.

In any event, the Warlock Lord recognized the importance of Eventine to the Elven people. He was the most revered and beloved leader the Elves had known since Jerle Shannara, and they would do almost anything to have him back safely. Dead, he would serve no purpose to the Spirit King, and his execution might so enrage the Elves that they would reunite in their common desire to destroy him. But alive, Eventine was of immeasurable worth, for the Elven people would not risk injury to their favorite son. Jon Lin Sandor and Breen Elessedil harbored no false illusions that Eventine would be safely returned to them, even if the army did not intervene in the Southland invasion. They were acting on their own initiative, gambling that they could find their friend and brother before his usefulness was ended—before the Southland fell.

"That's enough. Mount up!"

Jon Lin's impatient voice cut through the momentary stillness with biting sharpness, and the lounging riders leaped to their feet hurriedly in response. He stared a final time at the distant blackness, then turned and vaulted easily onto his waiting mount, gathering the reins in one swift motion. Breen was already at his side and seconds later the small body of horsemen was moving down the valley corridor at a fast trot. It was a gray morning, the air tinged with the pungent smell of last night's rain, still lingering on the plainlands. The tall grass was wet and yielding beneath the sharp hooves of the passing horses, muffling their impact. Far to the south a trace of deep blue sky could be seen beyond the clouds. It was a cool day, and the Elves rode comfortably in the moderate temperatures.

They reached the end of the valley quickly, pulling their eager mounts to a slow trot as they entered the eastern corridor of the pass. The riders talked among themselves, though in low tones, for the borders of the Northland lay just beyond the pass gateway. The line of horsemen wound snakelike through the high ridges framing the eastern entryway, and moments later emerged onto the vast expanse of the Plains of Streleheim. Jon Lin glanced almost casually across the emptiness that stretched out before him, and then abruptly reined in his horse.

"Breen—a horseman!"

Instantly the other was at his side and together they peered at the distant rider moving rapidly toward them. The Elves stared curiously, unable to make out the features of the advancing horseman in the hazy light. For one brief instant, Breen Elessedil was convinced it was his brother returning, but a moment later his hopes faded as he realized the man was too small to be Eventine. He was certainly no horseman. As he came up to them, he was hanging onto both the reins and the saddle horn for dear life, his broad face flushed and sweating from the effort. He was no Elf; he was a Southlander.

He brought his mount to a jolting halt in front of the Elven band, pausing to catch his breath before speaking. He studied the amused faces confronting him and his face turned a shade redder.

"I met a man a few days earlier," the stranger began. Then he hesitated to be certain he had their attention. "He asked me to seek out the right arm of the Elven King."

The looks of amusement faded instantly as the Elven riders leaned forward.

"I am Jon Lin Sandor," the patrol commander acknowledged quietly.

The exhausted rider sighed gratefully and nodded.

"I'm Flick Ohmsford, and I've come all the way from Callahorn to find you." With no little effort he dismounted and rubbed his aching backside. "If you'll give me a few minutes' rest, I'll take you to Eventine."

Shea marched in silence between two of his giant Troll captors, unable to shake the feeling that Keltset had betrayed them. The ambush had been cleverly sprung, but they might at least have attempted to fight their way clear. Instead, on Keltset's unexpected command, they had offered no resistance, allowing themselves to be willingly disarmed. Shea had hoped that Keltset might know one of the Trolls in the raiding party or that, being of the same race, he could reason with them and secure their release. But the giant Troll had not even tried to communicate with his captors, docilely permitting them to bind his hands without the slightest struggle. Panamon Creel and Shea had their weapons removed and their hands tied, and the three captives were marched northward into the barren flatlands. The little Valeman still had possession of the Elfstones, but they were useless against the Trolls.

He studied the broad back of Panamon, who was walking directly in front of him, wondering what the irascible thief's thoughts must be. The man had been so astonished at his companion's quick surrender that he had not spoken one word since. Obviously he could not bring himself to believe that he had so misjudged the silent giant, whose life he had saved and whose friendship he had valued. The Troll's behavior was a complete mystery to them both; but, whereas Shea was merely confused, Panamon Creel was deeply hurt. Whatever else there was between them, Keltset had been his friend—the one friend he felt he could depend on. The hardened adventurer's disbelief would quickly turn to hatred, and Shea had always known that whatever the circumstances, Panamon Creel was a dangerous man to make an enemy.

It was impossible to determine where they were being taken. The Northland night was a moonless black, and Shea was forced to turn his concentration to the task of finding his footing as the party wound its way northward through scattered boulders and high ridges strewn with loose earth and rock. The Troll tongue was completely foreign to the Valeman. Since Panamon had lapsed into brooding silence, Shea could learn nothing. If the Trolls had reason to suspect who he was, then they would be taken to the Warlock Lord. The fact that they had not bothered with the Elfstones might be an indication that his captors had seized them merely as intruders without realizing what had brought them to the Northland. The possibility offered little comfort; the Trolls would find him out quickly enough. He wondered suddenly what had become of the fleeing Orl Fane. His tracks had ended where they had been seized, so the Gnome must also be a prisoner. But where had they taken him? And what had become of the Sword of Shannara?

They marched for hours in the impenetrable darkness. Shea quickly lost all track of time, and finally became so exhausted that he collapsed and was carried like a sack of grain over the broad shoulder of one of his captors for the remainder of the journey. He awoke briefly to the flickering light of low-burning wood fires as the party entered an unfamiliar encampment, then felt himself lowered to the earth and led through the opening of a large tent. Inside his hands were checked to be certain the bonds were secure and his feet were bound. Moments later he was left alone. Panamon and Keltset had been taken elsewhere.

Briefly, he struggled with the leather thongs that held his hands and feet, but they would not loosen and finally he gave it up. He could feel himself drifting into sleep, the weariness from the long march flooding through his aching body. He tried to fight it, forcing himself to conceive a plan of escape. The harder he tried, the more difficult it became to think of anything, and everything in his tired mind grew steadily more hazy. He was asleep in five minutes.

It seemed only moments later that he was awakened by rough hands shaking him out of the deep slumber into which he had fallen. He rose dazedly as a heavyset Troll spoke something unintelligible to him and pointed to a plate of food before passing out of the tent into the sunlight beyond. Shea squinted in the darkness of the tent, absently noting the familiar grayness of the Northland morning that signaled the beginning of another day. Realizing with mild astonishment that the leather bonds had been removed, he briskly rubbed his wrists and ankles to restore the circulation and then ate quickly the meal prepared for him.

There appeared to be a great deal of excitement outside his tent, and the shouts and cries of Trolls moving hurriedly about the encampment filled the morning air. The Valeman finished his meal and had just determined to risk a glance through the closed flaps of the tent entrance, when they were abruptly whipped aside. A burly Troll guard stepped inside and motioned for Shea to come with him. With one hand tightly clenching his tunic front, where he could feel the reassuring bulk of the Elfstones, the Valeman reluctantly followed.

An escort of Trolls led the small Southlander through a large encampment consisting of various-sized tents and stone huts constructed on a wide bluff

surrounded by a series of low ridges. Glancing at the
distant horizon, he could tell that they were high
above the barren plainlands they had crossed the
previous night. The camp appeared deserted, and the
voices Shea had heard earlier had faded entirely. The
fires of the night before had died into ashes, and the
tents and huts were all empty. A sudden chill struck
the frightened captive, and it occurred to him that he
was probably being led to his own execution. There
was no sign of either Panamon or Keltset. Allanon,
Flick, Menion Leah and all the others were somewhere
in the Southland, unaware of his predicament. He was
alone, and he was going to die. He was so paralyzed
with fear that he could not even attempt to flee. He
moved woodenly between his captors as they wound
their way through the silent camp. A low ridge,
marking the boundary of the encampment, loomed
directly ahead of them, and then they were past the
huts and tents and standing in a broad, open clearing.
Shea stared in disbelief.

Dozens of Trolls were seated in a wide semicircle
facing the ridge, their heads turned toward him
momentarily as he entered the clearing. At the base of
the ridge sat three Trolls of varying sizes and, though
Shea could not be certain, probably of varying ages as
well, each holding a brightly colored staff with a black
pennant. Panamon Creel had been seated within the
wide circle to one side. He had a peculiarly pensive
look that did not alter as he caught sight of Shea. The
attention of everyone was focused on the massive
form of Keltset standing motionless in the center of the
expectant Trolls, his arms folded as he faced the three
staff bearers. He did not turn as Shea was led into the
circle and seated next to the thoughtful Panamon.
There was a long moment of complete silence. It was
the strangest spectacle Shea had ever witnessed. Then
one of the three Trolls seated at the apex of the circle
rose ceremoniously and tapped his staff lightly to the

earth. The assemblage rose as one, turned sharply to
face eastward, and spoke in unison several short lines
in their own tongue. Then quietly they sat down
again.

"Can you imagine? They were praying."

They were the first words Panamon had spoken,
and Shea started in surprise. He glanced quickly at the
thief, but the big man was looking at Keltset. Another
of the three Trolls presiding over the strange assembly
rose and spoke briefly to the attentive audience,
gesturing several times toward Panamon and Shea.
The little Valeman turned expectantly to his companion.

"This is a trial, Shea," the thief declared in a
strangely dispassionate tone. "Not for you or me,
however. We're to be taken to the Skull Mountain
beyond the Knife Edge, the Kingdom of the Warlock
Lord, where we'll be held for . . . whatever. I don't
think they know who we are yet. It is the command of
the Spirit Lord that all outlanders be brought to him,
and we're being treated no differently. There's hope
still."

"But a trial . . .?" Shea began doubtfully.

"For Keltset. He has demanded the right to be tried
by his own people rather than be turned over to Brona.
It's an ancient custom—the request cannot be refused.
He was found with us when his people were at war
with our race. Any Troll found with a Man is
presumed a traitor. There are no exceptions."

Shea glanced involuntarily at Keltset. The massive
Troll was seated with rocklike solidity in the center of
the waiting assemblage as the voice of the presiding
Troll continued to drone on. They had been mistaken,
the Valeman thought gratefully. Keltset had not
betrayed them; he had not given them away after all.
But why had he allowed them to be taken captive so
easily when he knew his own life would be forfeit as
well?

"What will they do to him if they decide he is a traitor?" he asked impulsively.

A slight smile appeared on the tall man's lips.

"I know what you must be thinking." There was a touch of irony in the mocking voice. "He is risking everything on this trial. If they find him guilty, he will be immediately thrown over the nearest cliff."

He paused meaningfully and for the first time looked directly at the Valeman.

"I don't understand it either."

They lapsed into silence once more as the speaker finished his lengthy statement and sat down. After a moment, a single Troll came to stand before the three presiding Trolls, whom Shea now realized must be judges, and made a brief statement. He was followed by several others, each of whom spoke briefly, responding to questions put to them by the judges. Shea could understand nothing of what was taking place, but supposed that the Trolls were members of the raiding party that had captured them the previous night. The examination seemed to drag on forever, and still Keltset had not moved a muscle.

Shea studied the impassive giant, unable to understand why he had chosen to allow matters to go this way. Both Shea and Panamon had known for some time that Keltset was no ordinary outcast, driven from his home and his people because he was unable to speak. Nor was he simply the thief and adventurer that Panamon had tried to make him. There was intelligence in those strangely gentle eyes. There was an unspoken knowledge of the Sword of Shannara, the Warlock Lord, and even Shea that had never been revealed. There was a past hidden deep within the giant's heart. He was Allanon all over again, Shea thought suddenly. Somehow both held the key to the secret of the power of the Sword of Shannara. It was a strange revelation, and the Valeman shook his head questioningly, doubtful of his own reasoning. But there was no more time to think.

The witnesses had finished, and the three judges had now called upon the accused to rise and defend himself. There was an impossibly long, agonizing moment of unbroken silence as the judges, the assembled Trolls, Panamon Creel, and Shea all waited expectantly for Keltset to rise. Still the giant Rock Troll sat motionless as if caught in an unbreakable trance. Shea was seized with an almost uncontrollable urge to shout wildly, if only to break the unbearable silence, but the sound caught in his throat. The seconds crawled by. Then without warning, Keltset rose.

He drew his massive frame erect, abruptly taking on the appearance of a creature who was somehow more than mortal. There was pride in his bearing as he faced the waiting tribunal, his eyes fixed on the three judges. Without shifting his gaze even slightly, he reached under the broad leather belt that bound his waist and drew forth a large black metal pendant and chain. For a moment he held it in his hands before the eyes of the judges, who leaned forward in obvious surprise. Shea caught a quick glimpse of a cross centered in a circle, and then the giant raised the chain ceremoniously above his head and settled it slowly about his great neck.

"By the gods that gave us life . . . I don't believe it!" Panamon gasped in startled disbelief.

The judges, too, rose in astonishment. As Keltset turned slowly about the circle of wondering Trolls, shouts of excitement broke from their mouths and they were on their feet instantly, gesturing wildly at the impassive giant in their midst. Shea stared with the rest of them, completely befuddled.

"Panamon, what's happening!?" he cried finally.

The intense roar of the aroused assemblage nearly drowned out his words, and Panamon Creel was suddenly on his feet, too, one broad hand clapping down on Shea's slim shoulder.

"I don't believe it," the thief repeated with unrestrained joy. "All these months I've never even suspected it. That's what he's been hiding from us all along, my young Valeman! That's why he allowed us to be taken without a fight. But there must be more still . . ."

"Will you tell me what's happening?" Shea demanded heatedly.

"The pendant, Shea—the cross and circle!" the other shouted wildly. "It's the Black Irix, the highest award, the greatest honor the Troll people can give to one of their own! If you see three given in your lifetime, it's unusual. To receive one, you must be the living image of everything the Troll nation cherishes and strives to attain. You must be the closest thing to a god that a mortal being can approach. Somewhere in his past, Keltset has earned this honor—and we never guessed!"

"But what about the fact that he was found with us . . .?" The little Valeman got only part of the query out.

"Anyone who wears the Irix would never betray his own people," Panamon cut in sharply. "The honor carries with it an unbreakable trust. The wearer would never breach the laws of his people—he's presumed incapable of even contemplating such a thing. They believe that violation of such a trust would mean an eternity of punishment too horrible to imagine. No Troll would consider it."

Shea stared dazedly back at Keltset as the shouting continued unchecked. The great Troll was again facing his judges while the three vainly attempted to restore order to the unheeding assembly. It took several minutes more before the noise abated enough for anyone to be heard. The Trolls reseated themselves, anxiously waiting for Keltset to speak. There was a brief pause as a Troll interpreter appeared at the side of the silent defendant, then Keltset began to communicate in sign language. His eyes on Keltset's massive hands, the interpreter translated the explanation to the judges in the Troll language. There was a brief exchange with one of the judges, none of which Shea was able to understand, but fortunately Panamon had already begun his own translation, whispering quietly to his anxious friend.

"He told them that he comes from Norbane, one of the larger Troll cities in the far northern Charnal Mountains. His family name is Mallicos—it belongs to a very old and honored family. But they were all killed, supposedly by Dwarfs who had attempted to loot their family home. That judge on the left was asking Keltset how he had escaped; they had thought him dead as well. It must have been a pretty grisly affair for even this distant village to hear about it. But then—wait til you hear this, Shea! Keltset says the emissaries of the Warlock Lord destroyed his family! The Skull Bearers came to Norbane almost a year ago, seizing control of the government and ordering the Troll armies to accept their command. They managed to convince most of the city that Brona had come back from the dead, that he had survived for thousands of years and could not be killed by mortal hands. The Mallicos family was one of the ruling families in Norbane, and they refused to submit, demanding that the city stand firm against the Warlock Lord. Keltset's word carried a lot of weight because he wore the Black Irix. The Warlock Lord had the entire Mallicos family decimated except for Keltset, whom he brought to his fortress in the Knife Edge. The story of the Dwarf looters was a deception to inflame the Troll citizenry to join in the Southland invasion.

"But Keltset managed to escape before they got him to the prisons, wandering southward until I found him. The Warlock Lord had ordered that his voice be burned out to prevent his communication with any living being, but he learned sign language. He waited for his chance to return to the Northland. . . ."

One of the judges suddenly interrupted and Panamon paused momentarily.

"The judge asked why he returned now. Our big friend says he learned of Brona's fear of the power of the Sword of Shannara and the legend that a son of the Elven house would appear to take up the Sword . . ."

Panamon trailed off abruptly as the interpreter turned back to Keltset. For the first time the giant Troll faced toward Shea, the strangely gentle eyes fixed intently on the little Valeman. An involuntary chill shook Shea. Then his massive companion gestured briefly to the waiting judges. Panamon hesitated, then spoke softly.

"He says they must go with him to the Skull Kingdom, and that once inside the fortress, you, Shea, will destroy the Warlock Lord!"

XXXI

alance Buckhannah died at dawn. Death came quietly, almost unexpectedly, as the first faint golden rays of sunlight crept searchingly into the darkness of the eastern horizon. He died without regaining consciousness. When Balinor was told, he merely nodded his head in acknowledgment and turned away. His friends stayed with him momentarily until Hendel silently motioned for them all to leave. In the hallway beyond the death room, they gathered quietly and spoke in hushed voices. Balinor was the last of the Buckhannahs. If he died in the coming battle, the family name would disappear from the earth. Only history would remember.

In the same hour, the assault on Tyrsis began. It, too, came quietly, born with the dying of the night. As the waiting soldiers of the entrenched Border Legion peered into the gray plains below the great city walls, the light from the slowly rising sun revealed the mammoth Northland army spread out all the way to the distant Mermidon, the carefully drawn formations giving a checkerboard appearance to the deep green of the grasslands. One moment the vast army stood silent, motionless on the plains below the city, shadows etched out of the darkness by dawn into figures of flesh and blood, iron and stone, and in the next they began to advance on the Tyrsian defenders. The silence broke sharply with the sudden booming of

Gnome war drums, the deep, throbbing beat ringing ominously against the stone walls of Tyrsis.

The Northlanders came slowly, steadily to the battle, the crashing of the drums matched by the thudding of booted feet marching in ragged time, metal clinking sharply against metal as weapons and armor braced for the assault. They came voicelessly, thousands and thousands of them, armored figures faceless in the deep morning gloom. Great hulking rampways made of timbers bound in iron creaked ponderously as they were pulled and pushed on metal-rimmed wheels through the half-light, mobile pathways to the heights of the fortified bluff.

The seconds ticked away as the massive attack force moved to within a hundred yards of the waiting Legion, and still the crashing drums maintained their unhurried pace. The rim of the sun became sharply visible in the east and the waning night faded entirely in the western horizon. The drums abruptly ceased, and the sprawling army came to a sudden halt. For an instant there was a deep, unbroken silence that hung in frightened hesitation on the morning air. Then a deafening roar rose from the throats of the Northland-ers; with a great surge, the massive juggernaut charged, wave upon wave rushing to grapple with the men of the Border Legion.

From beneath the closed gates of the towering Outer Wall, Balinor stared out at the awesome Northland assault, his broad face coolly impassive. His voice was calm and steady as he spoke briefly to his runners, sending one scurrying to find Acton and Fandwick on the left flank, the other to Messaline and Ginnisson on the right. His eyes returned instantly to the terrifying spectacle below the bulwarks as the wild charge drew closer. Behind the hastily constructed defenses, the Legion archers and spearmen waited patiently for his command. Balinor knew they could break even this massive charge from their superior defensive position, but they must first destroy the five broad rampways that were rolling slowly toward the base of the bluff. He had correctly anticipated that such devices would be used to scale the plateau and its low bulwarks, just as the enemy had foreseen that he would destroy the city rampway. The vanguard of the Northland rush was within fifty feet of the bluff, and still the new King of Callahorn watched and waited.

Then abruptly the ground opened beneath the feet of the charging enemy and great holes appeared as the attackers fell screaming into the ring of camouflaged pits concealed all along the base of the plateau. Two of the monstrous rolling rampways tumbled unchecked into the wide openings, the wheels snapping loose and the timbers shattering in splinters. The first wave of the mighty rush hesitated and from atop the low bulwarks the Legion archers rose on Balinor's long-awaited signal, to fire point-blank into the ranks of the suddenly confused enemy. The dead and wounded alike fell helplessly on the plainlands and were quickly trampled under as the second wave of the sustained charge pushed through, struggling to reach the entrenched Legion.

Three of the heavy rampways had avoided the concealed pits and continued to roll unhindered toward the low bulwarks. The Legion archers quickly loosed a flurry of burning arrows onto the vulnerable wooden backs of the ramps, but dozens of nimble yellow bodies were immediately seen to scramble atop the flaming timbers to smother the fires. The Gnome archers were also in position by this time, and for several minutes a concentrated barrage of arrows cut through the ranks of both sides. The completely exposed Gnomes crawling about on the rampways were cut to pieces. Everywhere men fell screaming in pain as the deadly missiles found their human targets. The wounded men of the Border Legion were sheltered in part from further injury by the low bulwarks and could be treated for their wounds. But the fallen Northlanders lay helpless and unprotected on the open field, and hundreds were killed before they could be removed to safety.

The three remaining rampways were still rolling toward the base of the fortified bluff, though one was now burning fiercely, great clouds of billowing smoke obscuring the vision of everyone passing within a hundred yards. When the two remaining ramps were within twenty yards of the bulwarks, Balinor signaled for his final defense. Huge caldrons of oil were lifted to the rim of the Southland defenses and the contents splashed down onto the grassland below, directly in the path of the rolling rampways. Before the charging Northlanders had time to veer in either direction, torches were dropped in the midst of the spreading oil and the entire area disappeared in a mass of flames and heavy black smoke.

The sustained enemy assault broke apart as the oncoming waves of attackers hesitated in fright at the wall of flames confronting them. The foremost ranks of the enemy had been burned alive; only a few managed to flee successfully from the terrible carnage at the base of the Legion defenses. The wind was blowing the dark smoke laterally across the open plains to the west, and for several moments the center and left flank of the two great armies were visually cut off from each other and from the wounded and dying who lay helplessly in the midst of the choking fumes.

Instantly Balinor saw his chance. A sharp counter-thrust now might break the assault completely and rout the Northland army. Leaping to his feet, he signaled to Janus Senpre atop the Outer Wall, who had been left in command of the city garrison. Immediately the massive ironbound gates swung ponderously outward, and the mounted regiment of the Border Legion, armed with short swords and long, hooked pikes, their leopard colors flying brightly, galloped onto the bluff, wheeling sharply left to follow the open pathway along the city wall. Within moments they had reached the left flank of the Legion defensive line where Acton and Fandwick had command of the entrenched Bordermen. A portable rampway was hastily lowered from the bluff rim onto the smoke-clouded plains below, and the Legion riders, led by Acton, thundered downward and swung left in a wide circle.

Balinor's instructions called for the famed regiment to cut around the wall of smoke and launch a sustained charge on the enemy's right flank. As the Northlanders turned to meet this counterattack, Balinor would bring a regiment of foot soldiers to strike at the exposed Northland front, driving the enemy back toward the Mermidon. If the counterthrust should falter, both commands were immediately to swing back into the covering smoke and return up the waiting rampways. It was a daring gamble. The Northlanders outnumbered the Legion soldiers at least twenty to one, and if the Tyrsians should be cut off, they would be completely decimated.

Small commands of Legion foot soldiers had already descended the mobile rampway on the left flank and staged a short counterattack into the enemy ranks as a defensive measure to protect the mounted regiment's only link with the besieged city. For the moment, the enemy seemed to have disappeared entirely on the left flank, totally obscured by the smoke which was blowing in blinding clouds from the burning rampways at the center of the defensive line.

On the right defensive flank, the fighting was ferocious. Only a light, drifting haze of smoke and dust obscured the vision of the two armies at this point, and the Northland assault continued unchecked. The entrenched Legion archers had decimated the first wave of attackers, but the second wave had reached the base of the bluff and was attempting to gain the fortified heights with the aid of rough-hewn scaling ladders. Lines of Gnome archers fired hundreds of arrows into the low bulwarks in an attempt to keep the defenders pinned down long enough to allow the exposed climbers to scramble over the Tyrsian defenses. The Legion archers returned the fire while their comrades used iron-tipped pikes from the rim of the defenses to push away the enemy assault.

It was a long, bloody fight during which neither side rested. At one point, a particularly fierce band of rangy Rock Trolls breached the Legion defenses and rushed onto the open bluff. A fierce battle raged for a short time as the bulky Legion commander Ginnisson, his florid face as red as his long hair, rallied his soldiers to resist the great Trolls; in bloody hand-to-hand combat, the Legionnaires killed the small band of attackers and closed the breach.

At the summit of the high Outer Wall, four old friends stood in silence with Janus Senpre and watched the terrible spectacle unfolding below them. Hendel, Menion Leah, Durin and Dayel had all been left inside the city, their assignment to observe the progress of the battle and to aid Balinor in coordinating the movements of the Legion. The rolling smoke clouds totally obscured the giant borderman's vision of the movements of his mounted regiment, and only those atop the towering city walls could advise him of its progress so that he could launch his own assault from the center of the defensive line at the proper moment. The King relied particularly on Hendel's judgment, for the taciturn Dwarf had been fighting nearly thirty years in the Anar border wars.

Now the grizzled hunter, the Southlander, and the Elven brothers stared anxiously at the panorama spread out on the plains beneath them. On the right defensive flank, the fighting was the heaviest, as the determined Northlanders continued to batter the entrenched Legion, struggling to scale the face of the bluff. The Border Legion was holding on, but it was taking everything it had to beat back the ferocious assault. The plains immediately below the city gates at the center of the bulwarks were obscured by the burning oil and wooden rampways, which had crumbled entirely into masses of flaming timbers. At the fringes of the smoke, the disorganized Northlanders were vainly attempting to draw up their confused battle lines to renew the shattered charge. On the left, the Legion horsemen had broken out of the cover of the rolling black smoke and were encountering their first signs of resistance.

A large squad of Gnome cavalry had been stationed on the right attack flank as a defensive measure against exactly the kind of maneuver that was under way. However, the Northlanders had anticipated some advance warning of any flanking assault and were caught completely by surprise. The poorly trained Gnome riders were quickly scattered by the Border Legion and the attack on the Northland army's exposed flank began in earnest. Fanning wide to the north, the fabled regiment lowered its hooked pikes and formed a wall three columns deep, charging into the center of the astonished enemy. Acton led his soldiers in a precision rush that cut deeply into the exposed flank and nearly routed the extreme right of the Northland army. As the little group atop the Outer Wall watched expectantly, the enemy instantly readjusted its lines to the right of center to meet this new attack; as they did so, Hendel immediately signaled down to Balinor. A second rampway was lowered from the center of the defensive lines, and the tall figure of Messaline was seen to appear at the head of a second regiment of Legion soldiers, who descended on foot onto the smoke-clouded grasslands. A rear guard remained posted at the foot of the mobile ramp as the second regiment disappeared into the dark haze. Balinor closed his defensive lines and hurriedly joined his friends atop the great wall to observe the outcome of his counterthrust.

It had been perfectly executed. Just as the surprised right flank of the massive Northland army wheeled to face the oncoming charge of the Border Legion's mounted regiment, the foot soldiers commanded by Messaline attacked from out of the smoke at the center of the defensive line. In a tightly drawn phalanx, with spears bristling through a wall of locked shields, the highly trained Legion advanced into the midst of the unprepared and confused enemy. Like cattle, the Northlanders were herded backward, scores dropping, dying and wounded every few paces. The horsemen of Acton continued to press in from the left. The entire right wing of the enemy line began to collapse, and the cries of terror grew so shrill that even the fierce assault on the right defensive flank wavered momentarily as the bewildered Northlanders stared westward in a vain effort to discover what had happened. From the summit of the Outer Wall, Menion Leah stared in amazement.

"It's unbelievable. The Legion is actually driving them back. They're beaten!"

"Not yet," breathed Hendel softly. "The real test comes in a moment."

The highlander's eyes returned to the battle. The Northlanders were still falling back before the onslaught of the attacking Legion, but there was fresh activity taking place behind the lines of the retreating enemy. The army of the Warlock Lord would not be defeated so easily; what it lacked in training, it made up for in size. Already a vast command of mounted Gnome horsemen was racing around the rear of the driven foot soldiers, called up to meet the attack of the Legion riders. The Gnomes drew up immediately north of Acton's advancing horsemen; supported by several lines of archers and slingers, they rushed to the attack. From the rear center of the enemy army, a vast body of tall figures sheathed entirely in armor had drawn into a tight, boxlike formation and had begun to advance through its own wilting army toward the Legion foot soldiers. For a moment, the men atop the Outer Wall stared speculatively, then started in astonishment as the armored warriors suddenly began to cut their way with pikes and swords through the retreating men of their own army. It was the most savage act Menion had ever witnessed.

"Rock Trolls!" Balinor exclaimed heatedly. "They'll slaughter Messaline and his whole command. Signal retreat, Janus."

Obediently, his newest commander hoisted a large red pennant on a nearby staff. Menion Leah stared curiously at the silent borderman. It seemed that the battle had been nearly won, and still he had called for a retreat. He caught the King's eye, and the borderman smiled grimly at the unspoken question in the highlander's eyes.

"Rock Trolls are trained to fight from birth—it's their way of life. In hand-to-hand combat, they are better fighters than the men of the Border Legion. They are better trained and much stronger physically. We have nothing to gain in pressing the attack. We've already hurt them badly, and we still hold the bluff. If we plan to defeat them, we must chip away at their strength a piece at a time."

Menion nodded in understanding. With a brief wave, Balinor left the battlements to return to his command below. His primary concern at the moment was protecting the path of retreat for his two regiments, and that meant a successful defense of the portable ramps, the soldiers' only link with the city. The highlander watched the broad figure disappear from view, then turned back to the wall. The carnage on the plains below was frightful. The bodies of slain and wounded men lay scattered all the way from the bluff face to the rear lines of the Northland army. It was the worst slaughter that any of the little group had ever witnessed, and they watched speechlessly as the terrible struggle continued.

In the distance, the Legion foot soldiers under Messaline's command had begun an orderly retreat back toward the city defenses, but the giant Rock Trolls had almost succeeded in forcing their way through the milling front ranks of their own army and were preparing to pursue the hated Tyrsians. While the foot soldiers were withdrawing without opposition, the mounted regiment had encountered unexpected resistance from the charging Gnome horsemen. The two forces were engaged in a fierce battle to the left of the advancing Trolls. Acton was apparently either unable or unwilling to break away from the persistent attackers, and his riders were being subjected to a withering cross fire from the double line of Gnome archers positioned directly to his north. A large mixed body of Gnome and Troll swordsmen had worked their way around behind the charging horsemen, and now Acton's command was boxed in on three sides.

Hendel began to mutter angrily to himself. For the first time, Menion became concerned. Even Janus Senpre was pacing the walkway nervously. Their worst fears were realized a moment later. The pursuing body of Trolls, fresh for the wearing chase, had rushed forward so rapidly that the retreating men of Tyrsis, tired and worn from their counterattack, had been unable to gain the safety of the bluff. Almost a hundred yards from the waiting rampway, they turned to fight. The billowing smoke from the scattered fires rolled like a black wall in front of the low bulwarks, completely obscuring Balinor's vision as he waited before the city gates, but the unexpected turn of events was clearly visible to the horrified men watching from atop the towering city wall.

"I've got to warn Balinor!" Hendel exclaimed abruptly, leaping down from his position on the parapets. "That whole command will be cut to pieces!"

Janus Senpre left with him, but Menion and the Elven brothers continued to stare helplessly, unable to tear themselves away as the giant Rock Trolls bore down on Messaline's weary men. The Legion soldiers had drawn together with shields locked and spears extended, the shafts braced against the hard earth for the rush. The Trolls, too, had gone into a phalanx formation, somewhat wider than it was long, their intention clearly to close in on the Southlanders from three sides and break their defense by sheer strength. Menion glanced hastily over the wall, but Balinor had not moved, still unaware that an entire regiment of the famed Border Legion was on the verge of annihilation. Even as the highlander shifted his glance back to the plainlands, he saw Hendel and Janus reach the tall borderman's side, gesturing wildly. It would not be in time, Menion shouted inwardly. They were going to be too late.

But suddenly a strange thing happened. Acton's entire mounted command, momentarily forgotten by the viewers on the city wall, unexpectedly broke away from the attacking Gnome horsemen with an abrupt surge and came together in perfect formation, swinging in a sharp arc directly east behind the pursuing Rock Trolls. At a full gallop, the superb horsemen cut through the Gnome riders who barred their way. Oblivious to the hail of arrows showered down from the enraged Gnome archers, they raced directly toward the Troll ranks. Pikes lowered, the regiment struck the rear lines of the Troll phalanx in a raking movement, continuing its sweep eastward across the plains. The giant warriors were caught by surprise and dozens crumpled to the ground as the pikes cut into them.

But these were the finest fighting men in the world, and they recovered instantly, closing their ranks and turning to meet this new threat. As Acton's horsemen swung westward once more, racing back at breakneck speed, raking across the rear of the Troll phalanx a second time, the Northlanders struck back viciously with hurled pikes and maces. Over a dozen riders fell lifelessly from their mounts, and an equal number slumped wounded in their saddles as the regiment charged eastward and then cut sharply south for the safety of Tyrsis.

Acton had accomplished his purpose; the timely diversion had permitted Messaline's besieged regiment to make a sudden break for the concealing smoke. It was a brilliantly executed maneuver, and atop the Outer Wall those watching shouted with unrestrained admiration.

Though pursued by the foremost ranks of the infuriated Trolls, the Legion foot soldiers had escaped into the concealing smoke, and most, with the aid of Balinor at the head of a relief squad, gained the safety of the waiting ramp. A sharp battle was fought at the foot of the bluff as the regiment struggled to withdraw the lowered bridge before the enemy could seize it. Finally, it was simply cast loose from the bulwarks and dropped onto the plain below, where it lay intact only moments before the Tyrsians set it ablaze and destroyed it.

On the left defensive flank, the embattled rear guard fought bravely to hold the other rampway, as Acton's command raced still another time within range of the maddened Gnome archers and still more died. It was a running battle all the way, and at one point the horsemen had to charge directly through the center of a thin line of swordsmen that rushed down to cut off their escape. But at last the harried riders reached the haven of the bluff, galloping up the rampway almost without slowing and swinging toward the opened gates of the city, where they were greeted by crowds of cheering soldiers and citizens. As the last of the returning cavalry gained the heights, the rear guard hastily withdrew behind their defenses and the rampway was hauled to safety.

It was midday by this time, and the heat of the noon sun settled like a humid blanket over the men of both armies. In sullen reluctance, the Northland army withdrew from the battle to regroup, dragging with it hundreds of dead and wounded. The smoke from the burning oil hung in an unmoving haze over the strangely silent grasslands as the morning wind faded quietly away. The ground before the bluff face was littered with the charred bodies of the dead, and small fires still burned persistently as the great timbers of the shattered rampways turned slowly to ashes. A foul stench began to rise from the terrible battlefield, and scavengers that flew and crawled appeared with shrill, eager cries to feast. Across the battered land, the armies watched each other with undisguised hatred, weary and racked with pain, but eager to resume the killing that had been thrust upon them. For several long hours, the once green land lay empty beneath the cloudless blue sky as its scarred surface baked and dried in the heat of the summer sun. It began to appear to those who allowed their reason to slip in favor of wishful thinking that the assault had ended—that the destruction was finished. Thoughts turned hopefully from killing and survival to family and loved ones. The shadow of death lifted momentarily.

Then in the late hours of the waning afternoon, the Northland army attacked again. As lines of Gnome archers showered the low bulwarks and the bluff beyond with a seemingly endless barrage of arrows, large bands of mixed swordsmen, Gnome and Troll, made sharp rushes at the Southland defenses, trying vainly to discover a weak point. Portable ramps, small scaling ladders, and grappling hooks with knotted ropes—all were tried to force a breach in the Legion lines, but each time the attackers were repelled. It was a wearing, vicious assault designed to tire and discourage the men of Tyrsis. The long day died slowly into dusk, and still the pitched battle wore on. It ended in darkness and tragedy for the Border Legion. As twilight descended on the bloodied land, the weary foes launched a final hail of spears and arrows at each other across the hazy void they could scarcely see through. A stray arrow caught Acton through the throat as the Legion cavalry commander was returning from his command on the left defensive flank, knocking the great fighter from his mount into the reaching arms of his attendants, where he died moments later.

The kingdom of the Warlock Lord was the single most desolate, forbidding piece of country in the known world—a barren, lifeless ring of impassable death traps. The tender, life-giving hand of nature had long since been driven from this thankless domain of darkness, and the wilderness that remained lay wrapped in silence. Its eastern borders were mired in the gloom and fetid stench of the vast Malg Swamp, a dismal, sprawling bog that no living creature had ever successfully traversed. Beneath the shallow waters, on which floated loose patches of colorless weeds that grew and died in the span of a day, the earth had turned to mud and quicksand, and all that came within its grip were sucked quickly from sight. The Malg was said to be bottomless, and while, scattered throughout its vast expanse, small bits of solid earth and great, skeletal limbs of dying trees could still be glimpsed, even these were fading one by one.

Across the far northern stretches, extending westward from the Malg, was a rambling series of low-backed mountains appropriately named the Razors. There were no passes through these mountains and their wide, sloped backs were craggy, jutting slabs of rock, seemingly pushed upward from the bowels of the earth. An experienced and determined climber might still have found the Razors passable—one or two men had even made the attempt—had it not been for the particularly venomous species of spider that nested in vast numbers throughout the barren mountains. The bleached bones of the dead, scattered in small white patches among the darkened rocks, gave mute testimony to their unavoidable presence.

There was a break in the deadly ring where the Razors tapered off into foothills at the northwest corner of the kingdom, and for over five miles southward the country was easily passable, opening directly into the center of the circle of barriers. Here there was no natural protection against intruders, but this small gateway to the interior of the kingdom was also the obvious approach, and hence the trapdoor to the cage through which the Lord and Master waited for the unwary to step. Eyes and ears responsive only to his command guarded the narrow strip of land carefully. The ring could be locked instantly. Directly below the foothills, a vast, arid wasteland called the Kierlak Desert ran southward for nearly fifty miles. A heavy, poisonous vapor hung invisibly over the sprawling, sand-covered plains, drawn from the waters of the River Lethe, a venomous stream that wound lazily into the fiery emptiness from the south and emptied into a small lake in the interior. Even birds chancing to fly too close to the deadly haze were killed in seconds. Creatures dying in the terrible furnace of sand and poisonous air decayed in a matter of hours and turned to dust, so that nothing remained to show their passing.

But the most formidable barrier of all stretched menacingly across the southern boundary of the forbidden domain, beginning at the southeasterly edges of the Kierlak Desert and running eastward to the marshy borders of the Malg Swamp. The Knife Edge. Like great stone spears driven into the hard earth by some monstrous giant, these mountains towered thousands of feet into the sky. They had the appearance not so much of mountains as a series of awesome peaks jutting in broken lines that blocked the dim horizon like fingers stretching painfully. At their base swirled the toxic waters of the River Lethe, which had its origin in the Malg Swamp and meandered westward at the base of the great rock barrier to disappear into the impregnable vapors of the Kierlak Desert. Only a man driven by an unexplainable madness would have attempted to scale the Knife Edge.

There was a passage through the barrier, a small, winding canyon that opened onto a series of craggy foothills which ran for several thousand yards to the base of a single, ominously solitary mountain just within the southern boundary of the ring. The scarred surface of this mountain was chipped and worn by time and the elements, lending the southern facing a singularly menacing appearance. On even the most casual inspection, one was immediately struck by the frightening similarity the south wall bore to a human skull, stripped of flesh and life, the pate rounded and gleaming above the empty sockets of the eyes, the cheeks sunken and the jaw a crooked line of bared teeth and bone. This was the home of the Lord and Master. This was the kingdom of Brona, the Warlock Lord. Everywhere it bore the stamp of the Skull, the indelible mark of death.

It was midday, but time seemed strangely suspended, and the vast, wasted fortress lay wrapped in a peculiar stillness. The familiar grayness screened the sun and sky, and the drab brownish terrain of rock and earth lay stripped of mortal life. Yet there was something more in the air this day, cutting through

the silence and the emptiness to the flesh and blood of
the men in the winding column passing through the
single gateway in the massive Knife Edge. It was a
pressing sense of urgency that hung poised over the
blasted face of the kingdom of the Warlock Lord, as if
events to come had rushed through time too quickly
and, jammed together in eager anticipation, waited for
their moment.

The Trolls shuffled guardedly through the twisting
canyon, their comparatively huge frames dwarfed by
the towering heights of the peaks so that they
appeared little more than ants in the sprawling,
ageless rock. They entered the kingdom of the dead
the way in which little children enter an unfamiliar
dark room, inwardly frightened, hesitant, but
nevertheless determined to see what lay beyond. They
marched unchallenged, though not unseen. They
were expected. Their appearance came as no surprise,
and they entered without danger of harm from the
minions of the Master. Their impassive faces disguised their true intentions or they would never have
passed the southern shores of the River Lethe. For in
their midst was the last of a blood line the Spirit King
had thought destroyed, the last son of the Elven house
of Shannara.

Shea marched directly behind the broad frame of
Keltset, his hands seemingly tied at his back. Panamon Creel followed, his arms similarly bound, the
gray eyes dangerous as they stared watchfully at the
great rock walls on either side of the winding column.
The ruse had worked perfectly. Apparent captives of
the Rock Trolls, the two Southlanders had been
marched to the shores of the River Lethe, the sluggish,
vile stream that flanked the southernmost borders of
the Skull Kingdom. The Trolls and their silent charges
had boarded a wide-backed raft of rotted wood and
rusted iron spikes, whose voiceless captain was a
bent, hooded creature who seemed more beast than

man, his face shielded in the folds of the musty black cloak, but his hooked, scale-covered hands clearly visible as they fastened tightly on the crooked leverage pole and guided the ancient craft across the tepid, poison waters. The uneasy passengers felt a growing sense of revulsion from the mere presence of their pilot and were openly relieved when, after finally permitting them to disembark on the far shore, he vanished with his ancient barge into the haze that lay across the dark river waters. The lower Northland was now entirely lost to them, the grayness so heavily disseminated through the stale, dry air that nothing beyond the river was visible. In contrast, the soaring, blackened cliffs of the Knife Edge loomed starkly before them, the great fingers of rock brushing the mist aside in the half-light of the northern midday. The party passed wordlessly through the corridor that split the vast heights, winding deeper into the forbidden domain of the Warlock Lord.

The Warlock Lord. Somehow Shea felt that he had known from the very beginning, from the day Allanon had told him of his remarkable ancestry, that it would happen this way—that circumstances would demand he face this awesome creature who was trying so desperately to destroy him. Time and events merged into a single instant, a flash of jumbled memories of the long days spent in flight, running to stay alive, running toward this frightening confrontation. Now the moment was drawing near, and he would face it virtually alone in the most savage land in the known world, his oldest, most trusted friends scattered, his only companions a band of Rock Trolls, an outcast thief and a vengeful, enigmatic giant. The latter had persuaded the tribunal to place under his command a detachment of Troll warriors, not so much because they believed that the insignificant Valeman accompanying him somehow possessed the ability to destroy the immortal Brona as because their massive kinsman was the holder of the honored Black Irix.

The three judges had also revealed the fate of Orl Fane. The Trolls had seized the little fugitive about an hour before his determined pursuers had been taken captive, and he had been marched under guard to the main encampment. The Maturen tribunal had quickly concluded that the Gnome was completely mad. He had babbled insanely to them of secrets and treasures, his wizened yellow face contorted in a hideous fixed grin. At times he had appeared to be talking to the air about him, brushing violently at his bare arms and legs as if living things had fastened there. His sole link with reality seemed to be the ancient sword that was his only possession, the sword he clung to so violently that his captors could not pry it free. They allowed him to keep the worthless piece of metal, binding his clenched yellow hands to its rusted sheath. Within the hour he was taken north to the dungeons of the Warlock Lord.

The canyon wound wickedly through the towering peaks of the Knife Edge, at times dwindling from a broad trailway to little more than a split in the rocks. The burly Trolls scrambled through the twisting passage without resting. A few had been there before, and they led the others at a steady, tiring pace. Speed was essential. If they delayed too long, the Spirit King would hear that Orl Fane and the ancient weapon he refused to release, even for the briefest moment, were safely shut away in the Warlock Lord's own dungeons.

Shea shuddered at the possibility. It might already have happened—they could be walking straight to their own execution. Each time before on the long journey from Culhaven, the Warlock Lord had seemed to know every move they had made; each time he had been waiting for them. It was madness—this terrible risk! And even if they did succeed, even if Shea finally held the Sword of Shannara within his grasp

. . . why, what then? Shea laughed inwardly. Could he face the Warlock Lord without Allanon beside him, without any idea what would trigger the hidden power of the legendary talisman? No one would even know he had the Sword.

The Valeman had no idea what the others intended, but he had already determined that if by some miracle he could get his hands on the elusive weapon, he was going to run for his life. Everyone else could do as he wished. He was certain that Panamon Creel would have approved of the plan, but the two had scarcely exchanged ten words since the journey to the Skull Kingdom had begun. Shea sensed that for the first time in Panamon's life, a life composed primarily of narrow escapes and hair-raising escapades, the scarlet-clad thief was frightened. But he had gone with Keltset and Shea—gone because they were his only friends, gone because his pride would let him do no less. His most basic instinct was to survive at any cost, but he would not permit himself to be shamed even to stay alive.

Keltset's reasons for this dangerous undertaking were less apparent. Shea thought he understood why the giant Troll had quietly insisted that they must retrieve the Sword of Shannara, and it was much more than personal vengeance for the slaughter of his family. There was something about Keltset that reminded Shea of Balinor—a quiet confidence that lent strength to those less certain. Shea had felt it when Keltset indicated that they must go after Orl Fane and the Sword. Those gentle, intelligent eyes told the Valeman that he believed in him, and while Shea could not explain it in rational terms, he knew he had to go with his giant friend. If he turned away now, after the long weeks spent searching for the Sword of Shannara, he would be betraying both his friends and himself.

The cliff walls on either side fell away abruptly, and

the canyon opened into a sloping valley that seemed like a wide depression in the rugged interior of the Skull Kingdom, its surface barren and dry, the earth broken by a scattering of rocky hillocks and dry riverbeds. The party halted silently, every pair of eyes involuntarily drawn to the solitary mountain in the bowl of the little valley, the southern face staring sightlessly at them from two huge, empty sockets that resembled the eyes of a skull. The blasted face waited in timeless anticipation for the coming of the Master. Standing at the mouth of the draw, Shea felt the hair on the back of his neck rise and a sudden chill surge through his small frame.

From out of the rocks to either side, a number of misshapen, lumbering creatures shuffled, their great bodies as drab as the dying land, their faces nearly featureless. Once they might have been human, but they were no longer so. They stood upright on two legs and two arms swung aimlessly at their sides, but the resemblance ended there. Their skin was the texture of chalky putty, almost rubbery in appearance, and they moved in the manner of mindless beings. Like apparitions out of some frightening nightmare, the strange creatures came all around the Trolls, staring blankly into their barklike faces as if to be certain of what manner of creatures had come to them. Keltset turned slightly and motioned to Panamon Creel.

"The Trolls call them Mutens," the adventurer whispered quietly. "Stand easy—remember that you are supposed to be a prisoner. Stay calm."

One of the misshapen beings spoke in rasping tones to the lead Trolls, gesturing briefly at the two bound men. There was a short exchange, and then one of the Trolls said something over his shoulder to Keltset, who immediately motioned for Shea and Panamon to follow him. The trio detached themselves from the main group. Accompanied by two other Trolls, they

silently followed one of the lumbering Mutens as he turned and moved rather unsteadily toward the inner cliff wall to their left.

Shea glanced back once and observed the Trolls scattering idly to either side of the canyon entrance, seemingly waiting for their companions to return. The remaining Mutens had not moved. Looking ahead once more, the Valeman saw that the cliff face was split by a long fissure that ran several hundred feet up and that this gap was a passage to something beyond. The little group moved into the rock wall, their eyes trying to adjust to the sudden darkness. There was a pause as their guide took a torch from a wall rack and lit it, handing it absently to one of the Trolls before proceeding. Apparently his own eyes were accustomed to the inky darkness, for he continued to lead them.

The party passed into a dank, foul-smelling cavern that branched out into several fathomless passageways. From somewhere far away, Shea thought he detected the faint, chilling sound of screams ringing over and over as echoes against the rock walls. Panamon cursed harshly in the flickering torchlight, his broad face streaked with sweat. The silent, heedless Muten shuffled ahead into one of the passages, and the faint light from the fissure opening faded into blackness.

The lingering echo of booted feet on rock was the only sound as the men moved down the darkened corridor, their eyes wandering briefly to the windowless iron doors bolted into the face of the rock on both sides of the passageway. The screams still rang faintly in their ears, but they seemed more distant now. There were no human sounds from the cells they were passing. Finally the guide halted before one of the heavy doors, gesturing briefly and speaking in the same guttural tones to the Trolls. He turned to continue down the passage and had taken his first step when the foremost Troll brought his great iron mace crashing down on the creature's bulky head. The Muten dropped lifelessly to the cave floor. Keltset moved to loosen the ropes binding Shea and Panamon as the two remaining Trolls stood watchfully before the cell door. When his friends were freed, the massive Northlander moved catlike to the iron door and slid the latches clear of their loops. Grasping the bars, he pulled on the ancient door. With a sharp grating sound, the heavy portal swung open.

"Now we shall see," breathed Panamon harshly. Taking the light from Keltset, he stepped cautiously into the tiny room, his two companions close behind.

Orl Fane sat hunched against the far wall, his scrawny legs shackled in chains that were bolted into the rock flooring, his clothing torn and dirtied almost beyond recognition. He was clearly not the same creature they had captured several days earlier on the Plains of Streleheim. He stared at the three faces with mindless disregard, his thin, yellow face fixed in a hideous grin as he babbled meaninglessly to himself. His eyes were strangely dilated in the bright torch-light, and he glanced all about as he talked, behaving as if there were others in the little cell, creatures invisible to all eyes but his own.

The two men and the giant Troll took in his condition at a glance, their eyes traveling instantly to the bony hands that still clutched possessively the battered leather and metal scabbard that sheathed the elusive object of their long pursuit. The ancient hilt flickered back dully in the torchlight, giving them a shadowy image of the raised hand holding the burning torch. They had found it. They had found the Sword of Shannara!

For a moment no one moved as the maddened Gnome clutched the Sword closer to his emaciated frame, his eyes showing a momentary flicker of recognition as he caught sight of the sharp pike glinting at the stumped end of Panamon's slowly raising arm. The adventurer stepped forward menacingly and bent close to the Gnome's thin face.

"I've come for you, Gnome," he said harshly.

Orl Fane seemed to undergo a sudden transformation at the sound of Panamon Creel's voice, and a frightened shriek escaped his lips as he struggled to move farther back.

"Give me the Sword, you treacherous rat!" the thief demanded.

Without waiting for a response, he seized the weapon, trying to wrest it from the now thoroughly terrified Gnome's astonishingly strong grip. But even with death staring him directly in the eye, Orl Fane would not give up his precious possession. His voice rose to a scream, and in sudden fury, Panamon brought the heavy iron binding on his piked hand down across the little fellow's unprotected skull. The Gnome crumpled unconscious to the cold floor.

"All those days we chased this miserable creature!" Panamon cried. He stopped abruptly and lowered his voice to a harsh whisper. "I thought I would at least have the pleasure of watching him die, but . . . it's no longer worth it."

In disgust, he reached for the hilt of the Sword, intent on drawing it from its binding, but Keltset stepped forward and placed a restraining hand on his shoulder. Still angered, the thief stared back coldly as the Rock Troll motioned silently toward the watching Shea, then both stepped back.

The Sword of Shannara was Shea's birthright, but he hesitated. He had come so far, been through so much, all for this moment—and now he found himself afraid. He felt cold inside as he looked at the ancient weapon. For an instant, he considered refusing, knowing that a part of him could not accept the awesome responsibility that he was being asked to assume—a responsibility that had been forced on him.

He recalled in a flash the terrible power of the three Elfstones. What then of the power of the Sword of Shannara? In his mind he pictured the faces of Flick and Menion and the others who had fought so hard to gain possession of the Sword for him. If he turned away now, he would have betrayed the trust they had extended him. In effect, he would be telling them that everything they had gone through for him had been pointless. He saw again the dark, enigmatic face of Allanon chastising him for his foolish ideals, his refusal to see men for what they were. He would have to answer to him as well, and Allanon would not be pleased. . . .

Woodenly he moved to the fallen Orl Fane and bent over him, his fingers closing firmly around the cold metal hilt of the weapon, feeling the raised image of the burning torch in his sweating palm. He paused. Then slowly he drew forth the Sword of Shannara.

XXXII

The second day of the battle for Tyrsis bore witness to the same wholesale slaughter of the men of the Northland army as the first. The giant invasion force attacked at dawn, marching toward the face of the bluff in precision formation to the deep booming of the Gnome war drums, pausing in silence within a hundred yards; then, with an earshattering yell, the army rushed headlong into the terrible struggle to gain the heights. With the same utter disregard for their own lives, the attackers threw themselves in wave after wave against the outer defenses of the entrenched Border Legion. They came without the aid of the monstrous rampways, which there had been no time to rebuild, relying instead on thousands of small scaling ladders and grappling irons. It was a ferocious, merciless, and bitter contest. Hundreds of the Northlanders died in the first few minutes.

With Acton gone, Balinor did not choose to risk the Legion mounted command a second time in counterattacking the massive enemy army. He decided instead to dig in on the bluff face and hold his position as long as possible. Burning oil and the Legion archers shredded the first waves of the assault, but this time the attackers did not break apart and run. They came in an endless, sustained charge, finally eluding both arrows and flames to reach the base of the wide plateau where scaling ladders were thrown against the bluff. Swarms of screaming Northlanders struggled upward and the fighting was reduced to basic hand-to-hand combat.

For nearly eight hours the valiant defenders of Tyrsis repelled an enemy twenty times its size. Scaling ladders and grappling hooks were methodically shattered and cut apart, Northlanders were pushed away as quickly as they gained the summit, and momentary holes in the defense lines were closed before a breach could be opened. The acts of bravery performed by individual members of the famed Legion were too numerous to recount. They fought against impossible odds without rest, without relief, knowing all the while that no quarter would be given them by the enemy, should they fail. For eight hours the enraged Northland army struggled to break through the Legion bulwarks without success. But finally a breach was opened on the defensive left flank. With a ragged shout of victory, the enemy rushed onto the bluff.

After the death of Acton, the aged Fandwick had been left in sole command of this section of the defensive lines. Calling on his diminished reserves, the Legion commander moved to block the Northland rush. An intense, fierce battle raged in the open breach for long minutes as the determined attackers battled to hold and enlarge the newly gained opening. Dozens died on both sides, including the valiant Fandwick.

Balinor rushed more reserves from the center of the line in an effort to close the breach, and he finally succeeded. But moments later a second and then a third hole opened in the left defensive flank, and the whole command began to waiver and break apart. The King of Callahorn realized his army could no longer hold the outer defenses, and passed the word to his remaining commanders to begin an orderly retreat into the city. Rallying the crumbling left flank, the giant borderman drew in his outermost defenses while holding the enemy at bay, and quickly moved the entire command into the city.

It was a bitter moment for the Southlanders, who now rushed to defend the great Outer Wall. But the Northland army did not advance to the attack. Instead, they began tearing down the defensive bulwarks and moving them inward on the bluff face, where they constructed their own defensive position, just out of range of the Legion archers. The weary soldiers of the Border Legion watched silently from atop the city walls as the sunlit afternoon turned slowly to dusk above the busy invaders. The Northland camp was moved forward to the plains below the city and the army began to light its watch fires as darkness closed in around them.

In the final moments of daylight, the enemy revealed a portion of its plan to scale the walls of Tyrsis. Great, sloping rampways from the plains to the bluff were hurriedly set in place, supported by stone and timber over the remains of the shattered walk-ways. Then from out of the twilight, three massive siege towers rolled into view, each one easily the height of the Outer Wall. The towers were moved to the rear of the enemy encampment within plain view of the city and anchored for the night. It was clearly a piece of psychological warfare designed to unnerve the besieged Border Legion.

From above the gates to the city, Balinor watched impassively with his Legion commanders and his companions from Culhaven. He toyed briefly with the idea of a night assault against the encamped North-landers for the express purpose of burning the siege towers, but quickly discarded it. They would expect him to try something like that, and the city gates would undoubtedly be under careful watch the entire night. Besides, it would be no problem for the Legion to set fire to these towers as easily as they had fired the rampways, once they were moved to the attack.

Balinor shook his head and frowned. There was something very wrong about the whole Northland attack concept but he couldn't put his finger on it. Surely they must be aware that the siege towers would never enable them to breach the city's Outer Wall. They had to have something else in mind. He wondered for the hundredth time whether the Elven army would reach the beleaguered city in time. He could not believe that Eventine would fail them. It was dark now and, after ordering a double watch on all sectors of the wall, he invited the men with him to share dinner.

Concealed in a grove of trees on the summit of a low ridge several miles west of Tyrsis, a small band of horsemen surveyed the carnage of the terrible battle below them as evening settled in. They watched silently as the huge siege towers were wheeled into position at the rear of the Northland army for the morning assault on the fortress city.

"We should get a message to them," Jon Lin Sandor whispered quietly. "Balinor will want to know that our army is on its way."

Flick glanced expectantly at the bandaged figure of Eventine. The strange eyes seemed to burn as he studied the besieged city.

"I trust the army is on its way," the Elven King muttered almost inaudibly. "Breen has been gone almost three days. If he has not returned by tomorrow, I'll go myself."

His friend placed an understanding hand on the King's good shoulder.

"You are in no condition to travel, Eventine. Your brother will not fail you. Balinor is a seasoned fighter and the walls of Tyrsis have never been breached by an invader in the lifetime of the city. The Legion can defend long enough."

There was a long moment of silence. Flick looked back at the darkened city and wondered if his friends were all right. Menion must be inside those walls, too. The highlander could not know what had befallen Flick, nor what had happened to Eventine. Nor for that matter what had become of the unpredictable Allanon, who for no apparent reason at all had disappeared shortly after the Valeman's return with the Elven search party. While the Druid had been purposely vague about a great many things since his appearance in Shady Vale, he had never gone off without an explanation. Perhaps he had spoken with Eventine. . . .

"The city is encircled and guarded." Eventine's voice broke out of the growing darkness. "It would be extremely difficult to get past their lines even long enough to get a message to Balinor. But you're right, Jon Lin—he should know we have not forgotten him."

"We don't have a large enough force to break through to Tyrsis or even to strike the rear guard of the Northlanders," his friend declared thoughtfully. "But . . ."

He looked quickly at the dark bulk of the siege towers standing deserted on the plains below.

"A small gesture," finished the King meaningfully.

It was not yet midnight when Balinor was hurriedly summoned to the watchtower above the gates to the city. Moments later he stood speechless on the ramparts in the company of Hendel, Menion, Durin, and Dayel and stared down upon the chaos spreading through the half-wakened enemy camp. To the rear of the sprawling encampment, the centermost of the three giant siege towers was a burning pyre that lit the grasslands for miles. Frantic Northlanders rushed wildly over the timbers of the adjoining towers, desperately trying to prevent the flames from spreading. It was obvious that the invader had been taken completely by surprise. Balinor looked at the others and smiled wryly. Help was not so distant after all.

The morning of the third day dawned with a sullen stillness that hung shroudlike over the land of Callahorn and the armies of the North and South. Gone was the mighty crashing of the Gnome drums, the muffled thudding of booted feet marching to the battle, and the thunderous yells of attack. The sun rose fiery red in the distant east, the dark hue spreading across the fading night like blood. A deep haze clouded the dew-covered face of the land. There was a complete absence of movement, of sound. On the walls of Tyrsis, the soldiers of the Border Legion waited nervously, their eyes peering blankly into the gloom for signs of the enemy.

Balinor was in command of the center section of the Outer Wall. Ginnisson held the right and Messaline the left. Janus Senpre again commanded the city garrison and the reserves. Menion, Hendel, and the Elven brothers stood silently at Balinor's side and shivered in the cold of early morning. They had rested poorly, but they felt unusually alert and strangely calm. They had quietly accepted their situation during the past forty-eight hours. They had seen men die by the thousands, and their own lives seemed almost insignificant compared to the terrible carnage that had engulfed this ancient land—yet very precious at the same time. The grasslands beneath the city were torn and rutted, the earth discolored with blood and littered with death. There was nothing to look forward to but more of the same, and still more, until one army or the other was destroyed. Forgotten for all the defenders of Tyrsis was the moral purpose behind the word survival; war had become a mechanical reflex that served as its own excuse for the acts men performed.

The bloodred of the morning sun grew sharper, and now the shapes of men and horses came into focus as the Northland army was rediscovered, a maze of carefully drawn formations spread all across the expanse of yesterday's battlefield from the bluff defenses to beyond the charred timbers of two fallen siege towers. They did not move; they did not speak. They simply waited. Hendel recognized what was happening and whispered hurriedly to Balinor. Swiftly, the Legion Commander sent runners along the walls to his subordinates, warning them of what was expected, cautioning them to keep their soldiers calm and in place.

Menion was about to ask what was happening when suddenly there was movement on the bluff immediately below the city gates. A single armored warrior walked slowly out of the gloom, tall, erect, to stand before the giant wall. In one hand he carried a long staff with a single red pennant. With slow, deliberate movements he planted the pole in the earth, then stepped back ceremoniously, turned and strode back into his lines. Again there was a moment of complete silence. The long, low, wailing cry of a distant horn sounded mournfully across the plains— once, twice, a third time. Then silence.

"The death watch." Hendel broke the stillness with a hushed whisper. "It means we're to be given no quarter. They intend to kill us all."

The air was rent violently by the sudden crashing of Gnome war drums, and everyone began moving at once. With a rush, thousands of Gnome arrows filled the sky, sweeping downward to the ramparts of the city walls. Spears, pikes, and maces flew upward from charging Northlanders. Out of the haze of the plains below appeared the bulk of the one remaining siege tower, groaning and creaking with its own ponderous weight as hundreds of the enemy pulled and pushed the towering monster up the newly constructed rampway toward the Outer Wall. From within the city, Legion archers fired down upon the darting forms of their attackers as the balance of the men of the Border Legion hugged the stone of the defenses and waited for Balinor's order.

The giant borderman waited until the massive siege tower was within twenty-five yards of the wall. Already the enemy was attempting to scale the great barrier with grappling hooks and ladders, and the rough stone was dotted with clinging figures vainly scrambling toward the summit. Abruptly the caldrons of oil poured downward from the ramparts, splashing over man and machine alike to saturate the bluff face immediately below. Burning torches followed, and instantly the entire front of the Northland assault force was engulfed in flames. The siege tower and the men around it simply disappeared as the black smoke billowed skyward, blotting out for the Legion defenders the carnage below them, but not the shrieks of terror and agony. The attackers attempting to scale the Outer Wall were trapped. A few managed to reach the ramparts where they were quickly dispatched, but most simply lost their hold or were overcome by the heavy smoke and dropped screaming into the fire. Within minutes the assault was broken and the entire Northland army had again completely disappeared from view. The men on the ramparts peered watchfully into the swirling smoke, vainly trying to discover what form the next assault would take. Balinor looked at his companions and shook his head doubtfully.

"That was utter foolishness. They must have known what would happen—yet they came ahead anyway. Are they mad?"

"Perhaps they did it to confuse us . . ." muttered Hendel quietly. "Like this smoke screen we so obligingly provided them with."

"All that dying just to get a smoke screen?" Menion exclaimed incredulously.

"If so, then they have something very definite in mind—something they are certain cannot fail," declared Balinor. "Keep an eye on things here. I'm going down to the gates."

He turned away abruptly and disappeared down

the winding stone stairway almost at a run. The others watched him go without comment and turned back to the wall. In front of them, thick clouds of the heavy black smoke still rose skyward as the oil on the plains continued to burn. The cries of death had ceased and there was a strange silence.

"What are they up to?" Menion voiced the question at last.

For a moment there was no response at all.

"I wish we had been able to catch Stenmin," Durin muttered at last. "I haven't felt safe even behind these walls with that madman running loose somewhere in the city."

"We almost had him," Dayel interjected quickly. "We followed him into that room, but he seemed to disappear into thin air. There must have been a secret passage."

Durin nodded in agreement and the conversation dropped off again. Menion stared into the smoke and thought about Shirl waiting for him at the palace, about Shea, Flick, his father, and his homeland—all in a rush of images that flooded his wandering mind. How was it all going to end for them?

"Shades!" Hendel jerked him around so sharply that he was momentarily startled. "I've been a fool. It was right in front of me all the time. A secret passage! In the basement of the palace, beneath the wine cellar, in the dungeons sealed off all these years—a passageway that leads through the mountains to the plain beyond. The old King spoke of it once to me, years and years ago. Stenmin must know of it!"

"A way into the city!" exclaimed Menion. "They'll catch us with our backs to them." He paused sharply. "Hendel! Shirl's back there!"

"We don't have much time." Hendel was already starting down the steps. "Menion, come with me. Dayel, find Janus Senpre and tell him to get help to us at the palace immediately. Durin, find Balinor and warn him. Hurry now, and pray we're not too late."

They were down the worn stairs in a rush, scattering across the barracks ground as if possessed. Hendel and Menion broke into a dead run, pushing their way heedlessly through clusters of soldiers toward the gates to the Tyrsian Way. Too slow, Menion's harried brain screamed at him! He nearly jerked Hendel off his feet in an effort to turn him toward a small group of saddled reserve mounts tethered to their right. Knocking an interfering attendant aside without pausing, the duo leaped into the saddles of the two nearest mounts and wheeled them toward the city. At a gallop, the horses tore through the open gateway, past the flustered guards, past swarms of reserves posted just inside the gates; with the path cleared, they raced at breakneck speed for the palace.

Everything that followed seemed to come in a rush that negated time and space. People and buildings flashed by them in a blur as the two horsemen galloped over the ancient stones of the Tyrsian Way. Precious moments were lost and then the wide arc of the Bridge of Sendic loomed in the distance, spanning the People's Park to the palace of the Buckhannahs. A train of baggage carts scattered wildly at the foot of the bridge as the two riders tore past them without slowing, racing their mounts across the stone arch toward the open gates of the monarchial home. Dashing into the garden-ringed courtyard, Hendel and Menion drew their sweating horses up sharply and vaulted to the ground.

Everything was silent. Nothing seemed amiss. A single attendant strolled almost leisurely out of the shadows of a great willow to take the reins from the heated riders, his eyes reflecting only mild curiosity. Hendel gave the man a sharp glance and dismissed him, beckoning Menion after him as he moved hurriedly toward the front doors. Still nothing. Maybe they were in time. Maybe they were even mistaken . . .

The hallways of the ancestral manor loomed empty

and silent as the two searchers paused once more in the foyer, casting quick glances at open doorways and deep alcoves, drawn tapestries and curtained windows. Menion turned to find Shirl, but his companion stopped him with a word. The red-haired daughter of kings would have to wait. Slowly now, on cat's feet, the little man led the anxious highlander down the opposite passageway toward the cellar door. At the bend in the corridor they hesitated, then flattening themselves against the polished woodwork, peered cautiously around the corner.

The massive, ironbound door to the now-familiar wine cellar stood ajar. In the open entryway, three armed men kept watch over the vacant hall. All bore the insignia of the falcon. Menion and Hendel drew back silently. For the first time, the Prince of Leah realized he was unarmed. He had left the sword of Leah hanging from the saddle pommel of his horse. Quickly he scanned the hall behind him, his eyes coming to rest at last on a set of crossed pikes fastened to the far wall. A pike was hardly the weapon he needed, but he had no other choice. Noiselessly, he retrieved one unwieldy lance and rejoined Hendel. A long look passed between them. They would have to be quick. If the cellar door were to be closed and fastened from within before they could reach it, they would have lost their chance at Stenmin and the passageway. In any event, they were only two. How many more of the enemy awaited them below?

They didn't stop to consider it further. In a sudden rush, they were out of hiding and down the hallway. The three guards barely had time to look around before their attackers were upon them. Menion shoved his lance through the man nearest the doorway and was on top of the second a moment later. The final guard dropped soundlessly before Hendel's great mace. It was over almost before it had started and the two fighters were through the cellar entryway, charging down the worn stone steps to meet the most deadly battle of their lives.

The ancient wine cellar was ablaze with torchlight. The small fires seemed to burn from every wall, cutting through the musty darkness like hazy sunlight in early morning. In the center of the vast chamber, the great stone trapdoor that led to the forgotten dungeons below was thrown open, and from out of the darkness of the pit came the distant sounds of metal striking stone. The cellar was swarming with armed men and they came at the two intruders from all directions.

Hendel and Menion met the rush with a ferocious counterassault that carried them into the very midst of their assailants. The highlander had retrieved a sword from one of the fallen guards at the top of the stairway. Standing back to back with Hendel, he began to cut away the number of his attackers. From the corner of his eye, he saw a familiar scarlet-robed figure emerging from the black pit of the dungeon; at the sight of the hated Stenmin, the Prince of Leah felt a savage rage well up inside. With renewed fury, he charged into the enemy guards, trying to cut through their ranks and reach the man who had betrayed them. An unmistakable look of fear crossed the mystic's lean features as he shrank from the terrible battle.

Back to back, the Dwarf and the highlander fought as if they had gone mad. Men lay dead and dying all about them. Both were wounded in a dozen places, but they didn't feel the pain. Twice Menion had slipped on the bloodied floor and gone down, and each time Hendel had driven off the attackers while the highlander scrambled back to his feet. Only five of the enemy were still standing, but Hendel and Menion Leah were nearly finished. They fought like mechanical creatures now, their bodies soaked in blood and sweat, their limbs leaden and nerveless. As if

suddenly regaining his wits, the terrified Stenmin
raced to the edge of the pit and began screaming for
help. The Prince of Leah responded instantly. With a
final burst of strength, he crashed into two of his
attackers, knocking both sprawling. A third rushed to
stop him, but the charging highlander put his sword
into the man up to the hilt and left it there. Grasping a
fallen lance, he pounced upon the cringing mystic and
stunned him with a sweeping blow from the great
weapon. As the lean frame crumpled to the stone
floor, Menion Leah gripped the edges of the heavy
trapdoor and heaved upward with the last of his
fading strength.

It was as if the stone had been chained in open
position to the cellar floor. It did not move. From far
below, the sounds of metal on stone ceased, replaced
by the thudding of booted feet as men raced toward
the trapdoor. Only seconds remained. If they reached
the stairs, Menion was a dead man. Bracing himself,
the wounded man again threw all of his weight into
lifting the massive piece of stone, and this time it rose.
Groaning with the terrible strain, the highlander
raised upward against the great trapdoor until at last it
came over and fell with a great booming thud into
place in the ancient floor. With numb, sweating hands
he bound the chain through the sealing rings and
fastened it with an iron bar. The passageway was
closed. If the Northland army sought entrance here,
they would have to cut their way through several feet
of stone and iron.

"Menion."

The sound of his name broke the sudden silence in a
cracked whisper. The highlander had fallen to his
hands and knees, but his groping hand found a
discarded sword and he raised his battered face.
Across a floor littered with a tangled mass of fallen
enemy guards, their twisted bodies either lifeless or in
their final death throes, the eyes of the Prince of Leah

found his friend. The Dwarf stood with his back to the wall near the bottom of the cellar stairway, the great mace still gripped tightly in one hand. There were dead bodies all about him. He had killed them all. No one had escaped. The hardened eyes met Menion's for just an instant, and it was as if they were again meeting for the first time in the lowlands beyond the Black Oaks. He was the old Hendel—taciturn, grim-faced, ever resourceful. Then the mace slipped from his hand, his eyes glazed over; with a long sigh, his body slid slowly, lifelessly to the death that had finally claimed him.

Hendel! The name raced through Menion's stunned, disbelieving mind as he struggled numbly to his feet and stood swaying unsteadily in the flickering shadows. Tears welled into his reddened eyes and ran in dark streams down his battered face. With leaden steps he picked his way over the lifeless bodies of the enemy dead, gasping now in unrestrained fury and helplessness. He was only dimly aware of Stenmin regaining consciousness somewhere behind him. He reached the Dwarf's side and knelt beside him, gently cradling the limp form next to his breast. How many times had Hendel saved his life? How many times had he saved them all, only to . . .? He couldn't finish the thought. He could only cry. Everything seemed to break inside of him at once.

Stenmin raised himself slowly to one knee and stared blankly about the cellar at the mass of tangled corpses. His men all dead, the stone trapdoor closed and chained, and . . . Fear surged up inside his pain-wracked body. One of the intruders was still alive—the highlander! He hated that man, hated him so badly he fleetingly considered trying to kill him, but then the fear returned even stronger than before and abruptly his thoughts turned to escape. Escape so that he could live! There was only one way out—up the stairs past the kneeling man and through the open cellar door. Already he was on his feet, moving noiselessly through the carnage, half walking, half slinking toward the unguarded steps.

The highlander's back was turned to him, still holding the body of the Dwarf. Sweat beads broke out on Stenmin's forehead and the thin lips curled menacingly—yet it was fear that kept him moving. Only a few more steps. He would be free again. The city was doomed; all of them would die—all of his enemies. But he would survive. He had to fight down the sudden impulse to laugh aloud. One hand touched the stone of the ancient stairway, one foot followed; the highlander was only feet away, still unsuspecting, the outer cellar door was ajar and unguarded. Freedom! Just steps . . .

Then Menion turned. A shriek of terror escaped the mystic's lips as his eyes viewed the terrible look on the face of the Prince of Leah. Stenmin clawed his way frantically toward the open doorway, stumbling blindly in the long red robes.

He was only halfway up the steps when Menion caught him.

At the walls of Tyrsis, the impossible was happening. Upon descending from the parapets of the Outer Wall, Balinor had moved quickly to the massive city gates. The Legion guardsmen stationed before the great iron portals had snapped quickly to attention. Everything appeared to be as it should. The series of inner lock bolts, controlled mechanically from the tower gatehouse, had been run firmly into place in the crease where the gates swung outward. The cumbersome iron bar that served as an additional safeguard lay snugly in its fittings across the width of both gates. Balinor stared fixedly at the great wall, a nagging doubt persisting. Something was going to happen; he could feel it. The gates were the key to the city, the one weak link in the otherwise impenetrable stone wall that bound Tyrsis. Siege towers, grappling hooks, scaling ladders—all these were futile attempts to breach that great wall, and the Warlock Lord had to know it. The gates were the key.

His eyes drifted skyward to the tower gatehouse, a squat, windowless stone enclosure which housed the mechanism that controlled the inner locks. Two Legion soldiers stood attentively at the single door. A picked squad of men had been given the responsibility of protecting that crucial mechanism, men selected by Balinor and commanded by Captain Sheelon. On both sides of the small housing, the men of the Border Legion defended the battlements. It seemed impossible that the Northlanders expected to seize the gatehouse. Still . . .

Already the tall borderman had moved to the foot of the narrow stairway that led to the gatehouse and had begun to climb the worn stone blocks. Sudden cries from the wall diverted his attention momentarily, and he paused as the air sounded with the deep humming of a thousand bowstrings, and a rush of arrows swept the ramparts of the Outer Wall. Hurriedly Balinor gained the battlements and in three short strides reached the wall. He peered carefully down at the face of the bluff, littered with bodies and debris and dotted with small oil fires that burned hazily in the morning mist. The Northlanders had temporarily abandoned any direct assault. Instead, lines of archers five men deep were raking the defenders on the ramparts with a concentrated barrage.

The reason for this new tactic was immediately obvious. At the rim of the bluff, a detachment of heavily armored Rock Trolls pushed forward a ponderous, mobile battering ram, shielded from the top and sides by a broad canopy of sheet iron. While the Border Legion was pinned down by heavy fire from the archers, the giant Trolls would move the great ram into place before the city gates and force an entry.

The plan appeared at first glance both preposterous

and unworkable. Yet if the gatehouse fell to the enemy, the inner lock bolts could be released and only the long, iron crossbar would hold the gates closed. The bar alone would not be enough to stand against the massive battering ram. Balinor ran toward the small gatehouse. The guards came silently to attention. He gave them a passing glance, his hand reaching anxiously for the door handle. Sheelon was nowhere in sight. The door swung inward, and he was a step into the closed room when he realized he had never seen either of the sentries.

The giant borderman reacted instinctively, side-stepping the noiseless rush of the guard behind him, seizing the outstretched lance that barely grazed his back and wrenching it free from the would-be assassin. His back to the wall, the King had only a moment to survey the dimly lighted room. The bodies of Sheelon and his men lay to one side, twisted in death, their stiffened corpses stripped naked of armor and clothing. From out of the shadows at the rear of the housing a group of faceless attackers rushed the borderman, daggers raised for the kill. Balinor threw the heavy lance crossways into their midst and broke for the open doorway. But the second sentry, who had remained just outside, saw him coming and quickly pulled the door shut from the other side. The trapped King had no time to force his way free. There was barely enough time to draw the great broadsword before his assailants were upon him. They bore him roughly to the floor, daggers chipping and glancing off the protective coat of chain mail that had saved his life so many times. With a mighty surge, Balinor shook himself free and regained his footing. In the faint light of the shuttered room, his attackers were only shadows, but his eyes were adjusting, and he cut at them as they moved toward him. Two of the dark forms screamed and dropped lifelessly as the great blade cut through them, but their companions had already broken past the sweeping sword and closed with the King.

For a second time, Balinor was wrestled down, but again he twisted free and the battle surged back across the little room. The din of the attack outside completely obscured the sounds of battle from within the stone housing; the borderman knew that unless he managed to get the door open, no one would come to his aid. He placed his back to the wall once more and swung the broadsword sharply as the shadowed enemies resumed the assault. Three were dead and several were wounded, but those who remained in the battle were beginning to wear him down with their repeated rushes. He had to get free quickly. Then an audible grinding of levers and gears filled the gatehouse, and he realized in horror that someone was releasing the inner lock bolts of the front gates. With a wild charge, he broke for the lock mechanism, but the determined attackers barred his path, and he was forced into a circling movement away from his objective. A moment later there was a sharp grating of metal on metal, followed by a series of hammering blows. They were jamming the release levers! In complete disregard for his own safety, the infuriated Balinor threw himself on the remaining enemies.

Then the gatehouse door burst open and the body of the traitorous sentry was thrust violently through the entryway. Gray daylight flooded the darkened room and the lean figure of Durin appeared from out of nowhere at the side of his friend. In grim silence they cut away at the few enemy attackers who remained, forcing them away from the jammed machinery, away from the open doorway and escape, and into the far corner of the small housing. There, locked together in ferocious hand-to-hand combat, they destroyed them. Without a second glance at the dead men, the bloodied King rushed back to the damaged lock mechanism, his face lined in fury as he surveyed the twisted mass of metal levers and gears. Angrily he threw his weight against the main release. It would not move. Durin turned pale as he realized what had happened.

"We don't have enough time!" Balinor exploded heatedly, wrenching violently at the jammed levers.

A great booming crash resounded through the stone housing, vibrating through the walls and shaking the two men ominously.

"The gates!" Durin exclaimed in dismay.

A second crash rocked the gatehouse, and a third. The rushing of booted feet sounded on the ramparts outside and a moment later Messaline's dark face appeared in the open doorway. He started to speak, but Balinor was already issuing commands and moving toward the battlements.

"Get this room cleared away and have our machinists try to free those gears. The gate locks are released and jammed!" Messaline looked as if he had received a mortal blow. "Fortify the gates with timbers and put your best regiment in phalanx formation fifty paces back and to either side. The Northlanders are not to break through. Put two lines of archers on the Inner Wall to bottle up the gate entrance. Reserves and the garrison command will defend the Inner Wall. All others will stay where they are at the Outer Wall. We will hold it as long as we can. If it falls, the Legion will retreat to the secondary defense and hold. If we lose that, we will regroup at the Bridge of Sendic. That will be the last line of defense. Anything else?"

Quickly Durin explained where Hendel had gone. Balinor shook his head wearily.

"We have been betrayed at every turn. Hendel will have to do what he can without our help for the moment. If the palace falls and they break through from the rear, we are finished anyway. Messaline, you'll hold the right flank of the phalanx, Ginnisson will take the left, and I'll be in the center. The enemy is not to break through! Pray that Eventine arrives before our strength fails us."

Messaline disappeared outside in a crouching run. The shattering thrusts of the massive battering ram continued to shake the great wall as Balinor and Durin faced each other across the little room. Already the gray light of day was growing dimmer as the shadow of the Warlock Lord continued to roll ominously closer to the doomed city. The giant borderman reached out slowly and gripped the slim hand of his Elven friend.

"Good-bye, my friend. This is the end for us. Time has just about run out."

"Eventine would not willingly fail us . . ." the Elf began earnestly.

"I know, I know," Balinor replied. "Nor would Allanon. He has not found the Sword or the heir of Shannara. His time has run out as well."

There was a brief silence between them, broken by the shouts of the men on the walls and the crashing of the ram against the gates of Tyrsis. Balinor wiped the blood away from a deep cut over one eye.

"Find your brother, Durin. But before you leave the Outer Wall, have the last of the oil poured onto that ram and fired. If we can't stop them altogether, we'll at least make it a hot place for them to work."

He smiled grimly and slipped quietly out of the gatehouse. Durin stared blankly after him, wondering what perverse fate had brought them to this unjust end. Balinor was the most remarkable man the Elf had ever met. Yet he had lost everything—his family, his city, his home, and now his life was to be taken from him as well. What kind of world permitted such terrible injustice, where good men were stripped of everything and soulless creatures of malice and hatred survived to glory in their pointless death? Once he had been so sure they would not fail, that somehow they would find a way to destroy the hated Warlock Lord and save the four lands. But that dream was ended.

Durin looked up dazedly as several burly Legion machinists entered the gatehouse to begin their hopeless work on the jammed lock mechanism. Quickly, the lean Elf moved out onto the ramparts. It was time to find Dayel.

The struggle to hold the Outer Wall was incredibly vicious. Despite the devastating barrage concentrated against the men of the Border Legion by the lines of Gnome archers below the bluff, the valiant defenders managed to cut away at the Trolls that manned the great battering ram before the weakened gates. The remaining caldrons of oil were moved to the fortifications above the ram and poured on the enemy machine and its handlers as they worked. Torches followed, and instantly the entire area was consumed in a mass of flames and rolling black smoke. Metal melted and smoldered and the Trolls were burned alive after the first few minutes of the terrible heat, their armor becoming a furnace they could not escape. But new enemy soldiers quickly filled the breach and the mighty ram continued to break against the city gates in crashing, booming blows that first bent, then split the crossbar and the timbers that held the tall portals secure.

The gray sky turned black from the oily smoke that rose above the burning grasslands to cloak the city walls and their defenders in a deep, murky haze. The smell of burnt flesh choked the nose and lungs of the Legion soldiers as the charred, blackened bodies of the Troll attackers lay in heaps before the Outer Wall. Desperately the two opponents strove to break one another's strength, but the stalemate continued. For a short time, it seemed that the day might end without any further change in the fortunes of either army.

But at last the great crossbar snapped in two, the supporting timbers sagged and splintered, and the giant battering ram forced a breach in the gates of Tyrsis. In a rush, the first Northlanders poured into the parade grounds and were dropped instantly by Legion archers positioned atop the Inner Wall. Drawn up in a three-sided box opening toward the Outer Wall gates, the Legion phalanx braced for the enemy rush, spears bristling through locked shields. The ram pushed forward and the gates opened further still, and then the foremost ranks of the Northland invasion force surged through the gap and threw themselves against the spears of the Border Legion. The Legion defenses wavered slightly, but held, thrusting the attackers backward, where they milled in confusion as they were cut to pieces by the archers on the walls both above and behind them. In seconds the parade ground was blanketed with Northland dead and wounded, and the breach in the gates had momentarily been bottled up so thoroughly that the great invasion forces could not advance farther.

Durin had positioned himself next to the gatehouse on the Outer Wall, and from there he watched the Northland assault break apart on the Legion phalanx. He had discovered that his brother had gone with Janus Senpre to the palace, and reluctantly he decided to remain with Balinor for as long as possible. The enemy was attempting to regain its momentum now; on the plains below, Maturens directed the great Rock Troll commands toward the breach in the gates of the besieged city. The Northland army was calling on the backbone of its strength in a determined effort to crush the Southlanders once and for all. The Outer Wall was under attack again from all angles, as hordes of Gnomes and lesser Trolls rushed forward with ladders, ropes, and grappling hooks. The thinned ranks of the Legion defenders who remained on the battlements fought desperately to prevent a break-through, but their men were dying and the numbers of the Northland army seemed limitless. The battle was turning into a telling war of attrition that the men of Tyrsis could not hope to win.

Then, into the growing blackness of the sky north of the besieged city, two winged figures rose and hovered menacingly, and Durin felt his blood turn cold. Skull Bearers! Were they so certain of victory that they dared reveal themselves in daylight? The Elf felt his heart sink. He had done all he could here; it was time to join his brother. Whatever fate awaited them, they would at least face it together.

Nimbly, he turned and moved along the wall in a crouching run until he was just behind the left flank of the Legion phalanx. A steep causeway led downward to the barracks grounds that lay between the walls of the city, several hundred feet behind the Legion rear lines. A deafening roar erupted from the men engaged in battle on the walls. As Durin neared the base of the rampway, he saw the tall, armored forms of the great Rock Trolls pouring through the breach in the gates of the Outer Wall. He paused involuntarily, sensing that the next few minutes would be crucial ones for the Border Legion.

The phalanx tightened its formation and braced for the assault as the massive Trolls drew up their ranks and moved slowly toward the center of the defensive line, where Balinor held command. Ten feet separated the combatants when, to everyone's surprise, the entire Troll regiment wheeled abruptly to the left and charged directly into the Legion flank. There was a crunching sound as the two forces joined and a terrific clash of metal as spear met mace and shield struck armor. For a moment the Legion phalanx held firmly and the foremost of the giant Trolls were killed and thrown down. But the superior strength and sheer weight of the Northlanders pressed back against the smaller men of the Border Legion until at last the right end of the phalanx began to break apart.

The commanding figure of Ginnisson moved quickly into the gap, his red hair flying as he fought to hold the line. The Trolls were driven back step by step as Balinor closed on the right and Messaline from the rear. It was the most ferocious man-to-man combat Durin had been witness to in this terrible conflict, and he watched in awe as the great Rock Trolls held off the men of the Border Legion and once again pressed forward. An instant later the breach in the phalanx was forced and Ginnisson disappeared from view entirely as a rush of massive attackers overwhelmed him and raced toward the barracks and the Inner Wall.

Durin was directly in their path. There might have been time to gain the safety of the walls, but the Elf was already on one knee, the ash bow armed and drawn back. The first Troll fell at fifty paces, the second ten closer, the third at twenty-five. Legion soldiers from the wall rushed to the attack, and archers from the lesser heights of the Inner Wall tried desperately to halt the Troll offensive. Everything in front of the Elf was confusion as Troll and Legionnaire surged toward him, locked together in desperate hand-to-hand combat. Still the massive Northlanders continued to come at him, and Durin fired the last of his arrows into their midst.

He threw down the bow, and for the first time thought about escape. But there was no time left, and he barely managed to seize a discarded sword before the surging mass of fighters was upon him. He struggled wildly to keep his balance as he was forced back against the barracks wall. A giant Rock Troll loomed directly over him, a black mass of barklike skin and armor, and the Elf twisted desperately to one side as a huge mace swung downward. He felt a blinding pain in his left shoulder, followed by a strange numbness. Grimly he fought to stay conscious, his pain abruptly returning in a flood that wracked his lean frame. But he was already falling. His face lay against the earth as he breathed in shallow gasps. A terrible heaviness pushed down on him as he felt the tide of the battle move beyond him. He tried to see, but the effort of looking was too great and he slipped quietly into unconsciousness, through which pain still seemed to penetrate in great bursts.

Menion Leah bent his blood-streaked face over the body of Hendel and carefully raised the inert form in his arms. With studied, mechanical steps, he threaded his way through the bodies of their fallen enemies to reach the stairs and climbed slowly toward the open doorway, stepping carefully, but without looking, over the headless lump tangled in a loose mass of reddened robes that sprawled grotesquely across the center of the ancient stairway. Dazedly, the highlander passed through the cellar entryway and moved down the vacant palace hall, gripping the lifeless form of the Dwarf close to him. He walked aimlessly, his eyes shockingly blank, his face stricken with a terrible stunned look that screamed in silent agony for release. He reached the palace foyer and there halted as the sound of running feet echoed hollowly from the eastern corridor. Gently he laid his burden on the polished floor and stood quietly as the slim, titian-haired girl slowed in front of him, sudden tears streaming down her beautiful face.

"Oh, Menion," she whispered faintly. "What have they done?"

His eyes flickered and his mouth moved dumbly as he fought for the words that would not come. Quickly Shirl reached for him, the slim arms coming tightly around his stooped frame, her face close to his own. A moment later she felt his strong arms come around her shoulders and the terrible agony trapped deep within him broke soundlessly and flooded over her to disappear in her silence and warmth.

On the ramparts of the Inner Wall, Balinor completed a final check of the Legion defenses and paused wearily above the heavily barricaded gates. The

Northlanders were already massing for a final rush. Just moments earlier, the impregnable Outer Wall had fallen and the courageous soldiers of the Border Legion had been forced back to the second line of defense. Balinor stared grimly at the enemy swarming over the heights of the towering wall and gripped the hilt of his great broadsword until his knuckles turned white beneath the chain mail. His cloak and tunic had been shredded in the terrible combat to hold the breach in the gates of the Outer Wall against the Troll assault. Balinor had held together the center of the Legion phalanx, but both wings had collapsed. Ginnisson had been killed, Messaline was severely wounded, and hundreds of Southlanders had died holding the Outer Wall until all hope was gone. Even Durin had disappeared in the fighting. Now the King of Callahorn stood alone.

He gestured sharply to the men bracing the timbers that supported the gates below, the chain mail on his arm glinting brightly in the graying light, showing where a dozen blows had chipped and nicked the protective metal. For a moment he allowed his courage to give way entirely to despair. They had failed him—all of them. Eventine and the Elven army. Allanon. The whole Southland. Tyrsis was on the brink of complete annihilation and with it the land of Callahorn, and still no one came to their aid. The Legion had fought alone to save them all—the final defense for the Southland. What purpose had it served? He caught himself quickly, roughly pushing down the doubts and despondency. There was no time to indulge himself. There were too many lives to be saved, and he was the one they depended upon.

The Northland army was drawing up its lines along the base of the Outer Wall, the familiar scaling ladders, ropes, and grappling irons held ready for the assault. Already scattered bands of the massive Rock Trolls had scaled the Inner Wall during the battle on the parade grounds and broken into the city proper. He wondered briefly what had become of the reliable Hendel and Menion Leah. Apparently they had secured the palace and prevented any rear assault, or the city would have already fallen. Now they would have to hold in the event isolated groups of the enemy breached the Inner Wall and broke for the palace.

Bits of soot from the rolling clouds of oil smoke stung his eyes, and he rubbed them until they watered freely. Everything seemed masked in a heavy gray haze as he glanced quickly at the wall fortifications. The Legion had been placed in an impossible defensive position against an enemy so vast that the loss of hundreds from their ranks was insignificant. He thought of Hendel's words after the deaths of his father and brother. The last Buckhannah. The name would die with him, die as Tyrsis and her people died. The familiar roar rose in thunderous echoes from the throats of the Northlanders, and they charged recklessly for the Legion's walled defense. The long scar on the giant borderman's cheek turned a deeper shade of purple, and he brought the broadsword up menacingly.

At almost the same moment, the first scattered remnants of the Troll advance force came together at the foot of the Bridge of Sendic and hesitated. A line of determined Legion soldiers spanned the center of the wide stone arch, barring all passage to the home of the Buckhannahs. Janus Senpre stood foremost, flanked on one side by Menion Leah, his battered frame erect as he gripped the sword of Leah with both hands, and on the other by Dayel, his youthful face drawn, but resolute. Behind the Rock Trolls, the air was thick with rolling smoke as fresh fires rose from the buildings of the city. Frightened cries sounded above the clamor of battle at the Inner Wall. In the distance, darting figures were seen scurrying across the deserted Tyrsian Way for the safety of their homes. Silently the forces faced one another, the number of Trolls growing quickly as others appeared to swell their ranks. They studied the Southlanders with the blank, experienced look of professional soldiers, confident in the knowledge that they were the best-trained fighting unit in the world. The defenders on the bridge numbered less than fifty.

The afternoon sky had gone suddenly black, and an eerie stillness settled over the two armies. From somewhere in the burning city, Menion caught the faint, clear cry of a small child. Several feet to his left, Dayel felt the cold north wind fade with a low, sighing whisper. Before them, the giant Trolls moved carefully into formation, the great maces held loosely; then as a unit, they lumbered forward. At the center of the bridge, the city's last line of defense braced for the Northland rush.

On the ridge west of the city, Flick Ohmsford and the little band of Elven horsemen watched helplessly as the destruction of Tyrsis mounted. Flanked by Eventine and Jon Lin Sandor, the Valeman felt the last trace of hope fade as the hordes of the mammoth Northland army poured unchecked through the breached gates of the Outer Wall. Clouds of dark smoke rose now from within Tyrsis, and the last remnants of the proud Border Legion had been driven from her walls. The city's defenses had been broken. He stared in horror as the grotesque figures of the Skull Bearers hovered in full view above the advancing enemy, black wings spread wide against the darkening noon sky. The worst that Allanon had foreseen had come to pass. The Warlock Lord had won.

Then a sharp cry sounded from a rider to his left, and Eventine's flushed countenance surged into view as he spurred his mount forward, crowding the Valeman aside in his eagerness. Across the wide expanse of the empty grassland, still many miles to the west, a faint, dark line grew against the grayness of the horizon. A low rumble of pounding hooves broke out of the distance to blend with the clamor and fury of the battle behind them.

The dark line grew quickly in size and became horsemen, thousands strong, banners and lances flashing color and iron. Strident and clear, the booming wail of a war horn sounded their. arrival. Cheers rose from the little band of Elves as the massive body of horsemen began to blanket the plains, sweeping at breakneck speed toward Tyrsis. Forewarned of their approach, the rear guard of the Northland army had already closed ranks and turned to face the advancing tide. It was the Elven army come at last—for the defenders of Tyrsis, for the beleaguered nations of three lands, for everything mankind had fought so hard to preserve through the ages. Come perhaps too late!

XXXIII

In a single smooth, silent motion, Shea slid the ancient blade free from its battered sheath. The metal gleamed in the faint torchlight with a deep bluish tint, the iron surface flawless as if the legendary Sword had never been carried in battle. It was unexpectedly light, a slim, balanced blade of exceptional workmanship, the handle carefully engraved with the now familiar crest of a raised hand holding forth a burning torch. Shea held the weapon guardedly, glancing quickly at Panamon Creel and Keltset, seeking their reassurance, afraid suddenly of what was going to happen. His grim-faced companions remained motionless, their expressions blank and impassive. He gripped the Sword tightly with both hands, bringing the blade around sharply until it pointed skyward. His palms were sweating freely, and he felt his body grow cold in the cell's darkness. There was a faint stirring to one side, and a feeble moan broke from the lips of Orl Fane. Moments passed, and Shea was conscious of the raised impression of the crest pressing into the palms of his clenched hands. Still nothing happened.

. . . In the gray half-light of the empty chamber at the peak of Skull Mountain, the dark waters of the stone basin were quiet and smooth. The power that was the Warlock Lord lay dormant. . . .

Abruptly the Sword of Shannara grew warm in

Shea's hands, and a strange, pulsating wave of heat coursed from the dark iron into the palms of the astonished Valeman and then disappeared. Startled, he took a quick step backward and lowered the blade slightly. An instant later, the sudden warmth was replaced by a sharp tingling sensation that surged out of the weapon into his body. Though there was no pain, the abruptness of the sensation caused him to wince reflexively, and he felt his muscles tighten. Instinctively, he sought to release the talisman; to his shock, he found that he could not let go. Something touched deeply into him to forbid it, and his hands locked securely around the ancient handle.

The tingling sensation rushed through him, and now he was conscious of a return flow of energy that pulled at his life-force, carrying it down through the cold metal of the Sword itself, until the weapon became a part of him. The gilt paint that coated the carved pommel began to strip away beneath the Valeman's hands, and the handle turned to polished silver, laced with reddish streaks of light that seemed to burn and twist in the bright metal like living things. Shea felt the first stirrings of something coming awake, something that was a part of him, yet foreign to everything he knew himself to be. It pulled at him, subtly but firmly, drawing him down deeper inside himself.

Several steps away, Panamon Creel and Keltset watched with growing concern as the little Valeman seemed to slip into a trance, his eyelids drooping heavily, his breathing slowing, his form turning statuelike in the dim torchlight of the cell. He held the Sword of Shannara before him in both hands, its blade raised and pointed skyward, the polished silver handle gleaming brightly. For an instant, Panamon considered taking hold of the Valeman and shaking him awake, but something restrained the thief. From out of the shadows, Orl Fane began crawling across

the smooth stones toward his precious sword. Panamon hesitated a moment and then nudged him back
roughly with his boot.

Shea felt himself being drawn inward, borne like a
cork caught in an undertow. Everything around him
began to fade from view. The walls, ceiling, and floor
of the stone cell disappeared first, then the cringing
whimpering figure of Orl Fane; finally even the granite
forms of Panamon and Keltset vanished. The strange
current seemed to wrap around him completely, and
he found that he could not resist it. Slowly he was
pulled into the innermost recesses of his being, until
all was blackness.

. . . A momentary shudder rippled the still basin
waters in the cavern depths at the crown of the solitary
death's head, and the frightened, crawling beings that
served the Master scampered from their places of
concealment in the stone walls. The Warlock Lord
stirred warily from his broken sleep. . . .

In the vortex of emotion and basic self that
comprised the centermost region of his being, the
bearer of the Sword of Shannara came face to face with
himself. For a moment, there was a chaos of uncertain
impressions; then the current seemed to reverse itself,
carrying him off in a new direction entirely. Pictures
and impressions loomed up before him. Thrust
suddenly before his eyes, the world that was his
birthplace and life source, from past to present, lay
open and revealed to him, stripped bare of his
carefully nurtured illusions, and he saw the reality of
existence in all its starkness. No soft dreams colored its
view of life, no wishful fantasies clothed the harshness
of its self-shaped choices, no self-conceived visions of
hope softened the rawness of its judgments. Amid its
sprawling vastness, he saw himself displayed for the
pitiful, insignificant spark of momentary life that he
represented.

Shea's mind seemed to explode within him, and he

was paralyzed by what he saw. He struggled wildly for his grasp of the vision of self that had always sustained him, for what had been his hold on sanity, fighting to shield himself from the awesome view of his inner nakedness and the weakness of the thing he was compelled to recognize as himself.

Then the force of the current seemed to diminish slightly. Shea forced his eyes open, avoiding for an instant the inner vision. Before him was the upright Sword, ablaze with a blinding white light that surged downward from the blade to the pommel. Beyond it, he could see Panamon and Keltset, standing motionless, their gaze fixed on him. Then the eyes of the giant Troll shifted slightly, centering on the Sword. There was a strange understanding and urgency in the gesture, and as Shea looked back to the Sword of Shannara, its light seemed to pulsate feverishly. There was a sense of impatience about its movement as it strained to advance from the blade into his body and was somehow thwarted in its efforts.

For a moment more, the Valeman struggled against this advance, then his eyes again closed and the inner vision returned. The first shock of revelation was past him now, and he made an effort to understand what was happening. He concentrated on the images of Shea Ohmsford, immersing himself completely in the thoughts, emotions, judgments, and motivations that made up this character that was both alien and familiar.

The images cleared with frightening sharpness, and abruptly he saw another side to himself, a side he had never been able to recognize—or perhaps had simply refused to accept. It revealed itself in an endless line of events, all caricatures of the memories he had believed in so strongly. Here was an accounting of every hurt he had caused to others, every petty jealousy he had felt, his deep-seated prejudices, his deliberate half-truths, his self-pity, his fears—all that was dark and hidden within himself. Here was the Shea Ohmsford who had fled the Vale, not to save and protect family and friends, but in fear of his own life, seeking any excuse for his panic—the Shea Ohmsford who had selfishly allowed Flick to share his nightmare and thereby ease the pain of it. Here was the Valeman who had sneered at and belittled the moral code of Panamon Creel, while at the same time allowing the thief to risk his own life to save Shea's. And here . . .

The images went on endlessly. Shea Ohmsford recoiled in horror from what he was seeing. He could not accept it. He could never accept it!

Yet drawing from some inner well of strength and understanding, his mind opened receptively to the images, expanding outward to embrace them, persuading him, or perhaps forcing him, to admit the reality of what he had been shown. He could not sensibly deny this other side of his character; like the limited image of the person he had always believed himself to be, this was only a part of the real Shea Ohmsford—but it was indeed a part, however difficult he found it to accept.

But he had to accept it. It was the truth.

. . . Filled with white-hot rage, the Warlock Lord came fully awake. . . .

Truth? Shea opened his eyes again to stare at the Sword of Shannara, gleaming whitely from blade to handle. A warm, pulsating feeling spread rapidly through him, bringing no new vision of self, but only a deep, inner awareness.

Abruptly, he realized that he knew the secret of the Sword. The Sword of Shannara possessed the power to reveal Truth—to force the man who held it to recognize the truth about himself; perhaps even to reveal the truth about others who might come in contact with it. For an instant, he could not bring himself to believe any of it. He hesitated in his analysis, trying desperately to follow up on this unexpected revelation—to find something more because there simply had to be more. But there was nothing else to discover. That was all there was to the Sword's vaunted magic. Beyond that, it was no more than what it appeared to be—a finely crafted weapon from another age.

The knowledge of what this meant ripped through his mind and left him stunned. No wonder Allanon had never revealed the secret of the Sword. What kind of weapon was this against the incredible power of the Warlock Lord? What possible defense could it offer against a being that could crush the life out of him with little more than a thought? With chilling certainty, Shea knew that he had been betrayed. The Sword's legendary power was a lie! He felt himself begin to panic, and he closed his eyes tightly against the chill he was feeling. The blackness about him began to churn violently until he grew dizzy with its sweep and seemed to lose consciousness altogether.

. . . In the bleak, gray emptiness of his mountain refuge, the Warlock Lord watched and listened. Slowly his rage began to subside, and the misty darkness within the hood nodded in satisfaction. The Valeman he had thought destroyed had survived. In spite of everything, he had found the Sword. But the man was pitifully weak, lacking the knowledge necessary to understand the talisman. He was already overcome with fear, and he would be vulnerable. Swiftly, noiselessly, the Master glided from the cavernous chamber. . . .

The tall figure of Allanon paused hesitantly at the crest of a barren, windswept hill, his dark eyes invisible beneath the heavy brow as they studied the stark, solitary line of mountains that rose hauntingly against the gray northern horizon. They seemed to stare back at him, their cavernous faces scarred and worn, reflecting the soul of the land that had spawned

them so many years ago. A deep silence hovered
expectantly over the whole of the vast wilderness that
was the Northland. Even the high mountain winds
had died into stillness. The Druid wrapped his black
robes about him and breathed sharply. There could be
no mistake; his extended mind sweep would not lie to
him about this. That which he had worked so hard to
achieve had finally come to pass. In the deep recesses
of the Knife Edge, still far distant from where the
mystic stood, Shea Ohmsford had drawn forth the
Sword of Shannara.

Yet it was all wrong! Even though the Valeman
might be able to withstand and accept the truth about
himself and perhaps recognize the secret of the
Sword, he was still not prepared to use the talisman
properly against the Warlock Lord. There would be no
time for him to grow into the necessary confidence
while he was alone and unaided, deprived of the
knowledge that only Allanon could give him. He
would be filled with self-doubt and torn by fear, easy
prey for Brona. Even now, the Druid could sense the
awakening of the enemy. The Dark Lord was beginning the descent from his mountain refuge, fully
confident that the bearer of the Sword was blind to the
full power of the talisman. His attack would come
quickly and savagely, and Shea would be destroyed
before he could learn to survive.

Only brief minutes remained before the confrontation, and Allanon knew that he could never arrive in
time to help. He had realized at last that Shea and the
Sword of Shannara had somehow both gone northward. Leaving the others in Callahorn, he had rushed
to the Valeman's aid. But matters had developed too
quickly. Now there was only one chance for him to be
of any use to Shea—if, indeed, there was any real
chance at all—and he was still too far away. Clutching
his robes about his spare frame, the Druid moved
swiftly down the hillside, scattering the dusty surface

in small clouds as he went, his features tight with determination.

Panamon Creel started forward as Shea crumpled to one knee, but Keltset's massive arm reached in front of him. The Troll was facing back toward the entrance to the caverns, listening. Panamon could hear nothing, but a sudden sensation of fear and growing horror reaching down inside him, halting his motion toward the Valeman. Keltset's eyes turned, as if marking the progress of someone passing through the corridor beyond the cell, and Panamon felt his fear deepen.

Then a shadow fell over everything. The torchlight that outlined the tiny cavern room dimmed sharply. Standing at the doorway of the cell was a tall form shrouded in black robes. Instinctively, Panamon Creel knew that this was the Warlock Lord. Where a face should have been, beneath the closely drawn hood, there was nothing but darkness and a deep, green mist that moved sluggishly about twin sparks of reddish fire. The sparks turned first toward Panamon and Keltset, freezing them instantly into motionless statues, sending all the fears and terrors they had ever known rushing through their paralyzed forms. The thief struggled to cry a warning to the little Valeman, but he found that he could not speak, and he watched helplessly as the faceless cowl shifted slowly toward Shea.

The Valeman felt himself drift back into consciousness in the shadowed dampness of the little cell. Everything seemed strangely distant to him, though there was a vague warning signal sounding somewhere in the back of his clouded mind. But he responded sluggishly, and for a time there was only the musty smell of stale air and rock and the faint flickering of a single torch. Through a haze, he saw the motionless forms of Panamon and Keltset no more than five feet from him, fear mirrored in their hard features. Orl Fane crouched at the rear of the cell, twisted into a small yellow ball that whimpered and mumbled incoherently. Before him, the blade of the Sword of Shannara gleamed brightly.

Then instantly, the secret of the Sword came back to him—and with it, the helplessness of his situation. He started to lift his head, but his eyes seemed locked in front of him. Sudden fear and despair washed over him like a river of ice, and he felt himself drowning in it. He began to sweat coldly and his hands were shaking. A single thought screamed in his mind: Escape! Flee, before the fearsome creature whose forbidden kingdom he had dared invade should discover his presence and destroy him! The purpose for which he had risked everything no longer mattered; all that remained in his mind was the compelling need to flee.

He staggered erect. Every fiber of his being screamed at him to break and dash for the doorway, to throw down the Sword and run. But he could not do it. Something inside him refused to release the Sword. Desperately he fought to control his fear, his hands closing tightly about the handle of the Sword, gripping the metal until the knuckles turned white with pain. It was all that he had left, all that stood between himself and complete panic. He clung to it in desperation, his sanity held together by a talisman he knew to be useless.

MORTAL CREATURE, I AM HERE!

The words were a chilling echo in the deep silence. Shea's eyes fought to look toward the doorway. At first he found only shadows; then the shadows tightened slowly, gathering together to form the cloaked figure of the Warlock Lord. It hovered menacingly at the chamber door, an impenetrable, dark, formless robe. From within the recesses of the cowl, the green mists swirled and the sparks of flame that were its eyes flashed and grew.

MORTAL CREATURE, I AM HERE. BOW DOWN BEFORE ME!

Shea turned white with fear. Something huge and black struck at his mind, and he balanced precariously on the thin edge of total panic. A bottomless chasm seemed to open before him. It would take only one small shove . . . He forced himself to concentrate on the Sword and his own desperate need to stay alive. A crimson haze slipped over his mind, bringing with it the voices of countless doomed creatures that cried for mercy without hope. Crawling, twisted things were clinging to his arms and legs, pulling at him, drawing him downward into the chasm. His courage turned to water. He was so small, so vulnerable. How could he resist a being as awesome as the Warlock Lord?

At the far side of the cell, Panamon Creel watched the black-robed figure draw nearer to Shea. The Warlock Lord seemed to be a thing of no substance, a faceless cowl, an empty robe. But he was obviously too much for Shea to handle alone, Sword or not. With a quick warning nod to Keltset, Panamon fought back against the sense of panic ripping at him and attacked, the piked arm coming up in a wicked sweep. Almost casually, the dark figure turned to him, now no longer seemingly empty, but filled with awesome power. An arm gestured, and the thief felt something ironlike grip his throat and hurl him back against the wall. He struggled once more to break free, but he was held fast and Keltset with him. Helplessly, they watched the Warlock Lord turn back toward the Valeman.

The struggle was almost over for Shea. He still held the Sword protectively before him, but the last of his resistance was breaking down before the assault of the Dark Lord. He could no longer think rationally. He was powerless against the emotions tearing him apart. From out of the darkness of the hood, a terrible command wrenched at him.

LAY DOWN THE SWORD, MORTAL CREATURE!

Desperately, Shea fought against the urge to obey.
Everything became hazy and he struggled to breathe.
Far back in his mind, a familiar voice seemed to be
calling his name. He tried to answer, screaming inside
himself for help. Then the voice of the Warlock Lord
ripped at him again.

LAY DOWN THE SWORD!

The blade dipped slightly. Shea felt his mind begin
to grow numb, and the darkness moved closer to him.
The Sword was of no use to him. Why not discard it
and be done? He was nothing to this awesome being.
He was only a frail, insignificant mortal.

The Sword dipped farther. Orl Fane suddenly
screamed in mindless terror and fell sobbing on the
floor of the darkened cell. Panamon had gone white.
Keltset's massive form seemed pressed into the cell
wall. The tip of the Sword of Shannara hovered just
inches from the stone floor, wavering slowly.

Then the voice in Shea's mind called out to him
again. From out of nowhere, the words reached him in
a whisper so faint that he could barely distinguish it.

"Shea! Have courage. Trust the Sword."

Allanon!

The Druid's voice pierced the fear and doubt that
tightened about the Valeman. But it was so distant—
so distant . . .

"Believe in the Sword, Shea. All else is illusion. . . ."

Allanon's words disappeared in a scream of rage
from the Warlock Lord as the creature shut the hated
Druid's voice from the Valeman's mind. But awareness came too late for Brona. Allanon had thrown a
lifeline, and Shea clung to it, pulling himself back from
the edge of defeat. The fear and doubt drew back. The
Sword came up slightly.

The Warlock Lord seemed to move backward a step,
and the faceless cowl turned slightly in the direction of
Orl Fane. Instantly the whimpering Gnome came
erect with the jerking motion of a wooden puppet. No

longer his own master, the pawn of the Dark Lord surged forward, the gnarled yellow hands grasping desperately for the Sword. His fingers closed about the exposed blade and wrenched futilely at it. Then abruptly Orl Fane screamed as if in agony, jerking his hands free of the talisman. His features twisted as he dropped to the floor, and his hands groped at his eyes, covering them as if to shut out some horrible vision.

Again the Warlock Lord gestured. The trembling form struggled to its feet, and the Gnome flung himself back into the battle, shrieking his dismay. Again he seized the flashing blade. Again he screamed in anguish and dropped to his knees, releasing the talisman a second time, his eyes streaming with tears.

Shea stared down at the crumpled form. He understood what was happening. Orl Fane had seen the truth about himself, just as Shea had done upon first touching the Sword. But for the Gnome, the truth was unbearable. Yet there was something strange in all this. Why had not Brona himself attempted to wrest the Sword away? It should have been a simple effort; instead, the Warlock Lord had first tried illusion to force Shea to release the Sword, then had used the already maddened Orl Fane as his cat's-paw. Master of so much power, Brona yet seemed unable to grasp the Sword away? It should have been a simple effort; groped for the answer, so close now—then there was the first small glimmer of understanding.

Orl Fane was on his feet once more, still hopelessly obedient to the commands of the Warlock Lord. He came at Shea in maddened desperation, his gnarled fingers groping wildly at the air before him. The Valeman tried to avoid the rush, but Orl Fane was beyond reason, his mind gone, his soul no longer his own. With a shriek of fear and frustration, he threw himself against the Sword. For an instant, the wiry form convulsed about the bright metal as the Gnome held himself wrapped about the one thing that still mattered to him in this world. For an instant, it was his at last. Then he died.

Stunned, Shea backed away, pulling the weapon free from the lifeless body. Instantly, the Warlock Lord renewed his assault, thrusting viciously at the Valeman's mind in an effort to crush all resistance. Brutal and direct, he employed no clever twists of doubt, no insinuation of uncertainty, no tricks of self-deception. There was only fear, overwhelming and devastating, hurled with the force of a sledgehammer blow. Visions swam through Shea's mind—the awesome power of the Warlock Lord pictured in a thousand horrible ways, all directed toward his extermination. He felt himself reduced down to the smallest, least significant living thing that crawled upon the earth; in another second, it seemed, the Warlock Lord would grind the helpless human into dust.

But Shea's courage held. He had almost succumbed to madness once, and this time he had to stand firm, to believe in himself and in Allanon. Both hands gripped the Sword as he forced himself to take one small step forward into the constricting haze, into the wall of fear assailing him. He tried to believe that it was only illusion, that the fear and growing panic he felt were not his own. The wall gave slightly, and he fought harder against it. He remembered the death of Orl Fane and built upon his memory a mental picture of all the others who must die should he fail them now. He remembered the whispered words of Allanon. And he concentrated on what he believed to be the Warlock Lord's own weakness, revealed in his strange refusal to grasp the Sword. Shea forced himself to believe that the real secret of the talisman's power was a simple law that affected even a creature as awesome as Brona.

The haze thinned suddenly and the wall of fear splintered. Shea stood again before the Warlock Lord, and the red sparks flashed wildly now in the dim green mists beneath the cowl. The cloaked arms came up quickly as if to ward off some pressing danger, and the dark figure shrank from him. From the dimness of the far wall, Panamon Creel and Keltset suddenly broke free and came rushing forward, weapons drawn. Shea felt the last traces of the Warlock Lord's resistance to his advance break apart and fade. Then the Sword of Shannara came down.

An eerie, soundless shriek of terror ripped from the convulsed shroud and a long, skeletal arm jerked wildly upward. The Valeman pressed the gleaming blade hard against the writhing form, forcing it back against the nearest wall. There would be no escape, he swore softly. There would be an end to the monstrous evil of this creature. Before him, the dark robes shuddered in response as the hooked fingers clawed painfully at the damp cell air. The Warlock Lord began to crumble, and he screamed his hatred of the thing destroying him. Behind his scream, the echo of a thousand other voices cried out for a vengeance that had been too long denied them.

Shea felt the horror of the creature rush through the Sword into his mind, but with it came strength from those other voices, and he did not relent. The touch of the Sword carried with it a truth that could not be denied by all the illusion and deceit of the Warlock Lord. It was a truth he could not admit, could not accept, could not abide—yet a truth against which he had no defense. For the Warlock Lord, the truth was death.

Brona's mortal existence was only an illusion. Long ago, whatever means he had employed to extend his mortal life had failed him, and his body had died. Yet his obsessive conviction that he could not perish kept a part of him alive, and he sustained himself through the very sorcery that had driven him to madness. Denying his own death, he held his lifeless body together to achieve the immortality that had escaped him. A creature existing as a part of two worlds, his power seemed awesome. But now the Sword was forcing him to behold himself as he really was—a decayed, lifeless shell sustained only by a misconceived belief in his own reality—a sham, a fantasy created by force of will alone, as ephemeral as the physical being he had made himself appear. He was a lie that had existed and grown in the fears and doubts of mortal men, a lie that he had created to hide the truth. But now the lie was exposed.

Shea Ohmsford had been able to accept the weakness and frailty that were a part of his human nature, as it was a part of all men. But the Warlock Lord could never accept what the Sword revealed, because the truth was that the creature he had supposed himself to be had ceased to exist almost a thousand years before. All that remained of Brona was the lie; and now that, too, was taken from him by the power of the Sword.

He cried out a final time, a whimper of protest that echoed mournfully through the cell, blending with a rising shout of triumph from a chorus of other wraithlike cries. Then all sound ceased. The outstretched arm began to wither and turn to dust, falling from his shuddering form like ash as his body broke apart beneath the robes. The tiny glints of red glimmered once in the thinning green mist and disappeared. The cloak crumpled and sank emptily, falling to the floor in a pile, with the hooded cowl gradually collapsing, until only a worn tangle of cloth remained.

An instant later, Shea began to sway unsteadily. Too many emotions had chased themselves through his nerves and too much tension over too long a time were demanding their price from his overstrained body. The floor seemed to tilt beneath his feet, and he was falling slowly, slowly into darkness.

In the city of Tyrsis, the long, terrible struggle

between earth-born mortal and spirit creature peaked with shocking suddenness. From deep within its rock-encrusted heart, the earth began to rumble, the tremors rippling to the scarred surface in steady, menacing shudders. On the low hills east of Tyrsis, the small band of Elven riders fought roughly to control their frightened mounts, and a haggard Flick Ohmsford stared in bewilderment as the land about him began to shake with the strange vibrations. Atop the Inner Wall, the giant, indestructible figure of Balinor repelled assault after assault as the Northland army sought vainly to breach the Southland defense, and for several minutes the tremors went entirely unnoticed in the ferocity of the battle. And on the Bridge of Sendic, the advancing Trolls halted and glanced uneasily about as the rumbling continued to build. Menion Leah started as long cracks appeared in the ancient stone, and the bridge defenders stood poised to run. The deep vibrations grew rapidly, building with frightening power into a titanic av-alanche of booming shudders that swept through the earth and rock. The wind broke over the land with ferocious thrusts that bore down upon and scattered the Elven army still racing to relieve Tyrsis. From Culhaven in the Anar to the farthest reaches of the vast Westland, the great wind roared. Massive forest trees splintered and snapped, and ragged sections of mountains were torn free and crumbled into dust as the blistering force of wind and earthquake gripped the four lands. The sky had deepened into a solid black—cloudless, sunless, and empty, as if the heavens had been obliterated with the single stroke of a massive brush. Huge, jagged streaks of red lightning cut through the darkness, spanning the sky from horizon to horizon in an impossible web of electrical energy. It was the end of the world. It was the end of all life. The holocaust promised since the beginning of the spoken word had finally arrived.

But a moment later it was over, dying instantly into

complete and utter stillness. The silence hung shroudlike and complete, until from out of the impenetrable
blackness the sound of wailing cries rose dismally,
turning quickly into screams of anguish. In the city of
Tyrsis, the battle was forgotten. Northlander and
Southlander watched in horror as the Skull Bearers
drifted skyward like formless wraiths, writhing in
unspeakable agony, their hooked limbs twisting as
they screamed. They hovered momentarily in full
view of the men below, who blanched in horror but
could not turn away. Then the winged forms began to
disintegrate, their dark bodies breaking slowly into
ashes and drifting earthward. Seconds later nothing
remained but the vast, empty blackness, which began
to move in a huge, rushing sweep that carried it
northward, pulling in its borders as if they were the
ends of a blanket. To the south first, and then the east
and west, blue sky shot into view and the sun swept
across the lands with dazzling brightness. In awe,
mortal men watched the impossible darkness fold into
a single black cloud far to the north, hover motionlessly above the horizon, and then sink downward
into the earth and disappear forever.

Time drifted away as Shea floated senselessly in a
vast, black, empty void.
"I don't think he made it."
A voice reached into his mind from somewhere far,
far away. His hands and face felt the sudden chill of
smooth stone against his heated skin.
"Wait a minute, his eyes are blinking. I think he's
coming around!"
Panamon Creel. Shea's eyes opened and he found
himself lying on the floor in the little cell, yellowish
torchlight flickering through the darkness in a hazy
glow. He was himself again. One hand still clenched
the Sword of Shannara, but the power of the talisman
had left him, and the strange bond that had briefly

joined them together was gone. He stumbled awkwardly to his hands and knees, but a deep, ominous rumbling shook the cavern and he pitched forward. Strong hands reached out to grab him as he fell.

"Easy now, slow down a minute." Panamon's rough voice sounded almost in his ear. "Let me take a look at you. Here now, look at me." He practically jerked the little Valeman about and their eyes locked. There was just a trace of fear in the thief's hard stare, and then he was smiling. "He's all right, Keltset. Now let's get out of here."

He brought Shea to his feet and started moving toward the open doorway. The massive form of Keltset lumbered several feet ahead. Shea took a few uncertain steps and halted. Something held him back.

"I'm all right," he muttered almost inaudibly.

Then abruptly everything came back to him—the power of the Sword coursing through his body to link them together, his inner visions of the truth about himself, the frightening battle against the Warlock Lord, the death of Orl Fane . . . He screamed and faltered.

Panamon Creel reached down impulsively with his good arm and held the little Valeman close.

"Easy, easy, it's all over, Shea. You've done it—you've won. The Warlock Lord is destroyed. But this whole mountain is shaking apart. We've got to get out of here before the whole place comes down around our ears!"

The low rumbling had grown steadily louder, and chunks of rock were being dislodged from the cavern walls and ceiling and falling in small showers of dust and gravel. Cracks were appearing along the ancient stone as the heavy shaking continued to mount. Shea looked at Panamon and nodded.

"You'll be all right." The scarlet-clad thief rose quickly. "I'm going to get you out of this. That's a promise."

Swiftly the three men moved into the dark passageway leading from the chamber. The craggy tunnel twisted and wound through the heart of the Knife Edge, the rough walls split by jagged seams and fissures. More breaks quickly appeared as the rumbling grew stronger and the walls began to crack and fall apart. The mountain shook as if the earth were threatening to open and swallow it whole, quaking with the force of the thunderous reverberations that echoed brokenly from the core of the earth. They passed through countless small passageways and connecting chambers, moving steadily, yet unable to find an exit to safety. Several times one or more went down under a cascade of rock and dust, but each time they worked themselves free. Huge chunks of rock fell crashing before them to block the tunnel passage, but the powerful Keltset heaved the boulders aside, and the small party continued quickly on. Shea began to lose all sense of what was happening to them, a strange weariness settling into his body, pressing remorselessly down and sapping the little stamina that remained. When he thought he could no longer continue, Panamon was at his side to support him, the strong arm alternately lifting him over and shoving him through the stone rubble.

They had reached a particularly narrow section of the passageway that angled sharply to the right when a violent, wrenching quake shook the dying mountain. The entire ceiling of the corridor cracked with a grating snap and began to settle slowly downward. Panamon yelled frantically and pulled Shea down in front of him, trying to protect the Valeman with his own body. Instantly Keltset was there, the giant frame bracing as the great shoulders hunched upward against the tons of breaking rock. Dust rose in blinding clouds and for a moment everything was obscured from view. Then Panamon Creel was pulling the Valeman to his feet, hastening him past the straining form of the Rock Troll. Shea glanced up once as he crawled and scrambled through the broken stone, and the gentle eyes met his own. The ceiling dropped several inches farther, and the massive human support threw all the awesome strength of a Rock Troll against it, the barklike body rigid with the tremendous strain. Shea hesitated, but Panamon's powerful grip closed over his shoulder, pulling him ahead, thrusting him beyond the tunnel angle into a wider corridor. They collapsed in a pile of loose rock and dust, gasping for air. They had just a glimpse of Keltset, his great frame still braced against the crumbling stone. Panamon made a sudden move to start back into the passage, but a deep rumble tore through the core of the mountain; with a groan of sliding, shifting rock, the tunnel behind them came apart and collapsed entirely. Tons of stone crashed downward and the way back disappeared altogether. Shea screamed and threw himself against the wall of rock, but Panamon pulled him back roughly, pushing the piked hand into his face.

"He's dead! We can't help him now."

The haggard face of the Valeman stared back in shock.

"Get moving—get out of here!" The thief was livid with rage. "Do you want him to have died for nothing? Move!"

He yanked Shea violently to his feet and thrust him toward the open section of the tunnel. The deep rumbling continued to vibrate through the mountain, and a series of sharp, wrenching quakes nearly threw the two men to the cavern floor as they stumbled ahead. Shea was running blindly now, his eyes clouded with dust and tears. It was becoming difficult to see clearly, and he blinked and squinted in an effort to clear his fading vision. Panamon's labored breathing was close in his ear, and he felt the iron stub of the piked hand shoving against his back, urging him to run faster. Shards of rock splintered from the passage walls and ceiling and rained down on his unprotected body, cutting and bruising it, tearing the forest clothing into tattered strips that hung from the thin, sweating form. In his hands he clutched the gleaming Sword, useless to him now except as proof that what had happened to him was more than an imagined madness.

Abruptly the tunnel dissolved in the gray light of the Northland sky, and they were free of the mountain. Before them, the scattered bodies of Troll and Muten lay broken in death. Without slowing, the two men raced for the mouth of the winding pass that split the monstrous Knife Edge. The hardened earth was quaking violently, long jagged cracks appearing from the base of Skull Mountain and snaking crookedly toward the ring of natural hazards that bound the forbidden land. A sudden, grating crash, louder than any that had preceded it, brought the two runners about. In speechless awe, they watched the gaunt face of the skull begin to sag and break apart. Everything seemed to shatter at once, and the mark of the Warlock Lord disappeared as tons of rock cascaded downward and Skull Mountain ceased to exist. A thick cloud of yellow dust surged skyward and a heavy booming sound burst from the bowels of the earth and echoed through the vast emptiness of the Northland. Violent winds swept over the remains of the dying mountain and the rumbling in the earth began to build once more. In horror Shea saw the monstrous Knife Edge begin to shake with the force of this new convulsion. The entire kingdom was disintegrating!

Already Panamon was running brokenly for the pass, pulling a dazed Shea with him. But the Valeman needed no urging this time and quickly picked up the pace on his own, his form flying through the tangle of dead bodies. From some final reservoir of courage and determination, he summoned the last of his strength, and a surprised Panamon Creel suddenly found himself running to keep up. By the time they reached the mouth of the mountain pass, pieces of the towering Knife Edge were beginning to break apart and fall, snapping free with piercing cracks as the booming quakes continued to shake the land. Massive boulders fell with crushing force into the winding canyon, and a heavy avalanche of loose stone slid steadily from the heights of the ancient peaks, building in force as the seconds slipped by. Through the center of this holocaust the two Southlanders dodged and twisted—the tattered half Elf, brandishing his ancient Sword, and the one-handed thief. The force of the wind broke over their backs, thrusting them faster through the hail of stone and dust. Twists and turns in the rock walls came and disappeared, and they knew they were closing on the far end of the canyon and the open foothills beyond. Shea was suddenly aware that his eyesight was blurring once more and he stumbled uncertainly, his free hand rubbing angrily to clear his vision.

Suddenly the entire west wall of the canyon seemed to break apart and come crashing down on both men, burying them in a choking rush of broken rock and dirt. Something sharp struck his exposed head, and for a moment Shea slipped into blackness. He lay partially covered by the mass of rubble, his groping mind trying to shake itself awake. Then Panamon was digging him free, the strong arm lifting him clear of the shattered stone and holding him upright. Through a gray haze, Shea saw blood on the big man's face. Slowly Shea rose to his feet, leaning heavily on the Sword of Shannara for support.

Panamon remained on his knees. His piked hand pointed to the pass behind them. Shea glanced anxiously past him. To his dismay, he caught sight of a misshapen, lumbering creature slowly bearing down on them from out of the rising clouds of dust. A

Muten! The formless, plastic face was turned toward them and the monster shuffled steadily forward. Panamon looked up at Shea and smiled grimly.

"He's been with us all the way from the other end. I thought we might lose him in the rocks, but he's persistent."

He rose slowly and drew free the long broadsword.

"Get going, Shea. I'll catch up shortly."

The startled Valeman shook his head speechlessly. He must have misunderstood.

"We can outrun him," he burst out finally. "We've almost reached the end of the pass anyway. We can fight him there—together!"

Panamon shook his head and smiled sadly.

"Not this time, I'm afraid. I've done something to my leg. I can't run anymore." He shook his head as Shea opened his mouth to speak. "I don't want to hear it, Shea. Now run—and keep running!"

Tears were streaming down the Valeman's face as he stared at the man.

"I can't do that!"

A sudden rumble shook the Knife Edge, throwing Panamon and Shea to their knees again. Boulders crashed down the crumbling mountainside as the heavy convulsions continued to build from deep within the earth. The Muten lumbered mindlessly toward them, unaffected by the tremors. Panamon climbed shakenly to his feet, pulling Shea after him.

"The whole pass is coming down," he stated quietly. "We don't have time to argue. I can take care of myself—just as I did long before I met you or Keltset. Now I want you to run—get clear of this pass!"

He put one hand on the Valeman's slim shoulder and gently shoved him away. Shea took several steps backward and hesitated, bringing the Sword of Shannara up almost threateningly. Panamon Creel's broad face showed a flicker of surprise, and then the familiar devilish grin appeared and the eyes turned to fire.

"We'll meet again, Shea Ohmsford. You watch for me."

He waved the piked hand once in farewell, and turned to meet the advancing Muten. Shea stared after him momentarily. His fading eyesight must be fooling him—for an instant it seemed that the scarlet thief was not limping, after all. Then the heavy tremors rippled through the mountain pass still another time, and the Valeman broke for the safety of the foothills. Slipping and stumbling through the loose rock and earth, dodging the cascade of stone and debris that tumbled from the heights of the Knife Edge into the narrow canyon, he ran on alone.

XXXIV

The afternoon was almost gone. Sunlight slipped in long, hazy streamers through the drifting white clouds, settling with warm touches over the barren, empty Northland terrain. Here and there the light fell providently on small patches of green—the first signs of a permanent life that one day soon would flourish in this earth that had lain parched and desolate for so many years. In the distance, the blunted tips of the shattered Knife Edge broke starkly against the northern horizon, and from the devastated valley beyond, the dust still hung suspended above the ruins of the Skull Kingdom.

Shea seemed to appear out of nowhere, wandering aimlessly through the tangle of ravines and ridges that carved out the foothills immediately below the Knife Edge. Half-blind and completely exhausted, the tattered figure was barely recognizable. He came toward Allanon without seeing him, both hands gripping tightly the silver-handled sword. For just an instant, the Druid stared speechlessly at the strange spectacle of the stumbling, ragged swordsman. Then with a sharp cry of relief, he rushed forward to gather in the thin, battered frame of Shea Ohmsford, and held him close.

The Valeman was asleep for a long time, and when he came awake again, it was night. He was lying in the shelter of a rock-encrusted overhang that opened into a deep, wide-bottomed ravine. A small wood fire crackled peacefully, lending added warmth to the cloak that was wrapped tightly about him. His troubled vision had begun to clear, and he found himself staring up into a bright, starlit night sky that stretched canopylike from ridge top to ridge top above him. He smiled in spite of himself. He could imagine himself in Shady Vale once again. A moment later Allanon's dark shadow moved into the dim firelight.

"Are you feeling better?" the Druid asked in greeting and seated himself. There was something strange about Allanon. He seemed more human, less forbidding, and there was an unusual warmth in his voice.

Shea nodded. "How did you find me?"

"You found me. Don't you remember anything?"

"No, none of it—nothing after . . ." Shea paused hesitantly. "Was there anybody . . . did you see anybody else?"

Allanon studied his anxious expression for a moment, as if debating his answer, then shook his dark face.

"You were alone."

Shea felt something catch in his throat, and he lay back in the warmth of the blankets, swallowing hard. So Panamon, too, was gone. Somehow, he had not expected it to end like this.

"Are you all right?" the Druid's deep voice reached out to him in the darkness. "Would you like to eat something now? I think it would be good for you if you did."

"Yes." Shea pushed himself up into a sitting position, the cloak still wrapped protectively about him. By the fire, Allanon was pouring soup into a small bowl. The aroma reached out to him invitingly, and he breathed it in. Then suddenly he thought of the Sword of Shannara and looked for it in the darkness. He saw it almost immediately, lying next to him, the bright metal gleaming faintly. As an afterthought, he felt through the pockets of his tunic for the Elfstones. He could not find them. Panicked, he began searching desperately through his clothing for the little pouch, but the result was the same. It was gone. A sinking sensation gripped him, and he lay back weakly for a moment. Perhaps Allanon . . .

"Allanon, I can't find the Elfstones," he said quickly. "Did you . . .?"

The Druid moved over to his side and handed him the steaming bowl of soup and a small wooden spoon. His face was an impenetrable black shadow.

"No, Shea. You must have lost them when you fled the Knife Edge." He saw the crestfallen look on the other's face and reached over to pat the slim shoulder reassuringly. "There's no point in worrying about them now. The stones have served their purpose. I want you to eat something and go back to sleep—you need to rest."

Mechanically, Shea sipped at the soup, unable to forget quite so easily the loss of the Elfstones. They had been with him from the beginning, protecting him every step of the way. Several times, they had saved his life. How could he have been so careless? He thought back for a moment, trying vainly to remember where he might have lost them, but it was useless. It could have happened anytime.

"I'm sorry about the Elfstones," he apologized quietly, feeling that he had to say something more.

Allanon shrugged and smiled faintly. He seemed weary and somehow older as he seated himself beside the Valeman.

"Maybe they'll turn up later."

Shea finished the bowl in silence, and Allanon refilled it without being asked. The warm liquid relaxed the still weary Valeman, and a numbing drowsiness began to seep slowly through his body. He was falling asleep again. It would have been so easy to give in to the feeling, but he could not. There were still

too many things bothering him, too many unanswered questions. He wanted those answers now
from the one man who could give them to him. He
deserved that much after everything he had been
through.

He struggled to a sitting position, aware that
Allanon was watching him closely from out of the
darkness beyond the little fire. In the distance, the
sharp cry of a night bird broke through the deep
silence. Shea paused in spite of himself. Life was
coming back to the Northland—after so long. He
placed the bowl of soup on the ground next to him and
turned to Allanon.

"Can we talk awhile?"

The Druid nodded silently.

"Why didn't you tell me the truth about the
Sword?" the Valeman asked softly. "Why didn't
you?"

"I told you all that you needed to know." Allanon's
dark face was impassive. "The Sword itself told you
the rest."

Shea stared at him incredulously.

"It was necessary for you to learn the secret of the
Sword of Shannara for yourself," the Druid continued
gently. "It was not something that I could explain to
you—it was something that you had to experience.
You had to learn to accept the truth about yourself first
before the Sword could be of any use to you as a
talisman against the Warlock Lord. It was a process in
which I could not involve myself directly."

"Well, could you not at least have told me why the
Sword would destroy Brona?" Shea persisted.

"And what would that have done to you, Shea?"

The Valeman frowned. "I don't understand."

"If I had told you everything that it was in my power
to tell you about the Sword—remembering now that
you would not have the benefit of hindsight, as you do
now, to enlighten you—would that have helped you
in practical terms? Would you have been able to

continue your search for the Sword? Would you have been able to draw the Sword against Brona, knowing that it would do no more than reveal to him the truth about himself? Would you have even believed me when I said that such a simple thing would destroy a monster with the power of the Warlock Lord?"

He hunched down closer to Shea in the dim firelight.

"Or would you have given up on yourself and the quest then and there? How much truth could you have withstood?"

"I don't know," Shea answered doubtfully.

"Then I will tell you something I could not tell you before. Jerle Shannara, five hundred years earlier, knew all these things—and still he failed."

"But I thought . . ."

"That he was successful?" Allanon finished the thought. "Yet if he had been successful, would not the Warlock Lord have been destroyed? No, Shea, Jerle Shannara did not succeed. Bremen confided in the Elven King the secret of the Sword because he, too, thought that knowing how the talisman would be used might better prepare the bearer for a confrontation with Brona. It did not. Even though he had been forewarned that he would be exposed to the truth about himself, Jerle Shannara was not prepared for what he discovered. Indeed, there was probably no way that he could have adequately prepared himself beforehand. We build too many walls to be completely honest with ourselves. And I don't think that he ever really believed Bremen's warning about what would happen when he finally held the Sword. Jerle Shannara was a warrior king, and his natural instinct was to rely on the Sword as a physical weapon, even though he had been told that it would not help him in that way. When he confronted the Warlock Lord and the talisman began to work on him exactly as Bremen had warned, he panicked. His physical strength, his fighting prowess, his battle experience—all of it useless to him. It was just too much for him to accept. As a result, the Warlock Lord managed to escape him."

Shea looked unconvinced.

"It might have been different with me."

But the Druid did not seem to hear him.

"I would have been with you when you found the Sword of Shannara, and when the secret of the talisman revealed itself to you, I would have explained then its significance as a weapon against the Warlock Lord. But then I lost you in the Dragon's Teeth, and it was only later that I realized you had found the Sword and gone northward without me. I came after you, but even so, I was almost too late. I could sense your panic when you discovered the secret of the Sword, and I knew the Warlock Lord could sense it as well. But I was still too far away to reach you in time. I tried to call out to you—to project my voice into your mind. There wasn't time enough to tell you what to do; the Warlock Lord prevented that. A few words, that was all."

He paused, almost as if he had gone into a trance, his dark gaze fixed on the air between them.

"But you discovered the answer on your own, Shea—and you survived."

The Valeman looked away, reminded suddenly that, although he was alive, it seemed that everyone who had gone with him into the kingdom of the Skull was dead.

"It might have been different," he repeated woodenly.

Allanon said nothing. At his feet, the small fire was dying slowly into reddish embers as the night closed about them. Shea picked up the bowl of soup and finished it quickly, feeling the drowsiness slip through him once more. He was nodding when Allanon stirred unexpectedly in the darkness and moved next to him.

"You believe me wrong in not telling you the secret of the Sword?" he murmured softly. It was more a statement of fact than a question. "Perhaps you are right. Perhaps it would have been better for everyone if I had revealed it all to you from the first."

Shea looked up at him. The lean face was a mask of dark hollows and angular lines that seemed the wrappings of some perpetual enigma.

"No, you were right," the Valeman replied slowly. "I'm not sure I could have handled the truth."

Allanon's head tilted slightly to one side, as if considering the possibility.

"I should have had more faith in you, Shea. But I was afraid." He paused as a trace of doubt clouded the Valeman's face. "You don't believe me, but it's true. To you, to the others as well, I have always been something more than human. It was necessary, or you would never have accepted your role as I gave it to you. But a Druid is still a human being, Shea. And you have forgotten something. Before he became the Warlock Lord, Brona was a Druid. Thus to some extent, at least, the Druids must bear responsibility for what he became. We permitted him to become the Warlock Lord. Our learning gave him the opportunity; our subsequent isolation from the rest of the world allowed him to evolve. The entire human race might have been enslaved or destroyed, and the guilt would have been ours. Twice the Druids had the opportunity to destroy him—and twice they failed to do so. I was the last of my people, and if I were to fail as well, then there would be no one left to protect the races against this monstrous evil. Yes, I was afraid. One small mistake and I might have left Brona free forever."

The Druid's voice dropped to a whisper and he looked down for an instant.

"There is one more thing you should know. Bremen was more to me than simply my ancestor. He was my father."

"Your father!" Shea came fully awake for an instant. "But that's not poss . . ."

He trailed off, unable to finish. Allanon smiled faintly.

"There must have been times when you guessed that I was older than any normal man could be, surely. The Druids discovered the secret of longevity following the First War of the Races. But there is a price—a price that Brona refused to pay. There are many demands and disciplines required, Shea. It is no great gift. And for our waking time, we pile up a debt that must be paid by a special kind of sleep that restores us from our aging. There are many steps to true longevity, and some are not—pleasant. Not one is easy. Brona searched for a way different from that of the Druids, a way that would not carry the same price, the same sacrifices; in the end, he found only illusion."

The Druid seemed to retreat into himself for a long moment, then continued.

"Bremen was my father. He had a chance to end the menace of the Warlock Lord, but he made too many mistakes and Brona escaped him. His escape was my father's responsibility—and if the Warlock Lord had succeeded in his plans, my father would have earned the blame. I lived with the fear of that happening until it was an obsession. I swore not to make the mistakes he had made. I'm afraid, Shea, that I never really had much faith in you. I feared you were too weak to do what had to be done, and I hid the truth to serve my own ends. In many ways, I was unfair to you. But you were my last chance to redeem my father, to purge my own sense of guilt for what he had done, and to erase forever the responsibility of the Druids for the creation of Brona."

He hesitated and looked directly into Shea's eyes. "I was wrong, Valeman. You were a better man than I gave you credit for being."

Shea smiled and shook his head slowly.

"No, Allanon. You were the one who so often spoke

to me of hindsight. Now heed your own words, historian."

In the darkness across from him, the Druid returned the smile wistfully.

"I wish . . . I wish we had more time, Shea Ohmsford. Time to learn to know each other better. But I have a debt that must be paid . . . all too soon . . ."

He trailed off almost sadly, the lean face lowering into shadow. The puzzled Valeman waited a moment, thinking that he would say something more. He did not.

"In the morning, then." Shea stretched wearily and burrowed deep into the cloak, warm and relaxed by the soup and the fire. "We've a long journey back to the Southland."

Allanon did not reply immediately.

"Your friends are close now, looking for you," he responded finally. "When they find you, will you relate to them all that I have told you?"

Shea barely heard him, his thoughts drifting to Shady Vale and the hope of going home again.

"You can do the job better than I," he murmured sleepily.

There was another long moment of silence. At last he heard Allanon moving in the darkness beyond, and when the tall man spoke again, his voice sounded strangely distant.

"I may not be able to, Shea. I'm very tired—I've exhausted myself physically. For a time now, I must . . . sleep."

"Tomorrow," Shea mumbled. "Good night."

The Druid's voice came back a whisper.

"Good-bye, my young friend. Good-bye, Shea."

But the Valeman was already sleeping.

Shea awoke with a start, the morning sunlight streaming down on him. His eyes snapped open at the sound of horses' hooves and booted feet, and he found himself surrounded by a cluster of lean, rangy figures clothed in forest green. Instinctively his hand dropped to the Sword of Shannara, and he struggled to a sitting position, squinting sharply to see their faces. They were Elves. A tall, hard-featured Elf detached himself from the group and bent down to him. Deep, penetrating green eyes locked into his own, and a firm hand came up to rest reassuringly on his shoulder.

"You're among friends, Shea Ohmsford. We are Eventine's men."

Shea climbed slowly to his feet, still grasping the Sword guardedly.

"Allanon . . .?" he asked, looking about for the Druid.

The tall man hesitated for a moment, then shook his head.

"There is no one else here. Only you."

Stunned, Shea moved past him and pushed his way through the ring of horsemen, his eyes quickly searching the length of the wide ravine. Gray rock and dust stared back at him, an empty, deserted passage that twisted and disappeared from sight. Except for the Elven riders and himself, there was no one else. Then something the Druid had said came back to him—and he knew then that Allanon was really gone.

"Sleeping . . ." he heard himself whisper.

Woodenly, he turned back to the waiting Elves, then hesitated as tears streamed down his haggard face. But Allanon would come back to them when he was needed, he told himself angrily. Just as he had always done before. He brushed away the tears, and glanced momentarily into the bright blueness of the Northland sky. For just an instant, he seemed to hear the Druid's voice calling to him from far, far away. A faint smile crossed his lips.

"Good-bye, Allanon," he answered softly.

XXXV

So it ended. Little more than ten days later, those who still remained of the little band that had journeyed forth from Culhaven so many weeks ago bade farewell to one another for the last time. It was a bright, clear day filled with sunshine and summer's freshness. From out of the west, a gentle breeze ruffled the emerald green carpet of the Tyrsian grasslands, and in the distance, the sluggish roar of the Mermidon floated softly through the early-morning stillness. They stood together by the roadway leading out from the walled city—Durin and Dayel, the former without the use of his left arm, which was splinted and wrapped. Dayel had found him among the wounded, and now he was healing rapidly. Balinor Buckhannah in chain mail and royal blue riding cloak, a still-pale Shea Ohmsford, the faithful Flick, and Menion Leah. They spoke in quiet tones for a time, smiling bravely, trying to appear amiable and relaxed without much success, glancing from time to time at the tethered horses that grazed contentedly behind them. At last there was an awkward silence, and hands were extended and taken, and mumbled promises to visit soon were quietly exchanged. It was a painful good-bye, and behind the smiles and the handshakes, there was sadness.

Then they rode away, each to his own home. Durin

722

and Dayel traveled west to Beleal, where Dayel would finally be reunited with his beloved Lynliss. The Ohmsfords turned south to Shady Vale and, as Flick had repeatedly announced to his brother, a well-deserved rest. As far as Flick was concerned, their traveling days were over. Menion Leah went with them to the Vale, determined to see to it personally that nothing further befell Shea. From there, he would return for a time to the highlands to be with his father, who would be missing him by now. But very soon, he knew he must come back again to the border country and to the red-haired daughter of kings who would be waiting.

Standing silently by the empty roadway, Balinor watched after his friends until they were no more than small shadows in the distant green of the flatlands. Then slowly he mounted his waiting horse and rode back into Tyrsis.

The Sword of Shannara remained in Callahorn. It had been Shea's firm decision to leave the talisman with the border people. No one had given more to preserve the freedom of the four lands. No one had a better right to be entrusted with its care and preservation. And so the legendary Sword was implanted blade downward in a block of red marble and placed in a vault in the center of the gardens of the People's Park in Tyrsis, sheltered by the wide, protective span of the Bridge of Sendic, there to remain for all time. Carved upon the stone facing of the vault was the inscription:

Herein lies the heart and soul of the nations.
Their right to be free men,
Their desire to live in peace,
Their courage to seek out truth.
Herein lies the Sword of Shannara.

Weeks later, Shea perched wearily on one of the tall wooden stools in the inn kitchen and studied blankly the plate of food on the counter in front of him. At his elbow, Flick was already starting on his second helping. It was early in the evening, and the Ohmsford brothers had spent the entire day repairing the veranda roof. The summer sun had been hot and the work had been tedious; yet, although he was tired and vaguely disgruntled, Shea found himself unable to locate his appetite. He was still picking at his food when his father appeared in the hall doorway, mumbling blackly to himself. Curzad Ohmsford came up to them without a word and tapped Shea on the shoulder.

"How much longer is this nonsense going to continue?" he demanded.

Shea looked up in surprise.

"I don't know what you mean," he answered truthfully, glancing at Flick, who shrugged blankly.

"Not eating much either, I see." His father spied the dinner plate. "How do you expect to get your strength back if you don't eat properly?"

He paused for a moment, and then seemed to recall that he had gotten off the subject entirely.

"Strangers, that's what I mean. Now I suppose you'll be off again. I thought that was all done with."

Shea stared at him.

"I'm not going anywhere. What in the world are you talking about?"

Curzad Ohmsford seated himself heavily on a vacant stool and eyed his foster son closely, apparently resigned to the fact that he was not going to get a straight answer without a little unnecessary effort.

"Shea, we have never lied to each other, have we? When you came back from your visit with the Prince of Leah, I never pressed you about what went on while you were there, even though you left in the middle of the night without a word to anyone, even though you came back looking like your own ghost and very carefully avoided telling me exactly how you got that way. Now answer me," he continued quickly when Shea tried to object. "I never once asked you to tell me anything, did I?"

Shea shook his head silently. His father nodded in satisfaction.

"No, because I happen to believe that a man's business is mostly his own affair. But I cannot forget that the last time you disappeared from the Vale was right after that other stranger appeared asking for you."

"Other stranger!" the brothers exclaimed together.

Instantly all the old memories came back to them—Allanon's mysterious appearance, Balinor's warning, the Skull Bearers, the running, the fear . . . Shea slid down from his stool slowly.

"There's someone here . . . looking for me?"

His father nodded, his broad face clouding darkly as he caught the look of concern mirrored in his son's furtive glance at the doorway.

"A stranger, like before. He got in several minutes ago, looking for you. He's waiting out in the lobby. But I don't see . . ."

"Shea, what can we do?" Flick interrupted hurriedly. "We don't even have the Elfstones to protect us anymore."

"I . . . I don't know," his brother mumbled, desperately trying to think through his confusion. "We could slip out the back way . . ."

"Now wait a minute!" Curzad Ohmsford had heard enough. He gripped their shoulders tightly and turned them about to face him, staring at them in disbelief.

"I did not raise my sons to run away from trouble." He studied their worried faces a moment and shook his head. "You must learn to face your problems, not run from them. Why, here you are in your own home, among family and friends who will stand by you, and you talk about running away."

He released them and stepped back a pace.

"Now we'll all go out there together and face this man. He looks a hard sort, but he seemed friendly enough when we talked. Besides, I don't think a one-handed man is any kind of a match physically for three whole men—even with that pike."

Shea started abruptly.

"One-handed . . .?"

"He looks like he traveled a long way to get here." The elder Ohmsford did not seem to have heard him. "He's carrying a little leather pouch that he claims belongs to you. I offered to take it, but he wouldn't give it to me. Said he wouldn't give it to anyone but you."

Now suddenly Flick understood.

"It must be something important," his father declared. "He told me you dropped it on your way home. Now how could that happen?"

Curzad Ohmsford had to wait awhile longer for his answer. In a rush, his sons were past him, through the kitchen door, and halfway down the hallway to the lobby of the inn.